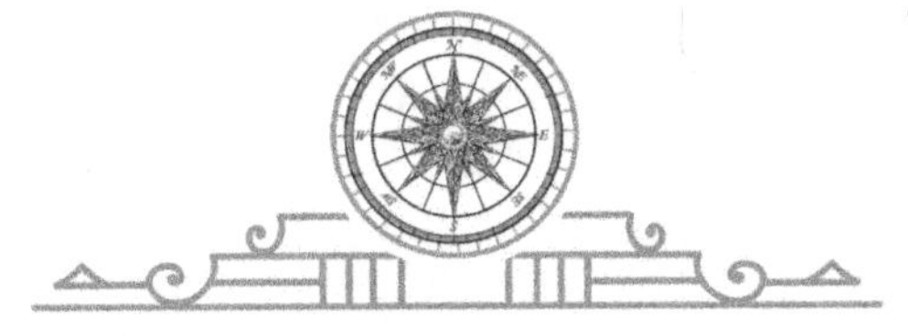

AETERNUM SAGA
J.C. KING

NO CHANCE FOR US

Love doesn't always need to be fanfare and fireworks. Sometimes it begins in the closest of friendships and hardest trials. We have definitely experienced that and more, Timothy. Thank you for everything I could never put properly to paper.

And to Joanna, who guards our characters with the same
diligent passion she brings to everything else in her life.
Thank you for preserving our William.

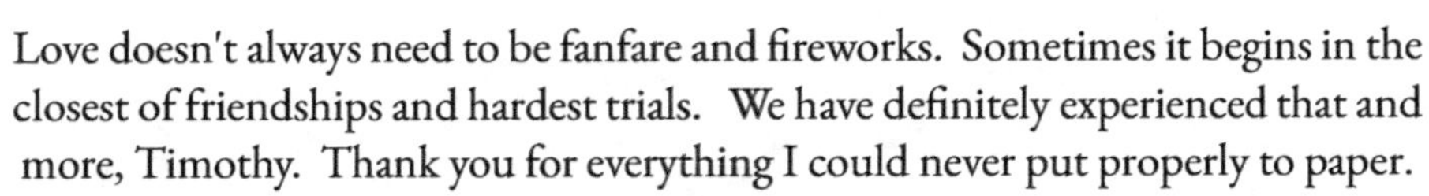

—Readers can find character bios, pictures of locations, author insights, chats about the book, and more on the author and book page—
https://www.facebook.com/profile.php?id=61572704312258

Chapter One

June 28th, 1808

Sebastian ran his calloused hand across the tops of the yellow husks and felt the smooth kernels pass between his fingertips. By all accounts, it had been another excellent year for the farm with nearly a hundred acres of wheat ready to be harvested and taken to the mill at the end of next month. "A bumper crop expected," was what the papers had proclaimed due to the excellent weather they had enjoyed since Christmas, but Sebastian knew it was more due to proper planning than anything else. The rain came and went as it always did, and the sun continued to shine. He had no control over any of that, but what he could regulate was how much work he put into the crop and how hard he needed to push his sons to get it harvested in time.

Jedidiah, his eldest son, had grown into quite a young man with a wife of his own and their first baby born just last fall, but that had not kept him from his work at the farm—quite the opposite in fact. Seeing his love for the land, Sebastian had freely given him half of the farm he owned as a wedding present last year and even helped to build the small homestead near the woods on the back corner of it. Of course, Jedidiah had initially refused the offered gift, but Sebastian had felt it was only right to do so, seeing as the land was purchased with his sons in mind before they had ever arrived in Philadelphia fifteen years ago. The other fifty acres would be Elijah's one day, if he could ever decide to sit still long enough to farm it, which at the moment was not looking too promising.

His second son was far less interested in wheat and animals than he was in helping him down at the forge. In the beginning, Sebastian had attributed his eagerness to be by his side each and every minute of the day to his absence when Elijah was younger, yet as the years passed by, it became easier and easier to see how skilled his son was becoming with every commission that came through their door. As genuinely talented as he was, it would not be long before his son would surpass even his own meager abilities and reach out to others more capable than he to learn _their_ skills.

Sebastian was fine with that. A man needed to be able to reach beyond his boundaries to motivate and stimulate both his mind and soul, or at least that was something William had told him once when he had asked for his advice on the matter. And though it was true that William had never been a father, nor was he ever likely to be so, Sebastian still relied on his wisdom on many things over the years, for the man had a keen insight into how people interacted with each other that he himself had never been able to master.

"Papa, will you be coming in for lunch?" Hope called sweetly from a few feet into the field just behind him. "Mama said to fetch you if you are."

Sebastian shaded his eyes to see her better from a distance and marveled at the way his daughter's hair almost matched the color of the summer wheat beside him. The girl had been his greatest treasure and biggest surprise fifteen years ago today and dismayed as he was at having missed even a moment of her time here on Earth, he cherished every day God had given him thereafter, as if time might wipe them all away just as quickly as they had been given him.

"I'm coming." He paid special attention to keep to the furrows between the rows so as to not upset the rich harvest that was sure to follow. "Did you come all this way just to pester me?"

Hope only smiled and laughed as she spun around within the wheat, allowing the wind to pull her long, light brown curls outward in a beautiful motion like golden waves upon a sea of honey. "Come. Dance with me, Papa, just like we used to."

Pleased beyond measure, Sebastian walked steadily towards the girl and stopped to take her hand when she spun back around to face him. "I'm afraid I am still not very skilled where dancing is concerned."

Afraid that he would stop and suddenly escape, Hope closed her hand over his calloused palm and put the other on his shoulder allowing him to take the lead. "Uncle Emile said that every woman should learn how to properly dance at least once in her life, even if we don't have the opportunity to attend any formal events like you were used to back in England."

"Uncle Emile thinks so, huh?" Sebastian rolled his eyes at the imposition but chuckled. "He would know best, I suppose, as he has had probably the most practice out of all of your uncles."

Hope laid her head on her father's shoulder and slowed down to a rhythmic sway. "All I need is for you to hold me forever, Papa. That will always be enough for me."

Sebastian wrapped his arms around the young girl and held her close as he prayed once again that God would forgive him for the decision he made years ago to support his family by his absence.

"What's wrong?" The girl within his arms prodded after turning her face suddenly upwards while examining his furrowed brow.

"Why does something have to be wrong? I was merely talking to God." Sebastian released his embrace and offered her his arm instead like any gentleman of their acquaintance would have done.

"Is that so…" The girl took his offered arm and began walking back to the whitewashed farmhouse off in the distance. "I thought that was Uncle Nathanael's job."

"What is his job?" Sebastian asked absentmindedly while walking and breathing in the warm summer air. "Praying? Well, I guess it is, but that shouldn't stop the rest of us from doing it, too."

"I know, Papa, but he just seems to do it so well, doesn't he?" The girl beamed with pride for her uncle. Out of the three, he was clearly her favorite currently as he had doted on her almost as much as Emile had done over the years. When she was little, he had kept his distance at first, not enjoying the chaotic lifestyle children often presented, but as she had matured and expanded her vocabulary, he had warmed up considerably to the girl. Probably more due to the fact that she was the only one of his children that delighted in asking him as many challenging questions as she could manage about the Bible and other random theological facts whenever he would visit.

"Nathanael does have his merits, that is true. They all do really, though I did not always think so in the past." Sebastian closed the wooden gate behind them and latched the rope around the top of the two posts securely so the cows would hopefully not escape again this week.

"Really?" The girl's eyes grew wide with astonishment. "You are all thick as thieves now. I find it rather hard to believe that you were ever <u>not</u> in agreement with the others."

"Well, the fault was entirely mine own in the beginning." Sebastian laughed at the girl's honest opinion, but also at her innocent naivety. "As you might expect,

I wasn't especially eager to make friends with any of them. All my mind cared about was getting my family to America and starting my life here."

"And so, you did." Charlotte stepped out onto the porch and wiped her hands off on her white apron before tucking the loose strands of her chestnut brown hair behind her ears. "And a wonderful life it has been, dear."

Sebastian mounted the steps in front of his wife and took her into his arms like the day they had married before turning her away from Hope to kiss her sweetly. "I would do it all over again if I had to, Mrs. Fabbri, minus a few unpleasant details along the way."

"As would I." Charlotte touched his cheek lovingly. "Now, come inside out of this heat and enjoy a cool glass of lemonade."

"Thank you." Sebastian tried his best to hide his reluctant grimace from Hope's view at the prospect of consuming yet another distasteful thing today, but he could not do so from Charlotte. Though it had indeed been years upon years since his initial transition into that of a vampire, food in any form still remained a torturous, albeit necessary normalcy, no matter how appealing Charlotte tried to make it.

"I know it is not your favorite, but it will at least wash away the dust from the fields," she tried to coax him quietly into accepting.

"Can we have a slice of my cake, too?" Hope begged her mother as she followed them into the homestead and through to the kitchen beyond. "It is my birthday, after all."

"I suppose so." Charlotte fingered the girl's loose curls and smiled. "I was saving it for tonight when everyone came for dinner, but if you are careful to take only a discreet piece, you may sneak some off the back of it. As delicious as it may be, I am sure none of your uncles would mind if you ate their share."

"Are they <u>all</u> coming for supper then?" Sebastian sat down lazily onto his favorite chair by the table and folded his hands on top of the clean linens she had placed in preparation for the evening's event.

"That is what William said in his letter. He and Nathanael will arrive around four and Emile and Emma will..." she started to explain when the door behind her opened dramatically in turn.

"They will arrive just in time for lunch." Emile took off his hat with a flip and held his hand outstretched lovingly behind Emma's waist.

"You're finally here!" The young girl almost squealed as she ran across the room and threw herself into the visitor's awaiting arms.

"I promised you I would." Emile's eyes sparkled at the welcome, obviously delighted in the reception. "The journey from Charleston took a bit longer than we had expected, but thankfully without all the calamity that occurred last time."

"That's good." Sebastian smiled weakly and stayed seated. "Anything is better than travelling here in a hurricane."

"It killed almost 500 people and destroyed thousands of dollars in crops. So, yes, I would say that was a tremendous storm," Emile replied matter-of-factly.

"And you brought Emma this time, too!" Hope hugged his wife just as tightly.

"As if he could keep me away." Emma hugged the girl right back, then used her free hand to push back the long curls from the girl's face. "You are growing into quite a beauty; you know that right?"

"I know," she said proudly and stood on her tiptoes to measure her height against that of her uncle. "See, I am almost as tall as you are now without your hat."

Sebastian shook his head at the overly dramatic display taking place in front of him and chided his guest severely, "She gets her vanity from you, I'm afraid."

"Oh, hush." Charlotte waved her husband off. "This is Hope's day, and I'll not have it ruined by the two of you battling it out verbally through supper."

"No offence taken whatsoever, Mrs. Fabbri." Emile took off his outer coat and hung it up by the door as if he had lived there all of his life. "I know when I am clearly beaten. Besides, I promised Emma I would be on my best behavior this time."

"This time...?" Sebastian grumbled and then smiled mischievously up at him over his lemonade. "I'll believe it when I see it."

"As will I," Emile shot back just as sarcastically. "Though to tell you the truth, I am personally looking forward to facing you at chess while I am here. Emma tries her best, but she lacks your vindictive spirit to crush me when it matters most and has even taken to hiding a few of the more essential pieces from time to time to discourage me from asking her to play."

"I unashamedly confess all, *Monsieur*, and I don't mind saying so. You can be a bear to live with when I manage to finally beat you," Emma replied tartly.

"Beat me?" Emile rolled his eyes in definite rebuttal. "More like compulsory surrender when you start chucking the pieces at me when you are angry with me for capturing your favorite rook."

"Please, stop." Emma placed her hand on his lower arm and smiled up at him with restrained admiration.

Sebastian smiled, too, though for very different reasons entirely. Once upon a time he had described all of his friends as being tied to one piece or another upon a great chessboard of life with their mentor, Señor Moretti, exemplifying the board itself. And for Emile, as complicated as he was back then, he had given him the distinction of being the rook. A satisfyingly complex choice, or so Señor Moretti had claimed, but one that Sebastian had initially refuted as truth. At the time, neither of them was very inclined towards seeing the worth of the other but knowing today that Emma also thought of Emile as her rook made him feel slightly vindicated now in saying so.

"Speaking of missing pieces, did I see Jedidiah out in the field as we were coming up or was that Elijah? It was too hard to tell from a distance." Emma diverted the subject curiously to another vein entirely. "Though I haven't seen either of them since Jedidiah's wedding two years ago."

"That would be Jedidiah if it was out in the pasture. Elijah is normally working in town at the forge with Thomas most days, either that or checking in the latest shipment of goods at the warehouse for William. He won't drag himself home until it is almost dark and too late to do any chores still left to be completed around the farm. That withstanding, I did make him promise me that he would be here for supper today, or else," Charlotte explained.

"I see," Emma answered sweetly and took off her dark grey cape and hung it up beside that of her husband.

"Well, speaking of town..." Sebastian began to speak slowly but then sped up his delivery considerably, hoping that the arriving visitors would provide the necessary deflection for his change of plans. "Now don't get cross with me, Charlotte, but I mistakenly told Thomas yesterday that I would tour the new building site with him this afternoon. As you know, it was supposed to be done last month, but now that it <u>is</u> nearly finished, the builders have a few questions for us that have to be decided upon today."

"Seriously, Bash... today?" Charlotte placed both of her hands upon her hips and stared him down incredulously. "Dear, we have been planning this supper for weeks. Promise me you will not miss it because you are running late <u>again</u>."

"I promise," Sebastian reassured her quickly, though his prior offenses spoke volumes otherwise.

"Hmm..." Charlotte studied him from across the room with a skeptical eye, but in the end threw her hands up in defeat as she picked up a bowl of fresh blueberries from the counter and placed it before him. "I might as well forgive you now as we both know you will be."

"Mrs. Fabbri," Sebastian seized his wife and pulled her onto his lap quickly before she could leave. "If I didn't know better, I would think you are full of spitfire and vinegar today."

"Perhaps I am." She smiled back at him playfully. "Just be sure to have an equally diverting excuse when you return, as you always do."

"<u>You</u> alone are the excuse for why I always return." Sebastian kissed her quickly then lifted her to her feet as he stood up.

"Well, see that you remember that when your dinner is cold tonight, and the cake is gone," she chided him though not harshly for she knew it was never his fault entirely when he was late. As diligent as the man was in paying the strictest attention to his responsibilities for his family and his work, he simply lacked the necessary fortitude to refuse any man his aid when something was asked of him.

"Emile... Emma... I thank you for coming all this way for Hope, but I best be off, or I will never make it back in time for the party." Sebastian walked towards the door, passing his guests on the way.

"A party? Oh, will there be dancing this time, Papa?" Hope asked eagerly from the kitchen. "Please say, yes!"

"As if we could have one without it," Emile assured her easily as he strode over to the girl, taking her quickly into his arms and spinning her around. "Have you been practicing what I taught you?"

"Just with Papa," Hope giggled.

"Then we had better put in some more practice now, so you won't embarrass yourself too terribly tonight." Emile winked at Sebastian and guided the girl easily as the two of them danced skillfully around the main room, avoiding various pieces of furniture in their way before stopping once or twice to adjust themselves when Hope forgot the next step.

"I'll make sure he behaves, Sebastian," Emma guaranteed him with a smile.

"That is a full-time job, isn't it?" He put on his lighter cloak and tightened the clasp, certain that he would need it now that the sun was high overhead.

"It can be some days." She sighed lightly, then laughed. "But I wouldn't have him any other way."

Emile only glanced back at her impishly and grinned through the various steps across the rug as he contemplated seizing her for the next round.

"Uh-oh, I've seen that look before. You had better run before you can't, Sebastian." She smiled back and shooed him out the door and off to his necessary appointment.

"Thank you, Emma. I will see you later this evening," he replied gratefully as he walked out the screen door, relieved at last to be away from the chaos unfolding behind him. With a little else on his mind other than finishing the task before him as promptly as possible, Sebastian strode down the stairs two at a time before walking briskly towards the main section of town, grateful for a bit of peace before the evening that was sure to be filled with a cacophony of noise within his home. The builders had told him earlier that day that they were finally ready for the last inspection of his new shop and with Thomas arriving last spring, he was more than ready to have the project finished and begin the new enterprise they had planned together with his former apprentice.

Besides the farm, he was already maintaining two successful businesses in town that served the community with their blacksmith services as it was. More than enough work to support one man, if not two in his estimation. Which was part of the reason why he had agreed to open the second shop to provide a path for his second oldest son, Elijah. On any given day, there was never a lack of horses needing to be shod, tools and other goods waiting to be created, and of course, nails to be steadily made to match the bursting growth of the city itself.

But this particular venture with Thomas was something surprisingly different and if he were honest, something he had been reluctant to entertain doing in the past as it went completely against his view that his trade should be more focused on the practical aspects of life. In creating specific commissions for new builders, Thomas had said that the growing population was simply begging for new adaptations of his trade, and in ways he had never contemplated before. Moreover, Elijah had agreed with this vision wholeheartedly, and together with his old apprentice, they had convinced him of its success. The only detail left to finish was to make sure the building that would house it would be completed by early fall so they could be safely inside before the harsh conditions of winter set in.

As optimistic as always, Thomas was certain that everything would be completed well ahead of schedule, but Sebastian was less inclined. The builders that they had hired had been slowing down in their progress as of late with countless excuses as to why the outer walls had not been finished per the designated schedule. Nevertheless, despite all of the countless setbacks that had plagued them for the bulk of the Spring, today was the day for the final inspection and payment in full for services rendered, which could not have come soon enough in Sebastian's mind. Just one more step before their next great adventure would begin, or at least that was what Thomas kept reminding him positively every day this month when they received yet another notice of delay.

"Have you been waiting long for me?" Sebastian asked politely as he rounded the corner and noticed Thomas leaning upon the open doorway to the newly constructed brick building behind him.

"Not terribly, only about thirty minutes. Just long enough to enjoy the view from my new window." Thomas made his way down the already worn front pathway a few feet to meet his master on the street's edge.

"So, it would appear that we have windows now." Sebastian nodded in definite approval. "Progress indeed!"

"I can't guarantee you that they will open like they should, but at least they are secure in the casements." Thomas chuckled lightly while trying to maintain his optimism.

"And you are sure this is what you want to do with your life in Philadelphia—make iron embellishments?" Sebastian held one hand over his eyes as he looked up and took in the full scope of the two-story building before him. In truth, it was not an overly large edifice like many of the newer buildings in town, but it was far grander than anything he had ever worked in, that was for sure.

"I wouldn't presume to speak of certainties under your watch, Mr. Fabbri, but I am sure I will be far more successful in this endeavor than I ever was at making swords. Though as you must know, I will always be grateful for everything that you taught me. Plus, from what I have heard from Doctor Wells, all the builders, both here and down the entire coastline, are already asking when we will be ready for them to put in their orders for this special type of enhancement. Their projects are quite literally waiting on us to be ready to begin and so the way I look at it, we will be able to ask top dollar for our work," Thomas assured him without hesitation.

"I see." Sebastian rubbed his hand along the edge of the wooden worktable in front of the building before inquiring once more. "What do they use them for again?"

"Churches, homes, stairs, gateways, government buildings—practically anything that would be augmented with a bit of flare. In fact, I've been thinking up some special designs with Hannah's help for some decorative gates and fencing. Maybe something that would feature a letter or something in nature." Thomas reached down and picked up the painted sign that had been created for the front of the building and lay it on the table before him. "Oh, and they dropped this off shortly after I arrived this afternoon. I thought you might want to see it first before I asked the men to hang it up properly on the front of the building."

Tilting his head to the side to read it better, he remarked. "At least they spelled my name right this time, though since you are going to be the majority owner of this business, perhaps they should have put your name on it first, then mine."

Sebastian held the sign up and scrutinized the angles of its construction before laying it back down once more upon the table.

"Oh, I don't know. Fabbri and Veriti has a good look to it on the sign, but honestly, maybe we should have given it a more American sounding name." Thomas' worried expression today reminded him of his own on so many other occasions in the past.

"No, Thomas," Sebastian placed one hand on the young man's shoulder with a sigh and advised him seriously, "If there is one thing I have learned in all the time I have known you, it is never to be ashamed of your heritage, man. You can run from it or even deny it, but at the end of the day, you are still who you are, so there is no use trying to hide it."

"I suppose you are right." Thomas nodded. "Besides, it's probably for the best. Hannah had a terrible time getting used to the last one. It took her months to respond when someone called her Mrs. Veriti. She kept thinking they were talking about someone else, and then people assumed she was ignoring them."

Sebastian chuckled once more at the amusing story because it suited their relationship perfectly. It was almost as enjoyable as watching the two of them interact together. Theirs had been a love match in every way even though she was a good five years older than the lad. Nevertheless, they had made it work, for what Thomas had lacked in years, he made up for in abject devotion. In every way that mattered, they rounded each other out as perfectly as anyone could have ever imagined as she kept him from most of his calamities and he protected her in her blindness.

"Well, shall we take the final tour then?" Sebastian offered, ready to be done with this task and on his way back home before he was missed too greatly.

"I thought you would never ask!" Thomas practically bubbled over with excitement and moved in front of him to lead the way towards the nearly completed building.

Hesitantly optimistic at last, Sebastian followed, but as he did, he began to feel the strangest of sensations overpower him as he glanced at the wall of the building in front of them. For the briefest moment his eyes refused to focus at all, as he studied the brick surface of the tall front but could not ascertain why. Then, with horror, he saw every facet of the calamity about to unfold as if God himself had sent him a vision.

The towering structure, which was meant to be as solidly secure as the foundation upon which it was fastened, was now swaying uncontrollably towards them. Unmistakably bowing and flexing outwards and slightly to the side as if being rocked back and forth like a toddling child.

"Thomas take care!" Sebastian shouted as he saw the entire brick facade of the outer wall waver, then begin to fall backwards towards them like a cascading waterfall of bricks and timbers.

"Sebastian!" The boy screamed, but his cries were almost muffled out completely by the groan of the beams as they pressed against each other and fractured under the weight of the sudden change.

In a short breath of a moment, Sebastian blinked twice then grasped the man by his shoulders and did the only thing he could think of to save him. Strong arms that had never wavered once in their ability to hammer down even the hardest pieces of iron steered and pushed the young man as far as they could into the space beyond the open doorway, away from the dust and debris descending rapidly on top of them both. Then, with a belch of dust and a horrible groan, the entire building collapsed around them, leaving behind only a horrible and agonizing muted quietness in its wake.

In the silence that quickly followed as the world took in its breath once more, calls from the other workers struggling to free themselves inside the building filled it for many minutes until once again the afternoon returned to the peaceful atmosphere it once held.

Surprisingly only covered in just a few pieces of debris and some broken glass that had caused a small gash that ran along his forehead, Thomas picked himself up from the wooden floor within and shook his head to clear it as the dust flew outwards in all directions from his hair. "Sebastian?"

Not a soul answered.

Dazed and more than a little disorientated, Thomas turned back towards the street from whence he had just come and surveyed the rubble in front of him for signs of his master but saw no one. Not even a hand or piece of fabric could be seen poking up through all the mangled beams and bricks. It was almost as if his master had vanished almost as quickly as he had appeared on the island years ago.

"Mr. Fabbri!" Thomas yelled frantically in panic and began digging through the heavy timbers from the building's second floor facade. "Someone help me please!"

Workers that were barely managing to remain vertical themselves and people passing by on the street who had seen the building fall now rushed to his aid and helped remove brick after brick until Thomas at last saw the first vestiges of the familiar black cloak and patched brown overcoat his master always wore. "He is over here! We need to dig here! Quickly!" Thomas shouted as he wiped away the tears that were now streaming down his dirty cheeks, causing long streaks in the dark grit on his face.

A large, ten-foot solid section of the wall that had remained for the most part oddly intact, was now lying horizontally to what was left of the building. Yet more importantly, it was also now covering at least two thirds of the man beneath it, no doubt crushing him under its weight. With blocks of wood and levers in hand, men raced frantically from the back of the property to prop it up just enough for Thomas to pull Sebastian's crumpled and contorted body out to safety from underneath it.

Once free and able to draw in oxygen at last, Sebastian's eyes opened only halfway in response as he stared up blankly at the sky and blinked. "Thomas? You're bleeding?"

"I'm fine, truly." Thomas coughed some of the dust out of his lungs and tried to push back a few clumps of hair that had fallen across the top of Sebastian's face.

"Good," Sebastian answered, but it was clear that he was still struggling just to take in a full breath. "I need Elijah."

"Of course. Go get Elijah Fabbri over at the forge down the street!" Thomas ordered the man next to him, then yelled again with even more force. "Run, man! Run!"

Without hesitation, the man took off at a dead sprint and returned only minutes later with a panting and visibly shaken Elijah. "I'm here, Papa. I'm here." Elijah took his father's large hand within his own and held it close to his chest, unable to control the fear rising within him at the obvious fragility of the man lying on the ground next to him.

"What a fine man you have become, my Elijah." Sebastian squeezed his hand once, then added more quietly, "I am so very proud of you."

"Oh. Papa," Elijah hung his head to hide the tears that were now flowing freely. "Just hold on. Someone will go fetch Uncle William, Papa." He turned to call someone to get a wagon, but Sebastian interrupted him by placing his weak hand on top of his own.

"Shhh... it's too late for all that, son." He drew in several ragged gasps and coughed as he strained to not choke on the fluid now filling his lungs. "Just stay with me for now. Keep me company."

"I'm so sorry, Mr. Fabbri. I didn't know..." Thomas apologized over and over again as he wept, feeling the guilt of Sebastian's sacrifice washing over him time and again.

"Oh, Thomas," Sebastian turned to him and smiled. "You remember what they used to say about you at the docks?" He asked slowly before coughing twice, bringing with it the horrible gurgling sound once more of his lungs trying to rake in more air without success.

"That the day hadn't begun until I fell down in some way." Thomas struggled to keep his composure remembering their long hours working together over the years.

"Guess today was my turn." Sebastian grinned and drew in another tortured, rasping jerk of air. "You said then that you would be surprised if you made it to twenty."

"I've managed to make it almost twice that long thanks to you and Hannah," Thomas tried to sound optimistic amidst his grief.

"Yes, you have." Sebastian closed his eyes slowly then opened them once more, only this time with a look of panic as he fought to remain conscious.

"Papa..." Elijah gripped his hand tightly and ran his other hand down the side of his head. "You can't die like this. You promised me you would never leave, remember?"

"I know." Sebastian tilted his head towards his son's hand and sighed at the love emanating from it. "Promises are meant to be kept, but not at the expense of hurting others, son. Tell your sister I am sorry, and that you three are the best thing I have _ever_ made in my lifetime. Will you do that?"

Elijah jerked his head up and down quickly but could not force himself to speak anymore.

"Good," Sebastian drew in another garbled breath halfway then relaxed as a remarkable look of peace finally came over all his features. "I love you, son. Never forget that. And tell your mother... I'll be waiting... for her... this time," he said as the last word trailed off into a whisper.

"I love you, too, Papa," Elijah pledged faithfully and watched as the light in his father's eyes finally left him, leaving behind only silence in its absence.

"Rest in peace, Mr. Fabbri," Thomas added mournfully as he placed Sebastian's other hand on top of his body and respectfully closed his eyes.

Chapter Two

June 28th, 1808

From the chair positioned just to the left of the wide screen door, William looked out it once more, expecting to see his friend casually walking up the worn road like he always did after a day of work, but still nothing was there but the long grasses that lined the road. When he had arrived with Nathanael just before supper, Charlotte had explained simply that her husband may be a little late due to some necessary business in town, but for some strange reason he could still not shake the foreboding feeling that had come over him since earlier that afternoon.

"Like someone walking on your grave," his grandmother used to call those ominous feelings when they hit her. Yet today, he prayed more than ever that the morbid sensation would just go away once and for all and leave him be. It wasn't like he had not felt them before, probably countless times over when walking the halls at the hospital and even a few times when he was back in Wakefield, but this time it was different somehow, for never before had it been so strong, or caused him more than a passing notice.

For the better part of the afternoon, he had spent his time busily making several crucial house calls, as was his required rotation for the hospital every Tuesday and had only bumped into Nathanael out of pure chance. As it had turned out, his friend was on his way back from a sympathy call himself and the two had most inadvertently met at the very same home. This funny coincidence <u>had</u> made it much easier for them to arrive together for Hope's birthday celebration as it did not necessitate going back to their flat before coming. Yet as convenient as that may be, it unfortunately had not also guaranteed that they would arrive on time.

As a rule, William hated being late in any form of the phrase, and Nathanael knew it, but his prayers could not be rushed. Thus, making the slight delay only marginally acceptable since God was the one instigating it.

"No sign of Sebastian?" Nathanael eyed him from across the room as he sat at the table waiting patiently for all to arrive so the party could commence properly.

"No." William shook his head and tried not to look too worried about his absence. It wasn't like this had never happened before, and no doubt, it would occur several times more in his lifetime, but today the lack of his presence coupled with the odd experience this afternoon unnerved him doubly so.

"Did you say that you and Emma had really decided to sell your bakery?" Nathanael asked Emile in an effort to distract everyone to a different topic of discussion.

"Yes, though a part of me will hate to leave it behind if we do. It has been extremely successful; much more than I had ever dreamt it could be. So much so that we have had a sincere difficulty in keeping up with the demand." Emile gave Nathanael what he thought the man was looking for, though it was not heartfelt. There were actually many reasons why they were considering selling, but most of them involved much more information than Emile was comfortable sharing, and all concerned his wife. It was his fault, after all, that she had been brought into this world of theirs in the first place, and if that meant a few sacrifices on his part to protect her along the way, so be it.

"Don't let him fool you, Nathanael." Emma broke in after him, placing a hand on the man's shoulder. "What my husband is not saying is how much he has missed all of _you_ over the years."

William smiled. "We've missed you, too, friend. Though probably more due to your witty sarcasm than your cooking."

"Hey, I managed to keep us all alive in Wakefield with no complaints," Emile defended.

"Barely," William mumbled, then cast another side glance out the window.

Still no Sebastian or even Elijah or Thomas.

"Don't take it too personally, Emile. The rest of us couldn't do any better," Nathanael admitted from his place at the table and studied the chessboard over Hope's shoulder. "Are you going to take your turn?"

Emile eyed his friend from across the way and raised one eyebrow in a poised response. "In time. I have to at least make it look like she is winning."

"Ugh," Hope huffed and narrowed her eyes at her uncle.

With a roll of his eyes, Emile ignored her antics and answered his friend more truthfully this time, "Fact is, I believe it is time to put away the apron and put on a different sort of costume for the moment." Emile played with his knight before moving it across the board and surreptitiously seized Hope's last pawn.

"That's not fair!" The young girl pouted. "I thought you were supposed to be nice to me on my birthday."

"*Au contraire*." Emile shook his head. "Would you prefer that I let you win so easily?"

"No... but I let you win on <u>your</u> birthday last year," the girl grumbled as she scrunched up her face and studied the board more intently before the light in her eyes suddenly shone as she moved her bishop in a diagonal line and seized his queen on the opposite side of the board. "Check!"

"Excellent, Hope." Emile smiled back at her fondly. "Bravo! And with your bishop no less."

"I thought it rather fitting to have my bishop bring you to ruin and shame." She raised her eyebrows roguishly in an absolute mimic of himself.

"He does always have a knack for coming out on top. Your bishop that is... or were you referring to your Uncle Nathanael?" Emile moved his king one square over but then toppled him onto his side. "I yield. A just win, after all."

"Maybe we should just start supper now. I am afraid if we wait much longer it will all be too cold," Charlotte said sadly and folded her arms across her chest in disappointment.

"Please don't be too put out on our account..." William began to comfort her but stopped as his ears picked up the unmistakable sound of a wagon along the road. Turning his head in its direction, he glanced back out the window towards it again to judge for himself but was surprised by what he saw. The wagon with the long bed in the back heading up the lane was not Sebastian's at all, but someone else entirely.

Confused, he studied the rig carefully and made out the distinct figures of Elijah and Thomas who both appeared to be slumped forward on the buckboard as they drove the team of horses slowly, not bothering to rush whatsoever in their approach to the house as if they had all the time in the world to reach it. "Well, at least the boys are here. Maybe that means Sebastian will be following close behind them."

"Good. I'm starved!" Jedidiah said finally and went to the kitchen to help his mother bring over the necessary plates and silverware.

Eager to see his favorite nephew and do anything but sit there in that chair any longer, William opened the door and stepped out onto the porch to greet him.

As busy as he had been at the hospital this week, he had not been able to fit in even a casual coffee break with Elijah as he stoked his forge in the morning, something he often did at least two times every week if not more, making him secretly hope that tonight would more than compensate for his absence.

The polar opposite of his father, Elijah, was always openly ecstatic to share every aspect of his life whenever they chatted, filling the conversation with lots of interesting stories about his patrons to distract William from the more tiresome aspects of his life at the hospital. Maybe tonight he would even have some news about the delayed shipment that was supposed to arrive from England last week, though he highly doubted it. The recent turmoil back home had caused more than a little wrinkle in the business the two of them shared. Nevertheless, despite all the annoying setbacks of late, they were managing it tolerably well at the present.

"Looks like you made it just in time," William called to him as he watched the wagon pull up across from him and the two men dismount—a marked heaviness controlling their every movement. "We almost had to eat the cake without you."

"No one is eating the cake before I do!" Hope's animated laughter echoed back to him through the screen door, filled with the pure joy she always seemed to possess no matter what occasion presented itself.

"See." William smiled at her effervescent spirit then stopped when the look on Elijah's face froze him cold. "Is something wrong, Elijah?" William inquired worriedly, the errant feeling of dread that had been plaguing him all day rushing up to him from the wagon.

Neither Elijah nor Thomas moved an inch in response.

"Um... Emile..."

"Yes?" Emile answered him casually from within the house.

"I think you had best come out here," William said calmly as he called back towards the door and slowly took the necessary two steps towards the porch stairs and walked down them.

Unable to say a word, Elijah finally looked up at him with a grave expression that told him everything he needed to know, something he never truly considered would happen to any of them, at least not this soon.

With an even greater hesitance, William glanced over the young man's shoulder and could see plainly now into the back of the wagon, the motionless Sebastian, half-covered with a woolen grey blanket, a grey pallor already covering his normally olive-tanned complexion. "Ohhh, Elijah..." He exhaled as he shook his head back and forth slowly in compassion.

"What's the matter now? Does Sebastian need help with the horses?" Emile asked as he exited the building before stopping dead in his tracks at the same shocking scene.

"Is Mama inside?" Elijah managed to finally say, though his throat was too constricted to utter anything more.

"I'll go fetch her," Emile replied quietly, a lump forming in his throat as he turned around to retrieve Sebastian's wife without delay.

"What happened?" William placed one hand on the boy's shoulder to comfort him, for he knew how close the young man had been with his father.

"There was... an accident in town. The new ironworks building collapsed on top of him," Thomas spoke up for him. "He pushed me out of the way in time, but he could not save himself."

"I see." William hung his head and closed his eyes thinking deeply about what he had just been told, while also realizing how appropriate the manner in which he had died had been to Sebastian's demeanor. "Loyal to the last, my friend," he whispered quietly as if he were speaking to his dear friend once more.

"Yes," Elijah's voice broke as he began to openly cry, completely unashamed about whoever might see him do it. It was the same gut-wrenching ache that had not left him for the past hour, nor could he manage to stop the racking sobs now that they had begun again.

Taking in fully the young man's unrestricted grief, William's heart instantly broke for him as his own sorrow matched it in tenor and compassion. "Come here, Eli." William drew him into a tight embrace and held him there as he cried, wishing that if by some miracle he could have swapped places with Elijah in some way and spared him even a fraction of the grief he was now enduring.

In the moments that followed, the screen door opened and closed behind him time after time again, signaling the arrival of the rest of the family as they joined them outside and hurried down to the wagon, shock and bewilderment filling their faces before the overwhelming spectre of grief and mourning replaced it again and again.

Only Hope remained steadfastly motionless on the porch with Emile close by her side, a solitary witness in the shadows as she chose to remain as far away from the very thing she obviously most dreaded.

"No! No! No!" Charlotte cried as she was helped into the wagon and held her husband's face close to her own, the sheer suddenness of his passing tearing at her like none other save perhaps that of her little Sarah's. "Please Bash, please no... not now..." She wept but knew the truth of it as the fingers that she longed would close over her hand and hold it once more never moved. Like most wives, she had often held an irrational fear that this day might someday occur before her own. She had even had more than a few nightmares about it while he had been away on the island. But now that the fateful moment had finally arrived, she found herself no less ready to accept it, though she had been given years to prepare herself for the inevitable event.

The grim scene and all the grief that went along with it unfolded itself many times over as the hours passed, each person making their peace with his untimely departure before Nathanael had been able to encourage everyone to bring his body into the barn for the night and wait until morning to prepare him for burial. Final arrangements would need to be made, and others notified of his passing, but for now, the party that everyone had been longing for was over. No food would be eaten. No laughter enjoyed. No dances given. No songs sung. Only heartache and tears had been commonly shared before everyone went off to their collective rooms or homes to try to sleep, as if that were even possible tonight. All that is except for Emile and Hope, who still sat in her father's favorite chair like a stunned deer, unable or rather unwilling to be persuaded to move anywhere.

"Hope, you must at least try to sleep. Your father wouldn't want you to make yourself sick at his expense," Emile tried to reason with her gently, to coax her with passive logic towards what he knew was best for the girl, yet she steadfastly resisted—not in outright stubbornness, but in shocked focus on the barn just outside, breathing so shallowly that Emile could scarcely tell if she was drawing in a breath at all.

With a drained sigh of true understanding, Emile stood and brought the prepared cake to the table along with a singular candle before lighting it unceremoniously, then pausing thereafter to allow its solitary flame to flicker in the darkness surrounding them as it illuminated only the two remaining at the table.

In the soft glow of the bright orange light, Hope only stared back at him with even wider, almost defiant eyes—staunchly incredulous as to the purpose for his actions.

"You might as well blow it out. No sense letting a perfectly good pastry go to waste, child," he said seriously, but firmly, the gentle command in his voice evident.

"Huh... you honestly expect me to make a wish?" The girl almost sneered at the mere suggestion and crossed her arms across her chest tightly, an action that might have looked confrontational on the surface, but in the dimly lit room, only served to make her look more fragile.

"No," Emile answered carefully, choosing to keep his conversation brief and casual. "We both know what our wish would be, but since that is not possible, perhaps we should just blow it out and leave it at that."

"Fine." The girl obeyed slowly like someone still stuck in a horrible trance and blinked twice as he followed the short action by handing her a fork after keeping one for himself.

Still appalled by the very thought of participating in whatever façade he was trying to support, she shook her head and at once her face returned to the cold, hard expression he had remembered her father wearing in the cave when he told him of his plans to go for a walk. "Happy birthday to me."

"Indeed, Hope." Emile pursed his lips at the curt sarcasm yet allowed the girl the necessary time to process her emotions for he knew she was not the least bit upset at her father for dying on her birthday, nor was she callous enough to blame him for it.

Choosing to ignore everything else that was taking place around him, he lifted his fork like the seasoned actor that he always was and dug it in slightly to the side of the cake before pulling out a small portion of the center and tasted it. "It's a little dry, but it's still edible."

"Seriously?" Hope rolled her eyes sullenly at the faulty assessment, knowing full-well that the cake was delicious because she had made it herself earlier that morning. "You only hate it because you did not bake it yourself." She took a forkful of the cake indignantly and tried it, wanting to prove her mentor wrong.

His ruse had worked as at least she was now talking, if only to argue. Patiently waiting thereafter for her honest response, Emile raised both his eyebrows in an unspoken question. "And...?"

Hope sighed in defeat. "Okay, you are right. It _is_ a little dry."

"I told you so." Emile smiled, but not out of satisfaction, more out of hopeful anticipation that she might be starting to come out of her slightly catatonic state.

"It doesn't really matter now anyway. No one is going to eat it after what happened today." She shook her head at his gloating and sampled another portion. "Besides, Papa wouldn't have complained even if it _was_ dry."

"Your father wasn't a cook," Emile replied quickly, wanting very much to smile at the memory of his friend, but everything inside of him felt more inclined to cry.

Hope sighed. "No, no he isn't." Her breath caught unexpectedly, her voice barely audible now as she quietly added, "...wasn't."

"Hope, dear, I know you may not believe this, coming from me, after all, but there are many things that I have admired about your father over the years, his baking notwithstanding. In fact, if I were to be completely honest, I would probably have to say that I have been most jealous of him many times over these past fifteen years, if not outright envious of everything he has accomplished." Emile licked his fork and placed it down upon the table, deciding he had had enough of the confection to please the girl.

"Jealous of Papa? Why? You are nothing like him at all. You have a successful business, a beautiful wife, you travel to lots of interesting places. What could Papa possibly have that you could ever want? Certainly not this farm, or even the forge. Do you even know how to milk a cow?" She laid her fork down on the table next to his and crossed her arms in front of her chest for warmth as the evening breeze had cooled considerably since Elijah had arrived.

Seeing the unmistakable shiver commencing across her shoulders, Emile stood and retrieved his suit coat from off its peg and wrapped it around the girl's shoulders. "Oh, I know my way around the bovine species well enough to get my milk and butter, young lady, but that was not why I was jealous."

"Then, why?" She asked innocently.

"He had you, silly." Emile affectionately tapped the tip of her nose lightly, then took a seat next to her once more.

"Thank you." Hope smiled. "I love you, too, Uncle Emile... as did Papa."

"Oh?" Emile's brow perked up at the very suggestion. "Are you sure?"

"Of course." Hope looked down at the table and then across the room until her eyes fell on her father's cherished guitar by the fireplace. "Since as far back as I can recall, I remember him playing that guitar for us in the evenings after supper. Sometimes he would even tell us stories about his life back in England or what his life was like on the island with Mr. Thomas. But on other occasions, I would just sit and watch him as he read one of your letters by the firelight after a long day at work and the smile that would come across his face as he read them was something so incredibly genuine, Uncle Emile. Something entirely different than the way his face looked when he talked with Uncle William or even Uncle Nathanael."

"He was probably humored more that I was still able to annoy him after all this time." Emile tried to deflect the intensity of what she was saying, but his throat felt tight and his chest equally heavy to hear it.

"No." Hope laid her hand on top of his gently. "He really <u>did</u> love you."

"It's kind of you to say, Hope." Emile grinned at the young woman's easy acceptance of him and her gift under such horrible circumstances. "Now, is there something <u>I</u> can do for you tonight, or are you planning on sitting at this table until sun-up? If so, I will happily remain here with you until then. I won't like it... but I will do it, for <u>you</u>," he playfully teased, but in a way that was endearing and sincere, hoping that she would accept his help and get the rest she so greatly needed.

For a long moment, Hope said nothing at all as she looked back out the screen door once more and over to the barn beyond dreading the pull that drew her to it. "He is really out there, isn't he? This isn't all just part of some horrible dream that I'll wake up from tomorrow?"

"Yes, he is there." Emile licked his dry lips and chose his words very carefully. "As much as I would love to tell you that he isn't, I can't." His heart tore in two just uttering the words out loud as if saying them made his friend's death more of a reality than it already was. "And no, I wouldn't wish this kind of dream on anyone, let alone you."

"Then..." She hesitated briefly before adding once more in an almost whispered tone, "Would you go with me to say good-bye? I couldn't do it in front of all the others. They wouldn't understand."

Without a word, Emile stood up and held his left hand out to her as he waited until she accepted it.

Instantly frightened once more at the possibility, even though she had just requested it, a single tear slid down Hope's cheek as she stared at the offered object for several long seconds, inwardly warring against herself to remain. "How do I even move?"

"By taking just one step at a time, Hope. We will go at your pace," Emile reassured her.

Hope nodded, then lifted her hand hesitantly to grasp his and allowed him to direct her slowly out of the house and across the yard over to the wooden barn opposite the house. Then, before pulling back the large door in front of the enclosed wagon, Emile paused and asked, "Are you ready?"

"No." Hope held her breath. "Can someone ever be ready for something like this?"

Emile pursed his lips and shook his head. "No. It is not a path anyone <u>wants</u> to take. I lost my own father when I was just a little older than yourself, and I still remember the moment I walked up to his bed and said goodbye like it was yesterday. Not a single second of it has ever left my memory, but it <u>has</u> gotten a little easier to bear since—not acceptable by any means, mind you. It never is. The ache that is left behind only becomes more manageable to endure as each day passes."

"So, you are saying that one day I won't feel like every breath I am taking is tearing me apart?" Hope held his hand firmly, trying to draw upon his strength with every beat of her heart.

"I wouldn't presume to say so. Every person is different in how they grieve. I can only speak for myself." Emile tried to comfort her just a little but remained entirely honest, for he knew how difficult it had been for Nathanael when Elsie had died and how much sorrow he had endured when his friend Jonathan had been killed during the revolution back in France. Not to mention the many other deaths he had witnessed over the years.

"I understand," Hope answered remotely then summoned the courage to pull back the door quickly and gasped as the light from their candle illuminated the darkness. Like being hit with a jolt of fresh anguish, Hope's breath caught at seeing her father lying there once more, unable to hold her in his tight embrace or feel the warmth of his smile from across the room as he read to her the letters from his friends both here and abroad. It was almost as if the joy she had once felt within her had suddenly been ripped from her along with his passing tonight, leaving only a hollow emptiness in its wake, like a shadow of who she once was or a precursor of what she would steadily become if she remained.

"Here, let me help you up." Emile lifted her easily into the back of the wagon and waited below as she approached her father and tentatively reached for his stiff hand before holding it close to her cheek at last. Then, as she had done on so many other occasions before when she would find him asleep while reading in his chair downstairs, Hope pulled the blanket higher up underneath his neck as if the action would help him in any way tonight and touched his cold cheek, the one which hours earlier, had been lovingly placed upon her head as they danced in the field. Running her hand along the contours of his loving arms, she felt the strong muscles they contained and longed for one more embrace, yet she knew it would never come.

"He was an excellent father, Hope," Emile comforted her quietly. "And you meant the world to him from the first moment he laid eyes on you. You all did. You know that, right?"

Hope nodded quickly and fought even harder against the tears that had been threatening to spill over since his body had arrived.

"Hope?" From the outer shadows of the yard, Elijah stepped silently into the barn behind them carrying a small lantern and climbed slowly into the buckboard next to her after handing it to his uncle. "I'm so sorry."

Desperate now for some kind of connection at last, Hope reached for his hand and clung to it on top of her father's chest. "There is nothing for you to apologize for, Eli." Hope sniffed and breathed in deeply. "You didn't do this."

"I know, but that is what Papa said to me before he died. Tell Hope I am sorry." Elijah drew the edges of his mouth back several times as he struggled to maintain his composure next to her.

"Really?" Hope's shoulders heaved up and down twice as she struggled under the weight of knowing that her father's last thoughts were of her. "Did he say anything else?" Hope's eyes brimmed over with ready tears.

"That we were the best thing he has ever made." Elijah began weeping once more as he remembered the look on his father's face as he passed. "He said 'I love you', too. He said it to me, but I know he meant it for all of us. Those were the last words he spoke on this Earth. His love for all of us, Hope."

Overwhelmed at last, Hope buried her face in her father's chest and sobbed. "I love you, too, Papa—always and forever. There will <u>never</u> be another man quite like you."

"No, there won't. He was the best of all of us." Elijah placed his hand upon her back to support her, but it did nothing to subside the racking sobs that were now finally overtaking her like waves of anguished despair. Consumed by his own grief, as well, Elijah moved down and allowed Emile the opportunity to climb up into the wagon beside Hope, knowing that he was the only other man beside his father who truly understood her.

"He is at peace now, Hope. We can take comfort in that at least." Emile tried to provide the guidance she needed at this time though everything inside of him also felt as unsteady as a vessel lost in a storm. Since the moment that he had stepped onto the porch tonight, a part of him that had always kept him feeling confident and resolute had disintegrated into the wind around him without his permission. To everyone else in their group, their strained friendship had seemed tense and guarded at times as they verbally taunted the other over the years, but in many ways, they had also shared a common fortitude together as if it were the two of them alone that were holding the four friends solidly together. In truth, it was a piece of him that he was desperately wanting to have back now, if for only a moment.

Sebastian would never have believed him if he had told him today when he had arrived that it was he who had inspired him in his marriage to Emma or that it was his faithful endurance through such a difficult past that had helped him to come to terms with his own failings. He probably would have even blown off the praise like he had for so many other things he was truly worthy of, but did not wish to be recognized. In many ways, Sebastian was his example for countless things in his life, though he would never have told the man of it. Yet with the finality of seeing him lying here so helplessly still in the wagon next to him, everything inside of him longed to pour it all out into the open along with Hope's flowing tears.

"I know...: Hope nodded several times hypnotically at his honest statement but continued to weep well after Elijah had long left them behind to return to his own bed, and the soft sounds of crickets and peepers in the pond beside the barn echoed loudly.

Sensing Hope was finally nearing the point of total exhaustion; Emile carefully pulled her away from Sebastian and coaxed gently. "Why don't you try to go inside and lie down for a little while, please. I promise, he will still be here when you wake up."

"Alright," her voice trailed off weakly, utterly spent both emotionally and physically by the ordeal. "I'll try." She grasped the wooden planks on the side of the wagon and attempted to stand up in a daze and leave the father she adored but tottered on her feet and almost fell in her fatigued state.

"No, you don't." Emile seized her quickly and steadied her before jumping easily down from the wagon and lifting the girl ably into his arms, not trusting her for a moment to allow her to leave his sight.

"I _can_ walk." She tried to protest feebly but was not convincing in any way towards her faulty assessment.

"I am sure you can, but you are not going to, not tonight anyways. You can exercise your superhuman strength tomorrow if you like." He stepped out of the barn and used his shoulder to close the door behind him as he carried her back to the house slowly.

"I can't..." Hope began to protest weakly once more several moments after they had passed the old water pump and were already almost back to the house.

"You can't what?" Emile continued walking without delay, putting the necessary distance between what felt like a chasm between life and death.

"I can't sleep in that house knowing he is all alone out there in the barn." She began weeping uncontrollably once more without any sign of abatement.

Conflicted as to what was the right thing to do under these unusual circumstances while also knowing that she would wake the whole house in this state, Emile stopped, looked down at the precious bundle in his arms, then turned around and walked back in the direction of the barn without reply.

"Where are we going now?" Hope asked faintly, afraid she had possibly said something that had finally upset him, after all.

"You're right. Your father shouldn't be alone tonight. We will simply have to sleep in the loft above him."

"Thank you, Uncle." Hope clung to his shirt and tried to control her ragged breathing to a more controlled state. "I'm sorry. I'm getting your fine shirt all wet."

"Really?" Emile laughed lightly, grateful that at least some of her humor had finally begun to return. "I dare say, it will dry soon enough, my dear."

Stepping inside the barn once more, he made his way past the wagon quickly on his path over to the ladder on the other side and climbed ably up after her before collapsing onto the pile of sweet hay that had been brought in last year for the cows, eager for just a moment to collect his many conflicting thoughts.

In the ensuing silence that followed thereafter, the two lay in the quietness of the loft side by side and stared up at the beams for almost an hour until Hope's soft voice drifted back to him once more in the moonlit darkness. "Did you and Papa really not get along when you first met?"

"Um-hmm," Emile chuckled, then looked over at the girl, trying very hard to be as discreet as possible with the truth that mattered very little now in the greater scheme of things. "What did your father tell you?"

"That he wasn't particularly interested in making friends when you all met." She replied simply leaving all judgement of the matter firmly behind her.

"Oh, Hope..." Emile laughed lightly once more at Sebastian's overly simplistic explanation and partial lie. "Let's just say we were both not interested in making friends when we first met. I wanted to get back to France just as soon as I could find a boat to take me, and your father was only interested in taking care of you or at least your mama and your brothers for he did not know you existed at the time."

"I see." She lay there for several quiet moments more before asking yet another question, only this time with a great more hesitancy, "Do you think Mama might let me come live with you and Emma for a little while? Maybe just until the fall?"

Surprised and more than a little bit concerned at her sudden change in subjects, Emile raised his eyebrows, contemplating the request warily before actually responding, "Don't you think it might be too hard for her to lose both of you at once? You wouldn't want her to grieve your father without you."

"No, I wouldn't." Hope closed her eyes and released a drawn-out sigh that sounded full of despair more than actual relief. "I know she needs all of us right now more than ever, but I just don't know how I can survive every day seeing him everywhere around me and yet knowing he is never coming back."

"I understand completely." Emile turned his head towards her and watched as she struggled to hold back her fresh grief at the prospect before finally adding, "Alright...I'll speak with your mother about it after the funeral, but I can't make any promises. And your aunt may have something to say, too, so don't make any plans as of yet."

Hope nodded and rolled onto her side to hide her fresh tears.

Emile did, too, but chose to lay one hand on the girl's shoulder as he soothed her at a distance. "Let it out, Hope. Let it all out."

With a final release of the guttural grief that was overwhelming them all, the girl obediently complied and spent the rest of the night crying until she eventually spent herself and drifted off to fitful sleep.

Chapter Three

June 29th, 1808

"Friends and family who have gathered today," Nathanael cleared his throat for the second time as he opened his Bible to the passage he had selected to read under the large oak tree and began. "In Thessalonians chapter four it says:

> *But I would not have you to be ignorant, brethren, concerning them which are asleep, that ye sorrow not, even as others which have no hope. For if we believe that Jesus died and rose again, even so them also which sleep in Jesus will God bring with him. For this we say unto you by the word of the Lord, that we which are alive and remain unto the coming of the Lord shall not prevent them which are asleep. For the Lord himself shall descend from heaven with a shout, with the voice of the archangel, and with the trump of God: and the dead in Christ shall rise first: Then we which are alive and remain shall be caught up together with them in the clouds, to meet the Lord in the air: and so shall we ever be with the Lord. Wherefore comfort one another with these words.*

And these words <u>are</u> a comfort to us indeed as we remember the life of Sebastiano Marcus Fabbri. A man who humbly served his family and friends each and every day of his short life to the fullest of his Earthly potential. A servant to his trade and a master to others, but also a loving encourager to all three of his children, not to mention a man who cared for his wife as dearly as his own soul."

Nathanael closed his Bible and looked at Emile and William who stood just behind Sebastian's family before continuing. "This life is indeed filled with great uncertainty. And from viewing this death today, we are reminded once more that we are not promised a day, nor even the briefest of moments on this Earth. Sebastian understood this truth better than most men, and he made the decision years ago to cherish the importance of each second God had given him through his hard work on this farm, as well as in all his other business endeavors.

It is also in times like these that we often consider other very difficult questions in our need to justify the sadness overwhelming our hearts: Where is God's justice in this death? Or why would a loving God allow this to happen? We are tempted to believe errantly that God has possibly forgotten our plight. That in His distraction, He has looked away from us in some way or is punishing our disobedience in another. But I encourage you not to dwell on seeking those futile answers or give place to those most unworthy of thoughts. We should instead focus on what we know about our God in Sebastian's death for He is also the Father to the fatherless. The Great Comforter to all those who are sorrowful. The Healer of our very souls. Moreover, He does not ask us to walk this difficult path ahead of us alone, nor does He seek vengeance for any wrong we might have committed against Him. No, He has promised to do as He has said in the Psalms. He will be our Shepherd. He will lead us in the times that are filled with blessings as well as in the times of great pain. And in doing so, He will also restore us. This gives us all the confidence that we need to not fear whatever death may bring."

He paused and looked up at William in earnest before continuing. "For though we walk in this dark valley but for a season, we shall fear no evil. Why? Because our God is with us. Because He has prepared a much better place for us when our journey is over. Because, as His children, we are assured of a home in Heaven with Him some day. These are the truths we claim about our God, and these are the things that comfort us most in light of the senseless tragedies that befall us."

Nathanael placed his Bible close to his chest as he reached down for a handful of rich brown dirt before tossing it gently upon the plain wooden coffin in the freshly dug hole beside him. "'Thou shalt come to thy grave in a full age, like as a shock of corn cometh in in his season.' I bid you farewell, my friend, but not in a forever kind of goodbye, but from one who knows beyond a shadow of a doubt that we <u>shall</u> see each other again once more in heaven. God speed the time between now and then, for I shall miss you greatly." He stepped aside and allowed everyone else that was attending the same moment to pay their respects, as well.

Like a silent moving line, one after the other they each filed by in unison: first his workers and acquaintances from back in town and Thomas and Hannah, then each of his children and Jedidiah's wife, Nancy, before Charlotte stepped forward and simply blew him a kiss then turned away quickly, unable to dwell any longer as Emma led her away in tears to comfort her back at the house. In the end, it was only William and Emile who stood in the silence next to him beside the grave, joining their friend in his reverent vigil.

"It was a good message, Nathanael," William said quietly through tightened lips while trying his best to control the quiver still present in the candor of his voice. "Sebastian would have been happy to hear it."

"Oh, I am sure he did." Nathanael set his Bible down a few steps away from where Charlotte and the others had been sitting and picked up one of the shovels from next to the tree. "Though oddly enough, I also could not help but be reminded of the last time all of us did this together not that long ago."

"Really?" William's head perked up in curiosity. "When was that?"

"Back at the castle, the day when we had to bury poor Rebecca." Nathanael's shovel dug deep into the loose soil and lifted it easily as he placed it on top of the pine box before him.

"Huh, I don't remember that at all." Emile walked over to the oak and picked up the other shovel to help him.

"You were unconscious at the time, I'm afraid." William did the same before adding more correctly, "It was just Sebastian and I that dug that grave. Nathanael waited with you by the wall in case you woke up and were suddenly... oh, how do I say this nicely?" He paused as he searched for the right word before continuing on in his work. "...unpredictable?"

Emile nodded, remembering the night he had killed the innocent girl down in the village and his time at the castle thereafter. "Well, then it is the least I can do to help you both today." He set to work piling shovel after shovel full of dirt on top of the grave like a man earnestly attacking his task. Or rather, as one who was trying to manage a war against something attacking him deep within.

Stunned at his sudden exuberance to the task before him, Nathanael and William both paused to watch him in intense concentration while also cautiously remaining to one side, allowing him the opportunity to do most of the work.

"Um, speaking of being unpredictable, would it be too dangerous to ask what is eating at you today, Emile?" William probed hesitantly, though he was partially certain he already knew at least some of the probable answer. "If it is about

Sebastian, I am sure he forgave you years ago for everything between you. Or is that not what is bothering you?"

"I wish." Emile appeared to ignore his question completely, focusing his efforts instead on shoveling feverishly for three minutes more before he finally hesitated and looked over at the two men with a shake of his head. "That is <u>not</u> it at all, quite the opposite in fact. I'd welcome the chance to banter with the man even in death if he would allow me." Emile chuckled darkly and dropped another shovel full of dirt into the mostly filled hole. "Isn't that right, old man?" He looked down at the final resting place of Sebastian, awaiting his friend's reply and laughed morosely once again. "He said, yes."

William and Nathanael both shook their heads in unison but still managed to grin just a little at his dark humor, despite it being a little ill-placed.

"Then what is it?" William scooped up another shovel and began helping him once more in his task.

"Something I have <u>no</u> idea what to do about as of yet." Emile sighed as he dropped another heavy shovel full of dirt then stopped, leaning both his arms on top of the spade now stuck into the earth in front of him.

"Oh?" Nathanael appeared equally perplexed. "Is it something we might be able to help you with?"

"Not unless you know how to solve the impossible now, Nathanael," Emile said sarcastically, then finally blurted out his dilemma, too drained to draw out the conversation any longer. "Last night, Hope asked me if I would talk to Charlotte about allowing her to come live with Emma and I for a time."

"What!" William halted his work abruptly and raised both his eyebrows in total astonishment. "I can see what you mean by the impossible. That is going to be extremely hard to ask it of Charlotte given the current situation."

"Not to mention, why would the girl want to leave now of all times? Shouldn't we be encouraging her to remain and help her mother here on the farm?" Nathanael drug brown dirt from the edges of the cut rectangle and patted it down firmly on top. "From my experience, big changes such as this are usually ill-advised, no matter the reason, even if they might seem noble or otherwise."

"Normally, I would agree with you." Emile nodded several times and did the same with his side of the pile of dirt next to him, making sure that the portion on top of Sebastian's grave was as level as possible. "But I promised Hope I would ask her just the same, even if I do not agree it is best. It was the <u>only</u> thing that would allow the girl to finally let go and sleep last night. As it was, I had to stay all night in the barn just to keep her from sobbing for hours."

"I'm sorry. I didn't realize. Though I guess I should have expected it when I didn't see either of you at breakfast this morning," William admitted awkwardly. "Was it that bad?"

Emile grimaced unconsciously, thinking back on the dreadful scene he had experienced in the hayloft and down below with Elijah and Hope. "There are no adequate words to describe it, William. That girl is undeniably broken in more ways than she is ready to admit, even to herself. And sadly, right now, I know exactly how she feels."

"Something the majority of us can relate to, no doubt," Nathanael admitted honestly. "My father passed when I was roughly her age, and shortly thereafter, my mother, too. It is something you never truly get used to no matter how many years have passed."

"As did mine," Emile answered quietly.

"And if Charlotte were to agree? What then?" William looked over at Emile with great concern for he knew how much Charlotte doted on the girl even before her husband died. Though in another light, he also knew, as much as she loved her daughter, Sebastian's wife would always do what she felt was best for her more than what she personally needed. And especially so, seeing as the girl was coming of age shortly and would one day entertain suitors and make a marriage match. In either scenario, Charlotte would soon be facing her life alone one way or another, just under better circumstances and not so close to her husband's death.

"I haven't the foggiest idea yet, William," Emile answered plainly.

"I imagine not. Well, that is definitely an uncomfortable predicament she has placed you in then, Emile." Nathanael picked up his Bible and sat down in the tall grass next to the grave to rest.

"Don't I know it," Emile sighed and stared out at the field of wheat beyond. "I may have been the one to help deliver her, but I have no earthly idea how to raise her, nor would I ever presume to take Sebastian's place for all the tea in China. Besides, I can barely keep myself out of trouble most days as it is. Let alone serve as an appropriate role model for a proper young lady."

"I thought that was Emma's job to keep you on the straight and narrow," William teased him lightly with a soft chuckle. "Or at least it used to be once upon a time."

Emile laughed, too. "Now that you mention it, I think I am more afraid that someday Emma will simply grow tired of the task and ask me to finally grow up."

"Not a chance." William took his seat next to Nathanael on the ground. "I think she rather fancies your sarcastic wit and playful demeanor. I know I do. It's part of the reason why I wish you both would change your mind about heading back to Charleston and move closer to Philadelphia. Letters just aren't the same and you know it."

"I do," Emile agreed easily with a smile. "Though I certainly haven't missed the magnetic pull of danger and drama that always seems to follow us whenever we are together."

"Agreed," William and Nathanael said in unison before Nathanael looked up at the tree with a curious expression.

"You know, William. I have often thought a lot about these solitary trees in the middle of fields as we have passed by them during our visits to various homes. Or more so, about the reasoning behind why a farmer would plant acres upon acres of crops all around them only to leave one, singular tree at their center." Nathanael picked up a long piece of grass and played with it before placing it between his teeth and chewing it several times. "It always seemed so out of place and wasteful, like an oversight on behalf of the farmer perhaps, but today, I think I have finally figured out why he does it."

"And why is that?" Emile took a seat near him in the grass, taking the time to lazily stretch out and lay down entirely to watch the leaves in the vast limbs move above him as he placed his arms folded up behind his head on the ground, fully relaxed.

"I believe it is to give him a place of rest for a time. The farmer's work is quite difficult, as we all know, unrelenting even. In his profession, he is utterly dependent on the weather at all times of the year. But with this magnificent oak, at any point in his work, he can simply take a short walk to a place of refuge for a time and then return once again with renewed strength and spirit. In that light, the tree is an oasis in the desert of plenty, I guess you could say."

William looked over at Nathanael and studied him for several moments with renewed appreciation at his insight. "Oddly enough, for someone who claims to be so simple-minded, you truly have a brilliant way of looking at things."

At first Nathanael did not say anything at all but chose instead to only give him an undeserving shrug, but then as the thought processed more in his head, he added more humbly, "You just say that because you are my friend."

"No." William shook his head, refuting his errant dismissal. "I say it because it is the truth, sir."

"Well, no matter what the lofty reason may be for it, I for one am glad for this oasis. It is a beautiful tree—as strong and as faithful as the man buried beneath it," Emile answered honestly. "And I am not ashamed to say it."

Nathanael chuckled. "I bet Sebastian is up in Heaven laughing at the three of us right about now."

"You are probably right. Either that or he would be telling me to get off his grass and do something useful with my life for a change," Emile replied sarcastically before laughing lightly at the image in his head of his recently departed friend. "He'd probably be right, too, as he usually was. Maybe, it's time I find something I can do here that will contribute to the betterment of this world around us in some way other than in simply earning money. Don't get me wrong, there is nothing wrong with wealth per say, but I would much rather be doing something that makes a difference than just spending my days watching the passage of time."

"It takes all kinds to keep this world running, Emile, but knowing Sebastian, if he were here, he would probably be back in the field or at the forge working as this funeral had probably taken up far too much time out of his busy day already. Either that or railing on the rest of us for wasting so much of ours in the process." William smiled as he remembered with a light laugh the look on his friend's face whenever he was especially annoyed.

Nathanael nodded his head in agreement. "He had an incredible work ethic, that is for sure. Something that should be a reminder to all of us to not grow weary in well doing. For we shall reap if we faint not. Sebastian is reaping his reward right now; we shall simply need to wait for ours a little bit longer."

"Ahem..." William cleared his throat and changed the subject dramatically before his emotions got the better of him once more. "Speaking of reaping... Jedidiah is going to need some extra help getting this harvest in at the end of next month. As proud as he is, I know he probably thinks he can do it on his own, but 100 acres is far more than any one man should tackle without assistance and hiring workers will only lessen the money they will all need moving forward."

"Don't worry, I am not planning on leaving Philadelphia any time soon," Emile assured him. "In fact, that may just be the answer to my other dilemma, after all."

"The one about Hope?" Nathanael asked curiously.

Emile nodded. "Emma and I were already contemplating moving closer in the next year or two, but with things being as they are, we can simply adjust the timing of those plans slightly and come now. Maybe even find a place closer to Charlotte's farm for the time being. Perhaps this way Hope can come stay with us when she needs to from time to time, and yet still be under Charlotte's roof, as well," he suggested and sat up, ready to discuss his new plan with his wife before talking it all over with Charlotte.

"Well, I can't speak for you, Nathanael, but I know I can give several days each week if Jedidiah needs the help. The hospital is in the process of building their new surgical theatre, but they will not be ready for me to train the new staff until it is completed at the end of the year. I will simply arrange my time there to accommodate helping him as I am able." William stood and brushed the debris from nature off the back of his pants. "Though he <u>will</u> need to give me plenty of instruction as I have never farmed a day in my life."

"Nor I. Still, the university does not keep me too busy that I cannot help, too, if required." Nathanael joined him.

"What are you teaching these days?" Emile rose and pulled his hands over his scalp to smooth out his long hair towards its tightly wrapped ponytail behind.

"Theology mostly, but more importantly, the practical application of those truths in their daily lives. Too many of my students are so full of head knowledge that they have forgotten that it must also be applied to their hearts and acted upon," Nathanael replied fervently looking rather distressed about his newest group of candidates at the college.

"What? You mean hellfire and damnation every Sunday is not the way to win souls for Christ? Inconceivable," Emile muttered as he began making his way back to the house off in the distance, well behind those who had already left ahead of them. An afternoon meal had been planned to bring a bit of comfort for the family, but despite his already formed dislike of food in general, this meal posed itself to be most likely of equally bitter and solemn endurance.

William only smiled at his friend's remark and placed an arm around the back of his preacher friend in knowledgeable appreciation. "Well, if anyone can make them see the value of living like one of Jesus' disciples it is you, my friend."

"Do you really think so?" Nathanael quickened his step to keep up with the other two men, for they walked much faster than he on any given day. With his shorter stature and less driven personality, he constantly felt the need to hurry to keep up with their much longer strides.

"We know so." Emile turned back to answer him before William could. "You turned two absolute pagans into believers, didn't you?"

"Please, you weren't <u>that</u> bad, Emile," Nathanael tried to defend him.

"Oh, yes, he was, Preacher, so stop trying to make him feel better about it." William playfully bumped his shoulder into Emile's to throw him off balance as he walked.

"Then it is a good thing we both acquiesced in the end, agreed?" Emile taunted him right back and recovered easily.

"I couldn't have said it better myself." William smiled at Emile and nodded. "Truth be told, you are a servant to many, Nathanael."

"Thank you, gentlemen," Nathanael replied meekly, and the three men walked the rest of the way in silence, each reflecting on the way in which their friendship had developed and making peace once more with the question that had forever plagued their existence.

Señor Moretti had once assured them all long ago that they could most certainly die, but when a person is given the gift of immortality, that certainty of death no longer shaped the importance of your every decision like it had when you were mortal. Yet, when the truth of it is also so shockingly revealed to you once more that your life is indeed not as eternal as you had once supposed, you are now forced to make your decisions with even greater care than ever before.

Clearly, Sebastian was not immortal, after all. In the end, he was merely blessed with a much longer time on this Earth to help others with his existence.

The only thing left for all of them now was to try to carry on the legacy he worked so hard to achieve, or at the very least, support his children in doing so.

Chapter Four

June 28th, 1811

"You know, there is such a thing as too perfect, right?" Emma asked as she walked into the kitchen for the second time that morning and leaned over her husband's shoulder to inspect his decorations on the cake.

Undeterred, Emile cast her a sideways glance but remained entirely focused on his work in front of him. "Today is probably one of the most important birthdays she will ever have. So, it must be just right." He added another small rosette to the edge and stood back to admire his work before slightly frowning. "Too much?"

"It is definitely made to impress." Emma judged the pastry with pink edged flowers that ran along one side and down to the bottom with white lacy strings of looped raised décor on the rest. "I think you would find it hard to purchase a better cake in all of France, let alone Philadelphia… but you already knew that, dear."

"Hmmm…" Emile picked up the cake and placed it in the cooled oven to protect it until supper.

"And what do you suppose Hope will be expecting for her 18th birthday?" Emma took a seat at the table and watched her husband as he cleaned up the various items he had used in the kitchen.

"Last year she wanted her own horse. Hopefully this year it will be something far more practical, and a little less inclined to drama." Emile raised his eyebrows, remembering the untamed stallion that had been delivered just in time for her birthday last year. It had taken him almost six months to train that beast, and even then, Hope seemed to be the only person he permitted to ride him. "I still don't know why you convinced me to buy that animal in the first place, Emma."

"Me? We both know that purchase was one hundred percent yours and yours alone," Emma deflected. "I bought her the dress, if you remember."

"Remember? How could I forget? That thing brought more destruction than the horse." Emile threw the semi-wet towel over his shoulder and joined his wife at the table.

"Oh, stop. I hardly think Hope views Mr. Adair as destructive, even if you do. Quite the opposite, in fact." Emma handed Emile his cup and saucer of milk tea and the plate of vanilla sugar cubes he always preferred.

"Indeed." Emile only shook his head in marked disdain. "That is precisely why he worries me, my love. The next thing we know he will be whisking her away from us entirely to some unknown land like... Boston or... Baltimore ... or..."

"Anywhere where you are not, is that correct?" Emma interrupted her husband as she voiced his only true fear in all the world right now... his niece marrying... or worse yet, growing up somewhere beyond his reach.

For several moments, Emile pursed his lips again and again and tried to smile, but Emma only laughed at the struggle it created. "You really do hate the thought of her leaving here, don't you?"

"I detest it almost as much as I do that idiot, Napoleon back in France." Emile gingerly sipped his tea and tried his best not to appear too affected by the sobering conversation.

"Astounding comparison! But unlike that short man with ambitions greater than his stature, you <u>will</u> have to let her go one day. He, you can ignore from a distance," Emma tried to reason with him gently, hoping this time her efforts would be more successful than in the past, though she highly doubted it.

"I do not." Emile clucked his tongue arrogantly. "And I can ignore Michael, as well," he said his name in a mocking tone, then held his head aloofly, allowing his pride to rise with his attitude.

"Oh, love, I fear she is too much like her father in that regard. If you do not relent soon in your dismissal of the boy, she will only hate you for it. And especially so if you stand in her way." Emma dropped a cube of sugar into his drink and stirred it for him.

"Who will hate Uncle Emile?" Hope asked as she bounded down the stairs behind them and into the small dining room directly adjacent to the front porch door. "I can't imagine anyone not liking him. Well, almost no one."

"And who is this no one?" Emile reached back and lovingly took the girl's hand before kissing it lightly and drawing her to the table with them. "I must see to speaking with him or her directly."

"Oh, you've already met, I am sure." Hope poured herself a cup of tea and plopped two cubes directly into the center of the cup.

"That is a lot of sugar, dear." Emile chided seriously at the action, unsure if allowing her yet another area of indulgence was entirely wise.

"Didn't you know? It's how I stay so sweet." She smiled unapologetically and turned her focus immediately on Emma. "I wanted to let you both know I will be going out this afternoon with Michael, if that is alright with the two of you. Mother says she will not need me until later this evening, and he has asked to take me to see Uncle William's new hospital. It is all the talk of the town, especially the new artwork displayed there. Uncle Nathanael says it is breathtaking, and that we should really see it in person."

"Uncle William does not own the hospital," Emile muttered, his mood suddenly soured by the mere mention of her supposed suitor and his plans for the afternoon.

"Breathe, my dear... be composed," Emma murmured quietly to her husband then placed her hand on top of his to try to soften his disposition further. "Don't spoil the day so quickly."

"Trying..." Emile mumbled back across his teacup unapologetically.

"Please Uncle," Hope's face instantly fell as she let out a quick sigh. "I know you disapprove of Michael, but if you would only give him a chance, you might find that you really do like him, after all. I know I do."

"I am sure he is quite delightful, Hope." Emma's eyes pleaded with her husband to at least accept his niece's opinion of her beau even if he did not.

"Well, it appears I am outnumbered once again." Emile set his cup down and threw his hands up in mock defeat. "Will Mr. Adair be joining us for supper tonight, as well?"

"Yes, if he is allowed. Mother said we should all arrive by five o'clock sharp." Hope drank the last of her tea and set it down carefully onto the saucer in front of her.

"Then you had best hurry, or you will not have time to see those fine paintings," Emile stated flatly, while secretly hoping the late hour of her departure would dissuade her plans.

It did not. On the contrary, Hope stood up, more exuberant and ready to leave than before, but paused first to kiss her aunt and then her uncle on the cheek. "I promised Elijah I would stop by his forge before lunch, but I'll see the two of you at supper. Oh, and I will be staying at Mama's this week. She has a few chores she needs help with, so I promised her I would do so."

"Of course," Emma replied. "Thank you for letting us know."

The two waved her on her way but continued to observe her as she left the house and walked down the street towards the hospital, a lighthearted skip to her step as always.

With a long-exhaled sigh that spoke volumes all on its own, Emile reached for Emma's hand and held it within his own as he watched Hope until she was no longer in sight. "I suddenly feel very old today, my love."

"Me, too, my darling... me, too." Emma sighed. "But we both knew this day would come eventually and now that it has, we must try our best to help her make wise decisions... just like you always have."

"Yes, except those were far easier to guide her in. 'Which dress shall I wear to church, Uncle? Does this hat make me look childish? Please say it doesn't. Can I drive the wagon into town by myself, Aunt?' I'd take any one of those to, 'Can I marry Michael Stuart Adair?' And what does the young man do all day anyway? He looks like he is barely able to lift a spade, let alone a hammer. Does he at least have a useful profession to support our niece?"

"Oh, I thought you knew. You know, for someone who cares so little about the man, you surely know a lot about him to remember his full name. I did not even know that."

"Hmmpf... it is important to know as much as one can about one's enemy," Emile muttered quietly and picked up the morning paper pretending to be suddenly interested in the front headline.

"Is that so..." Emma closed her eyes and shook her head painfully before continuing, "Well, you might be surprised to know that he actually writes for the very newspaper you are holding, Emile, *The Aurora General*. It's a decent occupation all things considered and from what Hope has told me, he is quite a talented author in his own right, though the editor is making him slowly work his way up through the ranks." Emma picked up the empty cups and saucers along with the towel that still lay over Emile's shoulder and made her way over to the sink behind him. "In fact, I overheard him say yesterday that the British Navy has attacked several of the merchant ships once again. They even took many of the men hostage and pressed them forcefully into the English Navy."

"Pressing them into service? Is that what they are calling it now?" Emile leaned back in his chair and huffed as he crossed his arms in irritation. "In my day it was called conscription. I guess they have not changed their tactics much over the years, though it does bother me that it is coming so close to home. Whether offensively or defensively meant, it all rather feels like piracy on the high seas, and I wouldn't wish that fate on any man... not even Mr. Adair."

"Yes, I suppose it does, now that you mention it. Well, Michael said you would want to know all the details before he printed so you could discuss them with the others in the War Office. Or maybe he is hoping you will even give him a comment or two tonight for his article."

"My dear, that is all <u>anyone</u> is talking about in the Capitol, that and the new construction of the building itself. You know, you should really come with me to see it one day. It is simply spectacular! It has rows upon rows of windows in the ceiling that illuminate the house perfectly. And the columns that line the outer room are all intricately carved with corn no less."

"Impressive, but will it stand the test of time, I wonder?" Emma cleaned the cups and dried them before placing them back in the cupboards behind her.

"It should. They even say that the entire building is supposed to be fireproof," Emile stated proudly and stood to help her. "I dare say, not many buildings today can boast that fact, nor do they cost as much as this one did."

"And all of it can withstand a fire?" Emma looked curiously surprised.

"Well," Emile placed one finger against his lips, as if contemplating fully the correct answer to her question, before adding, "All but the ceiling should be. They had to make that out of wood so that it could flex with the weather or for some sort of reason like that. I saw it in a memo the other day, but it was far less interesting than the news of the skirmishes along our border with the northern territories. Truth is, I find it terribly hard to believe that this country is still not satisfied with the vast quantity of land that it already has. And though my colleagues will be quite put out with me for doing so, I'm afraid that if this continues to a point of aggression I may end up siding with our northern colonies on this issue."

"What does Mr. Ingersoll say about it? Surely, he isn't in favor of the President's actions, not if it means war."

"You'd be wrong, yet again. And just as you might expect, I am <u>highly</u> encouraged daily to set aside my personal ideals and follow along with the rest of them with my vote along the party line. Yet the greed of this new country tends to shock me daily, Emma. So much so, that I don't think my conscience will allow it."

"Well, the last census did say there were now close to seven million people living here as of last year. That is a lot of individuals to house and provide for, not to mention have room for expansion." Emma crossed her arms and looked at her husband approvingly.

"I suppose, but it seems so unfair to provoke England again for only land. I wholly support the reasons for the last rebellion. Those were necessary and vital for this country to grow as it has, but not this." Emile scrunched his face up at the troubling thought.

"And the Indians, where do they stand in all of this?" Emma asked.

"Thankfully, many are still supporting us as a country, but other tribes have started forming a confederacy against any movement northward. And I truly don't blame them for doing it either. I mean how would you feel if someone just came in here and took our home as their own and said you have to move whether you wanted to do so or not?" Emile raised his eyebrows and shook his head at the possibility. "They say it may even come to a full-scale assault if one side were to instigate a fight."

"Let's pray it never comes to that, shall we? Oh, I almost forgot, Nathanael asked me to have you stop by today. Something about picking up a book he found for you." Emma handed him the note that had arrived just that morning addressed to her husband.

"Opening my mail now, Mrs. Deschamps?" Emile took the note and wrapped his arm around her waist, drawing her closer to him. "Some men might find that a bit scandalous."

"Well, someone has to fend off all the ladies you manage to charm in Congress." Emma playfully teased him but put both her hands upon his chest, taking hold of the sides of his shirt and drawing his face down to hers. "From the letters that I have read recently, you appear to have quite a few admirers in Washington."

"Do I now?" Emile's eyes stared deeply into hers before cupping his hand lovingly behind her neck, his fingers wrapping themselves delightedly into her soft hair. "Mrs. Deschamps, you are the <u>only</u> woman I will ever want, and you know that," Emile promised her once more and kissed her sweetly, just long enough to cause her to relax her body against him, but not long enough to delay his trip into town to see Nathanael.

"Now, I don't know. After that letter from the lady last week, I might need some more convincing, sir." Emma's eyes twinkled as she stared back into his own. "From what I read, she was most taken with your um, speech... your very eloquently dressed speech, I might add." Emma laughed lightly and continued to playfully spar with him about it. "In fact, I might still have it over here somewhere..." Emma tried to reach behind her for the folded letter, but Emile kept blocking her, constraining her reach every time as he held her fast.

"You're not jealous, are you?" Emile chuckled at the possibility, then groaned inwardly at the distasteful memory of his latest letter of adulation.

"Maybe a little," Emma teasingly admitted. "But the better question is, should I be?"

Emile rolled his eyes at her totally senseless reply, knowing she was not serious in any way. "Can I honestly help it if people think your husband looks dashing in a suit?"

It was Emma's turn to shake her head at his reply. "No, no you can't, and I wouldn't ask you to do otherwise. Besides, I have to admit that you <u>did</u> look quite excellent in the one you wore last week. The woman would have had to have been blind to not at least notice you, let alone dream about your, and I quote, 'finely cut figure'," Emma teased him mercilessly.

Emile had heard enough about the woman he scarcely remembered seeing, let alone spoke to. Placing both his hands on either side of Emma's face, Emile leaned in closer to her, so close that it made both of their hearts pick up their pace. "The only thing I will ever desire more than life itself is you, woman, nothing more. I promised you that when I wed you, and I will continue to promise you that until I draw my last breath." He kissed her deeply, then held her close. "Since the moment I first saw you, I knew you were what I needed, and I will forever be grateful you did not give up on me."

Content as always in her newfound life with Emile, Emma pulled back from his embrace and smiled. "Same here, and no, I am not jealous. I know no one knows what they are truly getting into with you, Emile Deschamps," she taunted him again before turning more serious. "So, what should we do with her many, many letters?"

"Burn them all," Emile replied wickedly, intensely satisfied with the very idea.

Emma couldn't help but chuckle at the tone of his voice, loving the fact that he adored her enough to refuse anyone who might try to vie for his affection. "Oh, and speaking of getting to know you, please promise me you will at least try to be pleasant tonight with Michael. For Hope's sake if for no other reason," Emma pleaded.

Emile rolled his eyes once more at the unwelcomed imposition and sighed heavily in disagreement.

"Call it your official birthday present to her, if nothing else," Emma begged further.

"Fine. I will try, but you will see, this will all lead to no good, I promise you." Emile released his wife and picked up his long suit coat from the post by the front door as he slid his arms into the black sleeves. "Mark my words, this infatuation will end up worse than the horse."

"We shall see." Emma handed him his father's hat with a light peck on the cheek and watched him leave before heading upstairs to retrieve the laundry.

Chapter Five

June 28th, 1811

Feeling brilliantly alive, Emile walked quickly down the street, taking in the many new buildings being constructed along his way to the seminary near the center of town. Probably over a dozen permits had already crossed his desk just this week alone that required his approval in some way or another. By all accounts, from the sheer magnitude of the pile that awaited him each morning, almost every business in the city was desiring to expand in some way as it fought to claim a small piece of the ever-burgeoning economy. Weeding through them all daily was demanding at best, but at least this kind of paperwork he did not mind one bit. Progress was progress, after all, and there was little anyone could do to stop it... provided it remained within the lines already drawn for the country. Everyone from the candlemakers to the new gunpowder works at the edge of town required a new, or rather, larger structure in which to meet the demand of their business and, with the upcoming possibility of the war with England, their coffers would only grow in its wake.

Glancing to his left, he passed by a small, two-storied building that used to house a bookstore of sorts, complete with two rather large bay windows that jutted out of the second-floor level. Like many others, it had also been replaced earlier this year by a more modern edifice next to William's hospital, making this one, the one whose roof and siding needed more than a little bit of repair, virtually obsolete.

With a sigh at its imminent demise, Emile stopped to examine the ruins of the older structure that was in the process of being torn down and frowned at the loss of it. "Why does everything have to be new all the time in order to grow? Why can't people simply appreciate the value of something old when they advance." He shook his head in frustration and continued walking until he reached the edge of Thomas' metalworks shop.

The recently constructed building with a brick front and all wooden sides, complete with large windows both above and below, was nowhere near as grand as its predecessor had been, nor did the current owner especially wish it to be so. In all, it had taken the man over a year to recover emotionally from the death of his former master and almost that long again to plan and rebuild it from the ground up, though with many required modifications to avoid any subsequent failure to the current structure.

"Once burned, twice shy," Thomas had said to him shakily one time as they were viewing the new blueprints for the building in his office and Emile could not fault him for being overly cautious. The man had gone through what most men would call their worst nightmare and lived to talk about it. They all had.

After deciding to remain in Philadelphia, Emile had made sure that there had been a thorough investigation given into the building's collapse shortly after Sebastian's death. In fact, his persistence towards the safety of the city's new structures was what had initially earned him his seat in office. Something he looked back on now as a gift from his friend, as well, as Sebastian's death had motivated him towards accomplishing something good from the ruin and rubble that had claimed his companion.

Thankfully for Thomas though, there <u>was</u> one ray of sunshine in the horrendous storm he had been forced to endure. The new building that currently housed his metalworks was completed this time at very little expense to him whatsoever, as the construction company had been forced to replace the edifice in its entirety free of charge and do so in less than three months' time, once the decision had been finally made.

And as it turned out, the older building was not wholly to blame for its unexpected collapse either. The true culprit had actually been the fault of the building company itself. Or more importantly, the greedy and poor decisions made by its owner. Nails, the very thing Sebastian said that he hated making most of all, ended up being the instrument of his untimely demise. Or rather, the use of a little more than half of the required amount was not sufficient by any means to shore up the building properly.

Moreover, Emile had learned later that the foreman had decided to 'cut a few corners', as they would say, to make up the difference in his lost profits and appease his failing pocketbook over his good sense and conscience. Upon feeling the mounting pressure of his continual delays on the project, and with the demand and prices soaring daily on the small bits of necessary metal, his fateful decision to use less of them to secure the necessary supports and crossbeams had created the inevitable demise.

As horrible and inexcusable as it was, the man had indeed erred on so many levels in his judgement and Sebastian had paid the ultimate price for the man's stupidity. Thomas, too, in that regard as the man almost did not return to his place of work at all, let alone seek to rebuild. In truth, it had taken all of them to convince him that the accident had not been the end of his future, but the beginning of something good, both for him and for his family.

And certainly, it had been a steep penalty to pay for any company to replace it, but one that Emile had seen on at least a few other occasions, as well. In just this year alone, there had been a recent spate of arson attacks around the city as desperate individuals sought to utilize the easy resource of empty buildings for the procurement of nails. Nails that they would then sell to others to make a quick income for their family. And it was no wonder why they did so when there seemed to be no shortage of older establishments that had been cast aside all in the name of progress.

In a way, they were also serving the advancement of expansion themselves in ridding the city of the dilapidated eyesores that resulted from yearly stagnation and neglect of such properties. Yet it also hurt Emile's heart to watch some of the finer relics, like the old bookstore, crumble and be replaced by the horrid, brick monstrosities they were building nowadays.

"Progress indeed." He paused in his walk under the shade of a nearby maple tree and contemplated once again whether or not she should stop to check on Thomas along his way but thought the better of it. The last thing the young man needed was the constant oversight of meddling uncles, no matter how good their intentions were otherwise. And since his family was always invited to their events, rain or shine, he would no doubt see him later tonight for supper. He could simply judge for himself then if the man needed further assistance and not step into his affairs unannounced and unwanted.

Suddenly catching a whiff of fresh bread mixed with something else not entirely sweet, Emile glanced across the street at the new bakery in town and smiled. From the long line outside the building, wrapping all the way down the street, the new owner, Robert Henderson, had quite obviously taken his suggestion to add a line of French breads and breakfast pastries to his daily offerings. The rich smell of buttery croissants that wafted over to him on the breeze, taunted him mercilessly, making him seriously consider joining the others in line but he decided against it for the time being. Nathanael's note had said that he needed to see him before lunch, and there was no telling how long it would take to get through that line today, and even if he did, if anything worthy of consumption would be left. Temptation aside, he would simply have to come earlier another day or arrange for Robert to save him a croissant or two ahead of time.

"Well, at least there is something in town that feels vaguely reminiscent of home now." Emile smiled as he continued onward until he found himself walking up the many stone stairs a short while later that led up to the large, four columned building in the center of town that was surrounded completely on the left by a rather stately walled park of sorts. The two-story edifice housed one of the nation's largest libraries next to Thomas Jefferson's own humble collection, but it also made Emile smile to think that his friend now taught at the very school that was founded by someone to whom his friend was most decidedly, spiritually opposed.

Oh, the many discussions they had enjoyed on this topic over the years and the jibes the poor man had endured at William's instigation, but Nathanael still remained characteristically steadfast. Like the rock of Gibraltar, he had staunchly stood against their storm and proved himself most vigilant in his instruction of the "new generation of thinkers," or so he called his students at Princeton Theological Seminary. Though in truth, from what Emile could tell, they were really just 21 spoiled young men from rich families whose heritage spanned the continent and beyond, the youngest being barely fifteen. Far too young in his estimation to be graduating from anything, but then again, his opinion was not consulted in these matters, nor should it have been.

Education was Nathanael's realm, and he would happily leave it to him. Emile had far more important things to worry about, like the upcoming war with Britain, the new coal industry in Philadelphia and countless other things a member of Congress had to oversee. Still, he loved his job as much as he hated it on any given day. After all, was it any different than what he had done back in Paris? In the place of his high society gatherings that were meant only as a means for diversion, the government was an undeniably well-coordinated society established to enact laws with each member playing his designated part behind a carefully created mask.

In fact, every man he had met since being elected three years ago had shown him in one meeting or another that they had some kind of hidden agenda for their constituents. Nevertheless, despite their cryptic facades, it was up to him, as a fellow participant in that game, to discover what their agenda truly was and how to compliment it or thwart it effectively. At present, he was currently enjoying thwarting it, but then again, that was his preferred, contrary disposition on any given day anyways, so why change any of that now.

Maybe that was why he despised Michael so. The man with his excellent manners was also a pleaser at heart. Someone who unpredictably played to the crowd, no matter whose company he was in. Or rather, a man who acted as if he was willing to do whatever it took to get what he wanted, no matter what the cost may be to others. In Emile's estimation, by the young man's recent reaction to him alone, he concluded that he obviously lacked the necessary backbone he required to marry his niece, though he had not garnered any true evidence to show Hope on that opinion as of yet.

More disappointingly, it also didn't help that the man was as dashing as they came in that regard, with no doubt more than a few ladies desiring his attention other than hers. Yet another reason to hate the man and his perfectly styled brown hair and neatly tailored clothes. He was too... flawless for her favor, too... Emile paused mentally in his deliberations to consider exactly what it was about him that irritated him so.

That man needs a little imperfection in his life, or at the very least an Achilles heel to torment mercilessly if I am to finally be rid of him. Emile's teeth ground hard upon themselves as he relished the possibility.

Yet, it was at that very moment that Emile abruptly stopped in the middle of the long hallway in complete shock at the sudden revelation that now dawned upon him. One singular realization alone that seized his entire being and left him now clearly shaken in its wake. In fact, why Emma had not mentioned it to him sooner was beyond him, but he was sure, as perceptive as she was, that she had already noticed what had taken him ages longer to see. Then again, perhaps she was merely being kind in not pointing it out since the very beginning. But shockingly enough, there it was staring at him right in the face like a horrible reflection looking back at him.

Michael was just like him! Or at least what he used to be at his age, which was not very old at just barely twenty-four. Old enough to have the courage to stand up for what he believed or cast it aside like yesterday's news. And yet not old enough to marry anyone, let alone Hope, in Emile's opinion, though he had certainly entertained probably a handful of ladies by that age, if not when he was younger.

"Argh!" He balled his hand into a fist then released it slowly. "Of course, Hope would find someone just like me!" He threw his hands up in disgust and grabbed the outer handle to the door of Nathanael's room and pulled, determined to let out his frustration immediately to the man on the other side.

"Good afternoon, Nathanael," Emile said as he entered, his focus turned downward in concentration as he walked.

"Mr. Deschamps?" Nathanael looked back at him from his position in front of his group of students and paused, suddenly surprised by the interruption. "I'll be with you directly. Please do take a seat."

"My apologies, of course." Emile nodded politely out of respect and watched as a few of the students whispered in turn to each other as he sat on the edge of the desk on the side of the room and crossed his arms patiently to wait for the end of the lecture. "Pray, please continue."

Nathanael only rolled his eyes at his cavalier attitude and began once more, "So what do you think Benjamin Franklin meant when he said, 'It is therefore that the older I grow the more apt I am to doubt my own judgement and to pay more respect to the judgement of others. Most men indeed, as well as most sects in religion, think themselves in possession of all truth, and that wherever others differ from them it is so far error... but I meet with nobody but myself that's always in the right.'"

One young man in the center of the gathered group of chairs raised his hand eagerly and stated, "He thinks he knows everything and that everyone else is less intelligent than he is."

"A very simplistic assessment, Mr. Biddle." Nathanael nodded. "But could there be more we might glean from his speech, something deeper perhaps?"

Another tentative hand rose from the taller boy on Nathanael's left, a markedly younger version of the first student that was almost as drably dressed as Nathanael used to be when Emile had first met him.

"Mr. Wylie?" Nathanael acknowledged him appropriately.

"He clearly speaks of one with growing humility because he recognizes that as he has aged, he finds himself more and more open to respecting the beliefs of others around him."

"Or at least he does in the beginning. He changes his tune entirely yet again by the end of his comment," another boy interjected cheekily without being called upon to answer.

Nathanael closed his book and smiled. "Yes, Mr. Barr, it is yet another example of the biblical truth that a double-minded man is unstable in all his ways. Now, I am not saying in any way that our Mr. Franklin was not a great man. In fact, we can all agree that he has done much for this country as well as for this college, being our founding father in more ways than one. But we _can_ also see how dualistic wisdom can deter our true message and purpose. Something to be considered for your future endeavors, gentlemen, as well as an admonition towards your studies as your summer finals are next week."

In the rustling of papers and closing of books that followed, the room all groaned in uniformed displeasure.

"You are all dismissed. Be sure to read the rest of Mr. Franklin's speech to the Continental Congress before class tomorrow. We will discuss it at length then. And don't forget to turn in your assignment from last night on my desk as you leave, please," Nathanael called above the din his reminder had created and watched as each one of his students passed by him after depositing their work.

From his place on the opposite side of the room, Emile couldn't help but smile as he watched them, chuckling inwardly. How glad he was that he never had to endure such examinations in his day. The worst he had been forced to undertake was learning how to ride a horse and even that was not judged too severely by anyone other than his father. Which was probably best because he had struggled to stay on top of his horse more than he had spent saddling it. Eventually giving up, his father had finally determined once and for all that his youngest son would make an excellent groom if he did not master the task sooner, but that only made Emile despise it all the more. In the end, Emile had much preferred walking to hassling himself with learning that skill, which suited him perfectly for after his family's financial demise, the horses all left along with the servants.

"Mr. Carroll..." Nathanael eyed a young man from his desk who looked more disheveled in his appearance than the others as he slunk from his chair towards the master of the class. "See to it that you try to arrive before class begins next time, please. It sets a bad example to your peers when you traipse in here half-asleep like you do," Nathanael chided him, then smiled genuinely in shared understanding. "As an over sleeper myself, it helps to have a friend wake you if necessary."

"I'll try." The man stifled a yawn and trudged out of the classroom looking like he was still sleepwalking at eleven o'clock in the morning respectively.

"Having trouble with the new graduating class of students?" Emile rose from his position sitting on the edge of one of the student desks and walked over to his friend.

"Hardly. They are a good bunch of lads, though still a little confirmed in their lines of thinking, but they will sort that out in time." Nathanael placed his copious notes on their recent discussion within his portfolio and closed it. "Now, what can I help you with today, Emile? I doubt I could teach you anything about our founding fathers that you don't already know."

"That much is true. I have made quite a study of them as of late, haven't I?" Emile checked the cleanliness of his fingernails, then placed his hand upon his hip, waiting for his friend's response.

"Yes, well, I have truthfully often wondered why that is." Nathanael looked up at him, a perplexed expression painting all of his features.

"Oh, I don't know. Maybe it is because they also fought in a revolution, I suppose. But from what I can see all around me, it has resulted in a far better outcome than my home country. France is still in a war with England as we speak, and there seems to be no end in sight for either of them. In a way, it makes me grateful that we came here when we did, or we might have all ended up having to choose sides."

"Or be forced into fighting, as well," Nathanael stated the obvious possibility.

"Not I," Emile refused him flatly.

"Nor I. After our brief encounter in Portsmouth, I do believe I have had enough of that kind of adventure for a lifetime, if not longer if you please."

"Indeed." Emile picked up one of the books from his desk and fingered through the pages. "You mean you would much rather battle wits than steel, my friend?"

"Any day, Emile... any day." Nathanael took the book away from him gingerly and tried once more to procure an answer to his previous question. "So again, how can I help you? You seem to be stalling, sir. Or did you need to give me a message for William, perhaps?"

Emile rolled his eyes at his friend's endearing forgetfulness and shook his head as he pulled the folded note from his pocket and held it up to Nathanael. "I believe it was <u>you</u> who wrote to <u>me</u>, sir."

"Oh, land's sake! I totally forgot!" Nathanael's entire countenance shifted to one of deep chagrin. "Just yesterday, I found a book in the archives of the library that you absolutely <u>must</u> read... immediately even." He searched his desk for the small tan book with the chocolate brown binding. "It is here somewhere... I just saw it."

"It wouldn't happen to be this one?" Emile picked up another of the small volumes that rested underneath a much larger copy of the Bible on the front corner of Nathanael's desk. "The one with <u>my</u> name upon the cover?" He chuckled.

"Precisely!" Nathanael almost shrieked with excitement. "When I saw it, I almost fell off my ladder at the discovery."

"Do you know what it is about?" Emile turned the book over twice, inspecting its simplistic creation before opening it to the front index page. "It is written by Rousseau! Someone few Frenchmen could not help but recognize, yet I have never seen this title in my life."

"Probably because the majority of his books were burned," Nathanael said enigmatically as the light of the long-ago fires danced within his eyes. "Shameful to think of it. This book was probably the most important thing that he ever wrote, but they burned it all the same."

"Sounds like the modus operandi of the current French society—destroy and eradicate what you do not understand." Emile shook his head, remembering his experience at the trials and subsequent flight from France. "Do you know what it is about?"

"Only a little from what I could make out. The majority of the book is in French, as you might well expect. My colleague said he read it before and thinks it is about a man and his teacher... something about the search for human goodness."

"A truly promising topic." Emile read the first page and smiled optimistically. "Looks interesting indeed, thank you. I shall return this when I am finished."

"Oh, no! It is yours to keep. The school has two copies and when I told them it was named after you, a Frenchman of equally significant distinction, they happily relinquished this copy to your personal library, provided you do not copy your countrymen's catastrophic lack of judgement regarding it." Nathanael reached for another book on the table and opened it to prepare for the next class that was due to arrive shortly.

"That is very generous of them and appreciated immensely," Emile thanked his friend warmly.

"They say our current educational system is actually based upon this book. So hopefully, you will find your namesake a better example than the one William found for me. The Vicar of Wakefield was quite a disappointment, I'm afraid."

"Well, then it is a good thing that his successor in that position was not. You were a very fine preacher in Wakefield. Something to be proud of, as I know I am of you." Emile placed a hand upon his shoulder and reassured him.

"As always, you are too kind." Nathanael smiled warmly back and nodded twice in gratitude. "Oh, before I forget, are you and Emma both coming tonight to Hope's birthday supper?"

Emile bristled once again at the thought of seeing his current nemesis before adding rather reluctantly, "It appears I cannot escape it, though I wish I could."

"Good, because Charlotte asked William and I to be there, as well. She said she wants all three of us to do something for her. What? I have no idea, but we both promised her we would be there, so please make an effort." Nathanael walked to the door and held it open for Emile to pass through before him. "Though I wish she had just said outright what it was. As you know, I have never done well with secrets, now or back in England." Nathanael walked out the door after him and paused before making his way down the hall.

"Well, you won't get any help from me. I haven't an inkling whatsoever what she might require. But I would like to ask you something along another vein entirely, if it wouldn't be too much of an imposition, Nathanael?"

"But of course, how can I assist?" Nathanael looked up suddenly from studying the text he had been carrying in his hand and appeared surprised, for he was not normally the one any of them consulted on delicate matters.

"Do you think eighteen is too young for Hope to marry?" Emile asked him bluntly.

For a minute, Nathanael seemed completely taken aback by the intimate question as much as Emile had been in his realization earlier. "Well, one would hope that whoever she does choose to marry will be much older than she and therefore be able to guide her in these matters more clearly. But to be frank, most people of her acquaintance are probably already courting someone or are otherwise betrothed, if not married, Emile. Age seems not to be the deciding factor in these types of situations, but rather maturity of character, and Hope has proven herself to be a worthy young woman by anyone's scope of the definition. Not that she needs our approval on the matter. Why? Is she seeking yours?"

"No... yes... maybe soon." Emile looked down at the book in his hands, pondering what Nathanael had just said but did not appear readily pleased with the man's honest reply.

"Emile," Nathanael walked closer to his friend and spoke slowly and carefully, wanting to encourage him as much as others had done for him many times over the years, "Allowing someone else to love Hope is not going to replace you in her life. It will only expand that love to others and allow God to bring you even more joy when grandchildren come along, should they be so blessed. If Sebastian's death has taught me anything, it is that each moment we have been given should be cherished, not imprisoned, for it is a rare gift that will never be given again."

"Grandchildren!" Emile tossed his head back and sighed dramatically. "Oh, Nathanael, I am <u>definitely</u> not ready for that yet."

"Men never are, I am afraid." Nathanael smirked. "But they arrive with or without our permission anyway."

Emile nodded in resigned acceptance. "Thank you for the book... and for your counsel. Even if I do not like the latter's inevitability."

"Pray about it, Emile. Let God give you the peace that you seek as He always does." Nathanael placed a comforting arm behind his back.

"I will and thank you once more," Emile bid his friend farewell and left the college to finish up a few things down at the office before supper. His clerk had told him yesterday that there were a several documents left to be signed and a new acquisition to approve before leaving for Washington next week. With any luck he would be able to finish them all early and arrive with plenty of time to spare.

As for what to do with Michael Adair...

Perhaps prayer truly <u>was</u> the only thing left for him to do.

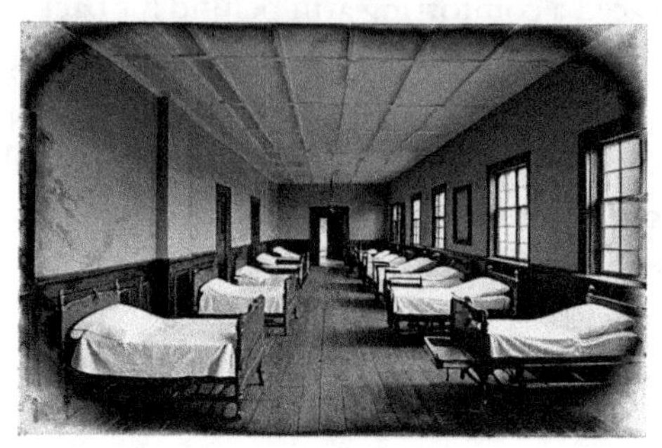

Chapter Six

June 28th, 1811

For several years after their arrival in 1793, William alone had struggled to find his own footing once more amidst the many choices afforded him in the new Colonies. With the war against England safely behind them, the cities within the framework of that liberated nation were beginning to truly thrive under their newfound freedom, making the opportunities endlessly available for anyone wishing to plant their roots and grow. This had certainly been true for Emile and Emma whose French-inspired bakery had soared beyond any of their expectations in Charleston, and for Sebastian's family, too, with their farm and the forge. Even Nathanael had managed to prosper in the new college that had been established as if his mind had been simply waiting to be awakened once more. But for William, every day he stepped out onto the tree-lined street with its passing wagons and busy citizens milling about at any given hour only made him feel even more lost than the day before and hopelessly lacking a clear sense of direction towards any path presented to him.

His decision years ago to begin an apothecary back in Wakefield had been something that had come completely natural to him at the time as if he were simply repeating a page of actions from his past, which in a way he was since he had done so at least once before with his father in London. It had even provided, for Nathanael and himself, a comfortable living in the peaceful village during the year that they had lived there. But Philadelphia, Pennsylvania was another place entirely, a world within itself, without a single comforting reminder of his past, much like a frighteningly blank slate that would forever dictate his uncertain future.

Yet the day he finally accepted a teaching position at the newly completed Pennsylvania Hospital would always be one he remembered fondly for years to follow. In truth, it was a rare opportunity that was not usually afforded to doctors of his presentable age, but also one that had initially filled him with a motivating drive to help others on a much grander scale than he had ever been offered in the past.

Located just a few blocks down the street from the two-level apartment he and Nathanael shared, it had been the perfect answer to all of his prayers. In fact, from his very first day working as one of the lead physicians, he had discovered a true love for everything about the grand location in which he was employed. From the color of the plaster on the ward walls to the smell of the floorboard stain as it wafted upwards during the summer heat, every aspect of its creation soothed him like nothing else he had ever experienced before in his life. What's more, each step that he took along those perpendicular halls filled him with a renewed form of energy and determination in his work as if it alone was driving him onward with an unseen force towards something he felt was equally fulfilling and meaningful.

In essence, the Pennsylvania Hospital quickly became his place of peace amidst the otherwise unpredictable world in which he lived. The one location to which he could always escape and find some form of normalcy when everything else felt upside down and foreign around him. It was nothing, of course, compared to his simple apothecary back home in Wakefield, and a part of him longed to return to it many times over the years, but in his new position he also enjoyed a steadily growing satisfaction that he never thought he would ever experience again.

Once upon a time, he had desired a small practice of his own, much like the kind his father had shared with him back in London, but over the years that had followed while living in America, he had learned that he much preferred the new teaching aspect afforded to him here to any form of self-gratifying acclaim he might experience in his field of work otherwise. The only part that remained regrettably disappointing at all about his current profession was that it had taken him much longer than any of his friends to see his true purpose in the world in which he was currently residing. But that fact aside, now that he had sufficiently committed to it, he was ready to take on the task with increased vigor to excel in it properly.

Or at least that had been his purpose in the beginning. All of that regrettably changed dramatically for the worse, however, the first day he encountered Miss

Charity Emiline Bentham, the oldest of the nurses in the most recent batch of hired professionals at the hospital. Though even saying that prejudicial characteristic alone sounded more than a bit disrespectful to her in that regard, as the young woman clearly looked not a day over twenty-four, maybe twenty-five, though he could not be for certain which as the woman barely spoke about anything regarding her personal life outside the hospital. Then again, neither did he unless it involved something that would alter his scheduled responsibilities.

Within just a short period of time after her arrival and subsequent assignment to his particular wing of the hospital, the calmness of spirit that treating patients always brought, left him completely. In its place instead, was an awful, denigrating feeling that almost always accompanied his constant need to walk on eggshells around her just to keep the peace. So much so that at present, he almost dreaded clocking in each morning, hesitantly fearful of what events might transpire next that would only lead to more unpleasantness between them.

As faithful as she usually was in diligently completing each and every one of the tasks assigned to her by some of his other colleagues, she was equally as eager to wait for him at her desk every morning at the precise strike of eight to go over his cases before beginning her day. With a folder in hand and a condescending expression on her face, he could almost predict to the letter what she was about to say from her posture as she waited, politely poised and dutifully ready to share with him her opinion on his newest barrage of errors and obvious misdeeds. Items which, in her opinion, far outweighed the logical deductions and treatments that would have been prescribed by his fellow staff members.

This unwelcome routine of daily degradation had, as one might expect, unexpectedly frustrated him in the beginning, and especially so when it came from someone he had felt a common affinity to as a fellow healer. But more importantly, it had taken an almost unbearable emotional toll on his total outlook on life, as well, as it sucked away a piece of the joy that he so often needed for his very survival.

And on the surface, this all would have been a mere inconvenience in the grand scope of things. Something which he could but endure for a season and then be done with entirely when she either left or found someone new to focus all her attention on. But when he started feeling equally chagrined about leaving at the end of the day, as if debating whether or not he had made any error she would notice and castigate him for the next morning, he knew it was time that something altered dramatically between them. As much as he appreciated the value of exactness in regard to anything medically related, her selective prejudice and scrutiny simply wasn't helpful for either him or his patients, and he knew it.

The only question that remained now was how he would ever be able to politely tell her to stop in a way that was not overly hurtful or condescending.

With a sigh after remembering the last encounter he had just had with the woman in question earlier this morning, William set down several of the folders he had been carrying with him onto the head nurse's desk and made his way into the first room of the East Wing to begin his rounds, optimistically positive for what the day might hold despite his recent run-in. If nothing prevented him from leaving at four o'clock today as planned, he would hopefully be celebrating Hope's 18th birthday with his friends tonight. An event which always promised to be a wonderful time of fellowship and laughter. Most definitely, something momentous to celebrate as the last of Sebastian's children officially crossed the threshold into adulthood, but also a night that would always draw itself to be slightly reflective in nature, as well, as it similarly marked the death of one of his cherished friends.

Losing Sebastian three years ago was something none of them had ever expected in their lifetime, let alone contemplated remotely possible for any of them at all. Nor had a single one of them fully recovered from it since. Oh, they had all gone through the expected motions of acceptance and faithfully helped his family whenever and however they needed it over the years, but each man had also inwardly worn the scar of his death, as well. In many ways, his death felt more like a horrible inward badge of honor that constantly reminded them at every turn by the pain it caused that every second of their lives was precarious at best, if not something that should never be taken for granted again.

For Emile, there was always an outwardly indifferent dismissal of his true emotion regarding the mentoring of Sebastian's daughter. A task that he had been ill-prepared for at first and yet seemed to be excelling in at the present.

For William, it was the deep loss of a close companion and the guidance he so often needed from someone with whom he had both trusted and sought many times over for his unique perspective or wisdom over the years. After all, Sebastian had been the <u>one</u> person with whom he had always been able to confide in completely without the need for veiled appearances or hopeful expectations. And William imagined it was the same for Sebastian, as well, as between the two of them, it was always the raw truth of the matter, as ugly and as naked as it always appeared, and not whatever strong countenance they had to show for the protection of others.

As for Nathanael, he was the most surprisingly accepting out of the three remaining friends, having dealt with his own chasm of doubt decades earlier. This was in no way saying that his connection with Sebastian was in any way less amicable or strong in its attachment. Quite the opposite, in fact. Rather, it was more due to the unique advantage he had garnered regarding the importance of keeping his grief in its proper perspective. And in the end, perhaps that singular understanding that he had learned from Elsie's passing was something the rest of them needed, too.

Yet today, William was more focused on just making it through the next hour plausibly still intact mentally and otherwise, emotionally unscathed. A task that was looking equally difficult to imagine with each passing minute of the clock.

Stopping at the first bed on his left after entering the large rectangular room with six beds on either side down the length of it, William picked up the chart that was hanging at the bottom of the patient's bed and read it once more, making sure he had diagnosed all of his issues correctly. The man in his mid-thirties had come in yesterday with terrible tremors and profuse sweating, all mixed with a cold greyness to his pallor from head to toe but had considerably perked back up to his mostly normal state with the administration of sugar water and some other nutritional supplementation in addition to the continuance of such treatment today. Other doctors before William had written their rather dismal suggestions in the margins following his patient's diagnosis, but a few of them made his head hurt considering the archaic methods some of them were still recommending that his patient follow.

"Do you still think it is diabetes insipidus, Doctor Wells?" The nurse, reaching almost his height, asked as she approached him carrying his patient's lunch on a short wooden tray much like the ones he might have seen at the café across town or back at the tavern in Wakefield. Though in that particular instance, it would have undoubtedly been also laden with fresh bread from Susan Summerfield's kitchen and not the sad sort of food they served here at the hospital most days. The carefully constructed meals provided by the institution were certainly edible and highly nutritious overall, but they were still a far cry from the hearty staple he had grown accustomed to back in England almost twenty years ago. In fact, just remembering now the distinct aroma that always wafted out of Susan Summerfield's kitchen every morning as he passed by on his way to Doctor Hadleigh's home filled him with a fresh longing to experience it all over again.

"Hmm??" William forced himself away from the familiar memories and back to the task in front of him. As distracted as he was in completing his notes as precisely as possible to avoid any further perceived mistakes, William barely looked up at the woman in question as he followed the writing out of his new orders by crossing out more than a few of the other side comments on the sheet before another doctor after him should happen to follow them. "What? Yes, it would appear so." He hung the chart back along the upper railing at the foot of the bed and eyed the assortment of food on her tray. "I'm sorry, Nurse Bentham. I know you probably mean well, but you will need to remove about half of the items on that tray if we do not wish to cause a relapse in our patient's recovery."

"What?" The young woman in the starched light blue and white uniformed dress that was worn by most of the nurses on the staff, glanced down in dubious agreement at the potatoes, carrots and roast beef stew that she carried, accompanied by a small bowl of fresh strawberries and a slice of pie on the side. "I don't understand. This is precisely what Doctor Brooks said to bring him this afternoon."

"That may be so. But he is incorrect, as he so often is." William reached over carefully and picked up the pie and the berries. "I am sure many of the doctors from the older order of things still hold tightly to the belief that the patient should be fed plenty of sugar-rich foods, but recent research has shown irrefutably that a diet of at least 65 percent fat, 32 percent protein and only 3 percent carbohydrates is better suited for sustainability of this condition." He shook his head as he struggled to shrug off the mounting dissatisfaction he felt yet again over the obvious intellectual disparity at the hospital. It was the same awful feeling that had always seemed to accompany situations such as this daily, despite his continued efforts to try to ignore it. After all, to the rest of those serving here he looked to be a little less than thirty years old, a mere beginner in his career as a physician and not the seasoned doctor who was quickly approaching his fifties.

And it wasn't the fault of the nurse who had just questioned him either. Due to her recent placement, she was probably still very new to the way they did things around here, or at least the way William was accustomed to how they were done. Not to mention the fact that it was probably his error entirely to have spouted off the reams of information he had just uttered in front of her as if he were speaking to one of his colleagues and not to a member of the lower staff.

During his years practicing in England, he had grown comfortable treating patients in a home setting by himself. Either that, or in collaboration with others like his father in London or even Doctor Hadleigh in Wakefield, if the case became more complicated or was outside his expertise. Yet in each of these instances, not once had he ever been placed in a position where he had to explain <u>why</u> he performed a particular treatment, nor were his methods ever questioned by anyone, save his own personal deliberations regarding something he viewed as a failure.

This was not to say that the staff at the Pennsylvania Hospital were not intelligent by any means, far from it. Despite their years of practically applied education, they simply lacked the decades of experience that he had acquired. Everyone around him, from the nurses to most of the doctors on staff, had been practicing medicine for far less time than he had boasted when he had first begun his apprenticeship on the Endeavor, much less the nineteen years that had passed since. What's more, at least half of those years had been spent learning from those individuals the doctors here had only read about in books. Which only made the firsthand knowledge he possessed doubly difficult to hide when he occasionally referred to those legendary predecessors in a familiar fashion, like the late John Hunter for example, or even some of the various treatments that were considered revolutionary during his time. In a way, he sometimes felt exactly the way Señor Moretti must have when he told his four weary guests that he had worked alongside the great Leonardo da Vinci, an equally stunning confession at the time, but also, still very much true.

Closing his eyes to focus better on how to restate the information that already seemed so rudimentary for him to give, he sighed and attempted to reply as politely as possible so as to diffuse the situation entirely, "What I meant to say is that a salad might be better suited for our patient than pie, Nurse Bentham. Though as far as sweets go, I don't mind the berries as much. The sugar they possess is natural in origin and will pass much more quickly than the boiled sugar in the pie."

"But, sir..." The young woman next to him pursed her lips in marked displeasure at his dismissal of the orders she quite obviously respected more than his own. "Doctor Brooks has worked in this city for far longer than both of us put together. All things considered, I think it would be wise for us to adhere to <u>his</u> wisdom on the matter and not circumvent his wishes." She reached out and took the berries and plate of pie away from William, placing them both back onto the tray in her other hand before turning around to hand them to the patient in question.

Watching her walk abruptly away from him in the opposite direction without so much as a pause to consider his own authority on the matter, William felt his blood pressure rise with the lack of respect she had given him in her curt reply and overstepping action but tried his best to endure patiently her outright dismissal in front of his patient. "That may be so..." He quickly took two steps forward without hesitation and surreptitiously seized the pie once more from her before he subsequently walked over to another bed on the opposite side of the room. Once there, he handed it directly to the elderly patient lying in the bed next to the draped window before smirking wittily at him. "Please, eat this quickly, Mr. Myers, before she steals it away from me again or worse... possibly decides to throw it in my direction. Someone did that once a long time ago, not at me, mind you, but it still took us weeks to remove the very colorful stain upon that wall just over there." He pointed to the end of the room and smiled, trying to add some much-needed levity to the increasingly tense situation.

"Then what, pray tell, am I supposed to say to Doctor Brooks when he questions me about why I changed his dietary orders for the patient?" She clicked her tongue behind him and stared at the doctor across from her with definite disapproval.

"Tell him whatever you like, I suppose. Blame me, if you must." William raised his eyebrows nonchalantly and confronted her with the same casual indifference that he gave to all the other instructions Doctor Brooks had ever written. "Just as long as you do not give my patient any more pie, please."

Making a habit of disrespecting a fellow colleague or even a nurse in any way was never his desired choice of action, nor did he relish the rebuke that was sure to follow from her because of it.   But in this particular instance, he felt more inclined to the necessity of such an action in order to control her actions or rather subversion to his requests. If it had been for his honor alone, he probably would have relented and let the patient in question eat whatever she wanted to feed him without any comment whatsoever about it, but in this case, he simply could not allow such an obvious error to occur when a patient's health was at risk

"As you wish then, Doctor Wells." She turned her back to him immediately without giving him even a moment to respond one way or the other and left the room to fetch another tray for the next patient.

"I'm afraid that you've made an enemy with that one, sir." His original patient in the bed looked up at him over his stew and bore the same worried expression William should have been wearing.

"Possibly, but I hope she will learn to forgive me in time. As you might expect in such a large establishment as this, not everyone agrees with the medical decisions of others, but rest assured, I feel I am right regarding yours, Mr. Miller. Besides, it has been my study that most of the nurses I have met over the years are just trying to impress the doctors they work with in whatever way they can." William paused when she entered the room and tracked her actions as she made her way over to the patient on the opposite side of the large room before continuing. "While the others are simply looking for one to marry," he added dryly, though the nurse who challenged him today did not seem like she fit into either of those categories.

If he had wanted to elaborate further, he could have said much more on the subject, volumes more. Oh, the stories he could have shared with the man about the dozens upon dozens of young nurses who had assaulted him with their attention over the past fifteen years, but he did not. As much as he wanted to do otherwise, he chose instead to remain professionally silent. After all, many of their actions appeared undoubtedly noble in the beginning. They always were on the surface. And they _did_ seem to truly wish to help the patients here. They may have even dreamt of making a difference with their choice of profession once upon a time. Yet in the end, most of them were not focused on the medicine at all. He had even seen a few nurses return months or even years later, looking equally dissatisfied with their previous choices, as they begged to be given a second chance.

Simply put, he had only seen but a handful of nurses who actually fit _his_ description of what their position actually entailed and even that felt close to an exaggeration compared to what the hospital viewed as acceptable behavior. But... like the gentleman he was trained to be, William simply kept the knowledge to himself as he studied the nurse who seemed to carry along with her a definite opinion about everything as she worked and wondered what it would take on his part to initiate a final ceasefire between them. Or really, anything that might conceivably resemble a peaceful coexistence daily instead of the farce they were currently enduring.

The man in the bed next to him, however, only shook his head at William's plight and went back to his food eagerly, trying his best to remain hidden from the brewing conversation unfolding quickly in front of him. In fact, twice in the span of two minutes, he glanced up and then over at William helplessly as he watched in tentative apprehension as Nurse Bentham suddenly stopped what she was doing and chose instead to storm back to his bedside once more, a fire evident behind her piercing green eyes.

"Can I help you further, Miss?" William looked up at the woman curiously as she waited, her blonde hair neatly arranged above her neck in a woven pattern to hold her evidently wavy curls up and out of the way of her duties.

"Unfortunately for both of us, Doctor Wells, I heard what you said just now, though I most definitely wish I had not. And while we are on _that_ subject, I'd prefer it if you would keep your erroneous assumptions regarding my personal life to yourself in the future. Despite what you have dismally surmised, I have not the slightest intention of marrying anyone here, much less an over-opinionated doctor like yourself." She folded her arms across her chest in clear perturbance.

"Now, you've done it," the man in the bed mumbled quietly, clearly more experienced in these matters of strategic avoidance than William was any day.

"Not helping..." William said out of the corner of his mouth to him as he tried futilely to think of a more diplomatic way out of his current conversation, but nothing materialized.

Although he had been raised with the social graces necessary to court a variety of women within his circle back in London, he had never been truly skilled when it came to conversing with any of them easily. A fact which only made matters infinitely worse with Nurse Bentham as he was constantly misjudged, or regrettably misunderstood by her, in his overly blunt remarks and inability to execute the proper amount of flattery to diffuse his fatal missteps. "What should I do?" He whispered quietly back to the man, eager for a little free advice.

"Beg, man... beg," the patient replied back quickly, which reminded William very much of the taunting his brother always initiated in situations where he was clearly in over his head. Which apparently, he was... again.

Trying to add some level of humility to the conversation at last, William cracked a smile, then huffed slightly, shaking his head in humored relief. He couldn't help it. The man was right. His manners had been atrocious and all of them knew it. "You are correct, Nurse Bentham. My sincerest apologies for slighting your character so openly in my inference. It was wrong, and it will not happen again."

"See that it doesn't, please." She held her head aloft with the confidence befitting a seasoned army colonel and left without another word to retrieve the next tray.

Unable to do otherwise, William examined her stride and stature intently as she went and couldn't help but admire the strength and poise she clearly possessed. Only his friend, Emile, had ever been as confident as she was in rebuking him. Not that he minded his often-times colorful comments, of course. On the whole, most of his remarks were constructive in nature or more or less humorous when he delivered them. Hers were, well... he wasn't exactly sure what it was that she was holding against him really, but whatever it was, she was undoubtedly, always ready for a fight with ample ammunition to spare.

"She truly hates me, doesn't she?" He asked the man honestly in the bed beside him before looking up once more to watch her walk across the room and to his left, the hair on the back of his neck lifting slightly at the sight of her as she passed, as if warning him of the danger she emitted by merely entering the room.

"Well, let's just say that between you and I, I would not be drinking anything she offered me today if I were you," the man joked at William's expense.

"Noted." William chuckled once more, though this time he was a bit more relaxed when doing so. All in all, the man was a delightful fellow to converse with indeed and certainly far more cautiously inclined when it came to sticky situations. "I'll be sure to heed your advice for the future. Now, as for you, I recommend that you continue exercising as much as possible when you are feeling better but be mindful not to do so when the tremors strike. That is when you should eat that pie I stole from you. The tremors are an excellent warning that your body needs you to stop and take care of yourself. Don't ignore them or the next time you might not be as fortunate."

"Is there not some kind of pill or tonic that might help instead?" The man finished his stew and allowed William to take away his empty tray.

"I am afraid not. Some doctors of my acquaintance have been known to treat this condition with opium, but in that case, the cure can be much worse than the illness. So, please do not try it. If you can manage to do as I say for the time being, that would be better overall for your family as the alternative can lead to very severe side effects and even dependency in many cases. Come to think of it, I have even heard recently that tobacco has shown some signs of helping, as does taking long baths—both cold and hot, but above all, you should avoid any form of stress if at all possible. A calmer lifestyle in general will aid in keeping your system more balanced and less prone to these attacks. Do you think you can manage that?" William walked over to the short desk in the corner of the room and began filling out the release paperwork for the patient.

"A calmer lifestyle? Doctor Wells, I have ten children and one more on the way this coming September. Stress comes with the territory in my life, I am afraid." The man shrugged.

"I imagine that it does." William laughed lightly. "But see that you encourage some of that brood to help you when you are able, at the very least."

"I will and thank you." The man fluffed his pillow and rolled onto his side. "No chance I can have you write that for a few more days of rest here, possibly? Might come in handy to build my strength up for what faces me at home later."

"That bad, eh?" William paused in his task, feeling a slight bit of sympathy for the man for though he had always wanted children of his own, ten seemed like quite an overwhelming number for any parent to raise.

"My wife makes Nurse Bentham look like an angel, sir," the man sheepishly admitted but did so without seeing the nurse in question walk through the doorway behind him.

With increasing irritation now over the second time that she had been demeaned in the span of twenty minutes alone, she cast a very dark stare at the man and then at William before choosing to ignore them both in a huff and instead uttered under her breath just one word before passing, "...children."

"Well, Mr. Miller, it appears that both of us are going thirsty today, if you remain." William smiled and signed his release papers. "Though all things considered, it might be safer for you at home."

"Probably so." The man laughed and threw his legs over the edge of the bed to begin getting dressed.

"But please do come back if you should have another episode like before." William patted the man's shoulder compassionately as he walked by and moved on to the next patient down the row. A very young-looking girl who couldn't have been much older than five or six by the tightly woven braids in her chocolate brown hair and the scattered spray of freckles across the tiny bridge of her nose. "And how is Miss Lily Mae feeling today? Is your throat any better?" William sat on the edge of the bed next to the little girl and placed the back of his fingers on his left hand gently upon her forehead.

Alone as she was at the time, the small girl did not move to speak at first, but only shook her head back and forth nervously, her expression quivering slightly as if she were about to cry at the thought of what might happen next if her answer was unfavorable.

"Come, come, now. It can't be all that bad. Here, let me look inside... I promise it won't hurt." He took the opportunity to tug gently on her chin so that he could angle her head just right to see deep into the back of her throat properly. "Actually, as it turns out, you may be wise in choosing not to speak today."

"Why?" The girl whispered hoarsely, her eyes suddenly growing wide in apprehension.

"I am no expert mind you, but from what I can see, there may just be a dragon inside of you, after all." William pretended to play along with the child as he attempted to cheer her up for neither of her parents had been able to sit with her for the past day at least.

"A dragon?" The girl fidgeted with her covers, pulling them higher up to her chin. "But I don't want a dragon inside of me. I want to go home to my mama and papa."

"Hmmm..." William nodded soberly and pursed his lips as if he were deep in thought as to how to rid a child of a dragon ingestion. "Well then, there is only one thing left for us to do, I suppose. If going home tomorrow is your desire, we will simply have to make him disappear today for good."

"But how will we do that?" The girl seemed intensely interested and keenly invested now in anything that might help her for she liked the manner in which he spoke to her very much, just like the way of her own dear papa.

"Well, you see... as a very old doctor... who has studied all there is to know about dragons and how they like to hide inside helpless little children, I happen to know the one and only weakness of dragons. Though to tell you the truth, it has taken me many years to discover it."

"How long?" The little girl's face was an absolute mixture of wonder and concern all combined into one delightful expression.

"Ages and ages... Can't you tell how old I am by my blondish white hair?" He continued to lead her along.

"Noooo..." The little girl giggled at his absurd description, as did several others in the room around her.

"Doctor Wells is known to be practically ancient, child. Much too old for the rest of us to fool him around here, let alone the dragons." Nurse Bentham quipped from the end of the bed as she passed.

"Quite right." William smiled at her humorous assessment for it had been the most truthful thing he had heard today. "But I tell you what, Lily Mae... if you promise not to tell anyone else, I will whisper it to you, as well." He paused dramatically to increase the suspense he had created. "Mind you... I can only tell you. I can't risk letting the secret out to all the other doctors here or it may not work again in the future. Dragons are smart, after all. So smart in fact, that they learn all of our tricks very quickly." William leaned back and crossed his arms across his chest leisurely as he waited to see if the little girl would take the bait.

"Oh, I promise, Doctor Wells. You can tell me. Mama says I am awfully good at keeping secrets when I have to." She studied William eagerly with her beautiful brown eyes, and it warmed his heart to see her enthusiasm for it meant her fever had most definitely subsided and she was certainly growing closer to being released from his care.

"Alright, but remember, you cannot tell a single soul." He looked down at her quite seriously for effect.

"I promise." The girl made an 'x' mark over her heart and kissed the two fingers on her right hand in pledge.

"Nope, I need a pinky promise," William demanded solemnly. "Us dragon doctors have a code to follow, you know."

The girl giggled then in immense satisfaction and held out her left pinky to the doctor beside her without hesitation.

"Alright, I accept your pledge, Lily Mae." William wrapped his pinky with her own and leaned down to whisper the secret very closely to her ear. So close in fact, that he could feel the tickle of her stray hairs that had escaped her braid against the edges of his lips. "The one weakness of all dragons is…" He looked around the room to make sure no one else was listening close by.

"Is what…?" The girl whispered back in focused concentration.

"Ice cream," he whispered swiftly, then leaned farther away from her once more and repeated his declaration even louder as if the news was never a secret at all, "It's ice cream, of course! Lots and lots of ice cream! We have to freeze him out of there."

The girl giggled again and the sound of it made William's heart soar. "You're silly, Doctor Wells."

"I know." William shrugged. "But it's true. Because you have been such a good patient during your stay with us, you can have all the ice cream you can eat today, and then tomorrow, you can probably go home. Now, how does that sound?"

"Really? Truly?" The girl's eyes lit up like he had just promised to give her all the gifts she had ever wanted on Christmas morning.

"If the dragon stays away for the rest of the day today, then, yes." William tapped the child's nose and made a note in the chart that the fever had left and to allow her as many cold treats as she would prefer to soothe the lingering effects of her sore throat.

"Thank you, Doctor Wells. You're the bestest doctor <u>ever</u>." The girl grinned up at him, obviously his new admirer, though on her account, this was one infatuation he did not mind enduring at all.

"No, thank you, Lily for keeping my secret. Now, why don't I go fetch you some of that ice cream before I forget." William stood and put the chart back on the end of the bed before turning to leave but instead ended up bumping right into Nurse Bentham who was standing silently behind him, a small bowl of vanilla ice cream waiting in her hands.

"Ooppss…" The girl laughed once more at the collision.

"I'm so sorry, Nurse Bentham. I should have been looking where I was going," William attempted to apologize sincerely but looked momentarily more flustered than apologetic by their sudden collision. On the surface, this singular contact, which took only seconds thereafter for the pair to move out of the path of the other, had surprised him more than anything else that had transpired that day or any other day in his existence so far. The startling feeling the connection with her hand had created as it accidentally brushed past the surface of William's skin sent a tremendously unsettling jolt of static through his entire being as if he had been suddenly struck with a miniscule bolt of energy.

Justifiably stunned, for the briefest of moments following their accidental encounter, Nurse Bentham met his gaze with the same look of hesitant alarm mixed with a healthy dose of definite confusion and concern but then quickly looked away once more as she kept walking over to their patient. "This is for you, Lily Mae. And just let me know when you would like more, Sweetheart, and I will fetch it for you—day or night." The young nurse handed her the small dish of ice cream and a spoon before turning to leave as if nothing of consequence had happened at all between them. "Doctor..."

Dazed and bewildered by what had just happened, as much as he was when it first occurred, William could not utter a reply in return but remained immoveable where he stood while trying his best to make sense of it all and sort out his inner deliberations.

"It's like I am a princess, here." Lily ate a large bite of the creamed dessert and smiled, the milk from the treat now layering the edges of her upper and bottom lip.

"As it should be." William shook his head to clear away the more troubling points of his curiosity and regained his sense of reality once more before he bowed politely towards the girl. "I will see her highness bright and early tomorrow morning. And I will send word to your mama and papa today that they can come get you shortly after breakfast tomorrow, if that suits you."

"Yes, please." The little girl beamed and continued to eat her dessert happily.

Feeling perfectly content with the exchange that had just transpired with his patient, William smiled genuinely at the way the child had been able to lighten his mood and walked out of the room towards the center hallway beyond, ready to sit down for a minute and simply collect his thoughts about what had just transpired. The conversation with Nurse Bentham today had not been his first encounter with the woman, but from the coolness of her countenance towards him through it, he prayed it might be his last or at least the last for a while.

And as to what he had just experienced at Lily Mae's bedside, William had not the faintest idea where to even begin in sorting all of that out. Nor was he particularly sure he was ready to either. As strange as it was, there was no doubt a litany of logical reasons for it had occurred and none of them involved anything nefarious in nature.

Maybe it was just... he began to deduce a possibility mentally as he walked but paused when he heard his name being called from the hallway behind him.

"Doctor Wells, may I have a word with you, please?" Nurse Bentham's impatient voice echoed off the surfaces around him where he stood, sending a fresh shudder of apprehensive fear up his spine in a learned reaction to it.

"Of course, Nurse Bentham." He forced himself to remain positive and professional as he turned around in his place to face her, just to the left of the main intersection of the two opposing wings. "How may I help you further?"

The woman across from him held her peace momentarily as she continued walking towards him, respectfully passing several of their other colleagues until she stood almost a foot away from him in the hall. Far enough to maintain a polite distance away from him, yet close enough to keep their conversation a tad more private. Yet in lieu of delivering whatever speech she had no doubt properly prepared during her short trek over to him, she instead shook her head in frustration as if she were taking the time allotted to her to thoroughly study him from afar.

"Are you looking for my weaknesses, Nurse Bentham?" William quipped wittily at her intense stare, attempting to lighten the mood between them with a little more honest frankness, or at least as much as he currently felt comfortable sharing.

"No," she stated flatly but did not shift her gaze in the slightest.

"Then what?" William countered casually. "My friends say I am more than an open book to them, though I'd like to think I still hold a few secrets that remain entirely mine own."

"I am sure you do... though I was merely trying to understand how you can be so kind and gentle with one patient, clever and almost endearingly diverting with others, and then a total shabbaroon to anyone else you don't prefer at the time, or outright rude even if they should dare to counterman your opinion in any way. It's almost like you are a myriad of conflicting personalities all at once—some delightful and charming, compassionate even, while others... to put it plainly, are quite offensive to experience."

"And that is unusual to you? I thought all men were faithfully described as an enigmatic mystery to women." William tried to hide the humor he was beginning to feel under her questioning for he had never heard himself ever described in such a manner. Not even Emile would have said so and that man never held back an opinion or sarcastic remark for any occasion.

"They might like to think so, but no. Still, I can't make you out, sir, but if you would be so inclined to try to explain it, I'd very much like to understand." She looked away from him at last and watched as another pair of doctors passed them by, allowing William the chance to study her in the same way.

In truth, William could still feel the lingering power of her previous gaze upon the surface of his skin even though her eyes were no longer trained directly on him anymore. "Well, I am not sure where to even begin." William raised one eyebrow in question, attempting to provide a concise answer to her simple request, but changed his approach entirely as a feeling of total amusement overtook him with her rather unique choice of words concerning his character. "Wait a minute... did I hear you correctly that you think I am a shabbaroon? Believe it or not, I haven't heard that term used in quite some time." He laughed lightly. "But I suppose if you think that it suits me... well, who am I to argue."

Nurse Bentham immediately blushed, noticing all too late her obviously outdated remark but deflected his jibe curtly as if he were continuing to mock her instead. "Oh, you know what I meant."

"Do I?" William leaned back casually against the wall behind him and laughed even harder, though quietly enough so as to not attract any attention from others passing by on their way to their given tasks.

Feeling utterly humiliated now by his nonsensical outburst, Nurse Bentham turned immediately to leave, thinking that despite his previous display of pleasant commonality, the man was just as eager to insult her in private as well as in public now. "Forget I even asked," she dismissed him promptly and shook her head in disapproval at her wasted effort on the man's behalf.

"Nurse Bentham, wait." William mimicked her actions quickly. Only instead of letting her leave as she had obviously wanted, he stepped in front of her to block her path and halt her escape entirely. "Let me ask <u>you</u> an alternate question instead, if I may."

"Fine. What?" Her reply came back cold and hard, spoken more as a statement of disgust than an actual question.

"What am I constantly doing that annoys you so greatly? I know you just alluded to the fact that it might have something to do with my capricious bedside manner, but is that truly all there is to it?" William asked sincerely, hoping to diffuse her anger further for he surmised that if he could just figure out what it was that he was doing that was annoying her so greatly, he had a hopeful chance of avoiding it altogether in the future.

For several moments, Nurse Bentham paused silently in patient deliberation next to him before she finally looked away from her focused attention on the wall beside her and back to the man in question. "Respectfully, sir, I don't think you fully realize the impact your words and actions have on the conduct of others. Or at least if you did, I would like to think that you would behave differently," she replied more cordially than he had expected possible with also a hint of something closer to an actually amiable form of conversation.

Stunned by the absolute truth of the words she had spoken, William's mouth fell open slightly as if he were about to speak then closed it again once more, as he suddenly felt the need to rub the excess anxiety away from the back of his neck that had collected there.

"I am sorry." Nurse Bentham looked away once more and collected herself swiftly. "I shouldn't have been so bold to say it, even though you asked. Please accept my apologies, Doctor Wells," she pleaded quietly but gave no further indication now that she was especially eager to leave his presence like before.

Finding his voice at last, William cleared his throat and answered softly, wanting nothing more than to put this whole awful situation behind them once and for all. "No, it is I who must apologize for you are entirely correct." William ran a hand nervously through his blond hair, trying to think of the most appropriate way to fix the situation he had quite obviously caused. "I should have been more sensitive as to what I was saying and who was listening. Please forgive me for my unprofessionalism at the very least and my sincere lack of manners in general," he said contritely and glanced back at her briefly, hoping to see at least some glimmer of hopeful resolution in her otherwise bright green eyes.

"Forgiven," she said just as quickly with a small nod and moved to turn her focus back to him to say something more but was instead, unexpectedly interrupted as they so often were in as busy a hospital as this.

"Doctor Wells, you are needed in the Receiving Room please," a voice coming from directly behind her in the doorway on her right instructed politely, the urgency clearly evident in her request.

"Thank you. I'll be there directly, Nurse Fitzpatrick." William nodded towards her respectfully and slowly held out the proverbial olive branch to the nurse in front of him. "Would you be possibly willing to work alongside me this afternoon? As I am sure I cannot change all of my habits sufficiently to avoid further offence in the area in question so soon, your help may save some other poor soul from going home crying because Doctor Wells was malicious to her again."

"Oh, dear." Charity only rolled her eyes, shaking her head for several moments before answering him with an equally sarcastic grin that matched his own. "So, let me see if I understand this properly. For the rest of the day, I alone am to receive the immense honor of being the main target of your torture?"

"Maybe..." William shrugged and held the door open for her to pass through first. "Or at the very least for this afternoon, perhaps tomorrow, too, if I can manage it? Though I suppose it all depends more on how long I can make this truce between us last."

"Wonderful," Charity muttered and turned around to follow him into Receiving while trying her best to obey his directions thereafter as he treated patient after patient until it was well after five o'clock.

Frankly, it was the first time that William had felt so utterly at peace while working with anyone in the hospital for a very long time. So much so, in fact, that the hours had passed by like mere minutes as they worked, instead of the relentless ticking of the clock in his ears as he completed task after task methodically.

"I think that should suffice to get them caught up for now," William claimed triumphantly when he had finally dispersed the last of its patients that required his immediate attention and looked up at the clock once more with a start. "I must be off, but if you need me, I will be at the home of Mrs. Charlotte Fabbri tonight. But please," he paused before placing the final chart he was holding onto the main desk by the front door. "<u>Please</u> do not need me unless it is an <u>utmost</u> emergency. We are celebrating a momentous occasion tonight, and I would <u>very</u> much like to be there if possible."

"Of course, sir." One of the new nurses at the desk nodded obediently towards him and picked up the chart he had just laid there to put it in the proper stack for filing later.

"Leaving so soon, Doctor Wells?" Nurse Bentham called out to him as he touched the handle of the outer door, obviously ready to leave, as well.

Looking more than a little surprised that she was still there and not already on her way home as she had left him over an hour ago, William turned back abruptly to answer. "Yes, I have a family supper to attend on the other side of town."

"I see. Well, I will have your charts waiting for you to amend in the morning. We can go over them then as usual." Charity nodded authoritatively once again and put on her short navy-blue cape to follow after him out the front door. "Provided there are any glaring errors in them at all this time."

"One can only hope not, Miss Bentham... one can only hope. Until tomorrow, then." William felt the irritation with her annoying habit of incessantly checking over his work, like a teacher grading his exams, flush over his skin once more but chose to bid her a polite farewell and began walking in the opposite direction to hire a carriage for he was already going to be dreadfully late as it was—much too late to contemplate taking the journey on foot as he normally did.

Still, as the carriage pulled up to the spot in front of him to collect its waiting passenger, William suddenly realized with a start what the brief surge of energy he had experienced earlier in the day reminded him of. The very same prickling sensation he was feeling now as he stood on the edge of the street and before in the East Wing, when Nurse Bentham had passed directly behind him, matched the one he had felt back at the Knole so many years ago. The one that had been associated with the late Doctor Clarke, though that man was most definitely not able to have caused it, nor were there many other people passing by him now, save the carriage driver alone, and a few others of little consequence. Or rather, certainly no one that made him instantly cautious as to their dangerous intentions.

With growing alarm at the strength of its intensity and what it may all mean going forward, he glanced back over his shoulder and watched as the young nurse from the hospital made her way down the walkway in the opposite direction towards his apartment. Never in all his life had he met someone so infuriating and yet so amiable as she was, all at the same time. As young as she seemed, she appeared to have the perfect balance of wit and tenacity to match his own, as if she had gleaned the knowledge of many more years than was blatantly obvious. Yet even more surprising was the way in which she had managed to keep step with him at every turn this afternoon, and especially so in the most difficult of situations that would have made other nurses cringe or look away.

Yet something was not right about her either. In fact, now that he finally had a moment to reflect upon it more at length, he realized that there had been an unusual imbalance between them since the very beginning that had been nagging him all afternoon as they worked.

But why?

Maybe it had all stemmed from the unusual sensation he had picked up when they had bumped into each other earlier. Or, quite possibly, it had originated from the stress of the day he had just endured. Either way, whatever it was, he did not have the time tonight to investigate it properly. Nor did he feel especially inclined that whatever he was experiencing was intended for harm. To be honest, it all felt akin to the same way his senses pricked to attention when Emile or Nathanael stopped by the hospital unannounced.

Still.... His eyes narrowed in concentration as he studied the beautifully annoying woman from a distance and contemplated once again if he should follow her instead.

Obviously sensing the weight of his stare upon her shoulders or possibly just as confused as he was right at that moment, the young nurse paused suddenly in her retreat and turned back to look at him before eyeing him with the same intense skepticism in which he was now examining her.

In the soft hues of the approaching sunset, time itself seemed to cautiously hesitate between their watchful gaze for the briefest of moments as it held its breath before resuming back into sequence once more with an uneasy jolt.

Rebuked and feeling suddenly awkward at being caught staring at the woman in question for such a great length of time, William chose to raise his hand in farewell instead, then turned abruptly to the waiting carriage and stepped inside.

Whatever strange occurrence was plausibly amiss between them, it would not be solved by going after her tonight. Nor would it do to be any later than he already was.

The only thing he needed most of all right now was time to think, and possibly a short discussion with both of his friends before he chose to act.

Chapter Seven

June 28th, 1811

"I hear the price per bushel of wheat is going as high as fourteen dollars this season."Jedidiah picked up the latest copy of the newspaper and handed it over to Elijah sitting next to him at the table, hoping to garner some kind of interest from his brother even though he had never shown more than a passing opinion on the subject before.

"That high? Well, that is certainly more than twice the cost of corn and much better than last year, too. Are you sure?" Elijah studied the paper casually for more details about the increase before turning to his brother and continuing, "But even with knowing that, you still plan on planting over twenty acres of corn like you always do, don't you?"

"Yes."

"That's crazy! I know it shouldn't, but it always baffles me as to why on earth you would waste your precious acreage and resources on something that won't yield the same in return?"

"It's for the livestock, of course, Elijah. Not every crop I plant is for sale. The cows depend on the corn during the winter months to survive just as much as the alfalfa and hay. In my opinion, it is wiser to lose the income from a few acres of corn if it helps me feed them properly. Either that or we will have to plant twice the amount of alfalfa to compensate, which will take even more acres away from the profitable wheat. Or worse yet, buy it elsewhere. Besides, it is far less detrimental to the land to grow it in small portions when it is needed than to use the same area year after year like I have seen other farmers doing," Jedidiah replied as he leaned back in his chair and crossed his arms. " always told me we needed to switch the crop locations every so often to keep the soil healthy. And though I do not understand the science behind it as much as say Uncle William or even Uncle Nathanael, since Papa said it, that is as good as gospel to me."

"Your brother has quite a lot of plans for the land this year and next. You should really hear them, Eli. You never know. You might even find them equally exciting as the forge," Charlotte encouraged her youngest son from the kitchen.

"I doubt that very highly," Elijah muttered, utterly unmotivated on the subject. "I think I'd much rather have my ears filled with wax then spend the evening discussing the price of seed and the current cycle of cow reproduction."

"You like milk, do you not?" Charlotte continued to try to draw her youngest son into some kind of involvement with the farm for Jedidiah's sake.

For the past three years, it had been quite an ordeal for her oldest son to manage the full one hundred acres on his own, but he had done so with little complaint. Moreover, watching him work in the place of his father, she had been forever grateful that he was as steady in nature as she was.

Each day that passed them by had turned into yet another that was equally difficult. Yet he simply went from one task to the next, completing whatever life threw at him as if it was always meant to be that way.

Though that did not also mean that Charlotte was ready to let his younger brother off the hook so easily either. In fact, with a little more help from Elijah, the farm, as a whole, would be more manageable for everyone, profitable even if they did not have to hire extra hands to bring in the harvest again this year. In truth, it was a necessary reality they had to consider time and again as situations arose where the required task demanded at least two men to be working steadily in tandem for a week, yet only one was willing to do so. Though all things considered, it had taken almost everyone's help to accomplish much of the farm's upkeep the months after Sebastian had died for none of them had truly realized the load that Sebastian had been silently carrying.

From the tightened lips that never seemed to smile anymore to the slightly hunched way Jedidiah now walked back home at the end of the day, Charlotte could plainly see that beyond menial chores, Elijah's refusal to help since his father's passing had grated on Jedidiah's nerves quite heavily, but he would never say so to her outright. Nor would he indulge his brother to appear weak in front of him either.

With little other choice than the one that placed more burden onto his mother than what she was already currently enduring, Jed was more the suffer in silence type, like his father. And just like her dearest Sebastian, as well, she knew he would not relent in the slightest until he was no longer able to physically do whatever it was he was currently tackling.

From the very first days of their arrival in Philadelphia, Elijah had made it undeniably clear where he was eager to pour all his energy, and it certainly wasn't at the farm. Day after day and month after month, Jedidiah had dutifully watched his father complete his tasks around the homestead and had chosen to follow after him in perfect mimic as he tried to emulate his actions to the letter and garner the love and attention he had so greatly missed the previous year.

Elijah, on the other hand, seemed completely bored with the life his father had suddenly thrust upon them, gravitating instead towards anything he could build with his hands. Whether that was iron or wood alike, it made no difference to him just as long as he had a hammer in his hand and a steady arm to drive it to completion.

The two boys, as different in nature now as they were in physical description, had only continued to drift even further apart in their understanding of the other when Sebastian had died. Without his daily reminders of the equal importance each of their trades held, each man had chosen to plant his roots on two very different sides of the street. Not in total opposition to the other's way of life, mind you, but rather, a bit too happily inclined to remain in their own sphere of existence for the time being.

As the eldest and obvious choice, Jedidiah had seen to the necessary management of the farm and to its livestock, continuing where his father had left off just like he had tried to do when Sebastian was on the island twenty years ago. Whereas Elijah had taken over the family business in town, creating his own version of his father's vision, complete with two liveries and a fully stocked forge that was nearly twice the size of the one his father had owned back in Portsmouth.

"Well, yes, I suppose I do enjoy cream in my coffee and maybe a glass for my supper, but I doubt I love it any more than the next person." Elijah shrugged.

"Then you should pay more attention to the manner in which we come by it." Charlotte set a plate full of fried chicken in the center of the table as well as a bowl of steaming hot green beans from the garden. "Food does not exactly appear out of nowhere like it does down at the café. If you want to eat, you must nurture and protect that crop—plan for its future even or someday you might starve."

Acting as if he had tuned his mother out completely on the subject, Elijah reached to steal one of the green beans from the bowl like he had on so many other occasions over the years but was stopped by a firm swat of her hand against his own... again. "Ow, Mama!"

"Hands off, young man. We are waiting for <u>everyone</u> please," Charlotte reminded him sternly.

"Who else is coming tonight, Mother?" Hope carried the bread and mashed potatoes carefully to the table and set them down in front of Michael who had chosen a seat closest to Jedidiah on the right side of the table nearest the kitchen.

"I think all of your uncles at the very least, but not Thomas and Hannah this time," Charlotte answered as she wiped her hands off on her short apron. "The baby has the sniffles, I believe. So, as you might expect, they are being understandably cautious that she doesn't excite herself unnecessarily."

"Aww, I was rather hoping to get a chance to hold little Abigail tonight," Hope pouted but not in a way that was overly dramatic. "She is such a lovely little thing."

"Yes, she is. It is a shame though that she was also born blind like her mother. Sadly, I have no real experience in these matters, but from what I have seen of the schools here, she may have a difficult time in finding a suitable education when she finally comes of age," Charlotte said politely before moving to the window to check on the progress of her other guests.

"You never know. She may surprise us all. People usually do," Jedidiah added positively. "Don't you agree, my dear?"

Jedidiah's wife, Nancy, who had been upstairs in one of the upper bedrooms nursing their new son, James, or Santiago, as his father liked to call him when they were anywhere other than in town, descended the stairs behind them and joined the family at the table. "What will people do, Jed?"

"Surprise us," Elijah repeated. "Speaking of surprises, are we waiting until after supper to give Hope her birthday presents?"

"Oh, please can we do it before! I am simply dying to see what you all have been hinting at this past month," Hope pleaded more earnestly.

"Well, maybe just one gift while we wait. The rest we will open after supper, <u>as usual</u>." Charlotte relinquished slightly, hoping that in doing so she would at least distract the rest of the group until the others had arrived.

Since the night of Sebastian's death, she had positively dreaded <u>any</u> activity that involved the watching of the long road for someone to arrive, and with good reason. Letting Hope stay occasionally at Emile and Emma's afterwards had actually turned out to be the easiest part of his passing, though also regrettably one that only added to her loneliness as it paved the way for a shockingly loud emptiness to creep into her home when her daughter was away.

Thankfully for all involved, Emile and Emma's home now lay not two miles from the edge of their current property line. Much closer than any other neighbor of their acquaintance, and yet also something that had, in God's great providence, been arranged irrefutably perfect for everyone involved. As a matter of fact, in a stroke of fortuitous luck, the owner of the small farmhouse to the west of their land had passed away shortly after Emile had mentioned the complicated request her daughter had made of him.

As divided as they all were at the time about the possibility of Hope moving all the way to Charleston, the now available property had provided the perfect answer to all of their prayers instantly as no one in the family seemed especially eager to sever any more ties so soon. Or as Nathanael had so properly put it during the rather lengthy discussion that had followed thereafter, "Now is the time to focus on family, not convenience." And he was exactly right.

The simple farmhouse next door was nothing compared to the large colonial monstrosity Emile and Emma had occupied back in Charleston, but neither of them seemed to mind the difference in the slightest. For the most part, it was probably even smaller than William and Nathanael's two-story flat in the center of town, with only two bedrooms on the upper floor to speak of and a small outer building they sometimes used for storage after they moved the rest of their belongings from their bakery after they sold it shortly thereafter. In all, it was just big enough for the two of them and one more yet still removed enough to provide them the necessary privacy when needed, while also allowing them the opportunity to be much closer to all of their friends, and of course, Hope.

And as with most farms, it also came with a healthy amount of acreage for some crops or pasture. At present, Emile was much too busy with his new position in the government to entertain anything in regard to its care and development in that way. So, as a gesture of goodwill, he had chosen to rent out his fields to the neighbor one farm over in exchange for a small, monetary compensation come harvest time from a percentage of the proceeds earned. This overly generous arrangement had suited the neighbor fine for there was little risk involved for him in doing so and precious little inconvenience in the end for Emile. In truth, it was the perfect solution by Charlotte's way of thinking and one that had allowed Hope the space she needed when she was feeling especially overwhelmed, without the expense and lengthy travel accommodation back and forth to another state, not to mention the added worry.

And yet, despite the overwhelming convenience the arrangement had provided, the long hours spent in isolation within a house that had once been filled with so much love had steadily grown to be some of the hardest in her existence. Without question, Sebastian was still everywhere here, just like he was in life, though she tried very hard to continue on without focusing on that unbearable truth. Even the sturdy walls themselves echoed back the soft tenor of his voice all around her at times when she climbed the steps to their bed at night or breathed out an exhausted sigh of stolid acceptance as she blew out the candles and slipped under the always-cold now covers.

Determined at last to pass the day this year without breaking down yet again at the absence of his touch, Charlotte chased away a tear from the corner of her eye quickly and tried her best to put on a convincing expression of the joy she knew Hope needed to see, but her heart was not ready to experience it for herself.

"Now, this is only a part of a much larger present, so please keep that in mind when you open it," Elijah explained as he watched the excitement on Hope's face grow with the suspense.

"Stop stalling, Eli! You make it seem like you are afraid I will be disappointed or something." Hope tried to contain her slight irritation at his repeated delays.

"So little patience for someone so old already." Elijah raised his eyebrows and shook his head at her teasingly as he reached inside his pocket and drew out a small box that fit just inside his palm before presenting it to her slowly.

"Oh...?" Hope frowned at seeing the rather dismally wrapped gift presented to her but reached for the box anyways and lifted the lid quickly, hesitantly still excited at the possibilities it might contain. Yet once the box that was wrapped with only a piece of crude twine and some slightly wrinkled brown paper was opened, the present inside confounded her even more, for within lay not a piece of jewelry she could wear, or a cleverly created metal comb for her hair, but a very ornately created metal key, complete with three beautifully entwined loops at the top that held the stem. "A key?"

"A key." Elijah nodded with no further explanation whatsoever regarding it.

"This is worse than having to wait for <u>all</u> of the presents as I have no idea what kind of thing this belongs to, or what is inside whatever it opens." Hope's bottom lip protruded into a definite pout.

"It is but the key to my heart and you, my dear, have it already," Michael said sweetly in an attempt to distract and impress her as he reached for her hand and looked up at her adoringly from across the table.

"Awww." Nancy placed one hand over her heart with sincere emotion. "That is probably the nicest thing I have heard in quite some time. Isn't it Jed?"

"Hmmm." Jedidiah eyed Hope's beau with skeptical acceptance.

"Uh-oh, perhaps you need to be taking some lessons from Michael now, brother, or he may sweep your wife off her feet next." Elijah laughed and practically pounced on the opportunity to tease his older brother who was not enjoying the focus in the least.

"Indeed," Jedidiah huffed in tired displeasure. Elijah, as he well knew, was quite the attraction in town with probably over a dozen or more girls vying for his favor currently. So much so, in fact, that there was probably not a single girl in their school growing up who had not secretly pined over putting her initials next to those of the strapping local young blacksmith, though Elijah had never shown interest in any one of them to date. Still, Jedidiah knew something that Elijah did not. Despite what his brother may profess loudly against it, it was only a matter of time before one of those girls eventually hooked him and reeled in her very prized catch, rough edges and all.

Annoyed tonight more than usual, Jedidiah eyed his brother from the head of the table, then shot back the best criticism he could manage, mercilessly attempting to draw his ire. "I already found me a wife, and a beautiful one at that." He winked at his wife and smiled when she blushed with pleasure at the compliment in return. "What do you have? A dirty old building and a bunch of cold tools to keep you company at night. A fine reality that is, or do you plan on being single forever, Eli?"

"Boys!" Charlotte warned sternly, afraid that the conversation might rise to an ill-advised level as it had on so many other occasions. "Be kind. We will not be spoiling today or any other day with that kind of talk no matter how much the other one annoys you."

"Fine." They both obeyed momentarily out of respect until Elijah shot his brother another dark look while his mother's back was turned, to which Jedidiah was only too happy to reciprocate in kind.

"I mean it, you two. Stop it or I will!" Charlotte commanded, though she had not turned around to see them, nor their subsequently provoking reactions.

"Wait! How did she…?" Jedidiah shrank back slightly in his chair, incredulously surprised once again.

"You know, Mama. It's a good thing we live in Philadelphia and not in Salem or someone might think you are a witch," Elijah quipped quickly at her uncanny ability to detect all of their mischief.

"Mother is not a witch, Elijah, and shame on you for even saying it." Hope defended her staunchly. "As rotten as you both are at times, she just knows you two better than you know yourselves."

"I ought to. I raised you. Though how I made it this long in life without dying of sheer exhaustion from having to keep you both in line is entirely beyond me," Charlotte replied as she shook her head and tried to fix the loose brown and white strands in her hairstyle. "The two of you gave me every single one of these white hairs that I proudly wear, and you know it. From almost drowning in the creek out back <u>twice</u>, nearly dying from the grippe back in Portsmouth, to who knows what other countless calamities you forced upon me over the years when your father was away at the forge. It's a wonder I survived to tell the tale. In fact, I shudder to even remember the worst of them for they were too numerous to count, though also thankfully miraculous in your recoveries. Or to put it more bluntly, if the two of you did not have your uncles so close to you in your lives, you both might not be here today. I know Hope wouldn't be."

Jedidiah and Elijah both grinned at each other delightedly as they mischievously remembered their many fortuitous adventures together with profound pleasure.

"And those are only the ones she knows about, brothers," Hope added the last word more scornfully while trying to secretly warn the two of them into silence with her eyes before she would be forced to divulge all.

Regarding her with slightly more respect now, as if he was keenly afraid of what she might reveal next, her eldest brother caught her suggestion immediately and stopped his teasing. "I'm sorry Mama... for then and for now."

"Don't give it another thought, Jed. Lord knows, I forgave it all years ago." Charlotte smiled adoringly at him and continued tidying up in the kitchen.

Elijah on the other hand was not the least bit inclined toward acquiescence, yet. "Oh, Hope, you were not the perfect child either by any means," Elijah warned her, in open defiance. "If we are sharing family secrets tonight, well, then we could always start by telling Mama all about the time you took her..."

"You will not!" Hope instantly interrupted him, true fear covering her face completely at his threat.

"Took my what, dear," Charlotte inquired patiently, not missing a beat of the conversation unfolding around her.

"Nothing, Mother. Elijah is mistaken." Hope kicked the young man as hard as she could under the table with the toe of her shoe, warning him further about sharing anything more. "Isn't he?"

"Ow, Hope!" Elijah rubbed his sore shin and threw the linen napkin his arm had been resting on at her.

Dodging the projectile as Hope stepped away just in time, Michael tried to step in and appease the growing excitement by changing the subject altogether to a less violent train of thought. "Mrs. Fabbri, I am sure all siblings have playful tales about things that went on during their childhood. Why I myself was known for stealing all the sweets from my grandmother's candy dish every time we would visit her. I'm sad to say, but my siblings are <u>still</u> rather upset with me 'til this day over that one."

"Oh, Michael…" Hope covered her mouth to stifle a small giggle at his rather meager confession. "I'm sorry, but that pales in comparison to what <u>we</u> have done."

"Maybe so, but the worth of our deeds is often judged not by us, but by the opinions of others in regard to their severity. In other words, what one man might feel is a slight, another may think is a mere diversion," Michael defended proudly.

"You sound a bit like my Uncle Nathanael." Hope smiled adoringly at him.

"Yes, well, speaking of your uncles, I think I hear them coming now," Charlotte interjected and walked gratefully over to the door before stepping out onto the porch to greet her guests. "Mr. Beckett, and Mr. and Mrs. Deschamps, thank you for coming all this way tonight for Hope's birthday."

"Mama, why are we being so formal, tonight? You know they have always been Uncle Emile and Aunt Emma to us." Elijah joined her on the porch; his face contorted in sincere confusion.

"I quite agree with Elijah this time." Emma walked up the stairs and kissed Charlotte on the cheek fondly. "Or are we putting on our best manners for our special guest tonight?"

"Perhaps," Charlotte nodded, hopeful that the woman would help her make a good impression on the man she hoped would be an acceptable match for her daughter soon.

"I'm sorry, Charlotte, but I am not pretending to be anyone tonight, Emile or otherwise. I have had quite enough of that down at the office already. Despite what they may purport or say otherwise, those men can play that game better than anyone else I know," Emile complained as he led the horses to the barn to rest for the duration of the meal.

"Oh, you know that you enjoy every minute of it, love." Emma shooed him off before placing a protective arm around Charlotte. "Come, let me look at you. As busy as I have been lately, I don't think I have seen you in weeks." She hugged her and laid her head on the shoulder of the woman who had served as her mentor for many years and was the only person besides her husband that had earned so much of her unconditional love and trust.

"I have missed you, too, Emma." She hugged the woman warmly back, then extended a hand out to Nathanael. "And how are the students treating you down at the college? Are you still enjoying teaching them this summer?"

"Very much so." Nathanael climbed the stairs and took her hand before raising it to his lips to kiss it fondly. "I have even decided to take up a rather unique hobby."

"Really? What hobby is that?" Charlotte inquired, sincerely interested in whatever the man might be studying, for he rarely tried new things unless especially prompted to do so.

"A few of us have chosen to amass a collection of local butterflies and moths for the students to study. Since the university lacks any boxed specimens at this time, I thought I might join them in this possibly enjoyable hobby or at least while the weather holds, as I doubt I will be able to encounter many such insects during the winter months." Nathanael took a few steps closer to her before offering her his arm, cautiously aware of the others on the porch beside him.

"Well, with that in mind, I _also_ have a surprise for you tonight, as well, but you need not wait for your present like our Hope must." Charlotte held onto his arm and patted it softly while they waited on the porch as if the arm itself was providing the strength she needed at the moment.

"Charlotte, you know that I will always appreciate any gesture you have made on my behalf, but I hate that I put you through all the trouble to do it when you already give us all so much already by your kindness." Nathanael looked over at her sympathetically. "Please tell me you did not overly stress yourself on my account today."

"Oh, stop..." Charlotte waved the man's concern off with a shake of her head and a slight smile. "It isn't anything that grand, I assure you. Just something you have been asking me for years to make for you."

Without another second passing between them, Nathanael's eyes lit up instantly as he realized immediately what she had done. "You made ratafia cakes, didn't you?!"

"Um-hmm." Charlotte nodded happily but tried to hold back the true smile his reaction had created as watching the joy spread across his face tonight was priceless all in itself and far worth the effort she had made.

"Since the moment your husband told me about them on the island, I have always wanted to try them. By the way he described them alone and the sheer longing he had for them that day, I knew they must be absolutely delicious!" Nathanael raved.

"Indeed." Charlotte blushed at his overly generous compliment. "Well, you shall taste them tonight, or as soon as your other companion arrives. Which begs the question, have you seen William today, yet?"

"Not since lunch, actually. But then again, he does tend to get tied up many times as the day progresses." Nathanael lifted his head slightly at the sound of horses approaching quickly at the end of the drive and waited to comment further as a hired carriage pulled up near the split rail fence near the road and deposited a frustrated-looking William. "Speak of the man and he appears it seems."

"And about time, too," Emile quipped as he strode back from the barn.

From his place on the porch, Nathanael eyed his friend and roommate from a distance and although William was not overly late per say, just tardy enough to cause the lines in his brow to furrow into two longer grooves upon the surface, Nathanael could already tell that the man looked bothered by something more than mere tardiness just by the way he had exited the carriage before paying his fare and walking towards them.

"Is the party outside this year, or am I just fashionably late, again?" He made his way all the way down the dirt-drive leading up to the house and joined Emile at the front.

"You are practically right on time if dinner was at six, but who is keeping tabs?" Emile smiled and placed a warm hand of friendship upon his back. Sadly, it had been over two weeks since the two of them had even spoken, given his rather complicated workload at the present, coupled with William's daunting teaching schedule at the hospital, making the absence of his friendship weigh heavily upon him. Undoubtedly, that was one of the many reasons as to why he had been so looking forward to tonight's meal. That, and the fact that all of them would be together once more, was always something to be celebrated, if not relished.

"Good evening to you, too, Emile." William grinned back at him, but the simple affirmation did not reach his eyes. Which upon further scrutiny, appeared more concerned than joyful, given the purpose of the occasion.

Slightly alarmed, seeing as his friend rarely displayed that particular kind of emotion unless it was warranted, Emile leaned in closer and whispered quietly near his ear as inconspicuously as possible. "Do we need to step aside and talk first before heading in with the others?"

"Later." William shook his head but managed to hold back his true thoughts with a grimace. "But yes."

"Of course," Emile nodded discreetly and turned back to his host, putting on his best smile for entertaining. With more troubling things obviously afoot, it would appear that acting was in order for him tonight, after all. "Shall we all join the others?"

Without further delay, the group followed Charlotte back into the house, while talking animatedly with each other as they always did, and soon the small farmhouse was filled with the laughter and merriment it had missed since Christmas. From one person to the next, warm embraces were given, laughter shared, and tears of happiness flowed freely amidst the wonderful meal Charlotte and Hope had prepared. It was almost as if the past six months had not happened at all. Or rather, that despite everything that had been transpiring in all their lives, they had never been separated for a single day, let alone many, as their paths normally led in various directions during the weeks and months. Yet there would also forever be only one thing that would always silently remain a constant, no matter when they all could finally gather. Whether at Charlotte's, Emile's or even at William's home, a single, empty wooden chair would forever stand vigil in the corner of the room as a silent witness of its former master in honored remembrance and dutiful respect.

As beloved as he was, Sebastian was most certainly not physically present in this world anymore, nor would he ever be absent either at any of their future gatherings. By this small token, he still held a piece of his family's heart in everything that they did. From the forge to the farm, to the very color of the walls around them, nothing at all had changed in the three years that had passed since, nor had anyone wished it to be otherwise. Moreover, not a single aspect of their lives had deviated from the expected series of events until tonight.

Tonight, there was an added feature to their party. A young man who appeared equally desirous to meet all of their expectations, while also nervously cognizant that he was most definitely, still the outsider.

At her request, Hope's beau, Michael Adair, had been cordially invited to attend her 18th birthday celebration, but more importantly, he was here to gain the family's approval of their courtship. A very eligible man in all respects to everyone else in town, but a stranger to those gathered here, nonetheless.

With the meal completed and the true festivities about to commence, Emile proudly brought the highly decorated cake he had created earlier that day to the table and lit the single candle placed prominently at its center. "Now remember, Hope, you may only have one wish, my dear. So, choose wisely," he cautioned her carefully. "And please do not waste it on another pony, for I shan't be buying one ever again."

"Uncle Emile," Hope looked up at her uncle and blushed as she shook her head in mortification at his remark and rolled her eyes in perfect mimic of him. "I'm not going to wish for anything like that, and you know it."

"Good." Emile nodded approvingly at her choice while looking down his nose at her and motioned with a flip of his hand towards the cake then for her to proceed.

Just as excited as she was to see her reach this momentous day, the group, including Emile, all sat in collective silence thereafter while they watched the young woman study the flame intently for several long seconds before closing her eyes for two or three moments more then blew it out.

With the action quickly completed, the room instantly erupted afterward with claps and proclamations of "Happy Birthday!" all at once around her as she took in each and every one of them in turn and smiled, knowing she was so very blessed by each person represented here today. Every one of them, from her dearest mother, who tended to dote on her more than she probably deserved, to little James, who was sitting delightedly on Nancy's lap, his cheeks dimpled rosily proclaiming the happiness he was experiencing, all were an integral part of her life story, and she loved them immensely for it.

"And what did you wish for this year, Hope?" Jedidiah asked curiously while holding his infant son in his arms. His second in almost three years.

"I did not wish more sons for you, if that helps," Hope teased, for she knew that her brother and his wife had their hands full already with their new, albeit growing family and taking care of the farm, as well.

"Thank you," Nancy added graciously. "Someday I would like to sleep again like Caleb is doing right now upstairs. As happy as I am for the brief interlude from chasing him endlessly around the room tonight, I'm afraid that will mean yet another sleepless night for me in a few hours."

"No doubt," Hope tried to smile empathetically while the others in the room laughed politely at their expense, knowing that only one of them in the room could adequately comprehend the struggle the young mother was going through.

"And eating hot food would be nice, too, wouldn't it?" Charlotte added with a gentle grin, understanding filling her features.

"Will that happen soon?" The woman pleaded.

"In about six more years, at least." Charlotte smiled. "But by the time it happens, you will wonder where all that time has flown to, and it will not matter as much as it used to. I know I do. Why, it seems like just the other day we were back in our cabin in Portsmouth and Uncle William was reading the two of you that book that he bought for you in town. What was it again?"

"Gulliver's Travels." William took a sip of his drink and leaned back in his chair, grateful for the levity the event was providing. "I thought they would never tire of hearing me read it to them."

"How could we?" Hope added, for he had read them many novels over the years during his weekly visits when they had first arrived in America. "I was always so fascinated by your library as a child. And it was absolutely amazing how you could make the characters literally come alive from off the pages themselves when you read it to us."

William grinned affectionately, too, as he remembered the cherished times when they were all much younger. "Well then, it seems that I will have to begin the tradition again with your two, Jedidiah. When they are older, perhaps, as I doubt they would remember much at this age."

"I agree, but you are welcome to come and care for them any time you like," Jedidiah offered freely to the man who had become like a second father to him over the years. "Maybe one of them will eventually want to be more than a farmer one day, perhaps a doctor or teacher, even." He looked over at Nathanael who smiled at the inclusion.

"I would be honored to teach them any day, Jed," Nathanael pledged most faithfully. "Just maybe not until they are old enough to talk in sentence, please."

The group of men all laughed together then, knowing full-well Nathanael's natural aversion to small children. Though it was inescapably true that he did not prefer their company as much as he did that of his friends gathered tonight, he did not outwardly dislike them as a whole either. The simple fact was, he was just not comfortable being in charge of "such a small specimen of humanity", or so he had once called Jedidiah's son shortly after his birth.

"So, Mr. Deschamps, what news do we have from the government these days? Will you be heading back to Washington soon?" Michael cleared his throat as he spoke up in the silence, obviously taking advantage of his privileged opportunity with Hope's second guardian to glean whatever insider information he could obtain for his newest publication while also keeping a safe distance away from the man. Despite what his rational mind always reminded him, it mostly scared him most days just to be in the same room with him if not as close as he was tonight.

And as a whole, Emile had never once desired to speak in her father's place in any way, nor did he ever purport to the others that he was anything more than a mentor to the young girl over the years, but from the way the man across from him squirmed in his chair, he might as well have been her father in many ways by the devotion Hope had for him and reverence for his wishes. "Though I am rarely told all the particulars until they are more solidified in nature, I expect that I will probably be called back by the end of next week. Why?" Emile eyed the man, trying to ascertain whether or not he was merely attempting to make a good impression on him or trick him into revealing more critical information.

"Uncle, Michael is only curious about what it is that you do there." Hope tried to defend her beau politely upon seeing her uncle's typically suspicious glare.

"Hmm..." Emile looked rather skeptically at him before continuing. "If it is not for the papers, then yes, I will be most happy to discuss what is happening at length with you. If it is, then the answer is always a resolute, 'no comment', as you might expect," Emile instructed quite severely, making sure the boy knew his boundaries plainly in regard to how far the young man was able to press him on the subject.

"Understood completely, sir." Michael fidgeted slightly in his chair at the sudden attention and looked as if he were about to break into a sweat.

"Relax, Mr. Adair." William couldn't help but chuckle while watching the poor man tie himself in knots. "Emile, I think you are making the poor boy unnecessarily worried."

"Yes, you don't want to scare away <u>every</u> suitor the girl receives," Nathanael added plainly and cast a quick glance in Charlotte's direction to judge her opinion on the matter.

"Don't I?" Emile challenged the two of them both equally, then turned his attention back to the man across the room from him at the table. "It's not like I am going to eat you, son. Speak up, man. What is on your mind?"

Oh, Emile... William tried once again to hide his obvious smile at his friend's ironic comment for he knew full-well that the thought had probably most definitely crossed the mind of his friend possibly more than once in the past six months, or at the very least this week, knowing he would be sharing a meal with him tonight. Though, if he <u>had</u> followed through on his darker musings, the man's unfortunate disappearance would have most definitely alleviated his current problem with Hope but would have also caused Emile many more headaches because of it.

Still, all things considered, William made a mental note to tease him about his assumptions later... much... much later, when he was in a more... amiable mood than he was at the present.

Suddenly wanting to garner her uncle's good opinion before the opportunity was lost forever, Hope squeezed her beau's arm and encouraged him onward in his conversation. "Go on."

For a moment, Michael appeared positively frightened at the idea of standing up to the man but then seized the last of his courage and began once more. "Sir, I was curious about where <u>you</u> stood on our advancement into Canada. General Hull says he plans to invade from Detroit by this time next year. Do you think that is a wise decision considering the situation with England and France right now? I mean, the blockades are growing by the day, and our ships are being boarded monthly without provocation."

"You <u>have</u> done your homework, Mr. Adair." Emile raised both of his eyebrows in approval of the man's painstakingly correct information. By the details alone that the young man had just shared, the boy had obviously taken more than a passing interest in the current situation unfolding. "It is true that our position is becoming quite tenuous at best. But even so, as a nation, we cannot simply declare war with another sovereign without a reason, and until Congress decides what that reason is, I am afraid the decision at the present will have to be to wait... watch but wait. The answer, I am sure, will reveal itself in time. As it always does."

"But shouldn't we act first? Be decisive. Stand our ground like we did years ago when England tried to take our liberties from us. What is there to gain by giving them more time to prepare an offensive against us?" Michael passionately gave his opinion finally on the subject, no longer merely content to be focusing on trying to remain objective anymore to please anyone gathered.

"Have you never heard of the phrase, "'Patience is a virtue?' Or are you so ready to throw down your life like the esteemed Mr. Hale in saying that his 'Only regret is that he had but one life to live for his country'?" Emile reminded him. "Thankfully for both you and for Hope, this saying, though motivational in nature, does not apply in this particular situation, nor should it."

"That's what I though you would say..." The young man shook his head in building frustration. "...politicians are all the same."

"The same? How so?" Emile's eyes narrowed slightly at the intended barb.

"It has been my experience that most are only focused on what <u>they</u> want and not what is best for the people they are supposed to be serving," Michael retorted just as quickly.

"And rashness of spirit and tongue is often the folly of fools." Emile flicked his eyebrows up just once in flagrant challenge, not backing down for an instant.

Feeling the temperature of the conversation suddenly shifting to an uncomfortable stalemate between them, William and Nathanael each placed a careful hand on either of Emile's knees to steady him in case he overreacted.

Suddenly amused, but not the least bit inclined towards violence... tonight... Emile only glanced down at each of their hands in turn and smiled ruefully at what must be passing through their minds before looking up with complete patience. For the better part of the past twenty years, he had been steadily tempering his impulsive reactions towards things that would normally upset him, and he was not about to let one insult throw all of that away. "Perhaps you would like to come with me when I go back to Washington, Mr. Adair. That way you can come and see for yourself firsthand how these decisions are made and why. Maybe even contribute some opinions of your own on the matters we discuss there."

"Is that allowed, Emile?" Emma glanced across the table at her husband, hopeful that he had found a peaceful solution at last.

"I don't see why not. The other members of Congress often bring <u>their</u> constituents to voice their opinion on the floor when topics arise that warrant their input. I see no reason why Mr. Adair cannot come and do the same, provided he can keep a civil tongue in his head when it is required."

"Is that a formal invitation, sir?" Michael stared directly into his eyes boldly, ready to literally leap at the opportunity afforded him.

"It is," Emile replied with the consummate calmness he had perfected for situations such as these. Ones where all he wanted to do was react violently but was required to maintain his sense of manners and decorum.

"Then I wholeheartedly accept." Michael's entire being now seemed excitedly poised for the journey to come, much more so than Emile.

"It is decided then. I will pick you up the Tuesday after next. Please pack light as the carriage normally takes several days. You will also need to let your editor know that you shall not be returning for a fortnight unless you arrange your own transportation to return. Will that be acceptable?"

The young man nodded and looked not the least bit concerned about missing his responsibilities for almost three weeks.

"Lovely." Emile smirked politely at the boy then turned back to Hope, eager for a distraction from his more focused and unpleasant thoughts. "Shall we open your presents, now?"

"Yes, please." The girl's eyes lit up with enthusiasm at the invitation before standing up and walking over to whisper in her uncle's ear. "Thank you for giving me my wish, Uncle."

"As I always do, my dear." Emile nodded once discreetly towards her then motioned for her to join her mother who was standing at the head of the table.

"Our gift is actually out in the barn, so we will need to bring it in if she is ready," Charlotte said enthusiastically as she motioned for her boys to go and fetch it.

"I'll help you clear the table then and make some room." Emma offered, and between the three older women, they managed to completely clear the table of the remaining food and plates just in time for Jedidiah and Elijah's loud return through the open door.

"A hope chest for our Hope!" Charlotte announced as they passed inside and placed both her hands upon her daughter's shoulders, eager to see her expression for herself.

"Really? Oh, it is positively stunning!" Hope exclaimed as they brought in the beautifully carved wooden trunk into the room and carefully set it down on top of the family table. "Did you both make this?" She inquired while looking over at her brothers.

"Well, sort of." Elijah shrugged.

"We all had a hand in its creation." Jedidiah placed a hand upon her back, too. "I planed the wood from the tree you used to swing from when we first arrived. A storm last winter knocked it down, so I saved several of the best planks for this. It _was_ hard at first, as I had not the least idea what I was doing, but I think it turned out really nice in the end."

"And as you know from earlier, I made the key." Elijah nudged her elbow, reminding her of the key in her pocket.

"Oh, that's right! I almost forgot." Hope finally noticed the small lock on the front and retrieved the key to open it. With a slight creak from the weight of boards used to create it, the top tipped upwards slowly to reveal not an empty wooden box, at all, but one that contained many treasures already stored safely inside.

"The quilt was made by Nancy and I from the clothes you wore when you were a child." Charlotte leaned in over the shoulders of her three children who were looking into the chest with admiration.

"Which was incredibly hard to do, I might add, as we had to hide it whenever you came back into the room." Jedidiah's wife smiled.

"I can only imagine." Hope touched the quilt's tiny lines and hexagons, allowing her fingers to caress slowly the fine stitching across its surface. "The book next to it is from Uncle Nathanael, I am certain, for it is the one he promised to give me last winter."

"Well, it was buried under some of my forgotten journals from long ago, so I couldn't find it until recently." He admitted sheepishly. "I'm only sorry it has taken me this long to get it to you."

"As you say, 'everything has a reason and a purpose.'" Hope smiled in appreciation and reached in next to pick up a small, white box that was lying almost underneath the quilt and opened it slowly before her mouth fell open in overwhelming astonishment. "Oh, Aunt Emma! No!"

"I think it's finally time that it should belong to you, now." Emma reached over and held her husband's hand fondly to keep her emotions contained. "Once upon a time, it was given to me with the same amount of love that I now pass on to you, and I pray you will cherish it as much as I do."

Lifting up the delicate charm carefully that Emma always wore, Hope clasped it around her neck securely before walking over to her aunt in a rush to wrap her arms around her. "I promise I will never take it off."

"That is precisely what she said to me when I gave it to her." Emile looked adoringly at his niece. "And I couldn't be happier that you are wearing it now, instead. Call it a remembrance from both of us, if you will."

She hugged him next then returned to the hope chest and clasped the lid to close it.

"Hold on, there's one more gift!" William stopped the girl as he patiently waited for his turn in the celebration.

"Where? There is nothing left in the chest, Uncle William." Hope looked up at him, confused. "Did you hide it somewhere inside?"

"No. Go ahead and shut the lid now, Hope." William pointed with his head and eyes towards the top of the chest while keeping his arms folded casually across his chest as he leaned back comfortably in his chair by the window.

Hope obeyed and when she did, she was utterly stunned as she finally took in fully the intricately carved scrollwork upon its surface. "Did _you_ do this, Uncle William?"

"Myself and your father, may he rest in peace. We were working on it several years ago when he was teaching me how to carve. To tell you the truth, I hadn't had the heart to finish it until recently." William tried to explain the process it had taken to carve it without giving in once again to the emotion he felt when he had finally completed it. In a way, a part of him had wanted to forever leave the piece unfinished as it had represented one of the last things he had enjoyed doing with Sebastian, but deep down he knew that it was finally time that it was passed on to someone who would appreciate it fully.

"It is incredible, Uncle William. Thank you." Hope replied, her own voice beginning to sound thick and strained.

"It seemed only right to give it to you today of all days." William said as he pursed his lips tightly and felt Emile's hand pat the top of his leg just once under the table.

As always, Emile was the only other person on this planet that truly understood even a fraction of the restraint it took for him daily to keep his struggles hidden from the notice of others. Not that anyone gathered today expected him to be any better than anyone else in the room. But rather, few people imagined that someone with his level of medical training would be falling apart emotionally whenever they saw a chisel or file on someone's workbench.

Nor would they know what to say when he sobbed, just remembering the smell of the oil they always used to treat the wood of their completed projects.

With deep respect at the level of love that had gone into its creation, Hope placed both of her hands upon the deep grooves and laid her arms and head on top of them, drinking in the warmth of the memories. "It is the finest thing I have ever been given… truly." She stood back up and tried to dry her eyes with the back of her hand. "Thank you all so very much. I am grateful beyond words."

Elijah, Jedidiah and Charlotte, all hugged her together, then broke out in happy laughter as they so often did in moments of deep emotion.

"I love you all." Charlotte touched each of her children's cheeks. "Now, let's eat some of that cake. It looks simply delicious, Emile!"

"It is," Emile stated proudly.

"Better be careful, friend. You know what they say. 'Pride goeth before destruction and a haughty spirit before a fall,'" Nathanael reminded him sternly in repetitive admonition.

"And yet… I have <u>never</u> once fallen." Emile held his hands up in defense, sincerely not sorry this time or for any of his hard-earned achievements.

"There is still time, Emile, there is still time. Not that I am wishing destruction upon anyone, mind you. Now how about that walk you promised me?" William pushed back his chair and stood, eager to discuss what he had experienced outside the hospital.

"Gladly." Emile did the same before placing one hand near his waist and bowing slightly. "If you will please excuse us, ladies."

"I think I will join you, too, actually." Nathanael chimed in. "I've been stuck in that classroom lecturing for the better part of the day. By all accounts, my legs could do for a bit of exercise, as well."

"Will I see you all before you leave, Uncle Nathanael?" Hope asked while still admiring her gifts within the chest.

"But of course," Nathanael replied. "You still owe me an answer from our last debate."

"I do." Hope blushed. "Though I thought you might have forgotten."

"Never. You are too quick-witted for that." Nathanael shook his head and answered from the doorway after the other men had passed through.

"Then be prepared to be humbled my fair teacher for I have been studying all week in preparation," Hope challenged him openly, with a look of true confidence.

"We shall see who reigns victorious in the end, dear child." Nathanael smiled in eager anticipation.

"Yes, we shall see," she countered right back and returned his smile.

"And hurry back so you can try your treat," Charlotte reminded him warmly, her eyes glinting with something Nathanael had not seen in quite some time.

"Absolutely," Nathanael promised and closed the screen door behind him to catch up with the others.

Chapter Eight

June 28th, 1811

By the time Nathanael had exited the farmhouse after his friends, the other two men had already made their way halfway across the yard and were lazily measuring their steps towards the great oak beyond, intent on putting some distance between themselves and the collected guests at the party before discussing anything.

"So, are you going to tell me what has been eating at you all evening, or do I have to guess." Emile opened the gate that stood between the main yard and the field and held it open for the others to pass.

"Huh, though I'd love to see if you could, I fear I am in no mood for any kind of divertive banter after the day I've just had." William stepped through the gate and waited patiently for Nathanael to rejoin them.

"That bad...?" Emile raised his eyebrows in response to indicate the right amount of obligatory compassion on the subject, but the feeling wasn't sincere. As much as he tried every time to empathize with his friend over his difficulties there, he simply could not imagine William's world being more trying than the countless stacks of papers he had to read and sign before he left the office every day. From what he could tell, the trials of war might indeed be fought by soldiers on the battlefield, but from his position, it seemed that they were also fought on paper, lots and lots of paper.

"Absolutely horrid, Emile, and the worst part is, I think she enjoyed it, or at least it looked like she did." William kept right on walking as if he intended on covering the whole of the globe tonight in his passage of needful distraction.

"She?" Emile immediately picked up on the one word that intrigued him the most as William had never once expressed an interest before in anyone of the fairer sex during the entire time of his acquaintance.

"Wait, I'm confused." Nathanael shook his head. "Who enjoyed what?"

"You caught that, too, eh, Nathanael." Emile glanced sideways at the man next to him in admiration of his friend's continually unique way of always seeing what others did not. "Did you have a problem with one of your patients today?"

"I wish it <u>had</u> been a patient, for if that were so, I could have merely sent her home and been done with the annoyance entirely. But no, this particular joy and daily irritation was most certainly sent by God to test my will to endure torture it seems." He sighed dramatically then slowed his pace considerably before speaking once more, "And as much as I might want to simply avoid another unpleasant encounter with the lady in question, I can't seem to find a way to escape it. Not unless I quit, that is." William stopped at the great oak and plopped himself down upon the ground as he rested his back firmly on the bark of the old tree before stretching out fully to face the house.

"Well, that is a rather bleak view of things, William." Nathanael joined him, too. "But all things considered, I do not think God works that way... even if it might seem otherwise for a time."

"No?" William challenged him irrefutably. "I beg to differ most vehemently, Preacher, or have you not met Miss Charity Emeline Bentham, nurse extraordinaire and resident doctor oppressor?"

"No." Nathanael chuckled at the overly expressive way in which William was describing someone who probably looked as ordinary as anyone else of their acquaintance, then added, "As far as I know, I do not think I have had the privilege as of yet. Wait! Is she the nurse with the blonde hair and green eyes that wears the navy-blue cape? The one that is always directing the other nurses at the main desk when I arrive?" Nathanael's eyes grew wide, realizing that he had seen just such a woman pass by their house several times when he was arriving home from school before supper, too.

"That would be the one. Though I do agree that she is probably not wholly bad as a person, per se, but Nurse Charity, as she is called by the other nurses, often prides herself on sharing exactly what she thinks is the best treatment for almost every patient that I see each day, whether I want her input or not." The look on William's face suddenly darkened slightly as he remembered the last words she had spoken to him that evening before coming here and gritted his teeth together slightly to control the deep-seated disdain that was now forming towards the woman the more he talked about her. "Oh, make no mistake, she will usually profess when she quite innocently does it, that her opinion is because another doctor wants it done in a certain way, but I <u>know</u> beyond a shadow of a doubt that she is just doing it to irritate me." William picked up several pieces of long grass and tied them around his fingers over and over again as he recalled his multiple interactions with the nurse that morning, wishing he could simply erase the whole lot of his interactions with the nurse and be done with it.

"Well, whatever she is doing, it seems to be working." Emile snickered quietly at his friend's expense. "I've never seen <u>anyone</u> get an emotional response out of you like this woman is obviously capable of doing."

"Thanks so much, Emile. Though it figures that you would take her side in this," William almost growled now at his friend's expected response.

Unable to control himself at all at that point in the conversation, Emile only smiled broader at the action. "Indeed, though it <u>does</u> make me curious to meet such a woman and get some pointers for the future, as she seems absolutely fabulous by the way you are describing her."

William stared back at him darkly, obviously displeased by his antics at his expense, yet again. "Well, next time you come to the hospital, I'll be only too happy to introduce you, but she would probably tell me I was doing that wrong, too." William looked off into the fields beyond the tree for several moments and tried to reign in the overflow of emotions that were washing over him again and again in the retelling of it.

"Well, I am sure she must have her reasons, William." Nathanael tried to be complimentary under the circumstances but stopped in his attempt to do so when William suddenly swung his head back to face him quickly.

"Don't count on it. In fact, do you know what she called me today, Nathanael?"

"I'm frightened to ask." Emile tried to hold back his growing merriment momentarily.

"A shabbaroon. I mean, what even <u>is</u> a shabbaroon? And who says that anyways?" William threw the crumbled grass away from him and picked up another three or four to mangle helplessly into submission.

"Not anyone from this century, or even the past decade to be sure." Nathanael interjected. "If you like, I can do a study on the word in the library this week and find out. Perhaps someone has heard of it there."

"Lovely." William grimaced at the very idea. "Lacking anything constructively current to say, it seems I am being mocked from antiquity now."

"Or... I can... just... let it be..." Nathanael said slowly in hesitation as he pursed his lips tightly shut in peaceable response after, cautiously concerned at how far William's frustration would progress under his current stress.

"So, what will you do?" Emile leaned one arm on the tree but did not sit down with the others to relax. Despite William's apparent need for diplomatic counsel at the moment, Emile was nowhere near ready to rest for the evening, nor was he inclined to share the recent revelations he had mistakenly discovered before his conversation earlier with Nathanael. The impulsive decision to include Michael on his upcoming trip to Washington had actually triggered the opposite reaction within him than what he had originally desired, as it was now sufficiently kindling a fire within him once more with fresh agitation towards the young man at being forced into a possibly ill-advised trip.

"What can I do? It's not like the woman is wrong all the time. On the whole, she is actually quite intelligent, perceptive even... for a nurse, which, as you know, is not my most relished form of interaction to date. Nor would it be justifiable, either, to move her to a different part of the hospital simply to avoid her presence." William thought carefully of other options available to him in his position once more before he then shook his head back and forth repeatedly in succession as his mind replayed with perfect recollection her very curt remarks from earlier regarding his actions. "Ugh! This would be so much easier if I didn't find her so.... so...." William struggled to find the right words to accurately describe the feeling he had felt all day working alongside side her.

"Interesting? Intriguing? Confusing? Pick one, though they most likely all apply, as women often are a myriad of the good and the bad all rolled up into one lovely ball of emotional turmoil." Emile sighed in learned understanding. "I remember quite vividly what a mess my head was in when I first arrived in Wakefield. Though thankfully, Nathanael was much worse than myself at the time, or I might have been tempted to do something rather rash to cope with the complexity of it all." Emile eyed the man next to him to judge his expression better. "Not that I am suggesting you do the same... please. We have walked that narrow road far too many times in our recent past to revisit it just yet."

"Very funny, Emile." Nathanael quipped disdainfully at the unpleasant memory.

"I meant no disrespect to you at all, Nathanael." Emile glanced over at the man fondly. "Surely you know by now that I would not have fared much better had our situations been reversed."

"Thank you. It is kind of you to say it," Nathanael acknowledged, then tried to reason with William in a way that might help him ascertain the true source of his problem and not merely his emotional response to it. "But William, do <u>all</u> the nurses still frustrate you in this way, or only this one young lady?"

"Just her." William threw the balled-up grass once more and flexed the muscles in his jaw twice in response. "As you are well-aware, the rest I try to remain professionally distant around for their own good, as well as mine. Besides, despite how irritating their amorous focus might be, I know that deep down, they are basically harmless as long as they do not receive any misleading attention from me. But she ... she is <u>certainly</u> in another category all on her own, though that is not entirely bad either... on the surface. Truth be told, if I were to be completely honest with you tonight, I'd have to say that we probably have a lot in common."

"I see." Emile nodded. "Then there is only one thing left for you to do. You are going to have to choose a path forward regarding your obstacle, like I have with Michael. Either face your problem head-on or let your problem control you. Either way, you win, or you lose, but at least in the end, it was your choice to make."

"Seriously?" William tried to smile, but it looked more like a controlled or rather, diligently concentrated effort than a genuine form of mirth in any way. "At this point I think the better course of action might be an absolute retreat for all parties involved just to keep the peace. Or in other words, it might be better to quit the fight altogether than to let our patients suffer because of it. Sadly, I don't know if I have the energy for another confrontation like I had this morning when I arrived. Though, thankfully, I did make it through this afternoon without a single argument. So, at least that was progress."

Nathanael shook his head at the incorrect decision and decided it was finally time to stick his oar in at last before William did anything he would ultimately regret. "That is not the William Wells I have come to know."

"Nor I," Emile added with a nod of approval in his direction. "Though I do understand why you might want to high tail it and run for the hills, you shouldn't choose to give up so easily. You've worked too hard to get where you are today to let one person ruin everything you have built for yourself here."

"Perhaps," William agreed reluctantly and allowed the calmness of the night to fall still around them once more as they listened to the grasshoppers tune their summer lyres.

Sensing that the conversation had finally stalled sufficiently enough on the topic of William's recent interpersonal entanglements, Nathanael focused intently on the ground in front of him before adding, "Um, there <u>is</u> one more unpleasant thing we all need to discuss tonight, if you will allow me."

"Really, something more dire than William's love life?" Emile quipped.

"Enough already, Emile... please, I'm begging you." William threw his head back against the tree slowly and groaned in displeasure.

"Alright, alright... I'll acquiesce." Emile tossed a loose acorn he had picked up playfully in William's direction but narrowly missed.

"What is on your mind, Nathanael?" William asked curiously before chucking the random projectile back in Emile's direction.

"Gentlemen... please," Nathanael chided them tiredly and waited for their antics to stop, so he could have their full attention before Emile waved a hand in his direction to continue.

"As I was saying, though I hate to even mention this tonight, seeing how lovely today has been already. But there is one thing we are going to have to decide upon, and fairly soon, before we are forced to make a decision about it unawares."

"Hmm... what is that?" William looked over at him, instantly curious as to which direction the conversation was now heading.

"Hope is eighteen now. The boys are twenty-three and twenty-six," Nathanael stated the obvious, hoping his two companions would see his point and step into the complicated conversation ahead of him.

"Yes?" Emile threw another acorn widely into the field next to him, feeling his impatience growing unnecessarily by him stating what was clearly common knowledge at this point, redundant even, if he were to put it more plainly.

Nathanael sighed, then plunged forward reluctantly, sincerely not wanting to be the one to even mention such a sensitive topic, let alone be the instigator of any more change in their finally settled lives. "As much as we love Sebastian's family, pretty soon we are going to have to either think of a convincing reason for why the three of us are not aging like everyone else around them or move on to some other location and communicate with them all from afar," Nathanael stated the very thing that made Emile's mouth run dry every time he even contemplated it.

"I know it," William admitted. "You aren't alone in this assumption, Nathanael. In fact, I've thought about that a lot the past few years, but I am also not ready to let go just yet. Mainly because I feel that we are finally able to do something good here. I know it has taken me a bit longer than the two of you, but I believe we have been given the chance to impact peoples' lives for the better in Philadelphia, and not merely passing the time trying to survive."

"That may be so, and a noble reason to be sure, but are we <u>also</u> putting the ones we love at risk of scrutiny when other individuals, less connected to the three of us, start asking questions? Questions that we do not have answers for, and neither do they," Nathanael spoke calmly and seriously.

"Surely, there <u>has</u> to be another way." William looked back at Nathanael once more, searching for some spark of a plan forward. "A way to steal maybe ten more years, perhaps? It's possible, right?"

"Maybe, but I am <u>not</u> wearing a wig for any price," Emile said resolutely. "Those idiots in Washington look ridiculous every time I see them, yet they cherish their ancient traditions just the same."

"No, not a wig." Nathanael chuckled at the very idea, then continued, "I think we can manage five years at least, possibly ten if we are careful by maybe changing our hairstyles and clothing choices. But after that, we <u>are</u> going to have to seriously consider where to move next." Nathanael stood and brushed off the collected dirt from the back of his trousers. "It will be sad, I'll grant you, and not anything I personally desire, but we always knew this day would come, gentlemen. We just didn't know how hard it would be when it did."

"Agreed." William stood, as well, and sighed deeply. "It kind of makes the situation with Nurse Bentham pale in comparison now, doesn't it?"

"Perspective usually does that to everyone," Emile answered bluntly, knowing that he was not ready today, in ten years or possibly ever to simply step out of his world with Hope. Since her father's death, she had become like the daughter he never had, nor had ever desired, but now that she existed in that role, he was not sure he could ever accept her leaving it. Undoubtedly, Emma would always be his sole reason for existing, but Hope had most definitely become his second.

"Well, while we are talking about unpleasant things, there is something else I need to tell you both. Something that I am not sure what to make of myself when I think back on it." William approached his guarded suspicions carefully.

"Hmm, what is that?" Emile tried very hard to focus on precisely what he was saying and not on his own scattered thoughts at the moment.

"Today, I felt something I have not experienced in eighteen years," William said slowly but deliberately.

"What?" Nathanael asked in building curiosity.

"Remember that time in the garden back in Kent when we all thought we were being watched?" William eyed Emile's and Nathanael's reaction carefully.

"Yes, why?" Emile was suddenly hyper-focused on the subject, attentive to the possible danger that might be possibly lurking around them.

"Well, I felt it again today, back in town before coming here, and again earlier this morning. It was only for a moment, mind you, but I can't deny its presence either." William looked back at the warm glow emanating from the house beyond, then continued, "Perhaps, I am just being paranoid, and it was nothing on consequence, but I don't think so."

"If it <u>was</u> a vampire, do you have any idea who it might be?" Nathanael seemed more than a little bit concerned, as he had very much hoped their time of adventure was safely and securely behind them.

"Maybe... Maybe not." William shifted his feet nervously, unwilling to admit what he knew deep down inside was the truth. "Whoever it was, they didn't necessarily wish to divulge their presence to me openly, <u>or</u> they were possibly hoping I would tip my hand first."

"I see. Well, there is little we can do about it tonight. If there is another one of our kind here in America, no doubt we will run into them again. Until then, we should really be heading back before we are missed too greatly." Nathanael motioned to the house and William nodded.

Tired from the day's activities and the stress that naturally came along with his position at the hospital, William began walking back to the house slowly to make his necessary goodbyes but stopped about ten or more feet away when Emile had not yet joined them in their retreat.

"You coming?" William called out to him nonchalantly, unfazed by the action as Emile was often lost in deeper introspection during the many instances that they were together.

"Not yet." Emile waved them off. "I need a minute or two with an old friend first."

"Alright." William replied, understanding completely, and turned back as he called over his shoulder to him. "I'll see you tomorrow night then?"

"Of course. I'll meet you and Nathanael for our monthly supper as planned." Emile looked over at the simple wooden cross that lay at the head of Sebastian's grave and waited until the other men were almost back at the house before he began to finally relax.

A few months after his passing, William had taken the time to carve their friend's name in bold letters upon it, but the flowers planted lovingly at its base were probably from Charlotte or Hope. "So, what do you think of Mr. Michael Adair, friend?" He looked out across the field, not expecting or wanting a reply in any way from the man occupying his space below, but it felt right to ask his opinion on the matter all the same. "If I know you, you'd probably not want him anywhere near your family, or your daughter, but you would most certainly have a far better reason than mere jealousy."

"Who?" An old barn owl above him called out into the night right at that exact moment, causing him to jump slightly at the clearly spoken response to his casual conversation.

"Who indeed?" Emile chuckled lightly at the uncanny coincidence. "Sebastian, I know that you and I did not always see eye to eye on things." He laughed lightly once more regarding the blatant honesty of that fact, and then added, "Alright, that is probably putting it too bluntly and you know it. But all I want to say is that I will always protect her _for_ you. Protect all of them, just as you would if you were still here and not me. As you can probably guess, William has the boys safely in tow. He always has. And Nathanael is well... Nathanael. He does his best work on their behalf from afar, but he _does_ help. You do not need to worry about their safety or their comfort anymore. They are whole. They are provided for. They are still immeasurably loved."

"Who?" The owl spoke up once again.

Emile only shook his head in amusement at the repeated gesture on the man's behalf for it felt like he was once again having the most irritatingly enjoyable conversation with his friend in death, as well as in life. "Oh, you know who, so stop it already. And I know... I know... I'll have to let her go someday, too. Just not today, Sebastian. And not to Michael Adair... not yet anyways." He kicked the last of the errant acorns at his feet farther into the field next to him, then bit his lip in deliberation slowly as if he were reasserting within himself once and for all his position on this most complicated of decisions. "I'll tell you what. I'll make you this promise today, then I will leave you in peace like you probably prefer after all of our senseless moaning about things you would probably love to have the chance to endure once more." He laughed again, remembering the way in which Sebastian would shake his head and roll his eyes at him when he was quite obviously fed up with all of the extra input his friends brought to the family gatherings. "When it does come time to let Hope go, you can rest assured, I will tell you first before I do."

He nodded in resolute decision and inner satisfaction while he touched the top of the cross next to him. "You can rest in peace, my friend. Just rest... we will join you soon enough, I am afraid. Just hopefully not for another century at least, alright. I'd like to see a few grandchildren before I join you, if you would be so inclined to wait." He pulled his mouth into a tight smile and wiped away one tear from the corner of his eye before turning to head back to the house, as well. "You are definitely heartily missed, Sebastian... but most certainly, never forgotten."

He walked away from the tree and the grave slowly towards the house in the distance, content as always, that he was precisely where he was always meant to be.

Chapter Nine

July 8th, 1811

Having finished the last of his home visits shortly before lunch, Nathanael climbed the short flight of stairs to the Pennsylvania hospital and paused before entering through the front door. Most states in the colonies did not possess anywhere close to as fine of an establishment as this one claimed to be. The yellow fever epidemic in 1793 had changed all of that for the better, directing measures to be taken by the esteemed Doctor Benjamin Rush to see that the necessary care for all citizens would never be lacking again.

The edifice that now stood almost as tall as the government offices in the center of town where Emile worked, included two wings on either side of the main portion that were designated for the division of patients and a large Receiving Room for new arrivals in the front. Having no area previously for surgeries and group lecture opportunities for apprenticing physicians, the new surgical wing had been constructed a short time later. And though it was also true that a building as large as this certainly came with greater purpose than merely meeting the medicinal needs of the people in Philadelphia and beyond, Nathanael reminded himself once again how important it was for him to be grateful that it also afforded <u>him</u> the opportunity every week to possible heal from his own afflictions there, despite his albeit abnormal state.

Before he had arrived in Philadelphia, he had spent the better part of his first year as a vampire avoiding any and all circumstances where he might encounter anything even close to a temptation for him. In fact, the only times he had been truly drawn to breaking that vow towards abstinence in a way that would endanger his fellow humans was the day Elsie had cut herself in the chapel and the day he proposed to her on Pasha. And although, ironically, both events involved the same dear woman, neither were her fault at all, nor did he eventually succumb to them in the end either. The power to resist the thing he wanted more than God itself, had taken a monumental effort on his part to do so, and a near death experience brought on by severe starvation on the second occasion, but he <u>had</u> done it.

And yet, as the years passed, he began to also see the true value of the necessity towards learning to temper his cravings by small exposures over time, rather than an outright avoidance, as both Emile and William had succeeded in doing. Like in other areas where he personally struggled, there would always be situations beyond his control. The very ones that might throw his system into total chaos just being close to blood in any way. But in his mind, it was better to be as prepared for them as much as possible ahead of time, than to wait helplessly for some kind of rescue... again.

Charlotte had told him once that conquering his fear of the attraction was all a matter of his personal perspective. Something she had focused on coaxing Sebastian through during their first years after his transition. And she was right in some regards, as she usually was, but that still did not mean that it made it any easier for him to step through the doors of the hospital every week for his routine appointment of torturous education.

For him, that fear of being overwhelmed unexpectedly by his nutritional desires far outweighed any of the other rational thoughts in his mind when it struck, allowing that distress to grow even broader and more intense as he fed it weekly with fresh anxiety and panic in contemplation of what he might encounter inside. Frankly speaking, it was one thing to pass the butcher shop on his way to class and smell the delicious aroma most others were often repulsed by. It was quite another to experience it sequestered by a patient's bedside with nowhere else to run and even less desire to do so. That particular feeling of being unconsciously compelled towards feeding on the weak and the vulnerable was something else entirely and most definitely something he wished to conquer once and for all.

On the whole, most of his visits to pray with the various patients receiving care there were pleasant interactions overall that filled him with as much hopeful contentment as his afternoons spent talking with Charlotte on the front porch of her farmhouse or the many long discussions he had enjoyed over the years with William after a long day at work. And each time he interceded on a patient's behalf to his Father in Heaven, he was optimistic that he was also giving as much peace and comfort to others as they were giving to him in return.

But on those few other occasions where things did not go according to his expectations, it was all he could do to make it back outside once more with his sanity and anonymity intact when another patient nearby became suddenly ill or in need of some serious medical intervention. These seemingly unpredictable anomalies were the very thing that filled his waking nightmares and forced his hand to tremble uncontrollably when he grasped the doorknob today. Or rather, it was the same trepidation he felt every day before he took a single step outside of the apartment on his way over to the seminary to teach his classes.

That singularly frightening contemplation of all the what ifs that might befall him on any given day had the ability to keep him rooted in his place just like it was doing now. In many ways, it had grown into its own entity of sorts over the years that very much resembled the mannerisms of an actual person as it steered him in whatever direction <u>it</u> felt was most comfortable. A person he very much wished to part ways with, given God's help, due to the controlling nature it always maintained.

After all, life itself would forever be completely beyond his ability to control, as it always was, even before becoming a vampire. Yet that still did not mean he was equipped any better now than he was before to meet the challenges facing him without at least a little bit of hesitancy. In fact, a success in his book might be simply not having a full-blown panic attack every time someone injured themselves accidentally around him, however minor.

William had explained to him once that there were always other doctors or nurses who could step in and take his place when treating a patient if his own temptation became too strong, but Nathanael still had no idea how his friend remained focused at work whatsoever. Unfazed as he always seemed about the imminent danger all around them when Nathanael's mind was about ready to revolt to the darker side of their existence, William reminded him that his quiet fortitude in the face of temptation medically was kind of like Nathanael's faith in that regard, as his desire to treat those who needed his help often overruled his desire to eat them. That and the fact that he would never want to do anything that would put a mark on the reputation of his place of work, or on his friends much like the way Nathanael associated his service to his Savior as a higher priority than his very life.

That simple explanation alone had somewhat encouraged Nathanael to reluctantly try pushing onward in his persistence towards embracing the opportunity that was being provided to him today with the calm assurance that his fear, more than his temptation, <u>would</u> eventually pass in time, as nothing short of moving Heaven and Earth would remove that other unpleasant fact of his current existence. Though all things considered, it still did not mean that he would not continue to marvel at his friend's daily restraint.

For the past twenty years, he had watched William encounter many tense situations that would have made most others shrink away, without the least bit of emotional response towards him actually doing so also. Yet that still did not mean those thoughts were not a part of him, all the same. Or at least Nathanael hoped so. Somewhere, deep inside the confident and self-assured William Harvey Wells that he always portrayed to everyone around him, there <u>had</u> to be a man that was probably just as broken as he was at times... just not as openly inclined to express it.

"Focus on the hope, Nathanael, not the fear," Nathanael whispered the last thing Charlotte had told him last night and opened the door in one swift motion, cautiously holding his breath momentarily as he stepped inside and addressed one of the nurses at the front desk politely. "Excuse me, please. I was wondering if you could direct me to any of the patients requiring spiritual guidance today." He smiled hesitantly and tried to appear more confident than he was currently feeling, even though every fiber of his being was busy calling him a liar.

"Of course, right this way, Mr. Beckett. I believe the young man you spoke to last week, Mr. Carter, went home already this past Friday, but there <u>are</u> a few people in the room on your left that might be interested in speaking with you." Nurse Fitzpatrick greeted him warmly and motioned for him to follow her across the hall.

"Thank you most kindly, Miss," Nathanael replied as took the opportunity to slip off his bothersome cloak and drape it across his arm while walking after her.

"For now, you can start with the patient on the end, a Mr. Everton. He came in earlier this morning, but I don't think any of his family have stopped by since he arrived. It's a sad thing, too, as he is so very sweet and patient with everyone he encounters... much like yourself, Mr. Beckett." She smiled in a way that felt charming to him every time he saw her and led the way confidently over the patient.

"I will take that as a high compliment indeed, Miss Fitzpatrick." He ducked his head bashfully and followed after her closely behind, taking great pains to hold his breath as much as possible when passing anyone with an open wound of any kind until he reached the end of the ward where the older gentleman lay completely covered up to his upper chest with crisp white linens and a navy-blue knitted blanket across the bottom of his bed, should he become cold.

The man in the grey and white striped pajamas with his head of rich brownish auburn hair that still maintained a slight wave to its texture bore a remarkable resemblance to his own dear father once upon a time, all the way down to the thickly extended sideburns that made his cheeks look fuller than they actually were. In truth, it was a style more or less familiar to most of those in the teaching profession, but even so, it had always made Nathanael liken the wearer to what an old sea captain might have looked like on one of his voyages with the East India Company. His father, too, had worn them probably for the majority of his life or at least as long as Nathanael could remember. But doing so himself was definitely not something Nathanael felt qualified to wear, given his consistently younger complexion, nor did he feel especially eager to embrace the more antiquated style.

In his heart, he was a man in the middle of his life, having survived a plethora of heartbreak and joy in his forty some years on this Earth, but to anyone else who might view him, he would forever remain a young man fresh out of seminary. Or to put it more plainly, he appeared to be someone who was on the very brink of discovering his life, like he had been on the Endeavor, and not a man who was eagerly awaiting his journey into the next... whenever that may come.

His father had once told him that despite what others might think, he wore his distinguished reddish-brown trails of facial hair for a nobler purpose than any of his other colleagues. Or rather, for a reason infinitely more sensible than a form of vanity alone. His cheeks, as perfectly plain as everything else about him, were simply cold, and the added piece of hair blocked some of the offending wind on his way to class. This had always made Nathanael's heart lighten when he remembered the way his father's rich blue eyes had twinkled in humor when he spoke it, but seeing it anew today brought many of the endearing conversations flooding back to him and some of the forgotten joy to his own eyes once more.

Taking a moment to glance over to the table next to the patient's bed, Nathanael spied a sturdy open satchel with several thick books of various sizes spilling out of it as if they were casually collected along his way to the hospital, each as different in its appearance and topic as the one above it. Intrigued, his eyes trained closer to examine them from afar, noticing that the collection in itself was most definitely worthy of his curiosity, as not a single book seemed to tie itself with the other, but rather all three were as unique as the man in the bed appeared to be.

Unable to do otherwise, or even speak a word, for the briefest of moments, Nathanael stood at the end of the bed in silent contemplation, his mind taking in fully the uncanny resemblance and strange happenstance of the coincidence, as if it was also completely frozen in time as he studied the man from afar. In many ways, his whole being was almost too uncertain to draw any closer to the patient in front of him should he suddenly open his eyes and reveal the same matching expression his father always wore.

Were there others who walked this Earth with identical features and habits as those who have passed on before them? And if so, what kind of miracle did God intend in creating two men so similar in quality as this? Nathanael wondered in shock, his mouth falling partially open in surprised consideration.

"Good afternoon, Cecil," Nurse Fitzpatrick said quickly when Nathanael did not greet the man outright as she walked over to the wall a few patients down and retrieved a small wooden chair before bringing it back and setting it down beside his bed for his visitor. "Do you feel up to a little bit of company today?" She jiggled his left arm slightly to awaken him further.

"Hmmm… what is this?" Cecil opened his eyes slightly and the wrinkles along the edges of them fanned out in a delightfully familiar pattern. "Ah, I see you have brought me company at last," he said weakly and tilted his head up to view his guest better. "And who might you be, son, to be bothered with an old codger such as I?"

"Um… Mr. Nathanael Beckett, sir." Nathanael drew a little closer to the bed in front of him and reached his hand out to cover the folded hand of the patient, feeling instantly how oddly unusual it was that the man's hands matched his own in temperature. "I was told you might like someone to talk to today."

"Is that so." The man's cobalt eyes practically sparkled at Nurse Fitzpatrick's arrangement as he cast her a doting glance of pure warmth. "I'm afraid that Nurse Fitzpatrick spoils me, Mr. Beckett, in preferring me above all others. But then again, she already knows <u>all</u> my weaknesses." His voice, though weaker in quality than most his age, still held a richness to it that far surpassed anything Nathanael had encountered in years.

"Only the ones that matter, Mr. Everton," she replied with a smile. "Now, just come and get me if I am needed, Mr. Beckett. And please see that he doesn't push himself too much. Though I feel I best warn you that he will talk your ear off if you get him discussing something in one of those books. I should know, I have heard many tales from most of them over the years."

"Oh, Bridget, don't scare him away so quickly. I have to reel my fish in slowly or they will never bite," he admonished her in jest and looked back to the visiting preacher. "Do you also like to read, Mr. Beckett?"

"Does a man breathe?" Nathanael answered back just as quickly, enjoying very much the candor and lightheartedness the man portrayed, even in his condition.

"I see I found you the perfect patient, indeed, then." She tipped her head in her patient's direction and turned around to see to her other chores.

"And what do you like to study in particular, Mr. Beckett? Latin? The sciences? Philosophy? History? What is your biggest temptation and greatest delight?" He motioned with his hand slowly for Nathanael to take a seat next to him and waited in patient expectation for his reply.

"Well," Nathanael almost choked on the question and its alternate response as he cleared his throat nervously. "Right now, I am working on a study of the Hebrew language, having already mastered Greek and Latin in Seminary."

"Is that so," the man replied. "And that interests you? Speaking other languages, I mean? Or do you just enjoy learning about them?"

"Both, I suppose," Nathanael answered honestly. "In many ways, I find it absolutely fascinating to be able to read the Bible in its original language without the need for someone else's interpretation."

"And is that your only topic of interest?" He prodded further, much like Nathanael's father would have also done, for he had always made it his practice to root out his son's perspective on a matter through inquisition and exposition than wait for his rather introverted son to finally share all his desires and details.

"No." Nathanael shifted nervously in his chair just like his students were known to do in his class. "I am also interested in: the various species of butterflies living in Philadelphia at the present, or the French culture before the recent revolution, how the world of trade even began, the famous explorers during Queen Elizabeth's reign-like Sir Francis Drake for example, Plato, Aristotle, and... oh, I'm sorry, you didn't really want a list, did you?" Nathanael added sheepishly. "I do tend to get a bit carried away sometimes when talking about books, too, I am afraid."

"Why do you think that is?" The man tapped the end of his folded-up glasses against the surface of his bottom lip curiously.

"I just find them so fascinating, I suppose." Nathanael crossed his right leg over his left knee and leaned back in his chair, placing his hands respectfully in his lap. "Ever since I was a little child, just opening the cover of any manuscript practically makes me feel transported somehow beyond what I am currently struggling with, even if that is a good thing."

"Me, too," he answered honestly. "Would you care to see what treasures I brought with me today, or would that be too much temptation?" The man tilted his head towards his bag on the table.

"I'd be only too delighted," Nathanael said a bit too eagerly and stood up to pick up the bag with reverence before taking his place once more to look through the various volumes contained within. "Well, the first one is an easy choice to understand. The Epic of Gilgamesh is a favorite among most scholars of any distinction, as is the Odyssey, but I am fairly certain you are aware of that as this is clearly an old copy <u>and</u> in the original text. Can you read it?"

"Yes," the man answered plainly with little annoyance whatsoever at being asked such a clearly impertinent question. "Like yourself, I am a man of many tongues, as well," he prodded Nathanael further with his eyes. "What else do you see?"

"The Travels Of Marco Polo! Now that is something I would most definitely be interested in reading any day, no matter the inducement. But what is this?" Nathanael picked up a rather strange looking text from out of the bag and held it up closer to his face to see it more clearly. "The Wakefield Master?"

"Yes, it is one of my newest discoveries to date. A book that is more of a collection of plays than anything else, for all of them have a more mysterious trend in their tone than what you might find in Mr. Shakespeare's repertoire. Thirty-two in all, and most take place in the town of Wakefield, England. Hence the origin of the title. Do you know of it?" Cecil asked him, his face and hands becoming more animated by the length of the discussion.

"The book or the place?" He tried his best to remain as calm and collected as possible given the fact that he most certainly knew of the place, very well in fact, as he had spent over a year pastoring a small church there back in 1793.

"Either. From what I can tell, each play found within the set is wonderfully written on various themes found within the Bible," he further explained.

"That sounds very interesting, indeed." Nathanael thumbed through the book quickly, perusing a few of the shorter passages that stood out to him as he went.

"And do you also have a deep faith that goes along with that interest in studying the Bible, Mr. Beckett?" He changed the subject to another vein entirely.

"I should hope so." Nathanael chuckled lightly. "I was blessed to maintain a small parish in the very town where your book takes place but have since moved here and now teach at the larger institution across town." He explained simply, while keeping to the most basic of facts, everything he had said was true, minus that part that it had happened almost twenty years ago.

"Is that so? Well, I am glad to hear it. I had a son once that I had hoped would follow in my footsteps, maybe even become a teacher one day, but alas, it was not meant to be." He closed his eyes momentarily, then opened them back up again slowly as he breathed in and out to calm the slight shaking his conversation had created. "He was around your age the last time I saw him, I suppose, but it's been nigh on close to thirty years since."

"Where is he now, if I might ask?" Nathanael leaned in closer, suddenly becoming even more invested in his story by the minute.

"He passed away years ago in the War for Independence. One of those few lads who did not make it through that horrible Christmas at Valley Forge. God rest his soul"

"Oh, I am so sorry to hear that." Nathanael put the bag of books back onto the table, then moved his chair closer to the man to hold his hand. "Was he your only child or were there others at the time?"

"Just him." The man nodded then tried to smile encouragingly. "But I learned long ago that a man must make the most out of every day he is given on this Earth to live. My son thought he had the rest of his life ahead of him, or rather, ages to accomplish whatever it was he wanted to do. In the end, he had but twenty-two short years. A mere drop in the ocean of eternity if you looked at it from that perspective." Cecil rubbed his hands together slowly.

"Death does have a way of giving us a different way of viewing things. I know for myself that I never fully understood grief until I walked that road, as well," he shared with him openly.

"That is true." The man picked up his spectacles from off of his chest pocket and put them on to see his visitor more clearly. "I hope you don't mind me saying this, but you do resemble my John very much, sir."

"I get that a lot, actually. I must have a face that is similar to many others." Nathanael felt instantly embarrassed at the remark, but it was the best he could manage under the circumstances, for speaking with the man today had brought him back to the Sunday afternoon discussions with his own father. The ones he would give anything on this Earth to return to once again, if for only a day.

"Hmmm... maybe so." He slid his spectacles farther down on his nose to be able to peer over them slightly. "Tell you what... why don't you borrow that book on the plays? You can return it when you come back to visit me as I doubt I will be going anywhere soon, or at least not for a few days I am told. Would that be enough time to finish it properly?"

"Plenty and thank you. I will return it promptly as requested or send it in care of my friend who works here if I am unable to come when it is completed." Nathanael fished out the book with the white linen cover that had definite signs of brown aging along all of its edges.

"Oh, who is your friend? Do I possibly know him?" He clasped the edge of his spectacles, took them off and held them against the edge of his lips once again.

"He is a doctor here actually," Nathanael began to explain before he felt a light tap on his right shoulder, interrupting him and drawing his attention upwards.

"I believe Mr. Everton and I are already well-acquainted, Mr. Beckett." William smiled easily, a chart in hand, though absorbed as he was in the conversation, Nathanael had strangely not heard him approach at all.

"Ah, my prison warden returns," Cecil joked again with him lightly, as if carrying on an inner joke between them. "Have you come to finally release me today, or will there be terms of surrender that have to be met before I resign myself to your absolute control?"

"Terms of surrender?" William laughed lightly at the rather amusing way the man described his most recent instructions but did not rebuke him in the slightest. "You know as well as I that you are free to go as soon as you can manage to walk out of here of your own accord. No questions asked." He raised his eyebrows once in sarcastic taunt. "But we both know that you can't do that, at least not yet anyways."

"You see, Mr. Beckett, I'm clearly his prisoner." Cecil winked at Nathanael in jest and shrugged helplessly at his predicament.

"I understand completely, more than you can possibly know, but since he is also a very good doctor, I think we should oblige him just this once and rest for the present," Nathanael reassured him politely. "No doubt you will be back home soon and enjoying the opportunity to collect more forgotten volumes on interesting topics."

"We shall see, though with all the extra attention I receive here, maybe I will just decide to stay a bit longer than is absolutely necessary." Cecil put his glasses back in his pocket for safekeeping.

"You are welcome to stay as long as you like, Mr. Everton," William affirmed genuinely. "But speaking of rest, are you about finished here, Nathanael?" William asked his friend directly while motioning with his eyes out the door to their left for a future conversation. "I am almost ready to go home for lunch if you wish to join me."

"Only just, I will make sure to come and find you before I go," Nathanael assured him and watched as he left out of the door immediately thereafter without another word one way or the other.

"Well, he seems to be a good friend." Cecil tilted his head in William's departed direction, then pulled the covers slightly higher up so that they touched the bottom of his neck.

"One of the best in my existence," Nathanael replied honestly. "May I take a moment to pray with you before I go?"

"Of course, I'd like nothing better," Cecil answered. "But only if I can pray for you, too."

"Um... certainly," Nathanael stammered out an awkward reply and for the second time today he was completely taken aback without the least idea what to say next. "Shall I begin?" Nathanael asked politely and waited until the man nodded and closed his eyes before he began. "Dear Lord, I ask that you give the doctors here the wisdom to help Mr. Everton in his recovery, and that you will see fit to give him the strength he needs so he may return home. Thank you for giving him such a full and long life on this Earth and I pray that you will direct his steps as he heals. Amen." Nathanael paused and tried to relax as he anticipated what Mr. Everton might pray for as very few of his acquaintances had ever offered to do so in the past.

"Heavenly Father, I thank you for my visitor today and the blessing he has brought to my soul just by his presence. I thank you for John and for his brief time here, but more importantly, for the joy he brought me every day of his life. Please continue to encourage, Mr. Beckett, in every word and deed he attempts to accomplish on this Earth as we wait for your heavenly welcome one day. I pray it will not be too much longer for either of us, though I suspect the day is much closer than either of us expects. And be with Doctor Wells, too. Please bless and guide his hands today. Amen," Cecil prayed sincerely as he held Nathanael's hands within his own.

"Amen," Nathanael whispered solemnly, his whole being so engrossed within the candor of his words that he almost did not open his eyes for a full half a minute after.

"Do you think I will see you before the end of the week, son?" Cecil turned his head sideways and laid it on his pillow to look at his visitor with less effort.

"I will do my best." Nathanael promised him and patted his hand gently. "Until then, make sure you follow the doctor's orders as much as you can, and I will try to bring you something new to read when I return."

"Now that is something to look forward to indeed." Cecil smiled and then closed his eyes to rest once more as Nathanael moved the chair slightly towards the wall behind him and carried the borrowed book reverently close to his chest as he walked out of the ward.

As he had expected, William was still patiently waiting for him on the other side of the walnut-colored door, though by all appearances he appeared thoroughly engaged in writing up a few copious notes of some kind on one of the sheets of parchment at the main desk.

In between the flow of people that was constantly coming and going out the front door to his right, nurses and other doctors mingled together in huddled conversations, apparently discussing various topics concerning their patients, while others chose to pass by him casually without making any comment at all. In truth, the inside of the great hospital resembled very much that of the street without, right on down to its busy foot traffic and deliveries going in all different directions throughout the day.

Intrigued once again by the scene he was witnessing, Nathanael leaned against the wall just outside the ward and paused to watch it all, endeavoring to understand the intricacies involved in running such a smoothly functioning facility. To his left and his right, several nurses passed him with food or medicine on neatly arranged wooden trays, only to disappear quickly thereafter through open doorways and corridors. An older man with almost no hair present on top of his rather round head looked to be as old as the sprawling tree out back in the middle of the large courtyard as he rubbed his shining balding patch and walked by reading a chart, obviously displaying how he had come by his physical malady over the years. Two animated pairs of students, not much older than some of his own pupils, laughed much too loudly for their environment from the end of the hall as they exited the lecture room, only to be shushed harshly thereafter by a stern-faced blonde woman who held herself perfectly rigid in posture as if she were possibly the one in charge of that section of the hospital.

That would be Nurse Bentham if I am not much mistaken.

Nathanael's eyes squinted to examine her more closely as she walked by but gripped his book tighter as she did, for as she passed, she brought along with her something more than the condemnation of improper behavior in her place of employment. Unaware to everyone else gathered around them, she carried also a sense of something he had not felt in years. That strangest sensation that pricked his skin from the top of his neck to the base of his spine moved throughout his being like an unwelcome guest and forced him to consider things he had thought were long forgotten. Events from his past that he wished never to relive again, even if they <u>did</u> have a satisfying outcome.

"Ah, Nathanael. Are you ready to finally go to lunch or do you have someone else to visit here today?" William called to him from a few feet away, practically startling him by his sudden announcement.

Shaking his head at least twice to clear away the rest of the fleeting feeling he had just experienced as the woman in question continued to walk away, he glanced back at his friend and attempted to look unaffected. "I'm done, and you?"

"Yes, but let me grab my cloak first." William walked over to the pegged wall by the door and picked up his lighter grey cloak and threw it over his shoulders easily, but paused when Nathanael did not readily join him. "What's the matter? You look like you've seen a ghost, man." He chuckled, though in their case, worse things <u>had</u> happened.

"Two possibly, though only one I am sure of." Nathanael put his brown cloak back on, as well, and followed him out the door.

"Oh, who?" William lifted his chin and smiled at the generally overcast sky, grateful that he would not need to put the hood of his cloak up and appear out of place among so many others enjoying the rather balmy day today.

"Your patient, Mr. Everton, to begin with." Nathanael kept his gaze turned downwards, watching the ground at his feet with great concentration. "By all accounts, he could be my father's twin, right down to the wire rimmed glasses he keeps in his pocket. I swear to you that had I not known my father was dead, I would have told you unashamedly that he was there in the flesh."

"Well, that is reassuring, and also a pleasant surprise for you, I am sure. Not many people get to see their loved ones come back to life in their lifetime. Was it just his looks that reminded you of your father or was it something more?" William turned the corner and headed down the street towards their home at the end of the block.

"All of it, actually. I'll have to dig out that old portrait I have of him tonight and show it to you. I'll let you be the judge." Nathanael swung his head back to view the hospital for just a moment, then returned his focus back in front of him. "And then there was this... I am not sure what to even call it, William."

"An unsettling feeling that makes you want to rub your hands over your skin to wipe it away?" William surmised quickly when they had finally reached their home and walked inside. "Something like what we experienced with Doctor Clarke maybe?"

"Yes, exactly," Nathanael agreed rather reluctantly and hung up his cape before plopping down onto the waiting settee, sending a few of the newspapers that were laid across it errantly to flutter down onto the floor. "Is that the same thing you were talking about after the party?"

"I'm afraid so. Though I am glad you felt it, too. With everything else that woman brings out in me, I was starting to think I was going crazy imagining it." William picked up the loose papers and put them into a neat pile on the table to the side.

"You're not crazy, William, or at least not any more so than the rest of us." Nathanael laid his head back against the top of the piece of furniture and closed his eyes to refocus.

"Well, that is reassuring... I think," William added dryly, then went straight to the kitchen to fix himself some much-needed coffee and something to eat. "Care for a sandwich?"

"Sure." Nathanael didn't budge to help him but rather remained where he was, enjoying this moment of stolen peace far too much to ruin it.

"Well, do you want to know my theory on the topic?" William laid four pieces of bread on the counter and began buttering one side of them in turn.

"Not especially. I know we shouldn't ignore anything that might be even remotely dangerous, but to tell you the truth, I am not ready for any more of that kind of adventure in my life, save that of existing within this family of ours at the present. If God sees fit to enlighten my future further, I can only hope He will do so within the more natural realm of things." Nathanael sighed and felt the last of the anxiety that had been lingering since the hospital finally dissipate.

"Fair enough. I suppose I will just keep an eye on it for the present then." William placed a few pieces of two different kinds of cheese between the two slices for each sandwich and brought the cast iron skillet over to the smoldering coals within the hearth before placing it on top carefully.

"That might be best for all involved." Nathanael rubbed the bridge of his nose for several moments, then sat up and rested his elbows on top of his knees. "So, if you don't mind me asking, what is wrong with Cecil that he can't escape your clutches?"

"My clutches? Oh, that's right... I'm supposed to be the terrible prison warden." William chuckled lightly as he flipped each of the sandwiches once and waited for the other side to brown to the same consistency as the first. "His heart actually. For the greater bulk of his life, he has worked at milking probably 100 cows at sunup and then the same again at even, not to mention plowing over 150 acres every summer to feed his family and the livestock. Work like that takes its toll on the body over time and especially so when you have to do it alone."

"I imagine so, but will he recover?" Nathanael eyed his friend with great interest, watching the way William's face shifted whenever he tried to be more reassuring than absolutely truthful.

For several moments William did not answer. Instead, he merely took the pan back over to the counter and deposited the two sandwiches onto the waiting plates, recognizing the deep connection his friend had already started forming with the man. "I think that question is beyond my purview, Preacher."

"I see." Nathanael stood and walked over to the kitchen to retrieve his lunch then took his seat at the table to join him. "So, there is nothing more to be done on his behalf, then."

"Oh, I wouldn't say that. He just needs more than medicine can give—rest, love and prayers." William took a seat across from him at last and handed him a glass of milk to go with his sandwich.

"Sounds like the perfect recipe for all of us." Nathanael swallowed hard once and tried not to sound too pathetic in the delivery of his declaration. "Will he be sent home soon or will he be available later this week to return something I borrowed?"

"We will keep him comfortable for a few more days at least. He doesn't have much help at home from what Nurse Fitzpatrick told me due to the fact that his wife died a few years back and he has no other children at home to speak of." William answered after wiping his mouth politely to clear away a few of the remaining crumbs. "But I did hear today that some distant family will be arriving shortly, so we will try to stall until they can arrive."

"He told me that his only son died in the war for independence." Nathanael leaned back in his chair and thought for a while about the man and his uncertain predicament. "Perhaps, once he is home, I can come by periodically and step in a little, possibly spend some time with him after teaching each day. It won't be much in the way of actual assistance, but maybe I can help him with odds and ends while I am there or at the very least offer a bit of company."

"I am sure whatever time you can spare will be greatly appreciated, friend. You about finished?" William nodded in question to his friend across from him.

"Yes." He handed him the empty plate and watched as he took them both to the kitchen. "I need to head back to the college now, but I should be back in time for supper. We can discuss your theories about Nurse Bentham then if you so choose."

"If it is all the same with you... I'd rather walk on coals of fire first," William answered him honestly and tried not to appear too reluctant to return to the hospital as the two of them went back to the door and picked up their cloaks before heading out onto the street, each turning in an opposite direction.

"Hmmm... and _he_ thinks all the talk of drama comes from Emile," Nathanael mused to himself humorously under his breath as he walked away.

With his borrowed book in hand, he made his way diligently over to the college several streets away, intending to spend the rest of his day focused on giving two lectures about the great speeches given by members of the founding fathers and their constituents, the primary focus being that famous speech given by Mr. Nathan Hale. A true patriot by any man's standards, but also one given to the same kind of dramatic expression that his friends so often slipped back into when their emotions got the better of them.

From Nathanael's brief existence, both here at the college and back in England, he knew that normal men on the street did not freely forfeit their lives in exchange for an ideal every day. Nor did they proclaim loudly that they would prefer death over the loss of that very same ideal. Those were things often reserved for the likes of Mr. Hale and Mr. Henry. And yet... Nathanael thought back to the man in the hospital and paused under a large oak tree on his way to take a small moment to reflect on the depth of the last statement in a new light.

_What _was_ he willing to die for if the situation ever presented itself?_
His newly formed family? His faith?

Once upon a time, he had stood up to a centuries old vampire to save the lives of two young children, but even in that, he felt more like it was a singular moment of self-defense than the heroic actions of someone defending a belief. Certainly nothing to write a whole speech about, nor would it motivate anyone else besides those in his direct family to hear it. Or was the real reason behind this unique difficulty of conviction something a bit more fantastical in nature?

Simply put, as far as Nathanael was aware, there was nothing of worth in his life that he could exchange in that way because he could no longer physically die. His immortality alone, which seemed to be a comfort to Emile and William, only made him even more lost than before when it came to discussions of passionate expression, as if a general spirit of apathy prevented him from feeling anything more.

The man at the hospital, to which he had become recently acquainted, had lived a full life already, and yet he did not appear the least bit ready to commit himself unto the grave like Nathanael seemed constantly eager to do. For Nathanael, it would take but a flash of a moment to freely accept any opportunity offered to him to return back to the man he once was, instead of the alternative of living for all of eternity with no purpose beyond that of teaching others and helping his friends navigate through their daily dilemmas.

Was that why he admired these speakers so much? The sheer fact that they had the <u>option</u> to give up their lives for their convictions?

Nathanael shook his head in measured frustration with himself. "You would think after twenty years this would get easier, but it doesn't, does it, God?" He looked up briefly to the heavens and nodded. "I know... I know... keep pressing onward. <u>Someday</u>, I will understand why." He sighed. "Just not today, it seems," he said with finality and walked up the ten steps of the front porch of his college and stepped inside.

Chapter Ten

August 15th, 1811

Like a heralder resigning his trumpet in sheer defeat at his called upon task, the final days of summer reluctantly chose to give up their hold upon the calendar and moved on to more pleasant options of a soon to be arriving fall. Or at least that was what everyone had hoped when the beginning of August arrived and moved through to the middle weeks before September. Yet unfortunately for everyone that was dragged along with them, that was not the case, as the passage of time brought no sooner relief from the incessant heatwave that the residents of Philadelphia had been enduring since May. From the man behind the counter of the General Store that was selling paper made fans to practically everyone that entered through his doors every day, to the young teen who always delivered the milk on his way down the street, daubing his forehead repeatedly with his rag as he went, the bulk of the citizens of this bustling thoroughfare had chosen to continue taking their retreat inside whenever possible to cope with it.

Yet for William and his friends, it had been a most welcome time of respite from the chill they constantly fought against every day of their lives, almost to the point that they were actually enjoying being anywhere outdoors where they could experience the added warmth, even if it did require them to take it in from a covered porch or shadowed lane.

This was not to say that the particularly annoying symptom of their vampirism had disappeared entirely, as nothing could accomplish that short of a miracle, or participation in one of their mentor's most recent experiments of transfusion. Rather, it was that the unusually hot temperatures had allowed them to feel slightly more comfortable in their given surroundings, pleasantly content even if they might go as far as to describe it, despite the fact that their relief was sadly, only temporary.

Yet the summer heat was not the only fire still brewing in William's world at the present. For the past two months, he had also been diligently placing all of his focus on heeding the wisdom his friends had given him on Hope's birthday. Not that it had been easy for him to do so... far from it. But Nathanael had indeed been correct, as well, when he said that it was unlike William to quit something he felt so passionate about once he had put his mind towards accomplishing it. Even if that meant abandoning the fact that he was also right in some regards, too.

In the beginning, a part of him made the uncomfortable effort towards a peaceful coexistence between himself and Nurse Bentham simply because he wanted to prove his friends wrong in their overly simplistic advice and taunting remarks. After all, what did <u>they</u> know about all that he was facing here daily? Not once had they personally interacted with the woman in question to know how infuriatingly direct she could be when she felt the need to countermand his orders, like she did every time he came in contact with her it seemed. Nor did they fully realize just how much he was having to endure mentally by negating or ignoring the other frustratingly antiquated directions by other doctors that he felt were entirely incorrect, but necessary to follow in order to avoid detection regarding his more thorough knowledge pertaining to a patient's particular malady. After all, he was only supposed to know maybe ten years of built-up knowledge and experience, not the almost thirty years of formal training he had already completed.

Though at the moment, it seemed in many ways that his job description had now changed to that of a more interpersonal mission towards keeping the rest of the staff pleasantly happy around him, despite how much it irked him to do it. And especially so since he gave Nurse Bentham his promise of personal remediation towards his treatment of her peers. That obligation alone demanded at least a small measure of his fullest attention towards its compliance, no matter the sacrifice. Because at the end of the day, William was still a gentleman in societal standing in spite of everything else that had changed about him, and as such, a part of him would forever be compelled to behave in a manner befitting his station—even if he were no longer obligated to do so by a bunch of centuries-old traditions.

Nevertheless, despite all of his carefully choreographed efforts, the strained form of peace that had existed between them after their in-depth discussion had only lasted a week, maybe ten days at most, if he were to be more accurate.

As quickly as the casual understanding between them had been made, as if it had meant something substantial to either of them, it had dissolved just as swiftly without the least acknowledgment or mourning of its passing, making the chance encounters with Nurse Bentham equally dissatisfying, if not outright impossible when they were required to do anything besides focus on the work in front of them. At the very least, the lingering absence of her overall good opinion when it had initially disintegrated should have affected him in some way, like it would have if he had offended Emma or even Charlotte, but instead he found himself hiding the fact that her dismissal of him daily was taking everything within him to ignore and remain professionally calm and collected in her presence for the hospital's sake alone. Or at least his vow of silence on the matter was noble in the beginning, if perhaps a little misguided in nature.

It was only when he had to work closely with the woman while discussing a patient's continued care afterwards that it became progressively difficult for him to hold his tongue sometimes and not react in retaliatory sarcasm to her sometimes-contrary replies and overreaching opinions. Which, unfortunately for both involved, was quite often, seeing as he was usually to blame where she was concerned, despite the monumental effort he was making to keep the peace. Something she clearly seemed to be hellbent on destroying.

Yet despite all of the drama they were personally creating on any given day, there was a reason why she had been hired to work there in the first place, beyond William's initial assumption that God had sent her to torment him into quitting. Without question, Nurse Bentham was an excellent nurse. Probably one of the best the hospital had ever added to its staff in the entire time William had been serving there. Maybe even better than some of the doctors William had become acquainted with over the years. And she <u>had</u> proven herself on many occasions to be more than a bit intelligently inclined and proactive in her nature, allowing the two of them to move from patient to patient without the least bit of unnecessary explanation one way or the other. In many instances, it was almost like the two of them were functioning at times as one healer instead of the apparent two. Which certainly made her the logical choice in William's mind to summon above all others in her station any time he had a difficult case. A preference that many others viewed as a possible enamoration with the woman, but one they were entirely in error to make—almost absurdly so.

For William and Charity, it was always less about the politics and politeness that the job also entailed, and more about the intense desire to help their patients recover as fully as possible, nothing more. And if being highly efficient at what you did in your profession came at a price neither of them were especially eager to pay, then so be it, if it also enabled them to accomplish something greater in the process.

Yet as the days continued to pass and the tension grew even higher between them outside of that realm of focused discipline, it started to become increasingly apparent to all who worked at the hospital, the true sentiment that existed between them. Secret or not, neither of them especially preferred the other's company whatsoever, or at least, not in the way everyone had initially suspected. Nor did they have any other interaction to speak of outside the hospital itself that might have further fueled that animosity or broken friendship, though many others of the staff did from time to time.

So, with little else to base their opinion on, the rumor mill of the Pennsylvania Hospital quickly began to shift its focus in another direction entirely, as each member of the staff soon formed their own opinion on the pair in question, favorably or otherwise. Sadly, the simple truth of the matter was that, whether anyone liked it or not, practically everyone in an establishment such as this was casually informed about the business of all the other members of its staff.

Due to the propensity of human nature to feed upon the theatrics occurring in the lives of others in order to block out their own troubles, people would always be inescapably drawn towards a desire to converse freely about the personal lives of those around them just as much as they probably talked about their neighbors or members of their distant family. William had known this better than most, maybe even more so, given his past life experiences.

And despite his initial desire to completely ignore the distracting comments and sometimes awkward stares he received daily, it soon became almost impossible to do so. Whether he was leaving for the day or simply going to another patient's bedside to check on them, not a single day passed where he was able to walk by any group casually gathered somewhere in the hospital and not be forced to endure the veiled discussion of snickering ladies with folders shielding their no doubt hurtful conversations or the mimicked dismissive behavior of others who thought Nurse Bentham's way of accomplishing her tasks were, in fact, the right way to do things. Or to put it more bluntly, it all reminded William very much of the many balls and social gatherings he had been compelled to attend back in England with their tittering chatter and nonsensical banter hidden behind decorative fans and smoking cigars. Pointless conversations from long ago that were still plaguing him in the present it seemed, forever feeling equally as annoying as the ones collecting all around him daily like rubbish needing to be thrown into the nearest bin.

Still, it would have been nice to have been able to peaceably exist, if only for a day, with the one person he felt oddly connected to at the hospital without some sort of flare up or another. If for no other reason than to silence the tales spreading like wildfire around their latest confrontation.

By all the mounting talk around them, it was almost as if the possible war that everyone was discussing outside the brick walls of their medical fortress was not with the British at all, but rather a carefully orchestrated dance between two opposing generals in the same army known as the Pennsylvania Hospital. Generals, who despite their actions otherwise, should have been colluding together towards the betterment of each other and the hospital itself and not pettily exchanging verbal barbs and snide remarks at the other's expense.

Worse still, if words alone could have killed the other combatant, Doctor William Wells and Nurse Charity Bentham would have most definitely been killed in action weeks ago and buried alongside their disdain and pride in the hospital graveyard due to friendly fire.

And yet, even with all of that transpiring around him, William refused to give up so easily. For almost two decades, he had put far too much effort into achieving where he was today, and this woman with an opinion about everything, knew nothing of the horrible things he had been forced to conquer just to practice medicine at all after his transition. The hours he had spent sitting alone on his bed in his room back in Wakefield that first winter just trying to acclimate himself once again to the smell of blood without devouring it completely in seconds <u>still</u> haunted him. As did the sleepless and shockingly debilitating nights he had spent since, as he sought to control his thoughts of self-denial, that the woman with barely a few years under her belt would know anything of, nor could ever hope to comprehend, though he had years to explain it all to her.

His passion to practice medicine was not merely the passing ambition that the mortal men of his acquaintance might seize upon for their livelihood like it was a distinguished profession in which to garner accolades and wealth. For him, it was his entire life and the single most worthy endeavor he was most proud of beyond his continued friendship with his friends, Emile and Nathanael. That gift of friendship given to him amidst his darkest trial would always be his most cherished possession, but helping others in this way would forever be his second... a very sacred second, he might add.

Shaking his head at his growing desire to desert yet again to the safety of his own home and avoid the rest of the unpleasantness that was surely to follow after him today, William reasserted his focus on remaining neutral in his tasks at hand. After all, this hospital had also become a part of his new life here in Philadelphia and as such, was as much his place of employ, as it was hers.

She would refute that claim, of course, but if both of them were to survive this ordeal by fire placed before them, there simply had to be a middle ground of concession somewhere in their fight. An attainable goal of possible concession, which only increased his desire today to find it, even if every emotion inside of him was poised for an all-out battle.

Like a general who had been pushed back several times in regrettable retreat, William decided once and for all that if he were to remain in good standing both with his conscience and the others he respected, he simply had to make some kind of peace with the woman. "Or die trying," William muttered quietly in sarcasm under his breath when the very nurse in question walked past him once more on her way to another patient's room, her blonde curls bobbing along behind her as she walked.

"I'm sorry?" Miss Bentham paused shortly thereafter, not more than five feet away from where he was currently standing, and looked over her shoulder at him, her face as unemotional as a stone. "Did you need something, Doctor Wells?"

"What?" William raised his eyebrows at her polite inquiry, surprised by her sudden willingness to be of assistance and shook his head. "No. Nothing at all, Nurse Bentham. Please feel free to carry on." He looked back down at the stack of folders he had been handed only moments earlier and tried his best not to peek back up in her direction to see her reaction after.

A small part of him, the childishly pettier side, simply didn't care what exactly was her issue with him today. The other half almost begged him to say something more encouraging. Or really, anything that he might think was humorously trite at all that would possibly lighten the mood between them just a little.

As he had half-expected, Nurse Bentham had been especially prickly this morning, even to Doctor Brooks, who had dismissed her actions outright just after checking in for the day and beginning his morning rounds. Something which William would not have consciously done to any of the staff, no matter the circumstances. Yet, the one man whose wisdom the nurse in front of him had seemed to revere above all others had done so with less care than he would have given to his pet hound. And to make matters even worse, the elder doctor had then chosen to arrogantly insult everyone else who was in the room, including the patient they had been treating.

Yet all of this was nothing William could discuss in her company at the moment either. Nor would it probably be proper to do so in front of other members of the staff who might be passing by at any given moment since Doctor Brooks was above him in authority, as well.

Like some of his own missteps of late, the callous action on the part of his superior had sent immediate waves of dissident discussion throughout the halls of the hospital afterwards, causing more than one of the nurses to give the elder doctor's needs the slower attention they deserved—an action that might have irritated William on any other given day, if it had been directed towards him. Yet today... Today he felt only the deserved pity for Nurse Bentham's plight. After all, from what he had overheard, her advice on the patient had actually been spot on. And if he had been the doctor on the case and not Doctor Brooks, he might have even accepted it and praised her quick thinking. But sadly, he was not, and the treatment handed down to her had only made matters worse... for everyone.

In fact, only an hour had passed since that unfortunate incident involving Doctor Brooks, and William had already had at least four unpleasant run-ins with Nurse Bentham thus far. One could not have been avoided as a heavily set man had needed to be lifted onto a bed for the remediation of some burns he had sustained while cleaning out the hearth in his home. An almost funny sort of circumstance to describe once again within his mind as the man had distractedly sat down upon some leftover coals within while he was busily trying to free up something stuck in the flue up above. On both sides of his upper thighs and all along the rather large and shockingly white backside of the man compared to his deeply tanned outer skin were angry polka-dotted blisters of various sizes and shapes that required the immediate application of several ointments to lessen their severity and curb off any future infection.

The other three patients were follow-ups to his previous medical orders. Which, again, was merely part of his job in the first place. Yet, as busy as the hospital usually became by the time lunch arrived, he was not assured whatsoever that her fleeting cordiality would remain anywhere past two, let alone endure until he left for his supper with Emile and Nathanael around four.

Since Emile's return from Charleston three years prior, the three friends had endeavored to plan, most faithfully, a once a month gathering at William and Nathanael's apartment to catch up on whatever was going on in their busy lives. Nothing distinguished or overly planned in any definition of the term, mind you, but a casual dinner where they could all simply relax and enjoy the unpretentious atmosphere while reminiscing with old friends.

Most of the time, William simply enjoyed passing the hours quietly listening to Emile's various stories about those he had encountered at the Capitol, or the funny tales Nathanael spun about his students' recent failures on test answers.

But recently, he had also taken to using the time in thoughtful examination of how the two men had managed to navigate through their own disappointments and challenges in their work, hoping to glean just a little bit of unique wisdom from his peers. Or really anything that would serve to be even remotely helpful in softening Miss Bentham's reactions, which under the circumstances, appeared as if he was still failing miserably at predicting or pacifying yet again.

And neither of the men would have thought that he of all people would have needed such instruction, as, by all outward appearances, he seemed perfectly in control of his sphere of existence on any given day. But William knew better. He had never once been a proud man like Emile always loved to portray, nor was he any closer to being as penitently humble as Nathanael forever seemed to be. Rather, he was a steady mix between the two. Though admittedly, that daily stabilization of his own life upon the emotional seesaw that bobbed up and down within him, did often require a great deal of careful balancing to remain perfectly settled in his own demeanor at times.

Oh, he knew his faults well enough by now. They were as plain as the nose on his face most days. He also understood the precarious situation he had placed himself in by concealing that inner struggle from others, for if one errant decision or emotion took over even a single aspect of his life, the entire system he had so delicately created might topple over because of it, causing a catastrophic reaction to the whole. Like a child's play tower built entirely from precariously placed blocks one on top of the other, his carefully constructed world and everything in it might tumble to the ground all around him, leaving a bigger mess for him to clean up than what he had originally been handed upon his arrival in the Colonies.

Well, thankfully for all involved, Nurse Bentham had chosen to leave him in the hallway just as quickly as she had entered and, for once, William was glad he had been so preoccupied with his own thoughts than to possibly make yet another inconsiderate error. Or simply put, his distracted state of casual contemplation had dulled his tongue just long enough to save him from further insult on this occasion alone. And for that, he thanked God quietly in prayer.

With a long exhale that spoke far more than any words he could have ever uttered, William closed his eyes and tried his best to relax once more, letting all the stress of the morning fall away from his heart, soul, and mind. Strained muscles in his jaw that were kept knitted tightly together from his terrible habit of constantly gritting his teeth to maintain his professional composure, all the way down to his cramped toes within his freshly polished boots, all stretched out happily in response, releasing the rest of the tautness and stress they had been holding onto so faithfully, as if doing so was their only job as they secured him together physically.

"Just a few hours more and it will be nothing but laughter and pleasantries for the rest of the night," William soothed himself into accepting the contentment that thought brought him and smiled as he breathed in the familiar smell of cleaner, mixed with the distinctly pungent odor from the stain used in the newly constructed surgical theater. This was indeed his home now as much as anywhere else in this world at present and there was no reason for retreat strong enough to make him ever want to leave it—at least not yet anyway. Someday it would be necessary to go, but that would only be by his own choosing in order to avoid detection, and not simply because he was not strong enough to endure a little discomfort... "Alright, maybe a lot more discomfort." He smirked to himself inwardly and shook his head at the decidedly non-humorous nature of it all.

"Doctor Wells, you are needed in Receiving please," Nurse Fitzpatrick said calmly as she walked over to him from the room beside him. "I believe your friend has brought along his wife this time to see you."

Opening his eyes in slight alarm at who the nurse might be actually talking about, he cocked his head to look through the glass window into the Receiving Room and squinted slightly at what he saw, expecting to see Emile and Emma walking through the door for some reason, or maybe even Thomas and Hannah, but neither were the case. There, near the door on the other side of the room was his unmarried friend, Nathanael, and what appeared to be an extremely pregnant woman who was obviously leaning quite heavily upon him as he walked, half-carrying and half-dragging the woman along with him.

Surprised and more than a little bit concerned at the unexpected turn of events before him, William placed the stack of folders he had been carrying on the elevated desk beside him and grasped the handle of the door firmly before entering the large room. "Did they only just arrive?"

"Yes," Nurse Fitzpatrick replied as they walked over together quickly and greeted the arriving couple.

"Hello... um, Mrs. ...?" William attempted to greet the woman warmly, extending his arm to support her in Nathanael's place.

"Armstrong." The woman panted several times thereafter and continued to lean greatly upon both men who were now supporting her fully. "Mrs. Jeremiah Armstrong."

"So, Mr. Beckett is not your husband, ma'am?" Nurse Fitzpatrick asked quickly while reaching for the woman's side to support her.

The look on Nathanael's now terrified face at the mere suggestion of such a thing was positively priceless. From the very shocked expression alone, it was clear now to everyone gathered around them that never in all his life would he have ever thought himself to be in such a position as the one he was in now, nor would he possibly be ready to raise anything more than a housecat... certainly not an actual child.

"Um, no. No, I am most certainly not," Nathanael practically stuttered back his reply, utterly panicked now that anyone would think something so implausibly startling as this of him.

"Relax, Nathanael." William chuckled quietly as he continued to help the woman next to him, for he could not help doing so under the circumstances. After everything he had been through today already, witnessing his friend's shocked discomfort at the misunderstanding was completely amusing, if not totally hysterical in so many ways. Though none of which he could disclose without offense in their current company.

"It's not funny, William, and you know it." Nathanael shot him a narrowed glance from behind him.

"No, I suppose it is not." William tried to remain professional and not laugh outright again at his friend's expense but watching him continue to struggle made it incredibly difficult to do so. After this rather unique experience, no doubt, the two of them would have <u>much</u> to talk about tonight, and William, for once, could barely contain his enthusiasm for it.

"I'm sorry for the confusion I have caused by my forward conduct on his behalf, but this is my husband's colleague at the Seminary." The woman allowed the two members of the hospital staff to guide her over to a waiting bed and laid down awkwardly upon it, grateful for the welcomed support of a stable surface. "I came to the school to find my husband shortly after lunch when my waters broke. And unfortunately for Mr. Beckett, my husband was away on a sick call at the time," she continued to explain through many pauses as her contractions seized her again and again without consent.

"Well, we do happen to have a few midwives on staff should you prefer one of them over Doctor Wells, dear. Some very excellent ones, I might add," the nurse next to William tried to explain helpfully, allowing the woman the opportunity to have someone more discreetly chosen attend to her needs, for a doctor of his caliber and experience was rarely called in for a delivery of this kind unless it was something more dire in nature or a complication that a midwife could not simply handle on her own.

Mrs. Armstrong shook her head. "No, Doctor Wells will do perfectly well, thank you. Mr. Beckett and my husband say he is the best doctor at this hospital and since I lost the last two babies before this one, that is who I want. I am not about to wait until it is too late to get help again, no matter what others might think of me for saying so."

"Too late for what, Mrs. Armstrong?" Like a true diagnostician, William was instantly engaged in the conversation presenting itself, as he began seeking out all the many details he needed to assist the woman in saving her child, if indeed there was any danger approaching them at all.

For several tense moments, the woman on the bed attempted to answer his question directly but was interrupted yet again by several concentrated contractions before Nathanael cleared his throat and tapped William on the shoulder politely. "If it is alright with you, I think it is time I take my leave and seek out her husband directly."

"Yes, please do, Mr. Beckett," the woman begged before a look of true appreciation crossed her face at last. "And thank you for the escort. I don't think I could have managed to get here without your help."

"My pleasure entirely, madame," Nathanael replied cordially and glanced back at William for his permission.

"Go on." William cocked his head towards the open door before adding, "I'll see you tonight for supper. And don't forget, it's your turn to cook, remember?"

Like a forlorn teenager who dreaded any task that required an effort on his part to do so, Nathanael groaned, "Why can't we just let Emile do it again. He far excels anything I could ever cook up any day, or even you for that matter."

"Nathanael..." William looked up at him patiently over his newest charge and cast him a glance like that of a stern father as he waited for him to acquiesce on the matter. "You promised."

"Fine..." The man waved him off reluctantly and trudged out of the hospital without another word on the matter, dejectedly consoled to his path of undesired destiny.

"He sounds as scared as my husband does at times." Mrs. Armstrong smiled at the exchange between the two men. "It's a wonder you men survive at all before marriage."

"Hah, in that you are probably right, Mrs. Armstrong, and my apologies for the interruption. You were about to explain to me what happened during the labor of your last two children." As pleasantly as his response had begun, William's seriousness returned in force once more as he concentrated the bulk of his attention on her care, while ignoring Nathanael's recent whining.

"Yes, that…" The woman tried to begin once again but instead closed her eyes momentarily as she gripped the sheets next to her, the contractions coming quicker this time with each one seemingly more intense than the last.

Sensing there was more to the situation than what was clearly being presented, William asked the nurse beside him politely, "Bridget, will you fetch a basin of hot water, some towels and something cool for Mrs. Armstrong to drink? I fear with this heat spell we have been having; she might need some added refreshment before we proceed any further." William studied the beads of sweat pooling up on the woman's brow and moved to dry them with the spare towel that was lying on the small table next to her.

"Right away, Doctor." Nurse Fitzpatrick complied dutifully and left William alone with his patient.

"Were your last two children both born full-term?" William asked quietly and calmly, attempting to soothe her concern with the current delivery.

The woman nodded. "Both girls and just as perfect as can be."

"I see." Feeling a deep sense of pity for the woman and the fear she must be currently experiencing, William reached down and picked up the woman's hand, allowing her to grip him instead of the sheets at her side. "And did the midwife also happen to say what might have caused their um, demise." William tried his best to be as gentle as possible in his necessary inquiry.

The woman shook her head several times and tried to keep herself as composed as possible through the strain. "No, but both were born with the cord wrapped around them tightly."

William's lips pursed immediately at the prophetic revelation as he searched mentally for the various means available to him to avoid such a recurrence. "May I take a moment to examine you and see how far along you are progressing with this child? I promise to be as gentle as possible."

Mrs. Armstrong nodded and attempted to remain as still as she could manage while William felt the various areas of her abdomen, trying her best not to pull away from him when he pushed and prodded on some of the more sensitive areas near her sides. "I'm sorry."

"Don't be," William reassured her. "I would imagine that trying to carry a baby into existence comes with more than a little bit of pain and discomfort."

"You have no idea, Doctor Wells," she breathed out slowly once again to temper her tolerance to the pain. "But they say it is all worth it when you hear that baby cry." She looked momentarily sad once again before she tried to hide the whimpered cry she was holding back as several contractions attacked.

"Just keeping holding onto my hand through it. We will get through this together."

Mrs. Armstrong jerked her head up and down in response and clutched the offered token desperately.

By the time that the next contraction had come and gone, Nurse Fitzpatrick had returned and set the customary ceramic basin and glass of water on the short table beside him before lifting Mrs. Armstrong slightly higher up on her pillows to assist her. "Here, dear, try sipping as much of this as you can. It will help." She offered the woman the glass of water and encouraged her to drink.

Tired as she was, the woman strained herself to sip as much of the liquid offered as possible, despite the surging cramps that stopped her more than once as she swallowed and before long she had finished that glass entirely and then another before she laid back down for a brief rest when the contractions seemed to lessen by some degree, though not to the point of actually stopping.

"If you will permit me, I will be right back, Mrs. Armstrong. I promise," William petitioned and motioned discreetly with his right hand for the young nurse to follow him to the other side of the room. "Nurse Fitzpatrick, I'm afraid our patient is going to need a bit more specialized care than what is normal under the circumstances."

"Why?" The more than capable nurse in front of him, whom he had worked with on many other occasions, stared back at him incredulously. "Women have been having babies for centuries, sir. It isn't precisely what I would label as a medical emergency."

"That may be so, but many of them have also died in the process which is what I fear might occur here if we do not take the proper precaution now." William looked over at his patient across the room and then back to the nurse once more before explaining, "What you might not have noticed because of her inclination on the bed is that the baby is presenting sideways still and therefore it is not in the proper position for a normal delivery. Yet from all other appearances otherwise, the mother is clearly approaching the last stages of labor and will soon begin to start pushing. That being said, my biggest fear is that if she were allowed to continue to progress to that stage in the state that she is currently in, we might be dealing with two deaths on our hands instead of the possible one. And even then, I would very much like to avoid that one, as well, if we can manage it."

"Then how do you wish to proceed, Doctor?" The nurse asked him seriously, clearly as uncertain as he was as to the proper course of action concerning their patient.

As if entirely lost in thought once more, William took a moment to contemplate several of the options available to him then frowned as he knew which one he was going to have to eventually choose. There was only one nurse, in his opinion, that could assist him properly in this case but requesting her after everything that had already transpired today made his skin crawl just considering it.

What he needed most of all was someone who could anticipate his patient's needs as they arose and only one person here had ever been able to do that effectively enough to warrant calling her now.

"Do we perchance have a midwife who is familiar with complicated births? Someone who might be able to think outside the box so to speak?" William searched tentatively for another possible alternative, though he could already tell by the look on the woman's face in front of him that his first assumption had been entirely correct.

"Only one, sir." The nurse looked back at him and smiled with a tip of her head. "Though she would not refer to herself as a midwife anymore, per se."

"I am assuming we are both referring to Nurse Bentham." William tried not to appear as displeased as he felt, while also eagerly desirous that the nurse in question might possibly have another solution for him other than the inevitable one he most feared.

The woman nodded.

William closed his eyes to build up his wall of defense once more against his overwhelming need to request her assistance and nodded, also. "Alright then. Please ask her to see me as soon as she is able. She does not need to rush through her duties if she is already engaged in a patient's care, but sooner than later would be overly preferred." He looked up over the nurse's shoulder at the other patients waiting to be seen, then continued, "And you might want to send for Doctor Baxter or his colleague Doctor Green, too, as we seem to be getting a backlog in here today."

"Right away, Doctor Wells." The woman left quickly to complete her errand as William made his way back over to his laboring patient.

"Mrs. Armstrong, if it is alright with you, I would like to have you moved to a more private room. Would that be suitable?" William picked up the woman's hand and tried to offer another possible comfort that might help her through her ordeal.

"Though I appreciate the consideration, the way I am feeling right now, I'd just as soon stay right here if it is all the same to you. Besides, I hate to be such a bother." The woman gripped his hand tightly once more, as if her life depended on her hold and attempted to smile back at him through the pain and discomfort.

"If that is your wish, though my patients are never a bother, ma'am. On the contrary, you must be pretty special for Mr. Beckett to have come all this way to convey you to me." William's heart yearned deeply once again to help the woman who had obviously been through so much trauma in her lifetime already.

On one hand, he could try to say that he sympathized with her in the loss she had experienced, but since he had never had the opportunity to have a child of his own, much less have it perish in that way, that did not seem even remotely authentic to say. Yet on the other hand, he <u>had</u> listened on several occasions to Sebastian as he related the story about his own child's death and how much it had affected him. By his very vivid description alone of his grief thereafter, as well as the memory of Susan Summerfield's face when she had told him of Elsie's final moments, William knew that such a death would be overwhelming for anyone experiencing it, crippling even should there be two such events to endure.

"Oh, no. It was Mr. Beckett who was most kind." Mrs. Armstrong tried to sit up for a moment but held her breath as another contraction hit her fully. "Though if truth be told, I didn't give him much of a choice in the matter. In my desperation to remain upright, I practically grabbed onto his coat when I saw him and wouldn't let go. Thankfully for both of us, he didn't need to carry me or bring you to the school, which would have been the second option if I could not manage to walk here of my accord." She paused for just a moment and laughed lightly, the mirth of the story now painting her delicate features. "Now <u>that</u> would have been dramatic for all of us."

"Most certainly." William chuckled just a little with her at the picture of what that would have most probably looked like and added, "Having a baby in the middle of an all-male university would have been something for the history books there to be sure."

The woman laughed a bit more, too, at his humorous description and definite fear she had already at least considered once. "No doubt, but I'd much rather make my news elsewhere, thank you. Oh, no! Here we go again!" She bore down hard several times once more but with each time that she did so, William noted that the pause between each subsequent contraction was lessening before the next.

Alarmed, more so than before, but with little else that he could do at the present without Nurse Bentham to assist him or offer another solution, William took his place next to Mrs. Armstrong on the bed and placed one hand upon her stomach during each push, searching for any changes in the baby's position or decline in the baby's movements. There were none. It was almost as if the child inside was arrogantly refusing to comply and leave his comfortable surroundings.

Searching for something to do in an attempt to be remotely useful, he took her wrist and felt her pulse, counting out the beats against the clock on the wall beside him. By all accounts, her heartrate was still steady, slightly elevated in its rate due to the added mental stress, but cautiously acceptable under the strain that she was currently exerting. Still, after hearing her foreboding revelations earlier, he wished more than ever before that he could have done the same action for the baby, as well. Or really anything that would have assured him of the baby's condition during the complicated labor it was enduring.

Yet it was at that very moment, in the middle of his anxious musings, that Nurse Bentham came into the room through the double doors behind him, crossing the short distance between them quickly before stopping to wait patiently beside him for his next instruction as if nothing at all of consequence had ever transpired between them. "I was told that you needed me, Doctor Wells. How can I be of service?"

Grateful once more for her keenly practiced professional demeanor in front of her patients, he glanced up, his face a perfect picture of the fresh concern filling his entire being. "The baby is not in the proper presentation for delivery, Nurse Bentham."

"I see. And about how many minutes apart are her contractions?" Nurse Bentham immediately moved to the other side of the bed and felt the woman's abdomen from top to bottom, then glanced up at William with the same look of worry before giving a silent nod of understanding.

"A little less than three minutes the last time I checked. Far too close together for my comfort at this stage in the delivery, and especially so under the circumstances. Can we slow it down possibly to allow the baby the time it needs to adjust to a better position?" William said quietly so as not to arouse too much concern on behalf of his patient.

Nurse Bentham shook her head in response several times slowly. "No."

With an exhausted exhale, Mrs. Armstrong fell back against her pillow once more, this time entirely spent by the last session of contractions she had just endured. "They have never been this hard before... not ever."

"I imagine not." Nurse Bentham tried to console her. "When did your waters break?"

"Around milking time this morning," she answered her quietly, overwhelmingly depleted by the continuing ordeal.

"Alright, then it has been a good eight hours since." The nurse remained consistently constant in her questioning. "Any other problems or issues to speak of before this child?"

William nodded silently. "This is not her first complication in delivery."

"How many others?" The nurse's face remained stoic, still entirely focused on the task at hand.

"Two."

"Certainly not ideal, no." Nurse Bentham clasped her hands together firmly and rubbed her fingers down to their tips in concentration. "Well, then with your permission, Mrs. Armstrong, I would like to try to do something that might help, if I can. But I must tell you that it will not be pleasant. In fact, it will be quite painful, but we <u>must</u> try it if we are to help this little one on its way."

From the mere description of the procedure and the firm tone with which the nurse had delivered it, Mrs. Armstrong's eyes became momentarily distressed, and even more so when she saw the same look of apprehension on Doctor Wells' face, also. "Will it hurt the baby?"

It was William's turn now to convince the frightened woman of the necessity of whatever Nurse Bentham was proposing to do. "I do not think so, but since I also believe that every patient deserves to know the absolute truth in order to make an informed decision, I will put the situation as plainly as I can." He paused and respectfully waited for her to have a short moment to absorb everything they were about to say to her. "At this point, though there is still very much we do not know, I believe it is worth whatever the risk involved will be to at least try. As much as I would like to tell you otherwise, there is simply no way you can deliver this baby with the way it is positioned right now, as trying to continue doing so will most likely kill you both."

Feeling nothing but admiration from her position on the other side of the bed, Nurse Bentham studied William with an expression that showed both a hint of surprise at his total honesty and also a great deal of respect for his desire to aid in his patient's understanding. In many ways, by this action alone, she now held a small bit of renewed appreciation for the man since he had seen the importance of taking the time to do something that other doctors of his caliber would have completely ignored.

"Then whatever we need to do, do it," the woman shot back at them resolutely, holding the determination of a hardened soldier as she refused to give in to anything that might result in the outcome she most feared.

"Doctor Wells, can we move those partitions over there around her for a little more privacy, perhaps?" Nurse Bentham motioned with her head to the folded wall-like curtains they sometimes used to divide up the patients into separate areas.

"Of course." William and the other nurses sprang into action immediately as they quickly moved three of the dividers over to where the woman was positioned and formed them into a makeshift room of sorts before only William and Nurse Bentham remained within its confines.

"Are you going to try to move the baby internally?" William whispered quietly to the nurse beside him when the two of them were huddled together cleaning their hands.

"Yes." Nurse Bentham nodded back to him slowly so as not to draw any additional attention to her movements. "But I'll need you to try and shift the baby from above while I am doing so," she instructed politely, but clearly.

"So, you think that by the gentle movements in a possibly clockwise direction, we might be able to coax the baby's head into a more favorable position?" William surmised quickly, yet even though he had spoken the words to describe her audacious plan, he still had no real idea how or if their efforts would eventually be successful.

"Yes. Have you done this before?"

"What?" William raised his eyebrows at the mere suggestion. "Never... you?"

"Only on two other occasions." She dried her hands off on the waiting towel and handed it over to him.

"Did it work?" William inquired politely, suddenly hopeful for a positive outcome for both the mother and the baby.

"No." Nurse Bentham shook her head sadly before adding, "But please do not tell her. This will be hard enough as it is."

"Do you mind if I ask what happened?" William finished drying his hands and stood close enough to her as to form a makeshift wall of sorts for their more private discussion.

Nurse Bentham pursed her lips and dreaded saying the two words she knew the doctor beside her had most likely already assumed since the beginning. "Both died."

William drew in a long breath and held it a moment longer before exhaling it out again more forcefully. "Can you think of anything else to try? Anything at all?"

Nurse Bentham shook her head once more and felt fresh empathy fill her as it always did in complicated decisions such as this. Ones that she would most happily wish to never be a part of, yet could not also avoid in her chosen profession. "Some things cannot be fixed, Doctor Wells, no matter how much we may want them to be so."

"I understand." The more learned doctor took in the information she was giving him respectfully, allowing the full weight of the matter to expand within his mind as he contemplated the bleak outlook for both of his patients. Nurse Bentham was entirely correct in her assessment, painfully so, but that did not also mean that he was willing to accept it, not yet anyways—not without at least trying. Endeavoring to change the mind of his colleague on the matter entirely, William resolved firmly, "No, Nurse Bentham, we _are_ going to save this child _and_ his mother. I refuse to allow defeat so easily, not yet anyways."

Shocked again at his sudden, though misplaced determination, Nurse Bentham did not speak at first. Instead, she only looked up at him with a pained yet reaching expression he had never seen before on the woman's face. In every feature and line that framed her face in that moment, it all tugged at the bitterness he had held towards her recently and struggled to remove whatever bricks were still remaining in his inner wall.

Cautiously reaching over to the man beside her, she uncharacteristically placed one hand upon his own and paused, both taking in the immensity of the moment between them. "William, please... you must know by now that sometimes it is out of our hands to save them."

"I do." William studied her green eyes intently, as if searching for something in particular to hold onto in his struggle. What exactly that was, he did not know. But standing there, in the midst of this situation unfolding around them, there was an almost tangible quality now to the weight of her stare. "But I need to at least try."

"I know, and I understand," she replied quietly and for the first time since their amicable conversation in the hallway weeks ago, William felt at ease in her presence once more. So much so that it was almost as if the energy between them had shifted dramatically in an opposite direction, though nothing had actually transpired to do so.

"After I am able to feel the baby properly from below, I will need you to use both of your hands on the side of her abdomen to move the baby around towards the bottom gently when she contracts. As you said, if we are successful, this will give us the presentment we desire, which will obviously be most favorable for a normal delivery. However, if that does not work, you can try maneuvering the baby from the other side. The baby will most likely be born breech then, but even that is better than how it is lying now," she explained thoroughly, detailing each of the necessary instructions for his part in the procedure. "It won't be ideal, but it <u>will</u> be better."

William nodded. "I understand. Let me fetch another nurse. We will need someone to tend to her needs directly while we work."

Charity agreed and moved to where her patient was groaning mildly on the bed. In any other state of mind, the woman would have most definitely heard their entire conversation and possibly objected to not being included in the decision-making process, but with her labor progressing as much as it was, she had not seemed to notice, nor would it have been especially helpful for all if she had. "Now, do you want me to tell you what we are going to do, ma'am, or do you wish me to simply do it?" Nurse Bentham asked politely.

The young mother did not say a word for several long and agonizing moments before her eyes fluttered suddenly open as she propped herself up on her elbows and leaned into another contraction. "Just do what you must. And if it is a choice between me and the baby... choose him," she demanded, slightly out of breath without the least bit of wavering whatsoever on such a dire decision.

"Let us pray it never comes to that, shall we?" Nurse Bentham seized her hand optimistically and stroked some of the loose hair back that had clung to the woman's face. "Have you picked out a name for the baby?" She asked, attempting to distract her further until William returned with the help they required.

"Daniel, after my father," the woman huffed. "I refuse to pick out a girl's name yet."

"Well then, let's see if Daniel wants to say hello to his mother, alright?" Nurse Bentham smiled back at her encouragingly and nodded to William and the other nurse who had just joined them.

For the better part of the next half hour, the three of them worked together in tandem to adjust the baby's position and within another two hours' time after that a healthy baby boy miraculously emerged, much to the delight and relief of all in the room who had worked so diligently for his safe delivery.

"Welcome to the world, Daniel!" William exclaimed proudly as he handed the small bundle up to the weary woman and focused the rest of his attention on finishing up with the last actions of the delivery.

Elated beyond the means of possible expression, the new mother clasped the wailing child to her chest and joined him in his tears, the exhilarating joy of the moment overwhelming her at last. "Thank you, Lord! Oh, thank you!" She whispered repeatedly as she clung to her miraculous gift. "And thank you, Doctor Wells... Miss Bentham."

"You are most welcome." Nurse Bentham smiled at the endearing scene and touched the small head of the tiny infant before remarking, "He has a full head of hair this one. Does red run in your family?"

"I sure hope so," a strong voice said behind the curtain before a man with an equally thick head of auburn hair peeked around it at her, obviously out of breath from his journey over there.

"You made it just in time, Mr. Armstrong." William laughed lightly and pulled a clean sheet up over the bottom half of his patient to make her more presentable. "We were beginning to think you might not be coming."

"What? Never!" The man quickly moved around the wall and over to his wife's waiting side, paying careful attention not to disturb her on the bed. "I wouldn't miss this for the world." His face bore the marks of tears sliding down his slightly tanned face, though the rest of his attire appeared equally damp as if he had been running for quite some distance as there was a thick layer of sweat collected in various places. "I was on the other side of the city, near the Wilson farm, so it took Nathanael quite some time to find me with the wagon, dear."

"I'm so glad he did." Mrs. Armstrong smiled up at him, unmeasured love in all of its many facets painted on all her features. "Come meet your son."

"Really? A son?" The man let out a controlled sob of happiness and held the child with her, both too involved in their quiet moment of blessing to notice much of anything else going on around them.

With their job satisfactorily finished for the time being, Nurse Bentham moved to the end of the bed and stood professionally next to William to enjoy the scene for just a moment before pulling back one of the partitions slightly to allow her the necessary room to leave.

Surprised, and suddenly unable to look away, William watched her closely as she left, then felt an intense impulse inside of him grow with his need to follow after her as if something was pulling him with some kind of force that was strangely compulsory and yet also desperate in nature. "Um, could I have just another moment of your time please, Nurse Bentham." William stepped around the curtain and over to where the woman had finally stopped, glancing around the small area around them for other members of the hospital staff.

"Yes." The woman stopped slowly at his request, then turned around to face him, but when she did William's mind fell instantly blank with what he had intended on saying as he took in the saddened expression she wore.

"I'm sorry. Are you alright?" He resisted the urge to reach forward and touch her arm, trying instead to appear guardedly helpful, though in his mind, he could not think of a single thing that had transpired in the past hour that might have brought out such a reaction in her. Certainly nothing he had said this time.

"I will be." The nurse looked away from him quickly, casting her gaze towards the door behind her as if contemplating once again her measured retreat as she struggled to compose herself more fully, then wiped away a stray tear from the corner of her eye. "Is there something in which I can assist you further, Doctor Wells?" She did her best to maintain the proper humility that was expected of someone in her position, but by the way in which she clasped her arms tightly across her chest alone, he could tell that the very action she had meant to be commonplace was the only thing holding her together at this point.

Enduring the pain of watching the woman struggle so in front of him, William glanced over his shoulder once again to make sure no one else was watching their interaction before he drew closer still, desiring to comfort her in some way, much like he might have done if she had been Charlotte. "What's wrong, Charity?"

"It's nothing, really." The normally composed woman beside him pursed her lips several times as she labored to stop the curling of the edges that escaped every time she tried to hold back her emotions. "Or rather, nothing that will not pass in time." She brushed anxiously at the non-existent wrinkles down the front of her blouse to smooth them out from nervous habit. "Besides, I am certain you have enough to worry about on your own to add my troubles to that very long list."

"Nothing as pressing as what I see before me now." William's brow furrowed instantly at her erroneous conclusion, thinking how very similar his thoughts were to her own at that moment, as well. "And before you go on the defensive and think I am trying to insult you, I wouldn't be a doctor worth his salt if I did not at least notice something was amiss. As you are probably aware, being overly observant about what everyone else thinks is inconsequential sort of comes with the territory... whether I like it or not." William paused and thought very seriously about what her reaction might be if he were to brush way the very small tear that was now resting above her cheek but decided quickly against it.

"You and I both know that you are an excellent doctor, William." Nurse Bentham half-smiled, then added more sarcastically, "Though you don't need me to tell you that."

Stunned by her honest admission instead of her usual criticism, William's mouth fell open slightly at the comment. "Well, I wouldn't go that far, not yet anyways, but I do know of a nurse here who works very hard to improve me daily. I'll have to let her know that her efforts are finally paying off," he finally managed to say cheerfully with a chuckle, allowing the action to clear away some of the tension that had begun to build during their conversation

"Well, she seems rather opinionated to think she needs to change you." Charity tilted her head in a more aloof manner like something he might have seen Emile do from time to time.

"Oh, I wouldn't go as far as to say that. I expect she is just a tad bit more passionate towards what she cares about than all the other nurses. That's all," William complimented her obscurely, wanting to bestow upon her the same kindness she had just afforded him.

Without another word, Nurse Bentham nodded and turned around to leave once more but the expected action made his heart almost stop completely. "Charity, wait." William touched her arm in the same gentle way she had done during their discussion earlier and held it there a moment in the silence that lingered—each sensing the overwhelming need to absorb the other's strength and composure, if for only a brief moment.

"I am very... grateful... for everything," William whispered quietly next to her, unable to form a single coherent sentence in the closeness building between them.

Without moving away in the slightest, the woman beside him, who had never once let her guard down even for a moment in his presence, looked up at him at last, her eyes searching his own carefully. "No, thank you for trusting my judgement this time." She finally said quietly back to him then squeezed his hand lightly and walked back out of the room and out of sight.

Firmly fixed to the floor at his feet, with no remaining ability to move anymore at all, William let her go and as much as he wanted to follow after her, his mind was now racing with a plethora of questions it had created regarding her actions. Questions that unfortunately needed answering before any other words, pleasant or otherwise, could be spoken.

What <u>was</u> so incredibly significant about this woman that made him want to be as near to her as he possibly could be right now? Yet more importantly, how could he avoid upsetting her in the future now that he obviously cared for what the woman thought of him? And last but not least, what did he truly want regarding her anyways? Amicable coexistence, a professional friendship or something more—much more?

Standing in the middle of the Receiving Room while others passed him by on their way to tend to their other patients, he considered the possible answers to all of his shockingly unexpected questions at once before his eyes widened with yet another more pressing question that trumped them all. One that quite possibly should have come before all the others.

What did <u>she</u> want?

That last question alone hung itself in his head for the remainder of the day and in every moment that his eyes trained the halls thereafter as if searching for her presence.

With the delivery an undeniably happy success, for the rest of the afternoon, he was subsequently pulled into several other, equally difficult cases and two more lengthy lectures about the importance of correct charting of patients, each held in an opposite wing of the hospital than was normally Nurse Betham's daily domain. Yet unlike other occurrences in the past, that fact pained him far more than it ever had before. On most days, the blessing of her absence would have given him a great deal of peace to have been finally rid of the woman for at least an entire afternoon, but after what he had just experienced by her side today, all he wanted now was another conversation with her, another glance in her direction, another second holding her hand—if only... just to make sure she was <u>still</u>... alright.

Why that was... he did not fully understand, not yet anyway, but whatever the reason, he knew now that he would most definitely be staying until he found out, even if it killed him.

Chapter Eleven

August 15th, 1811

"I'm telling you, Emile. You should have seen his face when the nurse assumed he was the father today." William laughed heartily at the table with his two other friends. "Pure mortification would have described it perfectly."

"Well, did the woman have a reason to believe him to be so or was it simply a misunderstanding on her part?" Emile took a sip of his wine and passed the bottle over to William sitting next to him. "I mean no disrespect, of course, but Nathanael doesn't exactly look like typical husband material."

"And you do?" Nathanael scoffed lightly at his errant remark.

"Maybe not, but I'd like to think that I look more the part than you do at least, and frightfully better than our dear William over here." Emile grinned at the humorous subject. "From his repetitively disparaging tales over the years, he seems to have perfected the process of scaring away even the most interested of parties at the hospital."

"Indeed." William rolled his eyes at the man and shook his head before filling up his glass half-way with the offered drink. "I assure you, the <u>last</u> thing that I need right now is a wife, Emile. Besides, I have my hands full enough already keeping track of the two of you. Which, at the moment, seems to be occupation enough for one lifetime, maybe even two. Besides, when would I ever have the time to afford towards entertaining a woman properly, much less marrying one?"

"What about that nurse from the hospital you have been talking about non-stop for the past few months?" Nathanael picked the most qualified example in his opinion and motioned with his spoon towards William. "By your rather colorful description of her veracity of character, she seems utterly perfect for you."

"Who? Nurse Bentham?" William swallowed reflexively and tried very hard to hide the newer feelings he had experienced just this afternoon in the hopes of deflecting his friend's assumption before he grew even more assured of its validity. "An excellent notion possibly on the surface, but I believe she has already professed to swearing off the idea of marriage entirely at the present. Or at least she has mentioned to me something of that kind awhile back."

"Ahhhh, but you <u>have</u> at least discussed the subject with her, William." Nathanael continued to pry intently. "Which gives me hope that she might also be open to other discussions should the temperature change someday."

"Please, Nathanael," William groaned inwardly and shook his head at the man's uncanny accuracy in his intuition but attempted to remain still utterly unfazed. "Miss Charity Bentham would no more consider me a suitor than Emile here will be elected our next president."

"Nice, William." Emile cocked his head sarcastically towards him, but did not seem to agree. "Though there are many reasons why I have not been considering such a position, vampirism aside, it does not mean I would not be well suited for it. Mr. Madison does a tolerable job overall, I suppose, but he is nothing compared to his predecessors... quite the contrary. In fact, many feel that should this war ever begin, it would be solely his fault alone."

"Why would they think that, Emile?" William took a few bites of the fried chicken on his plate and wiped his mouth politely.

"Well for starters, a president is supposed to think of his nation's needs first with a focus on its overall stability, not endeavor to reach for things it simply does not require nor even want." Emile paused and took a small bite of his potatoes, too, before adding, "Or at least most of us do not."

"Like the land in the Canadas, for example?" Nathanael asked curiously.

"Precisely so." Emile appreciated once again how very much Nathanael managed to remember everything he had ever said to the man. It was certainly true that his friend could be more than a tad bit scatterbrained at times, and most definitely a little overly emotional in others, but put them all together and they created a very fine specimen of a friend indeed. Moreover, in every way, he was as loyal as anyone Emile had ever known and twice as intelligent, though his friend would never admit that fact to anyone, nor to himself either for that matter. Simply put, his overabundance of humility prevented him from doing so, but to Emile, that was truly never a deficit in his character. It only made him the ever-incorrigible Nathanael Beckett. Which, in his opinion, was quite special indeed.

"Then what will you do when your term is up then, Emile? Run for another?" William asked openly, though he probably already knew the answer, as Emile had often needed a change of scenery from time to time to keep himself from becoming overly bored in his mundane existence.

"I am open to at least one more term in my current position, but not more beyond that. Then again, this may all be a mute discussion completely as I may not have the opportunity to run for re-election at all if I vote against the war preparations next month." Emile finished the last of the food on his plate and placed his fork and knife on top of it. "In government, I have learned that it is less about who you are and what you know and more about who you can please and what you can do for them."

"Sounds like a pretty sad existence, if you ask me," William said out of the corner of his mouth while sipping some of his wine.

"Only if I choose to let it be," Emile countered just as quickly. "Which I do not. For as long as I am able, I am determined to change at least some of their minds if it is the last thing I do, which by the looks of things, it just might be. Andrew Jackson is terribly fired up right now about it and with the amount of pull he has in the Senate, I doubt anything I say will make a difference in the slightest, but I <u>will</u> try. If only to prevent that windbag from silencing others."

"Yes, yes, you will," William agreed. "And who knows, maybe a miracle will happen, after all," he spoke the words to his friend, but deep down he felt them more profoundly for his own situation today. Truth be told, this morning had begun very much like his own personal war was continuing on over at the hospital, but as the day had progressed, he had found himself most surprisingly wishing he had never even signed up for the battle in the first place. Nothing in all the world was worth being at odds with someone almost every single day and especially when the person was someone like her.

But why was she so different to him than all of the others?

From what he saw today and at other times, she was indeed more like him than he cared to admit. So, if that were true, what was it about her that made him intensely intrigued about her every thought while also cautiously warning him to be hesitant at being in the same room with her alone?

William let his mind focus on that random question for quite some time before someone poked him in his arm and brought his attention back to the conversation transpiring without him. "I'm sorry, what?"

"I was just saying how very good this fried chicken was tonight and congratulating Nathanael on his triumphant success." Emile endeavored to catch his distracted friend back up to the discussion at hand.

"Yes, it was very good," William said quickly. But truthfully, he did not think he had even remembered anything remarkable about the meal at all besides maybe a slight smoky flavoring to the meat and the fact that there had been mashed potatoes instead of the usual roasted ones. "Where did you say you purchased the chicken, Nathanael?"

"I didn't say actually," Nathanael explained quickly and picked up his plate and William's, hoping his companions had not noticed anything more usual about the meal. "When I mentioned to Charlotte yesterday about tonight's meal, she graciously gave me one of the hens Jedidiah had put in the smokehouse last week." He kept his back towards the others and attempted to busy himself in tidying up the remnants of their meal for consumption at a later date.

"I see." Emile paused and allowed the silence to build just a little to an uncomfortable awkwardness between them. "And did she also happen to send over her cherry cobbler for dessert with the mashed potatoes she made?" Emile glanced up at him knowingly while wiping his mouth, effectively pinning the man to the floor where he stood.

Defeated once again, Nathanael sighed. "<u>How</u> did you know?"

"Oh, friend..." Emile tried to hold back his mirth at the man's obvious demise and beamed proudly in exultation once again for catching him in his delicate trap. "Who do you think gave her the recipe for this coating on the chicken in the first place?"

"I had to promise to help clean out the fireplace in exchange for this meal, and it's all for naught anyways it seems." Nathanael shook his head in dismay and ignored the man's antics as he trudged dutifully back towards the kitchen counter next to the table.

Watching the way in which the man across from them crumpled under the weight of his failure once again, William looked over at Emile beside him briefly as the two of them grinned widely, then shrugged together in unison.

"Face it, Mr. Beckett, you were bound to get caught eventually... just like last time. Still, all things considered, it might be best if you were to simply start confessing your sins before the meal begins next time so that you may repent of your sins outright and just be done with it." William toyed with the man's absolute affinity to the truth as he teased him right along with Emile on the subject.

"You both said this time that it was my turn to provide dinner." Nathanael turned around and hotly defended himself on the topic. "You did not specify exactly <u>how</u> it was to be procured."

"Crafty this one, isn't he?" Emile eyed Nathanael as he leaned back in his chair and mocked him freely. "Should we notify the Anglican preacher across town on his behalf? It's possible that his deceptive spirit might need to be dealt with, after all."

"I'd like to see you try... That man is an idiot, even by my standards... but his flock <u>does</u> love his sermons," Nathanael scoffed and practically threw the silverware into the washtub in front of him in disgust. "Glorified fairy tales more like it. There is barely a solid Scripture in any of them, more than maybe a verse or two thrown in for sheer effect."

"Whoa there, Nathanael." Emile raised his eyebrows just once quickly in definite concern at Nathanael's reaction to their incessant teasing.

"On second thought, it appears he may have some anger issues, too. You know, Emile, as long as we are calling the minister over, we might as well address everything all at once," William quipped and leaned in closer to Emile. "Then again, maybe we should be more concerned with the fact that we are in such close company with an unrepentant sinner? Might we be also tainted by the mere association by default?"

For several tense moments afterwards, Nathanael kept his gaze entirely focused on the dishes in front of him, refusing to even look their way, all in an attempt to cool his temper towards their denigrating comments. "Or maybe the two of you should hush your mouths and be grateful I haven't told the bulk of your secrets to everyone else of our acquaintance," he fumed quietly at the counter.

"Secrets?" William glanced over at Emile playfully, then motioned to him with the flip of his hand. "Do you have secrets?"

Without even stopping to consider his statement fully, or what his friend might think to reveal, Emile nonchalantly stared right back at him, incredulously amused. "Not that I am aware of. Though Emma might remember a few that I have forgotten recently."

Without drawing in another breath, Nathanael decided firmly once and for all that he had endured enough taunting insults for one evening at his expense. Choosing rather to grit his teeth together to curb the worst of what he feared would come out of him, the jovial mood with which he normally viewed his friends left him as he muttered darkly, "Where shall I begin, gentlemen...?" His eyes fixed first on William with his audacious *laze faire* expression still plastered across his face, then shifted over to Emile with a fire neither of them had seen before, nor would they probably ever hope to see again. "For many years Emile has pretended that what happened the night of Doctor Clarke's death has not affected him one iota… that he doesn't care a whit emotionally or otherwise about Hope staying with them even now. But deep down… all he has ever really wanted from the very beginning to be is her…"

"Alright, Nathanael… I think you have divulged enough on <u>my</u> behalf." Emile stood up instantly as he pushed back his chair loudly against the wooden floor to silence or cover up anything else that might come out of the man's mouth on the subject. "Please excuse our poor manners," he attempted to soothe the man's temper as he carried his plate over to the kitchen and placed it within the waiting water. "We are <u>both</u> extremely grateful you at least tried to furnish our dinner, and…" He held the word out longer for deeper accentuation. "That you dutifully keep whatever secrets we may possibly have left." He placed one hand upon his shoulder to garner his better opinion. "Truly."

Composing himself to a more even disposition, Nathanael relaxed slightly under his touch but not enough to negate giving the man a final word of warning, "Don't test me like that ever again, Emile or so help me…"

"Trust me… I won't," Emile replied quickly in response, then added, "And I <u>am</u> sincerely sorry. Please forgive the overstep," Emile apologized then cast William a sharp glance with the flick of his eyebrows and jerked his head in Nathanael's direction, knowing that the time for frivolity had sufficiently ceased, or at least where Nathanael was concerned.

"What?" William defended unrepentantly like a spoiled child waiting comfortably at the table before he grinned placidly back at them. "I have nothing to hide."

"Don't listen to him, Nathanael." Emile said quietly over the man's shoulder and crossed his arms casually across his chest. "We both know the man's true weakness, even if he is too afraid to admit it to himself."

"Just one? I can think of at least two or three right now." Nathanael nodded in agreement. "But one should suffice at the present to humble him into silence, as well."

"Really? What?" William held both hands up and leaned back in his chair, not the least bit concerned about anything he might utter thereafter.

"Well…" Nathanael began to speak again and share exactly what William was sure to refute after speaking it but just as he did a soft knock echoed back to them from the front door, effectively interrupting their increasingly tense banter.

"Are we expecting another guest?" Emile asked as he finished the last of his glass of wine and placed it on the counter beside the other dirty dishes.

"Not that I am aware of. Perhaps Emma is coming to collect you early," William replied nonchalantly, then stood up and made his way over to the front door before pausing to open it, not exactly sure who would be calling on them at this late hour.

"I doubt it," Emile mumbled sarcastically back at him. "She wouldn't give up her one evening alone with Charlotte for the queen herself, let alone me."

"Well, at least you can take comfort in knowing where you rank in _her_ priorities, Emile." William chuckled heartily at his friend's humorous marital predicament and then pulled back on the handle of the large door before shrinking back slightly in surprise at who he found standing there.

"Who is it?" Emile called from the kitchen, unable to see past William to the void beyond to discover for himself.

"Not... Emma," William replied hesitantly back to him, suddenly unable to comment further.

"I'm sorry. Please excuse the interruption, Doctor Wells, but might I find Mr. Beckett at home this evening?" Nurse Bentham asked politely from the brick sidewalk just below the two wider steps in front of their doorway down to it. "I was told at the hospital that he lived here with you."

"Why, yes, Miss Bentham. Please... do come in." He finally stepped aside awkwardly and graciously invited her into their home. "We just finished our supper actually, so your timing is rather perfect. Though if you would care for something to eat, we might have at least a plate or two left over to share."

"Thank you most kindly for the generous offer, but I had already planned to eat at home." Nurse Bentham entered through the front door next to him and lowered the hood of her soft navy-blue fabric cape that had been covering her head once she had stepped inside. "I was rather hoping I would not be disturbing you by stopping by unannounced, but I can see that you do have company."

"Oh, you are not bothering us in the least, I assure you." William bowed his head slightly in her direction out of politeness and waved his hand to his right to offer her a seat nearby. "Would you care to at least sit?"

Quickly noticing the importance of their new guest by William's more formal actions alone, Nathanael and Emile both stood more ceremoniously erect behind the counter at the other end of the apartment and smiled, having instantly put on their best manners on his behalf.

"No, thank you, but I appreciate the offer. I actually only stopped by because Mr. and Mrs. Armstrong asked me if I could find out tonight what your middle name was, Mr. Beckett," Nurse Bentham asked politely while mindlessly fingering the long ties on her cape that was draped across both of her shoulders so that it effectively covered most of her dress beneath to protect it from the elements.

"My middle name? Why on earth would they need that?" Nathanael appeared completely surprised by the seemingly unusual request.

"I believe they are simply looking for a possible use for their son. Since you were such an integral part of his birth, they both wish to acknowledge you in some way... if the name is suitable to them that is," she explained easily, delivering her called upon message as professionally as possible without the added need for a more complicated explanation.

"I am honored to be sure," Nathanael replied, seemingly stunned to be memorialized in such a fashion.

For several minutes more, the two of them continued on in their small talk on the subject while William kept his place standing casually behind their guest by the front door and slid his hand into the right pocket of his almost perfectly black breeches to control his pulsing nerves as he waited.

After their brief connection both before and after the delivery, everything inside of him now appeared to be incessantly begging him to reach out and hold her hand once more to experience it yet again, but doing so under the watchful gaze of his friends would not only embarrass her more than she would possibly accept but would also be highly discourteous, if not forbidden under most circumstances.

"You know, Nathanael..." William's curiosity finally perked up suddenly as he cleared his throat quickly and joined the conversation at last in sudden perplexion, "I have known you for simply ages and even I do not know that particular piece of information. Do you even have one?"

"Of course, he has one, William." Emile shook his head and rolled his eyes at his friend's utterly ridiculous insinuation.

"Actually, my father did not," Nathanael admitted rather sheepishly without any more explanation as if it simply was not necessary.

"Really?" Emile shot him an incredulous look, completely surprised that anyone would not have the proper identification, commoner or otherwise. "Nothing at all? Not even an initial?"

"Not even an initial, Emile." Nathanael pursed his lips and couldn't help but half-smile at his friend's apparent difficulty. "But I doubt he cared very much about it either way. I know my mother didn't."

"But do <u>you</u> have one, Sir?" Nurse Bentham asked politely, pressing him once again on the subject. "If not, I suppose you could merely suggest something appropriate for him as I doubt they would mind either way."

"Oh, I have one," Nathanael answered slowly but did not elaborate further as the rest of them thought he might.

"And... ?" William looked his way and cast him a glance of building frustration that was unseen by the woman in front of him, clearly trying to motivate him into wrapping up the rather lengthy discourse on the subject.

"My mother picked it out actually before my father named me Nathanael since she had always loved what it meant. 'Son of the right hand, favored or darling,' I think is what she told me. In fact, many people where I am from tend to use it if they are older and do not think they will be blessed with any other children. Kind of a final hurrah where names go, I should think. Though it was also the name used for the youngest of Jacob and Rachel's sons in the Bible, so that is probably where the favored definition came from," Nathanael explained in great detail as he was known to do for the simplest of questions.

"What?" Nurse Bentham glanced over at William beside her with great confusion filling her eyes. "Is he making any sense to you?"

"Actually, yes. He says that his middle name is Benjamin, Miss Bentham." William answered with confidence his interpretation of his friend's rather extended soliloquy. "Isn't that right, Nathanael?"

"Quite right." Nathanael smiled with great pride in his friend's astute accomplishment. "On second thought, I take back all the horrible things I thought about you tonight."

"Good." William shook his head, for he knew his friend had done nothing of the sort. He never could have, not ever. Oh, he and Emile might entertain a dark musing or two about the other over the years when an irritation struck. A few times they had even acted on it. Even Sebastian had been openly hostile to at least one, if not all of them, on more than a few occasions, but Nathanael... never.

"That is such a lovely name, Mr. Beckett. I am sure your parents were quite proud of you when it was given, and it will suit Daniel very well. Daniel Benjamin Armstrong, the name itself almost sounds prophetically robust, does it not?" Nurse Bentham looked upwards and considered the significant weight of the name once more. "If you are in agreement, I will be sure to let them know your answer in the morning."

"Of course, thank you," Nathanael added graciously.

Already bored with the lengthiness of the conversation taking place, Emile cleared his throat quietly by the counter and leaned one arm casually upon it to attract his friend's more distracted attention. "Aren't you going to introduce us, William?" He eyed his friend with an air of someone needing to be the center of attention, then switched his gaze to the woman by William's side. "You see, Miss, as a rule, we are rarely given the opportunity to meet any of his friends from work."

"He is ashamed of us, probably." Nathanael quipped right along with him, enjoying very much this side of the merriment instead of the teasing normally directed in his general direction.

Utterly delighted by their playful remarks, Nurse Bentham eyed the two men across the room and smirked slightly, doing her best to contain her quiet chuckle at the lighthearted banter between them. "I am not sure if that makes me feel concerned or incredibly privileged to finally meet you both properly."

"You can take your pick, as both are probably true where they are concerned." William shot his two closest companions a tired look but held out his hand in formal introduction to the only one in the room who truly needed one. "The man at the counter, whom you probably have not met previously, is Emile Bastien Deschamps of Charleston and formerly, Paris, France."

Emile took the given opportunity without delay to meet the woman William seemed utterly conflicted about and deftly strode over to the other side of the room to kiss her hand briefly. "A true pleasure to make your acquaintance, Miss."

"Ah, you must be the distinguished representative that was featured in *The Aurora* last week." Nurse Bentham nodded respectfully. "I didn't know our Doctor Wells was so well connected."

"Neither did I." William said under his breath in annoyance at what he perceived was the man's overly generous display of affection towards her. "And the other man you know from the hospital already, Mr. Nathanael Benjamin Beckett."

"And that, my dear, is why I never tell anyone my full name. When they know all, they do tend to wear out the uniqueness of it unnecessarily." Nathanael also came over to the woman and bowed slightly as he had seen William do on many other occasions. In truth, it was not a grandiose gesture in any way, but rather a slight inclination on his part to add a portion of his respect for her at the introduction.

"It is a pleasure, I am sure." Nurse Bentham smiled once again at the kindness the man always displayed and greeted him warmly. "I will endeavor to remember that in the future and only refer to you only as the illustrious, Mr. Beckett."

Nathanael shook his head at the overly gracious adjective and grinned at the woman who looked strikingly beautiful standing next to William this way. "You may also call me just Nathanael if you so wish. With my weekly visits to the hospital, I am certain I shall be entertaining your company again someday soon."

Nurse Bentham smiled back. "I truly hope so."

Suddenly conscious of the approaching late hour and her possible need to retire for the evening, William cleared his throat. "Speaking of company, may I walk you out?" William offered his arm to her formally and motioned with the top of his head to the door behind them.

"What? Leaving so soon? We haven't even had the chance to interrogate her about your behavior at work, yet," Emile taunted him mercilessly, knowing exactly what area in which to push the man if he wanted to annoy him effectively.

"On second thought, you had better escape while you can, Miss Bentham," Nathanael urged her politely. "I fear that if you remain any longer tonight, you may be exposed to an altogether different kind of atmosphere, and I for one, would much rather we kept our good impression for at least one visit."

With the delightful atmosphere of their endearing friendship filling the home all around her, Nurse Bentham absolutely hated that it was time to leave. It had been years since she had seen this kind of closeness and camaraderie, which only made the seclusion that she normally guarded in her own life all the more painful. Like a small band of brothers, the three men complimented the other perfectly from the easy repertoire of mischievous teasing right on down to the comfortable ease in which all of them maneuvered around the others in the room. "I appreciate the warning, Mr. Beckett, and agree. I think it might be best if I go for now... but I do promise to return on another occasion if you so wish, just maybe a tad bit more expected next time."

"You would be most welcome whenever you wish to stop by." Emile offered to her graciously. "With or without our dear William." He flashed her one of his best smiles to seal the deal before casting another taunting glance over to the man behind her.

Seeing his perfectly false performance like the day his friend had worked the room at the Knole ball, William quite literally scowled at Emile now but continued to wait patiently for her to take his arm, feeling that if she delayed any longer, he might say something to his friend in her company that they might both regret.

Though in William's defense, he knew beyond a shadow of a doubt that Emile was not in any way flirting with Nurse Bentham. Neither would the man wish her attention to be drawn to him at all in that way. But being who he was, he simply could not help himself when it came to a great display and especially so if it tortured someone else present.

"I appreciate the gesture, sir." She finally gave a curtsy slightly in their direction to announce her departure, then allowed William to direct her carefully out of the door and to the sidewalk below, towing her safely beside.

Chapter Twelve

August 15th, 1811

"Did you say that you were <u>only</u> <u>now</u> heading home from the hospital?" William held the young woman's arm casually adjacent to his side as he glanced back at the almost closed door over her shoulder to make sure his friends were otherwise occupied.

"Yes, only just. Why?" Nurse Bentham looked up at him cautiously for a moment, not exactly sure how she felt about taking a stroll on the arm of the man who had been making her life annoyingly miserable for the past few weeks.

"Merely curious, that is all," William tried to brush off the brief inquiry into her personal affairs and began walking in the direction he had seen her travel the night of Hope's birthday party.

"Well, I would have stopped by sooner, but I had a few patients that ran quite late. Thankfully, Doctor Brooks said I might come in later tomorrow because of it."

William nodded and continued walking calmly beside her, breathing in the smell of the lavender that lined the base of the hedges as they passed by them on their way. "I agree that it was quite generous of the man, and most definitely appropriate under the circumstances. Especially after how he treated you this morning. You know as well as I that it was not correct for him to do so." William paused and attempted to read her expression in the intermittent shadows that crossed her features. "I know this might seem a little too late to say it, but I feel that I must apologize on his behalf for his actions. They were not only overly cruel and demeaning, but they were also outright improper."

"You don't need to apologize, Doctor Wells. You didn't do anything wrong." Nurse Bentham tucked a stray strand of hair back behind her ear.

"Well, not today, anyways... Still, I had already planned earlier to speak with him about it tomorrow," William assured her and cast a glance in her direction to see if she approved.

"I appreciate the gesture, truly I do, but it isn't necessary." Nurse Bentham smiled slightly as she took in the full meaning behind his words, then just as quickly as it had appeared, it faded into obscurity from whence it came.

"Yes, it is," William defended staunchly once more. "You work exceptionally hard, Miss Bentham, and everyone knows it. It's not your fault if people do not want to listen to your suggestions."

Suddenly concerned by the possible change in the tenor of their professional relationship, Nurse Bentham stopped walking down the narrow pathway towards her home and held her breath, uncertain if she were ready to discuss with him the real reason why she had come tonight or if she should simply ignore everything altogether that had transpired between them today.

"What's the matter? Did I say something wrong again?" William's tone spoke of nothing more than friendship now, a very definite change from his earlier, and somewhat intimate, actions and expressions at the hospital.

"No, nothing is wrong... precisely." Nurse Bentham fixed her gaze on the pathway in front of her and began walking once more. "By the way, are you intending on walking me <u>all</u> the way to my apartment?"

"I don't know." William considered the possibility of her request, then added a hint of humor to the conversation at last. "Is it far? If it's more than a mile or two, I'd be happy to hire us a carriage. Not that I mind walking that distance tonight in the slightest, if it is. It's a fine night, and I find that I have grown quite accustomed to the exercise actually, as my practice back home in England was quite remote."

"Why on earth did you not use a horse then?" Nurse Bentham asked incredulously, very much confused by his description of his previous work.

"Horses cost money, and time, Miss Bentham. Both of which were in short supply when I first began my apothecary back in Wakefield," William admitted honestly. "Besides, the lack of it never really bothered me until I moved here. In fact, even when I lived in London, there was always some form of conveyance available at any given hour to never truly necessitate that kind of expense."

"I see." Nurse Bentham shook her head. "But aren't you entertaining guests back at your home? I wouldn't want to keep you away from them too long." She searched for yet another reason to allow herself the opportunity to flee to the solitude of her own home without him and avoid whatever it was that was beginning to breathe itself into life during their brief conversation tonight.

"Oh, them?" William laughed openly at her concern and the sound of his lighthearted joy made her smile, too... and maybe, even forget just a bit of the anxiousness and distrust she had been holding onto against him. "Trust me. They will still be there when I get back, I assure you. In fact, they will probably be waiting for me with bated breath for all of the many details they think they are entitled to. I will have little to tell them, I promise you, but that does not mean it will stop them from pestering me all the same."

"So, you <u>really</u> don't do this often with other women." Nurse Bentham grinned hesitantly, remembering the opinion he had shared previously and his definite aversion to all the other female staff at the hospital.

"Not a one. Social gatherings were my mother's affair, not mine. Though now that you mention it, maybe that is why I detest all the attention at the hospital." He guided them lightly around the roots of a tree jutting out into the path, then stopped when he felt her resistance to his next step.

"Is that the only reason?" Nurse Bentham placed her other hand unconsciously on top of the one holding his arm and waited, very much interested in the details he was sharing. From all that he had divulged already, it appeared to her more than ever that the two of them had lived quite similar lives in the past and held very identical aversions.

With a sigh of utter exhaustion on the topic in question, William flung his head upwards, resting it comfortably on the back of his neck for support as he suddenly decided to share much more with her than he had ever divulged to Emile or even Nathanael. "Every day that I walk through those doors I feel as if I am on display in some kind of shop. Like the tailors downtown that Emile loves or the milliners on the corner by the silversmith with the large glass window in front. And just like the people who walk by on the street and stop to peer over the goods for sale to find just the right one they are looking for, nurses pass me on their way to their patients and scrutinize my attire, my actions, you name it, all in an effort to see if I will fit into their plans for their future lives like they are selecting their next choice of dress or fashionable hat. On some days, it almost feels like every woman I speak to is anxiously waiting her turn to add me to her proverbial dance card or is secretly fighting for her opportunity to secure an understanding with me. Both of which are only subversive actions to achieve the very same end goal."

"And what pray tell would that be?" Nurse Bentham could hardly contain the absolute humor that was filling her being at the rather accurate description of her life, as well.

"Me securing their future happiness, of course." William rolled his eyes in definite sarcasm at the very idea. "As if I would know how to do that."

"I'm sorry, but don't most men want to marry one day?" Nurse Bentham asked him purely out of curiosity, though also tentatively hoping he would not infer that she was suddenly seeking to be included in the previously described group of candidates.

"Doubtful... Would you?" William countered just as hesitantly and started walking once more before she could even give an answer.

Without meaning to do so, Nurse Bentham unconsciously flinched at the simple question, the muscles in her jaw tensing imperceptibly, along with an almost tremor-like jerk in two of her fingertips.

As dark as it was on the moonlit path, William still saw her reaction plainly, but chose not to comment on it further, suddenly afraid she would stop talking altogether and end the first actual conversation they had enjoyed together in months.

"Well, to be honest, I don't know if the risk is truly worth all the effort involved," she finally added almost apathetically nearly a block later and the sound of her tone matched his own opinion on the subject whenever it was discussed.

"I couldn't agree more, Miss Bentham." He tilted his head in her direction and cast her an equally tired look. "Though I suppose someday I will be open to it when the right person comes along... maybe... but not right now. I guess I am a little like you in that regard. As much as everyone thinks I would be happier if I was finally settled down with the right person, I would much rather just focus on the medicine. And I can't do that if I am otherwise distracted trying to please others. Nor would a woman particularly want someone who wasn't focused on her needs alone, I would imagine."

"I wholeheartedly concur, Doctor Wells," Miss Bentham happily replied, then rubbed her fingers slightly along the fabric of his ivory shirt sleeve beneath her hand, enjoying very much the softness the fabric provided.

"Well, that is a first. You mean to tell me that we actually agree on something for a change?" William prodded further, almost playfully now in his tone and demeanor while using his other hand the push back a few of the tendrils of foliage that were reaching farther out into their path.

Nurse Bentham chuckled lightly. "That isn't too terribly shocking, is it? Why, I bet we would probably find out that we have a lot more in common if we weren't bickering all the time."

"True... But then again, what would we _ever_ talk about?" William joined her in her laughter briefly before trying to contain it to a slight grin.

"Oh, the weather, maybe? Your excellent health? Or other topics that mean next to nothing, but everyone thinks they need to discuss them anyway..." She rolled her eyes back at him in definite sarcasm.

"Exactly. When you look at it that way, our squabbles have probably allowed us to have the most thorough grasp of each other's opinions than anyone else we work with," William added wryly.

"Yes, and then some." Nurse Bentham nodded in agreement, then turned a bit more serious. "But that being said, Doctor Wells, I do hope I have not given you the wrong impression about my own intentions today. When I touched your arm during our discussion earlier, I was merely seeking comfort in a moment of weakness, nothing more," she admitted as emotionlessly as she could possibly manage under the circumstances, though she quite honestly felt very different. In fact, the entire experience this afternoon had left her thoughts quite scattered and disorganized as she struggled to deal with many things that she had thought were long forgotten. "I know other men might read more into such an action, so I want you to know that I do understand that it wasn't appropriate to motivate you in that way."

It was William's turn now not to appear affected by her honest admission. "I am sure I don't know what you mean. It was a rather complicated delivery, nothing more." He tried his best to say something that was as close to the truth as possible without causing her any more obvious regret in the matter. "It was only natural to be overwhelmed, both before and afterwards. I know I was."

"I agree, but I shouldn't have held your hand that way for any reason. Please forgive the overstep." She let go of his arm and walked a few feet closer to the brick red painted door next to her.

"Forgiven, though truthfully, I understand why you might have needed to do so, and I assure you that I thought nothing of the kind." William attempted to hide the hurt her words had surprisingly brought him, choosing instead to reply in the simplest way possible to cover his own feelings on the matter.

On the surface, William's words were the very thing she had expected to hear from a gentleman who obviously respected those with whom he worked, but the difference in his tone as he spoke them, so void of emotional connection, made her heart ache unexpectedly. "Doctor Wells, please don't be hurt."

Recovering his composure brilliantly before she could regret anything else about the incident in question, William looked up at her and held her gaze for a moment in the awkward silence building between them before answering. "I'm not... truly. You don't have to apologize for anything to me, Miss Bentham. Despite what you might assume, I don't think any less of you for it."

"Thank you." She looked down and away from him, feeling suddenly anxious about leaving their conversation unfinished in this way. "Well, this is my home, and I thank you kindly for the escort," Nurse Bentham eventually spoke up and tried to seem as unaffected as he apparently was, though from the way in which his eyes watched her every movement, she was sure she was failing miserably.

"I see... ummm..." William slid his arm out from under hers and stammered blankly for a second before his mind leapt five steps in front of him, pushing him to shift his body slightly between her and the door in an attempt to suddenly block what might be her desired route of escape.

"Doctor Wells, is there something else?" Nurse Betham held his gaze and waited patiently for him to settle his thoughts to completion.

Suddenly more alert than he had been all day, William began to speak all at once, the words coming fast on the heels of the ones before, "At the risk of ruining a perfectly pleasant conversation tonight, can I ask you for a favor before you retire for the evening... please?" He finally finished his question and waited for her permission to continue.

"Of course," she replied slowly and watched as the man in front of her cleared his throat twice.

"I know this is going to sound ludicrous... Trust me. It sounds crazy in my mind, too. But... Do you think we might... um... What I mean to say is... could we possibly try starting over again? You can even pretend for just a minute that I actually had the manners I was born with when we first met." He chuckled slightly again at the memory of their first real disagreement with the pie and the corner of his mouth curled up at the edges with the action as he fought against the nerves inside of him that were threatening to explode outward by even suggesting it. "Would that be too hard to do, or would there be a need for more penance involved in order to accept?"

For several moments, the stunningly beautiful woman across from him measured him skeptically, as if reasoning out the probability of such a feat. Then, without missing a beat, formally held out her hand to him in proper greeting at last with a discreet grin. "Alright, if you are going to try to be civil to me from now on, you may call me Charity like the others of my acquaintance, but if not, Nurse Bentham will still suffice."

"William... always." He took her hand for the first time in friendship as he greeted her formally and felt the immediate surge of energy the action brought him once again. Like a thousand tiny pricks of insatiable energy, the momentary touch between them created a surge of static that jolted all his senses into a faster motion in one unsettling and intoxicating burst.

What was that? He thought quizzically, then tried to deflect his concentration on the strangeness of it just like he had done before. Oddly enough, as brief as it was to experience it, it was the first touch he had encountered in quite some time that felt actually warm to him, pleasantly so, if he could describe it adequately.

Visibly confused once again, William cleared his throat and tried to continue on as if nothing had transpired between them whatsoever, "Charity, please know that I am sincerely sorry for the many times I have obviously hurt your feelings these past few weeks. If I could take it all back, I would, but I can't. As you have so properly put it already, my incorrectly placed cynicism and outright prejudices have regrettably clouded my vision in many ways and you, sadly, have paid the price."

Unable to meet his stare after such a humble declaration and obviously as affected by the sudden reaction as he was, Charity looked down and away from the man in front of her before taking a careful step back, feeling the absolute importance of putting as much space between them as she could possibly manage in the increasingly intimate conversation. "I assure you that I never meant to hurt you either, William. Your initial assumption aside, if I had wanted an eligible match, I would have simply remained back at home in England. My parents had plenty of men lined up for me there that I could have chosen from, whether I wanted them or not. Which I most certainly did not."

Feeling a bit more relaxed by her seemingly honest response, William took a seat on a nearby bench positioned under an absolutely enormous oak tree in front of her building and motioned casually for the young woman to join him on the adjacent one. "It seems we have a great deal more in common than medicine, Charity. In fact, just like you, my mother was ready to have me married off by my twentieth year. When that did not work out, she had the perfect prospect for me by my twenty-fifth year and was convinced I needed to marry a Miss Stapleton by my twenty-eighth. All would have been a rather eligible match by her way of thinking, but not so much for me."

Charity smirked pleasantly at the amusing revelation and tried to hold back a slight chuckle as she took her seat next to him. "So, despite the rumors at the hospital, there <u>really</u> has been no previous Mrs. Wells that met an untimely demise or some other such calamity that drove you away from wanting to ever remarry? By all of the talk recently, I was almost certain there was someone out there somewhere who was receiving far better treatment than the rest of us at the hospital."

William joined her in her comical wit and shook his head with a definitely playful quality to it. "No, there most certainly is not. Is that a problem?"

"Not for me." Charity shook her head, too. "Though without some kind of promised mate to speak of, you _are_ going to continue to have that same undivided attention you dread, as others will no doubt still attempt to vie for your good graces with or without your actual instigation to do so." She paused and for a moment, her face appeared utterly sympathetic in its contemplation of his imagined plight. "Then again, all things considered, I suppose I don't truly blame them either, William. I know you may not believe this, but in many instances, most women are not meaning to make your life as miserable as you might suspect. Some of them are just waiting cautiously nearby in case you should suddenly have a change of heart in their direction."

"Seriously? Waiting for me to change my mind? So, there really is no hope at all in this." William almost couldn't contain the tortured sigh that escaped his lips just envisioning the awkward and oftentimes uncomfortable entanglements that were surely to follow.

"Oh, you can sigh all you like tonight, sir, but just because I am not 'husband hunting', as you so properly described it... it does not also follow that you are undesirable to most of those women who walk through our doors. In fact, I think there would be many who see you as an eligible match by far compared to the others like Doctor Baxter and Mr. Thomas who delivers our weekly supplies. Why even that young man who runs the forge downtown has caught the eye of more than a few of the nurses. Yet where he is concerned, I think my friend Mary is quite smitten with him more."

"That would be Elijah Fabbri, and trust me when I tell you this, if you think I am difficult to lure into marriage, he is even worse." William felt instantly warmed by the lighthearted turn of the conversation at last.

"Well, that may be true, but your saving grace will probably be when those same nurses get to experience your unique bedside manner..." Charity left the last sentence drop off as she added in a bit of learned knowledge on the subject.

"Could there not be a way to avoid all of this completely? Maybe I could simply wear a small sign on my pocket that proclaimed clearly, 'stay away for your own good'?" William rolled his eyes and dreaded the future conversations with all of them.

"That would make it far easier for you, wouldn't it?" Charity huffed and smiled. "But I suppose with the lack of any other options, you will just have to keep being mean to all of them to scare them away sufficiently like I do."

"I hate doing that..." William leaned back against the trunk of the tree behind him and looked up at the gently swaying branches above. "It is always so exhausting and denigrating to everyone involved. But then again..." He pondered just a moment on another tantalizing possibility before uttering it lightly in jest, "I <u>could</u> always suggest that we covertly join forces to attack our mutual problem together, instead of trying to avoid it. Or rather, to put it more plainly, if they thought that we were otherwise connected in some way, even if it was false, then maybe…" He waited for her to add an expected witty remark in return like she had done on other occasions, but when he heard nothing but a brief inhale and silence thereafter like she was now suddenly holding her breath at the very possibility, he continued on as if nothing he had said meant anything at all, "But to do something so fantastical like that might take far more energy than either of us have to offer to keep the ruse up sufficiently."

"Undoubtedly." Her reply came back taut and strained, as if she had changed her chosen method of discourse with him entirely back into something far more distant and removed. In fact, in many ways the rigidness in which she sat now made her expression look even more utterly void of any emotion altogether and perfectly professionally detached. "Besides, as tempting an offer as that might be to consider it, I'm afraid that I much rather prefer my secret life of quiet anonymity, thank you." She copied his action of leaning back against the tree behind her and the two of them stayed that way for several minutes longer, apparently enjoying the peace and quiet afforded them before another couple passed by on the path in front of them quite unexpectedly, interrupting their moment of serene solitude.

"Well, I believe I have sufficiently taken up enough of your time for one evening, Miss Bentham. I should probably let you retire and return to my guests." William stood up and held out his hand to her to help her accomplish the same. "Though I do want you to know that I have thoroughly appreciated our discussion tonight." He looked over at her and the feeling he had felt all day in her presence pulled at his heart once more, though in many ways he was still as uncertain as ever as to why that was.

"And I appreciate your unusual candor, too, Doctor Wells." Charity stood and returned his gaze, but the only thing he saw behind her eyes now was not the compassion or even the guarded friendship he might have expected after their congenial conversation together this evening. Instead, he saw a very strange form of fear gripping the edges of her features as if it was now cautiously stepping in to control her every thought and action. A fear, that seemed not directed towards him as a person, per se, but looked more like a definite wariness about everything he represented. "I will see you tomorrow, Doctor Wells," she said politely in an almost clipped tone of voice and walked towards her front door without another glance back.

"Goodnight." He wished her a stunned, yet albeit polite farewell, but remained on the sidewalk where she had left him as he watched her enter the building in front of him and shut the door in total confusion at the unexpected change of countenance.

It was true that in everything she had divulged tonight, she had given him no pretense for expecting anything more from her than a professional ceasefire of sorts for the future. Neither had she expressed any desire towards a common friendship of any kind by anything she had uttered. That being said, none of that seemed to matter in William's estimation, given the fact that something had also undeniably changed in the span of time that had transpired between them.

And judging by her reaction alone just now, both of them knew it.

Though strangely enough, he would venture to say further that it would be hard to miss, even if they <u>did not</u> wish to acknowledge its existence in the first place.

But what exactly was it that he had said that had made her suddenly frightened? Or afraid enough to make her shut him out completely and walk away?

"I have no earthly idea..." He looked back at the door with a sigh of utter perplexity on the matter in question and turned around to begin walking the short distance back to the home he shared with Nathanael, sensing the beginning of yet another uneasy battle brewing in the wind.

Without question, Miss Charity Bentham was scared of something, make no mistake. In fact, by the look on her face just now, she appeared visibly terrified to the very core of her being, though try as he might to put together the limited pieces he had been given to her still mostly undisclosed past, he could not think of a single valid reason as to why that might be. Like a caged animal who has been hurt and forever distrusts any human touch thereafter because of it, she appeared just as panicked in her acceptance of his offered friendship and outwardly protective.

No... that wasn't the right description either.

She wasn't anxious like a child might be about some fearful event they were unsure might come to pass. No, she appeared almost petrified at the present to even consider letting someone into her area of personal comfort. Maybe even forcibly resistant to any person, man <u>or</u> woman, that might push her to the point of accepting that kind of human contact altogether, or at least one that might necessitate that level of trust on her part.

Sadly, he <u>had</u> seen that kind of reaction once before with a young child who had been abused and neglected by his new parents from the orphanage. To William's recollection, it had been one of the saddest cases in his history at the

Pennsylvania Hospital and certainly one he thought back on many times over the years as he strategized other creative ways he could have used to have made it easier for the child to accept their help.

In the end, it had taken the staff several days to garner the young boy's trust enough to properly set the bones in his broken arm and tend to the other lesser injuries he had incurred while in his new parents' dubious care. But seeing it on the face of someone as old as Charity was almost too startling to contemplate what events could have been so horrific in her life to have put it there in the first place.

Had she also been abused or neglected in her past? Or possibly abandoned maybe by those that should have lovingly cared for her? Or was she horribly denied any of the actual care and attention most parents normally freely dote on their children like Emma had experienced in her past?

He hoped not, for Charity's sake alone, if not for the thought of the many others who had suffered equally in similar situations without anyone to advocate for them against it.

Was that the real reason why she was forever pushing everyone away?
Maybe.
But if so, how would he <u>ever</u> earn her trust long enough to push past it?
How did Emile help Emma?

Feeling defeated and frustrated once again, only this time with a great deal more empathy than before, William shook his head at the inevitable events that were surely to follow. "She is going to make my life a living hell now after this, isn't she?" He murmured to himself quietly as he stopped abruptly and closed his eyes, breathing in and out slowly to prepare himself properly for what he was certain to face in their next encounter together.

As much as he cautiously hoped that he was wrong about what he had seen tonight, he was almost one hundred percent certain that he was not. Which only made that possibility more painful to contemplate than anything else she could have ever said to him tonight.

"Well, if Emile was able to save Emma from her dismal life back in France, I can certainly find a way to reach Charity..." He opened his eyes and glanced back at the now-lit window in the upper room of her small home. "And just like with , I <u>only</u> need to find a way to get her to see me as anything but the enemy... Or better yet... hopefully... I can manage to work a miracle before all of this kills us both."

Thinking heavily on all the definite possibilities that might have gone on in her past, William walked slowly back home and thanked God once again for his many, many blessings.

Chapter Thirteen

August 22nd, 1811

As on any other Thursday morning of his existence, the sun peeked its rays hesitantly through the bottom sill of William's bedroom window, declaring the arrival of yet another day to all that it touched. Almost a week had passed since he had offered to walk Charity home, and each day that had greeted him in that passage of time had only brought along with it no clearer resolution to the many perplexing questions constantly floating throughout his brain at any given minute.

Still, that disappointing fact aside, the only good thing of note that <u>had</u> transpired was that at least the constant bickering between the two of them had finally ceased. And yet, however wonderful that was for everyone at the hospital, including William, that also did not mean in any way that there existed an equally pleasant atmosphere between the pair either. On the contrary, the new, never-ending moments of professional silence that lingered after every answer she gave him, whether at a patient's bedside or on her way past him in the hall, felt even louder than any word she could have spoken... shockingly so.

"I can't believe I am saying this, but what I wouldn't give to have her just say, 'You need to adjust your notes here, Doctor Wells,' like she used to do." William sighed as he rolled over, away from the possible exposure of the sun near the foot of his bed and yawned.

To his right and out the usually cracked open door of his room, William could see all the way across the hall and into Nathanael's larger room. There, from the state of the many piles of scattered books upon his small table within, his friend had obviously spent most of his morning preparing for his classes. As a rule, Nathanael had always been a much earlier riser than William any day, even back in Wakefield. But thankfully, at least the man was quiet... when he was awake. When he was asleep, however, that was another matter entirely.

Since their very first night together under the same roof at the apothecary, William had often been awakened by the preacher's only real flaw as far as William was concerned. On the whole, Nathanael's entire personality from dawn until dusk appeared humble and reserved, or at least during his waking hours. His dreams each night were anything but calm and contained. In fact, if William had to explain it, he would say that it was almost as if there existed two completely opposite forms of the very same man in how he approached life and in his regimented filter concerning what he would or would not say.

Thankfully for all involved, the majority of his nocturnal rantings were more or less vague as to whom he was speaking, while others on the other hand, were far more painfully direct when they repeatedly referenced people both of them knew like his students for example, or Emile and Emma, and of late... even Charlotte. The latter being someone William would have quite happily been all too delighted to have been kept in the dark concerning his friend's increasingly ardent feelings about the woman.

Moreover, from the somewhat romantic tone of his recent ramblings, the man had quite obviously been entertaining the thought of some kind of relationship with Sebastian's wife of late, without the knowledge of his friends. Yet from the information William had learned from his lucidly accurate dreams just yesterday, Nathanael had yet to act.

For the better part of three years after they had first met, William had endured the chaotic rantings and narratives about the man's relationship with his first betrothed, Elsie Summerfield, with each night becoming more colorful than the next until they had gratefully started to dissipate along with the vividness of her memory. Still, even that had been welcomed compared to the night terrors he and Emile had been compelled to live through when she had died from the grippe around Easter of that first year.

That particular experience had almost broken all of them, though William would never admit it, neither would Emile. On the outside, they had both chosen to silently endeavor to help Nathanael come to terms with her passing in their own way. Yet on the inside, William had taken the whole experience they had endured as a clear warning to himself against forming <u>any</u> future romantic entanglements whatsoever.

This was not at all because he did not desire that kind of a relationship for himself or because there had not been more than a few young women who had tentatively caught his eye over the years. But rather, from the broken state in which the man had suffered thereafter, William could not see the overarching value in such an arrangement, no matter how beneficial it might appear for a time. After all, with his varied list of current restrictions and unusual aging abilities, living a lie with someone that he cared deeply for was not something he was especially eager to do either. On any given day, he had enough drama in his life already without the necessity of telling even more half-truths. And doing so day in and day out to someone who deserved his unlimited honesty, might just break him entirely.

"Coffee is ready, William!" Nathanael called up the stairs to him from the kitchen below. "I left it on the counter for you, but I have to leave for class."

"Thank you, Nathanael. I will be down presently!" William called back to him quickly, then suddenly realized he had a question. "Hey! Could you wait a minute, please?"

"Yes?" Nathanael answered hesitantly, cautiously poised to collect his satchel and books for class.

"Did Emile say he was going to be in Washington this week or next? I can't remember." William threw off the covers and walked over to the railing at the top of the stairs to view his friend better.

"Next, if I remember correctly. Though he did say something last night in prayer meeting about having several important consultations today that would absorb most of his morning downtown. Why? Did you need something?" Nathanael explained thoroughly what little information he had on the subject.

William shook his head. "Not from him, no."

"Alright... but William?" Nathanael took a hesitant step up the stairs so that he could see his face more clearly. "Are you certain you are feeling alright today? I hope you are not offended with me saying this, but I did notice that you were tossing and turning quite heavily for most of the night." His worried expression in the shadows below betrayed much more concern than William had intended to create.

"Quite, I assure you." William rubbed the sleep from off his face and pulled his hair back from it. "But truthfully, I should probably be honest and say that I don't think I have had a solid night's sleep for weeks, maybe months."

"Oh... well... why do you think that is?" Nathanael probed carefully. "Were you trying to spread out your supply a little longer again, or is there something else bothering you? Something... possibly to do with your work at the hospital... or Nurse Bentham perhaps?"

Instantly triggered by the mere mention of her name, the insides of William's stomach did a flip unconsciously, as the incessant fluttering of butterflies fanned at the edges to escape. "Probably both, though I have no idea why that would be as she barely speaks to me as it is."

"Hmmm... I see." Nathanael waited patiently for his friend to say more, but when he did not, he decided to offer his own piece of advice quietly, "I don't know what helps you to sort things out, but for me, I have always found that talking about it with someone who might remotely understand your current situation <u>can</u> aid you in seeing options you might not have previously contemplated. Mind you, it does not always provide the solution you are seeking in the beginning, but it may guide you to a clearer understanding when all else has evaded you."

"Maybe..." William considered the man's suggestion thoughtfully for several long moments before relenting. "Then again, I suppose you are right in that regard, as well, Nathanael."

"That's a first." Nathanael smiled, grateful to have been of some limited assistance to his friend today.

"Most definitely not," William replied quickly, so as to further prove his point. "Most days, you are the only sane one of the three of us, and far more even tempered overall."

"Four, actually," Nathanael interjected casually. "Emma is as much a part of our inner circle now as anyone else could ever be."

"Yes." William's mind seized instantly upon that pleasantly inclusive reality and realized once again who it was that he should visit. "Now that you mention it, I think I <u>will</u> take you up on your advice today, after all."

"Really?" Nathanael tilted his head, suddenly hopeful for the man.

"Fact is, I had already planned on working on the shipping logs at the warehouse this morning instead of the hospital anyway. Perhaps I will also stop by and pay Emma a visit before I do. Maybe even see if she is open to that conversation you mentioned earlier."

"Sounds about perfect." Nathanael walked back down the few stairs towards the kitchen table and from the sounds coming back to William from the room below, it appeared that he was almost at the door to leave.

"Will I see you at lunch?" William called back to him over the railing.

"Yes, Emile said to meet him around noon at the cafe," Nathanael yelled back discreetly from the doorway below. "Will you finish your errands by then?"

"I think so. Thank you, Nathanael." William turned to get dressed but paused as he considered just what he was going to say when he arrived at his friend's home unannounced. As a general rule, none of them had consistently bothered with the formalities most people of their acquaintance still maintained concerning guests and visitors alike, but that still did not mean his friend's wife would be prepared to entertain anyone so early in her day either.

Maybe, I should look over the books first before arriving and give her at least an hour to awaken properly before my arrival. He thought deductively as he contemplated just how much time he should delay to accommodate that supposition, then stopped himself mid-thought in growing frustration.

"Or perhaps you should stop stalling, William, and get it over with," he corrected himself with a grumble and went back to his room to get dressed. If anyone might understand what he was going through with Charity, it would be Emma. After all, Charlotte had married Sebastian almost nine years before the four of them had ever met and Nathanael's relationship with Elsie was nothing in comparison to William's own struggles. Emma was the only one of them who had truly experienced a rocky beginning with her husband to possibly have a common perspective to share, if not some kind of advice regarding what he might be facing with Charity's past.

Yet even with the wealth of her unique knowledge aside, William was still unsure if <u>he</u> was ready for her answers, today, or any day for that matter. Mainly, because he had still not decided firmly upon pursuing any real course of action concerning Charity to warrant bringing the unnecessary attention to his plight. And second, because he doubted the woman in question would invite his attention, even if he did.

Like a rebellious child preparing himself for a long day of educational torture at school, William trudged onward through the motions of getting dressed and drinking his morning coffee before setting out dutifully in the direction of Emma's home and his imminent conversation.

Horses and people, bustling this way and that, on their way to their intended destinations, all busily passed next to him in the street as he walked without the least bit of inclination as to what was milling around in his mind. Instead, every person seemed faithfully focused on the very same kind of mission that he had today, though none expressed it verbally to the other—escape in one form or another.

The sun, which seemed to never relent in its incessant torture daily, had been especially brutal again this week. Which, in itself, was not all that unusual for a day in late August, but the added dryness that had accompanied its glare had been even more debilitating to tolerate than ever before. Why, even the trees above him as he strode beneath were feeling the weight of its intensity as their leaves curled up to an unhealthy brown on all of the edges, begging helplessly for some kind of refreshment. Or really, anything that would help them endure just a day or two longer until they would eventually rain.

Lifting his eyes slightly within the shadowed safety of his dark, navy hood that remained his chosen staple rain or shine, William examined several stately maples and oaks as he walked past the hospital on his left and made his way across town past Thomas's new shop, the bakery and then at last, the back of the warehouse that Elijah and him owned, making sure to keep to the darker shadows of the path just in case the light breeze that was barely blowing today might rustle his cloak away from his body and render it momentarily useless.

With all the challenges from the constant blockades outside of port, their shipping business had experienced more than its share of ups and downs of late. Though thankfully, this month was an up with almost three fully-ladened ships arriving just this week alone. The largest one, all the way from the East Indies, was packed to the brim with silks and spices of varying kinds. While the other two were more practically based cargo vessels that contained things like wine and other textiles the shops in Philadelphia, as well as others along the coast, had been begging him for during the past two months.

All of which could not have come a day too soon for his friends either as William had drunk the last of his favorite coffee only just this morning and Nathanael's stack of parchment paper upon his desk had been almost exhausted entirely. Not to mention the fact that William had grown tired of Emile constantly pestering him for his favorite tea every morning for three weeks put together.

For the people of the Colonies, William hoped that this nonsense regarding England and France would be finally resolved and soon, so that all of them could put this unsettling turn of events behind them and return to some semblance of normality.

Rounding the corner at the end of the street where the city itself waned and the vast acres of rich farmland began; William waved to Jedidiah who was just now stepping out of the barn on his way to his mother's home with a large pail of fresh milk from his recently completed chores.

"Hello, there! How is the family, Jed?" William called cheerfully to him from the end of the drive, not wanting to pass all the way down the lane for fear that he would miss his opportunity to speak with Emma alone without the constant teasing of her oft-times sarcastic husband.

"Uncle William!" Jedidiah's face shone with delight at the unexpected visitor, a wide smile replacing the tiredness he had been displaying earlier. "They are all tolerably well, thank you. Where you off to this fine morning?"

"A few places actually, though nothing too momentous, I assure you." William contemplated quickly what he should say next to appease his sense of civility, then answered, "Right now, I am on my way over to Emile and Emma's to stop by and chat for a minute or two but after that, is there anything I can help you with when I return?" He paused and waited for the man to answer, conscious that Jedidiah often took on far more than he was physically able to do just to keep up with the ever-growing needs of the farm.

Jedidiah shook his head. "Not today, but maybe tomorrow. With all of this heat, I <u>could</u> use a hand weathering the guides and leads before the leather becomes any more brittle. Besides, I haven't gotten to talk to you in ages." He waited for his mentor to reply before entering the house.

"That sounds like a wonderful idea, Jed. I've missed our talks, too. If it suits you, I can come by after work around six," William offered.

"Six will be fine, and I'll be looking forward to it." He opened the front screen door with his free hand and left William to continue on in his trek without another word.

Nodding contentedly at the exchange between them, William continued on the short, two-mile stretch to Emile and Emma's home on the edge of the Fabbri property and climbed the steps to the small open porch before pausing to steel up his courage once more. Fresh fear, like the first time he had spoken to a woman at a ball, clung to the very fibers of his throat this morning, making his mouth instantly parched and constricted, quite unlike his normally calm countenance.

Not a single thing inside this home had ever once brought about such a change as this to overwhelm him before. Quite the opposite was true, in fact. Yet standing there listening to the cicadas play their hauntingly dissident music off in the field beyond the small pump next to him, he found that he could not even bring himself to lift his hand to knock on the frame of the outer screen door to the farmhouse, much less move to open it.

"Um, good morning! Is there anyone home?" He called out nervously at first, hoping very much that he had timed his arrival perfectly to have missed Emile altogether.

On any other day, he would have loved to see his friend and enjoy a plate of the breakfast that Emma would have created for them as she was probably one of the best cooks he had ever met, next to Mrs. Summerfield. But strangely enough, he simply did not have the energy this morning for the cryptic bantering at his expense that Emile would no doubt thrive on as he tried to ascertain why his friend was there in the first place.

In truth, William would forever feel the need to have Emile's company as close as humanly possible, as any other older brother might. Since the earliest days of their acquaintance, the two of them had often seemed like two opposite halves of a very fulfilling whole. Yet today, everything in him wished to sidestep the whole awkward explanation altogether, as the very need to be here in the first place was uncomfortable enough already.

"Ah, yes. Please do come in, William. I was just putting on a kettle for tea. Would you like some?" Emma cheerfully answered from deep within the kitchen assuming that her guest would take the opportunity to let himself in.

"No, but thank you for offering, Emma." William grasped the handle of the door finally and pulled it back to step inside the equally warm home. To his great relief, a small fire was already steadily ablaze in the hearth above the embers from the night before, letting him know instantly that he had most likely timed his arrival perfectly.

"Am I disturbing you?" He removed his cloak and hung it over the peg on the wall beside Emma's shorter cape and took a seat at the empty table.

"Not in the slightest, though if you were looking for Emile, you just missed him actually. With everything that he had to do today, I'm afraid he left over an hour ago for the office." Emma shook her head and placed a spoon within her porcelain cup and stirred its contents slowly.

"That's fine. I have plans to see him at lunch with Nathanael this afternoon anyway." William fingered the cotton tablecloth that was covering the wooden table in front of him and tried not to seem as flustered as he obviously felt.

"Good." Emma eyed the man sitting on the other side of the room and placed one hand upon her hip, in deep concentration. "I think." Her eyes narrowed slightly at the way in which William sat almost perfectly rigid and continued on as if the small talk alone might loosen whatever bundle of nerves the man had evidently brought along with him. "Well, what brings you all the way over here this morning? I doubt my simple life of tending to chores and the monthly mending is fascinating enough to tempt your interest alone as it is washing day today and a heavy one at that. With all of this dust that keeps piling up without fail, this city needs a good rain to wash it all away or at least convince it of the necessity of staying put where it belongs... <u>outside</u>. Come to think of it, a good gully washer, as my grandmother used to call it, would serve us nicely right about now, though it sounded much better in French."

"Most things do." William chuckled lightly at the unique way in which Emma always viewed things and the lightness of her spirit began working its magic through him, just like it always helped her husband. In every single facet of her personality, she was the perfect complement to his friend in every way and twice as essential. Furthermore, she had proved herself to be the truest foil to his complicated personality from start to finish, though it boggled William's mind even now to contemplate the odds his friend had defeated in finding such an absolute match as she. "Would it be too hard to imagine that I actually came to speak with <u>you</u> this morning?" He spoke hesitantly once more, afraid of what the next words might be that fell out of his mouth as his mind was an unhealthy jumble of emotions and confusion all at the same time.

"Me? Well, how can <u>I</u> help?" Emma filled her mug with two scoops of sugar then took her seat across from William. "Is there something wrong with Nathanael?"

William shook his head. "No, nothing like that. I was rather hoping we could talk about something else entirely... like maybe your courtship with Emile, if that isn't too sensitive of a matter to share without his permission."

Not exactly surprised in the least by his chosen topic of conversation, Emma stopped stirring her tea for a moment at his hesitant request and looked over at him seriously before smiling in the same way she always did when Emile teased her about something in public. "It is not a sensitive topic at all... at least not to me. Though mind you, I will probably have a very different view of things than my husband."

"You usually do... and I mean that in the best way possible, Emma," William admitted freely.

"I know you do." She took several sips of her tea, then offered the drink over to William. "Here. I know you said you didn't want any, but by the look on your face right now, I think you may need this far more than I do."

"Maybe so," William relented and took the offered drink before he sipped it gingerly, his mouth suddenly coming back to life from its parched state.

"Now, isn't that better?" Emma grinned, seeing William finally relax just a little by the action, then walked back to the kitchen to fix herself another cup, as well. "Well, what was it that you wished to know exactly?"

Like a flash of many memories all at once, William thought back instantly to the countless questions he had contemplated on his way over here as he prepared himself for their conversation, then settled on the one that seemed the most important to his current dilemma. "Can you tell me honestly... were you ever frightened of Emile? I mean... Were you ever truly scared to trust him at first?"

"Scared?" From her place beside the sink, Emma appeared briefly shocked by his unusual inquiry, then recovered just as quickly. "Well... I was never _really_ afraid he would hurt me, per se, at least not after the first night. But there _were_ a few times that I was apprehensive about what might lay behind his dark stares when I woke up and saw him watching me as I slept or studying me from across the room in the morning. I know now that he was fighting everything inside of him not to devour me for breakfast as you or I might be tempted to do, too, but I did not know that information at the time. Though looking back on it now, I think I knew even then just a little about what he was, even though he had not actually told me. But it did not frighten me away from him, no. In a way, it made me feel more compassionate towards his plight than afraid, almost like he needed me to help him breathe somehow. Which in a way, I suppose I did, too." Emma looked over William's shoulder with a far off look for several seconds, then returned her gaze back to him once more. "I'm not sure if I can explain it any better... but it was something like that at least."

"But _how_ did you know?" William drank some more of his tea and leaned back in his chair casually. "It's not like vampires are a commonplace sort of thing, or at least I had hoped they were not."

"Not commonplace, no, but definitely more plausibly possible in France than in England, or even here, it appears. You forget that the tales of those who walk the night looking for unsuspecting women to conquer in more ways than one are actually more of an urban legend in France. Of course, no one there has ever provided any true evidence of their existence or hunted them down like in other countries, but we are not something to be feared there like the spectres from Ireland or even the dark murderers in Romania. It is more like a seductive romance in our country, if you were to put it into a better definition... almost reverently so. Though, what I wouldn't give to have a cherished friend like Charlotte that was more inclined towards our challenges." Emma rejoined him at the table and cupped her fingers around the warm cup in her hands, stroking the finely sculpted lines of it up and down to warm her fingers.

"Why? Is it lonely for you in that way?"

"Sometimes... Why, just think of everything you share so freely with my husband or even Nathanael. It'd be nice if I could do that, too. Emile is a wonderful husband, and I wouldn't trade him for the entire world, but there is only so much the man will ever be able to fully understand or would even want to, I dare say. And Charlotte _is_ a truly wonderful person. She is a cherished friend who has more than graciously welcomed me without reservation into her trust over the years, but it's not the same, not really," Emma answered honestly.

"I imagine not." William pursed his lips once as he contemplated the value of what she was sharing. "But to go back to my previous question... even though you suspected what he was, you still chose to stay? Why? Didn't you have any shred of self-preservation left at that point?" William felt the terribly blunt words fall out of his mouth, then repented of the harshness of his delivery for they seemed more than a bit demeaning to be uttered. "What I mean to say is... um... I'm sorry, Emma. That wasn't kind."

"William, please..." Emma placed her hand over his to stop his awkward stammering and calm him further. "Stop over examining everything." She paused, then continued, "I am not offended that you asked and those _are_ deep questions to be sure... and ones I did truly struggle with in the beginning. But are you dealing with something similar, too?"

"I think so..." William thought about the moment when he had held Charity's hand in receiving and the way in which she had looked at him in the street and sighed, realizing he had placed himself right in the middle of his worst nightmare. "Oh, Emma, my mind is a horrible mess right now, and I don't mind saying it... to you."

Emma nodded several times quietly, then added a bit more encouragement, "Go on... I won't breathe a word to our mutual confidant unless you ask me to."

"Huh, he would be having a field day if he were here, Emma, and you know it." William almost couldn't stop the shaking of his head back and forth as he rolled his eyes while considering the delight Emile would have enjoyed in tormenting him.

"Well, he's not. So, why don't you start with why you look as though you are about ready to fall apart if I were to blow on you too hard, William?"

Considering the absolute accuracy of her spoken words, William gripped the cup he was holding even tighter, as if the tenseness of his fingertips against it would also somehow hold him tightly together, too. Either that or shatter them both completely asunder into every crevice of the house around them. Which was also almost a perfect representation of how he was feeling right about now.

"Breathe, William," Emma reminded him softly. "You might be a vampire, but you _still_ need oxygen to survive. Or at least last time I checked."

William nodded and did as she asked several times, then began to explain what he had been holding back, "One part of me feels like... like... like I need to do something impulsively stupid, or I will explode." He inhaled and exhaled once more, albeit this time much more slowly. "While the other more rational half of me knows there is nothing I can do even if I wanted to. Which in a way, feels almost like a an exhilarating relief ... or a justified excuse for doing nothing at all. Take your pick."

"I see... and I can only imagine how hard that might be to feel that way." Emma squeezed his hand and felt his own tighten around hers in turn. "Well, I can't say that I have the answers that you are wanting, William. I don't think anybody does, but what I can tell you is that no matter how difficult it may be to do so, honesty is the best course of action in the end, no matter how difficult it may be."

"What do you mean?" William looked up at her and stared deeply into her eyes to capture her full meaning.

"My <u>only</u> regret at all in my relationship with Emile is the time that we lost when we were both pretending to be something we were not." Emma released his hand and picked up her tea, pausing for just a moment before taking a sip. "As you already know, we were not always the happy couple we are today. That took years and years of hard work to create, like this farm for example. When we first purchased it, the fields were positively dreadful. No one had worked them for probably two years, and no upkeep had been maintained whatsoever on this house either for that matter. In every way, the property was left to be taken back by the wilderness from whence it came. But look at it now. When someone cares passionately about something, and puts their positive effort into its success, things change...crops grow... fences are mended... homes are filled with love and new memories. Not the same ones as before, and maybe not even in the same way, but restoration does take place, though only as much as the effort that is put into it."

"What do you mean?" William's brow furrowed as he concentrated harder.

"Look at those baskets over there, William." Emma nodded with her head in the direction of the stairs where two heaping piles of clothing lay inside two woven baskets. "Unless I am as certifiably mad as my husband claims I am at times, I can't expect that laundry to clean itself. It'd be nice if it would, but it's not going to happen short of a miracle, and I'll not waste my miracles on laundry." Emma laughed lightly once again. "If I want it done, <u>I</u> am the one who has to actively make a choice to sacrifice my time and energy to do it because I know in the end, the result will be a blessing to both Emile <u>and</u> me," Emma attempted to explain further.

"I understand," William finally nodded. "And so, I need to do the same with Charity."

"Is that who we are speaking of?" Emma sipped her tea once more. "The nurse Emile has been telling me about from the hospital?"

"Most likely." William shook his head slightly in fresh perturbance, for he might have known that Emile would have shared at least some of the more poignant details of his plight with his wife.

"Relax, William, he did not share anything you would be upset about, I assure you. He only said that she was making your life difficult right now. Nothing more." Emma immediately picked up the cues of his growing annoyance with Emile's possible overstep and moved swiftly to prevent it.

"'Difficult' would be a nice way of putting it. As it is, she barely speaks to me these days. But she is all I can seem to think about, too, whether I want to or not." William relaxed once again at her simple explanation and played with the few loose strands poking out here and there along the tablecloth's weave.

"And why do you think that is?" Emma finished her cup of tea and set it down carefully upon its matching saucer.

"Mostly because she is the one puzzle I cannot solve, I suppose." William did the same, then shook his head. "I want to... oh, how I want to, but I cannot get her to speak with me, much less listen to anything I might say, good or otherwise. So, what can I do?"

"Hmmm... that is a predicament." Emma tapped the table with one finger and thought a while on the answer. "Well, William, as hard as this may be to hear, I believe you will have to get creative if it is important to you," Emma suggested. "Or simply put, just like the process you normally use in trying to diagnose your patients, you will have to find out what is possibly holding her back in order to reach her. If you don't, you will just continue to be walking around helplessly blind through this, and you cannot hope to fix what you cannot see or understand."

"You are entirely correct, as always... and definitely not mad." William half-smiled, then released a drawn-out sigh. "Then there is nothing else to it, I guess, but to forge ahead towards certain destruction."

"Please..." Emma rolled her eyes and picked up both of their empty teacups in turn. "You men can be so dramatic at times. Or is it only because you are vampires?"

William laughed again lightly. "I would say the latter, but I really wouldn't know as I have never felt like this about anyone before in my life, human or otherwise." He stood up from his chair at the table and picked up his cloak to prepare to leave. "I'm not sure how I will succeed in implementing your advice, or how long it will take, but I'll let you know someday how it all works out."

"Please do, and I hope I was at least slightly helpful." Emma placed the dishes into the wash basin and wiped off her hands on the nearby towel.

"You were and thank you." William slid his cloak around his shoulders and walked out the door without another word, heading in the direction of the warehouse once more.

"*Bonne chance*, William." Emma sighed as he left, then returned to her chores.

Despite her definite aversion to the task that had long awaited her for the past two weeks, suddenly, conquering that pile of wash did not seem like such a monumental task, after all.

Chapter Fourteen

August 30th, 1811

"El Roi, as found in the story of Hagar in Genesis, is primarily used to describe God's quality of being able to see everything that is transpiring in the lives of His people. Or more importantly, that He knew what had happened to Hagar and her son when she had been sent away by Abraham after Sarah's jealous reaction." Nathanael scribbled his copious notes on the name in the portfolio that he kept concerning his studies of the Hebrew language. Since the moment that he had arrived shortly after breakfast this morning, Nathanael had been pouring himself fervently over a stack of books he had gathered, while continuing his studies towards a better understanding of the various names for God found within the pages of the Old Testament.

In several of the piles that had been left on his desk by the seminary's librarian, there were more than a few interesting volumes that highlighted the information he needed, but not all of them were in a language that he currently spoke, which only made his search all the more laborious when he had to translate them from their original Latin or Greek. The books written solely in the Hebrew tongue were in the farthest pile on his desk, reserved for when he had more time to confer with someone else as to their proper translation. For most of the summer, he had been endeavoring to obtain a better grasp of the language itself so that the consultations would no longer be necessary, but with few teachers of the older style of speaking among his peers, save one or two gentlemen who were far more ancient in mind and body than was cognitively wise to rely upon, his options still remained fairly limited.

On many occasions, William himself had been able to help reason out a few of the more complicated Latin texts for him when he was stuck, having also studied the language back in university, but he was no help in Hebrew at all.

"I suppose no one needed to speak Hebrew back when William was learning medicine in London. Or at least there were no journals written in it that might have tempted him to start learning." Nathanael tapped the feather of his quill against his lips in humor and contemplated the intriguing idea of finding such a journal for his friend, just so that he would have someone else with whom to study.

"That would probably take a miracle and far more time that I can afford to find it." He lifted his eyebrows up once in a contemplative sigh with the shake of his head and leaned back down over the book he had been reading. "Elyon is often used by the Israelites when they refer to God as being their Most High God..." He started to write but stopped when the door behind him suddenly opened.

"Professor Beckett, may I ask you a question about the homework that is due later this afternoon?" A slightly disheveled and partially out of breath, Mr. Carroll inquired as he hesitantly approached his desk.

"Good morning, Mr. Carroll..." Nathanael placed a hand on top of the Bible on his left and tried to hold back the sarcastic reply he wanted to utter but chose instead to say something a bit more admonishing. "Well, since it is almost time for it to be handed in, I suppose now is as good a time as any to make sure you understand all the parameters required for its submittal."

"Yes, well..." The young man stammered nervously while fidgeting with something he was searching for in the recesses of his leather bag. "I have the majority of my thesis done, but I heard this morning at breakfast that you were wanting us to include at least two quotes in it, as well. Did you happen to specify who those quotes needed to be from precisely?" He finally managed to withdraw the object of his search, a strangely compiled stack of loose parchments of various sizes and conditions, all arranged in some kind of order that was completely foreign to Nathanael.

"You mean to tell me that you actually made it to breakfast this morning?" Nathanael smiled in jest. "I don't believe it."

Mr. Carroll grinned too. "I suppose it helps to change your ways when your roommates decide it is suddenly time they quite literally start flipping you out of your bed promptly at six," he muttered disdainfully at the condition in which he had been treated, but Nathanael could tell that deep down, the young man was also, keenly grateful.

"I imagine it does. But if I were to be honest, as well, I've been told that one of my friends threatened to slap me one time to wake me up. Though thankfully for all involved, he did not," Nathanael admitted while trying to maintain a levity to the conversation.

"Why?" Mr. Carroll asked quickly. "If you don't mind me asking, that is?"

"Because he is a very strong man for the most part. If he had done so, I fear I might never have fallen asleep again out of concern for a second reprisal."

"I would be frightened, too, sir..." Mr. Carroll chuckled. "But the paper?"

"Yes, two quotes of your choice will suffice for this paper. Just be sure they are accurately documented when you submit it, or I will be forced to dock you ten points for the error." He leaned farther back in his chair and formed his fingers into a small triangle of sorts against his chest. "Come to think of it, you could always use a quote from someone living, too, if you have a notion to go interview someone down at the government offices. From what I hear from my friend, I think there are several representatives visiting today, so there should be at least one of two that might be able to help."

"That would be fantastic, sir." Mr. Carroll's eyes lit up immediately with the information offered. "I'd much rather feature someone living any day than someone who probably has no idea what we are all facing in today's world."

"Indeed, Mr. Caroll... indeed." Nathanael nodded slightly and tilted his head in his direction. "Will that be all?"

"Yes, sir, and thank you," Mr. Carroll replied as he shoved the papers back into his bag and headed out the door.

"Well, at least he has learned how to get up in the morning now." Nathanael laughed lightly again to himself at the image in his mind of what the young man had described and moved to pick up where he had left off before he had been interrupted. "Jehovah Nissi was used primarily after Moses's great victory in battle. God's name here signifies His presence as the flag that is carried into battle for His people. The one they rally around and defend. Or more appropriately, the God who is faithful to direct <u>and</u> protect." He continued on in his definition, attempting to capture fully what he had been reading. "In many ways it can also symbolize..." He began to write once more but was interrupted again by another visitor who burst through the door this time, not even five minutes after the departure of his last guest.

"Nathanael? Are you busy?" Emile strode across the short span from the door to his desk quickly as if he was on a mission of some great importance or was otherwise focused on many other tasks to complete.

Closing his eyes for just a moment to deter his irritation at being so rudely interrupted, he calmed his reflex reaction to say something more curt and possibly sarcastic but instead, endeavored to answer him politely. "Define... busy."

"Busy would entail not being actively involved in teaching at the moment." Emile took his father's hat from off his head and held it as he waited for him to look up.

"Then no, Emile, I am not busy." Nathanael smiled while placidly looking up at him and maintained his guarded composure.

"Good. I meant to ask you yesterday what _you_ were planning on getting William for his birthday next month. The man is a cryptic mystery when it comes to gifts, so I was rather hoping you might have a little insight. Has he mentioned anything he might have wanted or even hinted about doing?" His friend asked while he patiently tapped the top of the tallest set of books nearest to him with his fingertips.

"Well..." For several moments Nathanael seriously contemplated what kind of gift his friend of almost twenty years might actually want, then impetuously provided an alternative. "I think I did hear that he was looking for a medical journal in Hebrew actually." He smirked and attempted to keep an authentic expression, something that he struggled to do any time he was less than truthful.

"A journal in Hebrew?" Emile scoffed, utterly perplexed. "They are hard enough to find in English and Latin. Why would he want it in that language?"

"Oh, I don't know." Nathanael stood to stretch his legs just a little as he had been sitting for nigh over an hour already. "Perhaps it is for a particular patient. You know William, he always has the keenest attraction to everything we might label as strange."

"Yes... but in Hebrew?" Emile pondered the unusual request once more. "And nothing else comes to mind?" He probed even harder, obviously not ready to acquiesce to the necessity of such a difficult task as Nathanael had just proposed.

"He has also loved the shirt immensely that you got him in Charleston, a while back. The white one you gave him from the island is actually his favorite," Nathanael gave in and offered the best alternative he could think of on such short notice.

"Ah, the one made from King Cotton." Emile smirked proudly. "It figures that he would like it. They only use that fabric for royalty and Popes now. In fact, I had to barter pretty heavily to get the last one, but still..." He let the sentence drop off once more as he seemed to be lost in thought once again.

"Will that be all?" Nathanael asked a bit more authoritatively, eager to finish the chapter he was writing before the students for his afternoon lecture arrived.

"Yes, quite... and thank you." Emile placed his hat back upon his head and tipped it in his direction before he left just as quickly as he came.

"Well, it was worth a try," Nathanael sighed at his failed attempt to get his way with the medical journal and picked up one of the easier of the Hebrew texts. Thumbing his way through the worn pages with the loose sheets of written translations tucked safely inside for something that looked vaguely recognizable more than the gibberish his mind professed it contained, he yearned once more to be able to read the Bible completely in its original tongue. When he had been forced to learn Greek back in seminary he had done so initially only out of a scholarly obligation, but the world that it had opened to him thereafter had forever astounded and delighted him. Never in all of his life had he been so happy to connect with something in the way that he could do once he had mastered it.

"Someday, it will be the same with you, too." He promised the open book in front of him and moved to close it when the door of his room opened yet another time, only this time with less force and a great deal more attention to closing it afterwards.

"Good morning, Nathanael, how are your studies going this morning?" William asked warmly, though the expression on his face told quite a different story.

"Frightfully better than your morning it appears." He eyed his friend warily for several seconds, then inquired, "Are you feeling alright? Or did something happen at the hospital?" He watched William's changing expression for signs of distress as he was steadily becoming sufficiently worried for the man. Not once in their whole history together had he ever looked this out of sorts about anything transpiring in his life, let alone as positively dreadful as he truthfully appeared today.

"I have not had the chance to even check-in there as of yet. I was on my way over there this morning when I decided to come here first instead. For the second day in a row, I have woken up with this pounding headache that will <u>not</u> go away. And no matter how much I try to ignore it and attempt to push past it mentally, I just can't," William admitted honestly and sat down across from him in one of the student's chairs to collect himself.

"Have you tried anything else?"

"A few things, but I am struggling to hold off on what we both know will fix it." He placed both hands upon his temples and massaged the area on both sides of his eyes and forehead.

"Whyever for?" Nathanael set down the book and sat down beside him. "If your body needs it, you should listen to it."

"What my body needs is more than _it_ can give." William leaned his head back and closed his eyes to regain his focus, breathing in and out slowly to abate at least some of the throbbing that was attacking him.

"I see..." Nathanael nodded, then inquired more pointedly, "Then what does it need exactly, William?"

"Rest, Nathanael... one hundred percent, unconscious rest, but as long as my mind will not shut itself off, I cannot do that," William admitted reluctantly and looked at his friend for several long moments to the point that it almost made Nathanael want to cancel all of his classes today just to take care of the man.

"I think it might be time for the laudanum, again, William," Nathanael said quietly, not really wanting to suggest the only thing that seemed to give William any form of relief other than blood.

"I know." William closed his eyes and sighed a sigh that made his whole body shudder in response. "I just don't want to, not this time."

"Then why don't you go over to Charlotte's. I bet she might have a few things you haven't tried yet," he suggested optimistically.

"That actually sounds like a very good idea, Nathanael. And I may do that after lunch, but first, I am going home to lie down again. If I cannot fall asleep, I promise that I will do so then." William stood up warily and placed a hand on his friend's shoulder. "Thank you for the suggestion though."

"Any time, William... anytime." Nathanael smiled earnestly and walked him to the door before closing it once more with a soft thud.

When he came to his classroom this morning, the only thing on his mind at all was the desire to complete at least one, maybe two chapters in the guaranteed solitude his lecture hall normally provided. Yet the steady flow of visitors today had almost negated all facets of his logic in his decision to do so. In most cases, if he entertained one guest a week, other than his normally attentive students, that would have been commonplace for him, if not completely expected, but to have three in the space of ten minutes time was utterly boggling.

Glancing over at the pile of books and various parchments spread across his desk that still awaited him, Nathanael felt suddenly frustrated with the unexpected turn of events and his inability to finish his task properly. "Maybe I should take a few of these home to..." He began to surmise aloud before the door once again creaked on its hinges behind him to announce yet another unexpected guest's arrival. "For the love of all that is holy! Can't a man work in peace today?" He gritted his teeth slightly to contain the rest of his rising resentment towards the unwelcomed interruption and moved to turn around to face his newest disturbance but was in turn, humbled just as quickly.

"I'm so very sorry, Mr. Beckett. My sincerest apologies." Charlotte's normally self-assured voice stammered just a little as she attempted to make amends for her obvious intrusion and moved hastily to depart. "I will come back later." She turned instinctively to close the door behind her without completing her called-upon task but was stopped abruptly when Nathanael came immediately to the door and reached out his hand to touch her arm instead.

"Oh, please don't go, Charlotte." He tried to persuade her into staying and moved his other hand to fully open the door between them. "I had no idea it was you or I would never have behaved thus... truly." He ran a nervous hand through his shoulder length brown hair and tried to straighten it just a little from its slightly disheveled state.

Still unconvinced that she should remain when she was clearly disturbing his desire to study, Charlotte kept her eyes downward for the moment, her gaze firmly fixed on the basket in her hands that seemed to be the object of her mission. "Normally, I wouldn't dream of visiting you unannounced, Mr. Beckett, but I only wanted to stop by and give you these." She held the basket out to him and waited for him to accept it. "Emma and I have been baking all morning for the church picnic and since there were more than a dozen or so extra, I thought I might take them into town to cheer you and William up."

Observing the uncharacteristic hesitance in the woman's eyes brought on by his words alone, Nathanael felt instantly shamed in his careless outburst. "Thank you, Charlotte. I am so very grateful that you did. But what did you bring?"

Charlotte's expression softened just a little as he returned to his normally cordial state. "At first, I had a mind to make you some of those muffins you liked last month, but Emma reminded me of your love for cinnamon and how it is one of the few spices that is still remotely attractive to you and the others. So, I made you some of my snickerdoodles instead for dunking in your coffee."

"Once again, I am beyond appreciative of your efforts. William will be, too." Nathanael lifted the fabric that covered the still, slightly warm cookies and selected one from the top to sample. "The gesture was incredibly considerate, and as always, these are _very_ good, Charlotte."

"My boys used to think so, though I could never get Sebastian to eat even one of them either before or after he returned home to us. Oddly enough, he had a definite aversion to all things sweet." Charlotte smiled and watched with growing pleasure, Nathanael's joy as he consumed the treat.

"Would you care to take a minute to sit and talk? I have about an hour before I am expected at Mr. Everton's farm." Nathanael motioned with his hand to the chairs he and William had just occupied only moments earlier.

"You know I would love to, but actually, I can't." Charlotte shook her head sadly. "Truth is, Emma is waiting for me out in the wagon as we speak."

"Oh, I see." Nathanael fingered the handle of the basket anxiously. "Still, I feel as though I should at least do <u>something</u> to make amends for my rude behavior just now or else you might think I am normally given to a hot temper when the occasion suits me." He set the basket down in the center of his desk, then moved to offer her his arm to escort her back to the wagon. "In fact, surprisingly enough, I <u>did</u> just suggest to William that he should talk to you later today about his headaches if his current state does not improve."

"Oh? Is he still feeling poorly?" Charlotte took his arm and held it close to her as she walked. "Come to think of it, I did think he was looking rather pale the other day and not very talkative in the least."

"Feeling poorly would be the understatement of the year, I'm afraid. When he stopped by this morning, he looked positively dreadful." Nathanael opened the front door of the seminary and checked the position of the sun before sensing the need begrudgingly to allow her to continue on without him since his cloak was still back in his office.

Looking up in the same direction with the very same conclusion thereafter, Charlotte squeezed his arm encouragingly and reminded him, "The same sun which can prevent you from doing whatever it is you wish to do today is also the one that is a blessing to others." She beamed up at him and added, "Try not to think of it too harshly. Besides, I still remember tolerably well how to maneuver the rest of the way without your assistance... <u>today</u>, though I might forget a time or two when it is raining or am otherwise inclined for company, Mr. Beckett." She winked in his direction and released his arm readily.

Nathanael grinned, too at her intended humor. "I appreciate that very much, Mrs. Fabbri." He chose also to use her more formal name in public now that there were others passing by around them. "Though I <u>would</u> like to add a further bit of caution, too, if I may." He clasped his hands tightly together in front of him to keep them from nervously fidgeting with the encounter.

"Really? What?" Charlotte asked curiously as she turned around to view him once more.

"If you decide to stop by to see William on your way home, please <u>do</u> bring Emma with you inside, just in case. I would hate to even contemplate what might occur if William were to be strangely... um... more out of sorts than he would prefer in your company, as I am certain he may possibly be." Nathanael warned her as sternly and carefully as he could possibly manage while all the while believing beyond a shadow of a doubt that his friend would never hurt anyone of their acquaintance, let alone Charlotte. And yet, having that assurance aside, that did not also mean that he had not been tempted… they all had, whether they were so inclined or not. It was simply part of their nature now and keeping that darker self at bay was a full-time occupation some days.

"Would it make you feel better if I asked Emma to go in first instead and bring William out to me?" Charlotte prodded reassuringly.

"Immensely so." Nathanael sighed in grateful relief, appreciating once again her sincere understanding of their condition.

"Then that is what we will do," she affirmed. "Though I am not sure what you think I will know that he will not, but you never know." She continued on down the tall flight of steps in front of him and towards Emma who was waiting just below.

"Good day and thank you for the cookies!" Nathanael called after her from the doorway.

"Our pleasure, Nathanael," Emma called back and reached for Charlotte's hand to help her up into the wagon next to her.

Feeling suddenly much more anxious about an incredible list of things now that were freely flooding through his mind all at once, Nathanael watched them leave down the street, then turned around to fetch his cloak and another cookie. His appointment to help Cecil was not supposed to be until much closer to lunch, but for some odd reason, something inside of him was compelling him to head over there earlier.

Why that was… he did not know, but if there was one thing he had learned in almost half a century of existence, it was to heed the Holy Spirit's prompting when it happened, no matter the strangeness or inconvenience it created.

Chapter Fifteen

August 30th, 1811

Just like for every other trip across town to the farm occupied by Mr. Cecil Everton and his small group of farmhands, Nathanael had chosen to petition a ride from the wagon normally available at Elijah's forge. Thankfully for him, on any given day, he was always certain to find at least one, if not two, men milling about while delivering orders or picking up supplies for the young blacksmith, which usually made it terribly convenient to not traverse the many miles over to the farm on foot.

Nathanael never minded the exercise involved though. If truth be told, he rather enjoyed the splendid five-mile trek whenever the weather cooperated. But doing so on foot, often took just a bit too much of his available time when his visit was scheduled close to the middle of the day or after a lecture when William was also needing him to come along with him to a nearby sick call.

The Everton farmhouse, with its whitewashed horizontal boards and grass-green shutters, sat cheerily near the center of the large piece of property while also not that very far off from the main road, complete with an upper dormer and an especially worn grey roof. Moreover, a matching pair of equally faded white rocking chairs, that almost matched the home perfectly in their weathering, were always ready in silent vigil out front on the wooden porch that wrapped around almost to the side, inviting anyone to come sit and occupy them rain or shine.

Two large fields, one of corn and the other of lush light green alfalfa filled the horizon as far as the eye could see, stretching out in every direction, save that of the large barn to the house's right that was normally reserved for the storing of hay and the milking of his fifty cows twice daily. Nathanael had arrived more than a few times just before the nightly process had begun and, though he had endeavored to help the man as much as he was able, he was sure it cost Cecil far more time in his necessary instruction than it gave him in actual help. Still, the gentle farmer, with a heart as big as the fields he plowed every year without fail, was always grateful to see him whenever he could spare the sacrifice and told him so each and every time that he visited.

Because of the continual decline of his health, at least two other men were brought on recently to work the fields alongside the husband of Mr. Everton's niece, aiding him in completing at least some of the more arduous aspects of the farm. While his niece, , a very warm, middle-aged woman with bright red hair, the perfect color of a low fire or deepening sunset, often made sure to fix his meals whenever he would let her. And, for the most part, it was all proving to be a perfectly equitable arrangement for all involved, with very little of the concern Nathanael had initially felt when he discovered that William was allowing the man to return to his home after only a week in the hospital. Yet that fact aside, that still did not remove the sinking feeling Nathanael always experienced every time Cecil arrived late for Sunday services or not at all some weeks.

Nathanael would, of course, immediately visit him thereafter to ascertain whether he was in need of anything, but each time he would be told the very same assuring thing.

"God can't take me a minute before my time, Preacher. So, stop your fretting and sit a spell."

Knowing that he had surreptitiously captured his visitor's attention fully at last, Mr. Everton would then pick up his glasses and the latest book he was reading from the small table in the kitchen and the two of them would spend the next two hours at least in deep discussion before Nathanael would eventually leave to retire for the night, both feeling more hopeful than ever by the constant encouragement and shared fellowship.

As long as the time between them passed during each and every visit, it mattered not to either of them that the sun had long since set, or that neither of them had eaten any supper really to speak of. What they always shared instead was food for the soul, and no amount of nutrition could ever hope to match that.

"Hello!" Nathanael called as he hopped down from the wagon and thanked the young man for taking him so far out of his way.

Unsurprisingly, not a soul answered him in return, though that fact alone was not too overly concerning in itself as he doubted many would be able to hear him so far away from the house or the barn if they were inside.

"Cecil!" He cast his attention towards the field on his left and then to his right in search of any of the other farmhands, then started walking down the hardpacked, earthen drive that led up to the side of the house.

"Is anyone home?" He asked once more through the single screen door that had been left slightly ajar to create a cross-breeze through the house, but did not enter as he was still, more or less, waiting for someone to answer him.

The house within, with the large clock that pinged the hour just as loudly as William's favorite monstrosity, remained utterly silent other than the ticking that systematically accompanied it and what sounded like the wind fluttering the curtains in front of the front parlor window.

"Renee? Cecil? ?" He said each name with a long pause between as he beckoned to anyone who might be inside.

Not a single sound echoed back, human or otherwise. Not even the low mooing of the cows that should have been in the back pen waiting to be let out to pasture.

"Maybe he is in the barn... though I can't imagine why as it is most certainly far past milking time," Nathanael contemplated to himself aloud and placed his hand on the rough wood of the screen door to ground himself away from the aching dread that had been filling him since Charlotte had departed.

Why __did__ his mind always struggle so with its inability to stop worrying about the slightest of anomalies whenever they presented themselves? Was it merely a simple deficit in his human character alone that could eventually be conquered in time if given the right focus and practice? Or was it something more that was a direct result of his newer vampire senses that was meant to be aiding him towards knowing when he should fight whatever it was he was currently facing or giving him a warning that it was time to take cover and run?

Shaking his head twice to force away the darker shadows of the premonition that was still plaguing him, he pursed his lips and pushed himself forward off the porch in the direction of the stately barn on the right.

The massive structure that was quite easily twice the size of Mr. Everton's actual home had been built with pure efficiency in mind with an entire second level for the storage of hay and other goods necessary for feeding the various livestock on the farm. Though the area just below it, however, contained the real area for work, complete with countless stalls for milking, a large corral out back for the animals to wait their turn and a tack room that also doubled for where they sorted out the cream.

Just outside the brown-sided building and much closer to the main house was a vastly smaller home where Renee and her new husband had chosen to stay short-term in order to help Cecil. This petite version of the larger home behind him wasn't much to speak of overall, but was big enough for a tidy kitchen, one bedroom, and an equally cozy open space to enjoy some quality time with guests. On farms that were owned by some of the German families in town, this was usually referred to as a grandmother's house, but here, it was merely used for guests.

"Cecil..." Nathanael called out once more as he grasped the handle of one of the double doors on the front side of the barn and stepped inside, waiting anxiously for his eyes to adjust properly to the dimmer light it always contained. "Are you in here?"

"Nathanael..." A weak echo came back to him from somewhere near the other side of the building, far from a clear voice in any way, but something that was just loud enough to spark Nathanael's immediate attention and hasten his steps towards him.

"Cecil!" Nathanael exclaimed instantly when he reached the man's side at last and grasped his feeble hand tightly within his own as he examined the man's helpless condition on the floor. "What happened? Are you injured?"

"I don't really remember, son." Ceceil's hand trembled beneath his own and the vibration of its faint thrumming against his skin sent fresh shivers of fear through Nathanael, as well. "I was walking back to hang up the ropes from milking... and then... I woke up here." His eyes strained to fasten their focus once more onto anything close enough to him, but try as he might, they would not cooperate fully.

"Don't move. I am going to fetch more help." Nathanael's mind sprang immediately into motion, motivating him forward as he jumped up from the man's side and sprinted out of the barn towards Renee's small home before banging loudly on the outer door. "Renee! Mark!" He tried to catch his breath to compose himself at least slightly for when the door opened but despite his attempts to calm himself, he could only manage a slight slowing of his brisk panting.

"Nathanael!" Renee's eyes widened instantly in surprise at the man's impatient condition and opened the door for him to enter. "Whatever is the matter?"

"It's Cecil. I just found him collapsed in the barn. Is Mark around? I need him to go fetch someone at the hospital. <u>Now</u>," he implored fervently, the intensity of his delivery increasing considerably with every breath.

"Of course!" She turned around promptly to summon him and in no time at all, both husband and wife had exited the home with Mark swiftly mounting the brown quarter horse that had been kept tied to the railing in the corral.

"Tell them it is urgent and to hurry," Nathanael instructed feverishly and guided Renee back into the barn with him to where Cecil lay.

"Oh, Cecil!" Renee struggled to steady the wellspring of panic that overwhelmed her at seeing his dismal condition. "Why didn't you call for us?"

"Don't fuss so, child. I'll be fine. You'll see," Cecil answered just as weakly as he had done before, only this time with a great deal more difficulty breathing in-between his sentences.

"But you aren't fine, Uncle. Oh, I wish you had let me help you this morning with the milking. I knew you looked too tired at breakfast to do it by yourself." She used the back of her hand to wipe the tears from off her cheek but they returned just as quickly.

"Hush child. Don't cry." He patted her hand ever so slightly with his own but the whole comforting action appeared to be almost in a slower motion. "Though truthfully speaking... I don't even know... how long I have been lying here."

"Let me help you sit up, sir." Nathanael reached down and lifted the man carefully into a more comfortable position against a large mound of fresh hay that had been piled up beside him before taking the time to place both of the man's hands back upon his lap. Not surprisingly, each was almost as icy cold as his own were and already beginning to show the first signs of a stiffening of the joints. "Perhaps you could fetch him a glass of water, Renee, and some of that powder Doctor Wells left him? I think it is by his Bible on the counter," Nathanael suggested helpfully, knowing there was little either of them could do at this point until a more trained medical professional arrived.

"Certainly, I'll be right back." Renee's brow furrowed at the thought of leaving her uncle but went obediently over to the house to fetch it anyways.

"She's... a good... girl," Cecil acknowledged while taking in several quick breaths of air in-between each of his words as just the action of speaking was now starting to tire him immensely. "It is a shame.... she has to trouble... herself... on my account." He gasped even more so at the end, making his whole chest rise by the controlling action it required just to draw it in.

"You shouldn't try to talk, Cecil. Just rest until help arrives." Nathanael looked around the area in the barn beside them for anything that might have caused Cecil's sudden fall other than his heart but saw nothing out of the ordinary whatsoever.

"Oh, Preacher… the only help… I need right now… is… some of those prayers… you do so well." The man gasped wearily once more, then patted his hand twice upon Nathanael's to encourage him to do so.

"Actually… I have been praying for you all morning, though I didn't know why at the time. But, now that I do, I suppose I can pray even more directly while we wait," Nathanael promised faithfully and closed his eyes to petition his Father in Heaven for the help they required to arrive in time to make a difference. Or more importantly, that today would not be the last day he would get to enjoy a visit with his friend.

Lost in the awful silence that flowed all around them through his whispered words and fervent pleas, the fleeting minutes Nathanael most dreaded droned on, as they always had when there was nothing more he could physically do to help someone other than simply pray. Still, even with that trained knowledge aside, his penitent prayers felt nothing like those he said each night by his bedside or the ones he spoke passionately at church during the morning service. Not at all. This anxious form of petition between Earth and Heaven caused the very air around him to suddenly hum with an odd sort of calmness that he had experienced during only one other time in his life. Though in truth, the utter peacefulness of <u>that</u> particular moment had been brought on by one of the most difficult confrontations in his existence. Yet even then, he had known beyond a shadow of a doubt from whence it came, and had trusted the reasoning for it.

Today was no different, only yet it was.

The absolute quietness of the reflective moment that collected all around them had not been intended this time towards <u>his</u> comfort at all, but rather it had been created for the man breathing shallowly next to him. A wonderfully sweet stolen sequence of seconds, all carefully arranged in perfect order, was given imperceptibly in the silence to convey a sense of protection and longing that was quite unmistakable, matched perfectly with an almost joyful quality to its sad arrival.

"Nathanael… can I ask you a question, son?" Cecil eventually replied slowly in a whisper, his voice now appearing more controlled and even than it had been previously.

"Anything," Nathanael finished his prayer quickly and opened his eyes to concentrate on the man better.

"Anything at all?"

"Yes," Nathanael answered openly with little fear at all over what the man might ask him next.

"Hmmm…" Cecil hummed and for several quiet moments, his eyes traced the large wooden beams of the ceiling above him as if searching in them for the right way in which to form the question intended for his young friend before they moved gradually over to Nathanael and studied his face with the same intense but endearing concentration. "What is it… that makes you hesitate… every time… that you see me… Nathanael?"

"Hesitate, sir?" Nathanael shifted his position nervously on the ground next him as he tried to hide the initial shock his question had created. "I am not sure I know what you mean."

Cecil only smiled when he looked his way with steadfast endurance and the way it made the deep blue in his eyes seem to sparkle with true happiness forced Nathanael to smile, too. "We both… know that you do," he added in an exhale, then pulled out his wire rimmed spectacles and weakly put them on to see his friend's face better.

Nathanael nodded. "Guilty, once again." He glanced back over his shoulder and out the door, looking to see if the doctor had arrived as of yet, but was dismayed when still not a soul was present on the road or in the yard.

"Is it something bad?" Cecil inquired patiently. "Something that perhaps… our friend Doctor Wells told you… that you are afraid to tell me."

"Oh, no… nothing like that at all, I assure you." He shook his head once more and attempted to put his thoughts into a more logical form so as to not overwhelm the man unnecessarily. "My hesitation where you are involved is more due to the fact that you _very_ much resemble my own father, sir. Nothing more."

"Really… that poor man." Cecil tried to laugh lightly at the thought, but the motion of it only made him begin coughing repeatedly until in the end, he had to allow Nathanael to move behind him to support his body just to remain upright and be able to breathe fully. "I suppose… there are worse people… to resemble…. not many… but some."

Nathanael grinned widely at the man's intended humor, but every second that was passing between them also made his heart more anxious to see that time disappear. "Not at all, I assure you. I loved my father very much."

"Is he still alive?" Cecil barely whispered now, his eyes resting firmly closed to retain whatever strength he had left.

"No. Sadly, both of my parents joined their maker before I ever entered seminary. Still, if he was here, he would agree with me that you could be his twin, right on down to your glasses and hair color, Mr. Everton. I know it seems fantastical to claim it, but it is truly shocking how very similar you both are," Nathanael reassured him and placed his arms around the sides of his body to allow Cecil the room necessary to lean back on him fully as Nathanael leaned against one of the large poles that held up the second floor.

"I see." He sighed slowly and for several minutes more, Nathanael counted the breaths Cecil made as they waited.

"Nathanael?" Cecil finally found his voice once again and spoke even more confidently than Nathanael had probably heard him speak in weeks.

"Yes." Nathanael leaned his head back upon the pole behind him and distractedly trained his ears towards picking up any kind of sound off in the distance.

"If your father was here, what would you ask him?" Cecil asked hesitantly, unsure if the man would think it was improper of him to inquire.

"Oh, that is easy," Nathanael said without any hesitation at all. "In fact, it is the one question I have <u>always</u> thought of every time I remember him." Nathanael closed his eyes and concentrated heavily on his father once more: the smell of his hair when he used to carry him up to bed at night, the way his soft hands always felt like the perfect temperature between warm and cold, the light tenor of his voice when he would sing terribly off key with his mother, or the admonishing look he would give him when he finally found him hiding in the library. All were powerful memories within his mind, and the very essence of who his father was to him exactly, for he was much more than a mere remembrance or faded dream, he was a small piece of himself in many ways. "If he was here, I would ask him if he approved of the path I have chosen for my life, or if he would have directed differently." Nathanael opened his eyes and tried to envision his father's face once more, but oddly enough, all he could envision now was Mr. Everton's.

"I think your father would tell you how incredibly proud he is of you, Nathanael Beckett." Cecil placed just one of his colder hands on top of one of Nathanael's and held it there. "He would be most proud indeed."

"Really?" Nathanael almost choked back an unexpected sob. Within a guarded area of his heart, an emotion that had been long-kept dormant now flooded over Nathanael's entire being all at once, filling his eyes instantly with the tears he had managed to hold at bay for years. "How can you be so certain?" His voice cracked in several places through the strain the moment had created.

"Because oddly enough, you are like my John... as well... Nathanael." Cecil exhaled slowly and held his hand tighter still. "And <u>I</u> am proud of you, <u>both</u>."

The tears fell freely now from the corners of both of Nathanael's eyes all at once as he released them and allowed them to make their way down his face and onto the man's thick auburn hair. "And just like your John, I will tell you what he would say, sir." Nathanael sucked in a large gulp of air and tried to expel it out again, but it would not leave his chest. "He would probably say how very much he is looking forward to seeing you again." He let out the air completely and felt the true beginnings of a sob overtake him.

"Soon... Nathanael... soon." Cecil exhaled his reply almost like he was finally falling asleep, which in a way, he probably was as his body had become entirely relaxed from the exhaustion of the whole ordeal.

"I finally found it, Nathanael. It was in the drawer by the wash basin instead." Renee returned then with the cup of requested water and medicine for her uncle, but when she drew closer to hand it to him, Nathanael only shook his head slowly to dissuade her in her effort for it was becoming abundantly clear to him that no amount of intervention would save him today or any day.

Then, as if everything was suddenly playing out in line with Nathanael's last prophetic thought, a wagon pulled in quickly from the road beyond and one of William's fellow doctors dismounted along with Nurse Bentham who carried with them a large blanket, no doubt intended for transporting their patient over to the wagon.

"Mr. Beckett, how long has he been like this today?" The young man, about the same age as William appeared to be, felt the pulse on Mr. Everton's wrist and then reached inside his satchel for a remedy of some kind to give the man.

"I have no idea. I found him here when I arrived," Nathanael explained but did not move to change his position as he feared the sudden shift in the man's position would be more detrimental for him and take away what little time he had left.

"I am so sorry, Mr. Beckett, Renee," Nurse Bentham politely addressed each of them in turn. "We tried to get here as quickly as we could manage but there was a bit of a calamity in town that we had to drive around."

"It's not your fault, Miss Bentham." Nathanael wiped the remnants of the tears from off his cheeks and felt an almost familiar now callousness take the place of his previous emotion. "God alone decides these things for us here on Earth, whether we are ready for them or not." He brought his teeth together firmly at the formal declaration and felt the muscles in his cheek tighten even further with the action.

"If you'll allow me, I can give him something to make him more comfortable, but I am afraid that it is only a matter of time now," the doctor, who had been busy checking for any other possible signs of distress, affirmed and stood up to see to making the necessary preparations for moving his patient back into the house.

"I'll go fix his bed for him," Renee complied quietly as she was led out of the barn by her husband and the doctor, leaving only Charity and Nathanael waiting within for the others to return.

"Ah, Nurse Bentham... you've come to visit me... too." Cecil opened his eyes just enough then to view the woman in front of him and the corners of his mouth moved just a little upwards in response. "Seems like I am...quite the... nuisance today." He inhaled and exhaled out several times to compensate for the energy it had taken to say even that much.

"You are never a nuisance, and you know it, sir. Quite the opposite in fact." She knelt down next to him so that she could be closer still to his level and not require him to exert himself any more than necessary. "It has been terribly boring at the hospital today anyway with no one new to torture, so as you might expect, I practically jumped at the chance to come and visit you."

"Ah..." The man nodded twice, and Nathanael couldn't help but hold him tighter still as if doing so would transfer just a bit of the strength he possessed over to the man. "Well, then... I will give you a gift in return... for your sacrifice." He paused for several minutes.

"A gift... for me?" Charity smiled nervously.

Cecil waved his fingers slightly to dissuade her confusion then began again, "Every day... is a precious gift... and every breath... is yet another... They are not a right... so use them wisely." He drew in a long breath and exhaled it out again just as slowly.

"We will." Nathanael whispered with a nod and held him close until the others arrived once again and used the blanket to carry Cecil into the house to spend his final moments with his family.

Moving to stand outside now on the front porch, just staring into the lush fields in front of him, Nathanael finally took in the magnitude of everything that had transpired this morning and felt inexplicably numb in every way possible—physically, emotionally, but more importantly, mentally. For years he had compacted away his feelings concerning the death of his parents so that he could attempt to function in this world without them. Yet now that he had opened up that locked door, with all the grief and loss that it contained, he felt like he was experiencing their absence all over again. And in many ways, it was almost as if those same emotions he once hid from now refused to be shoved back into that very same space of dismissal once again.

"Mr. Beckett?" From the edge of the porch that faced the barn beside him, Charity walked over to where Nathanael stood and waited in the silence for him to speak, then chose hesitantly to offer the information she possessed quietly to him when he did not, "Renee's husband said that we can use the wagon we came in to head back into town and he'll hitch up another for Doctor Baxter to return later this afternoon, or whenever other arrangements can be made. I've already gone over and moved it to the house if you would like to go. If not, I can send someone back for you when you wish to leave."

"What I <u>wish</u> is for people that I care about to stop dying on me, Miss Bentham." Nathanael's voice came out far more hard and cynical than it had ever been uttered before, either to her or anyone else of his existence.

"Yes." Charity nodded politely but chose to remain quiet for several minutes to allow him the appropriate time to process his emotions fully. "That is probably all of our wish, Mr. Beckett." She glanced his way at last and watched him for several moments as she tried to make out just what exactly he was thinking.

Without wanting to converse about anything at all for the present, Nathanael remained precisely as he was, silent and unmovable, no longer concerned in the least about the students who were probably waiting for him back at the college or his friends who would, no doubt, be worried about him since he had not shown up for their prearranged lunch, either. Only Elijah, alone, had known of his impetuous trip out here this morning, but even then, he had been more than a bit distracted with his work when Nathanael had petitioned for the ride.

"Would you like to..." Charity began to ask again if he was ready to depart then stopped when she heard the sound of the family's weeping coming back to them through the screen door from somewhere deep inside the house behind them.

"Yes, we should leave, Miss Bentham. I don't think I have the appropriate words to pray with them today, though I know deep down that I should. Still... for Cecil's sake, I <u>could</u> try..." Nathanael cast a quick glance behind him and felt his body stiffen just contemplating entering the house once more and seeing his recently departed friend.

"No, I agree. I think it would be best if you came with me for the present. Call it being physically required to serve elsewhere if you must." Charity pulled on his arm gently but firmly as she directed him to take a few steps with her towards the waiting wagon, and away from the scene of sorrow he was most dreading. "Besides, I cannot drive the horses very well on my own, and with William not at the hospital today, I <u>am</u> needed there until he arrives." She walked him directly over to the waiting rig and stood resolutely near the side of it next to him until he mounted and took the reins.

"Fine." Nathanael complied sullenly but said nothing more.

In fact, for the majority of the drive back into town the two of them spoke very little other than the necessity of making sure they were heading in the right direction and asking whether or not he was pushing the horses too quickly or slowly for her comfort. As equally moved as both of them were by the words Mr. Everton had spoken to them shortly before his passing, neither of them had felt very compelled to offer much of anything that amounted to an actual conversation to speak of. Yet when Nathanael finally pulled up to the front of the hospital and moved to the side of the wagon to help her down, his mind began to slightly come back to life at last.

"Where did they say I should leave the wagon?" Nathanael offered her his hand and steadied her as she descended.

"We borrowed it from the livery that's by the forge, I believe. Do you know it?" Charity asked quickly and smoothed out the wrinkles in her dress that the travelling had created.

"Yes, I know it." Nathanael smiled at the irony of her question. "My friend's son owns it, actually."

"Oh, well that will make things infinitely easier for both of us then," she answered him lightly and turned to leave but stopped after taking a step away. "By the way, where _is_ Doctor Wells, anyway? When they said you had a desperate need of a doctor, I was quite worried that maybe something horrible had happened to him as he never misses a day of work, let alone two put together." Her brow furrowed considerably with the concern she obviously felt on the man's behalf. "Has he been unwell?"

For several moments, Nathanael contemplated very seriously what he should say to the woman seeing as she was indeed, the object of William's struggle at the present, but telling her that his friend had been losing sleep every night dealing with his conflicted emotions regarding her would not be an appropriate conversation, nor had William truly realized the full scope as to the origins of his distress either, it seemed.

The best he could do under the circumstances, was to give her a vague kind of response that would not only hopefully alleviate some of her concern about his welfare but also paint his friend in a possibly more favorable light for his absence.

"William has been suffering from a severe headache these past few days that has quite incapacitated him. But not to worry, a friend of ours stopped by with a few remedies this morning that I am sure will have him back working at the hospital in no time."

"Good. I was afraid I might need to come and tend to him myself, just to make sure he was still alive and well..." The corners of Charity's mouth turned upwards quickly as a humorous thought suddenly struck her, then moved back to a more serious expression as she tried to compose herself once again. "Well, in lieu of assaulting the man in private, too, would you please pass on my regards and tell him that he is missed greatly... even by me. Though all things considered, you might want to omit that last part, or it might make him stay home indefinitely."

"I doubt that very highly, but I <u>will</u> tell him everything and thank you once again for coming," Nathanael paid the appropriate respect she deserved for her efforts on the farm and climbed back up into the wagon.

With little else left to say, the two travelers subsequently parted ways and after depositing the borrowed rig and making his obligatory excuses at the seminary for his missed class this afternoon, Nathanael began to find his way back from the forge to the safety and solitude of his home downtown. Moreover, as much as he would have liked to remain perfectly at ease in his world for yet another day, William was not the only one whose mind was now a chaotic jumble of indecision and overwhelming emotions it seemed.

Today, had regrettably marked yet another death Nathanael would have quite happily never witnessed, though it had also been one of the most poignant of his life experiences to date, as well.

As immortally destined as he forever would be, no doubt there would be many more periods of grief to follow in his lifetime. And like it or not, each one of them would probably affect him in a similar way until he regrettably became so accustomed to the sorrow that it would be almost commonplace or expected. Yet having that intimate knowledge of his future did not necessarily mean that it would be any easier for him to accept the pain that accompanied it today... far from it.

Especially eager to sort out for himself just how he was going to cope with all the information that had flooded his brain this afternoon in the barn, not to mention the many complicated emotions Mr. Everton's conversation had stirred up within him, Nathanael opened the door to his apartment and closed it firmly behind him, cautiously cognizant once again how very alone he felt in his life, though he was constantly surrounded by quite literally hundreds of people.

Chapter Sixteen

September 5th, 1811

With a sigh of sudden relief, Charity closed the door quickly behind her and leaned her cheek against the smooth wood on the other side, hoping to erase the inexplicable embarrassment she had just experienced this morning. The flowing texture of the recently sanded and painted surface sent ripples of contentment through her every time she saw it, making her feel vaguely justified yet again in the expense she had gone through to refinish it this way. Having firmly decided almost a year ago that it was finally time she put down definite roots of her own, she had spent almost all of her free days in the past four months renovating her apartment just a short mile from the Pennsylvania hospital and now that it was almost finished, she could not wait to have a moment to enjoy it fully.

To the left side of the entry by the wonderfully carved front door was an entire wall completely surfaced with richly toned earthen bricks very similar to the ones on the great Independence Hall downtown, while the opposite side was adorned with the cream planks she had managed to salvage from the demolition of the old bookstore across town. The very one that had been her favorite place to stop during her lunch hour when she just needed a place to relax in the middle of her hectic day.

In the beginning, it had been a whim of a decision when she had seen the workers stacking up the beautiful boards near the side of the street for disposal. And the men who had brought them to her home had no doubt thought she was crazy to have requested them, too, as old and marked as they were from the years fighting off the elements, but when she had offered them twice the usual pay to install them for her, not a single man dared to contradict her vision.

Compared to the other, much larger homes on Pine Street, hers was a modest edifice with only two floors to speak of, with one bedroom on the second floor that took up the majority of the space above and a smaller area behind it for a garden, which suited her needs perfectly. After all, as busy as she was at the hospital, she much preferred living simply in this way without the need to be overly conversational after work or worse, forcibly required to be constantly replacing her things back to their proper location after they had been carelessly rearranged by a forgetful roommate. Only once in the past had she ever entertained that kind of aggravating arrangement, but thankfully, her new job now paid her much more than her last, making it most certainly enough to not necessitate doing so ever again. Or at least she hoped so.

Thoroughly soaked and more than a little bit flustered with herself by how the whole day had turned out, Charity climbed the steps to her room on the second floor and began changing out of her soggy attire one awful piece at a time.

When she had agreed to accompany her friend, Mary, on a stroll down by the docks this morning, she had initially thought it was a marvelous idea, accompanied by a genuine need to experience life in the great outdoors for at least one day this month. Yet her desire to feel the breeze against her face and drink in the diverse sights and sounds of the ships both unloading and taking on their newly created cargo could not have come on a more inopportune day. Not that there was <u>ever</u> a day that for someone to enjoy almost drowning on their only day off of work, but there it was.

Groaning inwardly at the mess she now saw in the mirror beside her, Charity released with great reluctance the only semi-dry strands of her otherwise damp hairstyle that had escaped being drenched completely by the Delaware River and tried her best to comb through the majority of the tangles before deciding in the end that a simple braid down the side would have to suffice for the evening or at least until she could clean it more properly. The only thing on her mind now, other than the battle against her total humiliation, was to heat some water for a much-deserved bath on land this time and forget that the whole day happened at all.

"As if that were even possible," Charity grumbled and lay back fully in her chemise on top of the quilt placed across her bed and closed her eyes. "Well, if he didn't have reason enough to dislike me before, he certainly does now." She threw her arm grumpily over her face and attempted to steady the nerves that had been threatening to force her to crumple in William's commanding presence and almost cried at the memory of how he had looked at her when they had pulled her to safety. "Just once I would love to not feel so helplessly insignificant around that man." She sighed once more as her lip quivered uncontrollably before adding quieter still, "One time please... would that be too much to ask, God?"

No one answered, though Charity was not truly waiting for an audible reply either. Frankly speaking, she already knew the answer He would give anyway, and it wasn't exactly something she was ready to accept... at least not yet.

Needing something to distract her away from the pity party that was more certain than ever to follow, Charity thought back to how happy she had been when she had awakened this morning, ready to embrace all that the day had in store for her. In many ways, her whole disposition had seemed perfectly poised on the precipice of accepting the hesitant optimism that was creeping into her bit by bit as she envisioned spending an entire day without the constant need to be strong and collected around all of her peers. She had even put on her new dress and bonnet that had only just arrived from the tailors yesterday, complete with a soft layer of yellow and white flowered fabric that covered the lower half of her full skirt all the way up to the matching embroidered top.

At that point, quite literally nothing in all the world could have properly prepared her for what she would encounter. Nor the way in which a simple sequence of events would thoroughly shift the paradigm existing between herself and Doctor Wells.

Just as she had promised, Mary had dutifully arrived shortly after breakfast, but not before Charity had finished the rest of her cup of coffee and the two of them had set out immediately thereafter on their way across town, intent on spending the day reading on the lawn or lazily picnicking nearer to the docks if the weather held out as from what she could tell from her bedroom window when she had finished dressing, the sky was already turning a definite shade of light gray. Many other citizens of the city had often spent their afternoons relaxing on the large grassy lawn that overlooked the busy pier with its large trees and thick bushes providing the perfect amount of shade, but this was the first time she had chosen to do so.

All the way down the street as she travelled from her home to the boardwalk with its warped boards and tall posts that moored the larger vessels docked there, her friend beside her was a virtual fountain of conversation. In fact, it was practically astounding to Charity once again, how the woman was able to seamlessly cover a litany of topics from the sermon last Sunday to the article about William's friend, Emile's, recent speech and even a few other uncommonly familiar anecdotes mixed in about someone's pig who had delivered only one piglet and a cow that had brazenly chosen to take up residence in a farmer's home while they were asleep. All were things Charity could have read for herself in *The Aurora General* if she had purchased it but hearing them from the point of view of her more comical friend made them even more interesting and vastly more entertaining to listen to.

"I suppose you have had a lot of patients this week with the heat being so intense, Charity." Mary's timid voice drew her friend's concentration back from where it had been lingering, staring down distractedly at the lane as they walked and back to the woman next to her.

"Not especially, but why do you ask?" Charity inquired, strangely deliberating as to the reason why the weather would be such a deciding factor for her workload at the hospital.

"Oh, no reason, really. It's just that a few fathers who came to collect their children from the school this past week seemed a bit overheated. Some even said that their fellow farmers were not working out in the fields at all for the time being because of it, and whenever the weather costs those men a day of work, I know it is severe." Mary leaned the handle of her parasol casually against her shoulder but made sure it still blocked the occasion gust of wind sufficiently as she walked so as to not upset her carefully styled hair.

Charity nodded. "That seems like a pretty logical way of looking at it now that you mention it." She glanced back to the path in front of her and then out to the open view before them. "My! Is it always this busy down at port?"

"Oh, yes!" Mary exclaimed quite happily. "Rain or shine, not a week goes by where there is not some kind of ship arriving. Most only carry cargo that you or I probably wouldn't care too much about, but a few also have foreign passengers, which makes them even more interesting."

"Why? I don't see you getting this excited when we go to the General Store? How is this any different?" Charity continued to walk down the busy path and paid even more attention to the men climbing on and off the vessel to her left as they seemed to be suddenly speeding up in their efforts. "They all look the same to me, though maybe some are in need of a hot meal and some rest probably."

"Not them, silly." Mary wrapped her arm within Charity's and pulled her closer to her as she turned in the direction of the smallest of the ships and pointed. "You see that one over there?"

"Yes."

"That one came all the way from the West Indies. And, from what I overheard the other day, they say she was almost torn to pieces in a storm last spring, but here she is once again," Mary explained with great animation. "And that one over there…" She pointed to a ship that looked more like an ancient pirate vessel than one that would be carrying precious cargo. "That one is owned by Mr. Elijah Fabbri and his uncle."

"His uncle?" Charity stopped walking then and glanced over at the vessel to take it in fully. "Does he have a name?"

"Oh, yes, but I thought you already knew him. Or at least I assumed so as he works with you at the hospital." Mary's shocked expression told far more than what the other woman had even requested.

"You mean, Doctor Wells, don't you?" Charity shook her head. "Though come to think of it, he and Mr. Beckett _did_ mention Mr. Fabbri the other day in passing. With all the casual connections they have spoken of late, I should have realized they were all related in some way."

"You'd think so, but no, not by blood anyways, or so I am told. But probably in all the other ways possible as Mr. Fabbri looks to him almost like his own father."

"Is that so." Charity pondered the information given to her out in her head for several minutes more before speaking once again, "Well, ships and their cargo aside, you seem to know a lot about Mr. Fabbri, Mary… Care to share why?" She smirked in the young woman's direction, knowing precisely why the young woman in question had discovered so much.

"Oh, no reason in particular," she tried to remain vague and yet still quite obviously interested. "Most of the girls in church say he isn't the marrying type, and even more so since his father's recent passing, but _I am_ still holding out hope. Who knows, maybe he just hasn't met the right girl yet to persuade him otherwise."

"You mean he hasn't met you, that is." Charity laughed lightly at the girl's blatantly hopeless predicament.

Mary blushed. "Oh, we _have_ met, actually."

"Did you speak?"

Mary blushed again. "Not even a squawk, Charity."

Both women laughed together then at her desperate state of infatuation.

"Well, if you want to woo the man, Mary, you are going to have to find your tongue sometime," she encouraged and noticed the very man they had been discussing standing next to his uncle near the large brick building in the middle of several other smaller, wooden ones off in the distance. "Speaking of the man himself…" Her voice trailed off as she began dragging her captive friend along with her down the boardwalk towards him. "There's no time like the present, I say," she declared firmly but humorously and continued to encourage her on in his direction.

"No... wait... Charity, stop!" Mary's shoe suddenly secured itself into one of the cracks of the boardwalk pathway not more than ten feet away from where they had been previously talking and threw her subsequently headlong onto it with an ungraceful thud. "Ouch!"

"Mary! I am so sorry!" Charity turned around instantly to help her friend and bent down next to her to assess her possible injuries. "What is the matter?"

"It's my shoe. It's stuck, I think." Mary tried to dust off the dirt that had gravitated to the front of her dress in the fall and stood once more but could not manage to remain fully erect. "Ugh, and I think I sprained my ankle, too, in the process." She pouted and painfully limped out of the way from where she had been previously lying to reveal her offending article of clothing still firmly fixed to the ground beneath her skirts.

"Well, that is a pickle of a problem to be sure." Charity shook her head and put her arm around her friend to help her over to one of the nearby wooden benches. "Here, let's find you a place to sit while I figure out a way to fetch it for you." She helped her a few paces over to a place that was partially protected from the wind that was beginning to pick up now and swung around to retrieve Mary's shoe when she saw Elijah Fabbri heading their way. "Um... Mary... You might want to compose yourself?"

"Why? What is the matter now?" Mary looked up, the tears still plainly visible near the corners of her eyes, then gasped when she suddenly realized what was happening. "Heaven help me. I'm finished for sure, now, Charity."

"Perhaps... but let's try to remain calm... maybe he prefers his wives to be a little clumsy," she endeavored to make light of the uncomfortable situation by adding in a bit of humor before she then put on her most professional expression to greet Elijah.

"Good morning, ladies. May I be of some assistance?" Elijah asked politely while nodding at each of them in turn.

Charity didn't answer, instead, she only smiled and waited for Mary to say anything of note first but decided in the end that it might be best to take control of the conversation when her friend seemed entirely too dumbstruck and horrified. "We seem to have met our match with one of your boards over there, sir. Do you think you could help us free it before it starts to rain?" She asked cordially and pointed to the area of the walkway that held the lost shoe.

"Of course." Elijah chuckled lightly at the predicament and the sound of it made Charity's heart warm even more towards him. "I think that is something I can manage, miss."

Without another word, he strode over quickly to the shoe in question and made sure to take the care necessary to remove it properly without adding further damage. "There. Good as new. Is there anything else? As you said, from the look of those clouds up above, I think you are right. We haven't had a good soaking in weeks, but those appear angry enough to drop buckets at any minute." He looked over at Mary, seeming to be more than a little bit concerned about her overall condition after her fall.

"Actually, now that you mention it. My friend here was just telling me about your shipping business and how fascinated she is by it. Could you possibly explain where that particular ship came from and what kind of things you might find it carrying on <u>this</u> journey?" Charity creatively constructed an excuse to make the man stay longer for Mary's sake.

"Um... sure, if she is interested. I think I have a few minutes to spare if you don't mind risking getting a little wet by the delay." Elijah ran his calloused hand through his longer brown curls that reached all the way down to his shoulders and stepped closer to Mary. "May I?" He motioned to the area of the bench next to her that was still empty and petitioned her permission to sit.

Mary nodded, still utterly interested and disappointingly silenced by her total adoration of him. "Please..."

"I'm Elijah Fabbri, by the way." He held his hand out to her and waited for her to accept it formally.

"Mary..." The young woman bit her lip anxiously, then swallowed when he did not release her hand but chose to hold it for a few seconds longer. "Mary Hoffman," she finally added more quietly after he had released it.

"Well, Miss Hoffman..." Elijah began to comfortably regale his attentive audience with many of the interesting facts about the ships around them while Charity furtively took the hidden opportunity to walk aimlessly away, allowing her friend the time she had dreamed of to enjoy her moment alone with him at last. Mary would no doubt playfully scold her later for abandoning her when she quite obviously looked ready to run if she were physically able, but Charity knew without question that Mary would also be playing this moment endlessly in her head for weeks if not for months to follow, too.

Content to merely drink in the solitude of her own thoughts at last as she ambled along the pathway next to the bobbing ships, Charity stepped around the various piles of crates and large sacks of goods along the way, attempting to navigate her way around them and continue on in her journey. A few had familiar markings that she recognized from her time aboard her own vessel when she had immigrated to the Colonies years ago, others had stamps written in other languages that were a complete mystery to her as to what they contained.

"And what might you hold, sir?" Charity wondered curiously while turning her back to the buildings behind her and the countless men rushing about in their tasks. No doubt, the sudden proclamation of a summer squall by the loud clap of thunder off in the distance moment earlier had spurred them on in their task of removing all the waiting cargo that might be ruined. Either that or they were all just terribly eager to be done with their work for the day.

"You are certainly not something from around here, that is for sure." She eyed the unfamiliar crate with the same sharp attention as she did for some of her patients and bent over to read the label more closely, tottering just a bit on the front of her feet to balance herself more properly. "Mo... lass... es." She made out the faded description finally on the worn wooden planking that wrapped it then began to move to stand back up when she was suddenly knocked completely off balance by a passing sailor carrying a rather bulky sack of sugar or some other kind of equally dense cargo. The unbalanced load with all of its traveling momentum instantly threw her headlong into the river in front of her and away from the safety she craved of dry land.

Powerless to catch herself and prevent the inevitable, Charity gasped as she sunk instantly into the warm water over her head and then emerged only seconds later with a piercing shriek, "Help!" She went under again, only this time, further weighed down by the many layers of her heavy dress. The very same one she had vainly thought made her blonde hair appear stunningly brilliant next to it.

Desperate now to reach the surface and the oxygen she so desperately needed, she fought furiously to drag herself back up to the somewhat brighter area up above the water. "Help!" She screamed in panicked despair before plunging back under once more without relent.

More than terrified this time that she would be unable to resurface in time to not perish by the very thing that had always been her secret fear, even as a child, Charity struggled against the constricting fabric until she felt a sudden rush of water move quickly around her along with a firm hand pushing its way through it to clasp her own.

"Charity! Hold on to me!" William's muffled choice shouted from a distance as he dragged her upwards and towards himself.

"William..." Charity choked once more on the water threatening to fill her lungs and coughed some of it back from whence it came. "I can't swim in this dress!"

"Don't worry, I've got you! Don't let go." He exclaimed confidently as he wrapped his free arm securely around her body and pulled her towards the edge of the wooden boardwalk where a group of deckhands and workers were already waiting nearby to assist.

"Take my hand, Miss," one of them offered over the even louder boom the nearing storm had created and reached down to help lift her with the two others who were bending down next to him, as well.

Exhausted by the ordeal and more than a little bit humiliated by the unexpected turn of events, Charity helplessly allowed them to raise her up out of the water and carry her over to William's shipping office nearby.

"Thank you. I'll take it from here, gentlemen." William's unusually worried tone directed from the doorway behind them, as he then waited for all to depart. "Oh, and please see to the sacks of dry goods first over the crates as they are much more susceptible to moisture at the present."

With murmured agreement, the men all nodded obediently as they passed. A few of them even snickered between them about her sudden excursion in the sea, but at the moment Charity could not have cared less if the King himself were talking about her as she was no longer cognitively interested in maintaining the customary forms of proprietary at this point. Nor did she presently have the necessary energy to even rebuff them if she <u>had</u> felt so insulted.

"Are you alright, Miss Bentham?" William stepped over quickly to where she was seated and put his hand upon the middle of her back to feel the tightness of the fabric around her bodice in case her corset had suddenly shrunk. "Can you still breathe in this state?"

Charity nodded silently, then surged forward as she violently expelled the rest of the water she had swallowed onto the floor at William's feet.

Content to merely sit there and hold her hair back away from her face until she was quite finished, William shook his head and grinned at the absolute irony of the moment. "Well, I would say that this was a first for me, but sadly... it is not."

"You mean you make it a practice to rescue damsels in distress every day?" Charity closed her eyes and tried to steady the incessant pounding that was beginning to resonate within her brain with every passing beat of her heart as it tried to get rid of the added adrenaline she had just fed it.

"No, I was actually referring to the..." William paused, remembering the time on the Endeavor when he had vomited all over his new boots in front of Doctor Clarke, then thought the better of it. "Actually, never mind." He stood up and walked over to the opposite side of the room before returning a short while later with a light blanket and a linen towel, his boots squishing humorously as he walked. "This should help a little. Though if you had wanted to go for a swim, I highly recommend doing so in the future without all of those layers... and maybe when it is a bit more sunny." He placed the opened blanket around her wet frame and held out the small rag for her to use.

With a roll of her eyes at his piece of rather useless advice under the circumstances, Charity accepted the towel happily and buried her face within it, longing to just disappear inside its various layers of fabric and magically reappear elsewhere, or really anywhere where he would not see her in such a state as this. "Unlike the fish I just met down below that I would like very much not to be reacquainted with, I don't swim, William," she replied wearily through the rag and then left it held along the side of her cheek, her will to just lie down and rest for a minute almost overtaking her.

Surprised and more than a little bit confused that someone as old as she would not know how to swim, William leaned closer to examine her vitals more accurately as if needing to satisfy himself once again that she was not impaired otherwise in any other way. "Then how <u>did</u> you end up in the water in the first place?" His face scrunched up in curiosity as he took her wrist and felt her pulse to quell the rest of his concern.

"An act of God, I believe, or Divine punishment... I leave it to you to choose this time." Charity watched his expression weakly without the energy to protest in any way about his overly cautious actions. "One minute I was on the docks reading the label on one of your pieces of cargo, the next I was meeting Davy Jones, or close enough to it."

"Is that so?" William laughed lightly at her dramatic way of describing it. "Well, thankfully, you did not, because if you had, I would have definitely missed your daily interrogations if you had perished."

"Uncle William, is Miss Bentham alright?" A very worried Elijah Fabbri appeared next in the open doorway of the shipping office with Charity's friend, Mary, awkwardly limping close behind him.

"I think she will be fine once she has a minute to collect herself properly." William replaced her hand back upon her lap and stood up to greet him. "Though it does seem like some of our crew were a bit careless on the docks this morning. It wouldn't hurt to warn them again that the citizens of Philadelphia have the right to enjoy them, too, without fear of being assaulted." William tried not to laugh at Charity's expense, but he almost couldn't help it.

It was true that his heart <u>had</u> almost stopped completely when he first heard her frantic scream for help coming from the river. But nothing could have properly prepared him for the jolt of panic he experienced when she did not resurface after. Nor did he even think twice about jumping in after her, even though it might not have ended well for either of them. Moreover, the only thing that had worked tremendously in his favor at all in the whole horrible accident was the fact that he had not been wearing his customary heavy cloak, as he had luckily, already taken it off when the first storm clouds arrived just a half hour before.

"And who is your new acquaintance, Eli?" William motioned with his hand towards the young lady waiting patiently in the open doorway by Elijah, attempting to draw his nephew's focus away and onto something else entirely.

"Oh, I almost forgot." Elijah moved quickly out of the way to introduce the young woman more formally. "Uncle William, this is Mary Hoffman. She teaches over at the school."

"Ah," William eyed the girl and crossed his wet sleeves over on top of each other. "Well, it is my pleasure to meet you, Miss Hoffman, though maybe we can do so again in far more agreeable circumstances."

"Thank you, sir." Mary gave a curtsy and cast a very worried glance over at Charity.

"I was actually just getting ready to come over and ask you if you would be able to excuse me for an hour to drive Miss Hoffman home when I saw all the commotion. It seems that she sprained her ankle when her shoe caught in the boardwalk." Elijah explained easily, not overly stressed at all about taking time out of his busy day.

"That sounds like an excellent suggestion as Miss Bentham will need an escort, as well. After what she has just endured, I am not about to send her home unaccompanied, no matter how much she is probably getting ready right about now to refuse me."

"Indeed, sir." Charity rolled her eyes once more at his accurate assessment and shook her head behind him. "Though all things considered, I'm too tired to fight you today, William. Feel free to command away... I'll obey you implicitly this time."

"Good," he replied just as quickly, justifiably pleased in his open victory, even if it was certain to be terribly short-lived.

"Here, let me help you to the wagon, Charity." Mary began to hobble over to Charity's side to assist her but was stopped instead when Elijah preemptively touched her arm.

"Let my uncle help her. You shouldn't be walking on that ankle either." Elijah looked over at her tentatively before asking, "May I?"

For almost two full seconds put together Elijah waited patiently for her to reply to his question, then smiled encouragingly at her when she was still too stunned to say anything at all. "Well, I suppose that is answer enough for the present." Elijah reached down and picked her up effortlessly before shifting her easily in his arms. "You can be mad at me later for taking liberties if you like, but at least by then you will be safely in the wagon." He smirked at her subsequent timid nod in return and walked away with the woman safely in tow.

"Huh, it looks like <u>someone</u> has been watching his uncle's way of doing things," Charity muttered, then almost frowned at the sarcastic tone in which she had just uttered it when she saw William flinch yet felt equally reluctant to take it back.

"Why don't we just focus on getting you home today, shall we? Between you and me, I fear neither of us enjoys discussing politics when we are cold and wet." William remained as diplomatic as ever. "Do you think you can walk?"

"I'd rather die than have you carry me out that way." Charity moved to stand up, then felt a wave of dizziness overtake her once again. Sensing the room spin suddenly around her, Charity instinctively reached out a hand towards the wall beside her to steady herself from falling but felt William's comforting hand seize her in its place.

"Well, death by vanity aside, I'll try to make it at least look like you are doing so under your own power. Alright?" William joked at her expense, but she could sense by the way in which his arm supported her, that he was far more invested in what was transpiring than he was letting on.

"Fine," Charity mumbled and walked slowly out the door and around to the back of the building where Mary was already seated in the front of the wagon.

"It is going to be bumpy and more than a little bit undignified riding back here, but it's the best I can do unless you would like me to hitch up another wagon," William apologized profusely and helped her up into the back of the waiting rig.

"Don't worry, I was planning on smothering myself with this blanket as soon as you leave," she quipped right back at him.

"No doubt." William laughed lightly again. "Well, at least your sense of humor is still intact."

"Sorry, I'm afraid it's the only thing you have left when your pride has set sail without you, dear sir," she replied just as easily.

Elijah laughed, too, then called over his shoulder to her. "Are you ready, Miss Bentham?"

"Aye, aye, captain. All aboard the calamity express." Charity held the side rail of the wagon behind her to steady herself for when they jerked into motion.

"Calamity indeed." William grinned and shook his head. "Maybe next time you can give me a little more warning when you plan to take an adventure so I can be properly prepared."

"Next time?" Charity looked back at him incredulously, obviously no longer interested in any activity that took her beyond the confines of her home or the hospital. "This was more adventure than I will require for a month, William."

"I'll agree with you on that point for both of us, and I'll see you in an hour, Eli. But please don't rush. I have plenty to do here without you, and especially so if it does indeed start to rain. Be sure to be mindful that the ladies do not get caught up in it if you can help it, or at least not any more wet than they currently are." William called out to his nephew.

With a tip of his head and two hands on the reins in front of him, Elijah encouraged the horses into motion and guided them into the street.

Chapter Seventeen

September 13th, 1811

Highly skeptical, but also intensely intrigued, Emile studied the recent dispatch in his hand carefully that had been given to him only just this morning along with several other direct correspondences from two of his more similarly minded contacts in Washington. By all accounts, the dissident factions within his party that had been trying to persuade the other Republicans against taking more aggressive action against the British embargo had been met with more difficulty than they had initially expected. So much so that Emile was more certain than ever that most would ultimately side with whatever their current president was proposing simply to save their own position within the party's framework.

Yet even with that disappointing knowledge aside, Emile knew the real reason for their outright dismissal of considering anything contrary was most likely due to the fact that England had, surprisingly enough, chosen to acquiesce slightly in its flagrant boarding of all vessels seeking to leave port as far as the exportation of goods were concerned and had even allowed many of the ships arriving to pass undeterred. Still, with all of the perceived munificence on their part, Emile remained equally skeptical as to their true motives as it did not also mean such actions would continue to be performed in the future, or at least not long-term.

"It is but the calm before the storm, I fear." Emile frowned decidedly and leaned back in his chair to consider whatever other possibilities were open to him in the fight.

"I've got your morning paper, sir. Hot off the press so to speak." A young man who was always smartly dressed in a grey overcoat and matching trousers entered his office and handed it to him directly.

"Excellent, Brian. I am grateful for your promptness... as always." Emile took the offered paper and opened it up fully to the front page without hesitation. "Anything especially interesting I should be aware of or is the majority of it advertisements and local flavor today."

"Oh, it's probably a bit of the usual... mostly." Brian shrugged and moved to leave the office swiftly, endeavoring to avoid the negative reaction that was surely to follow when the man across from him noticed the disparaging article on the inner pages but decided to stop at the door instead to add something a bit more hesitantly, "On second thought, you might want to just turn to page two, sir, and get it over with."

"Page two ... ?" Emile's one eyebrow lifted slightly as he flipped the first page back upon itself to the very next and tried not to look overly annoyed. "So, Mr. Adair has chosen a more centrally located official to torment this week with his lengthy diatribe." Emile perused the article briefly from top to bottom to judge the tenor of it, then looked back up at Brian to see his reaction.

"What do you expect, Mr. Deschamps? It's *The Aurora*, sir. They don't exactly sell papers by publishing articles about the weather and farming tables like Bache's grandfather used to do. Mr. Franklin could sell practically anything with his name on it, but today, things are different. People expect the truth from *The Aurora* and that is what they will get. After all, there's a reason why the officials in your government are trying to shut it down." The man shook his head at Emile's perceived lack of intelligence concerning the intricacies of his profession, then turned around. "Why do you even subscribe to it anyways, sir? Aren't you the least bit worried about what the other representatives will say when they see that you are clearly supporting the enemy?"

"The enemy?" Emile almost guffawed outwardly at the man's overly dramatic choice of words and outright audacity but chose to merely lightly chuckle instead. "My dear, Mr. Murphy, I highly doubt *The Aurora* is truly that dangerous, at least not at the present." Emile stood and laid the paper down article side up and walked around his desk before taking out the silver pocket watch Hope had given him for his last birthday and opened it to check the time. "Though perhaps if I were to put it more accurately, I suppose that I have always found in life that it pays to be keenly observant of one's adversary, no matter how inconvenient it may be... or irritating." He added the last two words with more disdain than he probably should have given the fact that he <u>was</u> attempting this week to give

Hope's chosen suitor the benefit of the doubt in his personally attacking opinions and comments.

"Well, that is certainly your choice, sir. Just don't shoot the messenger if it suddenly backfires on you one day." Mr. Murphy pleaded from his position by the doorway. "And don't expect that you will also escape unharmed in the end. I like you, Mr. Deschamps. In fact, I think you have much better ideas for this country than some of your other colleagues here, but you might do best to remember what the editors did to Washington and steer clear if you don't appreciate that kind of outcome."

"Indeed." Emile smiled and the thought of how concerned the man looked over something as trivial as his client's reputation and vanity made Emile feel partially apologetic. "Your safety is assured, Brian, and I thank you for the compliment <u>and</u> your free advice. It was kindly meant," Emile pledged most patiently, then added in a bit surlier tone thereafter, "...but Mr. Adair and I <u>will</u> need to chat before his next installment, should he wish to trespass on my good graces again."

"Understood. Do you want me to pass that on to him when I get back to the office?" The man's voice almost betrayed a hint of a quiver in it at the prospect.

"No." Emile shook his head slowly, then glanced back out the window to check the current state of the weather. "Let him enjoy his moment of perceived victory for the present. I'll battle wits with him later, if I need to."

"Very good, sir," the man said as quickly as he could manage and snuck out of the door before Emile could add anything further.

With a grin and a slight wave in his direction, Emile watched him leave and couldn't help but think back to the scathing letter President Washington had written regarding the facts that had been recorded about himself and his legacy during his years of service.

When their first president had chosen to retire from public life, *The Aurora's* editor at the time had found it perfectly fitting to publish an editorial declaring, most incorrectly, that the country's declining condition was solely due to Washington's inept ability to lead it efficiently. This was all entirely based on the ideas found in some forged letters that had been passed along to the newspaper that were supposed to be from the man himself, but they were not. And some poor clerk or otherwise <u>had</u> indeed discovered the counterfeit quality of them before they had been sent to printing, but that did not stop *The Aurora* from declaring the information they contained as truth anyway. Nor did it curb the overly critical sentiment expressed by the editor thereafter.

In the end, another editor altogether did eventually take over the newspaper, but even he had faced countless lawsuits for the libel his newspaper had brazenly printed. A tedious turn of events for all involved, but one that still did not remove the stain that had already been placed on Washington's otherwise respectable character.

Walking back across the room and picking up the newest edition of *The Aurora General*, Emile sat on the corner of his desk and studied it, unsure if he truly wanted to read it at all after Mr. Murphy's ominous warning before he left. "Mr. Adair, whatever did you decide to write about me today, I wonder?"

He reluctantly read the rather eye-catching title and the first few lines in the article twice, one right after the other, to make sure he had read them correctly before gritting his teeth to hold back his growing resentment. "That man definitely knows how to bite the hand that feeds him, that's for certain." Emile continued reading the rest of the article slowly and with great concentration like he had the other document he had received this morning until he had finished it completely, then folded the paper precisely into thirds and laid it on top of the others on the corner of his desk. "Well, that should make our Sunday dinner conversation extremely interesting this week." He chuckled slightly at the man's openly condescending opinion of his recent speech and suggestions about the upcoming vote and smiled. The young man, with aspirations much larger than his pen, certainly had a real talent for his profession, a natural when it came to writing. And he <u>was</u> correct in some of his opinions, though Emile could never outwardly say so without losing his support in the offices here, but that still did not mean that Emile appreciated the candor in which he had delivered those opinions.

"Well, there is a reason why people fought to free this nation. I will just have to hope that Mr. Adair doesn't hang himself with his own rope in the end." He mused audibly but stopped reading the front page from a distance when a knock sounded then on the door to his office, followed by the entry of all of his fellow party members for their morning meeting.

Without any more available time to devote to this particular line of mental deliberation, Emile turned his attention now away from the newspaper and to whatever other topics they all would be discussing today. No doubt, a few of the more controversial ones would also be in the next week's paper or would even be discussed at a family gathering or two in the future. Nevertheless, as much as he yearned for a week where no one was talking of anything related to war or unrest of any kind, today it was all he could do to focus on the present and let the future take care of itself... as it thankfully always did.

~   ~   ~   ~   ~

Arriving at the small room off the main hallway that held only two modestly fashioned chairs and a tiny table for sequestered consultations among the staff when needed, William opened the darkly stained door and entered, feeling suddenly drained in every way by the week's events. The space itself that he had chosen for his surreptitious escape from his usual duties at the hospital was in no way an official room, per se. Nor would two people within that same space find themselves pleasantly comfortable should they be forced to find themselves together in it for a longer period of time, as it was only really large enough for one person to stretch their legs out fully in one direction. Though to be honest, now that he was looking at it more closely through his tired eyes, the whole area felt more like a roomier closet or a large pantry back in London than an actual room to speak of, but it was also just what he needed any time his mind had decided that he had experienced enough input for the moment.

In every possible way, it was dark.

It was quiet.

It was devoid of... well... anything that made him feel even more unsteady or ill at ease, which at the moment... was pretty much everything it seemed, though William had no earthly idea why.

Grateful once again for the beautiful excellence of the waiting solitude he always found there, William smiled contentedly at the inviting prospect that awaited and closed the door behind him before sitting down in one of the two chairs it held and propped up his feet up on the other one in front of him to support his longer frame better. The only thing he needed now was a few minutes to lie back and rest his neck on its back. Not a full hour of rest mind you, or even a half hour of time, but just a small, selfishly simple pause in his day today would suffice if he could only take a moment to close his eyes, exhale slowly, and allow all the stress of the morning to fall away from him. In many ways it was the one thing he could always count on to rejuvenate his fortitude for the rounds to follow when everything else inside him begged him to quit.

What's more, William felt no remorse whatsoever for his reclusive desire today either. This hidden pause from his scheduled duties felt justifiably essential for his very survival, incredibly so. In fact, in his opinion, this stolen moment of isolation he was so eager to embrace today would provide him with exactly what he needed to relax completely. So much so that before his more rational mind could convince him to do otherwise, a few seconds after reclining his head, his mind found precisely what it had been desperately craving and blissfully drifted off to a light doze.

In his newly chosen position of total repose, his body had succumbed almost all too quickly to the opportunity afforded it to escape whatever it was that had been currently plaguing him, as if it had been distractedly seeking this all along. Or perhaps, he had not realized when he had entered the room in the first place, just how very exhausted he had become recently. The mere action of stepping away from the reality of his present duties and hiding here where nothing else seemed to exist had effectively drawn his body closer to that rest with absolute precision.

Whatever the reason, in many ways it truly did not matter, or at least not in the beginning. Like in so many other instances, his life was consistently full of stacked upon events that followed a set course of cause and effect. Or rather, to put it more plainly, without his consent, there would always be instances in his journey towards eternity where his chosen action preceded some complicated consequence to follow that was both undesired and unavoidable all at the same time. This was one of those moments, and one that would ultimately make William regret his decision entirely for as he lay there extended between the two chairs, almost completely in a state of absolute slumber and relaxation, the outer door that connected the room to the main hallway on the other side cautiously opened with a slight creak.

The swinging movement of its gentle swishing outward over the wooden flooring below was so quiet at first, and the disturbance so insignificantly unimportant to his mind's greater need for sleep, that he truly did not hear it. Nor did his body move in any way whatsoever to greet the person who had then entered thereafter. Which, in hindsight, only made the situation that was about to unfold around him infinitely worse.

"Doctor Wells, I would like an opportunity with you, if you please," Nurse Bentham spoke abruptly to him with her hands placed firmly upon her hips, as if expecting his immediate response.

Oddly enough, despite what she obviously thought was a terribly rude length of time to respond to her petition, William still did not answer.

Unbeknownst to the nurse waiting across from him, his body was instead, still feverishly fighting against the mental fog that had already begun to totally incapacitate his ability for rational thought and respectful conversation.

"Doctor Wells? Did you hear me?" The nurse repeated herself once more, clearly exasperated with him now since she had been thus compelled to do so.

"I'm sorry, what?" William struggled to become coherent once more and opened just one of his eyes to view his attacker better, then closed it once more in muddy confusion. "Oh, it's you... Nurse Betham... for a minute there, I thought I must have been dreaming it."

"Excuse me?" The nurse frowned immediately at the intimate insinuation and what that all might entail but chose to cross her arms across her chest impatiently in total frustration.

"Or what I meant to say is, how delightful to meet your acquaintance... again." He fought to remain plausibly polite to his unexpected visitor while his mind tried its best to ignore the woman's overly emotional outburst and relax once more, both sides hoping inwardly that she would get the hint and allow him his moment of sequestered peace or say whatever it was that was clearly bothering her to let it go entirely. After all, surely there were other men in this hospital she could irritate as much as him if she tried. Not that he wanted her to do so, for their sake, but a distant part of him that remained consistently hostile towards her repeated criticism couldn't help wishing it all the same.

"Sir, are you listening to me?" She tapped her foot impatiently still, obviously intent on receiving a reply before she subsequently departed.

"I am now." William sighed and removed his feet from the chair to face the woman who was demanding his attention and gave her his fullest in return. "What was it you wanted to know, again? I am sorry, but I missed the first part of it."

"Which part?"

"Well..." William looked skyward and contemplated the most peaceful response possible while wagging his head back and forth in front of her from his chair. "Probably everything from the words 'I would like an' to you tapping your foot over there." William admitted honestly, but though his response had been intended to be entirely lighthearted or playfully humorous in nature while measuring it all out carefully in his mind, having been half-asleep only moments earlier, his tone came back a bit flat and emotionless, instead.

"Oh, why do I even bother?" The woman groaned loudly at what she felt was yet another dismissive attitude being directed towards her once again and turned to leave before the conversation deteriorated even more.

Feeling suddenly alarmed by the obvious offense his mental struggles had apparently created, William cleared his throat and motioned with his other hand to the chair that sat across from his own in the very small room. "Please, Miss Bentham, don't go. I just need a minute to focus again properly. If you would be so disposed to give me that time, I will be happy to listen to whatever it is that you need." William stood and shook his head briefly, desiring more than ever that he could release the fog that had remained within it for months to no avail before adding quickly, "Would you care to sit? There <u>are</u> two chairs, after all."

"Hmmm…" Charity stood for several moments longer within the open doorway, seriously contemplating his rather unexpected offer, before deciding to close the door behind her fully. "I suppose a few minutes of peace and quiet wouldn't hurt either of us today, will it?" She took the only other available seat next to his and waited patiently for him as he did the same.

"My thoughts precisely." William ran a hand through his longer blonde hair and made sure it was all still carefully pulled back into its customary, thin black ribbon that gathered it at the base of his neck. "Overall, it <u>has</u> been a rather trying day for everyone with all of the recent admissions and lectures. By the way people keep flooding in here today, you'd think that it was a full moon or some other such nonsense." William leaned forward and rested the back of his arms along those of the chair to give her his fullest focus.

"You know that old wives' tale is actually true where laboring woman are concerned, right?" Charity laughed. "Though I have no idea how it applies to all the others who have come in lately."

"What?"

"Cross my heart," she replied just as easily. "It is a proven fact that women who are nowhere near ready to give birth, suddenly find themselves in labor during a full moon, and animals, too, I suppose."

"Huh? How very strange. But, since it happens as consistently as you say, I am sure there must be a scientific reason why that is. Though honestly, at this point, why does it matter. Sometimes in medicine, you just have to believe the facts of what has occurred because it is true, but not because you fully understand it." William raised both his eyebrows in simple acceptance of yet another interesting fact about his profession and shook his head slightly. "Now what was it you were wanting to know? Is there something wrong with a patient?"

"Yes, and yet no," Charity answered honestly, still focusing instead on his last statement far more closely than William thought it had warranted.

"You have my undivided attention, Miss Bentham. Though from what I have been hearing lately from all the rumors circulating through the hospital this week, the other nurses are calling you some kind of angel of mercy." William leaned slightly in his chair to view her expression better.

"Really?" Charity's head picked up immediately at the turn of the discussion, shifting her focus from one of annoyance to that of hesitant concern. "I wonder why that is. I'm certainly no different than any of them."

It was William's turn now to shirk back slightly at her dismissal. Nurse Bentham had been anything if not outwardly vehement to everyone about her right way of doing things. To go back on that point of view now felt almost foreign to him, if not an outright lie. "Um..." He searched for the right words to convey the most recent gossip he had heard in the most appropriate way possible but gave up. "I think the title stems more from some of your patients making a somewhat miraculously quick recovery, nothing more. I wouldn't make too much of it. It's just a silly rumor, and patients heal at their own rate with or without our intervention.""Quite. As you said, it could be one of them next who performs the marvel and receives the credit." Charity shifted nervously in her chair but remained almost rigidly seated across from him.

"Goodness... relax, already, Nurse Bentham." William tried to ease the woman's concern on the matter. "I expect it is probably something similar to the full moon phenomenon. After all, as long as our patients are restored, why should it matter how they arrived there."

"Precisely." Charity placed both her hands on top of her lap but also patted the corner of one of her pockets slightly, as if needing to check the contents of it once more. "Well, what I came in here to tell you was that the notes you left for the patient you saw this morning said he was to get plenty of robust extra flies when he returned back home, but as much as I would like to see that kind of unique approach to healing for humor sake alone, I can't imagine that was what you meant."

"Extra flies?" William repeated his erroneous inscription while chuckling, then laughed even harder still. "Now, I know I am finally losing it, Charity."

As contagious as his laughter was quickly becoming, Charity also began to giggle with him but moved thereafter to politely cover her mouth after to soften it. "I must admit, it <u>was</u> a rather unique prescription... even for you."

"Unique, indeed. Next thing you know I will be telling my patients to boil eye of newt, toe of frog, wool of bat and tongue of dog." He leaned back in his chair fully and crossed his arms over his chest just as casually as if he had been conversing freely with Emile or even Nathanael.

"Well, it worked for Shakespeare, so why not?" Charity joined him in his position, completely enjoying now their simple moment of lighthearted mirth.

"Oh, I don't know." William shook his head. "It did not end too well for poor Macbeth in the end."

"Yes. Well, witch's brew aside, should I change the orders to exercise and thus prevent Mr. Fleming from having to spend the majority of his day looking for ways to catch flies?"

"Please do." William laughed again so hard that the corners of his eyes almost cried.

"Oh, and there <u>was</u> one more thing." Charity hesitated to reveal the real reason for her sudden intrusion but dove right into the subject anyway knowing that she would never sleep tonight if she did not get this off of her chest once and for all. "I was informed by Doctor Brooks just now that you told him I was being, and I quote, 'hysterical', the other day when we were treating that woman that came in from the stagecoach. Is that true?" She seriously confronted him, as the rebuking conversation she had endured earlier today had been more than humiliating to experience in front of her peers, and especially so when she had no idea why that would have been said about her in the first place.

Stunned, for he had indeed used those very words in the conversation with the elder doctor, but nowhere in the same connotation or delivery that the man had clearly repeated them, William tried again and again to compel his mouth to form a sentence, but he could not answer her. Nor would she have assumed that he had been describing her character in general when he had spoken it if she had actually been there, but he doubted that mattered even slightly at this point.

"Um, truthfully speaking, I might have said something like that, yes..." He found his voice eventually at last and began to explain slowly his defense on the matter but was cut off instantly when she rose from her chair in disappointment and began to walk out of the room away from him, her mood justifiably changed from what it had been only moments earlier. "But in my defense, it wasn't like what he said, Miss Bentham, truly," he tried to convince her quickly of his total misstep in judgement and moved on thereafter to repeat the whole unfortunate conversation to her so she could judge it for herself but stopped when she turned back to face him head-on, the fire evident once more behind her piercing green eyes.

"I was a fool to have even asked. I am sorry that I disturbed your rest, sir. Clearly, we have different definitions of the word hysterical."

"Charity, please... just hear me out." He rose from his chair and took the hand closest to him in an attempt to stop her, not knowing exactly what else he could do to make her at least pause a moment to listen.

"No, thank you, sir. Now, will you please just let me go." She tried to pull her hand away from him and depart, but William would not release it, at least not yet anyways.

"I know that anything I might say to explain what happened won't make it any better. In truth, it was probably wrong no matter how the word was said. And I'm so desperately sorry for it." He said each word of the last sentence slower still, only this time stepping closer to her with each word as if being drawn towards her by an unseen force. So close in fact, that it felt practically improper to be doing so. And yet, despite what someone might think if they saw them together like this, he simply could not pull himself away, nor could he hope to explain why he had seized her hand in the first place.

This woman was nothing short of infuriating to him on most days, while on others, she was all he could possibly think of. Yet in this singular moment where nothing else mattered around them, the thought of her critical opinion of him now in the tiny room they had been occupying for less than ten minutes put together felt more suffocating to experience than if she were to suddenly leave and never come back.

In what looked like the same inner confusion and obvious pain painted clearly upon her face, as well, Charity only stared back at him intensely and bit the front half of her lower lip, the harshness that had been etching her features softening slightly. "Doctor Wells, you and I both know that this isn't about the fact that you and I might disagree. I can handle your opinions, even if we do not see eye to eye, but to dismiss me entirely like that when I have done nothing in return to deserve it was wrong."

Nodding at the accuracy of her statement William knew there was only one thing alone that would make the situation any better—absolute contrition. "You're one hundred percent correct, Nurse Bentham. I apologize freely for my error." William released the girl's hand immediately, feeling the growing self-consciousness of his impetuous actions and also the guilt for his rude behavior earlier. "But I also need you to know that I didn't say it like how it was relayed to you, Charity," he pledged faithfully the truth of the matter finally.

"Maybe not." Charity looked down with her eyes only at the hand that had been holding hers for several moments in the gathering silence before adding even quieter still. "But you didn't exactly stand up for me either, William, and in my book, that is almost as bad." She frowned and walked out of the room silently, leaving William alone once more to deliberate on everything she had just said.

Whatever it was that had been steadily building between them for the past few months, William knew now that it was something more than a mere professional relationship of any kind. Without a doubt, that singular reaction he had experienced on so many other occasions when one of them touched the other inadvertently, connected him more to her than any other person he had ever met on this Earth. Yet even more disappointingly, his more rational mind had also been trying repeatedly to attribute that need for its recurrence to a passing flirtation of some kind so he could dismiss what he felt outright. Yet as strong as it was every time he experienced it, he doubted it very much.

There <u>was</u> something remarkably different about this woman beyond the fact that she was as beautiful as she was intelligent. Something confusingly tangible existed in this transfer of energy that made him want to stay as far away from her as he possibly could, and yet also encouraged him to be close enough to take her into his arms if she would let him.

"This is pure madness, William Wells. One hundred percent, without description, madness, and you know it." William said to himself with a sigh but also remembered the way in which his heart had quickened when she was standing near to him just now and the manner in which the hair on the back of his neck had reacted when she had challenged him openly in the hall months before.

In the days that had followed Hope's birthday party, he had met the odd sensation at first with great focus, attempting to ascertain whether or not Nurse Bentham was indeed the source of it or if his oft-times overactive imagination had merely created the alarm as a reaction to his increasing feelings for the woman.

Yet now that he had grown more and more accustomed to its daily arrival and departure, he felt no additional concern regarding it than what he might think of any other passing individual on the street, or at least none where she was concerned as the woman posed no more apparent risk to him than another member of his staff.

If there was indeed something more sinister in nature regarding her and her life here in Philadelphia, he had yet to see it.

But why on earth <u>did</u> she constantly throw his mind into complete and utter chaos every time she but entered a room that he was in?

Was that the danger she truly presented? An awkward but enticing distraction that neither of them seemed ready to appreciate at the present?

Or was he so insecure in his desire to keep his life from constantly changing that he was willing to ignore his feelings completely regarding her?

"I have no idea." William sighed once more in defeat before he exited the room and closed the door securely behind him.

Chapter Eighteen

September 20th, 1811

"No, please tell Nurse Fitzpatrick that I do <u>not</u> wish to have Mrs. Smith in the same ward as the other patients that arrived this week. I can understand why she might have placed her there while you waited for me to examine her, as they do have similar symptoms, but from what I am reading here in this chart, Mrs. Smith should not even be in this establishment, let alone in this ward. Like it or not, there are rules against admitting people in her condition, even if it pains me to send her home," William declared sternly.

"But Nurse Bentham said she should be sent directly to you especially, sir." The young nurse trembled under his harsh rebuke, for she had been almost too frightened to be on his service today at all after the many mistakes she made the last time she had worked with him.

"Did she now?" Uncharacteristically bothered for some odd reason by everything this morning, whether it was mainly due to the incessantly sunny days that had prevented him from doing anything desirable outside whatsoever for almost two weeks now, or the way in which his very clothing had been rubbing roughly against his skin all morning like a knife's edge scraping along the surface of his arm, he couldn't say. The only thing he could do for the moment to cope with it adequately enough instead of simply walking out the door and finding a sequestered bench somewhere out in the courtyard under the large maple to clear his mind, was to silently shake his head to try to diminish the added irritation Nurse Bentham's negligence had placed upon him.

By his count, this was now his second patient today that should never have been admitted, leaving almost a full week open for her to do more harm than good at this rate if he did not stop her. "Nurse Sarah, I fully realize, with great compassion, that this patient may need to have a more hands-on approach to her care, but we are not the place to do such a thing. Nor should Nurse Bentham have taken it upon herself to admit her in the first place."

"Oh, I didn't realize. Should I send her home then?" The young girl asked him politely, but the hesitance in her voice still betrayed the slightest hint of a quiver as if the woman was nearly on the brink of tears at the mere prospect of disappointing him yet again.

"What are her symptoms now?" William placed one hand upon his hip and looked down carefully at the woman, waiting patiently for her answer so that he could finish writing his rather copious notes on his patient's prognosis and continued treatment... albeit preferably this time at home.

"Um... let me see, first there was the obvious f-fever... then the sweat-ting, and a r-r-racking c-cough, sir." The girl tried to answer hurriedly, flustered as she was, but ended up stuttering uncontrollably as she began relaying the few pieces of information that she had been given before approaching him.

"Alright." William picked up his quill and dipped it in the inkwell on the tall table at the end of the room as he wrote the basic symptoms she had just mentioned in the patient's paperwork and then proceeded to ask a necessary follow-up question, "And no blood is produced whatsoever when she coughs, correct?"

"Not that I have seen." The girl shook her head quickly back and forth in response.

"Good. Since she is stable at the present, we will observe her today only and provide whatever care she requires if it becomes necessary in the hope that I am wrong about her diagnosis, but she <u>must</u> be kept somewhere isolated for the time being. If she indeed has consumption as I suspect, direct access to the colder night air will be the best thing I can think of to help her lungs heal more quickly. And knowing this now, I am sure you will agree that she won't get that within <u>our</u> walls," William advised the nurse standing before him that had been helping him since earlier that morning.

From her petite appearance to her almost child-like demeanor towards him and simple vocabulary, she was quite possibly one of the most interesting choices the hospital had made in its yearly schedule of hiring. Yet all of that mattered very little to him as a doctor just as long as she could do the work that was required of her and tend to her patients' needs like the rest of her peers. In fact, when she had first started helping at the front desk, he had been told that despite her age, she was more than qualified for the position in which she held, though he had yet to see any true evidence of it. Moreover, upon seeing her severely shaken state just now, maybe he had been wrong in placing a little too much expectation on her already, given her current level of discomfort. After all, it wouldn't do to overwhelm the poor woman completely before she truly learned her duties, or worse yet, quit.

"Yes, D-d-doctor W-wells. Should I m-move Mr. T-t-t-hompson, also?" She picked up a stack of fresh linens to prepare two of the beds out on the second-floor summer porch of the hospital, as it was the only place available in her mind that would fit that particular criteria he had just specified for their care.

"That would be an excellent idea under the circumstances, but please do leave plenty of room between them as we do not wish to spread the illness if either of them is not carrying it in the first place. No one knows just yet how this disease is communicated from person to person, so to receive two such patients in one day definitely gives me pause for concern, if not great alarm." He wrote down a few more instructions on the paperwork and turned to leave without giving the girl another glance.

"I will d-do so directly, sir." She tried to reply quickly but looked more scared than obedient when she left.

Distracted as he was, William did not notice as he was far too preoccupied mentally now with the unexpected admissions and the very real possibility of more. Epidemics like this most certainly came and went in cities both small and great whether in England or the Colonies, but the thought that they might be beginning another such event worried him more than he cared to admit.

Why only twenty years ago, Philadelphia had been struck with one of the worst bouts of illness on this continent when the Yellow Fever came knocking at its door. Some had even blamed it on arriving passengers from France and closed the harbor. Others said it was due to the indomitably long summer that year which had also driven most of the government officials away to cities further north in fright. In the end, no one truly knew how it started, only that it took far too long to end.

Thankfully for him and the rest of his companions, it had struck shortly before they all had travelled here that year but few of the families that remained from that time appeared untouched. The ravages of the disease had changed the city indelibly for decades, but it had also motivated the remaining leadership to construct the very hospital in which he was now standing.

Still, despite how dangerous all of that was, this one staring him in the face today killed in a completely different manner with absolutely no rhyme or reason for whom it chose to infect. In many cases, sometimes whole households would succumb to the dreaded disease with all of the members passing very quickly, while other patients often rallied back to health with no apparent justification for doing so whatsoever. Some even lived for years with the symptoms constantly plaguing them.

Well, like it or not, if this illness that both of his patients seemed to share truly was consumption, and if it was indeed spreading, he would know soon enough. Though hopefully not by way of news from within the walls of this hospital, for their patients' sake and his.

Utterly deep in thought about what other possible cures were available to him in regard to treating the two people currently in his care, William stepped into the semi-busy hallway and made his way down past the new surgical wing, paying careful attention not to venture too near the linens area that was connected to it or the medical disposal on the other side for fear of the attraction they always brought him. For many years, several of his colleagues had thought him odd for passing up the tantalizing opportunity to enhance his skills and perform for the esteemed administration in the new surgical arena, but William knew enough about the limits of his restraint to know that exposing himself so recklessly for something like fame or prestige would be completely foolish if not fatal for all should he be suddenly overwhelmed.

Besides, after more than twenty years working as a physician, not counting the countless others spent serving under his father, he was far more content treating all the other ailments that walked through their doors than self-promotion any day. Well, he was mostly content. There <u>was</u> still one fly left in the ointment of his personal happiness that still remained, but try as he might, he had yet to discover a way to remove it or find any answer at all really to the myriad of questions his over inquisitive mind had proposed weeks ago. Nor had the lady in question seemed to change in her disposition towards him in a way that might encourage him past the guarded state in which they normally existed.

Feeling the need to pause and collect himself once more, William took a moment to peruse the view through the observation window just outside the surgery and watched with a smile as one of the older physicians began explaining to the attentive students the various intricacies of basic anatomy. The simplistic, yet necessary introductory lecture brought back a flood of fond memories from when his father had instructed him in the very same way decades earlier, though admittedly, with far less information than was currently available to them today.

How the field of medicine had truly changed for the better in just his short time of existence! Or more interestingly, what must it have also looked like when Señor Moretti had been present with Leonardo DaVinci, the man who first proposed many of the foundations upon which their current truths were based?

"Simply fascinating," William muttered aloud in total astonishment as he contemplated yet again the enormity of how much had transpired since and considered what kind of advances those who would be following after him might possibly achieve in time.

"What is fascinating?" A familiar voice asked from behind him, triggering his body to incoherently flinch at the sound of her greeting in unconscious preparation for the possible disapproval that might soon be to follow.

Adding to that reflexive sensation, as well, was the now customary rising of the hair on the back of his neck that always instinctively correlated with her arrival, as if already perfectly timed to the very second with his other reaction. In tandem, the two made for an equally rough experience every time she passed in the most unusual way, even if she never actually said anything negative at all.

"Nurse Bentham, a delight, as always." William remained facing the window to hide his initial reaction as much as possible but still couldn't help but cast a curious glance at the reflection of the woman's face in it to judge <u>her</u> response to his greeting.

For the past week, he had been endeavoring to be as amiable as possible around her in the hopes that it might soften her disposition towards him and make up for his careless error with Doctor Brooks. Yet until this moment, she had still been unwilling to converse openly with him about anything other than what they were currently doing at the time, choosing rather to avoid his presence whenever possible than to have a repeat experience.

"I wonder." She raised her eyebrows in definite rebuttal to his overstated truth, but in all other ways, remained placidly discreet. "I can see that you are obviously very busy today, but if you have a minute to spare, I do need to speak with you, please."

"Of course, how can I help?" William agreed easily, wanting very much to keep their conversation as positive as possible.

"I am afraid it is all rather complicated, sir," Charity explained but continued to study him from afar with the same hesitantly pained expression that had now become her newest form of greeting when he saw her approaching each morning.

"Why complicated?" William's expression shifted instantly to match her own in the reflection, confusion replacing his initial reluctance.

"Well, to begin... I just left a <u>very</u> emotional young lady over in the East Wing who told me she was considering leaving the nursing profession altogether after her encounter with you this morning. You would not happen to know why that might be by any chance?”

“Maybe, though I can already tell by the tone in your voice, that it is probably my fault.” William closed his eyes and felt a familiar instant regret for not taking the necessary pains of civility this morning with the nurse that was much more than half his age, though he did not look it. In his old practice, he would have been far more focused on the delicate balance such interactions with others entailed to have been so careless, and especially so when it came to something that might actually hurt anyone’s feelings in any way similar to what he had obviously done this morning and last week. But in this larger establishment, with countless doctors and nurses constantly coming and going on any given day, it was almost all too easy to become complacent in his address of those beneath him, negligent even... or so it appeared again. “I am assuming you are referring to Nurse Sarah who brought Mrs. Smith to me at your command, correct?”

“My command?” It was Charity’s turn to appear momentarily shocked at his particular choice of words but then managed to recover swiftly. “I did no such thing.”

“Didn’t you?” William turned around and faced the woman head on, ready to defend himself further on the subject, then thought the better of it. Given that she was actually talking to him again, the last thing he wanted to do now was frighten her into silent flight. Or worse yet, insult her even further on the subject and incur her wrath. A scenario neither of them would enjoy but were equally capable of reaching in any conversation... and quickly. “Pardon my bluntness in expressing the facts alone here, but I was told, and I quote, ‘Nurse Bentham said to bring her to you.’” He crossed his arms across his chest and viewed her seriously with the same expression she normally gave him. “Did you not know your patient had consumption when you made that decision?”

“Consumption?” Charity appeared equally stunned once more at the unexpected revelation yet managed to maintain her practiced composure in front of him anyway. “Mrs. Smith has the Kings Touch?”

“Yes....” William said the word slow and drawn out, his eyes narrowing immediately at the use of the unusually antiquated term, which only caused him to study her even more before replying as no one of his acquaintance in the year 1811 had referred to the illness as that for well over a decade, if not more. “From the symptoms listed on her chart, I believe that she does,” he said finally, then continued on with a question of his own, “Though oddly enough, not many people still use that name for it, Nurse Bentham. Something you picked up from one of Doctor Brook's lectures this month, perhaps?" He paused and waited for her reaction to his inquiry, but she gave him none.

"Perhaps... or it might have been from a journal I was reading the other night," Charity responded blankly to his given explanation without even pausing.

"Well," William shook his head to dispel his errant intrigue at the moment and moved on. "As troubling as it may be to have one patient with the disease, it is also quite possible that Mr. Thompson has it also."

"Mr. Thompson, too?" Charity asked, a genuine perplexion evident in all of her features. "He said he had been fighting what felt like an inability to draw in a full breath of air all month. At the time, I was not certain if it was his lungs or his heart that was the true problem, but I thought you might," Charity added, though in the process of giving her explanation, she had now started rubbing her fingers back and forth together in nervous habit as she contemplated the magnitude of the error.

"Relax, Nurse Bentham, please," William tried to reassure her away from the panicked thoughts he had also held just a short while ago. "No one else has been exposed to my knowledge, and though I know how terribly inconvenient it will be for all of your staff to accommodate both of them on the outdoor porch, that will just have to suffice for today. If I am wrong, the worst they will suffer from is an overabundance of fresh air. But if I am right, we may have saved our entire hospital from possible contamination."

"I'm so very sorry, Doctor Wells. I had no idea... truly," Charity's voice finally exhibited the depth of the concern she was obviously experiencing, either brought on by her error or by the extreme nervousness of something else entirely. Though on both accounts, he had not the foggiest idea as to which it was or even why. "When the woman came in this morning, she only said that she had been ill a short while and honestly, I have not seen a case of it in so long that I had forgotten to be wary of the symptoms." Charity struggled to maintain her hold upon her emotions, choosing suddenly instead to stop her fidgeting and simply fold her hands tightly in front of her, her fingers appearing whiter around the edges from the pressure. "Please accept my apologies, Doctor Wells, for overstepping my position in admitting her and in not seeing it sooner. I will be more careful next time so that it will not happen again."

It was William's turn now to be utterly shocked for he had yet to receive an apology so contritely given from anyone at the hospital, much less the woman in front of him. That was usually <u>his</u> preferred method of deflection to avoid further conflict, not hers. "It is quite alright, Nurse Bentham. Mistakes happen from time to time as we <u>are</u> only human, after all. And I suppose the fault is also mine in many respects with Nurse Sarah. In my concern to protect our patients from the possible spread, I did not pay her the proper attention she deserved and for that I am sorry. If you will ask her to come help me in Receiving this afternoon, I promise to behave much better and possibly change her mind about quitting."

"Thank you, that <u>would</u> help tremendously, sir." Charity nodded and turned to leave but stopped after going a few steps and turned back around, a true timidity covering her features for the first time since he had walked her home. Though admittedly, he could not be sure it had not been there all along, as he had ceased to have been given the opportunity to examine her more closely as of late. "Do you think it might be possible for us to start afresh and set things straight between us once and for all? Maybe even find a common ground so that we are not constantly wasting all of our energy on being professionally polite all the time." She paused for just a moment to collect her thoughts fully, then held her breath a moment to compose herself further when she could not. The entire interaction, from the moment she saw him standing off in the distance by the window to his eyes that were now reaching out to her imploringly, was taking a terrible toll on her, much more than she was obviously comfortable displaying. Which, from William's perspective, only bewildered him more.

"Of course, but what's wrong, Charity?" William pried, noticing the way in which the curls in her hair almost trembled in the shadows behind her.

Shocked once again at his extremely perceptive nature, Charity blinked twice, then opened her mouth to speak slowly, but the words tumbled out nervously instead, "Nothing of consequence, I assure you. It's just..." She bit the bottom of her lip in habit once again.

"It's just what?" William took a step closer. "I promise that I won't attack you this time... or at least not intentionally."

Charity nodded, then forced herself to proceed, "Despite what I may have led you to believe of late, I <u>do</u> much prefer your lighthearted banter over the deafening silence that exists now between us."

"Silence? I am not sure I know what you mean." William feigned confusion on the subject adeptly for though he had surely been affected by the woman's presence at every turn, he was not yet ready to discuss it at length with her in the hospital, let alone in so public a place as here in the hallway.

For weeks, this moment had been the very thing he had longed for in order to have just one brief conversation with the young woman, or maybe even one short exchange that might also lead to another if handled just right. Yet now that it had arrived, he had found himself utterly at a loss for words, lacking even the cognitive ability to compose more than a short sentence here and there in response, let alone express anything of actual worth.

"Doctor Wells, we both know that you do. You are just being kind in not saying so." The stunning woman across from him with the light dusting of tan freckles across the bridge of her nose that made him wonder more than once if they were painted on or had been created by the sun, raised her head in displayed determination at his easy dismissal.

"Alright then... lying aside, what do you propose?" William looked at her in the same manner, his eyes suddenly hopeful that she might release whatever it was she had been hiding from him for weeks. Or maybe, he was just pleasantly happy that she was now offering something that would allow them to fall back into the casual manner they occasionally enjoyed in each other's presence.

"A contract of eternal peace, perhaps?" She stated matter-of-factly but did not move an inch closer towards him, nor offered him any other form of olive branch for surrender.

"Oh, Miss Bentham..." William chuckled lightly at the humorous suggestion, for it was the funniest thing he had heard from someone this month. "For a white flag of concession and honorable discharge of weapons, we would have to have been at war," William joked easily, though the truth of his words could not have been more accurately stated by either of them.

"Aren't we at times?" Charity stared blankly back at him, daring him to contradict her at all as very few of their interactions had been agreeable of late save the sporadic conversations they had enjoyed when they had finally let their guard down.

Despite what either of them might prefer, in every instance, there always seemed to remain some form of physical barrier that prevented any kind of true friendship from forming, whether that had been real or merely something else entirely that both of them were either unwilling to acknowledge or too frightened to remove.

For several minutes, William couldn't help but focus his eyes twice on every detail of her strangely presented question, uncertain as always as to what the proper response might be in situations such as this—ones where his every word needed to be carefully measured and accurate. Yet in all of his mother's social instruction, not once had she covered <u>this</u> type of topic. Nor did she probably expect he would find someone so much alike to his own way of thinking that he often felt at odds with knowing how much of himself he should freely reveal and how much he still needed to keep safely hidden away. "I believe that in light of recent events, I am fully prepared to apologize for <u>all</u> of my actions if <u>you</u> are, though I might need you to remind me just what I am apologizing for." He issued the statement he thought was concise and mostly lighthearted in nature with an added slight grin at the end, intending it to be more humorous than sarcastic in his delivery, but from the look on her face after speaking it, he realized too late that she had assumed the latter.

"Fine. Have it your way then, Doctor Wells. I am sorry to have even bothered you." Charity shook her head in total disappointment as his selfishly perceived reply had not been the one she had been hopefully expecting. "As you have previously requested, I will tell Sarah to meet you after lunch. You can make whatever amends you deem appropriate then or find me a replacement for yet another one of my nurses."

Like a slap in the face that stung immediately after receiving it, her abrupt reply following what had seemed like a perfectly amiable conversation caused William's tight hold on his composure to suddenly snap at what he felt was her outright disrespect, if not unveiled rebuke. "Is that another command, Miss Bentham?" He blurted out unconsciously, allowing a bit of the childish pettiness within him to rise unchecked.

"You tell me. You seem to know everything else," she spat back at him without remorse before turning swiftly on her heels towards the way that she had come as if the entire conversation had never happened at all.

The distracting prickling sensation that had been humming along the surface of his skin left along with her once more as she strode away, but the immediate emptiness that filled the space behind her made William's throat constrict involuntarily. "Nurse Bentham... wait... please!" William called after her, and the sound of his somewhat raised voice in his attempt to halt her escape grated on his nerves to hear it, for it carried none of the warmth that he normally shared with all of his friends.

Like a pinned deer that had been suddenly startled from its desired path of flight, Charity froze at his command, as he knew that she would, but did not turn around to face him when she answered, "Is there something else you require... sir?"

William cringed inwardly at the way in which the last word echoed back to him from off the walls. "Charity... I think you misunderstood me," William tried to explain apologetically as he started to walk towards the woman, experiencing the same magnetic pull he had always felt in her presence. The one that cared not for the danger it was dragging him towards, but rather more like a man who was being compelled completely beyond his control by a strong current over a rather tall waterfall.

"No, I don't think that I did," she replied rather aloofly, still refusing to budge whatsoever in her decision to leave.

"Alright, but would you at least consider having coffee with me after our shift today to discuss this all properly? Maybe somewhere where we could both be as frank as necessary." He paused and glanced at the other staff around them that had continued to pass by during their brief discussion. "Look. I can't promise you that we will be able to sort <u>everything</u> out, at least not at first, but we can certainly try," he began to offer what he felt would be an acceptable invitation to the woman but stopped instantly when Charity finally swung around to face him in a movement that made him step back twice in response to it.

"I would rather drink with the pigs, Doctor Wells," she spat back at him defiantly and left him undeniably speechless where he stood—confounded and utterly flabbergasted by her sudden anger over something so trivial in his mind, though also... justifiably intrigued as to the real reason why.

Highly impressed, as always, of the strength she clearly possessed under pressure, he couldn't help but track her movements as she made her way all the way down the hall away from him and to the door that she subsequently flung open and walked through before he finally felt his shoulders slightly relax. "What in the world did I ever do to that woman to make her hate me so much?" William muttered under his breath numbly in pure astonishment as he struggled to grasp his guilt.

"You are alive and breathing, Doctor Wells," one of his colleagues interjected as he walked casually by, having been an unexpected spectator to their latest skirmish. "But don't take it too personally. I'm sure I don't."

"You're married," William said dryly, then chuckled, though nothing about the situation that had just occurred was funny to him in the slightest.

"I don't expect it would matter either way," he stated frankly without the least bit of professional courtesy towards the woman.

"Why?" William felt nothing but sincere regret for every dismally negative encounter he had ever had with her for the man's assumption was totally false. The attitude Charity had often displayed towards any man in a position of authority over her was not resentment or even arrogance as he had previously assumed, it was self-preservation. In her position, she was merely seeking to find a way that would protect herself from possible attack. And sadly, that oftentimes came out more overzealous in her delivery. Either that, or the men above her simply didn't think she was worthy enough to be understood.

Moreover, though it was true that she annoyed him so much at times that it actually made his teeth hurt thinking about it, that did not also excuse his flippant remark towards her just now either. In every possible way, he had been raised to treat women better than that... even aggravating ones like Miss Charity Bentham, and he knew it.

Besides, a part of him knew she wasn't doing all of this to intentionally hurt him. In fact, from the look in her eyes when they had parted that night on the sidewalk, he knew something more was undeniably lingering behind that gaze that she longed to tell him but could not. He was still uncertain, as always, what that particularly dark item from her past might be, but like what Emma had alluded to, it was obviously something she was desperate to keep hidden to everyone else but those in whom she trusted.

Her actions towards him today were merely a manifestation of that fear, as well, and nothing more.

"It was not her fault this time, Doctor Wilson. It was mine," he attempted to set right the facts for his colleague and possibly lift her up in the man's eyes.

"Maybe so, William. Look. I know you think very highly of her, but like it or not, she really does despise all of us equally. She always has." The man waved a folder in the air in farewell as he continued on his way down the hall without a second thought regarding the plight of the woman in question.

"Indeed," William muttered, then shook his head in renewed determination to put an end to their recent upheaval. "Well, we shall have to change that, won't we?" He turned back in the direction Nurse Bentham had just retreated and followed after her, intent on convincing the woman to at least entertain another discussion with him here if joining him for coffee was so obviously disagreeable.

Yet it was at the point where he reached the end of the hall that all of those plans suddenly shifted entirely as he stopped dead in his tracks when his senses picked up once again the acute odor of his greatest temptation and largest liability while working in a hospital. The strength of the odor as it emanated towards him from under the door that Nurse Bentham had just entered gave him pause for serious alarm as it undoubtedly meant that someone very close to his location was most definitely losing blood, and a lot of it by the way in which it had travelled so far to him.

Instantly concerned that something tragic might have possibly befallen Charity or anyone else on the other side of the closed wooden door in front of him, William braced himself for what he would most likely encounter therein and opened it swiftly, allowing the fresh air from the hallway behind him to flood into the room ahead as he entered and he prayed it would dispel it slightly away from him.

As he had dreaded, but thoroughly expected, the decidedly pleasureful, yet albeit dangerously tempting scent in all its intensity, immediately flew up his nostrils as soon as he crossed the threshold of the large room as it followed its easy path directly all the way down his throat and set his senses throbbing wildly in anticipation. So intense was it in fact, that it stole away his vision slightly for a second as his pupils dilated to accommodate for the sudden change in the rhythm of his heart. In every possible way, it was the very thing he had always tried to avoid if he was able, no matter where he was, as it often robbed him of the very focus he required for his survival.

Taking a moment to allow himself just a second to adjust to the changing atmosphere around him, William reached up unsteadily to place his left hand over his mouth to muffle the attack remotely and walked just a few steps forward in search of the disturbance. Nevertheless, what he witnessed once he lifted his eyes to scan the room, knocked the wind out of him entirely and sent his heart to pounding out of control.

"Are you quite alright, Doctor Wells?" Nurse Fitzpatrick met him immediately at the inner door and touched his arm, providing him just the right amount of necessary distraction from the incessantly long length of time that he had been holding his breath to avoid losing complete control of the various levels of mental protection he normally maintained.

"Yes, I just felt momentarily dizzy there a second," William gave an appropriate excuse for his odd behavior, then glanced across the room once again for Miss Bentham, seeking to solidify in his mind as quickly as possible as to her whereabouts and obvious safety.

"Well, it _is_ far past lunch, and from how busy it has been, I doubt you have eaten properly today," she surmised truthfully but, in many ways, it also made William chuckle inwardly at the poetic irony of it.

"You are probably correct, as always." William smiled gratefully but his mind still lacked its usual ability to form a clear plan of action away from the danger he anticipated, nor had he been able to find Charity anywhere. "I think someone has been injured very gravely, Nurse?" He nodded his head in the direction of the door, but his eyes fell instantly instead with intense concentration on the middle-aged man, dressed in the humble attire of a mason or a carpenter who was silently standing in the illuminated outer doorway while also cradling a young boy that looked not much older than Elijah had been when William had first met him years ago.

"Please someone! I need help!" The man finally cried as he snapped out of his semi-breathless state at the doorway in pitiful distress—a pool of deliciously rich, scarlet blood beginning to collect at his feet from the dangling arm of the limp child that he carried.

Thankfully for all involved, the man alone was the only source of William's new waking nightmare that he would carry with him for months to follow, but at least this disturbance would be something he could hopefully deal with and leave rather than the darker alternative he had already envisioned concerning Nurse Bentham. That scenario would have never left him, awake or in slumber, and he knew it. Though why his mind would not let it go either continued to distract him—which was, in a way, also useful.

Still, with every drop that splashed onto the puddle that was now amassing on the wooden floor below, the blood in all of its pungency and allure invited William closer to examine it properly for himself, but he would not.

Without the need of any instructions whatsoever from the doctor beside her, Nurse Fitzpatrick swung around to face their newest patient and flew swiftly into motion. "This way please, sir!" She called excitedly over to him, but the boy in his arms did not move or stir from the yell that his father or the nurse had uttered nor gave any other indication of his continued existence on this Earth.

Shaking his head once more to regain his wits completely in the midst of the overwhelming experience, William rushed to his patient instinctively, his desire to help him far outweighing the other fight he was currently enduring. "Place him over here," he directed abruptly, sensing the need to keep his sentences short and quick as he motioned to the bed just in front of the man. "And please tell me what happened exactly?"

"An accident, sir." The man took three steps over to the ready bed and nearly collapsed under the weight of the stress as he laid the child on top of it, staining the crisp white linens everywhere he touched. "My boy was working with me at the new General Store when he fell out of the upper window. I don't know how or why he fell, only that it happened so fast." The man's eyes were now brimming over with his falling tears as he looked down and staggered on his feet, noticing with fresh horror the large quantity of his child's blood that was now painted sporadically upon his tanned arms and the floor like a horrible watercolor of auburn brown and blackish red.

Seeing it as well, William tried to ignore everything his senses were telling him to do as he focused his attention instead on the examination of the boy, closely listening to the boy's heart and his lungs to make sure he was still alive. Then, when he was content that he was stable enough for the present, he set to work holding pressure upon the large gash running down the child's right arm.

By the vast loss of blood, he knew that he needed to stop the flow quickly if he was going to save his life and that meant that time was of the essence.

Noticing the doctor's obvious distress and swift actions thereafter, one of the younger nurses stepped over obediently to help him, handing him the necessary supplies as he asked for them until the bleeding had subsided considerably, allowing William the opportunity to finally address the severity of the wound itself and clean it up more suitably.

"I know many other doctors might prefer that a wound such as this to be left open to the elements to drain away any possible infection, but given the depth of the cut and the fact that this seems to be his dominant arm, I feel quite strongly that we should fully close the laceration if we can to allow it the chance to heal more effectively."

"Can you do that?" The boy's father asked hopefully, cautiously skeptical about everything that was transpiring beyond his ability to comprehend.

"Possibly. It will not be easy and truthfully, I've only done it for one other patient, but if your son can manage to keep his arm as immobile as possible for at least two weeks afterwards, so as not to re-open it further, the cut may have a chance for both sides to adhere to each other and seal themselves properly," William explained politely to the nurse beside him, but also loud enough for the boy's father to overhear what he was proposing. "If I am successful, would you permit him to stay overnight with us so that we can observe his progress and make sure there are no further complications in his care?"

"Of course." The man nodded and wrung his hands silently together in front of him, still too stunned for any more words to be uttered.

Confused by the increased shakiness in the tone of the man's responses across from him, William looked up from his work on the boy and paused momentarily, realizing by the wavering stance that the father was now exhibiting that the man in front of him had just as much need of his care as his son did at the moment. "Nurse Talbot, now that his son is more stable, can you wash the area completely here and prepare the necessary items I will need to close it?"

"What will you require, Doctor?" The nurse asked dutifully, uncertain as to what she should prepare as she had never seen this kind of treatment performed before.

"If you can manage it, I will require a strong sewing needle and some of your thinnest thread. Though it matters not what color."

"You mean to sew the boy shut like a pair of socks, sir!" The nurse exclaimed rudely without thinking, for the concept was entirely foreign to all of them gathered and, in her novice opinion, absolutely outrageous.

"Why not? It works for fabric. So, I am hopeful it will do the same for him. But since this is indeed a revolutionary idea, even for me, I cannot vouch for its effectiveness in all cases. However, all things considered, if we are to look at it in a different light, leaving a gash of that size exposed to the elements will most likely cripple him for life, if not take his arm entirely if it were to become possibly infected. I'm willing to take the risk if you are, sir?" William looked up at the father from across the child for his final permission on the matter, for at the end of the day, his was the only opinion that truly mattered.

Undeniably conflicted and still rather stunned from the whole terrible ordeal, the man stared back at him; trust mixing with an understandable amount of apprehension within his chocolate brown eyes. "You should do what you feel is best."

The nurse nodded obediently at the man's acceptance, then left to fetch the rather unorthodox things her superior needed as William finally stepped around the bed and over to the man before placing a reassuring hand on top of his arms to distract the man's attention from the blood covering them.

"You mustn't give up hope just yet. It's true that he <u>has</u> lost a lot of blood, but his heart is still amazingly strong," William tried to reassure him. "There is no reason yet to contemplate accepting what may never come to pass."

"But... it's all my fault, sir. I should have been watching him better," the man's voice broke as he used the back of one of his hands to wipe away the tears that were perfectly normal in this kind of situation. "My wife died last year or else he would have been home with her and not with me."

"Maybe so, but children are fast, sir. And they are often everywhere all at once. Not a single person here faults you in this, least of all me, as I am sure you were simply doing your best." William led the man over to the washing sink on the far side of the room, away from everything that was distressing behind him. "I myself was a troubling child for my own parents. In fact, there is no telling how many times I made my own father feel very much like you do today, and he was an even better doctor than myself. And yes, I sometimes got hurt, too. I even have a few scars to prove it, but I am still here today to tell the tale. And so will your son. Why, I bet this will all end up being quite the story for everyone."

"Yes, but he was <u>my</u> responsibility, sir. This boy is all I have left in this world." The man shook his head at his apparent failure. "I'll never forgive myself if he... if he..."

"Don't even put that thought into the air," William interrupted him carefully, pausing to pick up the pitcher and checking to see if it still had some water left in it. "My friend, Preacher Beckett, always says that God has a purpose in everything that happens to us... even our calamities. And we are only here on this Earth to serve him and to discover it. Yet even in that, I also know that all of this seems utterly terrifying right now, frightening even. And it is. I won't deny it. I would be scared, too, if I were you. But you <u>must</u> also hold onto that hope you are afraid is disappearing." He held out a clean towel to the man and waited for him to accept it.

"I'll help him." Nurse Bentham stepped closer to the two men and held out her hand for the pitcher William was still holding, choosing to patiently wait for his acceptance at last. "Now, why don't we see about getting you cleaned up first, shall we? Then you can sit with your son until he wakes up? It shouldn't be much longer. You'll see."

"Thank you, Nurse Bentham. I am much obliged," William finally exhaled a sigh of relief at seeing her once more and replied cordially without daring to meet her gaze, thankful once again for her calm and cheerful presence.

Then, not wanting to waste any more time in waiting for her reply, William crossed the floor to the other side of the room to return to his patient and set his mind in motion to sealing up the six-inch wound on the boy's forearm.

Mercifully, the whole procedure took a little less than thirty minutes time from the moment that he set himself to work, and surprisingly enough, had actually not been as complicated as William had initially anticipated as the cut was cleanly made as if it had been created by a shard of broken glass or something just as precise. In fact, his father would have been quite proud of his tiny line of neat stitches that now ran down the center of the boy's arm from his elbow to his wrist, seeing as his mother was the only one in their household that was plausibly capable of sewing.

And so, with the task completed, and the last of the puddle on the floor completely mopped up and the water disposed of, William finally drew in a steadying breath and exhaled it slowly out again, desiring nothing more than to escape the hellish torture he had been forcefully a part of for the past hour.

"I think that should suffice for now, Nurse Talbot. As soon as you are able, he can be moved into the East Wing. I will check on him later this evening when I do my rounds. Now, if you will please excuse me. I need to step out for a minute for a breath of fresh air and procure some lunch as I think Nurse Fitzpatrick was correct." William glanced down at his hands, grateful once again that the physical shaking that had been present earlier had thankfully subsided considerably once he had begun concentrating more fully on the work placed in front of him. Yet now that it was done, the inner tremors that had always accompanied this form of stress returned with a vengeance, and with them also came an altogether more unpleasant feeling of panic throughout his entire body that had yet to abate in the slightest.

"Should I expect you back this afternoon, Doctor Wells?" Nurse Charity asked him from closer to the doorway while tending to another patient, her face filled with a form of misplaced concern or preoccupation that William did not have the capacity at the moment to fully comprehend.

"Yes." William nodded shakily. "I will most likely return in an hour's time, maybe two." He gave the necessary qualifier to the rest of the staff who were waiting patiently in the area and walked directly out the door where the man had entered and all the way out to the street beyond without stopping.

As frantically desperate as he was feeling now with every step adding to the overflowing deluge of adrenaline that was already coursing through his veins, his mind could only focus on doing one thing and one thing alone—putting as much distance as humanly possible between himself and everyone else around him.

Chapter Nineteen

September 20th, 1811

Feeling the frantic pulsing of his heart quicken faster with every stride, William continued down the sidewalk at a brisk pace towards his lodgings and awaiting blood supply. The toll the emergent patient had required of his mental control had been more debilitating than he had ever experienced before, causing every muscle inside of him to twitch systematically as they begged him not to walk, but to sprint the short two blocks to his home in search of the one remedy alone that would alleviate the pain he was currently experiencing. Or rather, to do anything that would release the pent-up energy that was now threatening to spill over into something far more sinister, but he absolutely could not. After all, people on the street would notice if a doctor was running anywhere in Philadelphia and as such, would most likely stop him repeatedly to ask questions. Inconsequently, ridiculous questions he might add, that he would not be able to deflect politely in the state that he was currently in.

And so, as difficult as it was for him to continue doing so, he steadily forced his body to comply, taking step after painful step as he walked deliberately, but swiftly down the mostly vacant street towards the two-story brownstone in the distance—each second drawing him gratefully closer to his intended salvation. Yet it was only when he was within reach of a mere block from his home that the bright sunlight that had been casually hiding behind a group of clouds suddenly streamed out above him, halting his progress with its forceful burn upon the exposed skin of his left hand.

"Argh!" William shrank back from the unexpected attack to a still shaded area of the pathway next to him and examined his hand carefully. For the most part, there <u>was</u> a sudden sharpness to the burn he felt that still stung within the upper layer of the tissues, but as far as he could tell, no serious damage appeared to have been made further.

Suddenly panicked at his total ineptness for leaving his protective cloak behind him at the hospital, William tugged on the bottom edges of his sleeves to cover as much of his skin as possible, then froze as a fresh wave of fear washed over him immediately when he glanced back up.

From the small area where he had sought refuge, he realized in utter horror the true immensity of his error and regretted his most careless of decisions. As far his eye could see in any direction around him, there was now nowhere he could feasibly go to escape his current predicament short of certain injury. The illuminated path that led back to the hospital behind him was now fully exposed in every way to the searing rays coming down hard upon it with not a hint of a shadow on any part of the path whatsoever, nor was it any less brilliant in front of him on the narrow sidewalk that passed between the busy street and the long row of joined houses that led up to his home.

Alarmed even more so now by the increasingly shrinking shadow in which he now stood under a small sapling that was a mere six feet taller than himself, his wits returned, if only remotely, as he contemplated quickly any possibility available to him, but unfortunately, there was none. To his dismay, not even a conveniently placed overhang or ledge seemed alternately plausible as the nearest building to his current position was almost ten feet away. Nor did there exist on this side of the street, a large enough tree under which he could leap to and hide until the shadows returned once more as most of Main Street had been cleared of the much older specimens when the hospital had been built.

Casting a quick glance around him like a confined animal, William's heart pounded anew as his panic grew even higher, sufficiently replacing for the moment, the all-consuming thirst that had been caused by his bloodlust within. Never before had he so recklessly placed himself in such a predicament such as this. Since the day he travelled back to England from the island with Nathanael, his normally methodical nature had always prompted him to be almost religious about grabbing his cloak whenever he left any building, no matter the time of day. Which only made it even more shocking that he would find himself so vulnerable on a day like today, leaving him almost reeling with a rather new crippling anxiety that stunned him more than the fear it had created.

What was he going to do?

Whatever it was, he needed to do it quickly before it was too late...
...but what?
Think William... think...
"Doctor Wells!"

William's heart leapt unexpectedly as his ears picked up a familiar voice calling his name from a block directly behind him as Nurse Bentham emerged from the very door he had just left, carefully protected by a rather large parasol and her customary short navy-blue cape.

Undeniably shaken and almost unable to compose himself at all at this point, William struggled to take in a steadying breath but tried his best anyway to put on as normal of an expression as possible for her before he swung around and saw to his enormous relief that the nurse was indeed coming directly towards him. Yet even more providential than that fact alone, William could tell, even from a distance, that she was also carrying his hooded cloak draped over her left arm. The very one he had hastily left behind in his sudden escape.

"Blessed angel..." William whispered under his breath, then looked up and tried to remain calm and unaffected under the circumstances, but in the frazzled state he was in, it was becoming increasingly difficult to do so as the shadow continued to shrink all around him to less than a foot beyond the space his body currently occupied. "Nurse Bentham, so nice to see you again," William's voice came back thick and strained, obviously contorted from the stress he was under.

"I'm sorry, but I noticed that you forgot your cloak when you left, sir." Charity caught up with him easily a moment later and extended the garment out within his reach. "When I saw it still hanging up next to my own, I thought you might require it if you were heading home. After all, it <u>is</u> a bit sunny today."

"Yes, it is. Thank you most kindly. I totally forgot all about it when I left." William threw on the neglected piece of apparel gratefully around his shoulders and buttoned the clasp with slightly shaking fingers, feeling the immense relief the safety of the small token of fabric provided.

To everyone else who might be walking past them, the garment he now clutched the edges of was merely fabric, and an odd choice at that on a hot day like today. But to him, it felt like salvation—one hundred percent divinely-sent deliverance.

Watching William with what felt like a fleeting glimpse of mixed curiosity, Charity smiled and adjusted the large parasol she was carrying to cover them both before looking away from him towards a wagon that was loudly passing by. "You <u>did</u> say that you were heading home, correct?" She glanced back at him with an expression of true concern, judging whether or not the man was still cognitively capable to proceed the rest of the way home unattended.

"Yes, only just, though not for the day, as I mentioned before." William searched for a convincing enough alibi for his abrupt departure.

"Well, when I saw you with that boy's father, you looked as though you needed more than a minute to compose yourself. I did, too, when I saw him enter. But when you then left so quickly after, I became worried and with just cause as you look positively dreadful, Doctor Wells," she explained her justification in coming after him, as if she needed to have a reason for rescuing him so surreptitiously.

"Yes, um, sometimes I do find it difficult to see someone that young be hurt so gravely, I suppose." William fidgeted with the loose hair on the side of his head that had escaped his ribboned blonde ponytail and tried to dispel the uneasiness he felt growing between them once more, though this time it had nothing to do with Miss Bentham whatsoever. "I promise. I should only be gone long enough to grab something to eat, I assure you. As Nurse Fitzpatrick reminded me, I haven't had lunch as of yet, and I also need to change my clothes before I do my rounds later this afternoon."

"Oh, did you get much of his blood on you?" Charity scanned his body from his head to his neatly trimmed leather boots, then cocked her head slightly.

"Just a tad, but nothing that won't wash off eventually."

"I see." Charity nodded as she folded the parasol closed casually when the sun had finally slipped slightly back behind a cloud above them once more.

"Well, you probably remember where I live. It's that two-story brownstone on the corner." William felt the need to make incessantly ridiculous small talk as he kicked a stray pinecone at his feet and looked up at her in-between glances back to his place of sanctuary, wishing she would allow him a moment to flee for it was consuming all his residual energy left just to remain focused and polite.

"Yes, have you lived there long?" She continued the casual conversation between them like nothing in the world had ever transpired out of the ordinary today, not to mention in the past two months.

"A few years. Nathanael and I purchased it when we first moved to Philadelphia," William answered quickly, irritation now suddenly mixing with the building anxiety over the continued delay.

"Um-hmm... interesting..." She paused and shielded her eyes with her hand to see it more clearly. "Well, if you are sure you are alright, I will head back to the hospital." Charity studied the man next to her with renewed unease, her eyes declaring more than she was saying.

"I will be shortly but thank you for your concern." William smiled cordially back, yet in that moment he felt anything but desirous of pleasantries.

Without another word, Charity turned around to leave finally, but then unexpectedly paused yet again and spun back around towards him. "This may seem a bit forward of me for saying it, but it would make me feel immensely better if you would allow me to at least walk you back to your lodgings. Call it a professional courtesy if you will." She opened her parasol once more and stepped the necessary few feet over to the sidewalk next to him, purposefully waiting for him to join her.

"Fine." William pursed his lips at the unwelcomed inconvenience but agreed as it seemed the fastest way possible to be rid of the woman and retreat home to his place of solitude. "It is but four more houses down on the right."

"I remember," she said sweetly and continued walking in silence next to him, acting very much like they were just two normal people out for a casual stroll before William retrieved his key from his lower pocket and opened the front door of the anciently constructed building expecting to see Nathanael fixing his lunch, yet no one was present on the bottom floor inside.

Content that she had achieved her goal of securing his safety at last, Charity took her cue and turned quietly to leave but stopped when William called back to her from the doorway within.

"Nurse Bentham, I feel it would be rude of me now not to at least ask you if you would like to come in since you went through all the trouble of walking me here." He held the door open for her politely, hoping, in a way, that she would refuse him outright and leave as she had done so earlier. "As far as I am aware, Mr. Beckett is probably just upstairs, so you do not have to worry about wagging tongues, should you choose to accept."

"I couldn't care less if they _did_ talk." Charity closed her parasol and climbed the short step to walk inside. "After being dunked in the Delaware River fully clothed recently, I think I have learned my lesson that life is too short for nonsense such as that drabble."

"I quite agree, Miss Bentham." William offered her a chair next to the round table near the stairs and hung up his cloak on the coat stand that was positioned appropriately by the fireplace. "If you would please excuse me for a moment, I'd like to go change?" William asked politely before turning around to flee upstairs.

Charity nodded and took off her cape as well, carefully folding it in thirds before placing it on top of her lap. "Would you mind if I fixed us some coffee or tea perhaps while I wait? You did offer to discuss those terms of surrender earlier... or is now not a good time?"

Uncertain what would be the proper response in this kind of situation, as he very much wanted the end of hostilities to commence between them, William stopped halfway up the stairs and cast a wary look back in her direction.

"I promise not to poison you if that is what you are worried about." Charity smirked up at him remembering his previous patient's prophecy on the matter.

"Well, if that is the case, then I'd be delighted, of course. Though if I get a choice, I <u>would</u> prefer coffee over tea if you are so disposed. You will find what you need on the counter in the kitchen next to the kettle." William replied and continued up the stairs before practically throwing open the door to his room and grabbing his oldest supply of blood.

It had been only two days since he had last fed in this way, which normally was sufficient to sustain him for at least that long, if not several days more, but being unexpectedly exposed like he was today in the hospital negated all the logical reasons he had established for himself in fasting any longer.

In most cases, he didn't need a great deal of sustenance to perform his duties at the hospital without distraction, just something to take the edge off the pounding in his head so he could think straight amidst the many distractions, or at the very least focus enough to push through it, but today he didn't care how much of his supply that he drank. He would drink it all and savor every last drop if it allowed him to block out the lustful desire he felt right now about ravaging anyone and everyone that might cross his path. Even the beautiful young lady downstairs set his heart to pounding out of control just thinking about her being there, though he suspected that feeling was more due to a common physical attraction than actual thirst as oddly enough, he had never once been tempted in that way towards his attraction to her at all.

"William, you are home early. Is something the matter?" Nathanael peeked his head into the open doorway of his room, a rather thick volume of some forgotten lore or theology safely towed along with him in his left hand.

"Oh, Nathanael, where do I even begin...?" The young physician plopped down on his bed and massaged his temples carefully while sipping the reddish-brown liquid intermittently, relishing both its taste and ability to abate his debilitating symptoms. "There was an extremely bad incident at the hospital today, but I will be fine in a minute."

Sizing up the expression on the weary man's face and the state of his soiled apparel, a shadow of true concern crossed Nathanael's mind as well at the news, but he did not speak his worry audibly.

"Be at peace, Nathanael. Nothing like what you are envisioning, I assure you. Or at least nothing that would expose either of us to that kind of danger, but I still need a minute to collect myself before I can return."

With a studious face that resembled more like something Sebastian might have worn once or twice when William had met him in the morning to stoke the forge, Nathanael walked over to him and touched his bare forehead with the back of his hand before replying with more deduction than he normally displayed. "I know it is late August and everyone else on the street is probably drenched in this stifling heatwave that we are still having." He paused and tried to say the next sentence as carefully as he possibly could under the circumstances, "But William, you are sweating profusely, and as you know, we do not sweat."

"I know it." William took another sip and held it in his mouth a moment longer before swallowing it. "I was shaking too, but thankfully that particular unpleasantness has already subsided."

"Is this the first time this has happened to you? The shaking, that is..." Nathanael raised the book within his hands and held it against his chest casually.

"Not to this degree of severity, no, but when we first moved to Wakefield it happened quite often. I just didn't tell you about it," William admitted honestly, too exhausted from his current ordeal to cover his tracts with a more creative deception to soften its blow.

"Huh, and all this time I thought I alone was the only one struggling." Nathanael shook his head in total dismay. "You should have told me, William."

"I know, and I am sorry, Nathanael. At the time, our tentative friendship was just beginning, and I did not want <u>my</u> weakness to impede that bond. Besides, do you really think it would have helped?" William finished the last of the container of blood he held and picked up another one as his body had still not registered that he had drank any at all.

"Maybe... but we'll never know." His friend half-smiled, then cast him another disappointing look. "That was what all those letters to Sebastian were about, weren't they?"

William nodded again solemnly. "I wasn't going to say anything at all originally, but then I thought it would help him feel more normal if I shared my struggles. I suppose it did not. Though maybe the reason why it is hitting me so hard today is that I have grown so overly accustomed to the struggle within my own profession to heed the more subtle warnings before they grow into full-blown attacks like this one today." William shook his head once more to clear it, but it continued to throb mercilessly. "You don't have to say it. It was quite foolish of me, I know."

"Will you be going back then?" Nathanael eyed his friend with growing deliberation as to his current condition, care evidently returning behind his light blue eyes, the perfect color of faded calico.

"I have to." William closed his eyes and focused his attention on breathing in and out several times to steady himself and quell his trembling nerves. "In fact, Nurse Bentham is downstairs making coffee as we speak."

"Nurse Bentham? Here? Why did you not say so sooner?" Nathanael moved quickly over to the stairway and started descending rapidly. "You rest. I will entertain our guest until you have composed yourself more properly."

"Sure... do whatever you like, friend." William drank the last of the liquid and licked his lips twice to remove all traces of what it left behind. "But I appreciate you more than you know, Nathanael."

He laid there a few minutes longer waiting for the steady pounding in his head to relinquish its hold until he smelt the distinct odor of freshly brewed coffee wafting up the stairs towards him. The aroma of the inviting liquid, as completely opposite in quality as that of the blood in his hand, smelled heavenly compared to the musty air the humidity created all around him on the second floor.

As a vampire, there were few foods in all this world that appealed to him now that he had turned, but the richness of coffee was the one he could stand with little reservation or disgust. In many ways, he even liked it when it was prepared properly. Possibly this was due to its more acidic nature or the earthiness of the beans that created a closer relationship to the iron found in human blood, but either way he didn't much care about all the scientific reasoning right now. It was simply nice to have at least one comfort food amongst so many distasteful ones pressed upon him.

Peeling himself wearily from off the bed and standing upright, he glanced into the full-length mirror across from him and frowned at the man he saw reflected there. The robust physician of almost twenty-nine years looked nothing like the man he felt within who had aged over two thirds of those years since.

And yet... he pondered deeply. *Have I grown any wiser in all that time?*

He would like to think so, but today's incident on the way home had shaken him far greater than the pool of blood at the hospital.

What _would_ I have done if Miss Bentham had not sought me out when she did?

The answer to that question alone was too enormous to contemplate or even dare to mention to Nathanael, for if he did, it would undoubtedly upset the man into following him home after work every day like a lost puppy to assure his safety from future errors. Which he had every right to do when his flat mate had nearly maimed himself in one moment of sheer stupidity, or worse...

"Most definitely worse..." William muttered under his breath and contemplated morosely once again what it might be like to truly die as a vampire.

Would it be the same as what humans experience at the moment of their passing?

Would my body simply stop taking in the oxygen it required when my heart stopped beating? Or was there something more that took place within when our immortal bodies ceased to function?

Nathanael and Charity's combined laughter echoing back up the stairs beside him in the silence, distracted him sufficiently from his self-condemnation and dark musings, gratefully drawing him away from the mirror and to something his father had always said to him, "You can't change the past, son. You can only secure steps for the future when you fail." He heard his father's voice echo softly in the back of his mind from so many years ago during his years at the university. It was sound advice then as a struggling student, and especially true today, but only if he would continue to have the common sense to heed it more often and of course, apply it.

Nodding twice with a repaired strength of mind, William changed out of his stained shirt and into a deep navy-blue one before bounding down the wooden stairs to the two waiting below, not healed completely, but definitely far more stable on his feet and much more coherent.

"William, did you know that Miss Bentham knows how to paint almost as well as you can draw?" Nathanael exclaimed excitedly from his seat at the table across from Charity. "When you come next, you will simply have to show us some of your work, Miss Bentham. From what I have seen in the various homes I have visited here; it is rare to meet someone who professes to be as talented as you are for someone so young. Can you tell me, is this an acquired skill or have you always had this talent since birth?"

Charity shook her head and smiled as she sipped the steaming hot beverage in front of her. "Goodness, no. I had to spend years perfecting it until I finally managed to get something right it seems. Though if I were to be honest, I would not say that I am a master in any one interpretation as of yet. But someday I might be."

"Years? But Miss Bentham, you can't be more than twenty." Nathanael reached over and patted the woman's hand on the table. "Surely, you are just being modest."

"That is not a quality Nurse Bentham possesses, Nathanael," William stated frankly from the kitchen counter while pouring himself a cup of coffee, then felt the sting of instant regret after uttering it. "I am sorry, Miss Bentham. That was uncommonly rude and entirely uncalled for, even for me."

"Was it?" Charity raised her eyebrows and looked up from her mug at him in playful question. "To tell you the truth, I have grown so accustomed to how people treat me at the hospital that I hardly notice the insolence anymore."

"I find _that_ hard to believe," William mumbled as he added twice the amount of cream and sugar that he normally preferred and stirred the liquid loudly, his spoon clanking noisily against all the sides in the process.

"William, tell me that you haven't been treating this poor young lady harshly still, have you?"

William sighed at his expression and shook his head in annoyance at his meddling, but did not budge an inch.

"Well, shame on you if you have, as she seems like an absolute delight." Nathanael tilted his head to examine his friend's reaction and waited for his more contrite response like the scornful schoolmaster that he always was.

"Didn't you say that you had a tutoring lesson at two o'clock today, Mr. Beckett?" William motioned with a nod of his head towards the large clock on the wall that they had brought from their apothecary back in Wakefield. By the location of its hands, he could clearly see that it declared that it was just shy of ten minutes to the hour, barely enough time to arrive promptly for the start of his lesson, let alone arriving early to prepare his materials as his friend normally preferred. Which only begged to motivate William further in the fact that Nathanael needed to leave now and walk quite briskly at that if he was going to make it.

"Yes." Nathanael looked away from their guest and examined the clock with a quick glance but practically jumped out of his chair thereafter in response. "Glory be! You are correct, William, as always. Please do excuse me Miss Betham, William, my students await."

"I am sorry to have made you late, Nathanael." William took a sip of his coffee and motioned with his eyes to the door beyond. "Please pass on my apologies."

"Not at all," he replied back as he ran a hand through his hair to flatten down any wayward pieces.

"It _was_ nice to meet you again, Mr. Beckett." Charity extended her hand formally towards the man who took it readily and kissed it.

"The pleasure was all mine, I assure you, but please do remember to call me Nathanael, as I mentioned before." Nathanael deposited his large volume into his side bag and slung it over his shoulder quickly.

"Be sure to take your coat when you go. The sun is quite intense today," William warned him discreetly before walking over to hand him the deep, brown colored cloak he always wore.

"Thank you. I will see you at supper time," Nathanael called back from the doorway and shut the door behind him.

"Well, he seems like a congenial fellow." Charity took another large sip of her coffee and closed her eyes as she savored the aroma of it. "And this is especially good coffee, Doctor Wells. Did you purchase it locally?"

"In a way... We actually just got this in earlier last week from a ship carrying cocoa beans, amongst other things. As you might remember from the other day, my friend and I maintain a small shipping business down at the East End warehouses and one of those crates you were examining before your little excursion was one that held these very coffee beans. Though I think the two pieces of cargo might have been placed a bit too closely together in transit as they seem to have affected each other dramatically. The result, as you can see, is a much finer brew in my opinion, but I'll let you be the judge. Either way, it is delightful." William took a seat across from her and crossed one leg over his knee before leaning casually back. "And yes, to add to your other statement, Nathanael is probably one of the best friends I have ever had of my acquaintance. As humble as he is kind in every word that he utters, he would probably disagree, but I doubt that man has a single impolite bone in his entire body."

"That so... an admonishment for the rest of us." Charity scanned the room around her and finally took a minute to appreciate the simplicity of all the furnishings his home contained. From the simple kitchen in the back corner, to the longer living room with the adjoining open dining space connected to it before the stairs, not a single item that occupied the space was extravagant or flashy in their appearance by any means, but rather each seemed uniquely selected, as if they held a significance and importance all their own. Yet from all other appearances, they still all blended together to form a very inviting environment, cozy even to her way of thinking.

From the tufted brown settee in the center of the room which was the perfect distance between the fireplace and the outer wall to the two other wooden rocking chairs that were carefully positioned on either side of a rather stately, black-painted fireplace containing two large, silver candelabras positioned on the white mantle above it, each item was a perfect representation of the two men who lived here so casually. What's more, on the wall immediately to the left of the door where she had entered, a large assortment of carefully drawn portraits featuring several husband-and-wife pairs, as well as other individual images of children and young adults alike were each hung perfectly arranged in smaller groups in a long line across it, followed by a small, circular table by which they now sat that appeared to have been crafted recently with just three chairs surrounding it. An identical, fourth chair did also sit nearby, but oddly enough, it was not positioned alongside its mates at the table but appeared instead to be purposely set aside in the corner of the room to the right of the fireplace with a folded blanket draped upon its back, obviously not in use at the present, but faithfully positioned to remain close by in case it was ever required.

"Are those your family?" Charity motioned with her head to the wall behind William in building curiosity, for observing the man in his natural habitat had considerably softened her opinion of him and increased her desire to learn more about his background since he had remained fairly close-lipped at the hospital about anything besides his patients.

William shook his head. "No, but they might as well be."

"Oh?"

"It might be better to say that they are as close as I have to one here at the present," William clarified discreetly.

"Does that mean that your parents are deceased then?" Charity inquired quietly, not wanting to cause offence so soon with her line of questioning.

"Not as of yet, thankfully, though at a ripe old age of sixty-five, my mother often thinks she is on death's doorstep on any given day. Mind you, most of her friends _have_ already passed, which is probably why she thinks she will be next." William laughed lightly at the comedic and yet morbid truth of the statement given. "They both live in London right now. My siblings, too, or rather they live within an easy ten miles of my family home which is a rather slight distance compared to say... Philadelphia or even Charleston or Washington, for example. But I do hear from them monthly when the post arrives through the blockade so that is a great consolation, I suppose. From what they say, their families are growing as quickly as time is passing, with no stopping in sight it seems. In fact, it wouldn't surprise me if my sister were to have more children than my brother in the end if he does not start spending more of his time at home and less in the employ of King Regent."

"It _is_ always nice to have family to support you, even if it is from a distance." Charity grimaced at the comparison of the memory she held of her own rather complicated history but did not elaborate further as she did not wish to distract William away from sharing more.

"Sometimes family is better suited from afar, and sometimes close at hand. Or at least that has been my experience. What about you? Why did you not choose to remain closer to your parents? As independent as you may seem here, I am sure it has been quite difficult being on your own in such a large city as this. Or was it because of their meddling in your romantic life, as you mentioned earlier?" William recounted their previous conversation with detailed accuracy since he had thought back on it often over the past few months when the complicated reasoning behind her silence had kept him lying awake at night.

"Huh... that would be putting it in the nicest way possible, sir." Charity raised one eyebrow and scoffed at his inference, "For most people, leaving one's childhood home is always a more difficult decision than it would appear on the surface. But for me, I was to either leave or become someone I would have hated for the rest of my life. Though in the end, I guess I have landed somewhere in the middle, after all. Without a doubt, I love my life here, but I have yet to feel at peace within it. Which only makes me ask myself even more, 'why not?'"

William nodded in great understanding. "I think you will find that we are much the same in that regard, too."

"...and in a few other areas, as well, I am sure," Charity almost mumbled back.

"Really... how so?" William countered confidently, not exactly sure where the conversation was suddenly heading.

"To begin, we definitely share the same temper." Charity set down her half-finished mug and folded her hands politely in her lap.

"On that point, I wholeheartedly concede," William admitted easily. "And the second?"

"Well, before I tell you that one, I would very much like to know why you truly felt like you needed to leave the hospital in such a hurry this afternoon? I know what you said, but you didn't even remember your cloak when you left. The one that you clearly always wear for I have rarely seen you without it outside our hospital."

Instantly holding his breath in reaction to her probing question, William's sense of alarm rose within him once again at her perceptive nature, triggering the anxiety he had been quietly keeping at bay to slightly increase as he wondered what it would take for her to believe him if she was already this skeptical.

"As I said, I imagine it was just hard seeing someone that young be so near to death. I lost a close friend of mine recently, and I don't think I have properly recovered from his absence yet." William lifted his mug and drank a large gulp of the warm liquid to hide his fear of being exposed by his apparent carelessness and habits but chose to keep whatever he said as close to the truth as possible so that he would not falter into a lie.

"I see..." The young woman eyed him dubiously before deciding to continue on in as nonchalant a manner as if she were asking him to pass the salt to her from across the table. "Then how long would you say that it has been since you became a vampire?"

Utterly taken aback by her blatantly open question, William immediately spewed the coffee out from inside his mouth and coughed several times over, choking repeatedly on his response. "I'm sorry. What did you say?!"

"You... Doctor Wells... how long... have you... been... a vampire?" She said each word slowly and deliberately, making sure he heard her completely this time, though nothing in her initial question had changed whatsoever.

For almost a solid minute, William could do nothing but stare back incredulously at the young woman across from him, his mouth half-open in astonishment and half in fear. In just a few simple words, she had effectively trapped him in more ways than one. Worse than his momentary prison on the sidewalk and far more than anything he could have imagined her ever asking him.

Moreover, for the second time in his life, less than an hour apart from the other, he had not the foggiest idea how he could ever hope to escape unharmed.

Chapter Twenty

September 20th, 1811

"I am sorry. Please excuse the mess." William finally managed to say sporadically as he grabbed the spare napkin from the center of the table and tried his best to brush the brown liquid from off his clean shirt, not wanting it to stain it too irreparably before he attempted to wipe up the equally dotted table in front of him. "And what, pray tell, would make you think something so fantastical as that, Nurse Bentham?" He tried to remain as calm as possible under the circumstances, for he could not think of a single error he could have made that would have led this woman, or anyone else for that matter, to that kind of conclusion.

Charity did not respond. Instead, she waited patiently for the man across from her to compose himself fully, silently taking a keen delight in the struggle her question had created. Then, feeling a bit more empathetic towards the doctor who had clearly not told a living soul about his transformation, she finally added, "Would it make you feel better if I told you that this was the other item we also have in common among the things I've previously mentioned?" Charity confided in him slowly as if trying to ascertain whether or not the man was ready to bolt or battle—though hopefully neither. As old as she was, she had never disclosed this secret of hers to anyone else in her existence, either.

William coughed again, still trying ineffectively to clear the coffee from his otherwise unaffected throat and stared back at her with startled eyes. "What exactly, do you believe we have in common again? I think I need to actually hear the words once more."

Charity almost giggled now at his continued difficulty but stifled back as much of it as she could for his sake behind the palm of her right hand to hide her smile. "For someone as intelligent as I know you to be, you seem to be having a terrible time grasping the obvious today, William." Charity sipped her coffee again slowly, playfully ignoring the enormity of the conversation progressing between them.

"That would also be true on both accounts. It's just that I know I am hearing the words come out of your mouth but forgive me if my mind keeps thinking you are speaking in a foreign language." William stood and moved to the counter to pour himself another cup of coffee as the previous cup had been mostly wasted on the floor and the table. Then again, at the rate at which this day was proceeding, he was going to need at least two more cups to steady his nerves if not an uneven third.

"Well then, perhaps a more direct question might be to ask, when did you first realize that you had turned?" Charity tilted her head to view him better and eyed him from the table but also watched intently the pattern of his breathing to determine if she had made a horrible miscalculation in discussing something so sensitive this soon.

By her recollection, she had sensed her own draw to him months ago when she felt an unusual sensation whenever he walked into the same room where she was, and yet looking at him now, she could see that the man had either not experienced the same or had so deadened his senses to discerning it that he was denying it altogether. Either way, the result was the same. The man across from her still remained undeniably stunned into shocked silence. Which for her, seemed awfully amusing, endearing even, since it was happening to him and not her for a change.

William set down his newly filled cup of coffee and released a long sigh that spoke volumes all in itself, feeling a terrible weight suddenly fall off his shoulders at last. "I can't believe I am about to say this..." William shook his head in resignation, with his back still to the young woman seated at the table, his course finally chosen at last. "It was near the end of November, in 1792. And you?" He turned around slowly, crossed his arms across his chest and leaned with his waist back upon the counter but did not return to his place at the table as of yet. Open conversations, such as these, already made him feel antsy and ill-prepared in normal situations, not to mention the added necessity of having to share more than what he was ready to divulge. Both were something he disliked greatly, though he clearly, could not avoid either today.

Charity only giggled more at the sight of his tortured expression and the sound of it carrying through the silence around him was like a lightness had suddenly filled the room with its timbre and vivacity.

William chuckled and couldn't help but smile at her abrupt burst of merriment, too. Out of all the things the woman could have said or done in this moment of time where everything would direct their very lives thereafter, this was precisely what he had needed. In fact, it was almost as if the lighthearted action alone shifted something deep within him and worked to further calm the nerves that had been a jumbled mess for the better part of the summer. "How is any of that funny, Charity?"

"Because that means that I am actually older than you, sir." She laughed lightly once more and the way it moved her blonde hair loosely across the back of her neck made her appear even more charming. "I am your superior."

"How much older?" William released his arms and walked back to the table before motioning for her to join him over on the settee. "You don't look a day over twenty, though I have been known to be wrong before... or so you have frequently told me."

"Don't start." She cast him a reproving glance but was in no way annoyed with him by it. "I am more than almost fifty years older in that respect, though I stopped aging at twenty-four!" She stood up from her chair and brought her coffee over with her to the settee, grateful to be finally able to find a common ground with him.

"Then I am still older, as I transitioned at 28." William sat down casually.

"That is pure semantics only, and you know it," Charity countered just as cheekily.

"Agreed," William finally acquiesced, taking in the conversation between them easily, like two people who were now almost finishing the other's sentences.

"But seriously, William, how could you not have known I was a vampire all this time?"

"Honestly?" He cast her a slight tilt of his head. "In the past twenty years, I have only met two others like us, so I suppose I haven't really paid that much attention to it. Much of what I find around me causes a similarly unpleasant reaction, so why should this be any different." He leaned back farther onto the cushion and turned his hand palm side up in her direction. "You?"

"Oh, I've met more than my fair share of our kind over the years and let me assure you that none of them were as pleasant to be around as the three of you."

"Well, that makes me feel a little better."

"It should, the last one I met was positively dreadful. When I bumped into him near the port in London, all he kept talking about were his many travels at sea and how proud he was of the way he could use his profession to hide his activities. It makes my skin crawl just remembering him even now... hateful man." Charity shivered slightly at the memory and closed her eyes briefly while she shook it away. "Though I did hear later that he might have disappeared for good, so that almost makes me feel a little better."

"No doubt." William's brow furrowed considerably as he contemplated how very similar her tale was to his own experience with Doctor Clarke, then dismissed it just as quickly, thinking that the odds would be too astronomical to be so. "Well, since you said that you could tell I was a vampire, you have probably guessed the same about Emile and Nathanael?"

"Um-hmm." Charity nodded slightly. "But I feel that I <u>should</u> caution Mr. Deschamps. He may be a bit of a charmer, but his magical glare will not work on me, I am afraid. That particular power is exclusively effective on humans alone, though I have never used it for much more than to deal with what you would call a casual inconvenience when someone was drawing a bit too close to the truth."

"Well, that will definitely make it much safer for you, but seriously, Emile only pretends to be wooing other women to keep up the playful façade that he creates wherever he goes. He is never actually genuine about any of his advances," William defended his friend as easily as if he had been discussing this topic with her for years. "Oh, and while we are on that subject, there <u>is</u> one more of us, and when I tell her that you are a vampire, she will be absolutely thrilled to meet you."

"She? There is a woman in your group?" Charity's interest piqued considerably at the surprising admission.

"Yes, Emile has a wife named Emma." William answered as he took another sip of his coffee, his body beginning to relax more and more as the conversation unfolded.

"Huh..." Charity raised her right hand up to her lips and chewed on just one of her nails as if she were contemplating something very deeply. "Did <u>he</u> change her? By the way he romances a room, I would put money on it easily, but sometimes you never know."

William smirked again at how very close she was to the actual truth. "No, though you are not wrong either in some part. Someone else, who was not related to our group in any way, changed her. But that is yet another complicated story for some other time."

"I see, though I do suppose none of this would have even happened to me either had I chosen to remain with my family and follow their plan for my life, but as you already know, I did not." Charity set her cup down in her lap and ran just one of her fingers aimlessly around the upper lip.

"Knowing you, I am sure you had a very good reason, but if you don't mind me asking, why didn't you?" William tilted his head in her direction and stroked his thumb across his bottom lip thoughtfully.

"It was something more along the lines of your own escape, I imagine."

"Ah, parental entrapment into marriage... I know it well." William nodded in empathy. "Was he that bad of a choice, or did you just not like him?"

"Both. In the beginning, he wasn't all that horrible as a prospective match. You might have even said that there was nothing wrong with the man they had selected for me if you had judged him by his appearance alone. I know I was smitten when I first met him."

"Hmmm... then it was a match made more for your family's security than yours."

"Of course. Edward had a fairly large fortune, after all, and was quite debonaire and handsome. Or at least he certainly had the attention of all of the other young ladies at the time, much like you in that regard. But when I thought about the mindless activities I would be required to perform as his wife for his sole comfort alone, like keeping his home, embroidery, entertaining his many... many friends, hosting balls, planning the meals... Well, I wouldn't mind the last one so much, but the rest assured me that if I wanted to remain even plausibly sane, I simply could not accept his proposal no matter how many pieces of jewelry or romantic platitudes he threw at me." She took a sip of her drink and held it for a moment before swallowing as her mouth was suddenly becoming very dry with each sentence she spoke.

"I imagine from the look on your face that he did not take it well." William crossed his one leg over the other and leaned back calmly on the piece of furniture, finally at ease in the tranquil setting they were enjoying.

"Oh, William... does any man take something like that well?"

William chuckled softly at the admission. "No, I suppose not."

"Well, Edward was worse. When I told him no for the last time, he was absolutely livid, as you might expect, being a proud man from a very respectable family and all. And I dare say, I was probably the first person in his life that had ever refused him anything. But when his anger alone did not dissuade me back into accepting his proposal, nor did the fear he expected would sufficiently silence me into submission to his whims, he turned a bit petty, spreading unfounded rumors about my character as if I had done anything so unworthy. Things that would make you blush if I were to repeat them, William... which I won't.

Though, in a way... I suppose he felt I deserved whatever he said, since 'I had impugned his honor,' or some other such nonsense, but at that point, I didn't much care anymore. He had dug his grave with me, and now he was going to have to lie in it so to speak." Charity mimicked her old beau's tone of voice as she recounted his statement and laughed again nervously at the end before adding afterwards something that came out in a rather more disappointing tone, "As you might have guessed, being my father's only daughter and the one destined to raise our family's fortunes, my father did not take it well at all. In truth, the last thing I remember him saying to me was that he would never forgive me for shaming him in that way as he fully believed all the lies Edward had uttered. In <u>his</u> mind, my disrespect towards my own family only furthered to confirm the rumors, which in turn, made me dead to him, or something like that." She paused and held her breath and for several moments, suddenly looked more vulnerable and hurt than he had ever seen her before.

Sensing the pain she must be experiencing in recounting such a tragic tale, William almost considered reaching forward and taking her hand several times to comfort her but chose not to push her boundaries that far. "I believe I have heard more than enough to satisfy my opinion regarding your father, Charity. You don't have to keep explaining if you don't want to," William reassured her from his side of the settee.

Charity pursed her lips in response and nodded twice, but her eyes still remained fixed on her hands in her lap. "I appreciate that, William, truly." She said quietly, then unexpectedly half-chuckled, the corners of her eyes betraying just a hint of a small tear at the edges. "You'd think after all these years that those words would still be branded on my soul from the way I am describing them, but honestly, I have tried very hard to simply forget every word that was spoken and everything else that went along with it."

"Why?" William said the first question that came to mind before he instantly regretted it as the answer was quite obviously pointless.

"Why?" Charity blinked twice as if remembering afresh the sharp sting the word had created when it was first uttered by her father.

Why was she saying anything to William about her past at all? Her mind shouted back at her incredulously even louder.

When she came here today, she had <u>never</u> intended on sharing so much about herself, let alone the bulk of what had come out. Yet now that she had begun to open up her world to the man next to her, her whole horrible mess of a story seemed to be flowing out of her like escaping water. "Wouldn't <u>you</u> try to forget all of them if you could? I mean, what kind of father tells his only daughter things like that if he truly loved her?”

“You’re absolutely right.” William finally reached over instinctively and placed his hand tentatively on top of one of hers that was resting on the cushion beside him, much like he would have done in comforting any number of his patients, though never with the same inner yearning that this moment was creating inside of him. “I am so very sorry, Charity. I had no idea your life had been so difficult.”

Without thinking, Charity gripped her fingers slightly inward as if she also wanted to flip them over and grasp his own but chose only to hold them there instead and not shift her hand from beneath his. “I appreciate that, but all things considered, my life hasn’t been so dark and melancholy, either.” She tried to smile, but it lacked any true emotion behind it now. “In my younger years I had a fantastic childhood, great governesses, and many dear friends...” She paused, then looked up into his eyes once more. “...just no one who would stand up for me when it mattered most it seemed.”

“True. Which is why what I said to Doctor Brooks was so offensive.” William shook his head in complete frustration with himself for being so careless.

Charity nodded slightly, and it only pained him more to see how much he had hurt her inadvertently as it was clearly painted upon every feature of her delicate face.

“Please believe me when I say this, that as God is my witness, it will never happen again, Charity. I promise.” William pledged faithfully then turned his head somewhat to the side when another thought struck him. “But what did your mother say about all of this? Wasn’t she willing to do anything to persuade him?” William asked hesitantly, hoping nothing else had transpired worse than what her father had done.

“What could she say?” Charity’s voice came back flat, her eyes remaining fixed on the curvature of his hand as if in a trance-like state of remembrance. “In 1742, just as much as it is in 1811, a father’s word is law. And no one, not even my mother, would dare to cross him.”

“So, I suppose in the end, there really wasn’t any choice in the matter, was there?”

“No,” her voice came back quiet and reserved, without any hint of bitterness left in it.

Noticing her deep stare and increasingly distant focus, William apprehensively removed his hand and wrapped it back around his cup. The last thing he wanted to do now was add any more regret to what she already carried.

"It's a shame that there was not some way you could have appeased them both and make amends, if for your sake alone."

"Huh, after how they both treated me, I honestly didn't <u>want</u> to." Charity shook her head indignantly to clear it and half-smiled, a slight shiver of remembrance running down the length of both of her arms. "I realized then and there that I could not continue living under their roof as long as my future was in their hands, which it would be once again if I remained... so I left. Before they could stop me, I went to my room and packed a single bag of everything I felt was most precious to me, then walked out the door and never looked back, not even for a second. Besides, at that point, what exactly was I leaving behind? Everyone in their world looked at me as tainted goods now, whether it was true or not."

"And that was when you turned? Or was it much later?" William drank his coffee for several seconds before setting it back down in his lap.

"Actually, yes. Shortly after my first month working odd cleaning jobs wherever I could find work, I was on my way to church one fine Sunday morning, south of Oxfordshire, and I simply never arrived."

"Never arrived?" William's voice betrayed true concern amidst listening to the complicated story and a definite confusion at the sudden turn of events.

"Yes. From what I remember, which isn't much, one minute I was walking in the brilliant morning sunlight, looking up at the clouds and taking in the briskness of the cool autumn breeze, and the next thing I knew I was hiding in someone's barn, struggling to remain coherent and inescapably freezing from head to toe with no sense of time or desire to live in the beginning. It was there that some poor farmer found me in whatever horrible state that I was in and nursed me through the worst of it, but unfortunately for him, it might have been better if he had left me alone to die as that was what I had wanted most of all—a simple death free from the pain I was experiencing physically and the hurt my family had caused me."

"He didn't survive, did he?" William finished his coffee, deeply invested in her personal tale of transformation for it was almost the complete opposite of his own.

At least when he had turned, he had Nathanael and Sebastian to care for him and Emile was close by, though his travelling companion at the time had been in no condition to help him whatsoever either. Why, even afterwards, God had sent Señor Moretti to guide the four of them through the worst of things and helped each of them get back on their feet after.

He shuddered to think once again what might have transpired had Emile not taken that ill-advised trip into town after his transformation. The three of them who remained in the cave knew nothing about what to expect in regard to their limitations, or how to deal with the complexities of their new lifestyle. And as sad as it was about the young girl's demise that day, her death was really the inciting incident on which stemmed their entire survival, or the catalyst towards their ultimate salvation.

"Sadly, he did not." Charity looked at the fireplace and frowned. "It is the <u>one</u> thing I wish I could change most about my past, but I cannot and that is all there is to it. He died and I lived, or whatever this is called for us now. Though why the person who changed me did not kill me outright that day, I will never know. Perhaps he or she still doesn't realize I even survived or was not planning on transforming me in the first place. Or at least, that is what I try to think happened, as a random act of violence seems a bit less consoling to consider when you are lying awake, trying to push past those kinds of nightmares to sleep at night."

"I imagine so." William thought of his own vivid hallucinations of Doctor Clarke once again and shoved the images back away into the farthest recesses of his mind before they began to affect him in front of her, too.

For several moments, the two of them continued to sit together in silence while taking in their own thoughts before William leaned his head towards the fireplace next to them, noticing her lingering attention to it. "Would you like me to fix a fire for us? It's early, but I know how difficult the cold can be some days even if it is blazing hot outside for everyone else."

"I thank you, but no. As delightful as our discussion has been, we really should be getting back to the hospital before we are missed. Besides, I think we have exhausted the subject of my life sufficiently for one afternoon. It will be your turn to divulge all the details of your own on the next." Charity stood somewhat shakily from the stress the conversation had brought upon her and walked her now empty mug back to the kitchen before placing it in the basin to be washed later.

"That is a long story indeed, and one that cannot be simply shared over coffee." William sighed in mournful resignation, considering the many instances in his life where dutiful responsibility had won out over his own desires. *How many times had he selfishly wished he could simply choose what he wanted over the good of the many? A hundred? More?*

"I'll tell you what... I <u>will</u> leave all of this pleasantness around us and go back to the hospital with you on one condition." He cast her a glance without moving, waiting to see if she would take the bait.

"Go on." Charity retrieved her cape and put it casually over her shoulders but did not look the least bit swayed by his bargaining prowess.

"I'll go back, without complaint, if we each pledge to that truce you spoke of earlier, no matter <u>how much</u> we may irritate each other thereafter because we both know it <u>is</u> going to happen... and probably daily, if not hourly." William picked up his coffee cup and waited for her to respond while secretly also hoping she would change her mind entirely and stay just a little bit longer.

"I think I can manage that, if <u>you</u> can." Charity walked towards the door and waited for him to join her. "Besides, it was getting tiresome fighting with you all the time anyway, don't you agree?"

"Exhausting would be a better description for it. You know, you really do have an incredible wit about you when you are angry, Miss Bentham." William placed the empty mug on the table and picked up his cloak as well as her parasol that was lying next to it. "Here. You will want this for the next time you need to rescue me."

"Oh, does this happen often to you, too?" Charity opened the door and stepped out onto the bustling corner, aware of the stares of more than a few people who passed her by.

"Not usually, though I cannot promise it won't now that we are friends. In my experience, calamity does love company. And sadly, it also seems to follow after you to those you touch." William locked the door securely behind him and pocketed his key.

"That is <u>so</u> not fair, and you know it." She smiled back at him.

"Maybe not..." William grinned as he remembered precisely the way she had looked when he had been compelled to practically drag her to the wagon. "But that does not also mean it isn't true, or would you prefer to defend your recent swimming excursion?"

"No." Charity scowled instantly at the humiliating memory and started walking back the easy few blocks to the hospital in silence, both healers equally content to have finally found a common balance at last after the months of constant bickering.

"Nurse Bentham?" William finally paused in his path that led up to the Receiving Room of the hospital, summoning up his courage enough at last to ask her what had been on his mind the entire journey. "If it wouldn't be too much of an imposition, may I ask you something else?"

"Yes." Charity stopped walking momentarily and turned around to face him, confused as to why he had stopped so abruptly. "Though I do wish you would continue to call me Charity outside of the hospital. It has been so nice hearing someone use my name in a way that is far kinder than it is used here."

"That <u>would</u> be nice, but only if you will also agree to call me William, as well. I know it is my title, but Doctor Wells has always made me think someone was talking to my father." William felt a deep sense of peace wash over him finally at her honest acceptance and candor.

In many ways, he had almost forgotten how refreshing a meaningful relationship could be with someone on the same intellectual level as him since he had virtually no one he could think of to discuss topics of this kind here in America. It <u>was</u> true that he had enjoyed immensely his conversations with his father and Señor Moretti over the years, but in those brief discussion, he always felt more like the student in them than an equal peer, even though neither man ever intended to make him feel as such.

"Your father is a doctor, too?" Charity stepped closer to William to allow several people to pass by behind them on their way along the pathway. "Am I to presume that this has become a bit of a family tradition for you, then?"

"He is one of the best in London, in my opinion, but I am afraid that tradition may be ending with me as I will not be having any heirs to pass it on to." William explained frankly.

"Maybe, but I wouldn't lose hope for that just yet. You never know what all might be in your future."

"Indeed... an incredibly interesting thought, but I doubt that very highly, Charity. Though speaking of futures, I <u>was</u> wondering one more thing, if I may..." William felt like a young schoolboy again, too nervous now to control his stammer in front of the teacher. "My friends and I have a gathering each month at one of our homes to discuss the events going on in our lives and such. If you recall, you stumbled upon it the last time you visited."

"Yes, I remember."

"Well, for the most part it is a simple affair, I assure you, with no commitment on your part whatsoever. But should you wish to join us tonight, as well, you would be most welcome."

"And everyone who will be there will be...?" She replied quietly, letting the sentence drop off on purpose.

William opened his mouth and shut it again quickly realizing to what she was insinuating. "The ones that will be there tonight are, but the rest of my thrown together family will not. The rest are happily ignorant, save one. Charlotte was the wife of that friend of mine who passed away."

"I see, and I am sorry for your loss." Charity thought over the proposal for a few minutes before replying, "Then with that in mind, I would be only too delighted to attend, provided Mr. Deschamps can behave himself for one night."

William grinned widely and the way in which he shook his head in response to his friend's behavior looked positively comical. "I wish I could give you that kind of assurance, Charity, but Emile is nothing, if not pleasantly unpredictable. Though I <u>do</u> promise to keep him reined in as much as I can. Or at least I am fairly certain Emma will. As far as I am aware, she will be there tonight, as well, if you would like to meet her. Something about trying a new recipe for a desert she has created, I think."

"Really? What <u>is</u> Emma like exactly, and what does Nathanael do other than tutoring?" Charity folded her arms in front of her, suddenly curious about who she would be meeting that evening.

"Well, Nathanael teaches classess at the Theological Seminary over at Princeton. And Emile, spends much of his time between here and Washington now that Mr. Madison is gearing up for war with the Canadas. Emma and he met in Paris years ago but have owned a French bakery down in Charleston until recently when they sold it to move here. Since then, she has been helping Charlotte at their farm and... actually, now that you mention it... I don't have the foggiest idea what else she does with her time." William shook his head in utter confusion. "I suppose I never really asked. But she does always appear to be happy so... Or at least I think she is..." His brow furrowed once again at his apparent lack of knowledge or even conscious notice concerning Emma's daily life. "I'm sorry... since I obviously know shockingly little on the subject, I will simply let you be the judge and make it a point to pay more attention in the future."

"Judge? Oh, I doubt anyone wants that. Besides, believe it or not, most women prefer a little secrecy in their lives." Charity raised an eyebrow at the revelation but did not look overly chastising in the least.

"Clearly." William's expression matched her own and the two of them both smiled in renewed knowledge of the secret they had both been diligently keeping from the other.

"Well, with that in mind, they all sound extremely interesting, and yes, I can't wait to meet her," Charity agreed politely. "Do you think I will have time to change?"

"Yes, but please do not trouble yourself with anything overly extravagant. Most of us are certainly plainer than our professions suggest and come as we are, all that is, except for Emile. As you have already guessed, he resides in a category all his own and is quite content to remain so." William motioned with his hand for Charity to lead the way back inside the building.

"Clearly." Charity reached for the handle, then paused at the door before opening it, and began again, only this time with a bit more hesitancy, "But I do have just one follow up question to our previous conversation."

"Of course." William replied easily, letting his guard down once more for whatever it was that she may request as he simply did not care what it might cost him at this point. The past hour they had just shared at his home had probably been the most refreshing conversation he had enjoyed in months, and most likely something he would look back on fondly in the weeks to follow.

"Are you going to continue being brutal to me once we pass inside these doors, or does this truce between us only exist outside them?" She glanced back at the man severely, daring him to answer in a way that would make him regret it thereafter.

"Well…" William laughed lightly yet again, then added more respectfully, "Judging by the look on your face right now, I think I had better change my ways within, too. Furthermore, if I know that if I am suddenly nice to you, maybe the rest of the nurses will stop making advances in my direction." He sighed inwardly, grateful once again for the almost miraculous change that was transpiring between them.

"I doubt it. Despite what I might have led you to believe, you are a fine catch, Doctor Wells." She smirked and opened the door. "But it <u>might</u> be fun to see if we do make them all jealous… for a little while at least."

"You never know, it might be worth a try…" William shrugged as he followed her inside. "Or if anyone asks, you can just tell them you beat me into submission with your sharp wit."

"As if anyone would believe that." Charity rolled her eyes as she walked past the beds in Receiving. "By the way you always describe me, you make me look like a villain, Doctor."

"Hey, I thought that was my role, Nurse Betham." William smiled playfully and enjoyed very much the sarcastic look she cast back at him <u>this</u> time.

"Truce, remember?" She held her head slightly aloft as she took her place behind the head nurses' desk and handed him the stack of folders that contained the recent admissions.

"Truce, indeed." He raised his eyebrows at the disparaging look a passing nurse gave him and asked, "You think you can convince the rest of them that I am actually not that horrid, too?"

"Not a chance. I have a reputation to uphold, remember?" Charity smiled ruefully. "Like it or not, you are on your own, Doctor Wells."

"Thanks so much." He shook his head and opened the first folder before reading it as he walked to check on his last patient.

In the time it had taken William to change and return, the man and his son that he had treated earlier had already been made comfortable in one of the small rooms off the East Wing that held the patients merely needing observation. What's more, though the child seemed very tired and eager to rest within the arms of his father, he appeared to be well on the way to making a full recovery.

The only hurdle left for him now was to, of course, watch out for the dreaded signs of infection. But that being said, barring any future complications, William felt certain that the boy would retain the use of his limb for many more adventures to follow.

Chapter Twenty-One

October 1st, 1811

When the first light drizzle of the approaching storm began a little after supper, William had decided, like most of the other residents of Philadelphia, to retire early in the evening, almost lulled to sleep by the soft murmur of the rain's light pinging against the glass. Or at least, that had been his initial intention before the brilliant flashes of the sporadically increasing lightning awakened him around midnight, steadily lighting up his room and painting eerily foreboding shadows along the ceiling and floor beside his bed. Nor was it much longer thereafter before they were also accompanied occasionally by the loud rumbles of rolling thunder that then shook the sturdy walls around him.

The storm for which they had long-awaited had come quiet and steady in the beginning, as if following a rhythmic pattern, much like those in a musical score that Emile often enjoyed playing. Yet when the gentle gusts of wind that accompanied the crashing thunder increased in their ferocity and drove the rain into a hail-like torrent that threatened to gain entry through those very same windows, William's nerves sent waves of tremors throughout his whole being as they remembered with complete accuracy, the hurricane he had escaped years ago.

For the past fifteen years, his near-death experience at sea had been the <u>one</u> memory he could never seem to escape from no matter how hard he tried to forget it. Emile, too, for that matter as he had often shared with William his deep aversion to this type of weather, as well as the details of his almost tangibly accurate nightmares that always accompanied it. The ones that made both his friend and himself sweat profusely and set their heart to pounding just contemplating enduring it once more.

This type of traumatic response was probably the only thing they would forever have in common. Which was probably why they had both endured Nathanael's rantings after Elsie's death for as long as they did. At the time, Nathanael had thought they were doing so out of pure compassion, but William knew it was something much more than that, though he could not really explain it well then. In his mind, part of his path to dealing with the present was also the necessity of making his peace with the past. And although William had endured faithfully the long months that had turned into even longer years facing the immense difficulties brought on by those waking dreams, they <u>had</u> thankfully lessened in their severity over time.

Or at least they had for the most part. It was only on nights like tonight, when the conditions became so strangely similar to his realistic nightmares, that his body refused to obey logical reasoning. That night in the rowboat, battling the waves that almost capsized their small vessel many times over, was imprinted on his brain like a white-hot branding iron, searing it afresh with each new flash of lightning across the floorboards.

Unconsciously flinching once more and pulling the sheet tighter around him, he remembered anew how frightening the ocean had seemed every time a brief illumination from the lightning overhead revealed horrific waves that seemed taller than the very ship they had just escaped. Oddly enough, he probably would have preferred the total darkness of the roiling abyss compared to that. That blissful ignorance amidst their struggle could have blocked the repeated terror concerning their close proximity to certain death, making it infinitely better than being stunned repeatedly over and over again in paralyzing horror.

It had taken everything in them both to reach the safety of the island that day, leaving a scar deep within them far broader than the matching crescent shaped bite mark that lay upon the surface of their necks. In fact, looking back on it again, William needed no convincing at all to admit that those two nights put together were the worst by far in the totality of his existence. The intense stress he and Emile had endured in just trying to stay alive clung to him with every breath he took tonight, warning him against future excursions at sea.

Cowering in the darkness of his room once more, William felt trapped all over again, but not by an ocean of water at all, but rather by a vast sea of anxiety. With grasping fingers, it held him fast beneath the sheets, almost choking him, despite his inability to see or even attack it physically to find release.

Like a man that was certain to drown under the weight that he was currently carrying, William clasped his eyes tightly shut to block out the light that continued to assault him and tried to think of something else entirely. "It's just a storm, like all the others, William. It <u>will</u> pass," William whispered hoarsely to himself as his desperation to be finally free of the fear that begged to control him once more forced him now to search for anything that would distract his mind away from the darker thoughts that threatened to pull him under, just like those ferocious waves.

From his experience at the hospital, he knew that he was not alone in this unusual debilitation. Other men much older and wiser than himself had suffered from similar episodes, though most soldiers from the war would not speak of it to their families and friends for fear of their certain judgement. A few had even chosen to approach him discreetly at the hospital over the years, desirous of some kind of medical remediation to dull the worst of their symptoms. Others just needed to know they were not indeed going crazy. Or they merely required a confirmation from someone they trusted that what they were experiencing was actually normal for all that they had endured. And it was, in a way. In fact, as far as William could tell, it was at least as normal as anyone could call it, for he knew from personal experience that it was not a condition that could be necessarily cured.

Feeling empathetically inclined to the pain they were enduring; he had tried to help as much as he could, but the only treatments he could suggest in the medical realm were merely stop-gap measures for a much bigger problem. Or to put it more bluntly, like any other dam with a tiny crack upon its surface, he feared that with repeated pressure and lack of care, that dam, whether physical or mental, would most likely leak, if not fail entirely if pushed beyond its limitations eventually. A fear he held for himself, as well, when he longed to stop the nightmares altogether.

The only thing he had discovered to date that was far safer for his patients than the laudanum that most physicians prescribed were his own weekly conversations with his friends. Granted, their patient ears were not a cure entirely, as the fear never completely went away, like during severe storms like tonight. But their repeated counsel <u>did</u> help to appease the ocean of anxiety that periodically threatened to drown him, and Emile, too, for though his friend was less reticent to speak about it than William, William was certain he was also passing a sleepless night tonight.

On and on for another half an hour the storm raged without relent, threatening to topple their small abode into the same pile of rubble that had ended Sebastian, until, to his great relief, the wind eventually decided to die down an hour or two after midnight. Sheer thankfulness immediately flooded over him with its blissful passing, but the subsequent silence that settled all throughout the house afterwards began to unnerve him almost as much as the strobing brilliance.

Just like the cave, the entire world with which he was endeavoring to be at peace within seemed almost deathly still, suffocating him in the thick humidity it left behind. The ink-like darkness that felt just as real as a person he could actually see and touch, engulfed his room completely as it stole away with it the oxygen he required for life.

Maybe he had been wrong, after all, about desiring the darkness over the light that night so long ago. In the light, he could at least face his fears or consistently rationalize them into submission. But in the shadows, it was another world entirely. Here, time stood still, as if something was watching him from the corner, judging his reaction to it and patiently waiting... always waiting.

Trembling now, he sat up and threw off the covers, the motion of the abrupt action sending a swift gust of air outward into the darkness as it pushed back the corners of his fear just a little.

"Are you alright, William?" Nathanael called over to him from his room across the way, obviously not sleeping either.

"It's too quiet." William rubbed his face with both of his hands and tried to pull his unruly hair back fully from his face.

"Yes, it is, but if you need to talk... I'm awake," Nathanael offered tentatively, still sounding half-asleep but also managing to stifle a brief yawn so as to not offend him by insinuating that he was not entirely sincere.

William shook his head in the darkness and slid out of his undershirt that was now stuck to him in several places from the cold sweat he had just experienced. "No. I'll be fine in a minute. Go ahead and go back to bed, Nathanael. You have an early class tomorrow"

"As you wish," Nathanael spoke softly in return, but for the most part, he was otherwise quiet, no doubt in prayer, as William doubted he had fallen back asleep so quickly.

There _is_ one thing that will help you sleep tonight, and you know precisely where it is, William. His mind reasoned with him in the silence as it coaxed him closer to the remedy it most desired. In his rational mind, William knew that giving in to a medically induced escape was the last thing he needed to do to help him conquer the storm within his own mind. But at this point, what other options did he have? He couldn't lie awake all night but in the state that he was in now, nothing else would suffice to calm him.

Exhaling quietly as he rubbed the back of his neck in deliberation, William reached down into the drawer next to his bed and took out the small container of the liquid he tried almost never to use as it often made his dreams far more vivid than before and sometimes paralyzed him from waking. He would be lying if he said that he did not know the danger that surrounded this cure or that the use of the laudanum would actually dissipate what he was currently experiencing. Yet besides all of that, there <u>was</u> one thing it did quite nicely. It <u>would</u> at least grant him a few hours of sleep. Sleep that he desperately needed now if he was going to try to work at all tomorrow.

As a vampire, he had been granted the gift of many wonderful things after his transition, like increased strength, an immortal life, and the ability to hear and see things most others could not. But even with all of those tremendous blessings aside, that also did not mean that he held an immunity to every other human debilitation. Like everyone else, his body would forever be subject to the ills of stress, lack of sleep, pain, hunger and many other things that most people simply brushed off as being part of their daily lives.

That was his part of still being slightly human, too, he supposed.

Just this once... you know it is what you would tell others to do...

William nodded in agreement to the convincing mental advice once more and sighed heavily in the silence at his defeat yet again.

"Maybe... but only just a little..." William resigned himself finally and gave up with a low groan as he took a long sip of the bitter liquid, then closed the bottle, grateful to immediately feel the numbing sensation that the medicine always brought before he finally drifted back to sleep.

~   ~   ~   ~   ~

"William, did you want coffee with your eggs this morning or just toast?" Nathanael shook the shoulder of his friend gently, trying to revive him from his slumber.

"Huh?" William's mumbled reply came out slow and slurred before his eyes flew open in response as he sat up abruptly. "What time is it? Am I late already?"

Nathanael chuckled. "No. It is only seven in the morning, William. You still have plenty of time to share breakfast with me before you leave for the day... provided you can find anything clean to wear, that is." Nathanael cast a glance about the room that looked to be in a state of total disarray.

"Don't judge, Nathanael," William muttered grumpily as he began picking up the loose pieces of clothing that were lying on the floor here and there before placing them all within the straw basket in the corner of the room. "Happy?" He cocked his head towards his friend at the door, motioning with his hand towards the breadth of the tidied room for his final approval.

"It's not <u>my</u> room, so I care not how you keep it... or the lack thereof." Nathanael gave a funny look of mixed approval and dismay all in one. "I'll see you below."

"Fine." William ignored his antics and dressed quickly. Before he left work yesterday, he had promised Charity most faithfully that he would teach her how to properly stitch and clean out wounds this morning and he was not about to go back on his word so soon, despite how very spent he still felt from his ordeal.

Trudging down the stairs a few moments later, looking more than a little bit unkempt and wrinkled, William made his way over to the kitchen and picked up his already filled mug of coffee, grateful that his friend was fairing much better than he was this morning. "Thank you, Nathanael. This is precisely what I needed."

"Good." Nathanael moved around him and took his seat at the table with his plate of scrambled eggs and bacon. "By the almost catatonic state that you were in, I thought I was not going to be able to wake you this morning."

"Really?" William took a sip of his coffee and let the warmth spread all the way through him, hoping that it would remediate at least some of the lingering exhaustion he still felt.

"Yes, William. The first two times I shook you, you didn't budge at all."

"Didn't budge? I think you are exaggerating just a tad, Mr. Beckett." William furrowed his brow in definite sarcasm.

"I wish I was." Nathanael shook his head slowly back and forth. "From the state of drool upon your sincerely small pillow, you were sleeping like a stone. How much of that medicine did you take this time?" He scooped up a large portion of his eggs and took a bite.

"Regrettably, not enough to drive away the horrible dreams, but enough to finally get a few hours rest. If you can call it that." William's eyes still burned with the dryness they had felt upon waking. "Will you be teaching all day?"

"Um-hmm." Nathanael replied as he continued eating. "I have a pretty packed schedule, too. Why?"

"Oh, no reason. I was merely thinking it might be nice if I invited Charity over for supper." William finished his coffee and shook his head slightly to clear away the lingering fog.

"That seems like a very big reason to me." Nathanael studied him for several moments from the table before speaking carefully, "William, I know this might not be the right time for this kind of conversation, but you really <u>should</u> be more careful. Believe it or not, I don't want to encounter a corpse one morning instead of my friend."

"Me, neither…" William closed his eyes and then opened them again abruptly when a flash of a forgotten memory passed behind them. "I assure you that it is the farthest thing from my mind to do, but I <u>will</u> be more careful."

"Excellent." Nathanael accepted his sincere promise and brought his finished plate and cup to the counter. "I'll see you at supper then."

William nodded silently and followed him wearily to the door before picking up his cloak and strode in the opposite direction towards the hospital. Distracted as he was now with Nathanael's unintended prophecy of his possible demise, the gloomy weather around him matched the fog-like quality of his thoughts completely today with brief glimpses of sunshine and distant rumbles of thunder.

Taking a moment to stop in front of the hospital, William viewed the large edifice once more with great appreciation. His place of work was a marvel to be sure, with a prestigious draw that brought surgeons and physicians from all over the country just for the chance to be taught under the great Doctor Phillip Syng Physick in its surgical theatre. A man who, incidentally, came highly recommended and quickly hired. Some of the other doctors had even taken to calling him the "Father of American Surgery," though William had not seen anything so incredibly different as of yet that he had not witnessed back in London under Mr. John Hunter. But then again, few of his peers had lived long enough to have sat under both teachers to know <u>that</u> fact, and yet he had.

"Perspective is everything, I suppose," William mused tiredly as he walked through the darkly stained doors and absentmindedly picked up the newest list of recent admissions from the main desk, casually looking over it to see which needed his attention first, as was his custom almost every morning. At the top of the long list of names, there was a seemingly endless page of house calls still needing to be made this week, coupled with a few regular patients he had treated in the past. Yet it was a name near the bottom of the page that suddenly stopped his heart and made him drop the list quickly onto the desk as he rushed immediately down the hall of the West Wing and through the last door on his left—his mind instantly becoming alert.

There, cradling his screaming young son on the edge of the hospital bed was a very shaken Jedidiah and an even more worried Nancy Fabbri.

"What has happened, Jed?" William went immediately over to the child and began examining him methodically, though his first glance at the boy told him volumes more than he ever wanted to know, as it sent cold chills of dread all the way up his spine.

"James has been burning up for almost two days now, Uncle William. We tried everything you have ever shown us, but all he does is scream and cry for hours." Jedidiah handed his son desperately over to him, grateful that the man had been summoned, for he had no idea just what to expect from a stranger here. Nor was he sure he would trust whatever they would say without his uncle's final input either.

Almost as worried as Jedidiah was at the moment, William felt the boy's forehead first instinctively, noting how much hotter it was than any patient he had seen in quite some time. "You were right to bring him to me Jed. We need to get that fever down and fast." William advised quickly but tried the best he could not to show the intense alarm that poured over him at his touch. "Nurse Talbot, please go and prepare a lukewarm bath immediately. Not cold mind you, but as close to it as you can possibly manage. We don't want to shock his system too severely in the beginning or it could stop his heart entirely from the sudden change."

"Right away, Doctor." The young woman hurried out of the room obediently and went to prepare the necessary treatment without another word of discussion or question.

"Hey there, little man, what seems to be causing that fever? Do you have a tummy ache or a cold maybe?" William attempted to console the small child in his arms as he methodically moved on in his examination by lifting the center of his light cotton gown to ascertain what other symptoms he might be dealing with.

Without a word, the reflexive gasp that escaped involuntarily from his lips revealed the true fear that gripped him near the center of his chest. In fact, it was very akin to the same awful pressure he had experienced last night in the midst of his horrible recollections.

From the child's waist, all the way up to his neck and down both of his tiny arms and his legs, a distinctly ominous strawberry-colored rash covered the majority of his torso in bumpy splotches.

"Nancy, can you hold James for me while I look inside his mouth?" William tried to regain his professional demeanor once more through the fresh concern that was now spilling out into his voice.

Too stunned to speak, either that or too tired, the petite mother only nodded up and down quickly in response and took the wailing child from him carefully.

"I need to verify one last thing, though I already suspect what I will find." William snatched the mounted candle from the table next to the bed and used it to peer in closer, hoping with all his might that he was wrong about this particular diagnosis, yet from everything else that he had just witnessed, he was certain he was not.

Sadly, to his utter dismay, it was exactly as he had feared. Beyond the flushed red cheeks that looked as if the child had been slapped forcefully on both sides of his face, the boy's tongue was also bubbly and swollen with sporadic white patches down the center of it and well into his throat beyond.

"Has he had any other symptoms as of yet?" William set the candle back down upon the small table next to him and felt the child's glands along his neck. "Any vomiting, perhaps?"

"Yes, all day today, actually. Though the rash only started earlier this morning." Jedidiah's voice came thick and husky, obviously strained by the situation befalling him.

"And where is Caleb right now?" William asked discreetly while picking up the child's chart to scribble a few notes down feverishly.

"With my mother... why?" Jedidiah seemed taken aback, as his older son had shown no signs whatsoever of the illness that was currently plaguing his brother.

Suddenly feeling as if someone had struck him senseless from behind, William's whole body froze at the foreboding revelation, but then jolted back into sequence all at once as he pushed himself to explain everything plainly to them. "Because James has Scarlet Fever, I am afraid, and as such his brother is highly contagious to <u>anyone</u> he may come in contact with, as are the two of you for at least two weeks... maybe more." William stopped when he noticed the two parents begin to break down emotionally right in front of him. "Has Elijah or Hope seen any of you since this illness began? Or anyone else for that matter?"

Jedidiah shook his head. "No, no one, just Mama." His lips quivered at the immensity of what he was hearing, then appeared too overwhelmed to speak further, though the child continued to wail in his place.

"Is he going to die?" Nancy finally managed to say as she stroked her young son's head and held him as near as he would allow through his pain and confusion.

Feeling only a deep sense of compassion now as he struggled to come to grips with the terrible possibilities that might await them all very soon, William stepped closer to them and placed a comforting hand on the man's shoulder who was still seated on the bed. "I have never once lied to you Jedidiah, not when Elijah was sick with the Grippe, and not when your wife was giving birth to James or to

Caleb. You know by now that I firmly believe that a patient should be given all the information available regarding their condition so that they may make the best decision regarding their care. And so, as much as I know that this will frighten you both, I cannot withhold the fact that this illness is a very dangerous disease. And yes, some people do not survive it, especially when they are as young as James is here."

Jedidiah sucked in a large gulp of air around him and held it, as if stealing up his courage to face yet another funeral so soon, one that no parent was ever prepared to endure.

"Jedidiah... I need you to breathe for me..." William coaxed, certain that perhaps he had gone a bit too far in his blunt explanation, after seeing the marked despair now fixed firmly in every line across the top of Jedidiah's forehead. "This does not mean in any way that your son will not survive, Jed. It is merely a possibility, nothing more." William sat down next to him and chose his words more carefully this time, hoping to encourage the man away from his frightening thoughts, even though they were probably the same ones that were going through his mind right now, as well.

"But surely there is something else you can do? This is a hospital, after all. Don't they have new treatments or medicines for this?" The man stammered beside him, very close now to the brink of actual tears.

"Not for this type of illness, no."

"Then... did we just foolishly bring him here to die?" Jedidiah's demeanor was shifting more from his tortured state of sorrow and denial to one of pure frustration and possibly anger.

"Absolutely not. There is plenty we can still do to help your son in a small way, and you were right to come find me. I would have been hurt, if you had not. But for everyone's safety, we need to move you all into an isolation room until I can help you prepare something more suitable at home for his care. From there, we will work together to keep his fever at bay and make sure he drinks plenty of fluids—healthy broths mostly and whatever other foods he will accept. From what I know, the key in all of this is to keep him as cool as possible so that his body will have the time it needs to heal or it may affect his hearing or more importantly, his heart."

"What else can I do?" Nancy asked, desperate to do anything that might increase her son's chances of survival.

"You are doing it already, Nancy. For the moment, give James the love he needs, how he needs it. Do whatever it takes to help him rest. He is very young, but as Nathanael likes to say, there is always hope while there is a God in Heaven.

Trust in that and have faith." William tried to be as optimistic as possible, though he knew full-well the high mortality rate of the illness presented before him.

After all, it wouldn't help to scare the parents further. Especially when he had just recently read that roughly one in every ten people died from the disease even with the proper care and attention. James was already two days into that ten-day duration of the worst of the symptoms, and from what he could see, the child was still strong and otherwise holding his own... for now...

"Why don't you have a seat here next to Jed, too, Nancy. I need to give our staff a few more instructions before we proceed." William motioned with his hand to the place where he had been sitting beside Jedidiah.

"Will you stay with us?" Jedidah reached out desperately and clasped his hand in a vise like grip like he had done the night before William had returned to Wakefield over 18 years ago.

Stunned, the symbolism and depth of the simple action melted William's heart even more for the struggling father. "I'll only be a moment, Jed, but when we are done here, yes, I will return with you both and help at home. You are my first priority above all others, and I will not abandon my family now or ever. Now, if you will permit me, I need to get some things ready for James. Please rest just a minute if you can." He assured him and stepped out of the room before walking briskly to the center desk without stopping to talk to anyone.

"We need to move the Fabbri family immediately to isolation and clean thoroughly anything the family has touched since their arrival," William declared directly to Charity as soon as he saw her sitting at the main desk.

"Why? What is wrong?" Charity asked while retrieving the necessary supplies from the closet behind her.

"Scarlet Fever," William stated the two most horrid words he could think of at the moment without the emotion his heart was feeling at the declaration so as to not make a scene and watched as all the nurses around him froze in response, then jumped into action in multiple directions all at once.

"They will need to be moved out of the hospital as soon as possible, Doctor Wells. You are aware of that, correct?" Charity critiqued harshly, the tenor of her voice filling with the same level of fear and concern William had displayed when he first saw James.

"And they will, but first I would like to try to lower the child's fever with some salts and lukewarm water so that we can safely do so. When that is done, I will arrange for their transportation home thereafter," William explained, hoping the nurse would allow the family to remain for at least some remedial treatments though he knew that he was pushing the boundaries of the rules established for them far enough already. As fine a hospital as this was, he also had a responsibility to the other patients within its walls, patients like the hurt boy from the other day and others who were not expecting to leave this establishment with more than what they had arrived with. After all, something like this could ravage the whole hospital if it had not begun to spread already.

"You know that it is against my better judgement to allow it, but if we can isolate them until then, that will simply have to do." Charity pursed her lips in quiet deliberation, then relented. "Just like you, I won't turn someone out onto the street for a rule—valid or otherwise. And especially since they have been here for almost an hour already. Whatever possible spread may come from them being here, the damage has most likely already been done, so why not do what we can while they are here, correct?"

"My feelings precisely." William went to set down the chart but paused midway and thought the better of it. "On second thought, I will just hold onto this for the time being."

"A wise decision." Charity motioned for him to follow her down the hall to a small room across from where the couple was currently sitting. "The family can be treated here, if you think it will do." She opened the door to reveal a room that looked more like a small sitting area than an actual room of the hospital's wing. "It is big enough?"

"It will have to be." William placed the chart he was holding inside on the one wooden chair amidst the four whitewashed walls and retreated back to the family to direct them into it.

In a single file line, Charity and the other nurse entered after them with a somewhat shallow looking metal tub before placing it carefully upon a sturdy table in the center of the small room that was just big enough to allow one person to pass beside it and began filling it with the necessary water and salt.

"I am assuming you will need me to reassign your patients to Doctor Baxter when we are done?" Charity eyed William from the doorway as he stripped the child down and laid him cautiously in the water as much as he could manage without drowning the boy.

"You presume correctly," William agreed but did not look up to acknowledge her further as his focus was now entirely on the boy in front of him.

"On the whole, I do not believe that it will prove to be too difficult, as most of the patients you have been treating were discharged yesterday, save Mr. Clark and Mrs. Elliott. Though I do think Doctor Wilson might be a better choice for the young boy you helped the other day when he comes back in to have his sutures removed," Charity suggested as she moved across from him, taking a moment to admire the care with which he was using in treating the boy and the love so obviously displayed for his parents.

"Yes, he is probably the best choice out of the whole lot of them. Since he is the youngest doctor hired at this time, his mind does tend to be a tad bit more progressively inclined," William nodded at her choice, then advised the other staff present. "In light of the possible consequences we are all dreading, I would prefer it if only Nurse Bentham remained to help me, please." William instructed the other nurses to leave, in a conscious effort to contain whatever exposure the rest of them had with the family.

He would have preferred to also protect Charity, as well, if it had been indeed dangerous for either of them to remain, but after over eighteen years of being a vampire, he knew that only the two of them were immune to such exposure for he had never been sick a day since, though he had most definitely been exposed to countless illnesses and diseases during that timeframe. In many ways, it was almost as if the vampirism itself, as rare as it appeared to be, was protecting his system in some way from it. Which, as a doctor, was both fascinating to contemplate the reasons as to why and helpful, too. Though admittedly, there was nothing he could do at the moment to test that hypothesis outright to prove its validity or length of continuance, but perhaps someday, when he was a little less preoccupied with his work here he might.

Throughout his impromptu bath and into the many tense minutes that passed as the four anxious adults waited for any positive signs that their efforts were indeed working, James continued to howl at the shocking discomfort the water created against his feverish skin but quieted considerably after several more minutes resting within the water until his cries dulled to small, hiccupped sobs and sniffles. And as pathetic as the sound was for all in the room to hear, it was a welcome relief to the strained wails and thrashing he had been previously exhibiting.

Suddenly feeling the need to test the child's forehead once more, since William's hands were otherwise occupied in holding up the boy, Charity reached forward and smiled slightly with relief. "The fever <u>has</u> lowered considerably. Not to the normal range mind you, but anything less than how he arrived is an improvement and a definite blessing." She looked up at Nancy and replied directly to her alone, sensing that the mother needed a small bit of hope to hold onto as the young parents looked like they had not slept in days, "It means we are moving in the right direction at least."

"Praise the Lord." Nancy covered her face and sobbed openly with relief.

"Yes. Thank you," Jedidiah immediately added as he wrapped his arms around his wife and tried to support her, though he himself looked as if he needed the same action just as much as she did.

"He is not out of the woods, yet, Jed, but Nurse Bentham is right," William cautioned them sternly and gave a further admonishment, "If he is to fully recover, we will need to do this many more times over the next few days or at least until his fever breaks completely."

"Is there anything else I can do to help, Doctor Wells?" Charity asked, uncertain what other avenues of treatment he would like to explore before the family departed.

"Can you fetch me a towel, please, or a blanket."

"Certainly." Charity left, then returned with a long linen towel from the closet in the hallway but chose to wait carefully beside him until he requested it.

William, on the other hand, continued to soothe his patient further as he cupped some of the cool water in his left hand and bathed the top of James' head several times over to calm the child and couldn't help but relax just a little when he saw the edges of the little one's mouth curl up into a small smile of peaceful rest at last. "There now, little one," William soothed in wonder once again at how miraculously God could use His power to abate the worst of symptoms with a simple adjustment. "Jedidiah, I know all of this is a lot to take in, but I need you to listen to me closely and do precisely as I say. There are several things we need to do and quickly while your son remains stable." He looked up at the child's father once more, his mind switching immediately back to the urgency at hand.

"Of course." The man nodded. "Whatever you want me to do, I'll do it."

"Good. First, I want you to go down to your brother's shop and ask to borrow the wagon and then bring it here as quickly as you can. Do not go inside for any reason and do not in any way touch anything there if you can help it."

"But what should I tell him? He is not a child anymore, Uncle William. I can't just order him around to do anything I want just because I say so." Jedidiah guided his wife to the only chair in the room and crossed his arms, not in defiance, but almost as if he were at a total loss as to what he could do to accomplish what was being asked of him. "Wouldn't it be better if we just remained here?"

"No." William's head bent down a little farther, and Charity could tell from the tortured expression on his face then that he was dreading very much what he needed to say next.

"As much as we would like to help James, your son would receive far better care in his <u>own</u> home, Mr. Fabbri. Besides, I am sure Doctor Wells has already assured you that he will take over there once you arrive," Charity spoke up quickly and explained what William could not. "In my opinion, you have quite literally the best doctor our hospital has to offer as one of your own. So, it is only natural that you should use his skills to help your son improve as much as possible," she replied honestly for him.

Tilting his head to one side, so that only she could see his actions, William mouthed a grateful word of thanks to her before turning his head back upwards towards the boy's father and adding further, "Explain to Elijah that it was I who asked for it, and that he is not to go anywhere near you or the farmhouse until I tell him otherwise. He will not question it if it is coming from me and not you, nor will he hinder your return with pointless questions. And I will send your Uncle Emile a message, as well, to keep Hope away for the present."

Jedidiah nodded.

"Oh, and please ask Eli to stay with your Uncle Nathanael for the time being as I shan't have need of my room for the present." William picked up James from out of the water when the boy appeared to have started to fall asleep and handed him off to Charity as she wrapped James up securely in the towel before giving him to his mother for comfort.

"Come, I will show you the most direct route to the door." She motioned for Jedidiah afterwards to follow her out of the small room and led him to the outer doorway just beyond. "I will be watching for your return, so just pull up here and we will come out to meet you near the street. It will be easier for everyone involved, if you do not need to come back inside."

"Thank you most kindly, ma'am." The young man left obediently at her command as he jogged across the street and then turned so that he headed to the south, no doubt on his way to wherever his brother's shop was located.

"Thank you, Nurse Bentham. It seems I am indebted to you twice in one month," William said quietly while coming up to stand behind her, each allowing the solitude of the moment after so much stress to work its way through them.

"I am sure you don't need me to tell you that there is a good chance at least someone in their family may not make it through this, William," Charity replied while looking out the window, her every thought demanding that she not turn around and see the expression of dismay that was sure to be painted all along the contours of William's face.

"I know it." William exhaled slowly, holding his breath for just a moment, then inhaling once more. "But that doesn't mean that I have to like it, either. Sadly, we do not get to pick and choose who lives and who will die, though we may <u>very</u> much want to do so, and especially when it is people we love." He continued to stare out the window to the cloudy sky in front of them and wondered once again if the storm last night had been some kind of warning to him that an even greater threat was coming along with it.

"William?" Charity finally asked when the silence between them began to lengthen even farther.

"Hmmm..." William answered just as casually as he turned his attention to the people passing by on the street, his mind marveling at what it would be like to live his life like them in obscured darkness, ignorant of the waves and dangers around him.

"What if there <u>was</u> a way?" She remained fixed in her position, unmoving, as if waiting for the right moment to divulge something she had not felt ready to share with another soul until now.

"Well, unless you have suddenly discovered that you have received the power of performing miracles, I highly doubt anything <u>we</u> can do would make that much of a difference than what we are already doing." William finally stepped forward and leaned his back against the wall next to the window so that he could face her. "I know many people in our line of work profess that nurses are angelic, but that might be pushing it a little, don't you think?"

"Maybe..." Charity smiled at his playful expression, then laughed lightly at the humorous thought that had now entered her mind because of it. "You of all people already know that I am far from angelic."

William laughed, too, but then looked upwards and shook his head from side to side, as if contemplating his response very carefully. "I'd like very much to comment further, but I <u>did</u> make a promise to a rather striking young lady recently that I would not battle with her inside this hospital. And after all, I <u>am</u> a man of my word, if nothing else."

"Well, when you put it that way, it does sound rather controlling on the part of that striking young lady." Charity turned around and joined him at the window, leaning her head all the way back upon it to relax, her fingertips brushing slightly against his own when she did. "But striking?" Charity cocked her head in his direction once more and squinted slightly. "Do people even say that anymore?"

"Hey, you called me a Shabaroon," William countered quickly in jest. "I still have no idea what that means or if it was meant as a compliment, or a criticism."

Charity rolled her eyes at the joy his lack of understanding brought her, then added even more sarcastically, "Take your pick."

William laughed along with her once again but chose the side of peace over another equally acidic retort. "Truce, remember?"

"Truce," Charity replied. "And it was not a compliment, Doctor Wells... far from it."

"Wonderful." William closed one eye and leaned his head towards the woman next to him. "This is going to be a rather interesting friendship, isn't it?"

"Well, it will definitely be my first." She shook her head slightly, a lightness to the tone of her voice lifting the tense atmosphere that had been left behind them.

"Really?" William placed one hand over his heart in a mix of surprise and continued mischief. "Your first in almost a hundred years? I feel honored."

"You shouldn't." She chuckled once more and stood up to go back to the room with Nancy. "If you'll excuse me, I need to check on one more thing with James, but I will return shortly."

"Alright, I'll keep an eye out for Jed." William turned around to watch diligently for his hopefully imminent arrival.

"Better keep both eyes open. From what I hear, they tend to work better in pairs," she added even more levity to the already lighthearted conversation and stepped into the room.

Without being able to help himself, William smiled, too, at the exchange, and for the first time in his life he felt intimately connected with a woman other than someone in his own family and close friends.

Better yet... despite how much he had thought he would never have the chance to say this... he undeniably liked it.

Chapter Twenty-Two

October 20th, 1811

In the three weeks that followed James' arrival at the hospital, William found himself spread increasingly thin with both his duties at the home of Jedidiah and Nancy Fabbri and his necessary visits around the city. Despite his initial concern and obvious dread about the dire situation possibly unfolding for Sebastian's family, James did indeed make a fairly rapid recovery. A blessed miracle, in William's estimation, that caused everyone in the family to issue more than one prayer of gratitude on his behalf.

Yet it was not long before both Jedidiah and Nancy fell seriously ill, too, one right after the other. Even Charlotte had not managed to escape the illness that was now spreading like wildfire through the city streets, though William had seen fit to bring Caleb home on their way back from the hospital.

Soon, there were many other households around the city, wholly unconnected to the family, that had also been forced to put out the necessary white sheet on their fenceposts or doorways, indicating to all who passed by that they were under a strict quarantine. From the laborers down at the pier to the clerks and secretaries working in the government buildings and shops downtown, one by one, they all fell like soldiers in an open battle that were being picked off here and there by an enemy no one could see.

The dreaded Scarlet Fever quickly reached the level of epidemic within only a week's time, and there appeared to be nothing anyone could do to stop it except wait for it to burn itself out entirely and pick up the pieces to rebuild thereafter.

Sensing the need to take every precaution possible, Nathanael's college, as well as many of the other schools in the area, wisely chose to close their doors to students and faculty alike for the entire fall term in the hopes of preventing the possible spread among their students. While prominent businesses and shops alike took even more drastic measures by shuttering their doors and windows securely to prevent entry, preferring their sales to take place in an open market setting over those within the tight confines of their recently built establishments. The last thing anyone desired right now was to be the unintended cause of making an already tenuous situation any worse.

Nevertheless, despite however prudent those decisions were on the surface, that did not seem to deter in any way the near-constant stream of people that came to the hospital seeking care. At all hours of the day or night, patient after following patient was driven or carried to the stately edifice in desperation of a cure when the symptoms became too grave for them to treated at home. Yet, due to the specific nature of the illness and the lack of effective options available to treat it, the answer was always the same. Even with all the other medical advances the hospital could proudly boast of, there simply was nothing they could do there to help them. And as hard as it was to turn each one of them away, every person was instructed to return to their home and await the visit of one of the hospital's staff thereafter.

Doctors like William, and even some of the more seasoned staff like Charity and Nurse Talbot, who were naturally the first to be put at the top of this list of volunteers, given their recent exposure to the Fabbri family, would all go out daily to meet this request, each taking turns with other healers as they canvassed across the greater part of Philadelphia to the various patients and families alike. While others, who were older, remained dutifully behind the safety of the closed doors of the hospital to take care of the other patients within, all in an effort to alleviate the strain placed upon the dwindling level of available staff on any given day.

After all, this was not the first time the city had dealt with something on this large of a scale. But, thankfully, for all concerned, it was weathering the storm much better this time around, though the rising mortality rate had definitely kept Nathanael and some of his religious colleagues fairly busy conducting countless deathbed vigils and funerals alike.

Moreover, though it was a well-known fact to all of his friends, that Nathanael had never handled death very well in the past, he continued to push himself daily like everyone else. Whether it was with people he knew or those he did not, he had always seemed to struggle most with his inability to connect with those left behind in their grief, a definite deficit in Nathanael's opinion to someone of the cloth, though he could not seem to conquer it otherwise. Due to his more introverted temperament, or the scar that was caused by the untimely death of his own parents when he was younger, the sheer necessity of having to perform two to three funerals a day made his life indescribably daunting and overwhelmingly crushing. Though, that being said, even on trips where the only thing he could do was offer spiritual comfort to families drowning in their sorrow, Nathanael had not faltered in the slightest to be present, even if it was in body and prayer only.

Just like his peers serving alongside him, each day he had fought to remove that unusual reticence in his normally eager attitude to be a comfort to all and chose to faithfully dress once more in black, pushing himself daily to wait dutifully at the church down the street for the addresses of who he was to see next—no matter what it cost him to do so.

It was this singular, devoted responsibility alone that caused William the most concern this morning. Much more than he had been in years, if he were to honestly admit it, as he had never seen his friend this consistently melancholy since Elsie had died. Nor had Nathanael ever been this quiet for more than an afternoon in the past 18 years. In truth, they both added up to a justified reason, in William's mind, to lure him away from his penitent tasks in the city and redirect his thoughts elsewhere for a time.

"What do you think about going with me over to the farm this morning, instead of the church? We could maybe even spend part of the day under the large oak reading that book that arrived last week?" William suggested creatively when he watched his friend descend the wooden stairs and join him in the main room, looking more like a walking spectre than his usual bubbly self.

"I don't know, William..." Nathanael answered back in pace with his slow stride and moved the chair closest to him at the table slightly away to place his satchel upon it with a dissident thump. "To tell you the truth, I am not even sure what day of the week it is, let alone what the title of the book was that arrived."

Raising his eyebrows in surprise at the incredulous admission, William tried yet another tactic to persuade him. "Look, I know you feel compelled that you are needed there more, but it might do you a little good to get away from everything for just a day. 'Clear your head', as they say, so that you can be stronger on the next. It helps most people, or so I am told."

"Why? Do I look that bad that you are trying to coerce me into retreating?" Nathanael trudged to the kitchen where his friend was standing and reached for the kettle of coffee to pour a steady stream of the rich brown liquid into his favorite mug before adding two scoops of sugar and a dash of thick cream.

"A bit, but don't look at it so much as retreating, Nathanael. Look at it more like resting in-between the battles." He handed his friend a plate full of scrambled eggs and two pieces of mostly unburnt toast. "Besides, even God decided it was best to rest on the seventh day, and it has been over ten for you at least."

"Hmmpf, that is a very fitting analogy, William, but thankfully, the world's creation does not hinge on my ability to remain upright." He took his plate over to the table and plopped down onto the chair that faced the kitchen, as exhausted mentally as he had been the night before, despite having gotten over ten hours sleep.

"Nor do the people of Philadelphia, it would seem." William sighed in frustration and picked up his own plate to join him at the table. "Let the dead bury their dead today, friend. Go spend some time with the living for just this one day. If you still feel so disposed to continue as you have done, you can go back to your regular routine tomorrow, and I will say nothing more about it."

With a sigh of regret, mixed with more than an equal dose of utter exhaustion, Nathanael lifted a fork full of eggs and chewed them gingerly before slowly swallowing. "Honestly... I wish I felt like doing anything more than just sleeping right about now."

Not wanting to push the man away from the decision he was very close to making, William eyed the shadows beneath his friend's eyes from a distance and formed a stern expression before speaking again candidly, "Then sleep, man! Sleep all day if you need to do so. Do whatever it takes to rejuvenate your soul. I know this is probably the last thing you want to hear, but I am going to play the doctor card this one time and tell you that if you do not take today off, I am going to restrict you to bedrest for the remainder of the week."

"Is that so? Well, you might want to look in the mirror yourself this morning. I doubt you will find that you are fairing any better than I am at the present. Furthermore, being a little exhausted is not going to kill either of us today or any other day. You know that." Nathanael glanced up at the man across from him and narrowed his eyes in great consternation.

"Well, that may be, but I am not going to find you in the same state that you were in back in Wakefield." William couldn't help but chuckle a bit at the sarcasm Nathanael rarely shared before he took another sip of his coffee. "It took you months to recover from that, and even then, I doubt your body has ever regained the same bounce in your step that you once always carried. We may be immortal beings now, but we are not entirely invincible, Preacher Beckett."

"Ha... is that the pot calling the kettle black, Doctor Wells?" Nathanael finished his last bite of eggs and pushed the plate forward on the table, allowing them the opportunity to settle a little in his system before tackling the bread next.

"Maybe, but as they say, if the shoe fits...." William wrapped some of his eggs up within the slice of bread that he was holding and chewed them both in turn. "But truthfully, I was rather hoping to have a more relaxed day myself. Though I would be negligent if I did not at least stop by Jedidiah's house after breakfast. But that being said, you could come with me and see Charlotte, if you like. As you might have noticed, it always seems to brighten up her day considerably to have a little bit of your company when you can spare it."

"The fever has been difficult for her, but is she as bad as Nancy?" Nathanael reached forward and nibbled at the end of his piece of toast. "From what you were telling me the other day; you made it sound like Jed's poor wife could barely stand, let alone walk."

"Nancy has had a bad case of it from the start. Probably because she had already worn herself thin taking care of little James before she contracted the fever." William finished his eggs and toast and began drinking his coffee quickly in large gulps, so as to finish it sooner. "Speaking of taking care of the family, have you happened to see Elijah yet this morning?"

"Yes," Nathanael nodded. "I heard him leave just before dawn since it was his turn to milk the cows before breakfast."

"Huh, I bet he hated that." William shook his head and laughed lightly, remembering the incredible dislike the young man held for any work related to the farm. "I would send Emile over to give him some pointers, but I fear his days of milking livestock are over for the present."

Nathanael laughed, too. "Do you still remember him working at the Summerfields every morning?"

"I do."

"There was nothing that man wouldn't try to learn, if it would help Elsie's mother in the kitchen. In a way, it kind of makes me miss that simple life again." Nathanael closed his eyes and thought back to the most peaceful time of his existence. "Susan said in her letter last month that Gabe and Michael built a new addition to the barn. It was a pretty hefty investment, from what she explained, but he probably needed it after Simon and Levi encouraged him to buy all those cows after Matilda died."

"I'm sure he did, though I am glad Alice and her husband have been able to use the apothecary for the new bakery in town. It saves their family a tremendous amount of time not having to go to market every day to sell their wares. Still, all things considered, I'd give anything to be back there once more, enjoying the large expanses of fields as I walked home or just sitting by the pond and taking it all in. Who knows... maybe I will someday, though not for another century at least or people might still recognize us." William drank the last sip of his coffee and leaned back. "Life surely has changed for both of us since then, hasn't it?"

"Indeed." Nathanael finished his mug of coffee as well and stood to bring his dishes over to the counter. "On second thought, maybe you are right after all. If it won't be too much of an imposition, I think I <u>will</u> join you today."

William closed his eyes and breathed a silent prayer of thanksgiving, grateful once again that his friend had finally come around to his suggestion. "Good. Though I do need to stop by the hospital on the way and get a few things for the family before we go. Will that be acceptable?"

Nathanael shrugged. "My time is apparently yours, my friend."

"Excellent." William stood, plate and mug in hand and duplicated his friend's actions in the kitchen as he prepared to leave.

"Do you think Miss Bentham would like to join us?" Nathanael eyed William from the other side of the counter to judge the progress of their budding relationship.

"I doubt it. She is probably busy with her own patients today." William brushed the comment aside as he passed by him and picked up the two toys he had promised to bring Caleb and James.

"Is that so...."

"Stop pestering, Nathanael," William muttered gloomily, but did not otherwise engage. "Nurse Bentham does not see me presently as suitor material, I assure you."

"Interesting..." Nathanael frowned in concentration and pushed in the two chairs at the table beside him. "And yet, she does seem to spend a lot of her time over here when she is able."

"Nathanael Beckett, you can be worse than those nurses down at the hospital some days. As you are well aware, we have a commonality, that is all. You and I have Emile and Sebastian's family. She has no one, nothing more." William left his friend at the table and made his way over to the door to pick up the leather bad he always used to carry with him everywhere he went when he was back in England. While working at the hospital, he had stopped using it altogether. But since the epidemic had started, it had returned to being a near-constant piece of his daily attire.

"And you are not attracted to her in any way," Nathanael said the sentence more as a statement than a question and put on his chocolate brown and tan overcoat before draping his cloak over his arm in case he had need of it.

"Not in the slightest." William dodged his intrusion effectively as he buttoned his cloak around his neck, ignoring the obvious implications his friend was insinuating.

"Liar," Nathanael uttered more as an off-handed comment than an actual accusation.

"Stop meddling, Nathanael," William grumbled back, starting to get slightly annoyed now by his incessant prying.

"Stop ignoring the obvious, William," Nathanael replied in the same tone of voice in perfect mimic but showed little interest in relenting.

"Enough already... or I'll start asking you about Charlotte." William cast the man a dark look then that warned him of his building temper on the subject and noticeable discomfort.

"Go ahead, ask away. I have nothing to hide." Nathanael only smiled back and shook his head. "But that right there is proof that I am right."

"You're impossible today, you know that, right?" William opened the door and waited for the man to join him before locking it.

"And that is why you love me," Nathanael added lightly and continued on his way down the path to the hospital with an added skip in his step.

William only shook his head at the childish display but also couldn't help but smile at the sight of the man and his improving mental state. Though that encouraging fact aside, Nathanael had also been more than correct in his assumptions, much more, but he would ever admit it to him outright for though Nurse Bentham had been overly receptive of his attention as of late, on other occasions she had seemed almost cold and distant towards him in general. In fact, in many ways, it was almost as if he were acquainted with two completely different women—one warm and inviting with a hint of sarcastic humor that was wonderful to be around and funny. The other was cold and aloof, with a tongue as sharp as an icicle and just as deadly if you crossed her, which he normally could not help but do at least once or twice a week.

Even so, the real trouble that most often plagued his efforts was in knowing on any given day which Charity Emeline Bentham he was speaking to. Was it the one who welcomed his friendship to the point that she looked hurt at his lack of care towards her? Or did he mistakenly encounter the other version of her personality who thought every man should be burned at the stake merely for existing? So far, there simply was no way for him to predict which version he would meet on any given day, nor could he ever hope to explain all of that to his friend, as patient as he may be in wanting to absorb the details.

Nathanael was too undeniably simplistic in his view of love to understand the complexities that were often surrounding it. Passion, to him, was what he had with Elsie. It was two people finding each other and falling head over heels into an emotional bond that resulted in a happily ever after marriage. It wasn't what resulted from messy conversations, hurt feelings and awkward missteps. Nor could it ever hope to thrive in an environment of mistrust and uncertainty.

Yet William had seen all of that and more in the lives of Sebastian and Charlotte and Emile and Emma. Their relationships and resulting marriages had been anything but fairy tales and Greek lore. From what he had been told, Emma had once been seduced by Emile into an improper relationship before agreeing to marry him much later. Charlotte and Sebastian had both lied to each other for months thinking they were doing what was best for the other, when in the end, they were really just trying to protect themselves. Still, both pairs <u>had</u> managed to find a common ground amidst the turmoil in the end, which in a way, also supplied William with the hope he needed each day regarding Charity.

Given her rather turbulent past, William had already known their relationship might be fraught with many preconceived hostilities. It was just up to him to know how much he was willing to endure. Or maybe, the real question was whether or not he thought she was worth the constant arguments and pleasant conversations that hit him quicker than a whip across a horse's back some days. Or sadly, was it best for both of them to simply walk away before either of them was hurt and allow her the opportunity to resume her solitary life as if they had never met? He selfishly hoped not, but right now, he was not sure he knew the answer either way, and that held a unique set of problems all its own. Especially where Nathanael was concerned.

Arriving at the hospital a short while later, William strode up the stairs to the main door and met the nurse in charge who was standing dutifully at her post, though many other doctors and nurses were gathered on the lawn in groups awaiting their instructions. "Has Nurse Bentham stopped by yet today?"

"No, she has actually not checked in since last night when the two of you dropped off your completed list of patients. Is there something I can do for you, Doctor Wells?" Nurse Sarah asked him politely, folder in hand.

"Yes, please. There should be a package of supplies that were ordered for me. The courier sent a note yesterday that they would be waiting here this morning for me to pick up," William explained politely, remembering this time to offer her the kindness she deserved in her lower position. "Would it be too much to ask if you could check and see if they are ready?"

"No, of course not." The nurse opened the door and left for a few moments before returning with the requested supplies. "Here they are, and there appears to be a note on top that was left for you, as well." She motioned to the small calling card sized envelope that lay tucked under the rough twine securing the parcel.

"Thank you most kindly." William took the package from her and slid the note safely into his pocket to read later. "Can I leave a message for Miss Bentham, as well, before I depart?"

"Most certainly." The nurse reached for the quill placed within the ink well on the podium next to her and handed it to the doctor quickly, along with her folder full of loose sheets of parchment.

Knowing precisely what he needed to say, William scribbled a few instructions and a short salutation on one of the pieces quickly and handed it back to her. "I appreciate all that you are doing here, Nurse Sarah," William complimented her freely and turned around to rejoin Nathanael at the street.

"What is in the box?" Nathanael eyed the five-inch square parcel as they walked down the street and passed Thomas' business.

"A few medicinal treatments I would like to try on Nancy, if she will permit me. When I read about them, I thought they might give her some relief for her sore throat and allow her to finally eat. Despite what I might prefer, she is growing much thinner than I would like and that is probably due to malnutrition." William tucked the parcel underneath his arm and quickened his pace incoherently. He was walking so fast now, in fact, that it took them less than fifteen minutes to traverse the normally twenty-minute stretch between Thomas' shop and the old farmhouse on the edge of town.

To their surprise, however, Emma was already waiting for them on the porch, the look on her face drawing far more concern than anything she could have said, as she was not her normal, bubbly self in any way. Instead, her smile was taut in its offering and otherwise firm. "I cannot tell you how glad I am to see that you both came when you did."

"Why? Has something happened to Charlotte?" Nathanael asked immediately, his attention fully alerted to what she would say next.

"No... Elijah," Emma answered simply.

"Oh, did something go amiss with the milking this morning?" William glanced over at the barn whose door was left completely ajar. The chaotic commotion emanating from the animals within as it echoed off the worn, wood walls and out to where they stood warned all of them as to where the trouble had most likely originated.

"You could say that." Emma chuckled nervously, though nothing about what had happened this morning was humorous to her at all. "But before you get too worried, it's probably nothing a cold compress won't fix. Or at least I hope so." Emma hugged William when he reached the top stairs and then offered the same to Nathanael. "Though that being said, I'm sorry to have to say this, but the two of you look positively dreadful. Are you sure we can't catch the fever?"

"Positive," William reassured her.

"Well, Elijah fell, coming down from the hayloft a half an hour ago and hit his head pretty hard on the wagon in the process. As you can see, I just saddled my horse to head into town to fetch you, but you seem to have beaten me to it," Emma explained thoroughly and opened the outer door to the farmhouse for them to enter.

Without waiting for more explanation, William stepped inside the front door and took one look at the young man with his head leaning back on top of one of the chairs and smiled. "You're lucky you didn't crack open that thick skull of yours completely on the way down, Elijah. If you had, I might not have been able to help you this time."

"Is that so... well, right about now, I kind of wish it had split all the way open," Elijah answered gruffly but did not open his eyes to view his uncle. "Maybe then the guy beating the anvil inside of it would be allowed out."

"Hmm... I can definitely relate to that one." William chuckled lightly at his response, knowing precisely just how he was feeling. "I hit my head plenty of times when I was younger. Or at least definitely enough times to teach me to be more careful," William admonished him sternly, then turned his attention over to Emma. "Would you be so kind as to fetch me a small cup of water?" William requested as he searched within his satchel for some powder to relieve the worst of his symptoms. "If your head is hurting as much as I think it is, you will need to take a half teaspoon of this no more than every four to six hours. Mind you, it won't rid you of the man inside, but it will at least deaden his blows for a little while. The rest will just take time," William continued on with the story Elijah had concocted for it seemed quite humorous for him to do so.

"And how _is_ Charlotte today?" Nathanael asked cautiously, hoping she might have improved since his last visit.

"Resting mostly. She has had quite a fitful morning already, but I am glad that she is finally asleep now." Emma handed the half-full cup to William and moved to the kitchen to secure another cool, wet towel to exchange for the one already draped across Elijah's forehead.

"If you will permit me, I will go up to sit with her, now," Nathanael offered and waited for her permission before climbing the steps to the second-floor room.

Emma nodded. "I'm certain she would love that. Just be sure that you try to make her eat something when she wakes up. She drank some soup this morning after I practically threatened her, but I'd be best if she could try a little bit more if you can convince her."

"Of course," Nathanael agreed from the top of the stairs and paused as William added.

"I'll come back to look in on her after I finish at Jedidiah's."

"And what about you, young man? Are you ready to head back into town?" Emma asked seriously with her arms firmly folded across her chest.

"Town?" Elijah opened only one eye and stared back at her incredulously. "I think I'd prefer to die here if it is all the same with you—fever or otherwise."

"Oh, stop!" Emma playfully swatted him with her towel. "Did you at least finish milking the cows before you tried to meet your maker, or will I need to send for your uncle?"

"Yes, I milked those horrid beasts," the man groaned loudly. "Though if it was up to me, I'd make a juicy steak out of them rather than milk those cows another day more."

"Then how would you get your butter and ice cream, Elijah?" William examined the small lump forming on Elijah's forehead and grimaced. "You're not going to like this, but I'm afraid that is going to leave a mark for a little while for sure, son."

"Lovely..." Elijah closed both his eyes once more. "Though I think right about now it would be worth it to give up ice cream altogether than hunker down underneath them again in this heat. Did Uncle Nathanael forget to remind God that it is October already? Fall is supposed to be pleasant, not baking."

"All the more reason to milk those cows. After all, we have to have something to cool us off," William jested as he patted his arm and stood upright. "Well, I am happy to report that I think you'll survive to fight another day... this time, Elijah. For the moment, I have other more pressing patients to visit, but since you are otherwise incapacitated at the present, I <u>will</u> move the cows back to the pasture for you before I do."

"That would be excellent. Thank you, William." Emma picked up her lighter gray linen cape and headed out the door with him to the porch beyond. "I told Emile that I would return home as soon as I was able to finish hanging up the laundry before Charity stops by. Since Nathanael is here now to sit with Charlotte, I suppose I can leave earlier than I had planned. And with any luck, I will have it done before supper as it does look like it might rain, after all."

"That would be a blessing indeed, but speaking of Emile, I forgot to ask. Is Hope starting to wear on his nerves, yet?" William inquired as he had been assured by all that Emile had most certainly done his job well in setting strict guidelines for the girl in regard to visiting anyone outside of her aunt and uncles. A fact which had caused more than one confrontation between the two over the overly restrictive rules he had suddenly established. Though in truth, William was a little concerned that the whole ordeal might put a slight strain on their relationship for a little while, but the rest of the family knew the dire circumstances surrounding this decision far more than the eighteen-year-old girl could ever hope to comprehend.

"I don't think that is even possible. He has the patience of a saint with that girl." Emma put her cape over her shoulders and lifted the hood, attempting to hide the frown that followed thereafter just a little. "I wish I could say the same for myself."

"Well, it has been my experience that sainthood comes in many forms, Emma. Even ones that are responsible for two petulant children on occasion," William complimented her over his shoulder as he made his way over to the barn. "I will see the two of you tomorrow, if I can. Please pass on my regards to your husband and make sure Elijah leaves as soon as possible. I know he doesn't want to move, but he has spent far too much time in that house already. Since Charlotte has been primarily upstairs, I would think that his exposure should remain fairly minimal... or at least I hope so. With everyone seeming to be finally on the other side of this thing, I don't want yet another member of this family falling ill when we can avoid it."

"Agreed. I'll make sure that he heads out shortly," She answered back and made her way over to her horse and mounted him easily. "Elijah, come... it's time to go."

Chapter Twenty-Three

October 20th, 1811

"You don't understand, Uncle Emile. All I want to do is go over one time and just see how Mother is doing. I will be careful and stay outside the front door. Or, if that is too close, I won't even set foot on the porch, if that will make you happy," the girl begged for the second time that morning alone. "I'm truly worried about her. Elijah's note says that Mother has not left her bed for days. How is she supposed to get better if no one is there to help her?"

"Hope, dear, one of your uncles is there every night and your aunt has been taking care of her most of today already. From what I can see, Charlotte has more help than most people do in her condition, and far better care with your Uncle William checking on her twice a day. I dare say that not many other patients can boast that much attention." Emile looked up from his newspaper that he was reading and tried to reason with the girl, though he knew from their two previous conversations that it would be to no avail. Unless he gave in to her demands soon or provided an alternate solution to appease the girl in some way, this battle he was enduring would only end in yet another stalemate for both of them.

As passionate as she was stubborn, Hope had not ceased in her petitions daily to go over and help her mother, but despite how much it pained him to refuse her, he would not relent. First, because he loved the girl more than life itself and second, because Emma had reminded him just this morning before she left how entirely foolish it would be to do so. Their neighbor on just the next farm over had lost two of their children in one night, and it looked like the mother was likely to follow along behind them. Which in the end, only served to bolster his reserve even more with death so very near to their own doorstep. No matter how desperately the girl pleaded, there was simply too much risk to allow it.

"I'm not your prisoner here, you know. I am a grown woman, and as such, I can do whatever I want," the girl pouted like she had done when she was only five, arms crossed firmly across her chest, her face set firmly into a definite scowl.

It was cute then, and oh so easy to helplessly give her everything she ever asked of him at the time... But now... not so much.

"That is certainly true. As you say, you <u>do</u> have the freedom to do as you like... provided you remain anywhere <u>here</u> on this property when you do it." Emile continued to pretend to read whatever Michael had written about their recent trip to Washington together.

"Ugh..." Hope threw up her hands in total frustration at the consistency of his refusal on the subject. "Why are you always treating me like a child? You know as well as I that I can help Mother just as much as Aunt Emma can, maybe even better since I know what Mother likes." Hope tried a new tactic to possibly persuade him.

"Maybe so, but the answer is still, no, Hope." Emile summoned up the last of his patience for this particular conversation before setting down his paper onto his knee and stared pointedly at the girl. "And if you stopped acting like one, I wouldn't have to do it so often, now would I?"

With a roll of her eyes and a definitely insolent shake of her head, Hope turned away to look out the door beside her but continued muttering under her breath something that she probably should have kept completely to herself, "Well Michael says that you..." She suddenly stopped herself short mid-sentence, realizing that what she was about to say would only make the situation infinitely worse than it already was. "...never mind."

"Michael said what?" Emile instantly questioned without missing a beat, feeling a fresh bout of annoyance with the man's constant interference rising within him once more.

"Nothing... it's not important," she deflected quietly as if her uncle was the one who needed to be avoided on the subject and not her defiant behavior.

"Michael... says... what, my dear?" Emile said the words as calmly as he could possibly manage, though everything inside of him wanted to go out and personally murder the boy for stepping in where he wasn't wanted.

Killing the boy outright in a moment of uncontrolled temper wouldn't solve his current problem with Hope's looming independence, as no doubt some other, less desirable suitor, would eventually take his place in time. Yet all things considered, that did not also mean that he was not still incredibly tempted to do so.

"Fine. Michael said that the two of you just need to cut the apron strings finally," Hope said bluntly as she shook her head, upset with herself for even bringing it up for she had promised herself most faithfully when he had said it that she never would. "It wasn't kind of him to say such a thing because he doesn't know you two like I do. And you must know that I love you both so terribly, but it has been awfully hard trying to balance all of that with loving him, too."

"Hmm..." Emile set his paper down slightly, feeling a deep sense of regret upon hearing her honest confession of the turmoil raging within her. "Well, on that point, I can only say that I never intended for you to have to choose between any of us. You do understand that we are only trying to look out for your best interests, right?"

Hope nodded, "But I don't see how I can accept him any other way, especially when you detest him so, and don't say that you don't because you know as well as I that you cannot fool me like you do all the others."

Emile smiled in exultant satisfaction finally. There was a reason why she was his favorite person in all the world next to Emma. "Perhaps, I <u>have</u> been a little too hard on him of late." He tilted his head slightly and allowed his gaze to follow with a small sigh. "And truth be told, as a whole, he is not that bad a fellow, insightful even on certain topics when he tempers his emotion long enough to see the facts clearly."

"A little hard on him?" Hope guffawed slightly, then bit her lip at the unmistakable understatement of the century.

"Alright, a lot." Emile shook his head with a retiring expression. "But that is only because I do not feel he is completely worthy of you at the present... no matter how excellent of a writer he may be," Emile admitted honestly and fluffed the pages of the paper outward.

Hope sniffed, feeling the fresh pangs of defeat once again and the hopelessness of her current situation. "Will anyone ever be?"

"Probably not." He leaned back in his chair and crossed one leg over the other lazily. "You <u>are</u> pretty special. But then again, <u>you</u> already knew that."

"Special, huh? Papa used to say that you and I are cut from the same cloth even though we are not related. I guess that just means that you and I are more alike than we want to admit." Hope leaned on one of her hands on top of the table, propping up her chin as she looked out the side door once again to the beaming sunshine beyond. "Do you think he was right? About you and I, that is?"

"Maybe, but that is also a little funny, actually." Emile flipped open the paper once more and read the same line he had read at least five times already to distract him from the wave of fresh grief that suddenly attacked him.

"Why?" Hope fingered the design on the tablecloth in front of her.

"Because I think you are more like your father than anyone else, but I have told you all that before, too." Emile beamed back at her from over the top of the paper. "And that is most decidedly a better thing to be."

"Perhaps... but then again, I suppose at least one of his children needs to be. Though I think I could do without his stubborn streak, as it hasn't done me any good today at least." Hope looked back at her uncle hoping beyond hope that he might have suddenly changed his mind and decided to finally acquiesce.

"No, it has not. And the answer is still no, Hope...undeniably and unshakably... no." Emile lifted the paper higher still so as to not see the dismal expression the girl was sure to be making, for he had seen it all before. Witnessing it yet again today would only make it harder for him to remain steadfast in his resolve towards her.

"Fine." The girl sighed loudly. "Can I at least go for a short walk, or must I remain in this house all day, too?"

"But, of course. You may walk anywhere you like...." Emile said flippantly as the girl stood up quickly from the table to leave before he could put any other qualifiers on the statement. "...provided it is on this five-acre property and not a step outside of it. Don't force me, young lady, to show you what being a true prisoner can be like. I've done my time as one and let me assure you that it is most definitely not what you wish to experience, so do not test me on this."

"Prisoner or not, it wouldn't do me any good if I did..." Hope picked up her book from the chair beside the door and her favorite emerald cape. "I'll be out by the cherry tree if you need me."

"Sitting by it, up it, or chopping it down like our dear Mr. Washington... all will be acceptable, provided it is a tree on <u>our</u> property, dear." Emile raised his eyes slightly over the top to watch the young girl shuffle while grumbling out the front door before he allowed himself the opportunity to finally truly grin and let out an amusing laugh. "You are most definitely just like your father, Hope. Wonderfully and inexcusably endearing, but just like Sebastian in so many ways."

He finished reading the article before setting down the paper, remembering quite unexpectedly a post he had forgotten to send yesterday back at the office. In his haste to come home last night in time to fix supper for Emma and Hope, he had forgotten all about his need to send it and realizing it only now, a full twenty-four hours later, only frustrated him even more.

"Of course, it would be mostly sunny today, too." Emile placed his irritatingly necessary cloak on top of his overcoat and adorned his head with his favorite hat before picking up Emma's large parasol that she always preferred rain or shine. "It won't be stylish, but at least I will not get singed to a crisp." He frowned at the definite possibility and obvious spectacle he would be inviting before a brilliant idea abruptly occurred to him. One that would also bring a fantastic end to at least part of the war waging between them, as well.

"Hope?" He called from the front porch while silently praying that the girl was still within earshot.

"Yes, your majesty," came the half-muttered sarcastic reply back to him from behind the tree and nothing more.

Emile chuckled once again at the girl's incessantly witty humor. "What do you say about making a small trip into town instead? You can even visit that beau of yours along the way. He has not been exposed to anyone recently, correct?"

Immediately excited beyond words of possible expression, Hope practically jumped from her spot from under the cherry tree and hurried over to him. "That would be marvelous! And no, he has been holed up in that dismal office for almost a week. His editor won't even let him leave to go home for fear that he might lose his best writer since many of the others have not come back to work as of yet."

"Good. I need to step into my office for just a bit to handle something I left behind, but if you promise me that you will stay at the newspaper office alone, you can remain with him for the duration of the afternoon, providing that is agreeable to you. And then, if the café in town is still serving their meals al fresco, perhaps the three of us can enjoy an impromptu picnic on the green for our supper." Emile tried to make the day seem as inviting as possible under the limited circumstances before handing the girl the feminine-looking parasol and offering her his arm so that he could stand closely underneath its shadow.

"I'd like that very much, Uncle. Thank you!" She kissed him lightly on the cheek. "And I am sorry for my behavior earlier. I know you are just trying to protect me."

"Don't give it a second thought." He dismissed her apology easily and led the way down the brick path in front of the house and through the adjacent streets towards the offices of *The Aurora General*. "Would it be too much to assume that Michael may be considerably busy at work today? Maybe even too busy to have the time to entertain you properly?"

"I doubt he will be <u>that</u> busy, Uncle. From what he explained to me the other day in his letter, he normally has only one main article to write and then he is usually done for the week." Hope beamed with pride while discussing him.

"For the rest of the week! What does the man <u>do</u> with all his extra time?" Emile crossed the street and guided his niece towards the offices of *The Aurora* on the other side.

"Research mostly. Or sometimes he tries to interview people he thinks would have information for his articles. Like you, for example, when you took him to Washington. When he came back, he said that you had supplied him with enough meat for his articles to last him over a month."

"Well, the month is over, so that must be why he is eager for more." Emile opened the door of the building and held it ajar for her to pass through in front of him.

"May I help you, miss... sir," the young man, not much older than twelve, who sat on the high stool by the door, welcomed them politely.

"We are here to see a Mr. Michael Adair, if you please," Emile spoke in the same debonair fashion he was accustomed to using back in Paris, for it was something he had never been able to entirely remove from his personality.

"Yes, sir. If you can wait right here for a moment, I will bring him back presently." The boy lit off the stool and dashed out of the main room and into one of the smaller ones to the side.

"Maybe that is where Michael hides his mistresses." Emile leaned over and whispered in Hope's ear quietly, attempting to tease her viciously about the boy.

Perturbed at the mere insinuation he was making, Hope elbowed her uncle severely in the ribs in protest to remind him of her own position on the matter. "He had better not if he knows what is good for him and for you!"

"Ow!" Emile grimaced slightly, rubbing the area of her attack, though her sudden jab had not hurt him in the slightest.

"Now please, Uncle Emile, you know as well as I that you are embarrassing me," Hope hissed back but then composed herself once more, or at least as much as would be required for her to act in a manner which was proper for a young lady of eighteen.

True to what he had promised, the errand boy returned a few minutes later with a very delighted Mr. Adair close behind. "Miss Fabbri... Mr. Deschamps, to what do I owe this tremendous pleasure today?"

Feeling almost nauseated as soon as he heard the overly grandiose greeting and obvious attempt at flattery on his behalf, Emile tried his best to control the roll of his eyes to a slight upwards movement and struggled to remain placidly cordial. "Since I have a few things to finish up back at the office, I thought that perhaps you might like to spend the afternoon together."

"Really?" Michael's eyes lit up instantly at the possibility. "That would be most welcome, as I have not had the chance to see her in over a week, almost two."

"Yes, well, we have been endeavoring to keep our own Rapunzel safely locked away in her tower, but as you can see, she has been freed from her prison today... and the apron strings... cut," Emile said the last phrase curtly, purposely intending to make sure the young man realized that whatever he disclosed unfavorably in private about either Emma or himself, would most likely be divulged later and quite clearly, <u>not</u> in his favor.

Utterly humiliated now, Hope placed her palm across her face and hid behind it in embarrassment.

"I... I am still glad for the opportunity to see her, sir." The young man pulled at the center button of his collar, sensing the temperature in the room suddenly rising around him. "And I am sorry if I caused any offence, truly."

"Oh, relax, Michael... It's important to breathe, remember?" Hope tried to reassure him through her uncle's passive-aggressive attack.

"Right..." Michael released a nervous chuckle at her recommendation, then added, "Perhaps I will choose my words more carefully next time, Mr. Deschamps." Michael admitted rather apologetically.

"Perhaps," Emile replied, letting the end of the word drag out a bit in the silence before deciding he had tortured the man enough for one day. "Well, I must be off. Hope, I expect that I will be back in time to collect you around four. Will that be enough recreational time for the prisoner?"

"Actually..." Michael seized the opportunity quickly to plead his case, not wanting to miss his chance for more time. "Now that she is here, I was hoping that I might be able to steal her away for the rest of the day... if that is acceptable, that is? I promise that I will return her well before nightfall <u>and</u> keep her as isolated as possible."

"Please, may I? We can have that picnic you mentioned another day, Uncle," Hope begged while looking up at him and batted her eyes like a little child pleading with him for a piece of candy from the General Store.

"Oh, alright," Emile relented at last with a dramatic sigh. "But mind you, not a minute after sundown, and nothing more populated indoors than *The Aurora*."

"Most definitely, sir. You have my word." The man's worried expression assured Emile of his utmost sincerity.

"It is agreed then. I will see you tonight, dear," Emile reassured her casually and kissed her lightly on one of her cheeks.

"Yes, now please go, or you will never finish by supper." Hope giggled, her giddy excitement bubbling over at last.

"Mr. Adair..." With a polite nod in both of their directions, Emile turned to walk out the door behind them but then noticed the now overcast sky. "Here. You should hold onto this in case it should rain, my dear." He handed Hope the closed parasol he had been carrying for her.

"Thank you but go... please. You are stalling... again, and you know it." She took the offered protection and practically pushed him out the door before focusing her attention back on the handsome man in front of her.

With a long sigh, Emile only shook his head and continued walking down the street and into the government offices in the center of town.

Whether he liked it or not, Michael Stuart Adair was certainly here to stay. So, he might as well come to grips with that truth sooner than later. Besides, as much as he wanted to stand in their way, there were worse men that Hope could have chosen as a suitable mate. Men who might have wanted her for her beauty alone, or as a means to provide something for them in return, both equally plausible and also horrifying to even consider. Yet that being said, despite his personal opinion about the man, he would much rather her choice be someone he could easily manipulate when the occasion necessitated it, than a man that might take her away from him entirely.

A fact which meant one thing and one thing alone... he was going to have to tell her soon about the very difficult conversation all of her uncles had already had with her beau, and hope that in the end, they had all made the right decision regarding her future.

Chapter Twenty-Four

October 20th, 1811

For the first time that he could remember, Elijah had finally been given the chance to embrace a bit of independence in his life when his Uncle William had requested that he remain in the city for the duration of the illness at the farm. Something that appeared to be strictly a precautionary measure on the doctor's behalf, but really, had only served as a wonderful opportunity for Elijah to embrace the many possibilities he had long desired. Or at least he had thought so in the beginning. As in many other things in life, there were always a few exceptions to consider, but the momentary shift in his world to a different pace and atmosphere did not overly bother him like he thought that it might.

Like any other week in the year, work at the forge during the initial stages of the epidemic was consistently demanding, with many urgent orders still needing to be filled on any given day. Not to mention the other more mundane duties he had to accomplish like milking the cows more than a few times a week when Jedidiah became too ill to do so after James had recovered. Even Thomas had stepped in to lend a hand wherever it was needed, which helped immensely when William was called urgently to be elsewhere, and a ship had to be unloaded before the next tide. Though truthfully, that task was possibly a little bit self-serving in nature, as well, as Thomas and Elijah had as much use for the arriving materials for their own needs as anyone else at the moment.

This steady stream of daily activity provided an excellent means of keeping Elijah focused on the many tasks in front of him and not on the other more worrisome thoughts he refused to entertain when his mind became much more idle than he would have preferred. The biggest being the fact that slowly but surely, some of the customers he had known for years, at times, never picked up their paid orders. While others arrived upon his doorstep with money in hand, looking far more ghostlike and gaunter than he had ever seen another human being, alive or otherwise, and much too haggard for him to honestly charge them a fair price for his labor. From his limited scope of existence and firsthand knowledge of its common people trudging along the streets in front of his forge in search of something Elijah was infinitely unqualified to name, the city of Philadelphia appeared to be in a state of survival now, and every day carried with it something more terrifying than the next.

Though that being said, living with his Uncle Nathanael had brought about its own challenging complexities, too, as the man was always so extremely talkative no matter what the hour of the day. From dawn until dusk, it was almost infuriating to listen to the endless fountain of knowledge his uncle always loved to share when all Elijah wanted after a long day of work was to eat a solid meal and crawl into bed. Never once had it crossed his mind to discuss topics of spiritual and political themes or classical literature over his evening stew or morning pancakes. That was Hope's department, and he was more than happy to let her have it.

At this point, all he wanted now was his solitude. Or rather, just one single night of glorious peace and quiet and something to fill his stomach. Yet despite how much he wanted to pack up his things and move into the small storage area attached to the back of his forge, Uncle William <u>had</u> insisted that he remain with them for his own safety. And despite the incredible irritation that obedience required, if anyone knew the right decision to make in situations such as these, it was his uncle, and Elijah trusted him implicitly... even with his life.

Over the past eighteen years, he had never once felt the need to question his advice or logic on a matter. On the contrary, from the way in which his uncle had lovingly guided him through the worst of his grief after his father's death, he felt practically indebted to him.

Still, there <u>had</u> been times when he sensed that there was more to his uncle than what met the eye. The biggest being the fact that the man did not look like he had aged a day since the day he had met him back in England. Yet the wisdom he confided with him daily was incredibly rich with his years of experience, invaluable even as someone in whom he looked up to almost in the place of his real father on occasion. Which, in a way, mostly deflected any further questioning on his part that might have lingered. Though if Elijah were to be totally honest, he probably did so because it had been much more difficult for him to continue on without the presence of his father than he cared to admit—a loss both of them felt equally sharp at times when something would happen that reminded them both of Sebastian's presence.

Moreover, despite the burgeoning success of both his forge and the warehouse business he and his uncle were steadily managing, the joy he once felt every day when he picked up his hammer and stoked the fire higher had slowly begun to diminish. Since his very first lesson at the large anvil that stood in the center of his father's old forge back in Portsmouth, his desire to succeed in the very footsteps of his father was the one thing that had motivated him every day. In fact, each morning when he opened his eyes and pulled on the same tan cotton blouse with the small ties that ran up the center near his neck and threw on his darkly colored trousers that fit perfectly into the pair of soft leather boots that he loved to wear rain or shine, the singular drive he sensed all the way down to the depth of his soul pulled him physically towards a dream that he knew beyond a shadow of a doubt he <u>could</u> accomplish, if not excel in entirely, if given enough time.

Yet in the end... time was not what he was given... or rather... not enough of it.

He had the tools, yes. And the necessary knowledge to complete all the tasks that might ever be required of him in his trade, too. But that wasn't enough anymore, or at least he had yet to discover what truly was.

As everyone expected of him at the time, he had initially gone back to work each day more out of sheer obligation than actual desire, endeavoring to find his own pace in the silence left behind. And in some tasks, a part of him had begun to actually enjoy a few of the various aspects of his work once more, or as much as he could before this infernal illness had arrived. Or to use a more fitting analogy from <u>his</u> world, Uncle William had told him yesterday that most epidemics eventually burned themselves out in a few weeks' time. But sadly, for all involved, it had already been three and the numbers of people who were sick around him only seemed to be increasing, not abating. Like the wood in his stack that lay carefully piled up next to the fire, waiting to be used, the disease that was fueling the fire of possible death all around him made it feel like it was only a matter of time before the illness claimed someone else that he loved, or even him, should he allow it the chance to lick at his heels.

Which brought yet another unpleasant thought to his mind today among so many others that were crowding in line for his attention. Something he had been trying very hard to avoid thinking about all month. Since Jedidiah had fallen ill along with his wife, this meant no one would be able to bring in the crop in time for harvest if others did not offer to help there, as well. Neither was there a ready pool of people eager for work these days with most of the men hunkering down at home to care for their families.

"It's almost like when Papa died." Elijah sighed as he placed his tools back in their proper positions along the wall of his forge and untied his apron, preparing to hang it up for a pause in the late afternoon's work.

The whole family, the uncles and even Emma and Thomas had helped them bring in the wheat that year, but it had taken every last one of them to do it and with great physical effort, he might add.

How many times had he tried since then to dissuade Jedidiah from planting so many acres simply because of his fear that it all might happen again?

Regrettably, he had lost count, nor did his brother truly understand why he faithfully discouraged him at every juncture whenever the topic was brought up.

There were literally a hundred other logical reasons in Elijah's mind for not doing so, but true to what he expected, his brother had staunchly refused his counsel time and time again, arguing that they needed to plow every inch of dirt that they owned if they were to turn a profit of any kind whatsoever and keep the farm prosperous. A fact that also rubbed Elijah equally as raw today as the day when his father had informed him that half of the farm was his inherited responsibility, as well. A joint ownership of indentured torture to his way of thinking, that was deeded to Jedidiah and himself, along with their mother, since before they had ever moved across that blessed ocean.

Yet despite this incredibly generous gift that most men would have been overjoyed at receiving, there was not a single pebble on that land or blade of grass that held any attraction to Elijah whatsoever. To him, the farm was just another thing that made him feel undeniably trapped, like a restraint that held him captive, and an annoyingly demanding one at that. The last thing Elijah wanted in his life was to be forever strapped down to an unflinching schedule for every second of his day.

Unlike his brother, he rather preferred change... unpredictability... diversity... creative expression... the value of seeing something in his mind come to existence in front of him. The process of forging life into something that most people would probably throw away was an emotional high like none other and far more rewarding than anything he had seen from Jedidiah's life on the farm.

"A profit?" Elijah shook his head disdainfully once more at the enormous task ahead of him and felt almost nauseous. "How much profit can there possibly be in grains of wheat and ears of corn when it rots in the field during the late autumn rains."

Elijah placed one hand on the smooth beam supporting the front opening of his forge and watched the people pass slowly by during the late afternoon. Without even needing to contemplate what was most likely going to occur next, he knew exactly what his Uncle William would ask him to do soon, but that still did not mean that he would not dread hearing it all the same. With everyone sick except for Hope and himself, the whole family now depended on that harvest more than ever before, and like it or not, it would fall on his shoulders to come up with a plan for bringing in almost a hundred acres of grain, corn, and hay for the animals. An impossible task by any standard of measurement, yet one that could not be avoided, which only hurt his head even more than it had this morning when it connected with the wagon to even consider it.

"A hundred acres..." Elijah's eyes widened at the immensity of the task before him and grimaced as he accidentally touched the lump on his forehead when he rubbed his face to clear away the salt that had accumulated near the edges from his sweat. "I hate cows." Elijah shook his head once more in disgust and tried to loosen the accumulated grey ash from out of his loose curls.

"Good afternoon, Elijah! Are you closing shop early today?" Thomas waved a cheerful greeting as he crossed the busy street and rounded the corner in his direction.

"Not hardly. Though maybe I should, as I haven't had but a handful of paying customers today as it is." He sat down on the tall wooden stool and motioned for his friend and partner to join him. "How are Hannah and Abigail doing these days?"

"Oh, fine... fine... and yourself?" Thomas sat down with his back to the street and crossed his arms comfortably over themselves against his chest.

"Had a bit of a run in with a cow earlier this morning, but other than that, I am perfectly well as you can see. 'Utterly delightful', even." He gave a mockingly higher pitch imitation of the young lady who had flirted with him just this morning after he had arrived from his mother's home and tried to shake off the remaining cynicism the encounter had created.

"Ha! Is that so? Well, did this charming young lady you seem to have totally dismissed once again have a name?" Thomas inquired curiously.

"Probably, but my head was throbbing too loudly at the time to even ask."

"Hmm..." Thomas tilted his head slightly to eye the recently acquired injury. "Well, then maybe letting her go was the best thing for all involved. As preoccupied as you normally are with your work here, she has <u>no</u> idea what she would be getting herself into with <u>you</u> as a beau."

"No doubt..." Elijah answered back just as droll.

"By the way, whatever happened to that Mary girl? The one you had to drive home the other day?" Thomas rubbed his chin thoughtfully as he struggled to remember all the details that had been previously shared with him.

"Oh, I am sure that she is doing tolerably well, but you will have to inquire with Andrew in the future about her." Elijah pulled his thick brown hair back behind his neck and tied it with the leather strap he always kept hanging on his apron so that it fell down the center behind him. "When he saw her riding in the wagon with me, he made sure to let me know she was most definitely spoken for or soon would be."

"So, with no girl of your own yet, you have resorted to stealing the prospects of other men now, I see." Thomas smiled broadly at his expense. "Shockingly bold of you, I must say."

"Not really." Elijah rolled his eyes at his pointless assessment and just shook his head. "Did you come all the way over here, Thomas, to discuss my sorry love life, or did you actually need something today?"

"A little of both, perhaps." Thomas released his arms and leaned down on his hands that were now placed on top of both his knees. "As a matter of fact, Hannah sent me to find out if there has been any more word on Jedidiah's family? I love my wife, but she has been out of her mind with worry since she heard that little James was sick."

"Well, you can tell her to be at peace as far as James is concerned. He is more or less well now, thank you, but both of his parents have it, I'm afraid. In fact, from what Uncle William said to me at breakfast the other day, Jedidiah can't even pull himself out of bed, Nancy either for that matter." Elijah felt a deeper concern in regard to the health of his brother beginning to grow but knew there was nothing he could possibly do to help him more than what the others were already doing. In fact, his Uncle William had practically been living over there for the past four days this week already, and would no doubt continue to remain close by until they both recovered. Miss Bentham, too, as far as he could tell, as he often saw her heading in that direction every morning shortly after sunup and returning much later every evening well after his Uncle Nathanael had retired for the night.

"Is there anything I might be able to assist with that might lighten their load just a little?" Thomas asked cautiously, hoping he would not be asked to do anything that would risk his own family's safety by offering it.

"Well, actually there is, but I hesitate to even ask it at this point."

"Go on, you'll never know until you do," Thomas encouraged him onward.

"Alright, you asked for it," Elijah exhaled, dreading the refusal he felt certain would follow. "Do you think you could help me next week to bring in the harvest at the farm? I can't do it by myself, and with everyone either busy or sick, I don't know who else to even ask," Elijah admitted honestly.

"I think that would be doable, maybe Hannah can even come lend a hand with the food while we work. She knows her way around the place as well as I do by now, and it will give her a chance to get out of the house a little. I might even be able to bring a few other helpers from the shop if they are able since it will all be outdoor," Thomas offered eagerly.

"That would be incredibly generous of you. As you might expect, I can't pay you much for your labor though as I am practically working for free as it is." Elijah rubbed the thumb of his left hand across the smooth surface of his leather apron, allowing the motion of it to calm him.

"I would not have accepted it if you had. You've more than paid me back for anything I might do in your friendship over the years. Besides, it is the least I can do to repay that back to you and more," Thomas exclaimed. "Now, what is it that you are working on today?"

"What every other blacksmith in the area worth his salt is creating if he knows what is best for him," Elijah stated bluntly.

"Nails," the two said in unison and laughed lightly at the inside joke.

"Your father hated making those things with a passion when he lived on the island, but he also said that it supported you, so he did it anyways. When we first met, he would make hundreds upon hundreds every day for the men building the very ship that brought him home to you." Thomas thought back fondly to his time working under his old master.

"I would go mad in a week at that level, maybe even less."

"Oh, he had a trick for that, too, believe it or not," Thomas added confidently with a smirk.

"Really? What was that?" Elijah appeared suddenly surprised, for this story about his father felt completely new to him.

"He made swords—beautiful and wonderfully exquisite swords. He tried to teach me once, too, but I am afraid I was never as talented as he was. Come to think of it... I remember that he often called it his mental escape." Thomas looked across the room and pointed to one of the swords that hung proudly near the rafters out of view. "In fact, I was there the day he gave me that one. As clumsy as I am still, I knocked over a whole bin of metal and cut my arm terribly playing with it while he was working. Then, when he saw how badly I was injured, he wanted me to see the doctor immediately, but I was so poor that I could hardly pay for my lodging, much less the services of an actual doctor."

Elijah stood and picked up the sword from its hiding place, examining it closer as it glinted in the light. "So, what did you do?"

"He made me clean it with cold water and applied a dressing to it right away. Then, every morning before I was allowed to go to work down at the docks, he made certain that he checked that dressing for almost two weeks just to be sure no infection had set in."

"That sounds like my father—methodical to the last." Elijah handed the sword over to Thomas and nodded in his direction. "You should keep this one. It means far more to you than it will ever mean to me."

"But it was your fathers?" Thomas accepted the blade with extreme reverence, taking great care not to cut himself for a second time with the same blade.

"I have others, trust me. He made <u>many</u> nails during his time here in America, too." Elijah chuckled. "And thank you, Thomas. I am very grateful that you shared one of your memories with me. It will help me cherish the others more because of it. And who knows, maybe I will even start making a few more myself to find my own escape."

"I bet they would sell for a pretty penny these days. People shell out their money quickly for things of nostalgic quality." Thomas laid the blade across his lap and nodded.

"I bet they would," Elijah agreed. "So, do you think you could come to the farm next Friday morning? That way we can use the majority of the weekend to bring the wheat and hay in and lessen the time away from our work here in town."

"Sure, that will also give me a week to possibly round up a crew. Unless you suddenly change your mind and come up with a better plan, I will see you then." The man held out his hand and Elijah grasped it in a firm handshake.

"I doubt it, but thanks again," Elijah repeated once more.

"Any time." Thomas exited the forge and waved on his way back down the street towards his next destination.

With a curious desire now towards a bit of dubious experimentation, Elijah turned around and picked up a fresh piece of steel from the wooden barrel on his left, taking the time to eye it properly down its length to measure out its straightness before pumping his bellows several times to stoke the fire higher. Perhaps Thomas had been right about needing something to give him a mental escape like his father used to do.

Or maybe...

Maybe this was the very thing he had been looking for all along that would rekindle his passion and forgotten joy.

Well, there was only one way to find out.

Like the first day he worked the forge under his father's watchful gaze, Elijah picked up his father's hammer from the anvil and tossed the piece of metal halfway into the fire, waiting patiently for it to heat up.

From the yellow glow reflecting back in his eyes, he could almost feel the warmth of his father's hand pressed firmly on his shoulder once more as he waited. "I remember, Papa..." He closed his eyes and tied the straps of the apron tightly behind his back, wanting more than ever to have just one more conversation with him. "And no, I haven't forgotten..."

Elijah lifted the steel from the hot coals and began the process of possibly creating a masterpiece of his own.

Chapter Twenty-Five

October 20th, 1811

Almost twenty minutes had passed since the last time Emile had shuffled the papers on his desk casually, trying his best to pay attention to the other men surrounding his desk but his focus had returned time and time again to the discussion he had held with Hope earlier that morning and her stubborn dismissal of his authority now that she was an adult. That disappointing conversation alone, coupled with the almost nagging sensation that would not diminish in its pestering of him like an insect humming directly beside his ear, kept him from understanding the reasons behind anything that was transpiring around him.

When he had arrived shortly after lunch, his intention had been to simply pick up the correspondence he had forgotten, dispatch it and be on his way home as quickly as possible. Yet all of that was before he was stopped twice by three of his constituents and now his fellow house representatives were in his office bickering over which position he should take on the floor of Congress in a few weeks. An annoyingly pointless argument by his way of thinking as there was a very good chance it would all be tabled until a later date, yet again, due to the unpredictability of the epidemic.

"Surely you can see the valid reasoning behind such an advancement into the Canadas, Mr. Deschamps. According to the recent census alone, we can clearly see that the population is surging at an alarming rate. This means that we will eventually require that land, not to mention all the timber the Canadas possess to fortify our people," Representative William Anderson reasoned, puffing on the end of his cigar twice before blowing out the smoke in a direction away from his colleagues seated closely nearby. "Now, I know you favor the idea that our president is purely acting out of greed, but this is now about meeting the ever-burgeoning needs of our county and not purely personal opinion, sir."

"So, in that light, you think it is worth the risk we might face meeting a coalition of Indians there? No, thank you," Adam Seybert countered. "Crossing the border without provocation would be a suicide mission at best."

"Well, we already proved to them once that we were mightier than they. As savage as they are, do you honestly think a tomahawk will match a musket any day on the field?" Charles Ingersoll added proudly, his prejudice against them showing louder than his actual words.

"Gentlemen, please, I know these are emotionally driven issues, but we should at least consider the side Representative Clay has made. Great Britain, in all her superiority, may think they own the ocean and everything in it, but that does not mean that we own the Canadas also simply because we share a common border." Emile attempted to put the war into a more realistic perspective to persuade them further.

"I think you misunderstood him entirely, sir," Mr. Anderson corrected him sternly. "Henry Clay thinks rightly that God has given us the power to take the continent from them. It is not merely our desire. It is now our right."

"Even our brother in Kentucky, Mr. Johnson, agrees with him. In fact, he has often stated that the ownership of the Canadas is yet another step towards our greater destiny as a country." Mr. Ingersoll stood up and began pacing the room. "Should we not choose to side with Mr. Jackson in this fight for our national character?"

"Our national character?" Emile looked over the top of his hands which had been placed vertically into a triangle in front of him. "Are you saying that our character as citizens of this newly formed country is to steal whatever is not ours purely because we want it? That would make us no less than common thieves at best, if not opportunists at the very least. That is hardly anything any of us would call noble, or have we lost that distinction, as well, when we accepted our positions in the government?"

"Hmppff, when you put it that way, no." Mr. Anderson grumbled as he put out his spent cigar, realizing that continued discussion on the topic was useless, just as it had been on many other occasions previously.

"Then how <u>do</u> you intend to vote on the war, should it be taken up?" Mr. Seybert inquired, genuinely interested in what the man across from him would have to say.

For several long moments, Emile thought deeply about the subject in question, judging the weight of his answer and the ramifications it would bring before speaking carefully, "The calling up of the colonial militia in our nation's defense is not something any of us should be taking lightly. The conflict facing us is not the revolution of '76, and these men are not merely pawns in a great game of chess between two nations like you may suppose. Though, I will concede that on paper, they are only an army. But as most of us know, they are so much more than that, gentlemen. They are someone's father, brother, uncle or in Mr. Ingersoll's case, maybe even someone's grandfather."

The men chuckled lightly at the slight jibe for the man was almost twice their age if not more.

"And yes, I <u>do</u> agree that something should be done to stop the actions that Great Britain is taking in attacking our merchant ships. Our citizens are not pirates who are intent on looting and pillaging the high seas, nor should they be treated as such. And as representatives of this country, it is our job to protect our maritime citizens just as well as we protect those who walk the streets of Philadelphia," Emile continued. "It is not only just, but it is also their <u>right</u> to ask for our protection. So, I believe we <u>should</u> give it."

"And if that means going to war because of it?" Mr. Seybert raised his eyebrows, leading Emile farther down the path to war and destruction as a nation.

"Then I will re-evaluate that decision when the time comes, but not today, and not for the reward of something that does <u>not</u> truly belong to me in the first place," Emile stated firmly before looking up at the clock on the wall and shaking his head disappointingly at the late hour it had reached. "Gentlemen, it is already well after six, might we all retire for the evening and reconvene on Monday to finish our discourse? I fear, as weighty as it may be, the decision before us will not be made without <u>many</u> more discussions such as this."

With muffled words of agreement mixed with also a heavy bit of perturbance at his outright refusal to bend in the slightest, the men all stood and shook his hand politely before walking out of the room still in animated discussion between them.

"Why men are so eager to destroy one another I will never know." Emile shook his head as he watched them go before picking up the necessary dispatch and pushing in his chair before he made his way around his desk to the door. Then, in a moment of brief panic over the carelessness his distraction had suddenly caused, he returned once more to the fireplace mantle and blew out the four candles that had been illuminating it. "The last thing any of us need is for this place to go up in flames. Though it might be a fitting end for this day, that is for certain." he muttered sarcastically, then smiled at the irony of the statement for the very conversation he has just endured felt like the coals of Elijah & Sebastian's fires being blown upon repeatedly to stoke them.

The embers of the 1776 revolution still remained undeniably warm in the hearts of those who had fought so bravely for their liberties, dutifully kept near a dull red for the past thirty-five years as if waiting for the time to bring them to life again. Yet in all that time, it seemed that it would take very little oxygen at all to rekindle their fervor once more into a brighter flame. Though this time, he feared sincerely that the whatever message their passion eventually created, it would be nothing laudable to him whatsoever.

The rarity of what the people in this country had accomplished was something that drew both his admiration and terror all in the same breath. Or rather, how one nation could be so focused on a righteous determination for every aspect that freedom offered, and yet so staunchly blind to the havoc war created was beyond his understanding. How many soldiers had truly suffered in the freezing cold with Washington that winter at Valley Forge or in all the other battles for that matter? And for what? "For liberty!" They had all cried with the last breath of their existence. That transcendent theme was indeed something incredibly noble to die for, something he might have also chosen once upon a time if he had been in their position, but to die simply to gain a piece of property... that was a concept Emile could not comprehend, today or ever. Pieces of property could always be replaced. Homes rebuilt. Businesses re-established, but men, women, fathers, mothers, sons... never.

He placed his favorite hat on top of his head and bounded down the stairs quickly, dropping the correspondence quickly into the secured box when he reached the lobby for the courier to pick up in the morning. Being over a day late in his task might possibly cause him to be rebuked slightly by his superiors for the delay, but at least the message would get there and well before the time it was actually required... hopefully.

Opening the door at last to be on his way, he stepped out into the approaching twilight and smiled broadly at seeing his wife waiting for him in the wagon at the curb. "My, what a pleasant surprise! How did you know I was in town?" Emile walked over to the wagon and climbed up beside her before taking the reins in hand.

"I didn't." The look in Emma's eyes when he studied her immediately after her brief reply did not match his own mirth at all. Nor did she return his smile in any way. On the contrary, from the way in which she now clasped her hands in front of her, she appeared more than a little bit annoyed, or almost frightened.

"What is the matter, love?" Emile wrapped his free arm around her in protective reaction, instantly worried about what her silence might foretell. "Has something happened to Charlotte or Jedidiah's family?"

Emma shook her head, but her face reminded him of the one she wore back in the garden at Kent before he had asked her to marry him. It was the very same uncertain expression that carried with it all the tell-tale signs of someone deliberating inwardly about what to say next. So much so that it unnerved him even more. "Tell me. What is worrying you, Emma?"

"Where is Hope?" Emma bit her lip, afraid of what the obvious answer would bring out in her husband.

"I left her with Michael hours ago, why?" Emile's jovial disposition suddenly left him entirely, leaving behind only a dark skepticism in its place. "She isn't with Michael, is she?"

Emma shook her head quickly. "No, I went to *The Aurora* offices first on my way over here, thinking the same. Michael said he walked her home an hour ago. But Emile, I have been home all afternoon. She never arrived."

Emile leaned his head back and sighed in great displeasure at what he was most definitely going to have to say next to his quasi-adopted daughter before focusing again on the horses and calling them to a respectful attention. "I know precisely where she is, and so do you."

Emma nodded. "I would have fetched her myself, but at this point, if that is where she is, the damage has probably already been done. Maybe this way she will have gotten a bit of her stubbornness out of her system in the process."

"Ha! Don't count on that for a minute." Emile gritted his teeth as he drove the horses at a slight clip down the street past Elijah's closed shop and the bustling corner near the hospital but reigned them in when he saw Charity wave a hand from the curb to politely flag them down.

"Are you heading anywhere near the Fabbri home tonight?" Charity asked while secretly hoping that they would be able to assist her. "William left me a note that I was to meet him there when I was finished with my visits today."

"Yes, believe it or not, we were actually just on our way there. Would you care for a ride?" Emma offered freely and stepped down from the front to climb back up into the back of the wagon, taking her seat comfortably on the boards behind her husband.

"If it isn't too much of an imposition, but I could have ridden in the back, Emma, you know that," Charity offered, feeling suddenly awkward at the uniqueness of being given the position of preference.

"Nonsense." Emile reached out his hand to help her up next to him as he tried to remain courteous and pleasant outwardly despite the anger inside of him that was threatening to roil over. "Mrs. Deschamps and I have traveled in this fashion more than once over the years."

"Yes, well that is most definitely true," Emma mumbled back before continuing. "In fact, I believe the first time I was forced to hide under a very thick blanket because you were rescuing another woman."

"Another woman...?" Emile shot back incredulously at her irritatingly different view of their escape from Paris. "I was leaving because I was escaping a mob."

"True..." Emma concurred but stopped in discussing more as she realized that their story might also share a bit more information than what was prudent at their present location in town. "But perhaps that is a story for another time, love."

"Perhaps." Emile winked in her direction. "But it <u>is</u> a good story, *Mon Cherie*."

"Well, I have time if you do." Charity brushed out the wrinkles in her dress and held onto the side of the seat next to her as the horses leapt into motion once more. "And besides, you still owe me a good tale as payment for our trip last week to get those baking supplies you needed, Emma."

"Liar. You enjoyed escaping that hospital as much as I did this town, so I think we are even on that score," Emma countered just as quickly.

"You are right, but I <u>would</u> love to hear more about your past, if you are inclined to share it." Charity raised her eyebrows at Emma's husband to urge him on in his story.

"Suit yourself," Emile said casually. "But we shall tell it from <u>my</u> point of view as my wife seems to be a bit foggy on some of the more pertinent details." Emile cast her a playful glance and began regaling the newest member of their group with the tale of their escape from the French Revolution and subsequent trip across the channel to England.

The conversation, all the way up to the point where Emma left him to start a new life for herself in Kent, had been the perfect antidote in every way to distract him from the discussion that lay ahead for them at the farm. Yet when they had reached the outer fence of the Fabbri's farmhouse and pulled the wagon up to a complete stop, the anger he had been feeling earlier at Hope's outright disrespect had now been turned sufficiently into something more akin to actual worry for what all might lay ahead of them.

"Hope Larose Fabbri." Emile called firmly from his seat in the wagon, half-expecting the girl to come out to greet them, wearing the charmingly sheepish expression she normally bore when she knew she had gone against their established boundaries.

Not a soul answered.

Suddenly concerned even more than before by the silence all around them, Emile glanced over at the front porch of the house and squinted his eyes to peer deeper inside, for Hope was nowhere to be found outside either.

"Is Hope missing?" Charity asked curiously and scanned her side of the property beside the house for the girl in question.

"In a way, she was supposed to return home hours ago." Emma climbed out of the back of the wagon and straightened her skirt from the disruption of the journey. "I'll go look inside, Emile. Charity, did you wish to see Charlotte, too, or were you only looking for William?"

"Both, actually, but since you all are busy here at the moment, perhaps it would be better if I sought William out first to find out what he needed." Charity raised her eyebrows while observing the growing tension between the husband and wife next to her.

"At this late hour, you will probably find him at Jedidiah's. Just head through the gate, past the great oak, and it's probably not a hundred yards farther before the large tree line on the other side." Emile instructed her easily then chuckled. "If you don't return by morning, we will send out a search party for you."

"That doesn't seem too overly complicated to follow, Mr. Deschamps." Charity laughed lightly, as well, at the very suggestion. "Though admittedly, with my poor sense of direction, that might become necessary one day, but I don't think it will this time."

"Really? William did warn me that calamity liked to follow you. Maybe it would be better for all involved if I saved myself the time and took you part of the way... just to be sure." Emile offered politely, but everything in his body language spoke otherwise.

"No, please stay. I think I can manage on my own. Besides, I've been there a few times this week already, though normally from a different route." She replied and left the two of them by the house as she strode confidently across the yard and through the back gate.

"I like her, Emma." Emile watched the woman with interest. "She is open and honest, and a tad bit blunt, which in my opinion, is just what William needs."

"I agree. She _is_ a good match for him if he can only manage to get out of his head long enough to see her for what she is." Emma put her hand on the railing and climbed the front steps that led up to the house.

"Truer words have never been spoken, my dear." Emile waited by the wagon for her return while allowing the horses some freedom to munch on the grass near the porch.

Without another word, Emma walked inside to retrieve Hope but returned several moments later with an equally worried Nathanael instead. "Hope hasn't been here either, Emile."

"Not here!" Emile's head shot up immediately in alarm, for he had been certain beyond a shadow of a doubt that this was where he would find her.

"No, I have been with Charlotte since Emma left earlier today, and I promise you that she never once came by." Nathanael defended his niece though all the while knowing that her disobedience could also be a precursor to something even more dangerous.

"Come with me then." Emile motioned to Emma and watched as she climbed back onto the buckboard seat next to him. "We will check back at the house."

"But what if you do not find her there?" Nathanael asked with growing alarm, uncertain what actions they should take next to locate her should it become necessary.

"I will come back here to fetch you if we do not because that will mean that we will need your help searching for her, but until then, stay here and don't breathe a word of this to Charlotte." Emile slapped the horses briskly with both hands and felt the raw energy they were exerting as the same adrenaline rushed through his own veins all at once.

"I wouldn't dream of it." Nathanael's blank stare followed after them long after they had left the long driveway.

"Please God, let her be there." Emma prayed quietly over and over again beside him, her hands wringing in and out as she clasped them close to her chest.

"She has to be. She's naive, Emma, not a complete idiot." Emile growled with determination as he rounded the corner at a very fast pace before pulling up the horses to a halt a few miles later in front of their home.

Trying not to show the panic that was tearing at the edges of every breath that he swallowed, he paused for a moment to compose himself fully as he waited for anyone to exit the house at their arrival before his eyes anxiously scanned the outside yard and field just beyond, then stopped just as quickly as they fell on the cherry tree where she had retreated earlier. To his great surprise and most definite relief, there she sat, not twenty yards away, and perfectly intact, or at least she was faring far better than he was at the moment. The only thing that remained curiously amiss whatsoever now was the fact that she was also joined by two small, crying children who were hugging her skirts on either side just as tightly as he was now unconsciously gripping the reins in his hands.

"Hope!" Emma accepted the reins from her husband and watched helplessly as he strode indomitably in the girl's direction, his patience clearly spent.

Never before had she seen her husband this furious about anything to necessitate this kind of reaction, and a part of her felt justifiably frightened for the girl to experience it. Though if she were to be blatantly honest, she was more than a little bit relieved that he <u>was</u> there, as well, and not herself alone, as deep down, that same anger and disappointment he was displaying at almost losing the girl also churned inside of her, precariously teetering on the edge of lashing out every time she had to ignore the sullen looks and sarcastic replies Hope left behind her like lost toys. Emma's patience had felt ready to explode for weeks actually under the stress the epidemic had placed upon her, yet she had managed to keep it at bay solely with the knowledge that in the end, Hope's safety was far more important than her momentary irritation.

"Where have you been, young lady? Do you realize that you have made us all worried sick!" Emile commanded severely, daring her to defy him with any such nonsense as what he had heard only just that morning. "Don't you care about your aunt or myself, or were you only thinking about what you wanted?"

"I... I..." The young girl stammered uncontrollably under the heavy weight of his stare but could not manage to form a coherent sentence. In her whole life, she had never once heard him raise his voice towards her or anyone else for that matter, nor had another soul in her existence chastised her in such a fashion. All of which left her completely dumbstruck, too stunned to even contemplate what kind of response he truly wanted.

"Emile, please." Emma climbed down from the wagon at last and walked over to where he stood before touching his arm to calm him. "What happened, Hope? Michael said he walked you home hours ago, but I know <u>I</u> never saw you. Did you injure yourself along the way? Or did you go somewhere else?"

Overwhelmed completely now by everything that was happening so fast around her, Hope looked up at her aunt and then her uncle with wide eyes and started to whimper along with the children. "I did come home with Michael as we agreed upon, or at least most of the way, but then we argued when we reached Mother's. As you might have guessed, I tried to convince him into letting me see her through the window. Surely <u>that</u> would not have been dangerous in any way." She shuddered once more and sniffed but would not meet her uncle's gaze because she knew <u>exactly</u> what it would contain.

"Huh, I thought as much." Emile stiffened at her ludicrous defense but still remained steadfast as he looked down at her harshly with his arms crossed tightly across his chest, incredulous at her seemingly indifferent disregard for him.

In the long silence that followed after, Hope looked up slowly to check for any softening in his temper against her but then ducked her head once more, utterly ashamed of what she saw reflecting back at her in his eyes. "You should probably know that Michael was far too frightened of <u>you</u> to let me set one foot within the outer gate, Uncle Emile." Afraid to say more on the subject, she glanced back up at her uncle with the knowledge that she had disobeyed him in the worst way possible. In fact, seeing the level of disappointment with which he now viewed her literally tore at her to know how much of his trust she had lost by this one careless act alone—far more than anything else she had ever done before.

To his credit, Emile did not say a single word one way or the other. He didn't have to. His expression alone carried a wealth of conversation all on its own, even though his heart was inwardly singing for joy that she had not been injured or even worse.

"Then how on Earth did you end up here, Hope, and where did these... um... children come from?" Emma stepped closer to the boy and girl but stopped abruptly when she noticed the slight strawberry flecked rash beginning to show upon their cheeks. "Hope, whose children <u>are</u> these?"

It was then that Hope started to really cry. Yet, in between the ragged sobs that had finally overtaken her, she managed to sputter out the rest of her pathetic story. "It's not his fault, Emma. I left Michael at the farm and told him I was perfectly capable of walking myself the rest of the way home, but before I got here, one of the other doctors that works with Uncle William met me along the road. Doctor Baxter or Bailey, I don't recall which. I only remember that he said he needed me to come with him immediately, so I did. These are the neighbor's children from several farms over, though I have never met them before in my life."

"Was he talking about the Thomspon farm that was sold last Christmas down by the old mill?" Emile tilted his head slightly to view the children better.

Hope only shrugged. "From what he told me at their house, both of the parents passed this afternoon, leaving the two of them essentially... orphaned. As late as it was, he didn't know what else to do besides take them back with him to the hospital, which he couldn't do since they were also sick. So, with little else he could think of and since he expected there was no one else for miles who could care for them either, he asked us to do so until arrangements could be made." She held the girl even closer who was probably around three years old, if not a bit younger. Her older brother, likely by a year, maybe two, chose mostly to shrink behind her arm protectively, obviously frightened of the man who was now towering over them. "I don't even know their names."

"Thoughtless man!" Emile shook his head in dark irritation, wanting very much to march right down to the hospital tonight and give the man more than a piece of his mind on the subject. "He should be drawn and quartered for doing such a thing."

"Oh, don't be so dramatic, love. It wouldn't help even if you did." Emma touched the forehead of each of the children carefully. "Well, it appears that they are our responsibility now. So, why don't we start by trying to get them some supper first, shall we? I am sure they are probably famished and tired, aren't you? We can figure out the rest later once they are settled." She held one hand out to the boy and waited for him to accept it. "Would you like to try one of my biscuits? I hear they are pretty good."

Uncertain he was ready to leave the only other person he felt comfortable with at the present, the boy only eyed her hand from a distance, then nodded tentatively before getting up to follow her inside.

"I'll bring the girl," Emile said quietly as he walked over to Hope and picked up the young child gently into his able arms before speaking directly to Hope alone. "I expect you to remain here until I return, young lady." He glanced back once more over his shoulder with a look that meant far more than what he had uttered.

Unshakably obedient at last, Hope didn't dare budge. Instead, she buried her face in the arms that rested on top of her pulled up knees and waited for the punishment that was sure to follow, visibly overcome with the stress of the whole situation.

Emile and Emma, however, continued on their way into the house beyond and remained there for several minutes before only Emile returned and took a seat on the ground next to Hope, leaning his back against the tree behind him with a loud sigh as he finally let go of the last of the pent-up adrenaline he had been holding onto unconsciously. "What am I going to do with you, girl?"

"Forgive me, I hope?" Hope said with a question in her voice but from what he could tell, she was clearly still trying to contain the torrent of emotions threatening to escape and flood over her.

More relieved than anything else that she was indeed safe and sound, or at least for the time being, Emile glanced over at her, then reached his arm around her shoulders before drawing her into a close embrace. "Come here, little one," he cooed softly just like he had on so many other nights before when she had awakened from the recurring nightmares of her father's death.

"Oh, Uncle... I'm so sorry." Hope fell into his arms gladly, releasing her tears and sniffled jags between words of fervent apology and faithful promises never to do anything so foolish ever again.

In truth, there was really nothing Emile could do or say that would erase anything that had transpired that afternoon, nor could he possibly protect her from the consequences of what had been selfishly forced upon her. Instead, he chose to hold her close under the thick shadows of the hovering tree, gratefully taking in the moment as the two of them sat together in the silence of the night... just like they had in a hayloft so many years ago. And, by the time the apologies had finally subsided, and the last tear had been sufficiently wiped away, the fireflies beside their home had started to blink on and off across the pasture like a thousand sparkling dots of green and yellow light.

Mesmerized now by the peaceful picture beginning to form in front of her, Hope looked up at her uncle and wiped her eyes with the back of her hand. "Is the Scarlet Fever really as dangerous as everyone has been saying?"

"Um-hmm," Emile nodded slowly, but his gaze remained entirely fixed on the fireflies beyond.

Curious, as well, as to what it was that was suddenly holding his intense fascination, Hope joined him in his view and tried once more to restrain the fear she felt building within her. "Does that also mean that there is a good chance Mother and Jed might die, or maybe even the two of you?"

Emile shook his head slightly but replied in a way that displayed his careful contemplation of what he was eventually saying, "Probably not, but I can't promise you that they will be the same either."

"Oh, Uncle, I'm so scared." Hope's whole body shivered in response to the stress and shock she had endured over the past few hours.

"Shhhh..." Emile pulled her closer still, praying like he had never prayed before that God would not see fit to teach them all another unwanted lesson. "There is no sense being frightened of something that might never happen in the first place. Your father taught me that."

"That seems very wise." Hope whispered back with a sigh as she stared down at her favorite dress, thinking how sad it was to have spoiled such a fine day after everything he had tried to do for her to make it better.

"Yes, he was." Emile agreed easily but continued to trace the lighted paths of the bugs off in the distance.

"I know you might not believe this yet, but I truly never meant for any of this to happen." Hope bit her lip as it began to quiver once more.

"I know." Emile turned his head to watch her expression for several long moments before answering in a tone she often remembered from when she was a little girl. The one that held a special kind of sound to his voice that she had never heard him use with anyone else. "Do you know what I was just thinking?"

Hope shook her head slowly back and forth and waited.

"I was remembering back to when you were a little child. How you loved to try to catch those fireflies out there almost each and every night when I would come to visit."

"Really?" Hope blinked back at him in astonishment. "I don't remember that."

"Oh, you were probably not much older than that boy when you did it." Emile smiled patiently at her innocent reply but continued, "And twice as curious, I assure you." He touched the tip of her nose affectionately, remembering her cute freckles and dimpled cheeks that made her face come alive with energy whenever she smiled. "As I was saying, each evening you would pester your father all the way through supper to help you catch those bugs. At the time, you probably thought they were fairies or creatures from some magical realm out of one of your Uncle William's latest books, but that didn't stop you from being mesmerized by them as they danced in and out of the summer wheat and tall grasses like they were playing hide and seek."

He paused, recalling the light in her eyes as she chased them happily. "Your father and I did try our best to convince you that they were nothing of the kind, but you could not be persuaded. So, in the end, the three of us: your father, myself and you, caught probably twenty or more of those bugs in one night and placed them in a jar next to your bed just as you commanded."

"It was my summer nightlight! I do remember that!" Hope's eyes lit up with wonder once again at the memory she had once held.

"I am sure you do." Feeling the cool breeze of twilight settling all around them at last as the first stars began to appear up above, Emile took off his outer coat and wrapped it protectively around her before moving on in his story, "You loved your nightlight all that first night, and the night thereafter and the next after that. But then, one day you went up to your room after supper had finished and your nightlight was no more. Every one of those magical insects had met their untimely demise in the duty of your service."

"Awww, how sad! Poor things... I should have let them go." Hope snuggled up to her uncle, feeling once again the safety his arms always provided.

"Yes, you probably should have... or maybe, I should have done so for you and spared you the tears that followed for weeks afterwards and the very unnecessary funeral and burial you made us all hold." Emile answered honestly, then chuckled briefly as he remembered the hilariously eloquent speech he had made on their behalf. In truth, it would have put Nathanael's own sermons to shame had he been there to hear it.

"But Hope, I can see now that you are so much like those fireflies out there. Your light burns brightly for all to see: your wonder, your love, your optimism, your... well... hope. Which is why I think you are so appropriately named." He smiled down at her and felt the warmth of her smile back. "And best of all, you share that light so freely with others around you, not stopping to worry for a moment about what might happen if someone were to catch you and put you in a jar. It is what draws people to you, and it is what I love <u>most</u> about you. But it is also your greatest weakness, my dear, just like my pride is mine own."

"You aren't that proud, Uncle. You just have a way of doing things that is entirely your own." Hope tried to encourage him sweetly.

Emile chuckled once more at her totally biased assessment. "That is a very interesting way to put it, but I stand by my first statement. It is a good thing to acknowledge your failings openly, or at least to yourself. But... that being said, some pride <u>can</u> be a good thing. Yet it has also almost cost me the company of both your uncles and your father on more than one occasion in the past. As you say, it is something that makes me who I am, but it also a great challenge for me to keep it in its proper place or my weakness will overpower the good that I can accomplish in this life as it takes over and makes that strength even weaker."

"So, you think my light is my weakness? How can any of that be bad?" Hope tilted her head to see her uncle's face more clearly, trying to comprehend his rather confusing explanation.

"Because... out there in that field, there is no one to protect those fireflies from nature's destruction, or to defend them from mean little girls who want to use them for a nightlight. That is where I come in, and your Uncle William, your Uncle Nathanael, your mother, Emma..."

"I get the picture." Hope cut him off, then paused before saying something that very much needed to be said, "But someday it <u>will</u> have to be someone else's job to protect me. You can't do it forever, Uncle."

"I'd like to see you stop me." He huffed in sudden refusal before smiling and relinquishing his right on the matter. "Yes, <u>someday</u> Mr. Adair will whisk you away from us, and he will be right to do so, but that will <u>never</u> stop me from protecting my firefly."

"Just maybe not every second of the day... and maybe from a comfortable distance." Hope leaned her head against his chest once more.

"Yes, maybe from a distance, Hope." Emile considered the heavy probability of that thought, for he had always known he would one day outlive his little Hope, too. One day very soon, she would get married, have children, and grow old, yet he would still remain trapped in the state that he was currently in. Despite what he would ever truly desire now, he would forever be destined to be an unwilling spectator to her mortal departure, and that thought would always remain the only thing he would ever regret.

"Alright, enough already." Emile pushed the girl away slightly and stood up, trying to compose himself from the morosely defeating reflections. "Now that the worst has obviously happened, we must set our fears aside and do everything we can to help those children who are no doubt reeling from their unfortunate ordeal today."

"But I thought you said it would be too dangerous to be exposed?" Hope took his offered hand and stood up easily beside him.

"Well, fate has already decided that for us, hasn't it? Like it or not, we shall have to see where we land in all of this." Emile went to release her hand and head inside but stopped when she held it firmly, unmoving. "Is there something more we need to discuss?" He eyed her from several steps away, a definite apprehension returning to the peacefulness surrounding them.

"Only if you promise me that you will not be angry when I tell you this?" Hope's face bore the same worried expression Emma's always did when she was about to tell him some unpleasant news or detail he would be staunchly against.

Without being able to hide it, Emile sighed heavily once more, for he already knew exactly what words were going to come out of her mouth next. "Michael has finally asked you to marry him, hasn't he?"

The girl nodded soberly but did not say anything more.

"And have you formally accepted him?" He said calmly, not wanting to influence her decision in any way or make her rush into anything she was not prepared for just because she felt the need to defy him in this.

Hope shook her head. "Not as of yet. I told him I would need to speak with you first about it before I would."

"I bet he did not like <u>that</u> answer... apron strings and all."

Hope rolled her eyes like he always loved to do. "That was actually what we were arguing about, among other things."

"Good, girl." Emile smiled in definite approval of her strength of character.

"Uncle Emile, stop." Hope inclined her head and studied him with one hand upon her hip.

Seeing her slightly irritated expression, Emile couldn't help but laugh just a little before he chose to add an interesting detail that he knew would lighten the conversation even further, "Would it help if I told you that the young man in question had already spoken to your mother and your other uncles before he proposed?"

"Really?" Hope's mouth fell agape in astonishment. "All of them?"

Emile nodded. "He most certainly has more courage than I give him credit for."

"Well, I already know Mother approves of him, but what did you all decide?" She bit her bottom lip nervously, suddenly anxious about what they had said, for she knew they all stood in her father's place regarding matters such as this. It was true that for the most part, her mother might be in charge of her more basic decisions, but the three of them were the final say when it came down to anything more detrimental for the family.

"Well...." Emile leaned his head slightly to his left and stared out at the fireflies once more. "Your Uncle Nathanael said that Michael must promise to bring you to church every Sunday after you are married, or he would personally see you all for counselling thereafter."

"Of course he did, and Uncle William?"

"That Mr. Adair must prove he could support you financially first and also already have a home set up for you before you wed." Emile pushed back his loose hair towards his ponytail behind, thinking that their requirements sounded more like a contractual list than an actual marriage approval. "He is always the more practical of the three of us, I think."

"And... you?" She stepped closer, afraid of what he might have decided.

Emile scanned the field aimlessly for several seconds, then turned his attention back to her, realizing the moment he had dreaded for the past year had finally arrived. "I told him I would only let you go if he promised to love you as passionately and fully as we all do, for no one who would do less would ever be accepted."

"Oh, Uncle!" Hope threw her arms around him and held him tighter than she had ever done in her life.

Emile did the same before resting his head on top of hers. "Does this mean you will accept him?"

Hope nodded quickly. "I love him, Uncle, and I know he loves me, too."

"Then you had best go and tell your aunt as she has been dying inside trying to keep it a secret from you all this time," Emile instructed as he released the girl who then flew across the yard and up the steps, unable to contain her squeal of sheer delight.

The sound of the dissident joy against his own sorrow echoing across the yard back to him made Emile's heart ache even more and rejoice all at the same time. "Is this what you felt like all those years ago, Sebastian?" Emile gazed out across the field and thought back to all the conversations he had ever had with her father. "Loving your family so much that you are willing to die for them or being forced to choose a lifetime without them just as long as they are happy?"

He waited several more minutes, contemplating his friend's expected reply before nodding contentedly and making his way slowly back over to the horses to put them and the wagon away for the night.

Suddenly, despite feeling inexplicably and inescapably old in every fiber of his being tonight, he knew now that he would <u>never</u> forget a single detail of Hope's life, even though he lived for all eternity.

Chapter Twenty-Six

October 22nd, 1811

In the upstairs room, away from the comings and goings of those who might be passing through to drop things off or complete the necessary chores, Nathanael napped quietly in the large rocking chair set carefully next to Charlotte's bedside, unwilling to leave her side since the moment he saw her two days ago. The fever that had initially worried everyone so greatly with its intense ferocity had thankfully abated considerably during the previous night, but with it also slipped away the rest of her strength, as well. So much so that she could hardly lift her head from off the pillow now to shift her position in the bed, let alone walk much farther than a few steps if it was required. What she needed most of all now was constant assistance, but since there was no one else left amongst the family who could readily give it, Nathanael had, of course, seized upon the opportunity to eagerly volunteer.

When he had first come with William and witnessed the paleness of her normally robust countenance, he knew then where his place truly lay, and it was not with the dead. Though admittedly, he <u>did</u> have to try to be more than a little bit creative in how he explained all of that to the others, as being her only caregiver at the moment was not the perfect solution by any means, neither was he especially knowledgeable in how to tend to someone in her condition, yet he was certainly willing to try.

After all, Emile's family currently had their hands full with the two younger patients they had been given. And William and Charity simply couldn't be everywhere, nor did he especially wish them to be underfoot when he could certainly tend to the needs of one woman by himself... or at least he hoped so. Though honestly, she had not been awake long enough as of yet to truly test him.

From what Emma had explained when she dropped off dinner last night, both orphaned children did not seem to be showing any of the more troubling symptoms other than the telltale rash and sore throats, but that did not also mean that his two friends had not been kept extremely busy seeing to their many needs. No one had yet been able to find any relatives to speak of in the city, close friends or even acquaintances for that matter in any of the neighboring towns. Though thankfully, through some detective work of their own, they had fortuitously been able to at least discover the children's names.

Little Samuel, the oldest, was a stout, precocious sort of boy who had just turned four that past Spring according to the detailed family tree William had discovered in the front of the large family Bible at their home. His sister, Holly, was only a year younger, though the girl still did not possess a wide vocabulary of her own as of yet. Beyond that, they had found it extremely difficult to discover anything more about the family who seemed to have arrived here well before the revolution as indentured servants. And as old as the little lad may be, Samuel was not a talker, preferring to keep to himself most days or quietly play somewhere in an obscure corner of the room. Nevertheless, he certainly did have one exuberantly extroverted quality in a voracious appetite that had forced Hope and Emma to spend the majority of their waking hours trying to keep up with his likes and dislikes at any given moment, more than on his actual care.

In fact, Emile had sworn more than once that the boy must have been suffering from a tapeworm by the way in which he consumed things in rapid fashion, but William had assured him against it, adding that the age-old maxim was to feed the fever, not starve it. So, with little else he could do on the matter, Emile had chosen to placate the little tyrant for the present. The necessary instruction regarding his eventual use of moderation could be taught later, or at least later this month when the child was feeling more like himself and hopefully less resistant to their rules.

Adding more blessings to others this week was also the magnificent fact that Charity had told Nathanael even more promising news about Jedidiah and Nancy as both appeared to be improving more and more with each passing day. This in itself was probably the best news he had heard all week, even if neither of the young parents were able to do much more than survive at the present.

The dire, though positive explanation he received from his friend's assistant might have been viewed as dramatic in nature if it had come from Emile or even Elijah if they had delivered it. But after only days meeting Charlotte's needs,

Nathanael knew this was probably as close to an accurate assessment of their actual condition as she could have made. In every way possible, beyond what he could conceivably express to anyone else of his acquaintance, his heart ached with fresh pangs of guilt each time he looked over at the woman in the bed across from him, longing to take away the pain she was experiencing. From the way in which the soft candlelight highlighted the dark circles present beneath her eyes to the loose skin on the surface of her normally strong hands, he could tell that she had lost probably ten pounds if not more in the past week alone, if that were even possible.

Charity had suspected that it all might be due to her not getting the proper nutrition she normally received, but since neither the nurse nor Nathanael had been the best at making more than the basic provisions like eggs, oatmeal, and the occasional sandwich, which required practically no ability whatsoever to cook, the poor woman was certainly doomed to suffer in comparison to the others and would no doubt make a full recovery only by their generous failures in the kitchen. Still, as kind as she always was, Charlotte never once complained or spoke an unkind word about the dubious quality of the food she was served, nor did she make him feel like she was not pleased in any way that he had been the one who had chosen to remain by her side.

"I'm so thirsty." Charlotte stirred from beneath the heavy quilt as she rolled over onto her side with a groan.

Alarmed, for it was the first time she had spoken all evening, Nathanael jolted instantly at the request and opened his eyes, suddenly awake and ready to assist in any way she required. "Charlotte, you're awake."

"Yes, Nathanael." She licked her lips twice, trying to salve the cracks that had spread across them in her sleep.

"Can I bring you something to eat? Maybe some warm soup, perhaps?" He offered eagerly, knowing that Emma had brought over a fresh pot of chicken noodle soup earlier that evening and placed it carefully above the low fire in the large hearth below to keep it warm just after supper. Indeed, that had been hours ago, and well past the time everyone normally enjoyed their evening meal, but as far as he was aware, Nathanael felt certain that the warm coals that rested within were ample enough to have kept it simmering slowly for her.

"You made soup?" Charlotte opened her eyes and looked back at him incredulously through the glaze that covered them and restricted her from focusing properly.

"Ahem… no." Nathanael laughed lightly at the assumption. "Emma made the soup. I merely kept it warm, which is probably much better for you in the end."

Charlotte smiled. "Thank you. That sounds so nice right about now."

"Then I'll be back shortly." Nathanael got up quickly and returned a few moments later with a wide-mouthed bowl of soup, a wooden spoon, and a small linen cloth for any spills that might inadvertently occur.

Wanting to appear less of a burden to him after all of his efforts, Charlotte attempted to sit up higher on her pillow, but try as she might, she could only manage to move a few inches higher. "I'm pretty useless today, aren't I?"

"Not at all." Nathanael set down the items he was carrying onto the table beside her and turned back to her afterwards before asking her permission respectfully. "May I?"

Charlotte nodded and reached one arm weakly around his neck for support as he gently lifted her higher up on top of the pillows until she was almost in a sitting position.

The woman with the brown hair that had the slightest hint of white strands here and there around the edges that framed her face closed her eyes and placed her other hand upon her forehead to steady herself better.

"What is the matter? Do you have a headache? William left some powder if you should need it. I can go downstairs and make some up, if you think it will help." Nathanael used one hand to brush away the hair from off her face and held her hand protectively while still leaning close to her.

Charlotte shook her head. "Not a headache. Just incredibly dizzy at the moment. It will pass; I am sure." She slowly waved off his concern with her other hand, then tried once more to open her eyes and focus on the room around her.

"I'm not surprised that you might feel so. You haven't eaten anything substantial in over a week." He let go of her hand and sat down on the edge of the bed beside her, then set to work picking up the necessary napkin before placing it gingerly at the base of her neck and patting it down.

"A week? Are you sure? I barely remember the day I fell ill. Was it last Friday?"

"Actually, it has been almost two Sundays since, if one were to count the day before yesterday." He picked up the spoon and the bowl and lifted a portion of the contents up to her lips for her, allowing his patient to take as little or as much as she felt she was able.

For several tries, Charlotte attempted to open her mouth wide enough for the spoon to pass through unobstructed, but in the end, could only manage a small sliver in which to sip the broth away noisily. Grimacing at the painfully rude behavior, she stopped eating altogether but then smiled bashfully when she saw Nathanael try to hide his lighthearted laughter.

"Please forgive me. I was laughing at your expression, not the noise," Nathanael explained calmly. "There are no manners here, Charlotte. This is <u>your</u> home, after all, and you need to feel free to eat however you see fit. At this point, it is more important to get your strength up than it is to do what people might think is proper."

Feeling more at ease, she took several more, loud sips of the broth that was offered, then lay back against the pillows more fully for a brief rest. "Sebastian would be literally cringing in pain if he were here instead of you."

"Would he?" Nathanael cocked his head sideways in surprise. "I wouldn't have thought that of him at all."

"Yes, well, as provincial as he may have appeared on the surface, he had a keen focus on having the proper manners at the table. In fact, Sebastian especially hated it when people talked with food in their mouths more than if they slurped their food unnecessarily."

"Huh, I suppose that must have made things pretty difficult having two boys then." Nathanael smiled at the humorous tone of the conversation and returned his concentration back to chopping up the noodles into smaller pieces so that she might be able to consume some of them better.

"You have <u>no</u> idea. Ask Eli. He probably suffered the most in that area." Charlotte leaned forward once more and managed to eat four more bites, including some of the chicken, before she held up her hand to stop. "It tastes absolutely heavenly, but I had better pace myself. I don't want to even think about seeing that soup a second time."

Suddenly concerned that the quality of the soup might be to blame for her unexpected nausea, Nathanael smelled the aroma of the broth in his hands tentatively and closed his eyes, remembering the way his mother used to make a very similar style of soup every time he was sick.

"Do you despise food as much as Sebastian did?" Charlotte asked easily as if discussing the habits of a vampire were as common as discussing any other subject under the sun.

"Almost, though there are a few things that still taste acceptable, like cinnamon for example, or maybe even some of the fish they sell down by the docks. And I <u>do</u> rather enjoy a warm cup of coffee, for the most part, as long as it has lots of cream and sugar so that there is more of them than the actual coffee itself. But tea, on the other hand, is still entirely distasteful, and in a way, practically rancid to me just like some of the more intoxicating drinks they serve down at the tavern. I know Emile also prefers his wine on occasion, but I attribute that to the fact that fruit isn't so bad either as the sweetness far outweighs the acidic repulsion some foods bring. Yet all of that was nothing compared to the snails your husband and I ate our first night together on the beach, or the first cup of tea I was given at Señor Moretti's. Truthfully, between you and I, I almost could not swallow either of them. It was that bad." He eyed the soup one more time, debating as to whether or not he liked the scent of its rich herbs or staunchly hated it. "Still, William and Emma seem to like some of the newer blends that have arrived recently, so maybe there is hope in that for me in the future, as well."

"Then you should at least try the soup. It's not like you can catch anything from me in doing so." Charlotte waved her hand weakly in his direction, prompting him further.

"As much as I hate to refuse you... I think it might be best for both of us if I were to abstain," he admitted hesitantly, not especially desiring to cause a spectacle in front of her when he tried not to utterly vomit it up afterwards.

"Nathanael..." She encouraged him earnestly but did not try to push him further. "Remember... there are no manners here, right?"

"Right," he replied without the least bit of assurance that he actually believed her before he picked up a small spoonful of the soup and placed it into his mouth with great trepidation, holding it there for several minutes as he contemplated swallowing it.

"And?" Charlotte's eyebrows raised in question.

Nathanael swallowed, then halfway grinned. "It is not entirely horrible, and it does have a rather unique flavor that is vaguely appealing. However, it is most definitely not like my mother's, but... all things considered... that does not mean that it is not still somewhat enjoyable all the same." Nathanael tried another heaping spoonful before deciding to finish the rest of the bowl with increasing satisfaction. "On second thought, I think I shall have to get the recipe from Emma immediately." Nathanael licked the spoon when he had finished, then placed it politely back within its bowl, grateful for yet another culinary success.

Charlotte smiled. "I am glad that you tried it then. At least you have two things that you might love now."

"Precisely so."

"You know, I have often wondered so many times how difficult life must have been for all of you to have the things you enjoyed most of all stripped away with very little benefit given in return. I know Sebastian wouldn't talk about it very much, but it must have been so hard to deal with when you first changed." She tilted her head to study him closer.

Nathanael nodded. "It was at first, crushingly so... but Señor Moretti helped a great deal in aiding us to adjust to our new, um, diet and lifestyle. The rest I suppose we grew accustomed to along the way or learned to live without."

"But wasn't it as simple as just drinking blood in the beginning? I mean there had to be literally hundreds of people on the island you could have chosen from to meet your needs, if you had wished it." She stared back at him inquisitively with no judgement for his lifestyle whatsoever behind her eyes. "Sebastian never did share how he maintained his needs once we came to the Colonies, mostly because I think it embarrassed him to have to depend on something so savage." Charlotte tucked a loose piece of hair back behind one of her ears. "My guess is that he probably used the livestock like Emile showed him. But I suppose a part of him was also still trying to protect me in some way by keeping it all to himself, but I didn't care. Why should I? You don't judge me for eating a steak or fried chicken. Though I do also understand the moral question involved in all of that, too. It's not like I condone murdering someone to get what you want, but there <u>are</u> other ways."

"Well, Emile didn't seem to have a problem with it in the beginning. He killed a girl on his first day being a vampire. He was a different man then, of course, but it still happened. As you know, that was how we met Señor Moretti in the first place."

"But what about you? What did you do in the beginning?" She asked curiously, thoroughly invested in this version of the story that she had never heard.

"Starved mostly or tried to get by on whatever William could acquire from his patients in Wakefield. For myself, it was never a question that truly needed an answer... not really. No matter how hungry I ever became, I could simply never do what Emile did that night." Nathanael looked down and shook his head, remembering the look on the poor girl's face as she lay motionless on the cobblestone street before they had taken her up the mountain and buried her. "Though I also cannot say that I haven't been tempted... more than once actually..." He admitted truthfully and thought only of Elsie and the incident at Pasha when he had proposed.

"I'm sorry, but what could you never do? Take a life?" Charlotte said simply.

"No, take a soul," Nathanael corrected her quieter still.

"Oh...is that what you think you would be doing if you lived the life you have been given to live?" She studied him carefully, no judgement whatsoever behind her hazel and golden flecked eyes.

"Definitely." He leaned back in his chair and rubbed his hands together slowly, his skin crawling with the sensation of a thousand tiny insects walking upon it as his body began reacting involuntarily to the tenor of their conversation. "Once upon a time I would have given or done anything in my power if it would have saved my Elsie in some way, or to have at least been there to guide her through it to the other side. Instead, she faced it all alone while I cowered in fear, far away from the woman I loved."

"But would you have turned her into a vampire to save her life if you had been there?" She exhaled slowly, feeling already tired by the exertion of the rather lengthy conversation, yet still thoroughly engaged in what he had to say.

"Never," Nathanael shook his head slowly before he stared back at her seriously. "I could never take away someone's ability to choose their eternal stability merely so that I could be happy here on Earth. It would be... completely unfathomable."

"So, that is the real reason why you have chosen to never marry after all this time." Charlotte nodded, finally understanding the answer to much of her inner speculation. "It's not that you could not let go of Elsie. It's more that you just cannot let go of your humanity."

"Possibly." Nathanael smiled at the intuitiveness the woman always possessed. "But truthfully, I think I have just been inclined to believe so far that we <u>may</u> only be given one person in our lives to be completely whole with, whether that is for a lifetime here on Earth or for eternity—like you had with Sebastian and Emile has with Emma. I had my chance, too, I suppose, if only briefly. And it <u>was</u> glorious each and every day that it lasted, but the moment has since passed, and now I am determined more than ever to spend the rest of the time God has given to me now, honoring her life in some way by my service here."

"So, you don't think you will ever marry, Nathanael?" She looked over at him seriously, but her overall demeanor appeared still unaffected.

"Oh, I am sure I will someday when someone else unreservedly takes up residence next to her in my heart. And she will be equally as important as Elsie was to me, but that relationship will be different by design as all gardens are when you till them over and replant them for another year."

Pleased by his chosen analogy, the corners of Charlotte's mouth curved upwards slightly at the edges. "You know as well as I that I love my garden, Nathanael Beckett."

"I do," he admitted sheepishly, then cleared his throat afterwards. "Well, as you might expect, I am content to wait on God's direction for that choice, too. It will come in time, I am sure... if I am patient."

"That is an incredibly moving decision on your part, Nathanael." Charlotte patted his hand gently. "One that I think would make your Elsie very proud if she were here."

"Actually, now that you mention it, I don't know. She never did like to leave the town of Wakefield proper during the time that I knew her, so I doubt she would have followed me all the way to the Americas, let alone London."

"Could you tell me more about her? You already know everything there is to know about Sebastian."

"Not everything, I am sure, but enough to suffice my curiosity on the matter." Nathanael paused and took a long moment to glance out the window, uncertain how much he was comfortable sharing with her that would not also make her feel less important in his eyes, before he answered her in an almost dreamlike response. "She was like light itself in my darkest of times." He half smiled, remembering the way she would look up at him when she walked by on her way to market. "And just like you, everything she did brought joy to those around her until her very last breath. Why do you ask?"

"I was just trying to picture her. I think I feel more inclined to understand your heart more by seeing hers," she answered sweetly.

"Well, I only hope I don't live long enough that I'll eventually forget her. Though the letters I receive from her mother occasionally certainly do help." Nathanael tried to smile fully but the emotion of the conversation prevented it. "And what about you? Do you think you will ever marry again?" He held his breath expectantly at the answer he was most certainly dreading.

"Oh, I don't know." Charlotte turned slightly on her side so that her head could rest upon the pillow comfortably. "I'd probably have to find someone as stubborn as Sebastian since I am already accustomed to that or the man might think I am being too overbearing. Too bad Emile is taken." She tried to laugh but only ended up coughing several times before drawing in several deep breaths to recover from it.

"You are <u>never</u> overbearing, Charlotte, far from it. And yes, Emile and Sebastian were very much alike in that respect. Two men with similar dispositions that knew how to rile the other effectively like oil and water. Though I do believe they had finally managed to find a friendly alliance in the end," Nathanael admitted easily. "So, at least that was a blessing."

"You can thank Hope for that." Charlotte closed her eyes. "That was one of the main reasons why I let her stay with Emma and Emile after Sebastian died."

"Huh..." Nathanael's head lifted slightly as his mind contemplated many questions to follow. "Speaking of that, I have also wondered why you did so.

Though truth be told, it must have hurt tremendously to be here by yourself afterwards. If she had stayed, she could have at least been a comfort to you in your suffering."

"Yes, and no." Charlotte sighed and shook her head. "It <u>was</u> hard, make no mistake. It still is some days, but not as hard as watching your only daughter pining every day for a father that will never return to her. Sebastian did that when our little Sarah died, and it almost broke me. It was why I did not tell him I was pregnant with Hope all those years ago. As strong as I am, I know my limits, Nathanael, as I am sure so do you."

"I understand completely... more than you know. And do you still think you made the right decision?" Nathanael tilted his head to see if she was still awake, for she had since closed her eyes, and her breathing had slowed down considerably during the discussion.

"I'd like to think so. You and I both know that Emile loves her as if he is her own father and she has a deep love for him, as well... Emma, too. It is not the same love as it was for Sebastian, but it is still something very powerful and genuine every time I see it. They will protect her with their lives if it ever comes down to that so I am content that it is as it should be and that is enough for me," Charlotte answered easily with no remorse or regret whatsoever.

Sensing that perhaps it might be time that Charlotte rested more, Nathanael stood and lifted the quilt higher up on her body as he tucked her in more to its comforting warmth, then hesitated. "But are you sure you would never entertain a husband? From all that I have witnessed in the past three years, I am certain that you have so many years left to give someone and just as much wisdom to impart."

"Why? Are you finally asking me for my hand, sir?" Charlotte's eyes opened and blinked twice before she smiled warmly, intending only to lightly tease him. It had worked beautifully, for Nathanael looked almost completely flustered now as to how to reply.

Amused beyond measure at his uncomfortable reaction and inability to form a coherent sentence, Charlotte reached forward one hand from beneath the covers and grasped his own. "Be at peace, Nathanael. I was only teasing. You of all people should know that you will <u>always</u> be one of my dearest friends."

"Good." Nathanael sighed contentedly for he was not sure he was exactly ready yet for that kind of step in their relationship. Maybe someday soon, or at least he hoped so, but not until he had sorted out a great many other things in his mind first. "Now, if you will try to rest a little longer, perhaps we can see about getting you bathed and changed into something cleaner when Charity arrives.

You've been in that same nightgown for far too long already, but I believe both of us would feel better if she were the one to help you with all of that."

"Is she coming over, too? I hate being such a bother to everyone." Charlotte closed her eyes once more, as they were much too heavy to remain open for long periods. "And I absolutely despise just laying here doing nothing."

"You have never been a bother, Charlotte, not today, nor ever. Just sleep. I will be here when you wake up." Nathanael took his seat once more in the rocking chair and folded his hands politely in his lap intending to sleep for a few hours more if he were able.

"Nathanael?"

"Yes, Charlotte?" He replied, though he had also leaned his head back and closed his eyes, drinking in the comfort of the peacefulness all around him.

"You are a good man, and you deserve to be happy, too," Charlotte assured him sweetly before falling back to the measured silence that had passed between them for most of the night.

"Thank you, Charlotte. Despite all that has transpired, I think I have found a contentment that fills my soul, which is more than most men can boast."

"Oddly enough, that was something similar to what my Sebastian used to say." Charlotte remembered fondly.

"Hmm? What was that?" Nathanael kept his eyes closed but listened more intently.

"I asked him once before he passed what it had been like for him living as a vampire all these years, knowing that the rest of his family would most likely pass before he did. He told me that he had never once wanted to live forever like the lifestyle Emile and Señor Moretti had embraced. He just wanted as long of a life as possible with his family," Charlotte said with a sigh while feeling the deep love once more that Sebastian had always given her.

"Well then, that rather makes it all slightly ironic that he passed before any of us," Nathanael harrumphed softly while stating the obvious, as he was usually known to do.

"Yes." Charlotte joined him in a soft laugh. "All that senseless worrying about something that never came to pass—an admonishment to all of us. After all, he managed to survive being orphaned, apprenticing under a family that treated him lower than the servants, a shipwreck, and even being turned into a vampire, but despite all of that, he could not escape his own fate it would seem."

"Maybe that in itself was a mercy when you come to think of it," Nathanael admitted honestly. "I mean, if I had to choose to live forever or die in a way that saved someone else's life, I would hope that I would decide the same."

"Would you have done it for Elsie? Swapped places, I mean?" Charlotte asked as she stared at the man across from her who seemed so much more self-assured than the man she had met after her abduction. That man would have jumped at his own shadow in a dark alley and probably screamed like a little girl in the process. This one held a comforting wisdom well beyond his years and a calm reassurance to that fact every time she spoke with him. In fact, the two men were total opposites in every respect.

"If I was given the chance to do everything all over again, I would most definitely have traded places with her in a heartbeat. Even if that meant my life for hers. It would have been worth it." Nathanael opened his eyes once again and leaned his head back down to look at her seriously.

"Why?" Charlotte furrowed her brow, feeling slightly confused by his denigrating answer. "Why do you think that your soul is so much less worthy than another's?"

Nathanael shook his head and exhaled slowly. "I had to make my peace long ago that God had another purpose for my life than the one normally taken by mortal men, but I have yet to find what that purpose is. For me, some days I feel like I am here just passing the time while others are doing important things, making changes in the world, impacting others. Tell me seriously, what do I accomplish of any long-term worth? I teach young men to think for themselves. I go through my day just like the day before it, and for what? Emile has Emma to live his life for. Sebastian had his family. William has his work, and if we are all so fortunate, Miss Bentham quite possibly. God be praised. But what do I do that matters in the vastness of eternity that would warrant me spending the rest of it here on Earth? Sitting here now, I cannot think of a single, worthy thing to offer up in explanation."

"That is quite a big topic, Preacher." Charlotte looked back at him with endearing compassion.

Nathanael only stared back at her in the silence, then looked away and out the window once more to hide his disappointment. "I suppose that is why I never speak about it. Most people do not expect that a preacher can have the same despairing thoughts as their own. And yes, I did come very close to a point in my life once where all I wanted was to cease to exist. It was a dark place to be sure, and one I almost did not crawl out from. Yet here I am, though why, I could not tell you." He looked back at her and tried to lift the corners of his mouth into a smile, but it looked more like a constant struggle than an actual achievement.

"Oh, Nathanael...." Charlotte reached her hand towards the man who then slowly stood up and took his place once more upon the bed to hold it. "I will tell you the same thing I told Sebastian when he was in his own brooding moods, the ones that made him retreat to the corner of the barn and wish that by some mercy, God might intervene and end his suffering then and there. Every day you are here on this Earth is a blessing, whether that is to be a blessing to someone else or by His grace, to give it."

Nathanael looked down at the hand holding his own, unable to physically maintain his composure while looking at her. "I don't see how that is possible, Charlotte."

"Then maybe it is time you accept that being a vampire does not make you less of a child of God. It makes you more. It makes you specifically chosen, set apart. It gives you a unique opportunity to affect the lives of people not just for one day, or for one month, but for generations upon generations. Think of all the people you might be able to reach for Christ in a hundred years or two if God so allows. A mortal man is only granted forty-five of those years to serve him, maybe fifty if he is lucky. But you, Nathanael, you have been undeniably blessed." Charlotte touched his cheek with her fingers and wiped away a single tear that had slid down it. "Don't waste His blessing focusing on the wrong things. Look at your life through God's eyes and see a new perspective."

Feeling his heart so very close to bursting with the love he now held for the woman beside him, Nathanael lifted his chin higher to look at Charlotte and placed his hand over hers on his cheek. "You are a wise woman, Charlotte Fabbri."

"I know." She smiled and Nathanael couldn't help but grin, too, at her playful response and laugh lightly.

"And Sebastian was a very fortunate man, indeed."

"So was Miss Summerfield." Charlotte nodded in understanding and closed her eyes. "I think I'd like to rest now."

Nathanael nodded and placed her hand gently back on top of her other before leaning forward and kissing her lightly just once upon the forehead.

"What was that for?" Charlotte's lids fluttered open slightly at the unusual response from him for he had never done more than hold her hand, even when no one else was around.

"For never judging any of us." Nathanael said with a sigh and took his place once more across from her before closing his eyes contentedly at last.

Chapter Twenty-Seven

October 24th, 1811

Feeling an immense sense of calm despite the harried encounters he had endured since his arrival this morning, William took another sip of his coffee and looked out across the courtyard to the other doctors and nurses doing the same. Most were paired off with each other or in small groups assembled on various benches, but all were in animated discussion in one form or another, probably grateful that all of them had been given a brief respite on this rarest of days.

Only he was sitting alone under a large maple tree that had begun to flourish in the most brilliant of oranges and yellows throughout its lush foliage. In fact, it reminded him very much of a painting he had once seen in the King's House during one of his visits there with his father. The one in the alabaster frame that had been placed prominently at the end of the long dining room that few of the guests ever used, so many never had the opportunity to truly appreciate it. The mottled colors above him, just like the ones in the painting there, all blended together now to form a strange kind of impressionistic perspective when he viewed them swaying in the light breeze. And especially so under the crystal blue sky above that only highlighted further the spectacular weather they had been having all week. The only downside to any of it at all was being forced to enjoy it from the safety of the shadows.

Well, at least he could be glad that he was outside to appreciate it fully. That was more than he could say for Jedidiah, Nancy or even Charlotte, as they were mainly confined to their houses with the strictest order of total bedrest. Still, even with that being said, when he had time to visit them all tonight, he would suggest a thorough airing out of both houses to try to balance out the humors and rid them both of any lasting vestiges of the fever.

For the better part of the week, the late October nights had remained fairly temperate overall, given that November was less than a few days away, so that was a blessing, too, as far as William was concerned. The brisk weather that was likely to follow would no doubt bring with it a change of season and hopefully also a time of rest for all of them.

In every way he could possibly imagine, William was physically exhausted now beyond anything he had ever endured before. They all were. As a vampire, his body did not physically register the exertion at the same level that would make most others around him buckle under its weight, but that still did not mean that he could do so indefinitely. Like everyone else in Philadelphia, he had dutifully pressed on, stretching himself far too thin by the daunting schedule he had been steadily keeping. In fact, at this point, he did not know what his limits truly were anymore or if he even cared. From his feet that ached to be placed inside the leather shoes that he normally thought were entirely comfortable to the way in which he literally flinched every time someone woke him in the middle of the night because of some emergency on the other side of town, his entire body was more than ready for a long period of peaceful existence once more, if not a total holiday for at least a week... maybe two if the hospital could spare him that long.

Perhaps I could go visit that island Emile is always talking about over by Charleston. The one with the dolphins that like to play close to the inlet. Surely in November or even December, it will be overcast enough to have a chance to experience it for myself. William pondered excitedly the possibility when an equally intriguing thought occurred to him afterwards. *I might even try my hand at entering one of those Sunday races on the King's road down to the plantation while I am there.* He mused again thoughtfully, then tucked the glorious ideas back away for another day.

The only thing remaining that would make this day any more perfect by his standards would be the news that the epidemic was finally diminishing, if not gone entirely. Though regrettably, from the list of people he had yet to visit today with Charity, that possibility was highly unlikely. The miraculous news, that would seem almost too good to believe at this juncture in time, would certainly be welcomed by all of the staff, but everyone knew deep down that it would not be today or even this week, but hopefully soon.

Desiring nothing more at that moment than to simply lay his head back and peacefully relax against the stone wall behind him, William set his cup down on the bench beside him and closed his eyes to enjoy the cool sensation of the breeze as it blew over him and followed its path over the wall. It had been days since he had enjoyed a warm meal with Nathanael or even slept in his own bed for that matter as he had been compelled to spend the majority of his time over at Jedidiah and Nancy's. Not to mention the fact that it had probably been a week at least since he had the opportunity to clean his clothes properly enough to look even remotely presentable or arrange a well-earned hot bath. A fact which irked him far more than his clothing, if he were to be totally honest.

Though many of his acquaintances still held firm to the superstitious claim that an immersive washing of any kind would probably lead to some form of illness or chill if one were to do so more than once in a month, William, however, staunchly disagreed. The ridiculously antiquated notion seemed almost archaic in its creation as the mere thought of skipping even a week without soaking in the heavenly steam made his skin crawl to consider it. Since even before his transition, William had never much cared if others felt that doing so was dangerous, if not unhealthy. To him, the action of it felt justified as the sheer pleasure of the heated water pouring over his head and down his face calmed him better than anything else ever could.

"Well, maybe not everything..." William mumbled sarcastically to himself, secretly yearning once again for the one thing he <u>always</u> wanted most of all. There <u>was</u> one thing that was better, but the shockingly dangerous activity by everyone else's standards was certainly close enough to that to make it worth the negligible risk.

"Tonight... I just have to make it until tonight." William sighed happily in the shade just thinking about his rendezvous that evening with the large metal tub he had purchased with his first paycheck in the Colonies and smiled with absolute contentment at the possibility. In spite of everything that had happened this morning, maybe today was shaping up to be one of those perfect days of his existence, after all. Or rather, the day was quickly becoming the kind of day that he would think about often when he was unable to sleep at night or was too discouraged to choose a path ahead of him.

Well, if it was, he wanted to hold onto that feeling for as long as it lasted, as he probably knew better than most how very important that small action could be.

"Take no thought for the morrow, for the morrow shall take thought of the things of itself. Sufficient unto the day is the evil thereof." He quoted mentally in perfect repetition from Nathanael's sermon months ago.

At the time it had struck him profoundly with how utterly prophetic the verses were when they were applied to his life as a vampire. But after the past three weeks of not knowing how many souls each day he would usher into eternity ahead of him, he could also see how it applied to his life as a doctor, as well. Or to be honest, it would certainly be helpful to any man, woman or child if they were to also take it to heart as he did.

Certainly, he could go about his life worrying about every single thing that might befall him or one of his patients. That seemed perfectly logical, too, maybe even expected for the most part. Or... he could try something else. He could simply learn to trust that the good Lord had a plan, and nothing he could do ahead of time would prepare him for it until it actually happened. Simply put, as a child of God, he just needed to keep doing what he was doing and face each obstacle in methodical fashion as they presented themselves to him.

It was sound advice during Bible times, and William surmised that it applied to 1811 in the same way. Maybe that was one of the reasons why he had liked Nathanael's sermons so much of late. In the down to earth manner in which he was currently presenting them, God's Word felt more personally applicable than it had ever been before.

Or maybe... maybe it was him who had changed.

Most definitely me, as I do not think I was truly listening to him before, William admitted mentally and thought back to the way he was when he had set off on the Endeavor.

When the two of them had first discussed their differing views in Señor Moretti's library back on the island, William had no intention of ever considering God to be more than the great clockmaker who was callously intent only on watching His children scurry around from place to place like insects in a maze. Yet, through the man's humble example, he had soon discovered that God was much more than that. That despite how utterly ludicrous it was to even consider it, God truly did desire a relationship with His children, more than He wanted to hand out judgements.

That thought alone had been the one that had resounded the loudest in his heart when he had first heard it and had caused him to lie awake many a night contemplating the truth behind it just like he did with all of the other medical oddities he had encountered. In the end, he had been forced to concede that he would rather believe that God had created him with a specific purpose in mind than to waste whatever life he had been given for eternity aimlessly wandering around from accomplishment to accomplishment as he clung to his old self-serving drive towards goals he had intended for his future.

Not that he had ever had anything great that he had wished to achieve in the first place. Yet it <u>was</u> comforting just the same to know there existed something important he was supposed to do that mattered. Perhaps someday God would show it to him more plainly, but for now, he was content to merely sit under this glorious tree and enjoy the divinely given, robust surge of natural energy that he now felt flowing over him with each passing gust.

"Is this seat taken?" A quiet voice slightly above him asked, though they did not say more as they patiently waited for his reply.

Unwilling to move a muscle, William did not open a single lid but only exhaled slowly, taking great pains to reply just as carefully as he could manage to avoid further disruption, "It all depends..."

"Depends on what?" The young woman petitioned politely, her tone even and possibly inviting.

Understandably curious now, William opened his right eyelid and took in the gorgeous woman in front of him from her adorable black shoes to her light blue dress that was shaped close to her body near the waist, complete with navy-blue edging around both of the pockets and hem, all the way up to the smallest sprinkling of freckles that dotted themselves across her nose and green eyes, the exact hue of cut glass when held up to the bright sunshine. "It depends on which Miss Bentham I am currently entertaining at the moment. The one who takes my breath away just looking at her or the one that makes my blood boil when she speaks."

"Oh, please..." She took a seat next to him and mimicked his position, laying her hands casually on top of her lap. "You know perfectly well that you can be no picnic either most days. Though just from that description alone, it appears that the trouble may lie with you and not me in any way."

"Excuse me?" William turned his head and looked over at her sarcastically. "Are you sure someone hasn't switched you for someone else along the way?"

Charity laughed lightly. "Stop it, I'm warning you, William."

"Fine, Miss, whoever you are... Nice to meet you by the way." William put his head back to its original position for several more moments before he impetuously chose to reach over and place one hand on top of hers, waiting to see if she would push it away for it was the first time he had done so in public. "I've missed seeing you the past two days. Have things been busy for you, too?"

"A bit. I was over at Charlotte's house this morning and made sure to stop by Emma's to check on the children. As tired as I was from helping with a delivery last night, I almost fell asleep at their kitchen table right onto the pancakes Emma had fixed for me but decided I had better keep myself vertical, or at least until lunch. Besides, most of my patients are stable at the present, so I came out here looking for you." Charity held his hand in her lap for a moment, stroking his fingers in between her own casually, then released it with a slight squeeze. "How has your morning been going so far? Anything new?"

With a definite groan, William sat up and reached for his coffee before taking another sip. "Well, let me see..." He paused, then began again, "So far, I have dealt with a gangrenous big toe that Nurse Sarah had to help me sever, a patient who needed a rather nasty carbuncle excised and cleaned, and a young child who vomited all of her breakfast on my first set of clothes, not to mention on several of the nurses who were standing nearby while attending me, before we managed to fetch a bucket in time for her rather disgusting third, and thankfully last, explosion."

"Lovely." Charity remained leaning back, enjoying the moment of relaxation while she could capture it. "Remind me not to work with you in the future."

"Actually, now that you mention it..." William glanced over at the nurse in confusion before adding, "Why <u>aren't</u> you working with me at the hospital anymore? Did I do something wrong? I mean you normally have no problem telling me when I do. So, why avoid me altogether now?"

"Oh... that..." Charity scrunched her nose up and frowned at the necessity of having to answer him at all on the subject. Knowing how incredibly busy he had been, she had hoped he would not have noticed the change so soon, but she should have realized that he would have eventually. Though truthfully speaking, William hardly missed anything trivial, let alone an adjustment such as this. "I had to switch up the schedules a little last week."

"Why?" William appeared as equally befuddled as before.

"Well..." Charity sat up and smoothed out the wrinkles in her skirt, a marked look of resignation crossing her face. "Because I overheard that some of the nurses thought you are giving me preferential treatment. Or that I was somehow calling in favors that benefitted me over others. Though I don't see how anything you have done has advanced me in the slightest, quite the opposite in fact. I've done more work under your advisement than I ever did under Doctor Brooks. You know what he is like. As long as we allow him to take his afternoon nap in peace, he could care less what we decide to do with our patients."

"I see," William nodded in growing understanding. "That is a definite problem. I never imagined that our, um... friendship," he looked over at her and watched as the same smirk that he was wearing at the word lifted the corners of her mouth, too, "might cause your life to be more difficult by asking for your specific help when I need it."

"It is <u>only</u> an issue when it makes the rest of them jealous, William." She rolled her eyes at the drama that had been steadily building within the walls of the hospital. "Since we stopped fighting and actually started trying to work together, I have become the laughingstock of the whole hospital it seems. Worse yet, people are now gossiping rampantly to each other and to our very interested patients, about the spinster nurse who managed to seduce the good Doctor Wells like I am part of a dramatic novel of some kind."

"Oh, Charity, I seriously doubt it is as bad as you say." William shook his head at what he perceived was a gross over exaggeration on her part.

"Is it? You tell me. I walk into a room, and quite literally everyone stops talking, like I am some kind of pariah. It makes me so mad." Charity rubbed her hands together to rid them of the dust they had accumulated from leaning back on the bench.

Feeling more than a little empathetic about her uncomfortable plight, William took her hand once more between his own and turned his body to face hers more fully, blocking her view and his actions from the others in the courtyard. "Would you like me to stop? The last thing I <u>ever</u> wanted to do was cause you to have a reason to be embarrassed in front of your peers."

Charity helplessly blushed at his informal attention but gripped his hand tighter still, for it was the first kind of real advance towards her that he had made in weeks, or at least where others would be able to see it. During most of their visits with patients outside the hospital, William had endeavored to remain utterly professional, sensing that she might also be more comfortable doing the same. But on the rare occasion where they were too tired to keep up the formal façade any longer, she had found herself enjoying the moments where his hand had held hers on the way home in the wagon, the longer stares he focused on her when she read to Jedidiah's sons by the fire before bedtime, the occasional brush of his fingers against her cheek when he took the liberty to push back a piece of her hair that was bothering her when her hands were otherwise occupied, or the even more intimate moments where she could have sworn more than once that he had been on the verge of actually kissing her.

"No, of course not, William. As much as it scares me, I like being close to you. In fact, it is the first real thing I have felt in over half a century." She looked up and over his shoulder to see how many of the others were watching their interaction before clearing her throat. "But I just want to be recognized for what I do for my patients..." She lowered her voice and leaned in closer to speak for only his ears to hear. "Not for how well I am romanced by the most eligible doctor in this hospital."

"They think I'm the most eligible doctor, eh?" William smiled broadly but could seriously care less what the tittle-tattle was that being bantered about at the time.

"Oh, you knew that already." Charity beamed back at him. "You didn't need me to tell you."

"True." William let go of her hand unwillingly and turned back around to lean against the wall once more before grinning again. "But it is still nice to hear it all the same... when it is coming from your lips."

"And they call women vain." Charity shook her head, then proposed another topic of conversation more hesitantly, afraid of his response most of all, as most other doctors in his position had already rebuffed her sternly when she had approached them anywhere near the subject itself, let alone what she intended to ask him. "William?"

"Hmm...?" He kept his eyes closed, his breathing even and calm.

"What would you think of a woman becoming a doctor like yourself someday?" She bit the edge of her nail in apprehension, waiting for the expected explosion and flight.

"What? A woman doctor?" William's head shot up slightly at the absurd suggestion before he shook it twice in absolute bewilderment and laid it back down. "Why would you want to do that? I know we doctors make it look easy, glamorous even, but I assure you it is not. It is a lifetime of heartbreak and sacrifice with only a smattering of hope and joy mixed in-between. Far from anything a rational woman would want for her life." He paused and considered the possible consequences he was probably going to have to endure from her after sharing this much of his opinion. "But then again... if truth be told... you can be <u>far</u> from rational at times. And please... before you react violently and hit me over the head with a pinecone or something, I mean that only as a sincere compliment. In fact, I rather prefer your way of working out problems when you encounter them. That singular strength under pressure that few of your other colleagues possess was the first thing I truly admired about you."

"Thank you, and I am sure you mean well by it... pinecone attack and all." Charity laughed lightly at the hilariously tempting idea. "But don't you think that women should also have someone they can trust caring for them? In my time as a nurse both here and abroad, I've seen far too many patients refuse to seek the proper medical care they deserve simply because their husbands did not think it was serious enough to warrant treatment," Charity explained carefully, opening up just a small piece of her dream to him.

"Not all husbands are the scum of the Earth, Charity." William eyed the woman next to him. "Some actually love their wives."

"You'd probably like to think so..." Charity only eyed him with confident skepticism, then pressed further, "Did you know that a man can have his wife legally committed simply because he wants a divorce? She doesn't even have to be declared mentally incompetent to do it, William."

"No... but why would he do such a thing? It honestly doesn't seem worth all the hassle it would entail." William glanced over at her to judge her expression more fully and measured the weight of it for several minutes before asking in earnest, "This is something you are seriously considering for your future, isn't it, Charity?"

"Perhaps one day, yes. I know that our society today is not ready for anything so progressive, but I feel confident that one day that will all change. I just want to be ready for it when it does." Charity stared intently at William, hoping he would act differently than everyone else thus far.

"A woman doctor, huh?" William sat up and looked as if he were seriously considering the possibility for the very first time. "That does not seem like it would be that incredible of a dream. Not for today, mind you, but yes, I think someday that would be nice. After all, for centuries we have relied upon midwives for their knowledge of many things. So, when you look at it that way, they aren't doing anything all that different than what we do as doctors here."

"Probably not. And they are far more experienced in their specialty I would think since that is primarily what they do. I know I have personally had the opportunity to be present for over a hundred deliveries in my time, maybe a little more." Charity sighed in relief, feeling almost euphoric by the small victory. "But could you... I mean... um, would you be willing... to teach me someday?"

"Me? Teach you?" William's eyebrows lifted in sudden surprise. "I am not sure how good of a teacher I would be if I did. You should ask those nurses this morning that had to clean up all that vomit. They might have a different opinion to convey to you about my true capabilities."

Charity chuckled. "You are as open as you are humble, and that is good enough for me. Besides, everyone else thinks that I am crazy for even suggesting it."

"Asylum material for sure." William laughed lightly, then considered the possibility thoughtfully once more before responding. "I am not sure how we can do it, or when, but we can try... if that is what you are asking me. Believe it or not, I won't be the one who stands in your way if that is what you feel is God's purpose for your life." William paused, then chuckled once again. "And I'll not have you committed for suggesting it. That would be idiotic, and dangerous for both you <u>and</u> I."

"You know enough of my ire to never doubt that." Charity smirked.

"Most definitely," William reassured her and stood up from the bench after picking up his mug to take it back inside.

Doing the same, Charity could hardly contain the excitement she now felt at hearing his sincere and straightforward response. "This may be entirely improper of me to say this, but if we weren't in such a public place right now, Doctor Wells, I would absolutely kiss you."

William rolled his eyes and almost couldn't contain the low groan of frustration he now felt in every fiber of his being at possibly missing yet another perfect opportunity. "I really need to pick my timing much better in the future it seems, if I am ever to progress any further in this friendship of ours."

"Perhaps." Charity drew closer to him, so close in fact that it made both of them cautiously hold their breath for just a moment in response. "Or perhaps, we can go for a walk now and sort it all out along the way. It seemed to work perfectly well for us before."

"Before? The last time I walked you home, you shut me down as quick as blowing out a candle and closed the door before I could even say good-bye," William defended with perfect recollection.

"Indeed, you act like what I did mortally wounded you, Doctor." Charity mischievously grinned but also felt more than a little bit sorry she had treated him so curtly back then.

"Well, it appears that it was nothing permanent, as far as I can tell." William pursed his lips contemplatively, seriously considering her request once again, then thought the better of it. Today was the first time she had allowed him anywhere near her inner dreams and thoughts without the least bit of the careful protection she always maintained. Such a leap as finding somewhere more intimate to continue on in their conversation might set them back months if she regretted it later. "As much as I would love to go anywhere with you right now, I am afraid I have a lecture to give in ten minutes, Miss Bentham. I wouldn't want to disappoint my students so soon in their studies now that the hospital has finally opened up the lecture hall once more."

"Hmmm... but ten whole minutes, William..." She looked upward at the colorful leaves and tempted him further on the subject. "That seems like plenty of time to entertain even a small conversation alone."

William sighed, wanting nothing more than to take her into his arms right then and there in front of whoever saw them and kiss her until he could no longer think about who was watching them. But he could not. Not in 1793 and most definitely not in 1811 either. There were rules of propriety to follow, and rules, as he knew only too well, were always made for a reason. "How about supper tonight, instead. Maybe just the two of us this time? We can discuss whatever you wish at length then."

"Tonight? But aren't you supposed to go to Jedidiah's after work?"

"Yes, but you can come with me. It shouldn't take long. Then we can enjoy a quiet evening by the fire when we get back as Nathanael said he would be over at Charlotte's still this evening, something about helping her sort out some old letters and documents she had found from her husband, Sebastian."

"And Elijah?" Charity played with the rim of the cup in her hand absentmindedly.

William grinned broadly and remembered with perfect clarity the discussion he had enjoyed with his nephew that morning. The one where the young man had thrown a change of clothes and some money for something to eat into his satchel and trudged out the door in the grumpiest of tempers. "Elijah is sleeping at the forge tonight."

"The forge, whyever for? Doesn't he like a warm bed?" Her expression remained perfectly perplexed.

"Yes, but between you and I, I think Nathanael's talking is getting on his nerves." William attempted to hold back a light chuckle.

Charity smiled, too. "Oh, I see. That makes more sense, but Mr. Beckett is always so kind when he does it."

"Yes, but Elijah is more like his father in that regard than his mother. He isn't a people person, per se. He is more of a diligently leave me alone to work in silence kind of man." He glanced around the courtyard that had mostly emptied during their discussion, then back to the woman in front of him. "Well, what do you say?"

Looking up at him with an expression that drew him in as much as it cautioned him, Charity reached forward and fingered the lapel of his suitcoat before answering slowly, "That sounds nearly perfect."

"Good." He reached for her hand once more and held it just a moment against his chest before kissing her fingertips lightly. "I <u>do</u> have to be going now though, or I'll be late."

"Alright." Charity nodded politely and watched as he walked the rest of the way back to the hospital and through the large door of the West Wing.

Once inside, William let out the longest exhale he had ever released shakily, attempting to calm the quick uptick of his heart as he walked while also secretly hoping he had done the right thing in refusing her this once. After all, things had been going so smoothly of late. The last thing he wanted to do was step into another puddle of confusion or hole of destruction. Those things were hard to avoid and even more difficult to dig himself out of, but still they existed and waited around every corner, it seemed, when it came to Miss Charity Bentham.

Through their many discussions, he had almost grown accustomed to the barriers she placed protectively all around her to guard her from possible future pain. Though admittedly, those had been far easier to navigate than what had just happened out in the courtyard. Where matters of romance were concerned, he <u>never</u> knew precisely what to do, for it was never something he could predict and as he was quickly discovering, equally as difficult to methodically plan for.

For most of his life he had practiced the art of strategic diversion. And every woman that he had ever met along that journey had been a potential minefield of distraction that had to be carefully dealt with and or avoided. Most only wanted him for his position or his money, but since Charity knew of neither, he felt much safer around her than with the rest. Not that she would probably care that he was pretty close to nobility back in England. She only knew him as a doctor at the Pennsylvania Hospital, and an inept one at that, or so she had often told him. Though, after their conversation today, perhaps he had been wrong about that opinion, as well.

"Doctor Wells, we are ready for you now." One of the younger students met him outside the lecture hall and opened the door respectfully for him to enter.

Suddenly stunned, William paused where he stood, feeling the weight of the moment before him for really the first time in his life. Thirty students of varying ages were all seated behind that door, and every one of them was waiting for <u>him</u> to enter, as the teacher, the mentor, the guide. These students were coming to him for wisdom, like he had done when he sat under his father and others more distinguished than himself for so many years

And yet, *what unique knowledge did he have today that they did not?*

William pursed his lips and inhaled slowly again before exhaling once more.

"Is something the matter, Doctor Wells?" The student asked him politely as he waited for him to enter.

"No," William placed a hand upon his shoulder and smiled. "I was just taking in the moment, Doctor Stuart."

"Oh, I am not a doctor yet, though I <u>do</u> hope to be someday. Maybe as good as you are," he fumbled through his praise with barely a hint of the nervous stutter William had exhibited at his age.

"Well, if you keep up that humility, you will be soon. Never lose that and you will make a fine physician. One that people will be proud to know," William assured him and stepped into the lecture hall for his lesson.

Chapter Twenty-Eight

October 24th, 1811

An hour later, when the last of the students had exited the room, William stepped out into the long hallway feeling more assured of his calling than ever before. Although he had not spoken on anything during his lecture that was overly profound in any way, nor expounded on any new discoveries in the field of medical advancement beyond that which the staff at the hospital would already be aware of, his mere presence in front of them, speaking to his students as one of their peers, had motivated a sense of camaraderie within the group like he had never experienced before.

Perhaps, this in itself was the solution he had been searching for all along in regard to his bigger purpose here. After all, what had helped the most in his problems involving Charity was not the process of educating her or even the need to correct her repeated failings; it was his humility and openness to hear her ideas concerning his patients that had made all the difference. Which, in many ways, made him contemplate even further the idea that maybe, if he could give these students the same level of respect that he had received from his father and others, what all might each of them accomplish in turn for the world, or for mankind in their lifetime? William continued to contemplate deeply the possibilities in regard to how he could implement them effectively into the program here as he walked down the hall but stopped at the open doorway of one of the wards as he passed to observe Nurse Bentham treating one of their patients from a distance.

The woman who was lying in the bed beside her looked no older than her mid-twenties with a lighter shade of caramel colored hair that matched Charity's own in some ways, though hers was a bit darker and had already lost its proper containment from some experience she had endured before reaching the hospital. Moreover, as visibly injured as she appeared to be, she had been placed on top of the white linens of the bed, still attired in her tan dress that had splotches of black soot down the right side of her skirt and all the way up to the buttons of her splotched waistcoat until it reached her slim, but very tanned arms. Angry red burns that appeared to have been made less than a few hours ago, covered the majority of one side of her right arm down to the top of her hands, and most likely both of her palms from what he could tell from his position by the door, as both upper surfaces looked to be a deep shade of scarlet that begun to swell.

Intent on moving onto her next assignment, another nurse who was dropping off the fresh linens and supplies they would need throughout the day stepped through the doorway beside him and turned to the right before he stopped her with a questioning look filling his features. "Excuse me, Miss?"

The nurse with the tight black bun and severe features that always reminded him of his governess growing up pivoted in his direction and looked at him patiently. "Aye, Doctor Wells. Can I help you?"

"What seems to be the diagnosis with that young woman over there?" William glanced back at the patient in the bed and tried to petition the information as quietly as possible so as not to draw any further attention from those within. "The one Nurse Bentham is helping?" He nodded in her general direction.

Careful to make sure she was correct in the information she was about to relay to him; the young nurse walked back over to the doorway to verify exactly to whom he was referring and continued, "Oh, that woman came in just now with burns due to her customary fits."

"Customary fits? Does she suffer from some form of mental instability?" William thought back instantly to the conversation he had just had with Charity and couldn't help but sense the intense irony of the strange coincidence.

"No, nothing of that kind. Her injuries normally result from a physical condition that happened due to some kind of previous trauma as a child."

"Do you know what might have caused this trauma?" William continued to try to reason out a new form of alternate treatment that might help her, if only just a little.

"A fall or an accident, I believe. She has been here many times before, though ne'er as bad as this," the nurse's thick Scottish accent layered her assessment nicely.

"As bad as this? Does she often have these attacks?" William appeared genuinely shocked, for the woman seemed quite fragile for someone so young.

"Aye, and quite frequently to my understanding. I m'self have treated her probably ten times this year alone. She is what we call 'a regular visitor,' but there is little we can do for her here to stop them. She knows that. She just came today to have the burns treated," the nurse said very matter-of-factly as if unconcerned about the continued plight of the poor woman, either that or had become so overly accustomed to her unfortunate situation that it seemed almost commonplace that it was still occurring.

"Oh, I am so sorry... that must be incredibly difficult for her."

The nurse nodded and turned to leave again but was interrupted once more by William's following question.

"Just one last thing, I promise. If you do not mind me asking, how was she burned precisely?" William looked back at the nurse, trying to understand how someone could have been injured so severely and yet remain as calm as she was while lying there. In his recent past, he had seen many grown men, in far less serious condition as she was, sob uncontrollably and with more verbal exclamations that would shock everyone around them than the nearly composed woman on the other side of the room.

"From what I overheard, she said she was tending to the fireplace when she had one of her fits. Believe it or not, the poor thing used her own hands to put out the flames, as the fire was crawling up her skirts by the time she next awoke. No doubt, the burns on her legs were caused mostly from being too close to the fire when she fell in the first place," the nurse explained. "Her name is Joanna if'n you'd care to speak with her. She is fairly open about her condition and will not mind ans'ering whatever other questions you might have."

"Thank you, most kindly. It's Nurse Graham, correct?" Doctor Wells said gratefully, though he continued to remain by the doorway watching the pair interact.

"Aye, Doctor," she answered discreetly and continued on her way without another word or rebuke.

"I just might do that. Though I agree, there is probably not much I can do either." William said under his breath quietly to himself.

Without noticing William watching from afar, or hearing the conversation that had just taken place, Charity continued to work methodically and carefully with the small rag in her hands to clean the inflamed tissue on her patient's forearm, hoping that by doing so it would lessen the chances of scarring in the future, or at the very least, deter any infection from setting in. "I'm sorry, I know this probably hurts, but I will try to be as gentle as I possibly can."

"It's alright." The young woman winced but did not move to stop her. "I've grown accustomed to pain mostly. It's what helps you know that you are alive, right?"

"Right." Charity smiled. "But still, I am sure it must be hard enduring it all these years. Did you say how long this condition has affected you?"

Trying not to react to what the nurse was currently doing, Joanna looked up at the ceiling, attempting to distract herself from the pain each stroke of the rag created. "I suppose it all began when I was a little girl. My mother used to call me 'her little pixie girl' because I was always flitting to and fro with some happy thought in mind. Well, one Sunday, we were just arriving at church when I decided I wanted to skip all the way down the aisle to our pew near the front. I was so excited, in fact, that I made it almost the whole way there without my parents because they were still tying up the wagon for the service. As you might have guessed, I ended up tripping over something on the floor along the way, and before I could catch myself, I fell and hit my head pretty hard on something on the way down, probably the pew itself, I would imagine. I had my first fit right in the middle of the whole congregation that day."

"Oh, my! I bet that was scary, but how old were you when it happened?" Charity dipped her rag and wrung it out half-way.

"Oh, I couldn't have been more than four at the time, maybe five."

"Four? That young? That must have been so terrible for you," Charity sympathized openly.

"Probably more so for my parents than myself. I never remember anything that happens when it starts, during or after the fit occurs. Anyways, the people at church told my parents that God had struck me down for my wickedness in some way. Or that it was a punishment of some kind for either my sin or theirs because it kept happening again and again. Which, of course, it wasn't, but that did not stop the congregation from saying it," Joanna meekly explained.

"Ignorance," Charity chided, her cheeks flushing with the indignation she felt from her own brief encounters with simple-minded people.

"Maybe..." Joanna only smiled, suddenly grateful once again to have found such a compassionate ear. "Well, no one else corrected them when it was done so pretty soon, I was an outcast from there, as well as other places."

"Why?" Charity stopped what she was doing, suddenly surprised that someone would refuse anyone for a condition such as this—something that was entirely beyond their control and totally unaffecting to others around them.

Joanna shrugged. "I suppose people get scared when they see a woman flopping on the floor like a fish out of water."

Charity smiled and though a part of her wanted to laugh at the rather humorous analogy, she held it back. "I imagine so. But were you able to at least go to school?" Charity applied a mixture of vinegar, turpentine, and an egg white to the burn and spread it over the reddest of the areas before wrapping them all with some light linen strips she had cut.

"School?" The woman laughed. "That was a worse experience than the church. No teacher is prepared in teacher's college to maintain order in a class where one of her pupils randomly collapses every week or two without warning."

"I see." Charity frowned and for a few seconds she contemplated what a life like that must have been like.

Wanting very much to encourage the nurse away from the darker thoughts she was creating, Joanna touched Charity's hand and smiled sweetly, "Please do not pity me too much. My life hasn't been all that bad. I had two of the most wonderful parents in all the world. My mother taught me everything I know about gardening and sewing, and I even learned to knit tolerably well, or at least well enough to make a little extra money from time to time. And my father made sure I knew how very special I was to both of them and to God. Why, I wouldn't be who I am today if it were not for their love." The woman spoke quickly, feeling instantly self-conscious for making the poor nurse feel so badly.

"That is truly commendable of them. I cannot even fathom for an instant what that must have been like or to have that kind of unconditional love. My own parents do not even know that I am still alive. Much less bothered to look for me when I walked away from home." Charity stared at the woman, feeling the loss of that same accepting love in her own life more poignantly than before.

"How sad! I am so sorry for you." Joanna laid one of her newly bandaged hands upon one of the nurse's pristine arms and held it there. "It is a tremendous burden to bear when you become someone else's burden. But look where you are today? You have become a talented healer who is treating someone like me who has tried literally everything they have ever given me to no avail. Like it or not, the attacks keep happening and one day, who knows, they might even kill me if I am not more careful. I know this one almost did."

Charity felt the hot tears sting her eyes at witnessing the young woman's courage through her pain but held them back, as she struggled to remain professional in front of her. "Then there is no hope for you?"

"Not really. I have a liquid that sometimes lessens the fit when I place it on my handkerchief before it begins, but the pepper baths, vegetable diets and avoidance of anything remotely taxing haven't helped in the slightest. Life itself can be stressful, and you can't avoid life, so you might as well embrace it for as long as

God gives you breath." Joanna sighed but though her words had the candor of encouragement, her face spoke only of tempered despair, either that or apathetic resignation.

"It is still hard though, is it not?" Charity searched within her pocket for the small container of liquid she always kept close at hand and held it for just a moment in contemplation before letting it drop to the bottom of her pocket once more.

"Hard... would be an understatement. No man wants to be burdened with a wife like this. Or at least no man that I have ever met. I can't do anything useful without the threat of some calamity befalling me while doing it. Believe me, I know. I've tried countless things like gardening, painting, embroidery, you name it. Though I could share with you many of my humorous stories about my other failures. Some are funny enough to cheer even the saddest soul up to glory. But..." She paused and slowly shook her head from side to side as she exhaled. "Despite what I might like, I can only remain at home with my parents and hope they outlive me, for I don't know what I will do if they do not. I don't have any other relatives left that would step up for such a commitment as I would entail, let alone be willing to financially support me. I'm simply too much of a liability for life it seems." She sighed heavily before suddenly perking back up. "Still, I woke up on this side of the grass this morning, and I lived through setting myself on fire it appears, so there are two things in my most definite favor today, wouldn't you agree?"

Charity laughed lightly with her this time. "I would agree indeed. You have been very brave. Not many women would be in your position. But I wonder... just out of curiosity mind you, what would you do if you no longer had this disease? I mean... what if you could choose anything you wanted to do and just do it? What would you choose?"

"Oh, that's easy. I would try to help others who have illnesses like myself. Maybe set up some kind of home for them with like-minded people who could support them when it was needed." Joanna said with a smile. "It is a nice dream, is it not?"

"A very fine dream." Charity nodded, then excused herself for a moment to step over to the small table in the room near the corner, away from the view of the other patients who were either resting or being treated.

From his place in the hall, just outside the doorway, William watched with curiosity as Charity poured a very small amount of grape juice into a cup, then slid something out of her pocket and emptied the contents into it before stirring slightly. Alarmed at what he was witnessing transpire right before him, he continued to observe in horror as she handed the glass back to the woman on the bed and instructed her to drink.

Unaware that anything out of the ordinary had just transpired, the woman finished the glass completely, smiled, then handed it back to her. Charity, however, did not return the offered glass to the table, as she would have done with any other patient. Instead, William watched as she walked it over to the sink on the opposite side of the room and cleaned it out thoroughly with soap and water before setting it on a shelf that was higher up in the cupboard, away from the other cups as if it was reserved for a special purpose all its own.

Frightened that someone else might have seen her actions just as he had, William's eyes scanned the room quickly, thankful that only two other people were awaiting treatment. One was most assuredly asleep, and the other was a small boy who appeared more interested in talking to his toy horse in his lap than in watching anything else transpiring in the room.

Cautiously satisfied for the present of her immediate security, he entered the room silently before walking directly over in the nurse's direction and startled her when he came up to her from behind. "Nurse Bentham, may I have a word please."

"Doctor Wells! I'm sorry. I didn't see you there." Charity's eyes grew wide, as if appearing momentarily frightened by his sudden interruption.

"If you will please excuse us for a minute, Miss." He spoke calmly to the patient but tried to his best to contain the sheer panic that was now flowing through him.

"Of course." Joanna replied meekly and watched as he placed one arm firmly behind her nurse and guided her out of the room without another word and down the hall until they were outside the hospital and at least halfway down the front pathway as if they were taking no more than a casual stroll together.

"Where are we going, William?" Charity asked finally as she tried repeatedly to keep up with him. From the brisk pace he was setting, the only thing she could assume was that he was heading towards his home a few blocks away from the hospital. "When I said I wanted to go for a stroll earlier, I didn't mean right now."

Unwilling to discuss anything as of yet, William did not dare speak. Instead, he kept a firm hold upon her all the way, directing each of her steps skillfully around objects and people in their path until they reached his home and were safely inside.

"William, wait... I can explain." Charity began but stopped when William turned around and looked at her with one finger raised to his lips, his eyes filled with what looked like a healthy dose of anger mixed with an equally level spoonful of solid distrust.

"Stay there please." He left her by the fireplace as he strode up the stairs and returned a few minutes later, assuring himself completely that both Elijah and Nathanael were not going to be present for their conversation. Then, taking off his overcoat, as he was more than certain that this was going to be a very unpleasant discussion, he motioned for her to occupy the chair across from him at the table. "Please... sit and tell me what you put in that woman's drink and why you were trying to hide it from everyone. Were you giving her some kind of medication? You of all people should know that it has to be approved by one of the other doctors or you might end up poisoning her."

"Poisoning her? Seriously, William? You think I want to kill her?" Charity crossed her arms but refused to join him. "I was trying to help her, William."

"Help her? How? There is no known cure for her condition that I am aware of, or have you discovered something I have not?" William paced behind the settee instead, more distressed than upset, for if he had witnessed her actions, someone else surely might have, as well. "When I said this afternoon that I would teach you to be a doctor, I had no idea you would foolishly think I was giving you the permission to do so without me present, and in front of others no less. Do you realize the position you have placed yourself in? Or the very real danger to your patient if something awful happens? Worse yet, what if someone suspects you in her demise? You could be arrested at the very least, Charity, if not imprisoned or even hanged."

"They <u>aren't</u> going to hang me, William." Charity wrung her fingers in and out of her hands nervously in front of her before starting to explain several times what had actually occurred yet only managing to say next to nothing at all under his admonishing glare.

"By all that is holy, why would you do something so foolish, woman?" He leaned forward on the back of the settee with both of his hands, examining her seriously, true fear at what might occur because of her actions gripping his heart.

"I can't explain this to you, William, not when you are like this. Besides, you wouldn't understand it if I did."

"Of course, I won't understand it when you tell me next to nothing!" William exploded in obvious frustration, then felt his whole body react violently against him when he watched the woman shrink away from him.

Her near-panicked state as she leaned closely against the wall on the other side of the settee made his heart soften instantly, causing him more regret than he had ever experienced, knowing that he might have hurt her in some way. "I'm sorry, forgive me. That was too harsh and far too loud." He breathed out slowly and began once more, attempting to change his tone entirely. "Let's try this again, shall we?"

Fearing that she was now destroying the only friendship she had ever really cherished, hot tears began to flow freely down Charity's cheeks at the weight of his harsh condemnation. As much as she wanted to obey him, there was little she could say to explain her actions without revealing to him the whole terrible truth. "I would never do anything consciously to hurt one of my patients, William. The fact that you even think that... that anyone would think that I... that I..." Her words fell off at each syllable she uttered in a choked sob of sorts, not allowing anything she said thereafter to make much sense audibly.

"Charity, I'm sorry." William's heart melted as he stepped around the settee and over to the woman he had grown to admire in so many ways and placed one hand on the side of her waist, afraid that she would either leave or break down entirely. "But please... you <u>must</u> tell me." He begged as he lifted up her chin and looked deeply into her eyes. The same ones that pulled him in helplessly every time he dared stare into them. "Help me understand because what I saw today frightens me more than anything you might tell me here." He used his other hand's fingers to wipe away the tears from one of her cheeks.

"You sure you really want to know?" She whispered quietly, her voice far too strained by the struggle she was enduring to contain her emotions. "Even if it will change everything?"

William nodded silently, suddenly apprehensive about what she might divulge. Though at the moment, the required promise she was exacting from him made him feel more like he was quickly becoming an accomplice to a very complicated murder plot than an equal partner in their rather turbulent relationship.

"Alright." Charity stared back at him, still uncertain as ever if she could tell him what she had been doing all these years.

One part of her, the more vulnerable side of her personality, wanted to fall into his arms and tell him every detail of her entire life from start to finish, including all of the messy parts she would rather forget completely. In fact, having someone like him that she could trust so implicitly had been the one thing she had desired for years. Not just someone who was her friend and knew bits and pieces of her life, but someone who was safe with every facet of her being until there was nothing left that he did not know.

The other, more sensible side of her would always feel the need to protect her from being hurt the way she had been so many times before. This half was far more afraid that William would make her stop altogether or worse, change who she was if she were to confess all.

"But William, if I told you everything, you might not understand, or worse yet, hate me for doing it. Though right now, I am not sure which I am afraid of more." Charity fought the balance between her two selves and tried to be as honest as possible.

"Oh, Charity..." William wrapped his other arm around her and held her, breathing in the moment of closeness between them as they both settled. "I promise I will not judge you if I can, but you <u>have to tell me</u> what is going on. I cannot protect you if I do not understand you."

Instantly on the offensive, Charity let go of William and took a step back, the more rational side of her stepping out front and center at last. "I do not need you to protect me, William. I haven't done anything wrong."

Just like he had been practicing since the very first day that he had met her, William breathed in quickly at her sudden, yet not all that unexpected reaction, and exhaled it back out again slowly before taking a seat on the settee. "Alright... now that we have that established. What would you like me to do then? Hide your actions?"

"You could trust me." Charity sat down across from him on the far side and turned towards him. "Trust that you know me well enough to believe that I would never do such a thing. But mostly you should do it because all the preconceived ideas you have ever held about medicine are about to be unmistakably shattered when I tell you this."

"I'm listening." William waited patiently, for he knew from just his short time on this Earth that many things he had once felt were fantastical, were in reality, true, though he would never be able to tell another living soul about them.

"William, as vampires, we look at human blood as our means of sustaining ourselves. It is our nutrition. Though yes, animal blood will suffice in its place. However, it never truly satisfies what our bodies are craving like regular blood does, not really," Charity explained slowly, organizing her thoughts as best as possible to dissuade him away from his previous notion.

"So far, I am following you. Emile and Sebastian have been using the cows as a substitute for decades. It isn't a perfect solution, but it has allowed them to escape scrutiny and lessened the burden on me, as I can only provide for Nathanael in my current arrangement. Emile and Emma know that, and what they choose to do is their business. I try not to ask for many more details on the subject other than that. I assume you are probably the same," William clarified easily.

"Yes, it has not been hard to procure what I need through medicinal avenues at the hospital, and no one has been the wiser about my existence," Charity agreed. "Until you saw me do something today."

"Yes. What was that you put in her drink?" William asked curiously. "An herbal tonic of some kind?"

"No." Charity drew in a deep breath and held it before exhaling through the fateful answer. "It was my blood, William."

"Your blood? Why would you give that poor woman some of your blood? It's not like it will turn her into a vampire by doing so." William shook his head. "That seems like such a strange thing to do under the circumstances, and frankly, a risk not worth taking in the second."

"I am not trying to change her in that sense, no. But my blood, your blood, any vampire's blood does have a unique ability that you are not fully aware of." Charity bit her lip, trying her best to explain it quickly before she would lose his attention on the subject altogether.

"I would think our friend, Señor Moretti, would have told us if there was something <u>that</u> important. Or are you saying he does not know about this yet?" William scoffed openly, totally incredulous as to where this line of reasoning was taking them.

"Perhaps he hasn't been looking in this direction to know. Why would he be?" Charity began to grow a bit more annoyed by his outright dismissals and less interested in pleasing him. The emotion the whole incident had created now seemed to stir a growing fire within her that spurred her onward to the point of sheer bluntness. "For lack of better explanation, our blood heals people, William. In fact, from my experience, it has the ability to cure their ailments like they never happened in the first place. I have even seen it help people on the brink of death with only a few drops," she said boldly and waited a moment for him to take it all in. "Essentially, the very thing that is the means of our torment is actually a blessing to the people all around us, and you do not even know it."

"Hold on... wait a minute," William commanded as he stood and began pacing the room once more, suddenly energized, but not in a good way. "You are trying to tell me that you are using your blood as a cure?"

"Yes," Charity stated flatly. "You have witnessed it for yourself actually... though you did not know it at the time."

Suddenly assured of the very thing that had been nagging at him for the past three weeks, William stopped pacing immediately and swung around to face her, his eyes suddenly wide in apprehension, as if the realization of her statement had finally dawned on him. "You gave some to James before he left the hospital, didn't you?" The surprising truth of what she had obviously done without his consent, now stared its ugly face right back at him

"Yes." Charity nodded timidly, afraid of how he might respond next to the revelation. "Only a few drops. I didn't dare give him more than that, as I have never helped someone as young as him before."

"But why?"

Looking into his eyes, the same ones that always held a thousand hidden emotions all at once, Charity's heart felt the pangs of his grief all over again. "You looked so broken when you were treating him that day. I just couldn't let him die when there was something I could do to possibly stop it."

"Ugh!" William groaned and balled his hands up into fists, feeling the weight of his sheer stupidity wash over him again and again like a crashing wave. "I <u>knew</u> something was off when you left me at the window while I was waiting for Jed. Though I was grateful beyond words that he had gotten better so quickly, it never made any sense." William paused and tried to steady his breathing. "But how could you do something like that without even telling me. They are my family, Charity. Don't I get a say when you do something so reckless?"

"So reckless!" It was Charity's turn to be wholly offended. "You think saving a baby is reckless? You and I both know his chances of survival were minimal at best. Would you rather have been digging a grave right now or reassuring his parents that their child made a miraculous recovery?"

"What an utterly stupid question." William shook his head, his frustration with her winning out once again over his more logically calm side.

Pacing the floor while he absorbed what she had just divulged, his mind also devoured hungrily several more pressing questions among all of the others until he fought against them one by one, compacting them farther away from his decidedly emotional state. In this moment in time, he was far too committed to her now to simply walk away because they could not seem to spend a single day together without some kind of cataclysmic debate. That may have been who they were before, but that was not who they were now, nor was it how he felt they were destined to be. And, as hard as it might be to patch themselves up again after <u>this</u> dramatic event, she was what he thought he had needed for his life, what he had always needed according to Emile and Nathanael.

But how could they feasibly move forward after this?

HOW! His mind screamed back at him in the silence.

"You should have trusted me enough to ask me first, Charity. I would think that you owe me that much," he said quietly, the intense mental exertion he was currently experiencing weighing him down heavily.

"Maybe I should have." Charity stood up and took a few steps closer to William but stopped when he stepped farther away instead and shook his head, still reeling internally from her confession. "Don't you trust me?"

"I want to, but I feel like I don't even know you sometimes." William struggled to contain the emotions roiling inside of him—fear being the largest of all... but not fear for James or even for Charity's discovery, though both were definitely a part of his deliberations. Deep down, he was more afraid of making the wrong decision in this moment in time. His inner struggle concerning the dilemma before him tore at his heart to accept whatever it was that she needed of him, as if begging him to let go of his reservations against her, while also cautioning him to protect himself in some way against her eventual refusal. Something that was equally plausible on any given day.

"Of course, you know me." Fresh hurt crossed her face once more at his perceived rejection, only this time it bore along with it a sharp edge of cynicism from her past. "You probably know me better than anyone else I have ever known." She tried to reassure him, wanting very much to put this whole mess behind them once and for all and move forward, or rather, move anywhere beyond the disappointment he was now displaying towards her.

"Do I?" William shook his head slowly, refusing to relent. " Lord knows I have tried. Yet, every time I think that we are growing closer together in this relationship, you push me farther away, like today for example. One minute you want nothing more than to be near me, practically begging me to kiss you. The next you can't seem to stand anything I do. If you care for me at all, why do you keep fighting me every step of the way? Don't you trust _me_?"

"Maybe not." She said quietly and watched his wounded pride flash across his rich cobalt eyes back at her. "I'm afraid I never _have_ been very good at letting someone else control my life, but I _am_ trying, William." She paused and pleaded with him more earnestly. "I _want_ to trust you. I am just not sure I know how." She closed her eyes and shook her head slowly in resignation. "You'd think something so simple would be easy, but it's not."

Like two opposing soldiers contemplating which side of the battle they would eventually fight on, William and Charity stood five feet apart from each other and just stared, each unable to move closer, neither willing to move farther away.

Then, when the silence was finally reaching almost a breaking point between them, the clock on the wall suddenly chimed the three o'clock hour, making them both jump at the sound it produced as if a crack of thunder had just exploded in the middle of the room.

Looking away from her at last and to the pictures on the wall beside him, William reflected once more on the complicated versions of love that were displayed there. As upset as he was at that moment, he could ask her to leave and then move on to another hospital where they needed his skills more. He could even possibly pretend like the last four months had never happened at all. It <u>would</u> be hard to begin all over again somewhere new. But he had done it all before... twice, in fact. Or... he studied the pictures of Emile and Sebastian and felt the last of his reservations fall away one by one. Or he could simply accept what she was saying as the truth and let go of whatever prejudices he still held towards her. Either way, he had finally reached the point of the crossroads where a decision had to be made one way or the other.

Feeling suddenly at peace with his choice now that it had been made, William closed his eyes for a moment and sighed deeply before returning his gaze to the woman in front of him. "Miss Charity Emeline Bentham, when will you learn that loving me is not something to be afraid of?" He closed the gap between them and took one of her hands in his, his course firmly set. "Your father was a fool to throw you away like he did. It was thoughtless and wrong of him to do so. But Lord willing, I will not make the same mistake today, so you had better get used to discussions such as these because I am sure there will be <u>many</u> more to follow."

"Really... why do you think that?" Charity placed her other hand upon his chest and looked up at him, uncertain she knew anything that she wanted at the present save the love of the man standing in front of her.

"Because just thinking about you walking out that door right now made me realize that I am not ready to lose you so soon, Charity. And yes, I know that we may still have many more fights ahead of us, but I am more willing to stand my ground <u>by</u> your side any day, than let you go," William pledged faithfully. "As crazy as that may sound."

"Huh, then I guess I was right, after all; you do belong in an asylum, William Wells," Charity quipped lightly back.

"Perhaps." William laughed just once, as well, and the corners of his eyes lifted easily with it.

"Should I make you sign a contract to that effect for the next time something like this occurs." Charity laughed, too.

"A contract?" William leaned away slightly, the strangeness of such a witty notion humoring him more than it should. "I don't know if I am ready for any of that as of yet. At the moment, I am more focused on getting through this moment unscathed."

Growing more relieved by his easy acceptance and even demeanor once more, Charity reached up impetuously and kissed him on the cheek before lightly rubbing the spot she had just kissed with the thumb of her hand on his cheek. "I can definitely agree on that point."

Surprised by the deep emotion her simple action had sparked within him, William looked down at her and measured her reaction to the way in which he was holding her, searching for the minutest warning that he should let go.

There was nothing.

Nothing but an intense sense of longing between them and the same penetrating energy that always existed whenever they touched in any way.

As unbelievable as it was to even consider it, she _was_ his match in every way. The first thing he thought of when he opened his eyes every morning to the last voice he longed to hear each day when he closed the door to his home. And all of it was his... _if_ he wanted it... if he could manage to accept it along with everything else she might still be hiding.

Choosing to give in finally against everything that had been holding him back, he drew her closer and kissed her deeply, waiting to feel her resistance, but was pulled in more when she did not. From the way in which his fingers ran down the smoothness of her neck and took in the actual warmth of her skin next to his own, he felt as if some chemical reaction had shifted their usually cold exterior and sensed her tremble beneath his touch as his body reacted the same under hers.

She was the first woman he had ever kissed...

...and at that moment,

... he knew that she would be his last.

Clearly just as shaken as he was at her own reaction, Charity turned her face away at last, resting her head comfortably on his chest before sighing happily in defeat. "I think I am falling in love with you, William Wells."

"Really?" William couldn't help the broad smile that seemed to be now plastered across his face as his fingers wove within the edges of her soft blonde hair and played with the loose wisps between his fingertips. "Well, I hope so, Miss Bentham. Either that, or my other admirers at the hospital are going to be especially eager to take your place when we return."

"Oh? You think you can handle someone else better?" Charity shook her head playfully at the obvious tease.

"Not on your life, Charity... _you_ are quite enough." William assured her and leaned down to kiss her once more, only this time with the confidence that she was the only woman he would ever want to hold for the rest of his life.

Chapter Twenty-Nine

October 27th, 1811

In spite of the days and nights Elijah had spent positively dreading Friday's eventual arrival, there was no putting it off any longer. Even if there had been no epidemic or anything else he might have wanted to do, the crops had to come in today, and not a moment too soon, for any day was sure to bring with it the cold, driving rain and winds of November hard upon their backs, threatening to destroy any potential they might have for financial gain. Yet that being said, it still had not stopped Elijah from trudging his way all through the week in constant disgust of the imposition it was causing with every crash of his hammer against his anvil.

Thankfully, he would not be completely alone in his task today, like his father had often been before Jedidiah had volunteered to help him. Nor was he ever worried that he would be since Thomas had promised to come help earlier this week. What he had not expected, however, was just how many people would arrive.

"A regular barn raisin' crew," one of the men had cheerfully called it when he greeted him warmly at the farm, and he could believe it, too, for over forty men were already busy chatting as they waited near the barn with scythes in hand when he rounded the corner of the outer gate and walked down the long path towards his family's home. Though no edifice would need to be constructed today, each and every man present meant less work for the others and a quicker completion of the heavy task.

Hope and Emma had been in the kitchen busily cooking all morning as they prepared coffee for an army, sweet breads, cinnamon rolls, corn muffins and all other forms of temptations to fuel the men as they worked and would certainly have a full spread of sandwiches and cold lemonade ready under the large oak by noon. Even the two little ones, who were deemed no longer contagious, were toted along with the rest of the family and tucked carefully into their beds in the room that used to be Elijah's and Jedidiah's, or allowed to play calmly on the large, braided rug in front of the fire.

In the yard next to the house, just adjacent to the large barn that had been organized and readied to be filled by the soon-to-be harvest, Emile and Nathanael were already busily hitching up two wagons to the horses Charlotte owned and the one borrowed from Jedidiah before Emile moved to attach the large black stallion that had been Hope's birthday present to the last.

The latter, the one who had never seen a day of work for the majority of his young life, was understandably not happy about his current arrangement of unity, but Emile was steadily working to join them all together under their new assignment.

Because of an unexpected admittance, William would be along later around midday if he could be spared from the hospital in time for the afternoon turn at the fields, which seemed totally fine to Elijah now, given the large numbers assembled before him. Even his mother, as weak as she was, had insisted that Nathanael carry her out to the front porch and into her favorite rocking chair to watch the progress from a distance.

In every direction around him, the world hummed with activity and conversation like a great mass awaiting its orders, though the morning had barely started.

"How in the world did you manage to convince this many people to help us free of charge, Thomas?" Elijah clapped Thomas on the back incredulously as he shook his head in utter shock.

"I actually didn't have to do much convincing at all. I simply told them Sebastian's family needed help come sunup Friday, and the list filled itself. Would you believe that I actually had to turn men away and ask them to come over this afternoon if we still had work left to be done? Which they probably will from what I overheard them saying this morning," Thomas replied as he pulled on a pair of thick leather working gloves, the very same ones Sebastian had given him the Christmas after he had arrived in the Colonies.

"Turn men away?" Elijah's eyes widened, utterly dumbfounded at the possibility.

"Elijah, each man here could probably tell you five stories at least of a time when your father did the same for them. It is only fair to give them a chance to repay the favor and be a blessing to you in exchange," Emile said over his shoulder as he secured the last strap across the black stallion's back and latched it to the guide securely. "Whoa... steady there, Phillipe. We're doing this for Hope. Remember?" He soothed the horse calmly as he slowly caressed the side of the horse's neck under his mane down to his cheek. "She needs you to help <u>her</u> today."

With a bob of his head downward and a slight scraping of his foot in recognition of the man's words Phillipe complied, if only remotely.

"I had no idea." Elijah instantly felt ashamed once again at his ignorance, and the manner in which he had portrayed his displeasure for the better part of the week.

"Most people probably didn't. He was not a boastful man, your father. He just did what he knew was right, no matter what it cost him to do it," Nathanael added and walked around the second team of horses, checking their bits and leads carefully to make sure nothing was still loose. "It was what drew people to him—his simple sincerity. I believe you will find that if you treat people with the same level of respect that you would like in return, no matter what they can pay you, you will find the same, if not more. I know your Uncle William often helped people back in England who had next to nothing to pay for his services, but that never stopped him from trying to cure them when they needed him."

"Yes." Emile laughed at the distant memory. "I remember a woman offering me a dozen eggs and her best chicken for some headache powder one time. Of course, that was before I accidentally tried to poison her... poor woman." He shook his head and laughed once more. "That was one job, Elijah, that I was most definitely <u>not</u> suited for in the least."

"Poisoning people?" Nathanael joked. "I'd imagine not. People get hanged that way, Emile."

"Indeed." Emile looked over at him darkly, then smiled. "Then again, how would you know unless I was caught?"

Nathanael laughed. "On second thought, Eli, maybe we had better watch our food today," Nathanael teased lightly, then turned more serious again. "But truth be told, at least you gave it a fair try, my friend. That is all anyone can ask."

"Did you both know my father back then, too? Before Uncle William came to Portsmouth when I was sick?" Elijah walked into the barn and retrieved several of the pitchforks, scythes, and spools of twine they would need before throwing them all carelessly into the back of the wagon.

"Yes, though your Uncle William was probably the closest with him in the beginning... your Uncle Emile, not so much," Nathanael quipped as he climbed onto the buckboard and took the reins.

"From the way that he always talked about you, it seemed like all of you were friends since childhood." Elijah came to stand next to Emile and continued his questions seriously, for he had never heard his father speak a harsh word about any of his friends from back home.

"Not hardly but let us just say that we were more alike than different and leave it at that." Emile rolled his eyes and shook his head at the truth behind every word that he had just uttered.

Nathanael tried to hide the hearty chuckle that wanted very much to escape from behind his broad smile at the mirth the whole conversation was bringing. "Oh, don't let him fool you. The last time your father and Uncle Emile were together in England they were in a wrestling match across the floor of your house because your father thought Emile was some kind of an intruder."

"Seriously?" Elijah laughed. "I wish I had been there to see that."

"Actually, you were..." Emile raised one eyebrow in surprised gratitude that the young man had forgotten many of the more lurid details since. "You just probably don't remember it as vividly as <u>we</u> all do."

"That is for certain. Though come to think of it, do you still think you were the angel then, Emile?" Nathanael asked in jest, trying his best to keep the joy in the day alive.

"Most definitely," Emile echoed aloofly the forgotten truth. "That man could fight like a demon and was twice as strong, I assure you. In fact, I doubt many could best him in a fight."

Elijah laughed, too. "I wish I could remember all of that. Papa wouldn't hurt a fly if it landed on his best horse."

The two men nodded, though secretly they were both sincerely grateful he did not, for that was the day all of them almost perished. For months, the vampire who had turned them all had stalked them relentlessly, waiting for his opportunity to finish what he had started on the Endeavor. Yet in the end, he had only managed to help them as a group to grow stronger, and in turn met his own untimely demise.

Emma alone had paid the price for the man's schemes, but Emile had never been so grateful for something that was meant to be painful. In changing Emma as some form of punishment for him, Doctor Clarke had essentially taken away the hardest of decisions for Emile and opened the door to a happiness he had never dared dream of having. So, in that light, her capture had also been a blessing in disguise, even if it had meant her unwilling transition to vampirism.

It had also forced Sebastian's hand and brought him back home to his family at last—away from his work with Señor Moretti, but where he belonged all along... and present for the birth of his last child, too. Well, mostly present, as only Emile had been there to help Charlotte deliver Hope since William and Sebastian were busy trying to save the rest of their family at the time.

It all was a messy and confusing story to relate, but every facet of it shone in its own unique brilliance like that of the adeptly cut gem Emile had bought for Emma on their first anniversary together—beautiful in the eyes of the beholder, but incredibly difficult to create at the time.

"Are we about ready then?" Thomas asked as he walked over to the group standing by the wagons.

"Yes." Elijah nodded and jumped into the back of the wagon behind Nathanael. "We will start with the hay over by Jedidiah's first in the back pasture and make our way towards the front to bring in the wheat. With any luck we can finish at least half of it by lunch."

The men who were gathered in the courtyard around them all nodded in agreement and followed after them into the fields towards the south pasture beyond.

For the good part of the next three hours all the men worked relentlessly on the job they had volunteered to do. With long-bladed scythes in hand, they swung again and again as they swished through the wheat easily, while others spent hours bent over, tying up the sheaves on the ground into tight bundles with the twine. The last group, the men with the heaviest of burdens, heaved the bundles up into the waiting wagons for Emile and Nathanael to bring back to Jedidiah's barn and then Charlotte's for unloading. Throughout every inch of the field that stretched out to the horizon in all directions, not a single man was idle, as each one worked in their own way to accomplish the task. Knowing that at any minute it could open up on them and ruin the fruits of their labors if they did not hurry, they all kept their eyes focused downward and pressed on under the severely grey and foreboding sky.

Elijah was well-aware that the crop would normally have been brought in months ago as their wheat was usually harvested at the end of July like it had been the year his father had died. Yet the rains of spring had delayed Jedidiah's planting until May this year, making the harvest the latest it had ever been. Still, all things considered, from the manner in which the barns were filling by the hour, it was a good crop, and thankfully, all of it was being collected and stored safely for threshing later.

Almost halfway back to the house and finally approaching the middle of the day, a loud ringing of something metallic off in the distance alerted the men of the approaching meal. With no malice or complaint from anyone out in the field, everyone released a collective sigh of true gratitude for the much-needed break they all required. From the oldest to the youngest, each man was more than ready to drop his tools where they lay and plod gratefully back to the waiting benches and blankets already spread out all around the large oak near the edge of the field.

And what a feast greeted them indeed when they stepped out from the rushes! Sliced apples of various varieties, ice cold lemonade and tea, cucumber, egg and tomato sandwiches, not to mention hand pies, fried chicken, sliced up baked potatoes, a ham and even an assortment of cheeses lined the three long wooden tables around the tree, inviting them to rest beneath its shade and comfort.

"You have really have outdone yourself this time, ladies." Emile shook his head in astonishment at all the women had been able to accomplish in such a short time.

"Oh, it wasn't just us, I assure you. We had help," Emma admitted honestly while wiping her hands off on her white apron in front of her. "Some of the ladies from Nathanael's church brought over the chicken and pies. We only had to make the sandwiches and cut up the rest."

"And the ham?" Emile raised his eyebrows in curiosity. "I don't recall slaughtering an animal recently. I think I would have remembered that."

Emma chuckled. "You never miss anything do you?"

"Nope." He picked up a slice of the smoked ham and sampled it. "Though it _is_ very tasty. Hickory?"

"Um-hmm." Emma nodded. "Charlotte had it in the smokehouse. She said she had been saving it for a special occasion. I guess this was it."

"I suppose so." He fixed himself a small plate of cheese and a few sandwiches. Or at least enough to give the appearance of consuming a full meal without drawing unusual attention as every man there was heaping his plate full of the delicacies after a hard morning's work.

"How is Hope doing?" Emile glanced over at the girl fanning herself at the far edge of the group, trying to remain as inconspicuous as possible, but also very much the opposite of her usual bubbly self.

"Well..." Emma bit her lip nervously as she studied her again, then spoke, "I don't want you to read too much into this by saying it, but I sort of wish she had chosen to remain home today."

"Why?" Emile swallowed the last of his cheese and wiped his mouth politely. "She hasn't been a burden, has she? I can go talk with her if she has."

"No, nothing like that. She has been working just as hard as I have," Emma reassured him but scrutinized the girl once more before shaking her head with increasing worry. "But she doesn't seem right today either, Emile. It is almost like she is lost somewhere, perhaps. Or maybe I am just being paranoid."

Feeling a wave of fresh adoration for her all over again, Emile placed his free hand around the back of his wife and looked down at her lovingly before kissing her cheek. "Or maybe you are just being a mother," he spoke softly next to her ear, then pulled back and smiled.

"Maybe." Emma grinned, too. "I _do_ love that girl."

"I know you do." He sighed and felt the completeness the moment was bringing him. "Just keep an eye on her. That is the best we can do for the time being."

"Oh, I will. You can rest your mind on that point." Emma sat down on the grass and let out a sigh. "Goodness gracious! I think this is the first time I have sat down in nearly twenty-four hours. As strong as I usually am, my feet are absolutely killing me!"

"No doubt." Emile took a seat gingerly next to her before lying back on both of his palms behind him. "It kind of makes what we do out in the field look like child's play in comparison, I bet."

"Thank you, love." Emma sighed contentedly and looked over at her husband with sincere gratitude.

"For what?" Emile tried to look as innocent as possible, knowing full-well how much he already felt indebted to the woman beside him.

"For always appreciating me. Even back in Paris." Emma eyed the men spread happily across the grass. "Despite all of your perceived faults, you have never once in your life made me feel like anything I did was worthless, though many have before you."

"Worthless?" Emile scoffed. "Far from it! I quite enjoy our little rendezvous," Emile teased, though he knew precisely to what she was referring.

To Emma's family she had only been the means of making money for them through long hours cleaning houses and other odd jobs that often left her both physically and emotionally exhausted. Even her father had chosen not to work in lieu of reaping the benefits of her labors and that of his son. Though admittedly, there was not much work to be had back then even if the elder <u>had</u> chosen a profession. Before the revolution, money was scarce to come by and food even harder to acquire. And in some way, though gruesome to even admit it, the guillotine had spared so many a life of starvation and destitution, though he would never have chosen such a fate for anyone, let alone his worst enemy.

"That was not what I was thinking, and you know it." Emma poked him playfully in the ribs to bring him back to the present with her.

"I do." Emile smiled back cautiously, grateful for the distraction from his darker past. "You know, Emma, sometimes I think a lot about going back to those two people who lived life so free of death, the war with England, plague and countless other things we have to face today." He paused, his face turning more serious and worried as he looked over at Hope once more, who now appeared to be almost sleeping peacefully under the shade of the tree.

"But then we wouldn't have William, Nathanael, Hope and all of this wonderful life around us." Emma tried to remind him and draw him out of his deeper melancholy. "We have a lifetime to experience Paris again one day. Let's just enjoy the present for what it is."

"For today." Emile nodded, then reached for her hand and held it for just a moment before asking further with mixed emotions, "Would you ever want to return... to Paris that is? Maybe after Napoleon has decided to leave the country and everything has finally settled down again? Perhaps we can take up an apartment along the Seine this time. Or we could walk the streets at night and enjoy some of those cafes I have been telling you about?" Emile thought back nostalgically to everything he had missed so much in the past twenty years.

"Oh, I don't know... you forget that your Paris and mine were very different, love." Emma pushed back her hair behind her ear and played with his fingers within her hand.

Wanting very much to give her everything she had ever been neglected, Emile looked over at his wife with true adoration this time, a feeling of sheer satisfaction present in every fiber of his being. "Then maybe one day we can find a new Paris together? How does that sound?"

"I'd like that." Emma blushed at his intense focus in front of so many others, as the men around them were now starting to stand and prepare for a second turn at the fields. "But for now..." She skillfully led him away from the place they both wanted mentally to go and back to their present life for the time being.

"For now, we work." Emile brushed off his hands unceremoniously, stood, and then reached a hand down to help Emma up off the grass.

"For now, we work." She repeated before suddenly reaching up on her tiptoes to kiss him lightly on the cheek.

Surprised, but not the least bit perturbed by her sudden display of attention in public, Emile turned away from the men to stand in front of her and hid his expression meant only for her alone. "Be careful, Mrs. Deschamps, the rabble may see you and be jealous."

Utterly pleased by his brief insinuation, Emma giggled at the sudden look and playfully pulled at the buttons of the tan shirt he had chosen to wear. "Be careful yourself." She pursed her lips and wagged her eyebrows mischievously in impetuous invitation.

"Umm..." Emile groaned and turned himself around, away from the temptation standing right in front of him. "Later, Mrs. Deschamps... later."

"That had better be a promise, sir," she quipped right back as she started to make her way over to the tables to begin cleaning up.

"What do _you_ think?" Emile looked back at her briefly and smiled a smile only they understood between them, the urge he always felt to seize her and sneak away almost overpowering him completely.

Emma blushed and ducked her head yet again but stopped once more to admire the man she had chosen to marry so many years ago. Out of everything in her life, he had been the one thing that had been the easiest of decisions to make and the hardest one to let go. As complicated as she may be, he knew both her past, her present and future and all of it was his delight to treasure. An eternity of love and acceptance and none of it came at a price or had to be earned. Nor had she even once had the need to question his devotion to her.

One evening weeks ago, he had told Charity that he had been rescuing her from the hands of an angry mob back in Paris, but in reality, he had saved her many times over before any of that had ever happened. Though yes, their beginnings _had_ been under less than appropriate terms, but he had never once treated her the way every other man in her existence had. To him, she was _his_ Emma, and for that, she would always be forever grateful.

"Hope, Sweetheart, are you feeling alright?" Emma called from the table after the rest of the men had gone to the field, leaving very little for them left to put away.

"What?" Hope turned over and picked herself up sleepily from off the ground, her expression appearing more dazed than anything else. "Oh, I will be. Is it time to clean up so soon?"

"I'm afraid so." Emma looked over at the girl and paused, noticing the flush of pink on the girl's cheeks. "On second thought, why don't you go sit with your mother for a little while and keep her company? I think can handle this here without you."

"You don't have to tell me twice." Hope exhaled deeply and appeared to sway slightly on her feet as she tried to get her bearings.

"Will you need my help to get there?" Emma grew more concerned as she watched her take a few tentative steps towards the house and contemplated seriously calling out to her husband for his assistance.

"No, I think I can manage. It's not that far." Hope called back and walked slowly, but carefully to the main house, but did not take a seat on the front porch as they had discussed. Instead, she moved to walk inside and out of view.

"Hmm..." Emma tried to fight back the alarm that was increasing the adrenaline throughout her veins. "I think I had better send for William sooner than later." She decided and carried as many plates as she could manage back to the house before coming back out to ask Hannah to fetch William on her way home after lunch with Abigail.

With the late afternoon passing quickly by them, the rest of the men worked almost to sundown before every last bushel of wheat was bundled and stored within the barn both on Jedidiah's land and on Sebastian's. Ears of dried corn had been steadily plucked, grass bundled, and all the harvest tended securely in their places before each man respectfully passed by the worn cross beneath the oak and paid their respects before heading home. Nevertheless, not a single disparaging look was seen, though all of them were feeling the ache of muscles they had not realized even existed. Nor a word echoed by anyone in attendance that did not pay some kind of respect to the family they were serving. Instead, there was a steady thrum of overall merriment as they walked steadily out of the field, as if the day was a privilege and not the backbreaking strain that it truly was.

From dawn until dusk it had truly been a tiresome day, but Elijah could not help but smile watching the joy and contentment on each of their faces. By the way that they were acting, it was almost as if the work had been nothing at all, which was most definitely not the case. More than once he had even felt like quitting due to: the strain of the scythe, the aching blisters on his hands that had split just after lunch and the immensity of the burdens he carried to the wagon, yet he did not because the man next to him was encouraging him ever onward, forward, cheerfully pressing through yet another acre until every piece of wheat had been harvested.

And then there was his mother. Sitting there as weak as she was, she had kept watch throughout the whole day with abject appreciation for every person present. From her chair on the porch, she had prayed silently over them all through the morning and well into the afternoon hours just like she had done for each of her children over the years. Moreover, it was only as the group was finally heading back into town to their own homes for supper that she had timidly ventured down the stairs and into the pathway of the group to thank every single one of them for their fortitude and sacrifice on her behalf. In every way, she was beholden, and she needed them to physically feel her love and gratitude with every handshake and hug.

It all quite literally put him to shame watching her.

How many times had he taken her for granted all these years?

To him, she was always just his mother. The person who made the meals, cleaned the laundry, kept the house moving smoothly. Yet today had taught him volumes about so much in his life. About everything he had yet to learn it seemed.

Since he was a little child, Elijah knew that his father had wanted him to take over the other half of the farm, but even after being forced to work it for the past two weeks, Elijah knew that this life would <u>never</u> be the world of his choosing. That would feel like a prison. To have his day continually controlled by the milking of the cows, the sun in the sky and the rain upon the roof felt like torture to him—systematic and deliberate torture. And as much as he loved his father and wanted to please him in this, he knew now, more than ever, that he just couldn't bring himself to do it.

His brother obviously loved it. Or at least he had chosen to faithfully do it. Though now that Elijah had started contemplating it more fully from his perspective, maybe there was another reason why Jedidiah had worked in those fields with his father all those years.

Did Jed farm for the same reason why he worked in the forge?

Probably so.

In their own way, each man had chosen a different, however equally worthy path of closeness with their father, and Sebastian had not condemned them nor directed either of them towards what <u>he</u> had desired. Instead, he had blessed them with his guidance and love in whatever path they had chosen, no matter what it was.

"You were a truly wise and patient man, Papa." Elijah said quietly while looking out over the trimmed fields to the grave off in the distance. "I am only sorry that I did not see it or say it sooner," he admitted mournfully as he took the main straps off the two horses holding the empty wagon and led them by their halters into the barn. After all of their work today, they had certainly earned an extra ration of oats tonight, maybe even two after what they had endured, and a thorough cooling off. That would take buckets and buckets of water from the pump, but they had more than earned it.

Feeling almost as sore as the horses probably did right about now, he placed each gelding in the large corral on the other side of the barn and picked up the two buckets lying outside the fence to fill them.

"Care for a hand?" Nathanael asked, walking past him with the tackle from the other team.

"Gladly." Elijah handed him one of the metal buckets and picked up the other one that was lying nearby.

Without another word, the two men trudged over to the pump by the small windmill adjacent to the house and filled the three buckets easily before Elijah looked down at his reflection in one and paused, suddenly realizing with a start how very much he resembled his father now with his tan from working out in the fields today and muscled forearms from his work down at the forge.

"Everything okay, Eli?" Nathanael waited to lift his bucket from off of the hewn trough, watching the man beside him almost shudder as he gripped the rim of his own tightly.

"No." Elijah shook his head and leaned down, almost too overwhelmed to speak more.

Unsure what it was that was troubling the young man, Nathanael placed one hand upon the man's back and waited. Unlike his rather complicated father, the man beside him was an open book compared to his brother or even Hope. Still, Nathanael knew that if he waited until Elijah was truly ready to talk, he was sure to tell him sooner or later, for he was normally the easiest of Sebastian's children to decipher.

"I lived with my father for 20 years... and it took him dying for me to truly appreciate him," Elijah's voice came out in ragged gasps, completely choked with freshly discovered guilt and regret. "How can a son be that foolish?"

Nathanael nodded in final understanding. "Sadly, it does take that sometimes."

"But why?" Elijah leaned over farther still, his hands placed firmly upon his knees, struggling to take in a single breath of air under the strain of all of his emotions.

Knowing that the question had not been intended for him to answer. Nathanael leaned casually against the fence behind him and waited patiently. He leaned with his arms crossed calmly across his chest as Emile had nodded in their direction and put the other horses away in the corral and waited even more as William had walked up the stairs beside him before silently heading into the house with a concerned look upon his face.

Throughout it all, Nathanael only shook his head and waved them off, allowing Elijah the time he required to deal with what was hitting him, with the knowledge that whatever it was, it must be monumental for him to weep so.

"All these years I thought Jedidiah stayed on the farm because that was what he wanted, because that was what he was asked to do, when in reality... I know now that he was just trying to steal some quality time with my father. I was the one who was selfish in all of this. The one who <u>always</u> had to have things my way every time Jed asked for us to do something together. I worked at the forge from dawn until dusk. I encouraged my father to start up the second shop and invite Thomas to come to America with the rest of us. I tagged along everywhere the man went for most of my life, watching his every step. I monopolized as much time as I possibly could it seems, and when he died..."

"<u>You</u> couldn't stop it," Nathanael said quietly.

Elijah nodded. "I was too busy working on my own dreams to go with him that day."

Nathanael sighed. "I know from experience that it can be a tremendous burden trying to be in another man's shadow. You in your father's and Jedidiah in your own."

"In mine?" Elijah's face shot up quickly in confusion. "Why is Jed in <u>my</u> shadow?"

Nathanael chuckled lightly. "You said it yourself. I was, I had, I worked, I encouraged... where was Jedidiah in all of that?"

Elijah hung his head in shame once again. "Here... on the farm... waiting for me to be done with <u>my</u> father."

"Precisely. Someone had to do it. After all, your father had two sides, did he not? One that loved his craft in the forge just like you do and one that wanted to give his family everything he never could before. That part of him was what Jedidiah clasped onto, and you shouldn't feel too bad for him because of it. He knew a side of your father that you have probably never seen. A side you might want to learn about by asking him."

"Well, I learned a great deal today." Elijah stood up and breathed in deeply, composing himself once more.

"I am sure you did." Nathanael uncrossed his arms in front of him but did not move from his leaning position on the fence. "Elijah, your father knew from the very beginning that his sons were two completely different individuals. You were like two plants, each needing a different kind of soil and nutrients to grow, yet both requiring the same sunlight and rain. Your father planted you and allowed you to grow. He and your mother supplied the sunlight and rain along the way. And both of you have something unique to give to this world with your fruit."

"But..." Elijah paused before continuing, "I just can't help but feel like I am constantly letting him down all the time. I can't manage this farm like he could.

I barely milked the cows this week without total calamity. Two even managed to escape, despite my best efforts otherwise. Not to mention the knot on my head from falling out of the hayloft. I've lost countless tools somewhere in that tiny barn. Where? I have no idea. But they are gone, without a trace. You have no idea how much I just want to give it all up and sell my portion of the place to Jedidiah, but I can't. Something inside of me keeps me here no matter how much I hate it."

Nathanael chuckled. "The cows escaped plenty under your father's watch, too, Elijah. They're cows. They escape. It's what they do. Don't read more into it than that. Though I do know what you mean about feeling like you can never measure up to people's expectations. I've felt a little bit of that myself many times over the years. But there _is_ one important thing you are failing to consider in all of this."

"Really, what is that?" Elijah came over and leaned back onto the fence next to him.

"Who are you really trying to be enough for in the first place? God or your father? Your father certainly never intended you to be like your brother, just as Jedidiah could never be you. But more importantly, your Heavenly Father does not expect either of you to be like Sebastian. That man was too flawed to be emulated by anyone, and I say that in the kindest of ways possible. We all are, I am afraid, myself included."

"So, what is the point then?" Elijah kicked a stone at his feet several yards in front of him, feeling totally frustrated once more.

"Well... have you ever tried not looking at the bigger picture in order to fully understand it?" Nathanael asked plainly.

"What?"

"Many times in my life I have been overwhelmed by circumstances beyond my control. Things I have no way of predicting or avoiding, even if I wanted to. And you know what I do?"

"I am sure you are going to tell me," Elijah mumbled sarcastically, painfully remembering the many discussions he had already been unwillingly privy to this month.

Holding his breath slightly at the curt remark, Nathanael paused and waited.

"I'm sorry. That was rude, forgive me," Elijah acquiesced quickly, feeling justly rebuked by his poor behavior yet again.

"Forgiven," Nathanael replied easily without any malice, then continued on as if the man had not interrupted him in the slightest, "When my Elsie died, I felt like I could not even think to breathe, let alone get myself dressed every morning.

In fact, I spent the next two months sleepwalking my way through life until I finally realized that I did not <u>need</u> to see the bigger plan, not really. Even though I desperately wanted to know all of the details about why He had brought this sorrow into my life, in the end, I only had to trust God and do the next thing He placed in front of me. If I did anything else beyond that, my grief would swallow me whole."

"I think I understand what you mean, Uncle Nathanael." Elijah nodded. "And after a day like today, I believe I owe Jedidiah a monumental apology, though he probably won't think he is deserving one."

"Well, it never hurts to give it," Nathanael agreed. "Although you might be surprised. Perhaps he has been thinking the same about you and his own life the past three years, if not longer. Who knows? This might even be the door to a better understanding between the two of you. And that, Elijah, would most definitely make your father proud of you both."

"You're right... as always." Elijah sighed and stood up fully. "I best go finish watering down the horses before my body completely shuts down and I can't."

"Good idea. I will help, though I do have one favor to ask." Nathanael picked up two of the filled buckets and waited for Elijah to join him with his own.

"Sure, what is that?" Elijah lifted it up and started walking towards the barn close beside him.

"Don't tell your Uncle William I sorted the two of you out." Nathanael set his load down by the corral and stood up.

"Whyever not?" Elijah poured his bucket over the large gelding and started to brush him down vigorously.

"It might hurt his feelings." Nathanael shrugged. "He enjoys being the savior to all of us. I wouldn't want to steal that away from him. Besides, that is the kind of plant that God has called <u>him</u> to be, not me. Believe it or not, I am content in my own little garden on the side. And though I may not grow the biggest of flowers, they still grow."

Elijah laughed, then hefted another bucket of water and poured it over the back of the other horse. "Your secret is safe with me, Uncle Nathanael."

"Good." Nathanael picked up the empty buckets and moved to refill them at the pump.

"And thank you," Elijah called after him.

"You're welcome." Nathanael glanced over his shoulder at the man and thought for a moment he was looking back at Sebastian once more—the pleasant reminder making him smile. "And Eli, a piece of your father does live on wonderfully in each of you, never forget that."

"I won't," Elijah said seriously and continued brushing down the great bay in front of him who was only too happy to shake his head in satisfaction at his pampering.

Chapter Thirty

October 27th, 1811

Hungry for the fellowship of family and friends, Nathanael walked through the door of the farmhouse after helping Elijah with the horses and took his favorite seat at the far end of the table next to Michael, hoping to hear something interesting. As animated as he usually was, the young man was normally filled with fascinating tidbits to share and often tackled the more reticent silences by filling them with his tales of recent events. Nathanael would have been hanging on every piece of news or gossip intrigue Michael felt inclined to publish since Nathanael rarely heard anything even remotely obscure from his fellow professors at the college, but tonight he was hoping more to hear about how the young man had finally managed to propose to their Hope.

Given their recent blessing, Emile had told him earlier that the young man had already done so. Yet Hope had still to announce anything formally to the family as a whole. *Perhaps she is merely waiting for just the right moment after Jedidiah and his family are finally well? Or maybe she has not accepted him, after all?* Nathanael considered the confusing prospect worriedly, but in the end, decided that either way, he was certain something might be said tonight concerning it, as the family had not been gathered together as a whole since her birthday celebration back in July.

Regrettably for him, however, everyone, minus the man beside him, hardly looked ready for conversation of any kind, much less a joyful proclamation of future events. From Emile, whose dust-caked shirt looked far closer to a light brown now than the ivory from which it had started, right on down to Elijah at the opposite end of the table, who looked like he was about ready to lay his head right down upon it, they did all appear to be in dire need of a hot bath and a change of clothes, though the majority were too tired to care at this point in the day. The required work had taken its toll on all of them in more ways than one, but few were left feeling anything but grateful that the harvest was finally behind them for another season. Of course, there would still be threshing to be done later to prepare the wheat to be sold, but hopefully, they could take their time completing it when Jedidiah had fully regained his strength once more to help.

After all, was it the Bible or Benjamin Franklin that had once quoted, "Many hands make light work?" Well, the adage was undoubtedly true no matter who first penned it and most definitely displayed here.

"Did many people come out to help bring in the crops today?" Michael asked while pausing to take copious notes with a bit of charcoal upon a short parchment he had brought along with him to the gathering.

"Yes, plenty, why? Are you planning on writing about it?" Emile eyed the scribbled penmanship across from him with indifferent scrutiny, not particularly caring what the man would or would not write about him in the slightest. After the last article that had caused more than one impolite discussion between the two of them, the fledgling author of *The Aurora General* had already assured him that in the future, he would at least warn him before anything contrary would be printed about him without his foreknowledge. And since Emile was compelled to trust the man now for Hope's sake, he tried very hard not to do so with the same level of guarded protection that he normally gave to all others in his type of position.

"Perhaps. People do love a good personal interest story, especially with the epidemic and all. What the citizens need now is something that gives the city a sense of pride and hope that neighbors are still willing to take care of each other, despite everything that is happening around them," Michael replied easily, clearly confident in his ability to write what the public wanted. In fact, his editor had recently put him in charge of the Current Events portion of the paper, and he meant to impress him greatly in his inaugural issue.

"Well, we sure are grateful for every one of the men that came today, and I don't mind you quoting me on that one," Charlotte stated frankly from the kitchen, attempting to assemble a few leftovers for those who cared to eat them. "Though you might hear a longer story if you asked Elijah. He was out in the field with the workers from Thomas' shop for most of the day."

"Please don't remind me," Elijah groaned, his hands soaking carefully in a bowl of warm water and salts that he had been given to alleviate at least some of the swelling from the broken blisters and angry sores. "Even my hair feels tired, Mama. How in the world did Papa do this every year? There were forty men out there today, and back then, it was just him."

With a collective nod, the group all weakly laughed at his assessment, for the exhausted feeling was most definitely shared by all in attendance.

"He didn't do it all in one day, dear." Charlotte tried to fend off his assessment of his father's fortitude before further suspicion might arise.

"Yes, but how did he do it at all? It would have taken me at least a month to bring it in by myself." Elijah picked up one of his hands, turned it over to examine his palm, then placed it back within the water when the air began to create fresh pain. "He must have had superhuman strength. Either that, or he never slept."

"Maybe it was a little of both, Eli. Your father was used to working long hours, so it probably did not seem like that much of a burden to him." William looked over at Emile and then to Charlotte, unsure how much longer they would let Elijah deliberate on the topic.

"Perhaps the public would be more interested in an article about the doctors in Philadelphia, Michael. I hear from many at the church how they view them as the unsung heroes these days," Nathanael suggested quickly, suddenly interested in diverting the conversation to another vein altogether. "I bet not many citizens even know all the things that they do to keep this city functioning in the midst of the populace's daily calamities. By the way, how many of them are still visiting patients around the city, William?" He directed even more.

"Probably a dozen or so on any given day. Many of the nurses, too, when they are able." William leaned back in his chair and crossed his arms, grateful once again that Nathanael's quick wit had returned. It had taken almost a year to do so after Elsie's death, but once the fog had eventually lifted, William had delighted in the return of the lighthearted banter the man normally possessed.

Unlike the others at the table, William's day had thankfully been less strenuous than some recently. Yet, it had still been filled with two lectures, a few procedures requiring his supervision and a rather nasty compound fracture that had arrived shortly after his arrival that morning. Yet all of this was a welcome change to him compared to spending hours in fruitless efforts to decrease fevers that would not abate.

The man in question was lucky to keep his leg after such an injury, but William was still realistically cautious, given the severity of the break. With such an open presentation, that left the inner core of the bone exposed in several places, there was no telling if gangrene would eventually set in, and require the leg's removal, after all. A very real possibility whenever there was an injury of this nature. And sadly, one that often had no way of being predicted beyond instituting measures towards diligent care and cleanliness.

"And what do they do exactly when they go out on these calls, Doctor Wells?" Michael wrote feverishly all the details that were being freely shared around him.

Rubbing his thumb and forefinger along the length of his jaw as he leaned his chin upon one of his hands, William sighed in displeasure at some of the memories he would just as soon forget. "Things no one wants to read about, I would imagine. Sometimes we set bones and clean out infected wounds, but most of the time, a medical professional is called merely to help assure the family that they are indeed doing everything correctly, despite having nothing else they can physically do to ease their suffering. The Fever plaguing our city today can be hard to treat once it has started, but after that, the real struggle takes place, as the family tries to put everything back together again. Because the illness affects everyone so very differently, that is why it is one of the hardest to treat. And as a doctor, I can give some basic remedies or even a powder for the sore throat and pain, but beyond that, it is just a matter of making sure the patient has the proper fluids and balance."

"Balance?"

"Yes, if one humor becomes stronger than another, the whole system fails, and sometimes fairly quickly. When that happens, the patient can expire in less than one or two days sometimes, and many have, though it is not the norm. We are extremely fortunate if we can save nine out of ten of our patients with the proper care, but the number may be slightly lower this time around."

"Speaking of that, have there been any new deaths this week?" Michael asked curiously after glancing at Hope next to him for a brief moment before returning his attention back to William.

His hopefully, soon-to-be fiancé normally had plenty to contribute to any conversation he attended, yet tonight she had been uncharacteristically quiet. A fact which was beginning to worry him on the surface, but not enough to possibly embarrass her by drawing attention to it and making a scene.

"We average about five people on any given day at the present, which I know sounds like a shockingly high number, but when you remember that it was ten at least if not more in the beginning, I feel that we can safely say this whole horrible ordeal is finally diminishing. Or at least that is my hope." William looked over at his niece, as well, and tried to judge for himself just how she was feeling, as she appeared to be almost dozing off from time to time at the table.

"Can I quote you on that?" Michael asked respectfully, still thoroughly engaged in the present conversation.

"Quote away. It isn't a secret. Any doctor at the hospital will probably tell you the same but thank you for asking." William leaned his head down and strained it farther over to peer up into Hope's face across from him. "Hope, dear, are you awake?"

Startled, Michael looked over in her direction, suddenly completely focused on her alone. "Hope?" He touched her arm and shook it just a little to rouse her.

Seeming to wake up only slightly, Hope weakly lifted her head from where it had been resting on her left fist and elbow and looked up at him, her eyes clearly glazed over. "I'm sorry, did you say something?" She trailed off, her speech becoming more slurred and slower in its delivery as she tried to finish her sentence.

"Michael, move please." Emile stood up abruptly and motioned with his hand for Michael and Nathanael to allow his passage closer to the girl. "Hope, why don't you go upstairs and lie down? You have had a very hard day as it is."

"Alright." Hope nodded submissively, but it looked more like a drunken sailor's response than an actual nod. Leaning to one side to compensate for the world that was now helplessly spinning around her, she placed both of her hands firmly on the table and struggled to stand, but in the process fell in the opposite direction towards Emile as her legs buckled under her own weight.

"Hope!" Emile exclaimed in alarm as he scooped her up easily and hoisted her insignificant frame into his waiting arms. Looking over to William across from him, he saw in his eyes the same concern he and Emma had shared since the very beginning of the epidemic. "William... something is decidedly wrong."

"What's the matter? Is she alright?" Michael stood, ready to assist behind Emile.

"No, I'm afraid not." William was already on his way around the table to examine the girl, as his mind had thought the very same thing the moment he saw her lost expression.

With a tentative hand, he reached over and methodically placed it upon her forehead before staring back at his friend, his expression guarded and professionally careful, quite unlike the more relaxed state he had been enjoying only moments earlier. "She definitely has a fever, but for how long she has had it or how high it is, I couldn't tell you."

Feeling the awful rush of panic creep its way up his throat to finally strangle him, Emile drew the girl closer to him as if the action alone could protect her any more than he had already. "What do you want me to do?" He asked quietly, uncertain how long he could maintain his composure emotionally.

"Let's take her upstairs for the present and let me examine her more fully. Maybe her higher temperature is only from the exhaustion of the day, though I sincerely doubt it. By the red rash appearing along the base of her neck, there is little else it could be, but let's pray that I am wrong," William advised as he stepped aside to allow Emile the space to carry her up the stairs. Then moving as if in slow cadence, he reached over to the peg by the door and snatched up the strap of his medical satchel with one hand to follow after him, secretly dreading the next task at hand as much as he feared telling the others the disappointing results of his examinations.

William had endured enough deliveries of pessimistic news for two lifetimes already and having to do it more often did not make it any easier, quite the contrary. Beyond the distant apathy that grew on many of his more seasoned colleagues was the realization that this situation was entirely different. Hope was not merely another patient of his, she was the daughter of one of his closest friends, and that pressure alone, among others, clung to him with its icy claws of dread as it reached down his back with each step that he took up to the top of the stairs before entering the first bedroom on his right.

With little else left to say, all eyes in the room silently followed the pair as they disappeared, then focused back on the others gathered on the first floor. A few looked down at the table in front of them, contemplating the events that were surely to follow. While others appeared to be in silent prayer for the girl and her family.

"Would you like me to help you upstairs, Charlotte? I'm sure you will want to be with her," Emma asked politely while placing one of her arms carefully around the woman next to her for support.

From her place in the kitchen, Emma could tell from just reading her taunt expression and beads of cold sweat that Charlotte had been pushing herself far too much today already. Much more than she probably should have given her own recent bout with the illness.

Charlotte nodded twice feebly but pursed her lips in determination as Nathanael joined Emma by the stairs and took control. "I'll see that she makes it there safely or to bed, which might be a better idea in the end. William doesn't need two patients tonight."

"I want to see her first, Nathanael," Charlotte pleaded weakly and placed one hand of top of his own to help him see how much she truly needed this. "Though I promise that you can hover all you like while I do."

"Good, because I plan on being your very annoying shadow for quite some time, Charlotte. Or at least until you've had enough of me." Nathanael's eyes studied her discreetly, hoping she would change her mind and lay down instead.

"Well, that is never going to happen so far as I can tell, so I might as well give in to it now." Charlotte smiled warmly and allowed him to place his arm around her waist to assist her.

"Are you going to come back into town tonight, Uncle Nathanael?" Elijah inquired quickly before they left, wondering if he would need to sleep at the forge again or if a bed at the apartment would be available.

"No, but you should. As long as your mother is not recovered, I am not going anywhere," Nathanael stated firmly, then guided her up the stairs before she could dissuade him otherwise.

In the awkward silence that lingered behind them, the room fell back into an unexpected hush as the three remaining family and friends waited below, concern etching the majority of their faces.

"Do you think Hope is _very_ ill?" Michael asked Emma, his eyes filled with a worry and concern she had seen many times in the eyes of her husband on several other such occasions, though none as dire as this.

"We will know soon enough," Emma tried to reassure him. "The most important thing for her now is going to be plenty of rest. Would you care for a cup of coffee while you wait?"

Michael shook his head but remained fixed to his chair, as if he had glued himself to it. "My heart _wants_ to stay, but if it is as bad as you think, perhaps it would be wiser to give Miss Fabbri some space tonight. Besides, if I head home now, I can return before work tomorrow morning to check on her then. Would that be acceptable?" He tried to maintain whatever manners were appropriate in situations such as these for he had no idea how he was supposed to act or respond under the circumstances.

After all, Hope had made no confirmation whatsoever towards any form of acceptance to his proposal as of yet, nor was she certain to do so now after the verbal altercation they had endured. Since the day that he met her, he had always known her to be stubborn in her opinions when she felt strongly about them. It was something that originally drew her to him, in fact. But never in the entire time that they were courting had she ever not communicated with him in over a week. To him, the sheer absence of her daily correspondence shouted louder than any of their words that were uttered in anger.

However, that being said, when he had been specifically invited for dinner tonight along with the family, he _had_ hoped it had been a sign from her that she had softened in her opinion of him. That their words were just that, words, and that he would have a chance to speak to her about it before he retired for the evening. Yet with everything that had just transpired, he secretly feared along with the others that his previous conversation with her might be his last on this Earth.

That morbid thought alone was the one that filled him with the most apprehension and turmoil. Since he could not wind back the clocks and go back to ask her forgiveness, it also meant that he was just as unwilling to move forward without her.

Seeing the man's growing discomfort plainly written upon his face, Elijah answered him briefly for the rest, "Hope has been sick before, Michael. I wouldn't get too concerned just yet. At least not until Uncle William says so." Elijah attempted to downplay the severity of the situation for the man even though everyone in the room now stared at him in critical judgement. "What? What did I say now?"

"Perhaps now is not the best time for voicing opinions," Emma reminded him carefully. "This epidemic is not like anything else we have ever experienced. And yes, Michael, you should stay a bit longer if you are able. I'm sure my husband will allow you some time with her before you go."

"Is there anything else that is needing to be done tonight, or can I head back to town?" Elijah sighed grumpily at the correction, desiring more than anything to retire for the night to his bed and be done with the whole day entirely.

"No, I believe your uncles can handle the rest. But if you can toss that water outside, I will wrap your hands. It won't do much to deaden the pain beyond protecting them from further injury, but it will at least help. I'll not lie to you, Eli, as bad as those sores are now, you will probably not be able to do much hammering for the next few days until they heal." Emma walked to the kitchen and sought the torn linen rags they used for this kind of thing.

"It's the weekend. Besides, there hasn't been much work since last week other than the usual construction material requests." Elijah shrugged and stood up before walking out the front door to toss the salt water onto the dirt in front of the porch.

"In that case, I <u>would</u> like to say goodnight to her, if I am able." Michael petitioned hesitantly.

"Of course." Emma nodded and was about to answer him more when her husband suddenly thudded loudly back down the stairs behind her and out the front door as if the devil himself were closely chasing him at his heels.

"If you will excuse me, Michael. I will be right back." Emma followed after him, apprehension carrying her just as quickly.

Emile, however, did not notice anything transpiring around him whatsoever beyond the one thing his mind was centering on most—escape. With a look of indomitable determination, he strode purposefully without relent towards the barn and threw open the door in front of him, walking straight up to the corral on the other side before climbing through the railing to seize the bridle of Hope's cherished stallion.

Frightened by more than the action alone, the horse reared its head at the sight of him, ripping the leather straps free from his hands with a sudden jerk, as if he also was needing to get away.

"Stop, you foul beast!" Emile growled menacingly and grasped the reins once more. "You may not like it, but you <u>will</u> obey me or so help me I'll end you here and now."

Absolutely intent on total rebellion now, the horse brayed back at him in defense, pulling farther away as he sensed the danger Emile brought with his mere presence. The same energy he always held every time he was near the animal. Even when he appeared pleasantly calm to everyone else.

There was a reason why the horse had only let Hope ride him and never Emma or Emile. Despite the fact that he was regarded as only an animal meant for service and pleasure, he was also known to be highly intelligent, and keenly aware of the very real difference between his owners. One, the nicest of the three, was gentle and kind, and if he was good, she would always bestow a sugar cube or two before she saddled him. The other two were unlike anything the horse had ever encountered before, nor was the energy they emanated inviting in any way. In fact, just the mere proximity alone to one of them as they cleaned his stall would often make him instantly on edge and ready for flight, though they had never done a disparaging thing to him. Quite the contrary, their treats of apples and carrots were just as plenteous as the sugar was from the girl, but the scent of the hand that brought them made it almost not worth it.

"Emile, what are you doing!" Emma called frantically from the railing. "You know only Hope can ride him!"

"Not anymore, Emma! Tonight, he will learn that there are two masters on this property. The one he loves and the one he will learn to obey." Emile tied the reins to the rail of the corral roughly and hoisted the blanket and saddle up onto the horse's back with a jolting thud.

Uncertain if it was best to stop his sudden outburst of aggression or let him get out whatever frustration was currently building up inside him, Emma watched her husband in total confusion. Not once had he ever displayed a character of this kind towards anyone or was outwardly mean to any living beast, though he had been given plenty of opportunities to show it. Which only further drove home the point that whatever was happening here was infinitely more bewildering, and frankly, scary.

From what she could tell at a distance, Emile was uncharacteristically ignoring everything else that was spinning around him, including her, and focusing instead on methodically saddling the horse by tightening its girth as much as he deemed appropriate. Then, with an abrupt rush of motion that took her quickly off guard, he seized the reins and saddle in one hand before she could draw closer to stop him and placed one foot within the stirrup on the left side of the horse to mount.

This, however, quickly became his second fatal error of the night. The first was in coming out here and demanding it of the horse in the first place, as both of them knew the stallion could rid himself of any rider that he did not approve of, even ones that carried the determination and strength of the one holding his mane and bit.

And just like with all the others, the obstinate horse reared itself skyward on his hind legs almost doubling its height as he easily threw Emile off in one motion before he could react otherwise, sending him hard onto the packed dirt below before cantering away from him in triumphant retreat once more.

Disgusted and utterly incensed now, Emile murmured something in French Emma had not heard him speak in almost twenty years, then righted himself once more, standing to his full height to look insolently at the animal across from him, irritation evident in the tightened muscles that ran along the length of his jaw.

With a light toss of his mane and an equally tense flash of anger also in his eyes, the horse challenged him right back in open defiance but kept its distance, obviously not wanting him to come any closer.

"Emile, honey, you need to stop." Emma stepped through the railing at last and wrapped her arms tightly around her husband from behind to prevent him from moving closer. "Torturing Philippe will not help anyone tonight."

"He threw me off," Emile said darkly. "If anyone is torturing someone, it is him."

"Please..." Emma begged. "Look at me." She tried to turn her husband around and force him to focus his attention elsewhere, but he resisted only more as he struggled to pull away from her with a singular determination to complete his task, no matter how futile.

Sensing there was more at play here tonight than what the man was obviously doing, the horse steadily paced the area opposite them on the far side of the corral before openly relenting to his owner as he scraped the ground with his front hoof and bowed his head, appearing to show a small semblance of submission at last.

"That's better," Emile congratulated him, vaguely satisfied by the action, as he started to walk towards him to seize his reins once more but only managed to take three steps before he crumpled to the ground, overwhelmed by the crushing emotion and physical strain of the day.

"Oh, Emile..." Emma rushed to his side and cradled his head against her chest unaware of what was currently occurring back in the house behind them.

It was then at last that Emile finally wept, too weakened by his current failure to put anything into words.

"Let it all out, love... all of it," Emma's voice cooed like that of a mother comforting her young child as she held him there in the ensuing silence that followed.

Finally, wanting to make amends, the stallion stepped silently over to the pair in the middle of the corral and nuzzled the back of Emile's neck with the slightest bit of hesitant affection before using his teeth to flip Emile's long ponytail from off his back and onto his left shoulder.

"Not now, Philippe. He will say he is sorry, later. I promise." Emma shook her head at the animal's intended offer of support.

"I will not!" Emile replied ominously, his face, much like Samuel's had been when he was given some strange vegetable he was most certainly not going to consume.

"Are you going to tell me what is really going on or do I have to drag it out of you?" Emma pushed back the few pieces of his escaped hair and smoothed it down the side of his head towards the back of his neck.

"Oh Emma..." Emile's voice floated back up to her, thick with fear, and almost to the point of despair as he clung to his wife desperately. "I can't be in there right now. More than any other time in her life, Hope needs me... needs us... but I <u>can't</u> be in there."

"Whyever not?" Emma shook her head, deeply confused and disoriented by his previous display and actions for her husband had never once shown any violence towards a living soul, save his overly verbal rantings about Napoleon and Andrew Jackson, and those were nothing he would physically act upon.

Even on the night that Hope disappeared, his actions were driven more by panic than anger. Which made this altogether different... primal almost.

"William... is treating her, Emma," Emile tried to explain his worst fear regarding Hope, but every word was literally choking him to utter them. Or rather, maybe it was the knowledge of what was transpiring back at the house that was doing an efficient job all on its own. Either way, the result was still the same. In every possible way, he felt completely broken and useless, and far from the confident father she needed him to be.

"Oh," Emma finally realized to what he was referring and the gravity of his struggle. "How long <u>has</u> it been since you have had human blood, Emile?"

Suddenly exhausted by the struggle he had been enduring; Emile rubbed his face with both of his hands. "I can't even remember the last time. Maybe just before our trip to England after the trial."

"I see," Emma said quietly, taking a seat beside him. "I know you told me that deciding to feed on animals was something you chose to do for me, but may I ask why?"

Emile shook his head and sighed slowly before taking her hand in his and kissing it just once. "As strong as I may appear, I know where my weaknesses lie even if others do not. The man I was before in Paris is <u>always</u> one step behind me, Emma, just waiting to seize his opportunity to return if I allow him but an inch of room in my life. Which <u>I</u> will <u>not</u>," He said just as resolutely as the day he had first promised himself to abstain.

"And you think drinking human blood will draw you closer to that reality?" Emma stroked his hand, trying to continue to calm him.

"To tell you the truth, I don't know for certain anymore. It has been so very long since then. But what I <u>do</u> know is that back in that meadow in France, I promised to protect you and if that means this kind of a diet to do it, it is a small price to pay for the benefit I receive. Besides, it hasn't hurt me physically in any way to do so, and the risk far outweighs the inconvenience." He paused. "Until today."

"What happened upstairs, Emile?" Emma leaned closer to her husband, allowing him to wrap his arms fully around her this time.

"I really thought I could do it, Emma. After all, William is around blood all the time, and it has been years since I was last truly tempted."

"Oh? When was that? Back in Charleston?" Emma prodded curiously.

Emile shook his head. "No, it was the night William left me with Charlotte to help with the delivery. To this day, I <u>still</u> have no idea what that man was thinking, as out of the three of us there, I was the <u>only</u> one who had ever killed anyone. Why they both thought I could abstain from devouring Charlotte then, I'll never know."

Remembering the bits and pieces of his tortured voice begging her to live from her nightmarish dream of her transformation, Emma touched his arm and tried to reassure him, "But you did, and we have Hope now to prove that you can. So why is this any different?"

Emile exhaled deeply, a piece of his regret falling away with it as he spoke, "When Charlotte was delivering Hope, you were barely holding on by a thread. I was able to restrain myself then because the only thought my mind could fully focus on in that moment was <u>your</u> survival. As crazy as it sounds, I didn't care if Doctor Clarke came back and killed me or if any of us made it out alive, save you alone. So, as overconfidently stupid as I was, I just sat there tonight in Hope's room, thinking I still had that kind of fortitude against it. Like an idiot, I held her hand. I watched him start to cut her arm, and then..." He paused, his eyes blank with total recognition. "And then the next thing I knew I couldn't breathe. My worst nightmare in all of eternity was staring back at me... laughing. The entire room began to close in all around me, and I knew that if I did not leave at that very moment, something <u>very</u> bad was going to happen. Something for which I would hate myself for the rest of my life," Emile admitted honestly. "What kind of father lusts after the very thing that keeps his daughter alive?" His voice became strained once more to the point of breaking back into his sobs.

"One who is as unique as you are, my dear," Emma soothed him easily. "And if Hope knew the truth of who you were, I doubt she would even be upset with you for running away."

"You are probably right." Emile looked over at the horse resting casually across the corral from him and half chuckled. "Knowing Hope, she would probably offer herself up as a sacrifice to any idiot who needed it more than she did."

"Yes... that is the kind of person she is." Emma nodded in agreement with his assessment. "But if you want to be with her through this, you <u>are</u> going to have to feed properly, or at least daily, instead of this weekly nonsense you have been teaching yourself. I know you do it to make your trips to Washington more manageable, but you are not going anywhere soon so there is no harm in it at the present."

"I know." Emile laid his chin on his wife's shoulder and leaned the top of his head against hers. "But that horse <u>is</u> going to have to learn to mind someone other than Hope."

"Maybe so, love, but he will not learn it with anger." Emma reached up and placed a hand on her husband's cheek next to her. "And neither will you. Now go. Go out in that field and do what you need to do and then come back to me. We will both feel better when you return."

"Fine." Emile sighed, then picked himself up off the ground before reaching down to help his wife up. "I'll unsaddle Philippe first, then...." He trailed off with a wave of his hand to the field.

"Try not to think of it with such disappointment, love. It isn't a failure to take care of yourself if it helps you not to slaughter the whole village." Emma climbed back under the railing and waited for him to pass her the saddle and blanket.

"That is easy for you to say," Emile laid the saddle on top of the rail and waited for her to take it. "You have a ready supply with Charlotte whenever you have need of it."

"Oh, stop being so dramatic." Emma rolled her eyes in disapproval. "You and I both know that is a rare case and has only been done a few times in an emergency. As kind as she has been in offering it, I would never place her or her family in such jeopardy, not since the incident in Charleston."

"Indeed. And you're right... I'm just being petty." Emile slid easily between the railings and walked over to take his wife's hand as they left the barn.

"Forgiven... this time only," Emma replied sweetly.

"This time... huh, you know as well as I that you can be no picnic either when you are hungry... or discreet. If we are keeping tabs, there have been more than a few incidents that have left you open to scrutiny in the past twenty years," Emile shot back sarcastically, but not in a way that was overly mean or vindictive, he just knew the depth of her past much more than anyone else on this property.

"Maybe so." She glanced over at him, feeling suddenly apologetic once more about what they were both thinking, and then down at their swinging hands before adding in a bit of admonishment, "But I don't attack the animals, either when I am."

"Fair enough." Emile nodded. "It won't happen ever again."

"Good."

They walked a little further towards the field before Emile suddenly glanced back at the farmhouse next to them. "What do you think William will do with Hope's blood when he is done?" He turned his attention back to the ground below him, unable to do more than focus on where he was going at the present, as he could still smell the enticing odor of the delicious liquid coming over the breeze from Hope's ajar bedroom window.

"I'll ask William to take it with him when he leaves for the night. He can dispose of it at the hospital if need be when he heads back into town. Besides, I am sure neither he nor Nathanael is interested in it just as much as you and I are opposed to the thought."

Emile nodded and let go of her hand before heading in the direction of the pasture beyond the great oak. "Let <u>him</u> decide, but I want it off this property by the time that I get back, Emma. Vampire or not, I will not leave Hope to fight this alone... even if it kills me to do it."

"Emile..." Emma called after him, causing him to stop and turn back around towards her. "Please try to talk to Michael before he leaves, too. I think he could use some fatherly advice, or at the very least some encouragement. The boy is scared, and with good reason."

"Can't it wait for tonight?" Emile looked back at his wife, suddenly even more exhausted by the request. "I don't feel the least like doing either right now."

"We aren't doing it for us." Emma said in careful rebuke not wanting to push her husband over the edge he was teetering on so precariously.

"Fine." Emile sighed and turned back around before adding in a surlier tone. "We never do. I'll come find you shortly. If he is still there when I get back, I will say... something..." He said while shaking his head and continuing to walk off into the field in search of some cow or another to feed upon. Despite what he wanted more, he knew that at least this form of appeasement would allow him to push past the temptation, though not entirely. As controlled as he had been, he should have known after all these years as a vampire that he would never be strong enough to resist the pull of it completely.

Yet there <u>had</u> been at least one victory in his defeat tonight. As consumed as he had been on devouring it as soon as he smelt it, he <u>had</u> been able to flee, which is more than would have been said about many such encounters in his past.

During his time in France, he had welcomed that kind of cavalier lifestyle, feasting on anyone he so chose like he was sampling some new treat from his bakery back in Charleston. The old—like the time-honored baguettes, the young—as sweet as the macrons in their various flavors and just as delicate, the weak—often similar to the flaky layered delights the citizen would buy in droves when placed in the front window, and the very beautiful and enticing women at *Madame* Jeanette's who were just as satisfying as the buttery almond croissants. All were his to choose from, no matter the day of the week or the time. And those particular ladies were in a category all their own with an experience twice as nice as the unusual conquest on the street. As a whole, it was an intoxicatingly selfish game of cat and mouse back then with the mouse being the easiest to catch, and the cat the most eager to enjoy.

But that was not who he was anymore. True to his word, he had traded in his bachelor garb and reckless ways the day he saw Emma waiting for him in his apartment with Angelique before their flight. Weeks earlier he had asked

Madame Jeanette to locate a specific girl he had passed by in the street, and by some miraculous means, she had found her. Not only that, but the woman who waited before him that night was even more stunning standing in his apartment than she had been on the street, despite her dirty work clothes and slightly stained face.

In fact, while he had been conversing with her by the fire on their first night together, he had almost decided more than once to take her completely, as if his sole desire alone was to greedily drink every last drop of the mesmerizing blood that called to him like a siren as it washed over him time and time again—just like his first, fresh conquest. The one that happened long before he had met the woman with the stunningly beautiful strawberry blonde hair and crystal blue eyes that made him feel almost hypnotized looking into them. Yet even then, he could not bring himself to taste a single drop of her blood that night, or on any night thereafter. The sheer purity of her soul stopped him cold at every opportunity and chastised his every thought against taking her, at least not in that way, though she had been his in all of the others. And still, even in that, he had felt like the villain that he was, despite never feeling that way in the past.

Thinking back on that night and the many nights thereafter, Emile stopped and closed his eyes, remembering the rich aroma of lavender as he had unpinned her long tresses and could almost sense the way his whole body reacted when his hands passed through them softly. Without a doubt, it calmed him once again tonight, reimagining it, as much as it had done then.

What kind of supernatural hold did his wife truly have over him that made him desire to be whatever she wanted of him? Or what hidden ability did she always possess that allowed her to be able to change him from a monster to a man again merely by her presence? Try as he might, he never could understand, nor was it especially important for him to do so now. The only thing he knew for certain was that for the rest of his life, he would simply be eternally grateful beyond words that she was his and that she always would be.

In every way, she was his light in the darkness. The one who saw him for who he really was and never judged him for it. And as selfish as he usually acted, she accepted him completely. She believed in him then as much as she did today, though he did not deserve either. In every little thing that she did, her constant love and devotion amidst the storms raging in his life still humbled him and laid his soul bare before him as it spurred him onward to be a better man because of it... because of her.

Humbled and overwhelmed but the depth of gratitude flowing out of him, Emile breathed out slowly and knelt down in the middle of the freshly cut field, aware that no one in this world was watching him but the One above. In his own simple way, he thanked his maker once more for his wife and the way she had directed his life towards this world he was now enjoying.

Then, he paused in deep reflection, remembering all the ways God, Himself, had taken care of him throughout his life, even before becoming a vampire and began to praise Him for His protection through it.

Lastly, he cried out in desperation for his Hope. From the moment she took her first breath on this Earth in his waiting arms, he knew she was not his child by blood, and she never would be. But she <u>was</u> the closest thing he would ever have to that kind of connection in this world and the very thought of losing her made him think things he had never once considered—things no man should ever have to contemplate.

Could he do what must be done to save her life... if it was required of him? Even if that meant an entirely different path for her? Or should he acknowledge God's decision on the matter and allow the natural progression of events to occur as they must for all living things on this planet?

With the evidence piling up around him every day as he walked to his office downtown and witnessed the mourners at the cemetery, he knew that someone may have to decide soon.

Yet sitting there, bathed in the light of the full moon and the millions of stars up above, he knew one thing for certain more than he knew anything else in this life. His world was <u>nothing</u> without Emma. And if he were to be even more honest, he would be just as lost without Hope, too.

So, in the end, that meant only one thing.

If he had to turn Hope in order to save her, he would face that decision with the gratitude of a sinner and not with the condemnation of the self-righteous...

...no matter <u>who</u> had to do it.

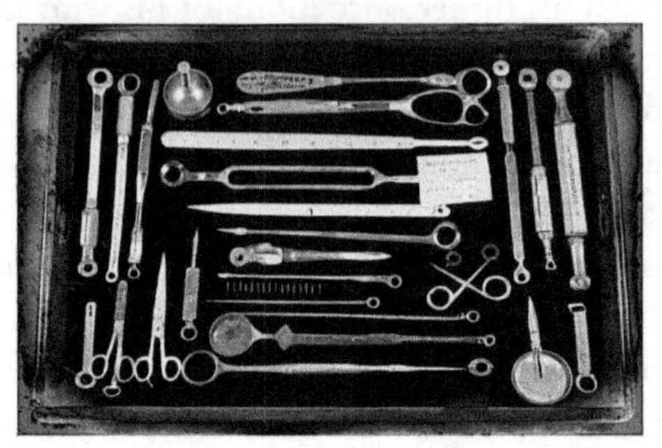

Chapter Thirty-One

October 31st, 1811

"I'd like to send Mr. Baker home today if we can. I think his wound has healed enough for him to tend to it at home. As for the break in his leg, he will need to keep it in the box for at least two months if he can manage it," William instructed the man's wife who was sitting dutifully next to him.

For the majority of the morning, their four little ones had been playing under the bed or dashing up and down the center aisle of the small room, causing a definite distraction to more than one of his staff, not to mention the other patients who were trying to peacefully rest. Sending the man home today was more of a courtesy to all of them than a true necessity for Mr. Baker. Nor would it change the outcome too greatly as far as William could tell. With everything healing as nicely as it had, his eventual recovery would be the same whether he was in the hospital or at home, though it might make things infinitely easier for his wife if it were done at home.

"Will he be able to walk again soon, Doctor? He makes his living at the mill bagging grain," the woman asked nervously as she bounced their youngest quickly up and down on her knee to keep the child distracted.

"I do not see why not. Though you might want to use this time of rest for carving a proper cane if you are able, Mr. Baker. The extra support will come in handy fairly soon, I would imagine." William motioned with one hand to Nurse Sarah to join them. "Would you help Mrs. Baker with the paperwork so her husband and his delightful family can return to their home?"

"Certainly." Nurse Sarah raised both her eyebrows and smiled at William, as eager as he was to be moving the boisterous crowd out of the ward and on their way. "I think that is a marvelous idea. Here. Let me show you some of the things that will help him recover more quickly."

"Thank you. And Mr. Baker, if you are any good with numbers, I would be very interested in hiring you during the interim to sort out my shipping logs, provided you are open to it," William offered, hoping that he might be able to aid their family in just a small way. Though if truth be told, it would be helping him out immensely, too, as he was at a loss as to where to even begin with the books now that he had been away from tending them properly for almost a month.

"Yes, I am excellent with numbers. If you will have me, I'd be ever so grateful for the work," the man responded quickly and exchanged a look of sheer gratitude with his wife across from him.

"Good. I will bring them over the day after next. You will not have to rush with them necessarily, but I would like to check in periodically with notes and arrival logs as they become available." William nodded in his direction and went to move on to the next patient down the hall but stopped along his way when he saw Charity speaking at the main nurse's desk with the young woman who had come in earlier with the fit-like seizures. From his view, more than ten feet away, Joanna's arm no longer held the bandages that Charity had applied. Nor did it even remotely appear that she had ever been burnt in her life before, much less to the severity that he had seen earlier.

Cautiously intrigued by the speed and thoroughness of her recovery, William stepped quietly over to the desk and picked up the folder that was resting on the flat counter behind Charity, trying to examine the woman more closely without being noticed.

"I wanted to stop by and thank you for everything that you did for me the other day. Your care was nothing short of miraculous. See, not even a scar! I wish you had seen my face when I took off the bandage yesterday. I could not believe my eyes! It has almost healed completely," Joanna exclaimed happily as she lifted her sleeve to show Charity her forearm and palms which were plainly as perfect as any he had ever witnessed before.

"I am so happy for you... truly," Charity said genuinely. "And have you had any more of your spells recently?"

"Now that you mention it... no." Joanna cocked her head to one side as if considering the rest of her answer. "In truth, I have been feeling so well of late that I hardly even noticed that I had not." The woman smiled broadly at the pleasant realization.

"That is wonderful news indeed. Then we shall pray that they will be gone for good." Charity placed one hand on the woman's bare arm and grinned.

"I could not even contemplate that kind of reality, Nurse Bentham." The woman looked nearly too moved for words. "That would be almost too miraculous."

Glancing upwards with deeply-seated chagrin at the use of the overly spiritual term where it clearly wasn't warranted, William tried not to show his obvious displeasure with the complicated situation and remain silent.

"Well, let us just take one day at a time, shall we? You can always come back here if you have another unfortunate incident. Since I am already familiar with your case, please do not hesitate to ask for me directly. Though anyone here can certainly treat you, it might lessen the time involved to receive the proper care," Charity encouraged the woman cordially.

"I will," Joanna said gratefully, then impetuously seized the nurse in a tight embrace. "And thank you once again."

Feeling suddenly awkward and uncomfortable by the overabundance of attention from her patient, Charity tried to reciprocate but the motion looked stiff and forced. "It was my pleasure, Miss."

Without another word, the woman let her go but still beamed at her with an expression of exultant relief. "Should you ever have need of something knitted for you, just say the word. I can't promise it will be perfect, as few of my projects ever are, but I would be so pleased to be able to do something to repay the favor."

"That is a very generous offer, and I will certainly keep that in mind," Charity answered politely though she had no idea what to say next. As kind as the gift was, the last thing she wanted to do was to cause more work for the woman or to possibly instigate another episode by adding on a stressful project.

Having achieved what she had originally intended, Joanna simply nodded discreetly in response, then turned around and left the hospital lighter than any patient William had ever seen exiting.

"Well, she definitely thinks <u>you're</u> angelic." William muttered sarcastically while still pretending to read the chart before him.

"Doctor Wells!" Charity jumped slightly, completely startled by his close proximity, for she had not heard him approaching, nor did she know how long he had truly been standing there. "Goodness gracious! You need to start wearing a cowbell, sir."

"Indeed." William attempted to hide his smile at her humorous suggestion. "Though if you really think so, I might know where to find one... should it become necessary."

"Well, you might want to if you want my nerves to remain intact." Charity shook her head and laid one hand upon her chest to calm herself. "You remember Miss Thompson, don't you? She came in the other day after a fall near her fireplace."

"The one with the seizures." William stared down his nose at the nurse before him, utterly unimpressed by her attempt at diversion and lack of transparency.

"Yes," Charity fidgeted anxiously with the stack of linens on the desk next to her, hoping beyond measure that the man across from her would drop the topic altogether and move along on his rounds.

"I remember who she is Charity. And what she means to both of us." William sighed heavily, not wanting to have this conversation yet again. Sadly, it was the same one they had already discussed at length several times this week alone. Yet despite her many, many attempts to logically persuade him, he was not any more convinced towards her way of thinking than he had been in the first.

"You still won't accept the benefit of what I did, will you?" Charity's eyes narrowed slightly, though she was trying very hard not to be perturbed with him today. After all, it had been over a week since their first kiss and not a day had gone by that she had not thought back to it at least once, if not more often if she were to be honest. On the surface, it was just one of the happy little distractions in her life at the present, but as nice as it had been, the intensity of the unexpected experience had also scared her more than she had thought possible.

William shook his head in disapproval at her overly simplistic assessment. "Until I can verify medically that no other ill effects occur because of it, I would like you to at least promise me you will not do so again without my knowledge. If for your safety alone, please."

"If that will make you feel more comfortable," Charity quipped curtly as she pursed her lips in disappointment, still seeking a peaceful solution, though she far knew better than him that nothing she had done in the past fifty years had caused any deficit to anyone she had treated... or at least not to her knowledge.

"It would." William sighed yet again but still could not manage to physically relax standing this close to her. The building tension that always seemed to exist between them, though positive in nature now, was almost palpable today. Which only made focusing on his work even that much more difficult.

"Then I promise that I will not do so again without your permission. Or as long as it is not a matter of life or death," Charity pledged solemnly without a hint of dissatisfaction towards him for asking it of her.

"Thank you. I appreciate that," William said mechanically, though her abject compliance was the last thing on his mind today.

Feeling consumed with the need to do something constructively useful, he had spent the majority of the night with Hope, attempting every method he was familiar with to help the poor girl. Yet nothing had worked. Nor had any of his efforts managed to lower her fever in the slightest. Moreover, for the past four days, he had tried countless forms of remedies from every medical journal he possessed, from cooling tamarind and marshmallow root liquors on her tongue to opening all the windows to bring in the colder night air. He had even placed heavy blankets on top of her to sweat the fever out, yet the uncontrollable tremors and unrelenting delirium remained constant. As inhuman as most diseases were, it still felt as if the illness itself was tormenting him personally, mocking his every effort, and not the other way around.

Worse still, it was driving him literally mad watching Emile pace the floor beside him without relent. His long strides within the tiny room and ever-present brooding in the corner as he stood vigil over the girl were utterly maddening to witness. Not to mention the repetitive prayers whispered from the young girl's mother across the hall.

In all, it made the house that was virtually empty of people seem eerily haunted by the ghosts that waited just outside the bedroom door to take the girl at any minute should he fail.

"Hello?" Charity waved her hand in front of his face and for the first time since she had stopped talking, he realized he had not heard a single word the woman had uttered in the past five minutes, if not more. "I'm sorry, could you repeat what you just said? I wasn't listening."

"Apparently not. I was asking you how Hope was doing."

"Really? Why? Other than the obvious, of course," William replied but still looked dazed and lost in his own thoughts.

Suddenly concerned for the man, who never failed to catch every detail of the conversations he was privy to, Charity inched into the conversation again slowly, "Emma came by the hospital this morning looking for you, but I wasn't sure where you were at the time."

"Did she happen to mention <u>why</u> she came? It might be important." The hair on the back of his neck rose to attention at the possible threat of imminent defeat so soon.

"Goodness... take a breath, William. She was only asking me if I knew anyone at the hospital who might be able to care for the two children they are caring for." Charity took the folder away from him and placed it back upon the stacked pile of other folders, then led him away from the main desk and over to a quieter area. "Given that Hope has not been improving as of yet, she thought it might be possible that she would need someone to watch Samuel and Holly for the next few days. Or at the very least until they are certain she will turn the corner. Now that the children are doing so much better health wise, Emma wanted to give Hope as much peace and quiet as possible under the circumstances."

"A wise decision, as always." William rubbed the palm of one of his hands with his thumb methodically for several minutes, a nervous energy running through them as he contemplated another subject entirely. Something he was still not sure where he stood particularly. Or if he should even be seriously considering it. "Speaking of Samuel and Holly... have you had the chance to properly meet them yet?" William tentatively searched for her opinion, too conflicted mentally to even look up at her while doing so.

In their time spent helping Jedidiah and Nancy, William could tell already that Charity had a sincere love for children in general. But how she felt about these two particular children felt a bit more important to William now that they were actually discussing it.

"Oh, yes! Aren't they positively delightful?" Charity exclaimed happily, unable to hide her excitement From the very first time that Holly had placed her little palm in her hand at the table to the way Samuel kept bringing her whatever he was abundantly proud of that day, she knew she adored them both immensely. "I was just over there the other day talking with Emma and the three of us girls had a pleasant little tea party of sorts. Well, I should probably say four or five as I think there were a few other toys that joined us at the table, too."

"Most likely Anna Grace Bunny and Wilber the frog. I had the unique pleasure of making their acquaintance when the children and I fetched their things from their home." William nodded at the memory, but he couldn't hide the smile that always filled his face whenever he thought of them. "They are precisely the perfect ages and both so very intelligent. It's a shame that they do not have any other family to speak of that could take them in. Without another blood relative, as much as I hate to even suggest it, they will most likely have to be taken to the foundling home at the end of the month."

"Oh... I didn't realize the decision had already been made. But that being said, some of those places are run very well, William," Charity tried to reassure him, though both of them knew the dark reputation a few of the lesser funded establishments held. "I am sure there are many other parents who would jump at the chance to adopt them, given the opportunity."

"I doubt it." William shook his head sadly. "I expect that one of the children will find a home fairly quickly, but most likely they will not be living together.

And even then, many adoptive families view those that they take in as pieces of property, not as actual members of their family."

"You speak as if you know a bit more about this than what you are letting on, William. Or is there a specific reason behind what you are saying?" Charity pried gently, hoping to see just why he held such a strong prejudice.

"I don't have any firsthand knowledge outside the few children I have treated here, but Charlotte's husband, who died three years ago, lived a very similar life. Something he never really recovered from in many ways, as the family who took him in was very opportunistic. It was only when he married Charlotte and had his own family that Sebastian truly experienced what it meant to be loved." William inhaled deeply and thought back to the many times his friend would watch the people passing by his forge and the way he would grimace sadly at how they were speaking to their children or each other. Being forced to abandon his family after his transition was the one scar that had never left him, no matter how much he had tried to make amends for it. And seeing others so casually dismissing something that was so infinitely valuable in his opinion, only made him cherish his own family all the more. "You know that I don't like to speak ill of people out of turn, but the truth of the matter is that despite how possible a positive scenario might be, the opposite has been my experience more times than I would like to say over the years."

"So... by your own admission, it sounds like you would quite possibly be in favor of someone you are acquainted with keeping them. Someone like Jedidiah or Nancy perhaps? Or even Charlotte?" Charity sat down in a chair closest to the wall and folded her hands in her lap, grateful for a moment to rest her feet.

"Probably not them." In truth, William had already thought over the very short list of people he felt would be suitable parents for the two children but had come up empty-handed <u>every</u> time. With two little ones of their own, there was no way Jedidiah and Nancy were ready for more, nor could they financially afford the extra burden so soon after being sick. And Charlotte, as eager as she always was to see them, had not yet recovered from the Fever to be well enough to care for herself, let alone two small children. Though with her self-sacrificing nature, William also knew she would undoubtedly have been more than happy to try.

Then there was Emile and Emma. For the past three years, they had been helping to mentor Hope but though the children seemed to be a daily blessing to Emma, she did not seem as attached to them as she was with Jedidiah's children or even Thomas' Abigail. That left only Elijah and Nathanael and that was even more comical to consider—most definitely not a solution in the slightest.

"What about yourself then?" Charity prodded deeper. "Could you see yourself caring for them? I mean, you obviously think the world of them, or you would not be troubling yourself on their behalf."

"Me?" William tried to sound vaguely surprised, but he could not even manage a false expression. In so many instances, the thought <u>had</u> crossed his mind more than a time or two since he met them, but knowing how very implausible the scenario would be, he had dismissed it just as quickly. Or at least he had tried. "With my schedule around here, how would I ever manage it? I never know from one day to the next where I will be, and that is no life for these children either. They need a family, Charity. And as much as I don't want to choose it, they might be better off taking their chances at the foundling home and allowing fate to control the situation as it has for so many others before them."

"You can't mean that!" Charity appeared totally shocked now by his outright refusal.

William shrugged, his heart aching just thinking about the moment he would have to let them finally go but could offer up no more than a disappointing reply to an equally sad decision, "I feel at this point, there is little else we can do."

"Oh, I think you could arrange a nanny during the day if you really wanted to make it work. Most children don't need a parent hovering over them day and night. They just need to know that they are properly loved and cared for. Besides, I should imagine that a stable home environment is more important than hours of time, no matter who raises them," Charity continued to coerce him on their behalf. "And Samuel will be attending school in a year, so that will occupy at least a portion of his time while you work, as well."

"But what about you?" William shot back quickly, seizing upon yet another possibility he had been hesitant to suggest at first. The very same one had been secretly dreading asking her for the past ten minutes. "Aren't women supposed to make better mothers than someone like me? As learned as I might appear, I wouldn't know the first thing to do about anything. They'd probably eat me alive."

"And you think I would know more? Just because I am a woman doesn't make me any more qualified than you." Charity laughed freely. "Though I <u>would</u> help someone raise them if I was asked, under the right provisions, of course."

"Now there is an idea... perhaps a group of the nurses could form a party of caregivers of some kind. Or take turns helping with them on various days of the week as their schedules allowed," William suggested feebly, finally running out of ideas at last.

"These children aren't new clothing to try on, William." Charity sighed in defeat at his lack of understanding.

"Then what would <u>you</u> propose?" William took the other seat next to her along the wall and leaned forward, resting his elbows on top of the arms of the chair.

Resisting the urge to utterly throttle him at his ineptness, the woman next to him rolled her eyes instead. "If I have to spell it out for you... it truly isn't worth it."

"What's not worth it?" William answered quickly, not following in the slightest the direction the conversation was suddenly taking.

"<u>We</u> could take care of them <u>together</u>, William. Not in the same house, mind you, or at least not in the beginning, but as a shared responsibility of sorts while they are young. I fully realize that it would not be the perfect solution by any means, and we would have to arrange our schedules to accommodate it in the beginning, but it would at least offer them..." She tried to explain in detail the only logical solution she could think of but stopped when William took her hand in his and held it tightly within his own without any regard whatsoever as to who might possibly see it. "What?"

"Are you certain you would not mind?" His mind raced ahead of him onto a literal volume of new and exciting questions. "I know there would be definite complications for us as they grew older, but it is also possible that we might find some of their family by then." William's heart seemed ready to burst at the possibility, as he had been drawn to their plight from the very first day he had met them.

Charity nodded, feeling the slight tinge of fear begin to rise within her once more at his closeness and excitement.

"I think it is my turn to say that I could kiss <u>you</u>, Miss Charity Bentham... but I won't, because we both know that neither of us would be able to focus for the rest of the day if I do and our patients deserve better than that," William admitted honestly. "Though to tell you the truth, I <u>have</u> been an absolute wreck this entire week just remembering it."

Suddenly just as eager to find some obscure corner of the hospital with him, as well, Charity pushed a strand of loose hair behind her ear and leaned in closer to speak quietly. "I haven't been able to concentrate either."

Without needing to say more, the two sat together in silence, each knowing precisely what the other was thinking, yet both straining to resist acting upon it.

"Well, then..." William finally cleared his throat several times before standing up awkwardly to compose himself once more. "If you can arrange for someone to help this week with Samuel and Holly, I will see about making the other necessary arrangements for afterwards. Nathanael has already approached me with the idea of him lodging with Charlotte and Elijah for the time being to help more at the farm, so it looks like my home would be..."

"Available and easily accessible, being so close to the hospital." Charity finished his sentence, then stood up, too, trying her best to keep a respectable distance away from him for both their sakes.

"Precisely, that was why I initially chose that particular home in the first place. And it providentially already has three rooms on the upper floor. So, that should work nicely, too." William rubbed the back of his neck, contemplating already how he would arrange the children's rooms once Nathanael's things had been carefully stored elsewhere.

"If I can find a few people to care for them during our shifts this week, do you think they could stay there for the time being? It might be easier doing that than finding someone with room for both." Charity stepped around several other doctors who were passing by in the spacious hallway and picked up the next patient's chart from the desk before handing it over to him.

"I don't see why not but let me discuss it all with Nathanael and Elijah first during lunch to make sure. Elijah will need to bunk at Emile's for the present, or at least until Hope is no longer sick. Since he has shown no other signs of transmittal after being exposed at the workday, or anyone else who was present for that matter, I would rather not risk exposing him daily if there is an alternate solution available." He followed after Charity as she started back down the hall, walking at an easy pace to the main hallway and towards the patient he was originally stopping to check.

"That should work out fine..." Charity began to agree but was interrupted when they finally reached the merging of the two long hallways by a loud crash that echoed back to them from the room directly to their left. As loud as it was, the jarring commotion caused both of them to focus solely on it alone now and almost run to assist, uncertain as to its origin.

"What has happened?" William entered the room first and strode up to the woman on the floor beside her bed who was doubled over in pain, her arms tightly wound across her stomach as she writhed on the floor beside it.

Reacting to the commotion, as well, two nurses were already huddled over her, but neither of them had a ready explanation for him.

"I don't know. We were both over there helping Mrs. Walker when I heard the crash," Nurse Sarah replied at last as she struggled to keep the woman from hitting her legs on the broken pieces of pottery that had been scattered all around her when she fell.

"Argghhhh!" The woman on the floor twisted in pain as she clutched her side, obviously in agony, though in all other ways, she remained oblivious to everything transpiring around her. Tiny rivers of sweat, like raised streaks across her forehead, now poured from her temple and down the sides of her face as they wet the base of her neck near her blouse in many places.

"Let's get her back up on the bed. We can assess her better there," Charity instructed the other nurses as William moved the fallen tray and dishes out of their path to allow them clear access.

With a yell of agony that escaped her lips the moment she was shifted from her place on the floor, the woman's unfortunate predicament caused more than a few patients in the ward to peer over in her direction from their beds in concern.

Assuming the worst, William instinctively grabbed her chart, quickly scanning the notes before walking over and checking the woman's pupils. "It says here that she was admitted for abdominal pain almost twelve hours ago. Has no one treated her since?" He demanded, his eyes reflecting back the horror of the mistake he was seeing.

"No," the two other nurses said in unison and shook their heads silently. "Doctor Brooks said it was most likely gas and that it would pass."

"Imbecile! Gas does not cause these kinds of symptoms." William shook his head in anger, a true distaste forming in his mouth from the ineptness that had caused so much suffering. "She should have at least been given some laudanum for the pain if the man had any compassion at all for his patient."

Clearly just as moved as he was, Charity took a seat near the woman's head and attempted to comfort her by stroking her hair while the woman, who looked to be only slightly older than herself, still thrashed about in pain next to her. "What do you think it could be, Doctor Wells?"

"It's not gas." William flexed the muscles in his jaw at the condemnation and lifted the woman's loose blouse, tapping several areas of her stomach until he reached a point where the woman let out a gut-wrenching scream in protest and jerked away from him. An area, about the size of his fist in her lower right pelvic region was already turning a bright pink and was very warm to the touch. "Have you sustained any kind of an injury before arriving here Miss? Did you fall perhaps? Or were you kicked by a horse?"

"No," the woman managed to say through her gritted teeth. "Help me... please!"

"I am trying. Charity, would you ..." William began to instruct her to give the woman the needed pain medication, but she had already moved to retrieve the amber bottle and spoon, ready to administer the dosage he requested. The action, as simple as it was, startled him completely as he realized how very much the two of them were in sync with each other now that they were no longer fighting.

"How many spoons, Doctor Wells?" Charity asked him respectfully, using his formal name in front of the others.

"At least two at the present should suffice." He turned to hold the woman's arms still against her side so he could steady her movements a little for Charity to give the proper dosage and not spill.

Unable to do otherwise, the woman continued to writhe uncontrollably even under his gentle restraint but managed to swallow the bitter liquid in spurts and little by little her spasms calmed as she relaxed, though the ever-present low groan was still audible like a dull hum in the distance across the room.

"We will need to administer this sedative in a few more hours if the pain returns, which I expect that it will under the circumstances." William respectfully tucked the covering blanket around the woman and raised it up over her chest.

"Of course. But what do you think is wrong with her? I've never seen anything create this much pain." Charity used her hand to smooth back the woman's hair, trying to help her regain at least some of her dignity.

"Doctor Brooks is an idiot, and his total lack of consideration probably signed this woman's death notice today." William took his stub of charcoal out from his pocket and crossed out the man's previous instructions and assumptions. "Any first-year student could have diagnosed her more accurately than he did." William paused, then looked over at the three nurses before offering an opportunity to them inquisitively with an outstretched hand. "You three have been here just as long as most of them. Be honest. What do you think she is suffering from?"

Unsure if the doctor was really serious about his invitation, Nurse Sarah glanced nervously over at the other nurse beside her but held her tongue respectfully.

"I'll let you two guess first," Charity said confidently. "I already know exactly what is wrong, and it isn't good."

"Alright." The nurse next to Nurse Sarah raised her hand timidly.

William nodded. "Go on. I am sure both of you have as much training as the students do, maybe even more so since you actually treat the patients they are only reading about in their journals."

"Since her child was born a few months ago, this is most likely not a complication from her recent pregnancy, and a gas build up would have dissipated by now," she surmised quietly, still considering the unique chance that had been afforded them.

"I think her appendix may be ready to burst," Nurse Sarah declared unceremoniously, confident that she was right and desiring to impress.

"Do you concur, Nurse Bentham?" William eyed Charity, who was still sitting at the top of bed stroking her patient's hair, speaking to her in the same way he would address any of his peers.

"I believe Sarah is undoubtedly correct and yet incorrect, as well. From the high fever, chills, obvious sweating, and now the intense abdominal pain, there can be little else to blame," Charity said with the self-assurance afforded to most doctors.

"Excellent, both of you. And where was she incorrect?" William asked just as respectfully.

"It has already burst, hasn't it?" Nurse Sarah placed a hand over her mouth to contain her small gasp thereafter. "That was why she fell to the floor moments ago, wasn't it?"

Charity nodded solemnly. "Most likely."

"You are both correct, again." William smiled with true admiration. "And what would you propose for her treatment then?"

"Treatment?" Nurse Sarah cocked her head in sudden confusion. "Is there a treatment yet for this?"

"Sadly, no." William frowned and shook his head. "It has already progressed beyond the stage of any medicinal intervention, and any experimental surgery at this point would be out of the question. From the moment she arrived at our doors, it was only a matter of time."

"A matter of time before what?" Charity asked him seriously.

"Before we notified the next of kin." William sighed quietly. In every way, situations like these and the one Hope was currently facing were never easy, and seeing it occur in one so young made it doubly so.

"But she has a new husband and a baby. Isn't there something we can do to help her? Something radical since there is no other alternative treatment?" The more timid nurse petitioned politely.

"I wish there was... truly, but there simply isn't. In my lifetime, I have only seen one doctor attempt to cure this. He did so by placing a small cut in the abdomen to allow the infection to pass out of the body, but only one of his patients survived such a procedure and it was excruciating for them to endure. In her current state, I do not think our patient would live through such an ordeal if we tried it." William placed a reassuring hand on the small woman's shoulder. "The best thing we can do for our patient now is to offer her a dignified passing. We should, of course, provide as much support for her as possible, manage her pain until that time arrives, and someone should send for her family now. They will want what little time they have left with her."

The two nurses nodded and scurried out of the room silently to send a messenger for the woman's husband. As dire as she currently was, there was no way to know just how much longer the woman had left to live and as such, both of them knew how very precious every minute was quickly becoming.

"There _is_ something we _could_ try, Doctor Wells." Charity lifted one of the woman's hands and placed it on top of the other slowly. "I'm almost certain that it will not work at this stage, but there is nothing left to lose if we try."

"Charity... no." William looked down at her and frowned, not out of anger or even resentment that she would bring up the same tiresome idea yet again, but more out of a sincere desire to guide her through something that was equally difficult for him, too. "We cannot use our gift, as wonderful as it may be, to save every one of our patients."

"No, but we _could_ try to save _her_." Charity attempted to reason with him gently. "Look at her, William. She is so young. She has her whole life ahead of her."

Wanting to please her in every way but knowing he would never be able to do so in this, William walked around to the other side of the bed to be closer to her, finding a place where prying eyes and ears would not be privy to their conversation. "You have to stop looking at this in that way, Charity. Didn't you tell me once that 'sometimes it is out of our hands to save them'? I believe with Nathanael that everything in our lives happens for a reason. You and I know that better than anyone else. Besides, how do _we_ know if God hasn't already ordained that this man will one day meet his new wife somewhere down the road, someone who will very much need him just as much as he needs her, and you saving this woman here would stop all of that from happening as it should? Or to put it in another light, what about Samuel and Holly. They would not even exist in our realm of thought if their parents had not also died. Their untimely death has provided a rare opportunity for the two of us that we would never be able to physically have." He paused and tried to calm the racing of his heart that the conversation had created back to its original cadence, then began again, "I know you have the purest of intentions concerning her, but we aren't meant to play God, and He hasn't called us to go around saving all the people who are sick around us. There isn't enough blood in this world for all of that and you know it."

"I'm not asking you to save the world, William. I'm asking you to let me help this one woman," Charity pleaded earnestly, her eyes yearning for him to give in just a little. "Just like you were desperate to try anything for Mrs. Armstrong, something in me needs to at least try."

"And what about the next patient, Charity? And the one after that? When will it stop? When you have run out of blood yourself?" William reasoned flatly. "We don't understand exactly how our systems work, at least not completely, but I doubt that we have an endless supply to be giving it out freely."

"I don't have all the answers you want, William... but just like you have been called to help people at this hospital, I believe this something I have been given to do in my life. Yet I do also comprehend your logic, and because I respect you, I won't go against you. I promised you that I would not, and I intend on keeping that promise if I must." Charity bit her lip to hold back her disappointment on the topic.

With a wealth of emotions now fighting to expose her true feelings about all of this, half of her wished she had never told him about what their blood could do. The other half was grateful that someone else was around to finally protect her, as there had been more than one close call over the years. As tender as her heart always was, someone was bound to discover in time what she had been doing and when they did, they might not handle the situation as gracefully as William had or as peacefully.

"Charity, I can see how much this is upsetting you." William reached for her hand, then stopped, afraid that she would pull away from him in her displeasure. "It distresses me, too... every time someone dies. And, you have no idea how much I want to say the things that will please you, but I beg you to believe me when I say that everything inside of me wants to let you do this, but I just can't. There are lines here that have to be considered, Charity, and some of those lines should not be broken, no matter how noble the reasons."

"I understand." Charity nodded soberly. "Then this poor woman will die."

"Yes, and probably before the end of the day, if not by morning. It has been my experience that most patients do not last very long once the organ has ruptured. From what I have read, whatever causes the appendix to fail in the first place, soon spreads to the rest of the body and with it, the infection. It is only a matter of time before the lungs and heart are too damaged to function properly because of it. Still, though it is of little consolation, the laudanum will help her pass peacefully." William watched Charity's reaction closely and struggled to gauge her dissatisfaction with him at the moment.

"Alright. Since there is nothing left for me to do here," Charity stood, a complete look of controlled apathy spreading across her features at last, "may I be excused please, Doctor Wells?"

"Charity..." William glanced up at her, his heart breaking to see how quickly she had closed herself off to him.

"Please, William... I just need a minute, if you will allow me," Charity said coldly, no longer able to look at him directly.

William shook his head and released her, "Of course, you may go."

"Thank you," Charity replied mechanically and left the room, feeling the need to put as much distance between him and herself as she struggled to maintain her composure until she was safely in another room.

"Why do I feel like that was not a win for either of us?" William sighed and studied the woman beside him, increasingly miserable about her eventual fate. "I wish I could do more for you, Miss. You deserve <u>so</u> much more."

The woman's shallow breathing as she slept assured him of her inability to remember anything that had just been uttered around her, much less continue to endure any of the pain she had been experiencing just moments earlier. Despite how much he might have liked to lessen the burden on her more, it would still take many more hours before her final moment on this Earth would arrive. Yet when it did, she would at least pass as peacefully as he could provide. Maybe someday there would be more he could do, something phenomenally helpful beyond using Charity's cure, but for the present, there was not, and wishing for a miracle wouldn't help anyone either.

Studying the woman's face more closely and the remarkable way it resembled many of the other souls he had helped usher into eternity, William thought once again about Charity's very tempting suggestion and pictured himself in the place of his patient's husband with a new baby to care for and no wife to comfort him. The very vivid image his mind began to create caused him to remember anew Nathanael's overwhelming grief when Elise had died and the many months of tortured solitude thereafter. The trials of life could be so unfair at times, debilitating even when they did not match with our understanding, and it all made his heart ache for the man even more just to contemplate it.

In the span of twenty-five years, he had lost many patients in his short tenure as a physician, each one of them leaving their mark on his soul like an etching on a prison wall. Twenty-three in just this year alone had carved their line upon his wall, in fact, all joining the hundreds more that were already waiting there for them.

Yet despite that disappointing fact aside, he still could not force himself to relent. God, in His great wisdom, had given their lives specific parameters, and it was not up to them to change them simply because they felt they knew better than He who deserved a different path. The practice of medicine that he had dedicated his life to was not about balancing risks and worth. It was about managing the rules of life and death, and that line, though blurred where he and his friends were concerned, was not supposed to be crossed... no matter the person, intent, or reason.

Chapter Thirty-Two

October 31st, 1811

Feeling utterly exhausted from the past two days of keeping vigil silently by her bedside, Michael sat on the edge of his chair but dozed off in-between groans from the girl in the bed. It had been hours since Doctor Wells had left for the hospital and even Mrs. Fabbri had finally relented to Mr. Beckett and laid down for a short nap, though it had taken more than a great deal of convincing by both of them for her to do so.

At long last, he had finally been given a moment of peace and quiet with the girl that he loved, and now, as tired as he was from sitting there all night worrying about her, he could not seem to stay awake long enough to say anything, much less provide any comfort to her in some tangible way.

With a jarring thud, a door shut hard beneath him, startling him out of his slumber momentarily and alerting him once again to the passage of time that he was wasting.

If only there was something he could do to help lower her fever in some way, or some small occupation that would make a difference...

If only...

Fighting back the exhaustion he felt in every pore, he rubbed the sleep out of his eyes with both his hands and reached forward to push a lock of damp hair out of Hope's. "Can you hear me, Hope?" Michael asked tentatively, first barely above a whisper, then much louder again when he thought he saw the girl's face twitch in some way in reaction to his voice.

"It's Michael. Of course, you know it's Michael." He shook his head in frustration at his stupid statement. "Who else would it be?"

The corners of the girl's mouth moved slightly upwards at hearing it, as if she were attempting the smallest part of a smile.

Oh, how he missed that smile that she always wore. Everything in his world could be falling apart, but Hope would bound through his door at *The Aurora* with a beaming smile, eager to share with him whatever wonderful thing that had happened to her that day and all would be well again.

But will it be well again? Michael's throat constricted tightly at the fear that was threatening to choke him.

Like any other man, he had often been too distracted to listen to all the details she had wanted to share at the time, but if he had known then how precious little time they might have left, he would go back and pay her the closest attention possible. With raptured attention, he would hang on her every word, giggle and joke that she wanted to tell him. He wouldn't care that his articles needed to be written. Or that his editor would be cross with him come deadline time. It all wouldn't matter. Nothing but <u>her</u> would matter.

Suddenly feeling the need to stand up and stretch his legs, he paced the room once more, regretting all the many missed opportunities that had passed between them over the last year. Oh, the countless hours they had spent in pointless arguments over topics that mattered next to nothing at all compared to living an eternity without her. In fact, thinking about it now, it quite literally drove him mad as he contemplated how wasteful it all was, causing his blood to boil remembering how angry he had been at her recently.

Although it was true that he knew what her uncle, her father, or whatever the relationship was that she clung to so deeply, thought of him, he still couldn't help the deep animosity he felt towards him at times. After all, the man was utterly demeaning of him at every turn and not the least bit encouraging of their relationship as a whole. Though to be equally honest, he had not made it exactly easy for her uncle to like him either. From the very beginning, he had never cared for the man and his French mannerisms. Or the way in which he always looked like he owned the place, even though it was <u>he</u> who was the visitor. There were even times while watching him look down at him aloofly from across the room, that he had wanted to go right up and... well, he knew both now and then how foolish and detrimental those thoughts could be in the mind of an ambitious suitor—fateful even if he wanted to stick around, which he most certainly did.

Still... he looked over at the pale form of his first love and shuddered. He would fight any man before him right now if it meant giving her the slightest chance that she might actually beat this illness. That she would come back to him and be the cheerful, oft-times childish woman that he had grown to love so dearly. Yet there was no way he could fight anything so inhumanely invisible as this disease as there was nothing of flesh and blood for his hands to find purchase.

With a sigh of defeat on <u>both</u> subjects, he trudged back over to the bed and took a seat next to her on top of the quilt, paying careful attention not to jostle her in any way. Deep purple streaks, the color of the sky just before twilight, crossed both of her inner arms where they had removed blood twice in the past few days. Though oddly enough, the shade had complemented perfectly the scarlet flush upon both of her cheeks and neck as it wound its way down her arms towards him as if reaching for its next victim. At the moment, he did not particularly care if that <u>was</u> him. He would gladly accept death in her place if it came down to it—not only accept it but be grateful that she would no longer be suffering and was whole once more.

"Hope..." He tried to speak but his voice caught in his throat each time he started. "Hope, can you hear me?" He cleared away the stress within it and annunciated every syllable slowly.

Hope's eyes fluttered slightly and opened just a little. "Michael?"

"Yes, yes, it's me! Are you in pain?" A rush of adrenaline flooded him instantly.

Hope shook her head slightly. "I'm... just... tired..."

"I know you are, but please, you <u>have</u> to fight a little longer for me, for all of us." Michael picked up her limp hand and held it close to his cheek. "It isn't time to rest just yet. Not for a long, long time, let me assure you."

Hope smiled again and seemed to take him in visually just a little. "You... look... worried."

Michael tried to laugh at her insanely ridiculous understatement through his running tears, but the sound of it in his ears sounded utterly pathetic, like something closer to that of a wounded bird or flapping fish on the pier. "Of course I do, silly. You are making me a nervous wreck. You know that, right?"

"I'm...sorry." She moved her finger on her hand marginally to touch his tears. "Don't cry."

Wanting nothing more than to obey her every command happily, Michael wiped the back of his hand across his face quickly. "There, is that better?"

Hope grinned even wider, but it was still not her full smile. "Much."

"Your uncles have been here all night and so have many of the others. They will be absolutely furious with me when I tell them that I have stolen all of your time today." He continued to caress her hand in his own while keeping it laid carefully across one of his legs.

"They'll live," Hope said softly. "Maybe not father... but... the rest... will understand. Father... needs... me, Michael."

"Hope, your father passed away several years ago. Please don't tell me you have been seeing him. I am not ready for that kind of discussion just yet," Michael admitted nervously.

"Not him..." Hope weakly shook her head, "my other father... the one who likes... to torture you."

Michael laughed lightly once more. "That he does... and quite well, I might add. Though he might be disappointed that he will not have that pleasure anymore after you are better."

"Why?" Hope looked back at him, suddenly confused. "Are you leaving?"

"Me?" He pointed to himself. "No, but I wouldn't blame you if you still hated me after that last argument we had."

Hope sighed. "I... could never hate you... Michael. I love you."

"Really?" Michael's heart surged with relief and sadness all at the same time. "Are you sure?"

"Papa said I could marry you... didn't he?" Hope said slowly and carefully.

Michael nodded though his throat felt almost too constricted to speak once more.

"Then, I say yes," Hope added weakly. "In sickness ... and in health... right?"

"Right." Michael finally managed to say despite the tears that had begun to flow freely once more down both of his cheeks. "Though you had better get to the health part pretty quick because I don't know how much more of this I can stand." He motioned with his free hand, the breadth of the room, and tried to add humor to the situation that was already far more dire than he preferred.

"I'll try." Hope exhaled a long sigh, then closed her eyes slowly as if she had completed the last thing she was supposed to accomplish in this life, giving him what he had wanted more than anything else in this world—her forgiveness.

In truth, it frightened Michael instantly when she did it, for it sounded like her last breath being exhaled out into the room around him. "Hope!"

"I'm... still... here..."

"Praise God," Michael whispered as he looked to the ceiling and thanked God immediately while he subsequently tried also to calm the racing of his heart. "I thought you had decided to leave me there for a minute."

"Not yet," Hope breathed out once more.

"Not ever, Hope. Do you hear me?" Michael spoke harshly before wiping away his tears once more.

"I hear."

Overwhelmed by the dismal reality she had just barely suggested, Michael leaned forward and kissed her forehead just once before also kissing her hand. "Would you like to see the ring?"

Hope opened her eyes slowly, like she was again having the worst difficulty in focusing on him again. "Maybe later... Michael. I'm too tired..."

Michael nodded. "Just rest. It will be on your nightstand when you wake up."

"Okay," she said slowly, then appeared to drift off to sleep once more with a peacefulness that appeared both angelic and frightening all at the same time. In many ways, the expression was like that in the paintings of the Lady Of Shallot or Hamlet's Ophelia, two ladies that were forever frozen in their youth as they passed on to the next world beyond.

Steeling himself for what may possibly lie ahead, Michael placed her arm lovingly across her chest before lifting up the blanket higher until it reached the base of her neck. Doctor Wells had given him strict instructions not to let her catch a chill from the open window and as hot as her skin had been a moment ago, he didn't want to risk another minute of exposure.

From the half-closed door across the room behind him, Emile watched the entire scene unfold, wincing in marked displeasure more than once throughout it, yet not for the reasons he might have expected. In this moment, while hiding in the silence, he felt only a sense of regret and not a fatherly reticence for his part in delaying their eventual union. Since the very first Sunday that he had noticed her favoring the boy after church, he had adeptly stood in the way of the happiness that Hope rightly deserved, and for far less noble reasons than he probably should have. In fact, for months he had congratulated himself to William and Nathanael for the way in which he had always managed to stall them at every turn. But today... today that false sense of self-righteousness alone embarrassed him most to admit it.

Michael was not the enemy any more than he was, and the young man had not deserved the deep censure he had always given him, either. Nor had either of them warranted the purposeful obstacles that he had placed between the two of them on many occasions just to be petty. From watching them interact just now, Emile knew full-well that the lengths in which he had gone to were totally indefensible compared to what he had faced when he reached the door of this room.

Emma knew it. As kind as she always was, she had tried to lovingly guide him through it every step of the way for the past year, waiting for him to warm up to the idea. Yet true to his usual ways, he had resisted her, as well, like an insolent child. In all of his indomitable stubbornness, he had confidently ignored her pleas, thinking he knew much better than she did on the subject and rebuffed the poignantly truthful advice she had given as if it had meant very little, when, in reality, she was the one who had been right all along.

With a heavy heart, he looked at the young couple holding hands so intimately and knew then beyond a shadow of a doubt, that if <u>he</u> had been the suitor instead of Michael, he probably would have convinced Hope to elope already months ago and been done with it than deal with her father's antics a day longer. Yet his Hope had chosen to lovingly wait until <u>he</u> was ready to let go.

Not only that, but she had persevered through his harsh remarks and curt assessments and still loved him through it. And to make matters even more convicting, Emile had to also admit that not once had she ever gone around his authoritative guidelines concerning Michael, except for the day she visited this farm weeks ago. Nor had she made him feel unworthy of her respect through it, despite the fact that she most definitely had fallen in love with this boy from the very beginning.

And though it pained him to his very core to admit it even today. She had also been right. Michael Stuart Adair <u>was</u> the perfect match for her life. From his fortitude against rebuke, to the gentle way in which he cared for her even now, the man was as much Emile's equal in so many ways if not more where Hope was concerned. Michael Stuart Adair was the best of what <u>he</u> could have been once upon a time, and she deserved that. Just like his Emma, she was worthy of him and then some, if only they would be given a second chance to explore it.

With a desire to put to right everything he had tried to destroy for months, Emile reached one hand up to the side of the doorframe and tentatively knocked before entering, trying his best this time not to smirk as he watched the man on the other side of the room practically jump off the bed in response. At one time, that action alone would have pleased him to have that kind of effect on the boy, but today, it only chastened him further to know how much he was feared instead of respected.

"Sit... please, Mr. Adair," Emile instructed casually and took a seat in the chair on the opposite side of the bed, instead, allowing the man to remain as close as he wanted to the girl on the other side.

"I'm sorry, I should have been more discreet in where I chose to sit," Michael apologized from his position on the bed and began to move back to his chair. "I promise I have not been taking any liberties, sir."

"Just stay as you are and relax, please," Emile replied in as casual a manner as if he were discussing the weather with someone on the street. "I am not offended in the slightest, nor should you be under the circumstances."

For several minutes, Michael's shoulders tried to relax in a valiant attempt to faithfully obey the words coming out of Emile's mouth, but his body still fought against him to remain respectfully rigid in the man's presence.

"I mean it, Michael. I'm not here to rebuke you. Be composed, for goodness sake."

"You're not?" Michael's chest slumped just a little.

"No. I think it is high time that you and I had the talk we should have had months ago." Emile smoothed out the wrinkles that had formed in his vest when he had sat down, hoping that his honest reply might begin to repair at least some of the damage he had caused for so many months.

"Which talk is that?" Michael looked over at the man across from him, feeling more than a little bit skeptical of his markedly changed behavior.

"The one where I admit that I was wrong, and you graciously forgive me, of course." Emile folded his hands in front of him, pensively waiting for Michael's next reply.

In truth, he would have to wait for quite some time. The man, as direct and passionate as he usually was, appeared to be so steadfastly shocked at what had just been requested of him that time itself decided to take a pause in his presence.

"I'm sorry... what?" Michael finally managed to say, though he did shake his head several times back and forth, just to be sure he was still awake or at least competent enough to be having this kind of conversation.

"I believe it is time we made a pact, you and I, for Hope's sake, if for nothing else. From what I just overheard from the doorway, the two of us have reached the time in our relationship where I tell you that perhaps I have been too hasty in my judgement of your character, and you say that you would be honored to care for our Hope for the rest of eternity," Emile tried to sound distantly official but remorseful all at the same time.

"Well, the last part is a given, unreservedly so. Hope is my life, sir. It's the first part I am having a little trouble understanding." Michael continued to resist the concept that the man might have finally accepted him into his family.

Emile sighed. "I am afraid there is nothing I can say today that is going to change that for you. So, we shall simply have to shake hands with the assurance that I promise to behave better hereafter should you wish to continue this association.”

“Seriously? Oh, I most definitely plan on it, sir. As soon as she is better, we can announce our intention to marry. After that, it will be up to her to merely set the date,” Michael promised him fervently.

“And did I hear you mention a ring?” Emile cocked his head, suddenly curious what kind of token the young man might have been able to acquire on such a meager pay as that of an assistant editor.

“Oh... yes.” Michael fumbled around nervously inside his top, inner pocket for the small box he had been carrying around with him for weeks. “It belonged to my grandmother. I would have bought her a new one, but Hope said that she loved pearls the most since they reminded her of a story her father once told her when she was little. Something about a little girl who collected them from the fairies. I don’t know.” He shrugged. “Either way, my grandfather had this ring made for my grandmother out of the pearls he found during his travels abroad. I have been holding onto it for ages, but I think she will like it. Or at least I hope so.” He held the opened box out to Emile to view and waited for his approval.

Emile nodded in satisfaction. The silver ring in all of its simplicity and charm, glinted in the scant sunlight shining in from the window, showing off the slim row of four perfectly round pearls all in various hues of iridescent white and pinks. Tiny swirls of elegant metal wove around them like feathery wisps, holding the pearls in place while adding an almost wistful charm to its overall features. “I think she will love it.”

“Thank you. That means a great deal, especially coming from you.” Michael shut the box and started to place it carefully on the nightstand. “As does your approval.”

“Yes... Well, speaking of approval...” Emile hesitated, then pushed himself to encourage him further. “Why don’t you go ahead and put it on her now. I would hate for something that precious to be misplaced mistakenly by someone who was paying a visit.” Emile tried to appear as accepting as possible under the circumstances.

“You don’t mind?” Michael looked over at him, suddenly more overwhelmed than he had been before.

“Not as long as you are the one doing it,” Emile said seriously. “But just know one thing only and that will be the last thing I will say on the matter.” He stared at him severely, measuring the strength of the man before him. “The only man who will ever take it off her had better be you, sir. Once it is on her hand, she no longer belongs to me.”

Michael returned his gaze for several moments, taking in the seriousness of the decision properly before answering him without the least bit of hesitation, "You have my word, Mr. Deschamps... today, and always."

Emile nodded once. "Then never look back, son. You have your whole future right in front of you, so seize it."

Michael nodded as well, then turned to Hope before pulling back the covers carefully to place the ring upon her left finger and kissed it in pledge.

"My job is finished then." Emile stood, suddenly feeling the need to take a walk once more to clear his head.

"Thank you," Michael's voice cast back to him quickly when he had reached the door.

"For what? I have done nothing but make your life miserable, Michael," Emile said plainly.

"No. You made me cherish her all the more because of it," Michael replied honestly, the slightest bit of gratitude starting to form.

"Then it served a fruitful purpose, after all." Emile smiled, though not genuinely. As hard as it had been to do it, his heart felt almost too heavy now to beat in his chest. "I'll give you a few more minutes in peace, then I believe Emma and I would like to try to get her to drink some soup. As you already know, she hasn't eaten enough to keep a bird alive, let alone a young girl."

Michael nodded. "I will be down presently to fetch it."

"Take your time." Emile closed the door behind him, knowing that nothing would transpire behind it, and even if it did, he was certain it was no longer his business to know it.

"Is Hope awake?" Emma asked him hopefully when he reached the bottom of the stairs. For the past hour, she had been busying herself in the kitchen preparing the soup for the afternoon meal, and with the voices echoing back above her, she was prayerful that maybe, the girl might have turned a corner at last.

"She was, though I think she is resting once more. She has had a busy morning, love." Emile looked over at his wife and shook his head, his whole being flooded with the dread of the unknown, mixed with the satisfaction of his recent redemption.

"A busy morning?" Emma's head popped up from her concentration while cutting the remaining carrots and celery. "What do you mean? She hasn't moved an inch from that bed in days."

Emile sighed loudly at his wife's confusion and walked over to her in the kitchen, taking great pains to wrap his arms around her tightly from behind as he sensed the need to draw on her strength now more than ever before. "She has finally accepted Michael, Emma."

"She has!" Emma's face shone with delight. "And you are still okay with this?"

"I practically told the man to take her." Emile threw his head back and tried to remember how to breathe again. "Tell me. When did I become so old, love? I don't remember feeling any of this the day I married you, quite the opposite in fact. All the way from England to the Colonies, I couldn't wait to show you off to everyone, to take you anywhere you wanted, to be anything you desired. I wanted to give you the world back then."

"That was eighteen years ago! And even then, we were far more intimate than Michael and Hope are at the present, or at least they had better be," Emma warned, the knife still held firmly within her hand.

Slightly amused by her vague attempt at a feeble threat, Emile took the blade from her with a raise of his eyebrows and released her to lean his back upon the counter. "I don't think you are understanding me, wife." Emile looked over at her sternly. "I... have given Michael... my consent. Whatever happens from here on out is between God and them now."

"Oh," Emma finally caught up to where he was headed. "And you think that is wise?"

Emile shook his head. "I am trying very hard <u>not</u> to think about it right now, Emma."

"I see." Emma wiped her hands off on her apron and took two steps over to her husband, wrapping her arms around him before placing her head against his chest. "Well, you made the right decision... even if it was hard to do so."

"I know it." Emile ran his fingers across her back as he rested his chin on top of her head. "I also know that we are never certain how much time we will have left with Hope, even if she does survive this illness." He let out another long sigh and held Emma closer. "I just want to stop being the reason for her unhappiness all the time."

"Finally." Emma hugged him back, enjoying the brief moment of closeness between them.

"Yes, finally." Emile chuckled and let his wife go before offering her back the sharp knife. "I am sorry I have been such a bear in all of this."

"Well... I would have been more surprised if you had accepted him outright." Emma finished cutting the vegetables and placed them together with the chicken in the pot in front of her.

"Indeed." Emile picked up one of the orange medallions and sampled it. "Do you remember what time William said he would be coming back here tonight?"

"I have no idea, actually. I tried to speak with him at the hospital this morning, but the nurses said he was extremely busy today."

"I am sure he is," Emile said with a toss of his head. "We can't monopolize all of his time."

"Are you sure you are my husband today? I think perhaps a stranger has suddenly taken his place somehow." Emma chuckled at his expense.

"Odder things <u>have</u> happened." Emile raised both eyebrows and ate another carrot. "Look at you and me."

"Yes." Emma laughed once more, then stopped suddenly as the sound of someone charging down the stairs interrupted them.

With a gasp and a flurry of activity, Michael flew around the corner in their direction, his eyes wide with fear. "You need to come upstairs... <u>now</u>!"

Not willing to waste a single second for him to explain further, Emile and Emma pushed past him immediately, leaving the young man reeling in shock at what he had just witnessed above.

When they finally entered the room, Hope, who had been quietly resting for the past twenty-four hours, was now deliriously thrashing about on the bed, pulling at her clothes and tossing herself almost off the bed without any consciousness whatsoever.

"Nathanael! Come Quick!" Emma yelled as she reached for the girl's arms and struggled to hold her.

As if already on his way from the commotion transpiring out in the hall, Nathanael came rushing into the room behind them. "What is the matter?"

"Go get, William, man! Hurry!" Emile shouted from the other side of the bed; his usual composure shattered beyond containment. "Take my horse out front. He's already saddled."

Without another word, Nathanael left immediately, leaving the two of them to keep Hope from injuring herself further.

"Emile, can you carry her?" Emma threw off the covers on top of her and gasped at the darker, deep red rash that had now spread all the way down both of her legs.

Emile did not pause to respond, but rather scooped the girl up into his arms, allowing himself to be pummeled mercilessly by the movements of her arms as she thrashed. "She's positively on fire, Emma." He pushed past her ably, directing each of his steps out of the room and towards the awaiting stairs.

Casting a frightened glance in Charlotte's direction as she passed her in the hall and begged her to follow, Emma trailed close behind him barking out orders to Michael at the base of the stairs like a general preparing for battle. "Get a bucket from the barn and meet us at the pump, Michael!"

Grateful to finally have something he could do to help, Michael did as she commanded and ran out the front door and over to the building beyond, jumping over the corral railing easily to grab one of the metal pails they used for milking.

Emile, however, continued walking as quickly as he could possibly manage, pushing through the swinging screen door and down the front steps until he was within a few feet of the spring pump at the end of the porch. "Emma, I know what you are thinking, but this may be too cold for her? I heard William say in the past that the water must be slightly warm, too."

Emma shook her head. "It's a risk we'll have to take. At this point, I fear that if we do not get her fever down and fast, she may not survive at all."

Michael returned then with the buckets clattering by his side and began feverishly pumping the handle of the metal pump until bucket after bucket had been filled and poured over the body and head of the young girl in Emile's arms.

As close as he was to her, it had thoroughly soaked Emile, too, as he held her, but he never flinched once. The only thing his racing mind could concentrate on now was the girl in front of him as she shivered uncontrollably under the strain of the fever. "Hand me that stick over there, Michael. The one as big around as your finger," he asked finally when he was certain the constant chattering might possibly hurt her. "Place it here, between her teeth."

The young man obeyed quickly. "I'm so sorry, Hope," he whimpered softly as he stroked her wet hair down to the long strands that hung limply in the air beneath her.

"Don't stop now, Michael. Keep that water coming. We aren't finished yet," Emma encouraged, entirely focused on the task at hand.

"Yes, ma'am." He left the girl and obeyed without question.

For almost a quarter hour, he pumped, and he poured relentlessly without stopping while Emma and Charlotte worked together rubbing the girl's arms and legs to provoke the needed stimulation as William had taught them how to do earlier.

"Is it working?" Charlotte clutched at the knitted shawl haphazardly covering her shoulders, a slight shiver passing over her in the process from the wet spray.

"I think so... Look," Emile directed his head towards the less chaotic thrashing that had preceded the ritual as it abated little by little in the evening light, leaving in its wake, instead, a frightening racking shiver throughout her whole body that seemed almost as bad as the convulsions had been.

The angry, red flush that had painted all the surfaces of her arms and legs for the better part of week had almost completely vanished now. Though the alabaster skin on her hands and fingertips that was the perfect hue of cream and white now displayed the faintest hint of lavender also—a shade that was beautiful to behold but spoke more of warning to all of them than relief.

"Now go fetch me the quilt by the table inside, Michael, as fast as you can," Emma instructed him calmly as she rang the excess water out of Hope's long, light brown hair, true fear gripping her heart at last.

"I'll be right back." He took off at a run up the stairs, but in the stillness behind him, Hope's body finally became tranquil and limp, motionlessly declaring the illness' final defeat.

Alarmed, Emile instinctively felt Hope's forehead with his cheek. "She _is_ much cooler now. Almost too cold, Emma." His eyes flashed with the same level of fear that was shining back at him in hers. "Is she still breathing?"

"Yes... but that is what the quilt is for. We are going to need several more and some hot tea next." Emma continued to rub the girl's arms from the top to her fingertips.

"I'll go put a pot on now," Charlotte said quickly and went inside to place it on the fire.

"Maybe put on two, Charlotte." Emile's teeth chattered now as he spoke, though not from the cold, at all, or at least not in that way. It was more from the sudden dump of the adrenaline that had been consistently holding him together.

Beginning to feel a strange sort of tremor overtaking the length of his legs and back from remaining essentially frozen in his kneeling position, Emile tried to stand but nearly buckled under the strain the experience had placed upon him.

"Steady there, love. I can only deal with one issue at a time please." Emma braced him easily with one arm, helping to guide them both back into the house.

"I'll be fine in a minute," Emile gasped at the shivers presenting themselves violently in his own body from the stress he endured and pressed onward towards the house before he eyed William and Nathanael as they galloped up the path in front of them, their horses shaking their heads at the sudden stop.

"Nathanael said it was urgent!" William dismounted quickly and left the horse for Nathanael to care for.

"Thank you for coming so fast. Hope was practically incoherent twenty minutes ago," Emile replied without stopping.

"I will go find you and Hope something to change into." Charlotte held the door open for them to pass through easily, then headed upstairs to retrieve some of her husband's old clothing and another nightgown for Hope before returning shortly thereafter with a rather Spanish-looking light tan blouse and dark brown breeches for Emile, the very ones that reminded him exactly of the outfit Sebastian had been wearing when they had first met, and, of course, a light blue nightgown for Hope. "Will these do?" She handed the clothes intended for Emile out to him.

Emile accepted them gratefully without reservation. "I am sure they will be fine." He turned around and met Michael near the door before taking the man by his elbow as he walked in the direction of the barn to change. "Come walk with me for a minute please."

Michael nodded, suddenly appreciative of the man beside him.

In their absence, Nathanael set to work immediately stoking the fire to a considerably higher level that even the three vampires could sense was toastier than what was normally deemed appropriate for an indoor room. Yet not a single one of them breathed a sigh of relief until the purple color that had spread across her lips during their dousing began to be replaced once again by the light pink hue they normally held.

"Is she conscious, yet?" Emile asked when he entered the room and rolled up the longer than normal sleeves, intending to leave his forearms slightly exposed.

"Not really, though thankfully, she <u>has</u> stopped chattering." Emma tried to sound optimistic despite the very real danger before them.

"Well, from what I can see, she still has a very slight fever, though you all probably saved her life tonight by doing what you did. I don't know if she could have lasted until I got here if you had not stepped in," William admitted seriously. "I'm not going to lie to you all; this is probably the worst case I have ever experienced, and I have seen many."

"Oh, William... no." Charlotte tried to hold back a sob as she placed the back of her hand across her mouth to stifle it.

Instinctively in tandem with what had seemed like a completely nature thing for him to do now, Nathanael reached over and drew the woman closer to him in an embrace, concern for both her and her daughter filling his expression. "Is there anything else <u>we</u> can do?"

"Maybe." William thought for a moment, then replied just as hesitantly. "There is one thing, though I do not know if it will help to reduce her fever any more than everything else we have tried to this point. I only know that many other patients have shown significant improvement after doing so, even if it is a bit archaic to contemplate."

"What?" Emma asked eagerly. "Whatever it is, we shouldn't delay."

With a sigh, William glanced over at Emile, knowing that his friend was teetering on the edge of his composure, as well. "I'll need you to fetch me the sharpest pair of scissors you can find."

"Scissors?" Emile looked taken aback by the odd request.

"Yes, please." William's face appeared more downtrodden than hopeful, but he did not elaborate more.

"Fine." Emile obediently went to the kitchen and pulled the shears from the center drawer before returning to his friend by the fire and handing them over to him like he was one of his nurses. "You aren't going to bleed her with these are you? That would finish her for sure."

"No." William shook his head and stood before exhaling just once as he gathered Hope's richly colored hair in his fist and cut it as close to the base of her neck as possible. With the ear-shattering first snip, an audible gasp filled the room as the scissors cut through her hair easily, leaving only a ragged edge behind in their wake.

The action itself, as simple as it was to complete, took all of fifteen seconds to do, but the effect on everyone gathered there appeared to have shaved off years from their lives.

"Here." He offered the two-foot-long bundle of caramel to Emma, who was standing beside him, without daring to meet any of their gazes for fear of seeing their judgement against him.

Like a cherished treasure that had been recently discovered, Emma took it reverently. "I'll go find a ribbon to tie it up."

"Let me." Charlotte stepped away from Nathanael at last and turned around to go back into the kitchen to retrieve something from out of the same drawer from where the scissors had originated. A bright blue satin ribbon, like the most brilliant shade of a summer sky, now shone in her hands, as if by magic, and almost as long as the hair it would soon hold.

"That should work nicely. Thank you," Emma said quietly as she and Charlotte worked to tie the bundle up securely about five inches from the top. Hope would no doubt be sad for its passing in time, but prayerfully, the insignificant sacrifice of something so inconsequentially important would allow her the chance to watch it regrow.

"And I know <u>precisely</u> where to put that for now." Emile said as he drew in a breath and blew it out slowly once more before nodding in the direction of the stairs.

"Alright." Emma handed him the hair like she was handing off a newborn baby and watched with yearning as he carried it slowly up to the room above.

Inside Hope's room, and far away from the eyes of the others, Emile found the hope chest that she had been given on her last birthday. The one she had said was the best gift she had ever received after she opened it. As he expected, everything was still exactly as it had been inside, just as he knew it would be, with only a small stack of letters added on top of the folded hat that he had made for her out of one of Michael's newspapers, though those letters were also most likely from Michael, too.

Reaching down, his hand now physically shook as he laid the long hair on top of all of her other treasures, then placed his other hand upon it, too, fearing that this might be all he would ever have left of his Hope—nothing but mementos and trinkets given in love, and safely stored away for all eternity.

With a sob that tore at the very fiber of his being all the way down to his selfish soul, he fell to his knees and leaned fully upon its closed cover, the weight of the world suddenly crushing upon his shoulders.

Chapter Thirty-Three

November 2nd, 1811

I n the early morning hours of the following day, the fever they had battled against at every turn gratefully chose to leave Hope's body, just as swiftly as it had appeared, along with all of its horrible side effects. Yet even with that joyous news, the relief that it should have brought along with its passing was fleeting, as the girl had not grown any stronger in its absence. On the contrary, every hour that had passed onto the next only brought with it the same dreaded confirmation to everyone that their Hope was either not going to make it through this battle, or if she did, she would be a fraction of the woman she used to be because of it.

Sadly, Emma had seen it all before, both here and back in France years ago. For the first two weeks after James' recovery, Jedidiah had not been able to pull himself out of bed, much less muster up the strength that was necessary to care for his wife when she fell ill right alongside him, not to mention provide any assistance towards the needs of their two children. William, of course, had kept a constant vigil over all of them until the fever had abated. Charity, too, for that matter, though her efforts had been mainly directed more towards distracting the children and arranging whatever meals the family required or delivering supplies when William was too busy to get them for himself.

Yet it was when the two healers had needed to turn their focus onto other patients who now needed them more, that Emma had witnessed firsthand the young mother's daily struggle as the simplest action of merely putting a kettle of water on to boil had exhausted her entirely. Still, though the two of them had been nowhere near as bad as Hope from the very beginning, the fever had still managed to leave its ugly mark upon their family like a lasting scar of hateful remembrance. Eerily similar to the silent soldiers who painfully drug themselves home after a particularly gruesome war, they had both managed to survive their ordeal, and they <u>were</u> getting marginally better by the day... but Hope was not.

Sensing that the direness of Hope's illness was quickly approaching, the family had all chosen to gather today for a noonday meal, intent on merely deliberating whether or not it was worth the risk of having Elijah come to sit with the girl before it was too late. But despite the fact that everyone had initially seemed almost mentally numb to discuss anything of worth whatsoever, the five of them had already endured two rather heated discussions in the span of twenty minutes. Most definitely one more than they had probably had in a year, if not two.

The <u>only</u> blessed part of any of it was that Michael had finally gone home to rest after much convincing that they would alert him if anything changed one way or the other. Though Emma highly doubted that he would be able to do so, as most of those waiting in the main room below had probably not slept well either. Still, that being said, getting the young man to at least concede to leave the farm for a few hours today had provided the opportunity they all needed to speak frankly about things they could not have done in his presence. Conversations like the one that had almost come to blows moments earlier.

In the beginning, it had not started out as an argument at all. In fact, when Nathanael had arrived earlier this morning, he and Emile had simply been discussing scenarios for possibly helping the girl get some nutrition in her since she was now refusing any substance at all. While William, on the other hand, was staunchly refusing all notions that the girl should be forced to do anything. His opinion, which was viewed with a bit more respect and weight to it than all the others, was that because of her fragile state, she needed to maintain whatever strength she still had left and not waste it in fighting them.

Yet it was Charlotte's meeker suggestion at the end of their many curt replies and overly short answers that had brought them all to a sudden, respectful silence when she uttered it and caused everyone to seriously contemplate the magnitude of what she was asking.

"What if someone were to change her?" Charlotte had said with a resolute confidence over their heated debate, her expression firm and unwavering, unlike most in her very rare position. "Would <u>that</u> save her life?"

Stunned that it had been she who had offered it before anyone else, Emma had only stared back at first in total disbelief, shocked beyond any kind of possible utterance to even hope for a sensible reply. Instead, she had chosen to merely keep a respectful silence on the matter and focused her gaze on the vegetables she had been cutting for the evening meal, knowing that whatever Emile would say on the matter would probably be what was in her heart, as well.

To no one's surprise, William had been the first to object, outwardly defiant of the very suggestion. Though he always was the one who was overly controlling when it came to matters that he deemed were too risky or ill-advised if they compromised the safety of their necessary obscurity.

In that past, it had bothered Emma very much to witness the way he always seemed to try to steer her husband around to his way of thinking. But over the years, she had come to a better understanding that his perceived hesitancy was not a direct opposition to what anyone wanted to do, far from it. It was merely his way of covering up his fear over what he could not control. Which, in the end, was probably much scarier for him, having been raised in a world of high affluence back in London than it was for her or even her husband and Nathanael. None of them had been given any options more than the choice of whether or not to fight for their survival in many ways, and even then, it had come at a great cost.

And as much as she had learned about Nathanael's past, she doubted the young preacher had ever truly considered what <u>he</u> might have wanted to do with his life after both his parents had died. From his earlier education to his elders' dictates over what parish he would pastor after seminary, every step along his life's journey had been laid out for miles without any space for his own personal input whatsoever. Even the career he was now exceptionally proud of only needed him to take the first step and carry the burden that went along with it in silence, as if that chosen responsibility did not bother him in the slightest. A fact which Emma knew was anything but the truth.

In fact, when he had been asked his opinion about Charlotte's suggestion concerning Hope, Nathanael had only looked away and stared at the oak tree far in the distance, almost too uncomfortable with the knowledge that he was probably going to have to choose a side, one way or the other, though neither would be what he personally desired.

But Emile... Emile had only shook his head slowly and said the one thing that sounded like the most logical sentence anyone had said all day. "Charlotte, though it pains me to say this, I do not believe it would be a viable solution at this point in her illness. As weak as she currently is, the transition that you hope will save her will not take place."

"But I... I thought it would heal her?" Charlotte had appeared then as if she were finally grasping for any fragment of hope that was still possibly remaining.

"Yes, it would have, if she were more or less healthy when she was bitten or even just injured or slightly sick," William had explained seriously. "But in the state that she is in now, it would most likely kill her instead, and painfully at that."

"Oh," Charlotte had said quietly in response. "Forgive me for even suggesting it then. I didn't know."

Feeling only empathy for the woman beside him and the strength it must have taken to even suggest such a thing for her only daughter, Emile had placed his hand over hers and squeezed it gently within his own, his heart reaching out to her through the gesture. "There is <u>nothing</u> to forgive. You are not alone in this line of thinking... quite the contrary. I myself had already contemplated it earlier, yet I had hoped we would never be required to discuss it."

Charlotte had then smiled up at him for his easy acceptance and added a further consolation to everyone, "I know you all would never have chosen this path for yourselves, but if given the choice, I would rather my daughter survive as one of you, than meet her father once again in eternity, at least not right now."

William and Emile both had nodded their heads in shared understanding.

"There is nothing to be ashamed of, Charlotte... truly," Nathanael had reassured her lovingly, speaking the words all of them felt deep in their hearts. "None of us judge you at all for asking it. In fact, in many ways, the request seems far more logical from that point of view when there is little else that can be done otherwise."

The group had then echoed a collective agreement to his statement and had returned thereafter to their own thoughts and muted conversations as Emma remembered how she had reached over and placed one hand upon the shoulder of her husband who sat stiffly in the chair nearest the base of the stairs next to Charlotte before walking past him to go back up to sit with Hope.

All of that had happened hours ago, yet the scene had continued to play itself relentlessly again and again within her mind as it pressured her to take some kind of action. What that could possibly be that would make a difference between the chasm of life and death she was now facing with every shallow breath that Hope took beside her, she had no idea, but anything would be better than watching her slip farther and farther away from her like rhythmic waves pulling at the sand beneath her feet.

~   ~   ~   ~   ~

For the rest of the afternoon and well until after the time for the evening meal, Emma and Charlotte had taken turns sitting faithfully across from the girl who had managed to make it almost two weeks since the beginning of her illness, while the atmosphere below in the home took on a more somber feel as each person seemed to be praying for Hope's miraculous survival, while also reluctantly preparing themselves for a crushing inevitability.

From Sebastian's large chair where Emile sat glaring into the fire across from him, the flames flickering their dancing reflection across his eyes with each burst from the logs within to Nathanael and Charlotte, who merely stood in the corner of the kitchen in a quiet moment of gentle support, both giving the other what they needed most in that moment, not a single person felt the desire to speak or even move much more than the constant flipping of yet another page as William searched through his journals relentlessly for some kind of cure he had missed. In truth, they were all held captive now in a strange sort of limbo by the thinnest of life thread, cautiously frightened to do anything that might cause it to suddenly snap out of their hands.

Making her way down the long drive towards the white and grey farmhouse near the end, Charity glanced upwards at the windows on the second story above her, noticing the warm glow emanating from the one on the far left. Without a doubt, her stomach churned with the building anxiety she had been keeping at bay like a thousand butterflies desperately trying to escape every time she took yet another step closer. It was the same feeling she had endured all morning, as her mind mulled over the mostly rational reasons William had provided for his opposition. In spite of her many failed attempts to change his view, he had still chosen to remain dogmatically opposed, maintaining the sincere belief that what they would be doing was morally wrong, almost to the point of an actual reverence to that view.

"Misguided reverence," Charity mumbled sourly, then frowned at her negative comment. *Though I suppose I would rather have him fight for what he believes wholeheartedly than blindly follow after the next best thing if I had to choose.* She decided mentally and continued walking closer, closing the gap in front of her quickly as she went.

When she had accidentally discovered that their blood could heal people, she had been intensely skeptical, just like William and, quite frankly, more than a little bit afraid to do so again, since she had no medical training whatsoever at the time. After all, the last thing she had wanted was to compel someone into the same kind of existence that had been forced so violently upon her. Yet over time she had begun to see its unique value. Or rather, she eventually came to the ironic perspective that something most people viewed as an aberration sent from Satan himself could be used for a higher purpose. In truth, this shocking revelation had not frightened her like it probably should have, it astounded her. It still did.

If only she could find a way to make William see it that way, too.

Narrowing her eyes with renewed determination at last, Charity stepped onto the porch and knocked tentatively on the screen door twice while she waited for the family inside to answer. "Hello? May I come in?"

Like a clap of thunder that followed an equally bright burst of lightning in the middle of a dark ocean of grief, every person in the home instantly jolted.

"Of course, Miss Bentham." William stood and opened the door graciously for her. "Though I am afraid you will find all of us terrible company at present."

"Oh," Charity's face fell at the news. "I was rather hoping that Hope might have improved during the night."

"I'm afraid not," William answered quietly what no one else wanted to say, as everyone who had gathered around the bottom level of the home all shook their heads solemnly in response but remained in their chosen places.

"I see. Well, would it be alright if I went up to see Emma for a minute? I am assuming she is upstairs?" Charity nodded towards the stairs politely since she did not see her friend anywhere on the main floor with the others.

"Yes, she is. I can take you up to her, if you like," William offered briefly, trying to give her his best manners despite his definite desire to be left to face his imminent failure without the need of more witnesses.

"Oh, no. Please sit, William. You should be here with your friends. I think I can manage to find my own way this time." Charity motioned for the man to remain with his family as she made her way confidently up the stairs and into Hope's room without him.

The white walls surrounding the bed that greeted her inside the modestly decorated room now seemed utterly changed from the cheery brightness they once reflected with the yellow flowered curtains and light blue covering on the small table that matched the eyelet bedspread in design. In contrast, the muted hues now displayed with perfect accuracy the paleness of the one within, not to mention the matching weariness in the expression of the woman who sat close beside her.

With a heavy heart, Charity reached for the door behind her and closed it silently, not wanting to disturb anyone else in the room below with their conversation before she took two steps nearer the bed. "Oh, Emma... I am so sorry."

"Charity?" Emma looked up in delighted relief, her eyes red from the hours she had spent crying or the sheer lack of nutrition and sleep. "Am I glad to see you."

Charity smiled at the warm welcome she always received whenever she and Emma had a chance to talk. In fact, the friendship that had consistently blossomed between them had probably been the most significant in her life, next to that of William's, and something she had never truly contemplated as a possibility, let alone her newly discovered necessity. "I had rather hoped you would be, though I wish it was under better circumstances."

"So do I." Emma reached out for the woman's hand instinctively and held it tight, her grip suddenly becoming more desperate than someone who was trying very hard not to fall off a precariously high cliff. "I am afraid you are about to see us at our worst, as I don't think Hope is going to survive this."

"I see." Charity touched the vial within her pocket and felt the warmth of it like fire against her leg. What she was about to do for her friend was going to change everything between her and William beyond reparation but knowing what she would have wanted if their situations had been reversed, she simply could not stand by a moment longer without offering. "Emma, I came here today because I need to speak to you about something." She paused and held her breath a few moments before deciding to suddenly start again. "Or rather, there is something very important that you should know concerning William and Hope and I suppose James, too."

"Okay." Emma wiped the corners of her eyes and sat up straighter to look at the woman across from her better. "What is it? Has William done something wrong? Something we should know about?" Emma stared back at the woman, incredulous that her husband's friend could have made an error so grievous in nature, no matter who his patient was, that would cause her friend to come to her in secret, but there was little else that came to her mind to explain it.

Charity blinked twice, instantly aware of the false assumption Emma had made and moved quickly to defend him. "Oh, no! Nothing like that at all, I assure you. Quite the opposite, William has done everything he has been trained to do for the better part of half a century without the slightest bit of deviation."

"Then what?" Emma prodded, still just as confused as before.

Deliberating whether or not what she was going to say was worth the price she would ultimately pay to do it, Charity looked away and out the window to the fields beyond that seemed to stretch out until the horizon, then turned back to the still form of the young woman beside her. William's niece was very near to the age of the woman who had died in the hospital only yesterday from her appendicitis. A difficult thing to witness for everyone involved, but Charity alone had been the one on shift that was forced against her will to comfort the grieving husband all through his eventual loss and departure.

William had been here with his family the entire time and though she did not despise him for doing so, his absence had felt more like a selective escape to her than his necessary duty. With full knowledge of what could have been possibly tried to save his patient, he had still made the conscious decision to restrict her actions and then opted not to witness the consequences of that decision.

"Charity?" Emma drew her back to the time and place in which she was now. "What are you not telling me?"

For several minutes, Charity could do nothing more than look deeply into Emma's eyes as she deliberated the choice placed before her but then realized there was no other way. For better or worse, she needed to make the decision <u>for him</u>, even if he hated her for it. "Has William told you about the woman at the hospital?"

Emma shook her head twice. "William tells us next to nothing about his work there, why? Is she important?"

She was important to someone.... Charity sighed and felt a sudden surge of fresh irritation more than regret at the position he had placed her in once again. That man, as much as she loved him, was not going to make this any easier for her. "I need to tell you something. Something that will make William extremely angry with me for telling you, but I have to."

"Go on..." Emma began to encourage but was suddenly interrupted as the door behind them unexpectedly opened and permitted the entry of a rather stern-faced William.

"Charity, don't," he warned harshly, attempting to silence the woman on the topic completely before more damage could be done.

"Don't what, William?" Emma asked. "If she knows something that will help Hope, I want her to say it."

"No... no, you don't," William stated flatly yet again, but refused to explain any further.

Hearing the commotion and suspecting the worst, Emile stepped into the room next, followed by Nathanael close at his heels, and then Charlotte.

"My, it is turning into quite the party in here tonight," Charity joked nervously, the lilt in her voice raising it almost half an octave as she spoke.

"Nathanael, would you be so kind as to fetch my coat from the barn? I think I left it there last night when I slept in the loft," William spoke to his friend behind him, but did not otherwise acknowledge his presence.

Totally confused as to why he would be sent on such an errand now of all times, Nathanael pushed back incredulously. "Whyever for?"

"I believe Miss Bentham might need it when she leaves shortly," William retorted with controlled politeness, his gaze remaining constant on the woman in front of him.

"Um, sure, if it's that important... I will be back directly," Nathanael answered obediently with a nod towards Charlotte and left the others in the awkward silence that was building behind him.

"Emma? Is something wrong?" Charlotte asked her from across the room.

"I'm not sure," Emma replied, but she could already feel the same irritation she had tried to keep at bay concerning William's overstepping nature start to rise within her just like before.

"Emile, close the door and do not open it again until I tell you," William commanded severely, not caring what the others might think of him for ordering them around in such a fashion.

"William, what is going on?" Emma asked him once more as she heard the click of the lock on the outer door.

"Go ahead and tell her, Charity. Tell her all of it," William scolded her like someone who had caught his wife in the embrace of another man, without the least bit of tender regard towards her or their mutual understanding. Moreover, by the way that his eyes were now attacking her, not a single thing about his presence at the end of the bed welcomed her interventions into his personal life in the slightest, nor spoke of anything more than how he might deal with her as a casual acquaintance.

Stunned at the calloused reversal of everything they had fought so hard to overcome, Charity blinked back at him, pleading earnestly with her expression alone for William to relent, as the hurt he was causing started replacing the love for him behind her eyes. "If that is what you wish," she finally stated quietly in complete submission to his spoken desire, then began the long story of how she had discovered that their blood could heal people and how she had used it in the past. She even admitted giving some to James at the hospital without William's knowledge and told them about the day when William had finally caught her with the epileptic woman, but understandably, had left out the part where he had kissed her thereafter.

"So, you mean to tell me that all this time you had a possible cure for Hope, and you refused to use it!" Emile almost shook with the rage he was now feeling for all that Hope had endured... for everything that she could have been possibly spared... for all that could have been blissfully different... for everyone.

"Emile, it's not like that at all. I love Hope, too, but as a doctor I'm held to a higher standard than what I personally desire. I can't, under good conscience, knowingly give her something that I am not certain will do her more harm than good in the long run," William defended himself against the man who he looked to almost like his own brother, unafraid of what Emile might eventually do to him for standing in his way this time.

"She is dying, William! How much worse can things be?" Emile's face contorted in pain and despair. "Isn't _that_ worth the risk?"

"Oh, it can be worse, my friend... much worse and you know it." William's eyes flashed with the agony of the many things he had witnessed over the last few decades. "I have seen things no man should ever have to witness, things no one would wish on their worst enemy, all because of something a doctor thought would be some new kind of miracle. And do you know what I have learned?"

"No... enlighten me," Emile snarled back.

"A cure can be worse than the illness, Emile, and twice as debilitating, if not life-ending at times. I've watched men physically heal from one dreaded disease only to take their lives with the very thing that helped them conquer it. Would you want that for Hope?" William shot back without the least bit of reservation.

"Of course not. But I _was_ willing to change her to save her from all of this if I had to," Emile defended, feeling justly vindicated in his chosen decision, even if it was now too late.

"As if that would have been _so_ much better?" William shook his head in total disbelief. "You assume that because all of us have managed to remain remotely civilized, that she would have done the same. Or have your forgotten the man you were back in Paris? The man who killed that poor girl without thinking twice about whose daughter _she_ was and what _they_ would be suffering because of it. Would she still be your Hope if she were like Doctor Clarke... evil and bloodthirsty, killing anyone she wanted?"

"Argh, man! You can be so arrogant sometimes!" Emile shouted, though also knowing William spoke the truth none of them were willing to contemplate.

"Speak for yourself, Emile!" William countered quickly. "You haven't been humble a day in your life, have you?!"

"Stop it! Both of you!" Emma intervened finally in a volume above both of them that commanded their respect. "I hear what you are saying, William, truly I do, but right now I do not care about all of your reasons behind it. I only want to know from Charity if it will work. _Will_ it save her life?"

"I think..." Charity tried to answer, but William cut her off quickly before she could finish.

"At this point, she will tell you anything you want to hear, Emma. Everyone at the hospital already believes that she is some kind of angel of mercy," William mocked disdainfully, knowing full-well the hurt he was causing by his every word and action. Yet the truth of the matter was... as disrespected as he was feeling at that very moment by everyone in the room around him, he simply no longer cared who he hurt now, or how much. Like the water that had threatened to drown Charity months earlier, he was also thrashing away with his words, frantically desperate to stay on top of the surface before it all sucked him under.

"At least I wouldn't have let that poor woman die at the hospital without even trying to save her. What are you <u>really</u> afraid of, sir?" Charity finally spat back rudely the one question that had been repeating itself over and over inside her head for days, finally fed up with the manner in which he was consistently treating her.

"The better question is, why are all of you <u>not</u> afraid?" William said just as forcefully. "Why am I the only rational person in this room?"

A knock on the bedroom door in the tense silence that followed after reminded them all quickly of Nathanael's return and drew their attention to the door on the opposite side of the room. "Is everyone okay in there?" His muffled question came through from the other side of the locked door.

"Could you give us a minute please, Nathanael," Charlotte pleaded as nicely as she possibly could under the circumstances and waited to see what the rest would do.

"Not a word of this to..." William pointed in the direction of the door behind him, true concern finally evident on his face for the first time since he had entered the room.

"Agreed." Emile's eyes widened with fear and unity on the subject. "Trust us on this one."

The women all nodded.

"Please forgive me, Emma. I never meant to cause a problem between all of you." Charity looked over at Emma and then to Emile and Charlotte. "But you needed to know that you had an option, even if it is not what everyone personally feels comfortable with."

"<u>You</u> aren't the problem, Charity," Emma reassured her but did not say more as her husband quickly finished her sentence for her.

"<u>He</u> is," Emile added darkly with his arms firmly crossed over his chest, not willing to give an inch in his opinion towards the other man's point of view.

"Emile, stop being so childish," William rebuked him harshly back. "I didn't judge you downstairs or even now when you said you considered changing her yourself."

"This is <u>not</u> the same and you <u>know</u> it." Emile threw his hands up in frustration with the man.

"Do I? I don't know anything about this, Emile! I don't know if it will cure her today only to kill her tomorrow. I don't know if it will eventually change her into what we are or shorten her lifespan altogether. I don't know..." William continued to try and list all the many possibilities behind his reasoning that he had already considered since Charity had first told him about the cure but was effectively silenced by Emile talking over him with yet another criticism.

"We get it... _you_ don't know." Emile rolled his eyes. "And that is most definitely a first for the great Doctor Wells. Admit it. It makes your blood boil that someone else might actually know more than you do on a subject?"

It was William's turn now to look back at him menacingly. "Don't push me today, Emile. I am in no humor to be tempted by your sarcasm _or_ your ridicule."

"Sir..." Emile raised his eyebrows in a definite challenge as if waiting for the man to lash out at him physically next.

"Out! Both of you! Now!" Emma ordered, her face staring down at Hope alone.

Emile nodded obediently, fearing his wife far more than his friend any day, and opened the door to find a very bewildered Nathanael holding William's coat on the other side of the hall, his back leaning casually on the door to Charlotte's room behind him. "As it turns out, our dear William will not be needing his coat after all, Nathanael." He glanced back at his friend audaciously who had still not left the room as of yet, then added more authoritatively, "Miss Bentham will be staying as long as she likes."

"Oh," the man glanced back at the others inside the room before whistling aloud nervously. "Whatever you all are discussing in there, I probably want no part of anyway. If you need anything else, you can find me downstairs."

"Fine. I'll be with you presently, Nathanael," William said politely back to him before looking more intensely at Charity and giving her a final word of caution, "Don't forget what you promised me, or is your word no longer valid between us?"

"I haven't forgotten as much as you have it seems," Charity rebuked him resolutely and held her head up with the confidence she had gained from years of dealing with men that were far more opinionated than he was.

"Indeed," William spat out in anger and left the three women in the room behind him to cool off, assured remotely of her compliance, if not at least her respect.

He was wrong about both. Then again, he had been wrong so many times before. His disregard and harsh words towards Charity had only served to further solidify her hesitancy about their relationship. Apparently, they really were water and oil, two opposite and completely incompatible substances that would forever refuse to join no matter how many times they had forced them together.

Why continue to fight? Why should we endeavor to struggle against the very nature we both possess if nothing good will ever come of it? Charity frowned and for the briefest of moments almost allowed herself to cry.

"I want to do it, Charity," Emma said quietly as soon as William had left the room and his footsteps on the stairs had finally ceased.

"Yes, please," Charlotte added and drew closer still, feeling the tiniest bit of hope slowly returning to her.

"But you heard him just now." Charity tried to hold back the pain she felt just thinking about the way he had spoken to her. The way he had dismissed everything they had meant to each other so quickly without even a pause to acknowledge its passing. It was almost as if another man entirely had walked into the room tonight and had begun speaking... just like her father and Edward... all over again.

"You know as well as I that he will never forgive me if we do, though honestly, I am not sure that even matters anymore in comparison." Charity looked down at the girl in the bed and the ache in her heart pleaded deeply once more for her to help her. And still, as much as she wanted to, her hands were always tied when it came to the girl's uncle one way or another.

"I know he may think that now. But I also believe beyond a shadow of a doubt that he will <u>never</u> forgive himself if she does die," Emma stated flatly, knowing the truth of that statement more than the man himself knew it. "No matter where the fault may be placed otherwise, <u>he</u> will shoulder this burden for centuries, letting it slowly destroy him from the inside out. As God is my witness, I will <u>not</u> let that happen either. He is too good a man for that, and if I can spare him that burden by saving Hope myself, then I'll do it. Not to mention the fact that her death will drive a wedge between my husband and him that may never be repaired, if it hasn't already. As much as we may wish to think otherwise, this is no longer about saving one life for another, Charity. They <u>all</u> need our help, so we must do what we must."

"Alright." Charity nodded and pulled the small container out from deep within her pocket that held her blood. For over a week, she had been hoping that William would suddenly change his mind after she had explained her reasoning yet again to him and allowed her the chance to use it willingly. Yet even in that, she had scarcely believed that he would. "Then we are all agreed?"

"Yes," Emma and Charlotte replied in unison, before Emma then placed her hand over Charity's to stop her. "But if we are doing this, we will use my blood, not yours. You are taking enough of the blame for this already by telling us. Let me shoulder the rest. This girl is my husband's life, and so the decision is mine alone to make."

"Are you certain?" Charlotte asked Emma tentatively, knowing the dynamic between the men almost as well as she did.

"Yes, I don't want William to have anything else to hold against Charity should this go wrong in any way," Emma declared resolutely, her mind firmly set in the matter.

"It won't," Charity assured her and reached over to pick up the small blade and bowl from the table beside her that had been used to bloodlet the girl days earlier and nicked a small area on Emma's arm. Little by little, the deep red blood that came from it poured slowly into the small bowl on the bed until it had filled it a third of the way from the bottom. "I think that should be more than enough, but you will have to get her to swallow it. It won't do her any good if she does not ingest it fully."

"Alright." Emma stepped aside to tie her handkerchief around her wrist securely, allowing Charlotte and Charity the opportunity to lift Hope higher up to drink the small container that held Emma's blood.

Then, as if unable to even breathe while they waited, they all collectively tensed in apprehension, searching for any change in her condition whatsoever. In fact, for almost the entire evening and most of the night they continued to hope and fervently prayed beyond reason that the miraculous might be the possible. Yet nevertheless, when it seemed at last that nothing would transpire at all like what Charity had initially promised, it finally happened... so slowly at first that the untrained eye would have hardly noticed it occurring.

Without any other reason to do otherwise, the young woman's heart picked up its rhythm just a half a second faster and her breathing became increasingly less shallow. Before another hour had passed, the beads of perspiration that had been accumulating along her forehead for days vanished entirely, leaving in their place only large accumulations of salt along the edges of her hairline.

Cautiously optimistic at what might be happening, Emma reached for Hope's hand and squeezed, dreaming beyond comprehension that whatever they had done had been successful.

Hope's fingers flexed slightly in return. Not enough to grip Emma's back fully, but certainly enough for both Charlotte and Emma to notice the vague movement on top of the quilt.

"Hope, can you hear me, darling?" Charlotte leaned in closer to her daughter and stroked her shortened light-brown hair.

"Ma ...mmm... mother...?" The girl's eyes twitched back and forth for a second behind her closed lids, then fluttered open momentarily.

Tears of exultant gratitude now flowed down both of Emma's cheeks freely as she kissed the back of Hope's other hand repeatedly. "That's right. We are all here, sweetheart."

"Where is Papa?" Hope asked weakly, still not totally coherent, though decidedly breathing much better overall.

For the space of a full minute, Emma froze, fearing that the fever had caused permanent damage to her fragile mind. "Hope, your father died several years ago. You remember that, right?"

"I know... but where is Papa?" Hope pulled at the covers on top of her body as she struggled to sit up just a little to find him.

"Stay, Hope. I'll go fetch the others." Charlotte got up quickly from her side of the bed and returned with Emile and William who appeared almost as in glorious shock as the women had been moments earlier.

With the jaded skepticism they had already expected, William took Charlotte's place on the other side of the bed and listened to Hope's heart and lungs before exhaling the loudest sigh he had ever given in his life. "Praise God! I think she is finally starting to pull through this!" He reached for her other hand and counted several times more with the ticking of the clock on the wall beside her before closing his eyes and smiling broadly. "Her heart remains steady and true, strong even." He glanced back at Charity in growing suspicion, studying her intently as her body hugged the corner of the room by the window, away from all of the others.

To her credit, Charity only shook her head and held her peace. From the look in his eyes, she knew exactly what he was thinking, and whether he would admit it or not, she did not deserve his censure today or ever again.

Utterly overwhelmed now by the sudden turn of events into everything he had steadily prayed for, Emile tried to take a step closer to his wife, but fell onto the end of the bed in front of him instead and sobbed openly at Hope's feet, holding them as carefully in his hands as he would a fine piece of porcelain, the true weight of his relief washing over him again and again.

"Papa?" Hope called for him again without any hesitation at all in her voice this time.

Hearing the word he had always longed for her to call him, Emile's head lifted in surprise, but he did not move to correct her. "I'm here, little one," he used his pet name for her once again.

"You were yelling earlier... you were not being unkind again... were you?" Hope tried to reach for his hand but could not, for he was too far away.

Still feeling the sting of his friend's hurtful accusations earlier, William stood and motioned for his friend to take his place closer to her but still remained bitterly distant towards everyone gathered in the room around him.

"I would never dream of it, not for the world." Emile sat down quickly and clasped her hand in his before laying it lovingly against his cheek.

"Good." Hope squeezed his hand and then flexed her fingers backwards to caress his cheek. "I love you, Papa... always and forever."

"I love you, too, Hope." Emile gasped several times as tears streamed down his face onto the fingers of her hand.

"You are going to get <u>my</u> shirt wet this time," she murmured weakly before giving him the same endearing smile she had always given him on so many other occasions.

"It will dry," he repeated the words he had uttered the night her real father had passed and laughed lightly at the welcomed lightness to the banter between them once more.

Still afraid to accept the miracle they had all be cautiously praying for, Emma looked up at William before asking in a voice strained with emotion, "She is going to be alright, isn't she, William?"

"I think so," William answered, though as grateful as he was, he could still accept that something had not transpired outside the realm of normal medical intervention. "We will know more in the morning."

Sensing it was time to allow Charlotte her own moment with Hope, the group all moved to leave the room and went downstairs to notify the rest of the family and of course, Michael. No doubt, he would want to see her as soon as possible, as would Elijah, but the others knew it was only right to allow her mother the first opportunity to reconnect with her daughter before anyone else.

"Goodnight, Mrs. Fabbri. I'm so glad Hope is finally awake." Charity bid her host a kind farewell from the doorway, feeling more than a little out of place now that the crisis was finally over.

"So am I, Miss Bentham." Charlotte smiled genuinely, grateful beyond words for God's intervention at last. "And thank you."

"You're welcome," she said as she closed the door behind her and walked quietly down the stairs, hoping to avoid any more of William's scrutiny for one evening. "Goodnight, Mr. Beckett, Mr. Deschamps."

"May God be with you," Nathanael replied methodically but also in prayer, as he was certain there was much more going on upstairs than he ever wanted to know. Much that should to be brought before his Father more than it needed to be spoken.

"Oh, Charity, wait…" Emma rushed over to her from the kitchen and took her into her embrace, her arms firmly holding onto her with all the love she could ever express. "<u>You</u> are my miracle, Miss Bentham. And I don't care what William says, you will always be an angel to me, too," she whispered in her ear before releasing her.

"Indeed," Emile stepped closer behind his wife and placed his hand on the upper part of Charity's arm. "There will never be enough words to express our gratitude," his voice broke at the end of the sentence and Charity almost joined him in his tears.

"I only did what I could, nothing more." Charity looked back over her shoulder to search for the only other person who was no longer present, then added after glancing in Nathanael's direction, "God took care of the rest."

"As He always does." Nathanael grinned broadly at her choice of affirmation and moved to shake her hand in farewell.

"I'll see you tomorrow," Emma called in a tired voice from behind her, making sure she knew once and for all that she was always welcome at her house, if not here, as well.

"Perhaps," Charity tried to sound reassuring, but moved to step out the door as quickly as she could to avoid saying any more promises she might not be able to keep.

"Miss Bentham, may I have a word with you please before you go?" William stepped out of the darkness on the front porch beside her like a common thug and opened the door the rest of the way for her to pass, attempting at last to show her the briefest of kindness towards her journey.

"Thank you, Doctor Wells, but I believe I would like to retire for the evening. I fear that in my current state of mind; I am much too tired now for any kind of conversation with you." Charity tied her cape around her shoulders and tried to ignore the sour expression on his face as she passed.

"That is rather rude, even coming from you," William replied sarcastically, the hurt at being so cast aside by her without any remorse whatsoever spurring his growing resentment and ire to an even higher level.

"Is it? I don't remember impugning your honor at <u>any</u> moment today, or am I mistaken? I usually am where you are concerned," she answered easily, not caring for one minute if she hurt his feelings by it or not. After all, he had made it perfectly clear upstairs in front of everyone exactly where things stood between them and now that the crisis was over, it was time to pay the piper.

"Honor? Do you even know what that word means? You disrespect me every time you speak!" William balled his fists up in anger, then released them as he tried to calm his temper.

"Then let me make it easier for you, Doctor Wells. We won't have to do this ever again. I am leaving," Charity affirmed seriously, her voice empty and cold.

"What?" William stopped pacing, suddenly shocked by her unexpected revelation. "Leaving this farm or leaving Philadelphia?"

"Does it matter?" Charity shot back, clipping each syllable crisply, no longer resolved to care about his feelings on the matter.

"Not really? Have a good life, Miss Bentham. I wish you well." William turned his back to her and walked back up the stairs without giving her a second glance.

Stunned once again by the ease in which she had been dismissed and forgotten, Charity called out to him, her voice as calm and collected as the first day that she had challenged him at the hospital. "Oh, and William..."

"What!" William almost glared back at her as he swung around to face her.

"I kept my promise," Charity declared resolutely, tossing the unopened vial of blood in his direction. "And you, dear sir, have done far worse than anything Edward was ever guilty of," she attacked him with the most honest thing she could have ever said about him and walked away, not looking back for a second to see his expression. At this point, she simply didn't care what the man thought of her. After all, he was only one man in a rather long list of disappointments she had been forced to endure during her lifetime. And just like the rest of them and her family, he would be forgotten just as quickly. It was only a matter of time.

Unbeknownst to him, she had thankfully already received an offer of employment months ago for a position over in Washington. Though when it had arrived, she had not intended to accept it at all. Yet after his behavior tonight, the offer was looking more appealing by the second.

With the strength of her determination and stubborn resentment building with every step, she walked all the way back to her apartment, packed her bags and carried herself to the General Store to check the transportation schedule. As she had expected, a coach would not be leaving for a few more hours at least, but there would be one ready and waiting come sunup.

With luck, she would be on it.

More importantly, she would be away from the most self-entitled man she had ever met.

Incensed with the betrayal she felt with every breath she drew in, hot tears stung her eyes as she sat down on the bench near the General Store and waited, but try as she might, she could not stop them. In letting herself trust someone so implicitly, she had broken her number one rule for survival and allowed herself to care for the man above all sense of reason and inner caution. Yet now that she had, she was just going to have to deal with the regret she would forever feel in regard to her total negligence concerning him.

As hard as it had been every time that she had dared to trust anyone in the past, she <u>had</u> managed to pull herself through it all before... and as equally difficult as it was destined to be to forget William entirely and the love she still felt for him in every ragged breath, she would do so again.

As much as he might like to think so, Doctor Wells was not the only intelligent man in this world, and she was not beholden to anyone... least of all him.

Chapter Thirty-Four

November 25th, 1811

Over three weeks had passed since the night of Hope's miraculous revival and with them not a moment of William's time had been free for a single minute of errant thought, good or otherwise. From the countless patients still needing his attention at the hospital to the hours spent caring for Samuel and Holly over at Charlotte's, every minute of his day from the moment he awoke to the hour that he placed his head wearily back upon his pillow once more had been allocated to work, or really to anything that would keep his mind fully occupied and off the departure of a certain young woman of his most recent acquaintance.

And as hastily as he had needed to do it, he had not even had the time to properly move his things over to the farmhouse. Not that he cared particularly if they remained wherever they were at the present, or even if they had been stored in the barn with the rest of the harvest for that matter. Almost every aspect of his life was now sufficiently turned upside down, far from the orderly way he normally liked things, so worrying about where his favorite Sunday overcoat might have been placed seemed like the least of his worries, if not pointless to even consider it.

Seeking to be flexibly helpful, Nathanael had agreed to occupy the house in the center of town with Elijah until other arrangements could be made that would be more suitable for all involved, as well as volunteered reluctantly to help Charlotte watch the children for William during his day at the hospital. Which, in the end, had made it all a rather haphazard adjustment for all of them. But thankfully, one that they were all managing to cope with just the same.

The only thing William did miss most were his daily chats with Emile during their lunch every afternoon. As he had sadly expected, his friend had not spoken with him since that night weeks ago. Partially due to his sudden trip to Washington, and also somewhat because of their rather heated discussion. Adding to that was the overwhelming dismay that followed when not a single letter or note had passed between them in that span. A sad realization in every way imaginable, that caused him to pause more than once when another day had passed, and he still had not received any word from the Frenchman.

Both men, though brothers in many a trial, seemed to be stubbornly holding a grudge against the other now with neither willing to give an inch in either direction. A fact that brought more than a little bit of disappointment to the others around them and even more sorrow to Hope at being the apparent cause of their current separation.

And yet, if William had stopped for just a minute in his sullenness to view the situation from a different point of view, he might have realized that it wasn't Emile's fault entirely that the government had suddenly called the standing members of Congress back to Washington for a special summit. As a representative from Pennsylvania for his party, Emile had been legally required to go, despite how much he may have been needed elsewhere.

But William did not. Secretly, he had felt deep down that the man was only trying to avoid running into him by going. Either that or punish him further by his continued absence.

"They were a family, after all, and families forgave each other, even if they did not understand them." Or at least that was something to the fact of what Nathanael had told him just last night before he had left Charlotte's to head back into town. Unlike his usually passive ways of dealing with problems, the man had been quite severe in his criticism of William's behavior of late, not only towards Emile and Emma, but also towards Charity herself, who neither deserved his rebuke nor harsh treatment of her that night. In the preacher's eyes and most of the others, the woman had done nothing wrong whatsoever, or at least nothing that he knew of that warranted the reaction William was giving.

William begged to differ.

Charity was beyond insightful; she was undeniably intelligent. And as such, she knew precisely what she was doing when she had set foot in that house, and how it would affect him by doing it. Which, in his opinion, meant volumes more than the actual sin she had committed against him.

No matter what Nathanael might think otherwise, she was not some innocent party that was being unfairly scorned because of her desire to help Hope. Not in the slightest. In William's mind, she was the real enemy here, not him, and she always would be.

And despite whatever Nathanael had said in her favor, William had completely tuned out his words last night almost as soon as he had begun speaking them, just like he had during the many other times he had spoken to him over the past few days, as well. Mainly because, at this point, he was not especially interested in forgiveness from Emile today or even in the near future. And he most certainly did not require anything from Miss Bentham. As strange as it may be to say it, it appeared as if he alone was the righteous one in this whole mess and incidentally, the only one who had done the right thing.

Sooner or later, his friends would simply have to accept it. It may take a few years for Emile, given the level of anger he had displayed when William had tried to talk to him the next day, but he had time for him to finally come around. They all did it seemed.

As for the nurse who had been the singular catalyst for all of this upheaval in his present world, not a single person in Philadelphia had heard a word from her since that night so many weeks ago, not that he had been eagerly inquiring. As methodical as she always was, she <u>had</u> left a brief note at the hospital for the staff announcing her departure, as if everything she had decided upon had been previously planned and not the unexpected flight the rest of them assumed. Yet other than the statement of her necessary trip, no other details were given as to where or what she would be doing there, or if she would ever return.

"Gracious to William to the last," Nathanael said in her favor, as if her actions were highly indicative of her pureness of character and high regard for him, even in the face of his error.

Yet William had refuted that assumption as well. To him, they were anything but. Her rash decision and secretive actions merely displayed yet another manipulating reason to despise her all the more. Because of her decision to leave, many of the nurses were no longer speaking to him because of it. In fact, all of them, right on down to the newest hire that had just started last week, were absolutely certain that <u>he</u> was the true cause of her untimely flight. But in the end, that mattered little to him, too. Here or in another country, tearing some other family apart, he simply didn't care. The lower staff hardly spoke to him before she left, so having more enemies now made little difference to him whatsoever. After all, his job overall was to help his patients, not participate in the various social aspects of the hospital.

For far too long his every thought and action had been dictated by the candor of their gossip, and fed-up as he was with the lot of it, he was done playing their game. The only thing he required now of each of those beneath him was their dutiful obedience to his directions, nothing more. Anything beyond that was up to them. And if they suddenly decided to quit because of that request, then so be it. There were plenty of other fine establishments that would surely hire them, maybe even ones that did not require their nurses to like every staff member they worked alongside.

Or maybe, William pondered more remotely. *Maybe it was him that should leave next.* Go back to England and start over under another name or in some distant countryside village where life was simpler, and far less complicated than it was here. With nothing else important enough to hold him here other than the family he arrived with, the new year might be as good a time as any to do it. Besides, Charlotte could help Nathanael now just as much as him, if he was truly struggling. Or Emile could finally teach their friend how to feed as Sebastian had done in the past.

Either way, all William wanted now was a few weeks of peaceful existence until Christmas. Having been pushed beyond all of his physical limitations for months, the storm that was still constantly churning within him, forever threatened to spill over at any moment, demanding at least a small period of earned respite from all of the drama brewing around him.

"Would you like to read the bedtime story tonight or should I do it?" Charlotte asked him politely at the dinner table after their evening meal, her eyes diligently analyzing his overall expression and demeanor for any spark of a change whatsoever.

Setting his fork down and reaching over to pick up little Holly who was sitting beside him playing with the remaining beans on her plate, William tried to answer her in as pleasant a way as possible, but it came out regrettably far more drained. Though if she were to describe him more accurately, his whole countenance lately seemed to lack any of the vitality it once held. "I think I can manage tonight but thank you for offering."

"You know, William, Sebastian and I had a few fights in our time, as well. Some really big ones come to think of it. I didn't think we would ever mend those fences in the beginning, but we did... in time." Charlotte picked up the dirty plates from the table and walked them over to the kitchen to wash them.

"I know you mean well, Charlotte, truly I do, but I am not especially interested in mending anything right now," William retorted tersely and pushed his chair back from the table. "I'd much rather just go read them a story and go to bed."

"Suit yourself," Charlotte acknowledged sweetly and walked back over to the table, but not before touching his arm to stop him as he passed. "I know you think

I am meddling to say this, and maybe I am, but you need your friends more than you realize. Don't let your pride drive them away or push them beyond reach of your redemption."

"I'm not doing anything of the kind." William kept his gaze firmly on the steps in front of him and motioned for Samuel to head up the stairs for bed. "When they want to apologize to me, I'll be waiting." He paused and waited for her to release her hold.

"Oh William, you may be waiting a long time, if that is your intention. Are you sure you are willing to do that?" She cautioned him once more before picking up the dirty cups, too.

"Right now, I am simply too tired to care, Charlotte," William replied firmly and walked up the stairs without another word to tend to the two children. At least they always had a ready smile waiting for him. They didn't care why Miss Charity left or what heinous action he might have committed to send her packing. They did not even question why he was so angry at any of their new aunts and uncles. They only wanted his love, and he was one hundred percent happy to give it. In fact, as strange as it all seemed, right now they were the one glimmer of joy left in his life, and he intended to fan it fully.

"Knock, knock," Nathanael called from outside the screen door to the woman inside. "Care for some company?"

"Of course," Charlotte smiled and motioned for him to enter. "You know you are always welcome, Nathanael."

Without hesitation, Nathanael opened the outer door carefully and entered, scanning the room briefly first for his friend. "Is he up with the children already?"

Charlotte nodded as she washed the various trappings from dinner. "You only just missed him."

"I see. Well, maybe that is for the best as I doubt he wants to talk to me tonight anyway." Nathanael retrieved the rest of the items from the table and carried them over to the kitchen to put them away. "Has he said anything else about Charity?"

"No, and I don't think he will. That one is ready to dig his heels in for eternity if he has to. As kind as he always is, I fear he will let this bitterness hold him to the grave, if he isn't careful." Charlotte set two of the cups down on the towel and waited for Nathanael to dry them. "Do you even know why she left? I assume it was because of the disagreement they all had about Hope, but I have never seen him get this angry about anything, let alone something medical. It doesn't seem like that would be enough to send the girl flying across the country to get away from him."

"Indeed. Sadly, I've learned many times over the years that there are some things I simply do not wish to know when it comes to William. This being one of them." Nathanael placed the dry dishes back in the cupboard and leaned back against the counter, his hands firmly propping him up upon it on either side. "From what I have been able to piece together from what Hope and Emma have let slip, I gather William felt his authority was breached in some way, either that or the girl outright refused to do as she was told. Either way, the result is still the same. She is gone, and William might as well be, too, for the way he is carrying on without her. In truth, I've never seen him hold so much disdain towards anyone in my life, except for Doctor Clarke maybe, and even then, it looked <u>very</u> different. To be frank, it kind of scares me to witness it and be powerless to help him find his way out of it."

"Oh, but that is where you are wrong, Nathanael. It isn't hatred that he is holding onto. It's guilt. Raw and unabated guilt at not being able to stop what happened in the first place. Or maybe it is more about his actions towards her or something he accused her falsely about. Either way, the result is still the same. Until he lets go of that piece of his heart that he is holding back from everyone around him, it will continue to burn a hole inside of him until it chars him completely from the inside out," Charlotte explained slowly.

"You are probably right." Nathanael nodded. "I have to remember that people need to make their peace at their own pace, I suppose. I just miss the old William. The one before this horrible epidemic happened. Though I would not wish to repeat any of the events that transpired therein."

"Nor would I. But that being said, I for one am glad that Miss Bentham did whatever it was she did that upset him, as I could never express my gratitude enough to her for giving me back my child." Charlotte hung up the towel to dry and turned back to the man across from her knowing she would never once reveal to him the real reason why Hope had survived. "I'd walk on coals of fire if it meant saving one of my children, maybe worse."

"Huh," Nathanael chuckled lightly and reached one hand out to her, waiting patiently for her to accept it, as calm and unassuming as ever in his approach. "A mother's devotion is definitely greater than anything else <u>I</u> have ever seen on this Earth, and much stronger than any vampire. That is for sure."

Suddenly experiencing a strange sort of peace about doing so, as if the action had been something she had <u>always</u> been intended to do, Charlotte took it readily and grasped it within her own before smiling up at him warmly. "I am grateful for you, too, Nathanael, more than you will ever know. I don't think I would have had the strength to face any of this if it hadn't been for you."

Feeling surprisingly just as connected as she was at that moment, Nathanael stood back upright and stepped closer to her in the kitchen. "Would it be too soon to say that I very much hope to continue in garnering that service to you in the future?"

"No." Charlotte shook her head and looked down timidly and then back up, fixing her gaze completely on his own, the rich indigo in his eyes contrasting handsomely to his almost coffee-colored tones in his otherwise chestnut brown hair. "Nothing would bring me greater pleasure. But you know that already, or at least I hope you do. Still, I thank you for asking me all the same. In truth, it is probably one of the things I love most about you."

"Really? What is that?" Nathanael rubbed the fingers of her hand slowly, his mind recording each and every small detail of them as he did so.

"Your quiet patience," she said softly and placed her other hand upon his chest. "Your respectful silence is not a deficit in your character. It is your gift." She smiled and patted her hand softly upon it.

Nathanael smiled, too, knowing that he felt the very same about the woman across from him, as well. "Thank you."

In the quietness that the farmhouse provided, Charlotte continued to study him for several moments before reaching one hand up to move a lock of hair away from the center of his face and to the left, the same stray group of strands that always seemed to find its way playfully into the center.

Mesmerized, Nathanael could not look away. As simple as the movement was, it stirred within him feelings he had not experienced in many years. Something not at all like what he had ever felt with Elsie, but in a way, he preferred that, too. Whatever it was that had started forming more strongly between the two of them weeks ago, had stemmed originally from years of close friendship and interactions. And as essential as her wisdom was whenever she shared it, she was not someone who ignited a passionate response from him whenever she entered the room. She was instead a warm fire that drew him closer to her, just to enjoy that warmth with her.

Concentrating on everything that the other found essentially important in that moment, they stayed that way for several minutes more before Nathanael eventually cleared his throat and took a step backwards, allowing Charlotte the opportunity to do the same. "Well, I had best do what I came for before it gets too dark to see out in the barn."

Charlotte nodded quietly, then stepped slightly aside to allow him the room necessary to pass by. "Of course, will I see you in the morning?"

"Actually..." Nathanael reached for the screen door but paused before opening it. "Would you be interested in taking a walk with me tomorrow, perhaps? Maybe just to the back pasture or around the garden? I wouldn't want you to exhaust yourself too soon."

"I would like that very much." Charlotte grinned back at him. "I'll pack a picnic lunch for me as I know you probably wouldn't enjoy anything I might fix."

Without meaning to do so, Nathanael's brow furrowed somewhat at the comment. "You know that I'll eat anything <u>you</u> make for me, Charlotte. I just can't promise that I will like it."

"True." Charlotte laughed gently in response. "But there is no sense wasting good food."

"Thank you." Nathanael nodded sheepishly back. "Can I call for you around ten?"

Charlotte agreed, "I'll ask Hope to watch the children for me. Would an hour suffice? I wouldn't want her to do more than that."

Feeling suddenly self-conscious about what he was essentially proposing, Nathanael glanced hesitantly behind him out the door to the large oak in the distance. "An hour will be plenty. Goodnight, Charlotte."

"Goodnight, Nathanael." Charlotte stepped closer and kissed him lightly on the cheek in farewell. "I'll see you then."

Utterly stunned and completely delighted all at once, Nathanael could hardly close the door behind him after that. Of all the things she could have done or said to him tonight, that singular, spontaneous gift was nothing for which he had been prepared for, at least not yet anyways. He had thought it would be years before either of them felt anything more than the compassionate friendship that the two of them shared, or decades before a lasting attachment was made at all.

After everything that she had been through, he was prepared to accept whatever Charlotte would be willing to give. But something in the way that she had looked at him tonight had changed all of that. Or maybe it was him that had changed. Either way, he knew now that there was one more thing he needed to do tonight before he finished feeding the livestock for the family. Though perhaps it was something he should have thought to do much earlier.

Either way, it made no matter now.

Turning up the collar of his coat to block the steady wind that had started to pick up since yesterday morning, he made his way out to the large oak and the grave beneath. As nervous as he was quickly becoming, he needed to have a conversation with his friend tonight, and if he was ready, maybe also ask for his permission to care for his wife.

Chapter Thirty-Five

November 28th, 1811

"Is it really true that Uncle Emile will be back in time for the feast tonight, Auntie Hope?" Samuel asked excitedly as he stacked block after block on top of themselves at the table, intent on constructing the tallest tower possible with them.

"Yes, it is, Samuel," Hope answered him happily, her shorter hair with its loosely woven curls bouncing as she spoke was held back from her face neatly with a single black ribbon on top of her head. One that, incidentally, matched the band around her neck that held her charm from Emma that had been given to her earlier that year.

"I like Uncle Emile. He is funny." Samuel giggled and watched as his tower tumbled before him. "Opps! I'll have to start again."

"Yes, I think you will," Hope beamed. Life had been simply a joy when she was watching the two of these children every day for Uncle William, and much more entertaining than she had expected. When she was younger, she had often wondered if she had ever wanted to raise any children of her own, but after this experience, she was convinced of it completely. Having been the baby of her own family, she had little experience in caring for those younger than herself over the years. In fact, it had not been until Jedidiah's son, Caleb, arrived that she had ever even held a baby, much less cared for one personally. Yet now, every time she hugged little Holly, she couldn't help but feel drawn more and more towards that path in front of her. How many children she would eventually desire, she did not know, but however many God would decide to bless her and Michael with, even if it was only one, she knew she was ready to accept them.

"Have you and Michael set a date for your wedding yet?" Charlotte inquired from the kitchen, eager to be talking about anything related to the upcoming nuptials between the two and not the uncertain row between friends that would most likely occur later that evening when Emile and William finally saw each other again. After all, it was high time some joy returned to this property and maybe Hope's wedding would be the catalyst for it.

"I was thinking maybe we could schedule it for after the new year. What do you think about February?" Hope said tentatively, as if feeling out her mother's opinion on the date she and Michael had been recently contemplating.

"How about April?" Charlotte countered quickly, then arranged the slices of apple on top of the pie that she was making. "I don't think there is enough time for the two of you to be ready by February."

"What all do we need to do? Don't we just need to say, 'I do'?" The girl giggled nervously. "How much more is there to plan?"

"Oh, ye of little knowledge," Charlotte huffed with a smile and shook her head. "There will be plenty, let me assure you, starting with: the church, the food, the decorations, what dress you might wish to wear... shall I continue?"

"Well," Hope bit the nail on one of her fingers, contemplating the various answers to her mother's suggestions. "I was rather hoping we could have the wedding here, right in this house like you and Papa did back in England. I don't need anything lavish and expensive like all the other girls in town. Besides, just the thought of having to stand in front of all of those people and not make any mistakes, kind of makes me anxious."

"And Michael would be okay with not getting married in the church?" Charlotte placed the pie within its place inside the mouth of the large fireplace just to the left of the flames where it would be able to cook but not burn the edges.

"Michael doesn't care if we get married in the barn, just as long as we are married and preferably soon. I know he might look patient on the outside, but I don't think he wants to wait a minute longer than he has to." Hope laughed once more due to the sensitive topic.

"Men <u>are</u> like that, I suppose." Charlotte chuckled, too, then continued to consider her request seriously with a roll of her eyes as she turned around and examined the size of the room around her. "Well, thankfully our home <u>is</u> much bigger than the barn, and far less pungent come spring."

"Agreed. Though it might be time to take Holly upstairs for a change, Mother." Hope smelled the air and thought she picked up the odor of something very unpleasant.

"That is probably a good idea, too." Charlotte walked over to the little girl and reached down her hand. "Why don't we go upstairs, little lady, and give you a fresh change?"

The young girl who was playing with a stuffed doll on the large, braided rug nodded, then put her pudgy little hand sweetly in Charlotte's before tottering after her.

"Hope, if you will come upstairs with me, I think I might have an answer to one of your other requests, too."

"Alright, Mother. Samuel, will you promise me that you'll stay inside until I return?" Hope asked seriously of the boy before wiping off her hands on the apron at her waist and taking it off to hang over the back of the chair at the table.

The little boy nodded. "Uncle William said I was not to go outside until he returns, unless I need to go use the privy," he said obediently as if reciting every word that the man had said to him before he had left for the hospital that morning.

Hope grinned. "That is precisely what Uncle William said. I need to go help my mother for a minute, but I will be back down soon to help you clean up. And if you need to use the privy, I will take you. The wind is blowing far too hard outside to let you go out there on your own. In fact, I wouldn't be surprised if we got a little snow tonight by the look of those clouds."

"Snow? Oh, really, Auntie Hope?" Samuel exclaimed excitedly and ran to place his face upon the glass of the large window on the opposite side of the room, utterly thrilled by the possibility.

"Uh-hmm. Just you wait until morning, it will probably look like Christmas very soon," Hope declared optimistically and followed her mother up the stairs and over to her parents' bedroom on the second floor.

In the short time that it had taken for her to arrive, Little Holly had already been placed comfortably in the center of the great four-posted wooden bed, the one her father had carved for them shortly after their arrival. From the rich hickory headboard with the patterns of leaves and small berries carved into its edges to the ropelike pillars that stood guard at each of its corners and stretched all the way up to the ceiling, Hope had never seen its match anywhere. Unsurprisingly, it had been her mother's pride and joy for so many years, though the wood had darkened and smoothed with the love it had protected and the overall passage of time.

Yet speaking of her mother, as much as Hope had expected her to be changing the small child as she had originally intended, she was nowhere to be found. Instead, she was busily searching for something underneath the large bed, like a raccoon searching for an apple at the edge of the trees.

Unable to contain her delight at such a humorous spectacle, Hope laughed lightly at the scene and arranged the new cloth nappy for Holly on the bed, making sure to fasten it securely on both sides afterwards. In her haste to be done with the decidedly unpleasant chore, she had forgotten to do so once before when she had been just learning. But after that near disaster that had required her to change the poor girl's clothing altogether due to her own ineptness, she had been careful to double check it every time thereafter.

Grunts and muffled words, that sounded more like the frustrated rantings of her brother, Jedidiah, when he didn't want to get out of bed in the morning, floated back up to Hope from her mother under the thick mattress as she waited, causing the young child on the bed to peer over the edge with Hope to make sure the woman was definitely okay. "What on earth are you doing under there, Mother? Did you lose a pin or something?"

"No... I know it has to be here somewhere... Maybe it is behind the... Aha!" Charlotte cried triumphantly at last and pulled herself and a long rectangular box out from underneath the bed, her hair now in a total state of disarray.

"Oh, Mother..." Hope tried her best to hide her amusement at the sight behind her hands when she took her in, but it couldn't be helped. "What forgotten treasure did you manage to locate under all of that dust?" She peered across the bed at the long box in her mother's hands and shook her head. "As hard as it was to dig it out of there, it probably has not seen the light of day in half a century."

"Ha, ha." Charlotte rolled her eyes in mockery. "I am not <u>that</u> old, young lady. Neither am I that poor of a housekeeper. Mind your tongue," Charlotte corrected her, though Hope could tell that she was speaking more in sarcasm than in parental rebuke.

"Alright, but what is <u>in</u> the box anyways?" Hope placed the protective bloomers back onto the girl and handed her dolly back to her to play with.

"Something that I think you might like to see. Though believe it or not, I haven't looked upon it in probably 20 years. I hope the moths have not gotten to it." Charlotte's face softened immediately as she opened the box and fingered the soft material inside with the tiny lavender rosettes and green leaves embroidered upon the fabric like tiny dots.

"What is that!" Hope gasped while moving to the other side of the bed to view it better.

Like a clerk displaying to her client the finest silks available for her to purchase, Charlotte lifted the delicate dress up with both hands into the light from the nearby window at last and beamed at the sight of it once more, remembering all of the wonderful memories she still cherished from that memorable day.

"Pretty..." The little girl exclaimed as she pointed one finger at it in the dancing sunlight.

"Yes, it is, Holly," Hope agreed with immense curiosity and wonder while taking a moment to marvel at the fabric that was still just as stunning today as it had been when it was created.

"This was my wedding dress, Hope. It isn't as fancy as the ones they wear nowadays. It wasn't even fancy the day that I wore it back then, but your father said it was the most beautiful thing he had ever seen." A small tear of happiness fell from the corner of her eye before the emotions of her cherished memories caused her to lightly laugh. "He was probably blind even back then, too. Then again, he always was where I was concerned. But the compliment was the best thing he could have ever said to me that day, and I have never forgotten it."

"Oh, Mother, it is absolutely beautiful, but how did you ever afford it?" Hope touched a few of the small flowers and marveled at the softness of the material in her hand.

"Well, since your grandfather never had much money to part with, being a dairy farmer and all, I had to pay for it myself," she explained without the least bit of offence at the necessary requirement. "Still, he helped in so many other ways though, like making sure we all had enough milk and butter over the years when you were little, which certainly came in handy in the months when your father's forge struggled."

"Did you make this yourself? You must have worked your hands to the bone to buy it."

"Not hardly. After your father proposed, I sold a few of my shawls that I had knitted over the years down at the docks to some of the newer arrivals and with the savings I had squirreled away over the years, I went to the store down in town to buy the fabric. Oddly enough, four shillings and six pence went a lot farther back then than it does today." She held the dress up to her body just once to imagine herself in it again before offering it up to her daughter.

Seeing a piece of the finest chiffon she had ever set eyes on; Hope took the dress carefully from her mother and held it up to her body to check the sizing.

"We may have to take it in a little here and there, but it might do if you would like to use it, as well. Though it will not offend me whatsoever if you do not. A woman should choose for herself what she will wear on the most important day of her life and if this is not this dress, I will not fault you for it. Since I no longer have a use for it, I will simply turn it into a christening dress for your first child or maybe something else just as special in the future," Charlotte prattled on nervously, yet it was more than the woman had said to her in weeks, as she was normally a woman of little conversation even though Hope knew she had much to share.

Overwhelmed by the dress and the story that she had just shared, a single tear slid down Hope's face as she studied her reflection in the mirror on her mother's wall and could not make herself move or speak.

"Don't you like it at all?" Charlotte stood up from the bed, suddenly ashamed for even suggesting it from the lack of words from her normally verbose daughter.

"Not like it?" Hope instantly turned to her mother and seized her in a tight embrace, the dress crushing helplessly between them. "It is <u>exactly</u> what I would have picked out, and it will be like having a piece of my Father with me, too." She released her and both women laughed as they wiped the tears away from each other's eyes.

A playful spectator to the scene unfolding around her, Holly squealed with delight at the entertainment from upon the bed and clapped her hands together happily.

Hope and Charlotte clapped, too, and hugged each other once more until a knock on the door behind them surprised them all.

"I'm sorry, but I thought I heard crying up here and came to make sure everyone was alright," Emma said carefully from the doorway, not wanting to intrude on so private a moment.

"Of course, it's just us two biddies bawling our eyes out." Charlotte wiped the sides of her eyes with the back of her hands.

"Look, Aunt Emma!" Hope turned around and showed Emma that beautiful floor length gown with the high empire waist and flowing sleeves that her mother had offered her.

"Hope!" Emma gasped. "Is that your wedding dress?"

Hope shook her head. "No, it was my mother's." She looked in the mirror once more and spun around.

"It's absolutely perfect, Charlotte," Emma exclaimed. "I bet Sebastian could barely speak when he saw you in it."

"He could barely speak whether I was in it or out of it," Charlotte joked uncharacteristically.

Emma laughed, as well, and shook her head. "We _do_ control our husbands in many ways, don't we?"

Charlotte nodded. "But we cannot change them. We may desire to. We may even want to wring their necks in our frustration with them, but we will never be able to make them more than what the good Lord intended them to be."

"Tell me about it." Emma rolled her eyes. "Emile refuses to even write William a letter after..." Emma stopped herself mid-sentence, suddenly feeling rebuked for speaking about something so sensitive in front of Hope.

"Why _isn't_ Papa speaking to Uncle William, Mother? Have they had some kind of a fight?" Hope asked innocently before handing the dress back to her mother momentarily.

"You could call it that. Though truthfully it is more about them being too stubborn to see the other person's point of view." Emma placed a hand of affection on the girl's arm and grimaced with concern as the girl's skin still felt far cooler than her normal body temperature, not as cold as her own, mind you, but certainly cooler than it had been in the past. "I wouldn't fret too much over it. One of them will give in eventually and then they will both be thick as thieves once again. You'll see."

"My only hope is that they do so before either of them does something rash," Charlotte admitted her biggest fear out loud. "Nathanael said William was checking the passage costs to England yesterday."

"To England!" Emma appeared instantly taken aback at the sudden news. "You are joking, right? William wouldn't leave, would he?"

"I wish I was." Charlotte shrugged and sat down on the bed, allowing the little girl next to her to finger the dress she was holding. "Let's hope for all our sakes that Emile will be able to talk some sense into him tonight. A rift, no matter the size, that is left un-mended bears many scars, and sometimes those are impossible to remove over time."

"Uncle William _can't_ leave. He's family," Hope staunchly defended his position within the very fabric of her life, unwilling to let a single thread of it go so easily.

"Well... that is not actually true..." Emma and Charlotte exchanged knowing glances before Charlotte cleared her throat and spoke up again softly, "Hope, if I shared something with you that you could not share with another soul as long as you lived, do you think you could do that? Not even to Michael, if he asked?" Charlotte looked up at the girl seriously and waited for her to consider her question with the same level of respect that she was asking it of her.

Increasingly alarmed at the abrupt turn in the conversation, Hope looked over at Emma and then to Charlotte in intense concentration, then agreed, "I think so. Is it something that affects Uncle William and the family?"

Charlotte nodded solemnly. "But I do not need to burden you with it if you are not able. Though if you are, it will allow your world to be infinitely wider in its scope and hopefully give you many more years with your uncle and Emma," Charlotte explained slowly before folding the dress up with the greatest of care and placed it back within its box on the bed.

"What could possibly be so serious that you look like you are about to tell me that someone has died. No one has died right?" Hope's eyes grew wide in sudden apprehension. "Uncle Emile is just away in Washington, correct? Uncle William didn't kill him or something dreadful like that?"

Emma laughed lightly. "No, no one has killed anyone... not yet anyways."

Hope appeared even more confused, almost to the point of growing a tad bit frustrated by the vagueness of their answers. "What aren't you two telling me?"

With a sigh that had been held back for almost twenty years, Charlotte motioned for her daughter to join her on the bed and waited a few moments longer as she collected her thoughts into the best way to approach the subject she wanted to share. "Hope, on the day that you were born, it was also the birth of someone else, though not her first in this world. Yet it <u>was</u> the beginning of many more for her thereafter." She paused and looked over at Emma who nodded approvingly and moved to stand on the other side of the girl by the bed, cautiously away from the light that was bathing the two of them from the window.

"In this world around us we know there will always be a greater good striving for all that is right. A light, just as bright as this one, that has been sent from God to be continually struggling for the truth He has placed therein as they help others to find it. Your Uncle Nathanael has spent years telling you about this light. Remember?" Charlotte described carefully in detail.

"Yes, go on." Hope kept her attention focused entirely on her mother.

"There is also a tremendous evil fighting against it, too, Hope. A darkness that would love nothing more than to blot out all the light it encounters. And sometimes this darkness has created creatures to do its bidding. We call them demons or fallen angels in our bedtime stories and in other places in the Bible. As evil as they are, they want nothing more than to destroy anything God has given to His children and distract others from finding God in the first place." Charlotte paused then and reached over to take Emma's hand before holding it tightly in the shadows. "But there are others in this world that God has placed here to fight that evil, too. They are not people like you and I, but they do have a greater purpose than we can <u>ever</u> hold."

"Mother, this all sounds like the strangest fairytale you have ever told me." Hope looked over at her mother in bewilderment. "By the way that you are telling it, I don't know if I should be frightened or surprised because none of this makes any sense."

Charlotte nodded. "I know exactly how you feel." Charlotte inhaled slowly, then breathed it out into her next sentence, "I felt the same way when your Uncle William told me all about it. It was on the day that you were born, in fact, but he wasn't speaking of himself at the time, he was talking about your father and why he had been away from us for so long before you arrived."

"Wait... Father wasn't with you when you were pregnant? Why not?" Hope appeared totally shocked by the neglected revelation.

"Before anyone even knew you existed, your father was already aboard a ship named the Endeavor. It was taking him here to start a new life for all of you... but that wasn't all it was carrying. That ship also contained something very evil, as well," Emma explained another part of the rather long story. "A man named Doctor Malcom Clarke."

"That was the ship on Uncle William's shelf, the one that Uncle Nathanael said he carved for him their first Christmas together. But they said it sank years ago. Were they on it when it went down?"

The two women nodded.

"Then how did they all manage to survive?" Hope asked quickly. "Uncle Emile told me once that Uncle William saved him twice in his life. Was he on the ship, too?"

Both women nodded once again.

"So, according to what Uncle Nathanael described, the ship went down in a hurricane. If that is so, then how did they manage to survive?" She replied in confusion.

"Your Uncle William and Emile rowed a boat to shore with your father and Nathanael unconscious inside. When they finally made it to land, the four of them helped each other survive, or at least learn to adjust to their new circumstances."

"Their new circumstances? This is not making any sense at all." Hope shook her head. "Was that on the island where our grandfather lives?"

"Yes, but they did not know him at the time," Emma answered softly.

"But I thought Señor Moretti was just our grandfather?" Hope stared back at them blankly.

"He is," Charlotte assured her. "But not in the way my father is to you, not by blood. Though he is much closer to us in all other respects. Señor Moretti helped save your father and actually gave us the money to buy this land and the house that sits upon it. We wouldn't even be here if it were not for him, nor would your father, as he guided Sebastian for many months."

"Then what happened to them?" Hope said finally, growing more agitated by the lengthiness of the explanation.

"Remember the evil I spoke of?" Charlotte asked her in a serious tone.

"Yes."

"That man was a vampire, Hope, and he was the one who changed everything for them," Emma tried to keep the truth as simple as possible.

"What is... a vampire?" Hope asked, her brow intensely furrowed and taut.

"Someone who can either help others, or someone who chooses to live within the darkness he has been created to enjoy. Doctor Clarke was the later. He didn't change them to help them. He only wanted to use them or kill them, I suppose. Your Uncle William stopped him from doing so on the ship, however, and your father ended Doctor Clarke's reign of destruction later while saving your brothers," Emma elaborated quickly while keeping the details brief but truthful. "From that day on, the four of them were never the same and they have had to live in secrecy just to survive."

Hope's mouth finally fell open in shock at the revelation. So much so that for several moments she sat stock still, just staring out the window of the bedroom and out into the fields beyond.

"I don't expect you to understand everything we are saying, dear. But I will not always be here to care for you, and they will, as long as you can manage to keep their secret." Charlotte reached for her hand to touch it but stopped herself, afraid that her daughter might not react in the way she was hoping.

"So, Uncle Emile, Uncle Nathanael, Uncle William and my father are all these... good... kind of vampires?" Hope inquired quietly, still staring out the window in intense concentration.

"Yes," Charlotte replied, her one word carrying a weight all its own.

"And you, too?" Hope looked back at Emma who only nodded her head three times quickly.

Justifiably stunned, Hope turned back to the window and gazed out of it once more before standing up and walking over to the frame, fingering the edges of the wood against her smooth fingers. "Then why tell anyone at all if it is too secretive to share?"

"Because we can't stay here forever, dear," Emma informed her bluntly. "In case you haven't noticed, we don't age like the rest of you, and sooner or later we will have to move on to escape someone's curiosity."

"Then why tell me?" Hope swung around slowly and faced the two people she cared about more than anything else in this world. "Why burden me with the secret after all these years? If father couldn't tell us, then why should I know now?"

"Because your brothers will not give it a second thought if any of them were to suddenly choose to move away and distance themselves from us for our protection. But you..." Charlotte defended her decision.

"I... would be crushed," Hope whispered slowly, then closed her eyes and sighed. "I'll keep your secret, Emma." She opened them again and saw the fresh tears glinting in her aunt's eyes. "I won't lose another father or you, if I can do anything to prevent it."

"Thank you," Emma replied in almost a whisper, the emotion she had long kept at bay filling her voice completely. "You can tell your Uncle Nathanael when you are ready, as none of them besides Emile know that we are telling you, but please..."

"You don't have to say it. I understand. I will guard it better than anything else in my life," Hope promised, then walked over to Emma and hugged her tightly. "You are too important to disappear, so stay a little longer, please."

Emma broke down and really cried now as she hugged the girl closely. "I promise to stay as long as I can. After that, you will have to come visit me, alright?"

"Alright."

"Goodness me! So much weeping going on up there. You'd think someone was having a funeral or something," Emile called up the stairs from the main floor below, trying to add the slightest bit of humor to the tense conversation he knew they were having. "Oh, and I brought the item you asked for, Emma, if you want to come and get it."

"Just wait here a minute please." Emma tried to dry her eyes and compose herself once more, then left them only to return a few moments later with a small parcel tied with a simple piece of brown twine.

"What did Papa bring you?" Hope took the offered package from her and turned it over once in her hands to judge the weight of it.

"You'll have to open it and find out, silly," Emma encouraged eagerly and watched as the girl pulled at the twine excitedly in an attempt to open it but failed when the knot would not release itself.

"Here, allow me." Emile stepped into the small room and extended his short knife forward to cut the taunt string easily before sheathing it once more and walking back behind Emma to watch from his place by the doorway.

"Thank you, Papa." Hope smiled appreciatively in his direction and Emile's eyes twinkled at the newer reference as he watched Hope lift the crisp corners of the brown parchment to reveal a beautiful piece of French lace that tumbled all the way down to the floor in front of her.

"Oh, Emma!" Charlotte gasped in reaction to seeing it once more.

"Hope, your Uncle William bought this for me to use on my wedding day. At the time, I didn't want a fancy affair, but he insisted that I needed to have something special to mark the occasion." Emma reached forward and gently picked up the portion of the veil that held a small silver comb near the middle and stood behind her to place it in front of the black ribbon in her hair. The intricately patterned lace with a light dusting of small seed pearls here and there flowed gracefully around her entire body and enveloped her fully in its beauty, just like it had Emma so many years ago.

"Your Uncle Nathanael even performed the ceremony in the same church where your father and I met in Portsmouth," Charlotte added quietly. "I think it was probably his first wedding, too, as he had a terrible time recalling all the things he was supposed to say and do."

"I remember." Emma chuckled. "I felt so bad watching him stumble through the vows. I suppose he was probably more afraid that we would be mad at him that it wasn't perfect."

"Truthfully, he could have said anything he wanted, and I would have been happy just as long as he ended it with man and wife." Emile shook his head at the man's struggle. "He did say that, didn't he, love?" Emile appeared momentarily concerned at the very thought.

"Of course." Emma rolled her eyes at him dramatically. "You don't think I would have endured your teasing this long without it, do you? Besides, don't let him fool you for a minute, Hope. Your uncle is well aware of every detail from that day." Emma walked back to her husband and pulled on the lapel of his coat with one hand. "You were as dashing then, standing in the front of the chapel with William by your side as you are today. Well, maybe a little more so now."

"A small benefit of immortality, I assure you, Mrs. Deschamps." Emile grinned at the memory and kissed his wife lightly on her cheek with a look of deep affection in his eyes. "Though I'd marry you all over again if I had to and you know it. You are just as beautiful standing here now as you were on the day you wore it, too."

"Maybe to you, but I do think William's veil looks twice as nice on our Hope," Emma declared resolutely.

"She's right. You _are_ positively breathtaking in it," Charlotte beamed.

Wanting to see the entire view of her wearing it for herself, Hope looked at her reflection in the mirror and blossomed the veil out from her body to watch it float back to her. "It is the most beautiful thing I have ever seen next to your dress, Mother!"

"I am so very glad you like it. Your Uncle William will be, too, when I tell him," Emma said easily, her heart overflowing with the emotion she felt in seeing her wearing it.

"But don't you want to keep this? Maybe you could…" Hope started to advise but was interrupted by her mother's soft hand.

"This is her way of passing her dress on to you, dear. You are the only daughter she is likely to ever have, so it is only natural for her to want to give it to you," Charlotte advised sweetly.

"Thank you, Charlotte. I don't deserve a friend like you." Emma tried to maintain her composure, but was quickly starting to fall apart emotionally, watching the scene unfold.

"None of us do," Emile added even more resolutely.

Charlotte nodded, for the sentiment was also shared by her, as well.

Completely absorbed by the reflection staring back at her, Hope laughed giddily at it all at once. "Wait until Michael sees me in this." She hid her face behind the corner of the veil and glanced back at the others playfully before batting her eyes. "Your bride awaits Monsieur…" She laughed once more, then looked in her uncle's direction entirely.

With a low, but muted groan, Emile turned around and left the room without further comment, suddenly uncomfortable watching her, and especially so given her reference. The last thing he wanted in his mind now was yet another reason to despise the man for taking her away from them.

"What's eating him?" Hope dropped the veil suddenly, peering around Emma after her uncle.

"Probably something with Uncle William." Emma waved her concern off with a bat off her hand. "I sent him a note on Emile's behalf, inviting him to join us for supper tonight, and I don't think your Uncle Emile is eager for that conversation just yet. Nor is he especially happy that I stepped in for him."

From the other side of the bed, Charlotte raised just one of her eyebrows and sighed. "They <u>will</u> have to make up eventually. God says not to let the sun go down upon your wrath. Remember that Hope. You will need that more than you realize once you are married."

"When I am married? Ha, I need it now." Hope removed the veil and carefully folded it with Emma's help before handing it over to her. "Michael and I seem to have a different opinion about everything these days, but especially on where we are to live. Because he works in the city, he wants me to join him in town, but I would rather live farther out in the country, maybe even build a small home here on this land like Jedidiah did."

"You'd have to get Elijah's permission for his portion to do it," Charlotte reminded her. "Deeds of property are not handed down to the daughters of the family, only sons, my dear."

"Well, wherever you decide to live, Hope, just remember that you have the same opinion about what matters most. You both love each other, and that is far more important than anything else you might face together," Emma added.

"Yes." Hope nodded before she hugged and kissed both of them in turn and picked up the young child as she left to pester her uncle more on the subject of her Uncle William.

"Are you still sure we should have told her?" Emma handed the veil over to Charlotte to place in the box along with the dress.

"Without a doubt." Charlotte took it from her and opened the lid. "Someday she will be your responsibility, and I cannot think of another woman I would trust more." She closed the lid and slid it back under the bed.

"I don't think you fully realize how much I love you, Charlotte." Emma embraced her as Hope had done earlier and the two women reveled in the closeness their relationship and trials had brought them through. In so many ways, they were as far apart as two people could possibly be, and their backgrounds did not have a single thing in common. Yet the two could not have been described as anything less than sisters, despite the fact that they had not been born together in the same cradle.

"And I love you, too, Emma... until my last breath," Charlotte promised.

"Or until mine," she pledged just as faithfully and walked out of the room together to finish the meal.

Chapter Thirty-Six

November 28th, 1811

"Uncle William is here." Hope called up the stairs to the women above from the living area down below. "And he has Elijah with him, too."

"Supper calls." The women said in unison and walked down the stairs towards her.

"And not a moment too soon, either." Elijah exclaimed as he pulled back the screen door and entered his childhood home, tilting his head back to drink in the rich aroma of cinnamon that seemed to coat everything within. "Did you make the same apple pie that you made last year, Mama?" His eyes searched the opening across from him in the open hearth to confirm his suspicions, then took a seat across from the young boy at the table. "I hope so because I haven't eaten anything since breakfast."

"Yes, but you will have to share the pie with the others. I don't make it only for you alone. You know that, right?" Charlotte admonished him sternly, though also inwardly grateful that her son still appreciated her cooking that much.

"I only have to share it with Jedidiah. The rest of the uncles say they don't like desserts, or they never finish them. Either way it seems like a terrible waste to offer such a delicious pie to anyone not decidedly eager to eat it," Elijah stated confidently his point of view with little regret whatsoever.

"Hey! I like pie, Uncle Eli!" Samuel defended staunchly from across the table as if he was suddenly scared he would not receive a slice of the treat he had been smelling as it cooked for the past hour.

"I am sure you do, little man." Elijah grinned. "I'll tell you what. How about we split it? Does that sound fair enough?" Elijah tapped the tip of the young child's nose just like his Uncle Emile used to do whenever he sampled his many culinary delights over the years.

"Alright." The boy nodded resolutely. "I'll eat four slices. You can have two."

"Hey!" Elijah protested loudly. "That doesn't seem very fair to me. I was thinking more like half for you and half for me, with maybe a small sliver from both for your Uncle Jed."

"Your math sounds perfect to me, Samuel." Hope laughed lightly at his lopsided deduction. "From the look of how tight your breeches have been of late, Eli, you could probably stand to lose a few pounds this year after all of those meals down at the café with Uncle Nathanael."

"Talk about not fair..." Elijah looked heartily offended. "We can't all be thin like Jedidiah. He probably works off the majority of his food before breakfast. Either that or he is not eating enough in the first place. Are you sure Nancy knows how to cook?"

"Mind your tongue, young man," Charlotte scolded him once again before he went any farther in that direction. "You would hurt her feelings terribly if she overheard you say that because number one, it isn't true, and number two, it isn't kind. Now go fetch me some more wood for the fire before I give your <u>only</u> slice of pie to the crows out of spite."

"Yes ma'am," Elijah answered more respectfully.

"Don't worry, Eli, you can have my piece if she does as I don't think I will be having any pie today either. In fact, just the smell of it all morning has been kind of making me nauseous," Hope said politely. "Though I am sure it will still be delicious, Mother."

"It smells fine to me. Are you sure you are feeling alright today?" Charlotte asked cautiously and looked over at Emma with fresh concern, as Hope had still not gotten her appetite back fully after her recent illness.

Equally alarmed, Emma reached a steady hand over and felt Hope's forehead to confirm or deny their assumptions before shaking her head gratefully. "Nope, still no fever."

"See, I am fine.... Please stop babying me, both of you. I am just not that hungry for pie, that is all." Hope sighed. "But now that you mention it, I <u>could</u> go for a nice juicy steak, slightly on the rare side maybe."

"Mmmm... me, too, and I know just the cow to give it." Elijah raised his eyebrows knowingly at the suggestion, then scooted out the door without another word to fetch the wood that had been requested, sheepishly avoiding further comment on his sister-in-law's household or his mother's cooking.

"I thought you said your uncle had arrived. Do you know where he went?" Emma asked from the kitchen as she placed the remaining cut vegetables on the counter into a large cast iron pot and carried them over to the fire to place them over the flames to boil.

"Which one?" Hope adjusted the ribbon that held her thick curls out of her face and picked up a few of the random toys that had been scattered across the large, braided rug. "If you mean Uncle William, I think both him and Uncle Emile went over to the barn as soon as Uncle William arrived. Though judging by the look on Uncle Emile's face when he walked out that door to greet him, I know _I_ wouldn't want to be alone with him in that barn. He was _not_ happy." Hope replied honestly as she played on the floor with the little girl.

"Were they at least talking?" Emma pried further, cautiously hopeful that William might have suddenly had a change of heart from his antagonistic attitude towards everyone lately.

Hope shook her head. "More like scowling, and that is never good."

"No, it is not." Emma lifted the lid to verify the position of the vegetables once more within the pan now that it had been placed over the fire and excused herself to check on the two men, heading out the front door and making her way quickly over to the barn beyond. The last thing anyone wanted today was for the already tense situation to escalate into something far uglier. Though at this point, Emma wasn't sure how much worse things could possibly become.

Just like a kettle that was placed too long over the fire, leaving the two men to sort it out on their own did not sound like a fully rational idea either since it had never worked out too well for them in the past. In each of those equally difficult instances, where things had gotten much too tense for a plausible solution, she had learned that sometimes a mediator of sorts was always good to help the other person see things more clearly when they were being characteristically stubborn. And especially so, when either of those men were as obstinate as the two of them could be.

Drawing in a full breath of the crisp air gathering around her, the biting breeze played with her apron strings as she walked and clawed at the edges of her hair as it wisped by in a great exhale across her full skirt and bodice, reminding her once again of the very quickly approaching winter to follow and the snow that usually came close behind. Christmas would be here soon and with it the festivities she always loved.

Oddly enough, it had been the one thing she had enjoyed most about her time here in the Colonies. With every day leading up to Christmas being like a celebration of sorts, there was always something to look forward to in each approaching morning. Cookies would be crafted with etched images and spices decorating their surfaces. Special gifts carefully sewn or new family heirlooms created like quilts and other handmade items. Toys and treats were soon to be hidden inside hanging stockings or shoes placed neatly by the fire. And beautiful cards would be intricately written or poems penned that were meant to delight the reader with their endearing descriptions.

But those were just the initial preparations. The actual day itself was something more out of a dream for most people as the farmhouse was always filled with the family stuffing their faces endlessly with homemade delights and dancing around the family room while making sure not to knock over any of the chairs along the way. And of course, there would always be the abundant laughter that reverberated off every wall as the whole group shared stories from their past and warm remembrances. Something that she feared would be greatly hindered this year if the two men did not patch things up and soon.

Oh, and then there was the music. Oh, how she loved the music! On every Christmas Eve since the very first that they had shared together at Señor Moretti's, the entire family would gather around the large fireplace at Charlotte's home and listen adoringly as Sebastian played familiar carols and songs on his guitar, his rich tenor voice blending in with those who joined him. In fact, there was nothing else in all the world like it next to her husband's piano concertos from time to time when he thought no one else was listening.

And although Sebastian was no longer here to continue the tradition now, Elijah had dutifully stepped in for the past few years to do so in his place. Equally as talented as his father before him, Emma had known how incredibly difficult it had been for him to play those familiar songs that Christmas while also grieving the deep loss of the man who had created the tradition. Yet though he had often made excuses throughout the night that he was not up to the task musically, everyone would simply not let him bow out since he had carried on the tradition so beautifully.

Rubbing her arms to defend herself against the cold attacking her both outside and the one she expected to find within the barn, she opened the large door quietly and slipped inside before following the voices she heard at a distance, making sure to keep to the shadows as much as possible. If the two men could work things out on their own, she was more than happy to let them do it. But short of hogtying them to the corral and forcing them to do so, neither of them were leaving today without a peaceful resolution, and that was that. Despite all that had happened that night, she owed that much to Charity and to the two of them. After all, it had been her decision alone to use her blood to save Hope, and she would not allow that choice to tear this family apart any longer.

"She has told you everything, hasn't she?" Emile stated flatly without the usual warmth he normally held for his friend across from him. "I told Emma you didn't need to know every detail of what happened in that room, but she insisted that you would want all the facts anyway. That woman can be nothing but persistent when she sets her mind to something, God bless her."

Instantly perturbed, Emma's eyes narrowed considerably at the possible slight even if she knew her husband did not mean anything truly by it, but chose to remain silent, carefully holding onto the tall beam that held up a portion of the hayloft above her.

"Yes, she told me, Emile." William shook his head in disapproval at the fact that his friend had chosen to keep something so decisively significant from him. "Though the more important question should be how long have you known?"

"Since the day Hope almost died, of course. Emma was so overwhelmed with joy by the girl's miraculous survival that she couldn't keep the secret from me, and I would never expect her to, William. She is my wife, and I would support her even if she asked the devil himself to do something," Emile quipped emphatically before looking over at the man in disbelief. "Is that why you have been so angry with me? Because I didn't stand with you to stop her... or because I called you arrogant?" His reply came out more flippantly than he had initially intended, but he did not move to correct it, as the entire situation he was now living through felt solely based on his friend's inability to see reason.

"No." William held his breath and scowled inwardly as he tried to clear away just a bit of the resentment that had been building within him for weeks. "I am more or less angry with her than anything else. You were just collateral damage, Emile," William admitted ruefully, then glanced quickly at his friend with an expression that spoke completely of the war that had been waging within him before looking away just as quickly as he kicked at the small clods of dirt next to the posts at his feet.

"Well, thanks so much," Emile scoffed with a sour smirk, endeavoring to utterly dismiss his hurt feelings that had been created by their rather heated conversation and his friend's overly rude silence towards him afterwards.

Hesitantly hopeful at last of what might just be a final ceasefire in this terrible battle between them, Emma held her breath in the silence that followed and waited a safe distance away, afraid to do anything that would interrupt their restorative conversation and possibly derail everything.

"But you're angry... at Emma?" Emile looked at William incredulously once again, ready to defend his wife to his last breath if he needed to but hoped that his friend would eventually relent and forgo that given necessary action. "By all that is holy man, how could you possibly fault a woman for trying to save her daughter!" Emile attempted to reason with him once again, but hearing the elevated volume in his words as they left his mouth made him realize too late that they probably sounded more like he was vehemently preaching at him instead.

"Not Emma, Emile... Charity. Out of everyone in that room, she was the <u>only</u> one who knew precisely where I stood, yet she came anyway and offered it to you as if it meant nothing to do so. How is a man supposed to trust a woman who does that? For the past three weeks, I've tried to see it her way. I really have. But I can't seem to find a way to reason around that level of disrespect?" William threw the pitchfork he was using to feed the horses back into the stack of hay in front of him and leaned both of his arms across the corral's top beam. "In the back of mind, I know that I <u>should</u> forgive her as Nathanael has been preaching to me... <u>daily</u>... I assure you. But there is nothing my mind can wrap itself around to get to that point, or that even compares to how I feel about her right now. Or maybe it's because I don't especially wish to, if I were to be totally honest. In a way, the only thing a part of me wants to do is to simply erase <u>everything</u> we ever did or said to each other if I could, but you and I both know that I can't. So, there it is."

"Oh, William... you should forgive her because you love her, man. Nothing more. Or is that not a good enough reason anymore?" Emile cocked his head slightly to view his friend's face next to him. "Besides, doesn't Nathanael also say that love covers a multitude of sins? You could start there if you are looking for a first step back to redemption. Though from what I have seen and heard, it might take a sight more than that to repair this rift, even if all you want is a continued friendship with the woman... which I doubt."

Closing his eyes for several moments to stop the inward spinning going on inside his head, William pursed his lips and inhaled slowly to temper his response, then opened them once again before speaking. "Yes, but this was not merely an oversight on her part, Emile. That I could understand easily. I'm not that petty, at least not yet. But that was not the case. Like it or not, despite the promises she made to me, she willfully marched over here and started this whole problem between us all, knowing full-well I would not have approved," William defended hotly, still incensed with the woman's audacity towards him that night as if it had just happened this morning.

"So, by your own admission, <u>you</u> would have done nothing and let Hope die then," Emile snapped curtly back at him as he shook his head in total astonishment, his ire building once more to an unhealthy level. "Unbelievable..."

"Well... we will never know now, will we?" William replied just as tersely under the weight of Emile's glare, but his voice, by all accounts, had lost the sudden fervor of his previous statement. "That decision was ultimately made <u>for</u> me... like so many others before it," he muttered the last part almost despondently, as if his answer had carried with it the complexity of things far deeper than their current dilemma, as well. Things he had not really divulged to anyone on this Earth really, save in his prayers alone.

"Oh, we do know, Doctor Wells. And your continued stubbornness is going to cost you the only thing worth living for in this life." Emile threw his hands up in sudden exasperation and started to walk away from him, back to the house, having had enough of this endless circle of torture, but stopped when he saw Emma's raised hands in the darkness pleading with him to remain.

"Ughh..." With a tortured groan at what she was compelling him to do, he turned back around to face his friend and began his reasoning all over again, only this time in a manner that was far calmer than admonishing, as if needing to try a different type of tactic altogether than what he had used to persuade him before. "William, I can deal with you not speaking to me. It <u>has not</u> been pleasant, let me assure you, but I <u>was</u> fairly confident that we would sort it all out in the end. We always do. And I can even excuse your idiotic behavior at the hospital towards the other staff there and even your harshness towards Nathanael of late, not to mention Charlotte. He <u>can</u> grate on my nerves, too, from time to time, but come on man, you need to at least try to be reasonable."

"Alright, then what, pray tell, do you think it is costing me, o wise one, since you seem to have all the answers tonight?" William looked over at him, obviously mocking him with his own previous statement.

"Miss Charity Bentham, you daft man, or have you not been listening to me?" Emile placed both hands upon his hips then lowered them as he walked back over to William and put one arm across the man's shoulders. "If you refuse to accept my word for it, then look at it this way instead... have you never done anything even remotely similar, even though it might be dangerous to try."

"A few times, yes..." William relented just a little in his position but still did not look at him as he focused all of his attention instead on something that appeared insignificantly important to him on the ground in front of him. "But most of those instances were calculated risks that were backed up with a great deal of research first, Emile. <u>This</u>..." He glanced back in the direction of the house behind them with its glowing windows and humming activity. "This is not about that at all. This is more about being ten feet away from the danger that none of us can anticipate and not carelessly playing near the edge."

"Fine, I'll concede on that point." Emile exhaled loudly and tried his best to temper his growing frustration with his friend's repeated refusal of his patient efforts to make him see things more clearly. "But William... do you know how many things in my life I would have missed out on simply because I did not step out in faith? Hundreds. And I also know by your character alone, that you are not overly cautious in everything you do because you are a coward, William." He raised his eyebrows at his friend just once as he saw his friend begin to shake his head in denial. "No, it is true, and you will not persuade me otherwise. You, William Wells, are one of the bravest men I know, and I am acquainted with a great many distinguished gentlemen who claim to have done far more than you have in your lifetime. To begin, you saved me from Doctor Clarke when he would have utterly finished me on the Endeavor. You even got every one of us off that ship when I could scarcely move, much less help you. You nurtured Nathanael for months after he almost slaughtered the whole village of Wakefield. And you never once gave up while encouraging Sebastian to return to his family. Do I need to go on, or are the deeds that happened in just 1793 enough to prove it to you?"

"No, you can stop there." William shook his head slowly, then glanced up at him with a look of pure regret and denial. "But that was so long ago, Emile. Things are different now... I am different now."

"That we can both agree on wholeheartedly." Emile removed his arm and looked like he was about to begin pacing next to him but threw his head back for a moment and cleared his throat instead. "For several years, I knew something had changed after you arrived in Philadelphia, but just like the rest of us, I had hoped you would learn to adjust to everything in time. Yet the one thing I want to know most of all is how long will you continue running from your own distorted expectations, William? A century? Learning to deal with the chaos that life throws at us doesn't have a time limit to it, and Charity might not be willing to wait until you finally sort it all out." He stared him down seriously, hoping that he had not been too harsh in his delivery that William would walk away from them once again. "Besides, everything that transpired in that room wasn't about you at all. And if you stopped to look at it from someone else's perspective, you might agree that Emma wasn't trying to hurt you personally by giving Hope her blood. Neither was Charity usurping your authority by telling us about the possible treatment, either. They both only did what they felt was right at the time, just as you do every day in countless other situations, and no one questions your actions when <u>you</u> do it. So, why can't you trust <u>them</u> in this? Or is that so unreasonable to ask it of you?"

"Unreasonable or unacceptable?" William held his gaze with a look that appeared more on the verge of a total emotional release than anger of any kind. "At this point, I am still not sure what I am capable of accepting and as you know, there is so much about this situation that has been beyond my scope of understanding from the very beginning," William admitted faintly.

"But William... Do you <u>need</u> to understand everything in order to accept it?" Emile asked him honestly. "Isn't that what Nathanael calls faith?"

William nodded in agreement. "Yes, but a part of me still does." William answered him honestly, then shook his head, the disappointment at where his life was suddenly heading rushing back to him like a horse who had been trained to run headlong back to the barn no matter who was riding him or what awaited. "Look, I know you mean well, Emile. Truly, I do, but not everyone is as fortunate as you to have found their soulmate as you have in Emma. Some of us might just have to be content with living a bachelor's life it seems. Either that or learn to change who they truly are."

"You're an idiot. You know that right?" Emile mocked him openly, folding his arms on top of the corral's railing once more in sheer incredulity of the man's overly despondent assessment.

"So, you keep reminding me." William smiled as he looked over at his friend and squinted one eye. "Truce?"

"Truce." Emile nodded approvingly, grateful to have put at least that unpleasantness behind them. "Just as long as you remain here on this continent and stop all this foolish nonsense about going back to England. Nathanael can't keep the smallest of secrets it appears, and I am glad he can't because I am not going to keep up our friendship through pieces of paper when I can have the man himself beside me. Agreed?"

"Agreed." William sighed before adding more truthfully, "Besides, I wasn't especially looking forward to another six weeks of seasickness anyways."

"I imagine not." Emile chuckled lightly at his expense. "You were sick on our voyage here, too, if I remember correctly. You know, for someone so steeped in volumes of medical knowledge, you truly looked pathetic... both times."

"Thanks so much." William frowned, then laughed, too, feeling the joy of their memories together once more. "That last voyage really <u>was</u> quite horrid."

"Quite... buckets of vomit everywhere, not to mention the absolute stench," Emile agreed easily. "And yet," Emile paused and played with the grooves in the wood under his fingertips for just a minute before hesitantly speaking once again, "as much as it pains me to bring up anything else tonight that might set you off again towards that unhappy future, there _is_ one more thing I need to tell you before we go any further. Something that might make you equally as mad when I tell you, though at this point, I am exhausted trying to walk on eggshells around you."

"Seriously, Emile... stop already." William rolled his eyes at Emile in a time-honored tired expression that was now utterly characteristic of their common exchanges.

"Stop yourself..." Emile did the same to him in mimicked fashion, as well, and shook his head. "Since we seem to be on the path towards total reconciliation tonight, we might as well work this last thing out now, too, and be done with everything once and for all. It is Thanksgiving, after all."

"Well, as long as you haven't told Nathanael any of this, I doubt anything you are going to say to me right now will pale in comparison. The man would never forgive himself if he knew there was something he could have done years ago to save Elsie, and we both know it," William replied casually while watching the horses feast upon the hay beside him.

"That we do, and he shan't hear it from me... _ever_. But you must promise me that you will be calm and hear me out until I am finished. I need you to actually say it, out loud," Emile commanded firmly with one raised brow in his direction.

"Is it that bad?" William looked back at him with the same worried expression he always wore when topics such as this came up.

"I don't think so, but then again, it all depends on your point of view," Emile added flatly and looked away from William towards where Emma was waiting in the shadows, pausing patiently for his reply.

"Fine, I promise to listen before acting. Now, out with it, Emile. I won't be angry with you or anyone else, no matter what you say," William finally blurted out in agreement.

Knowing it was finally time that she joined their conversation at last, Emma took a decidedly hesitant step forward from behind him and spoke up quickly to unleash the heavy burden she had been carrying with her for weeks. "Charlotte and I told Hope about everything today, William. Like it or not, she knows our whole terrible story and has agreed to keep our secret."

"Emma... no..." Hearing her voice and yet another thing that might throw everything in his carefully constructed world upside down once more, William swung around, instantly on the defensive though he truly had no idea why. Sadly, despite how much he very much wanted it to stop, the compulsive action now seemed to be his knee-jerk response of late about everything and anything that caught him off guard.

"William…" Emile watched him cautiously, ready to intervene between the two of them if it came down to it but chose to offer him a calm reminder instead, "You promised, remember."

"Huh… I think I am starting to understand how Charity must have felt when I made her pledge not to do something I felt strongly about." William tried to compose himself once more, feeling utterly unjust now for what he had done to Charity. "Did you do this to entrap me, Emile? 'Cuz, if you did, it worked."

"Again, this decision, like the one before, had nothing to do with you personally, William," Emile said matter-of-factly, further driving home his point from earlier.

"But I thought we had agreed not to tell anyone else because it would compromise their safety?"

Emile nodded but did not speak at first as he waited for his friend's temper to cool slightly in the moments that followed before he added more hesitantly, "We did, but the parameters have since changed."

Hearing his now most hated word among all the many others in his vast vocabulary of many languages, William grimaced sourly, "I hate change, Emile."

"I know you do, William, and I am sorry to have caused you more discomfort. But are you truly angry with me for doing so?" Emma asked sincerely, knowing that the man needed Emile's friendship much more than hers any day. In fact, even if he chose to hate her for the rest of his life because of it, it would be worth it if her husband still retained his best friend in spite of her actions.

William shook his head. "I'm not angry, Emma, not at you anyways, and I suppose after that, I shouldn't be mad at Charity either. I seems that I have only myself to blame for this whole horrible mess I've created."

"Yes. Yes, you do," Emile agreed wholeheartedly, placidly content at last that his friend had finally relented.

In the safety of the barn around them, the man beside him sighed even deeper still and felt the weight of all his anger finally falling off him. "I suppose, maybe relieved would be a better word for it, Emma. In a way, I feel fantastically satisfied that none of us will have to make another pointless excuse around Hope ever again."

Emma smiled tentatively back at Emile. "I want you to know that we didn't do it to inconvenience you, and you do not need to tell Nathanael if you don't want to. But we felt you should know, and that it should come from us since we were the ones who made the decision to do it."

"No, don't tell him. Nathanael is in a good place right now. He has a wonderful job that he loves doing. And he has formed a growing friendship with Charlotte that has greatly benefitted them both, though I personally don't know if it will ever progress farther than that. All things considered, it <u>has</u> been hopeful watching them interacting and seeing the happiness they bring to each other when they do. I see no reason to upset any of that."

"Yes, Charlotte has told me that they have been spending more time together of late. So, that is something to be grateful for, for both of them," Emma said politely. "She has been so lonely since Sebastian's passing. It has been nice seeing a light back in her eyes again."

"Yes, well, Hope can tell him if she likes but let us leave that up to her to do for the present. It isn't something that has to be rushed unnecessarily," William instructed easily.

"I agree," Emile approved of his decision emphatically. "So, what do you intend to do about Miss Bentham then?"

"Huh... I have absolutely no idea, Emile." William looked at the ground and held his breath, suddenly feeling as if he could not release it, then exhaled. "For once I do not have a single... solitary... thought. That woman drives me as mad as a hatter and is twice as confusing to understand. Besides, I doubt she would even speak to me if she were still here."

"Well, I have one," Emile piped up sarcastically before William could change the subject.

"I'm sure you have," William agreed with a smile. "Arrogant people normally do."

"Ha!" Emile laughed lightly at his intended quip. "You should know."

"I do. Haven't you heard? I know everything." William laughed right along with him as they replayed their final argument, but in a much lighter tone and atmosphere and with far more merriment of spirit.

"Well, if the two of you are finished building each other up for the evening, I best go back and finish making the dinner that none of us will eat." Emma smiled at the terrible irony of the situation.

"Oh, you love doing it, so stop your complaining, Mrs. Deschamps," Emile teased her right back.

Playfully minded as always with her husband, Emma stuck her tongue out at Emile as she exited the barn and left the men behind, grateful at seeing things return to normal once again, or at least as normal as anything could be under the circumstances.

"So, do you even know where she went?" Emile asked William after his wife had passed on ahead of them and the two of them had also started walking back to the house for the meal. "Miss Bentham, I mean."

"Not a clue. You?" William shuffled towards the house next to him, appearing to be not in the least bit of a hurry now to arrive.

"Actually... I might," Emile said teasingly, trying to repetitively torture his friend for as long as he was able with a playful glint of mischief in his eyes after the weeks of harsh silence.

"Are you serious? How?" William looked back at him in total amazement.

"She <u>may</u> have been walking across the street in front of the Capitol last week while I was enjoying my coffee... and she <u>might</u> have entered into the establishment of a Mr. Benjamin Rush shortly thereafter."

"What! The man who started my hospital hired her at another?" William threw up his hands in utter disbelief. "No wonder all the nurses hate me. That place is all they ever talk about. Here I was thinking she was off somewhere begging for a job, but it would seem that Charity has left us for much greener pastures."

"It would appear so, but why would that matter to you?" Emile replied casually knowing how very much it meant to the man next to him, though from what Emma had told him, William had spent the past three weeks denying it in every way possible.

For the briefest of moments, William stared at the man beside him in total disbelief at his friend's openly audacious remark before true realization finally dawned on him at last. "You already talked with her, didn't you?"

Emile nodded just once and watched his friend carefully as the man froze instantly in shock. Moreover, from what he could see of his face next to him, not a single feature even flinched for a full second, maybe three.

Then, as if all of his systems had finally been jolted back into movement all at once, he blinked twice and gasped, "Well... what did she say, Emile?" William begged tentatively, not really sure if he wanted to know if it was not pleasant, yet also certain that whatever it was she had divulged in anger to his friend, he had probably more than deserved it.

"Something about hell freezing over before she would ever..." Emile started to torment him further before William moved to stand directly in front of him, daring him to continue on in his jest if it wasn't really true.

"Relax, William." Emile sighed slowly and smiled affectionately at him instead, choosing to relinquish his final piece of hidden information at last. "She is arriving tomorrow on the next coach. So, you had best go prepare the greatest

'I am sorry' speech that you have ever given before she arrives. If she is anything like my Emma, no doubt she will be expecting a monumental apology after the tantrum you threw at her, if not more... <u>much</u> more, if you get my meaning."

William chuckled, though his mouth only managed a half-smile in doing so. "It sounds a bit like you are overly experienced in situations such as these."

"I could write volumes on the subject, friend, but that is between my wife and myself. Marriage is work, William. Don't think for a second that everything is always pleasant just because it looks that way on the surface. Sometimes it is bending to someone else's point of view and accepting their failures simply because you know that they have forgiven you of so much more already. But that is me... what are <u>you</u> going to do?" Emile eyed the man in front of him skeptically, hoping he had made the right decision in convincing Charity to come, after all. In fact, it had been almost as hard to do as his conversation had just been with William... immensely so, but he <u>had</u> managed to accomplish it, yet only barely. And with a great deal of promises that Emma had sincerely missed her.

With a sudden burst of energy that Emile had not quite expected, William grabbed him by both of his arms and hugged him powerfully, a surge of life flowing through his friend once more.

"Whoa there, Doctor! So much emotion for a man who doesn't love someone." Emile grinned and hugged him briefly back.

"You know exactly how I feel about Miss Bentham." William let him go and then looked down the path towards town, his attention totally unfocused now on the meal that awaited him inside with the others.

"I do... I've known it for months. So, go on, William. Go prepare your speech, man. I'll make your excuses to the others." Emile patted him lightly on the back and walked up the stairs in front of them without him.

"Thank you, Emile." William waved in his direction and took off almost at a jog back into town.

"Go get her, William." Emile smiled with great delight at the hopeful expectation to follow, then walked confidently back into the house.

Chapter Thirty-Seven

November 29th, 1811

With increasing irritation at the necessity of having to wait a full night in preparation for Charity's imminent arrival, William paced the bottom floor of his apartment for the past hour at least. Since the moment that Emile had told him that Charity was already on her way, his mind had become a state of total disarray as he arranged and rearranged his thoughts frantically over and over again to make them as perfect as they could be, though he doubted anything he would say would make up for the way he had treated her weeks ago.

The posted schedule outside the General Store last night had said that the coach would arrive slightly before supper today, but that did nothing to help him pass the tormenting hours since. For almost the entire night, every sound around him had made him jump in reaction to it and even the normally relaxing breathing of Nathanael in the other room irked him in its never-ending incessancy. In fact, more than once, he had considered throwing his pillow at his door across the hall just to make him change his rhythm, but instead, he had chosen to cover his head and focus on something else, anything but what he was going to say or do when she finally arrived.

Is this what love did to people? Drove them incomprehensibly mad? William shook his head and walked over to the counter for his third cup of coffee today.

"Are you meeting Charity at the Mercantile?" Nathanael asked as he came down the stairs while buttoning the small brown buttons on his left sleeve.

"'Are you meeting Charity at the Mercantile?'" William repeated him in mimicked, albeit mocking tone. "Of course I am, Nathanael. What else would I be doing today?" His reply came back sour and curt, laced with every bit of the anxiety he was now feeling.

With a great deal of justified hesitancy, Nathanael eyed William from across the room and raised both eyebrows in response to his overly rude behavior, quite unlike the way William normally guarded his tongue, even when he was feeling poorly. "How much coffee <u>have</u> you drunk today, might I ask?"

"Not enough... <u>clearly</u>." William downed another cup and slammed the empty vessel forcefully back onto the counter next to him.

"Or maybe too much," Nathanael said slowly, scared to step any closer to the brewing storm already taking place within the kitchen. *Nobody needs food that badly,* Nathanael thought and looked for something around him to occupy himself until William had moved into another area of the room.

Instantly on the defensive, William looked over at the man darkly, as if he had just read his thoughts. Yet thankfully, for all of their sakes, it was a good thing that they did not possess that unique ability. For the most part, they were extremely cognizant of each other's moods, almost to the point of annoyance at times like today. But that kind of supernatural phenomenon probably would have come in handy a time or two over the years... or been an extreme nuisance in others.

"What?" Nathanael held his hands up in his defense.

"Nothing," William replied out of habit, then shook his head in frustration. "I hate waiting around for the inevitable. It is like methodical torture." He ran one of his hands over the surface of his hair to the back and adjusted the ribbon that held it tightly behind, his fingers searching for something constructive to distract them from shaking slightly. "By the way, when you see Emile next, you can let him know that if the army is looking for a way to torment people effectively into submission, I have a few excellent suggestions to offer them."

Nathanael laughed lightly at the very idea, then corrected him, "No, you just don't like anything or anyone that controls your life for you, that's all."

Surprised by his incredible accuracy, William glanced back up at him and smiled halfway. "You might be right about that, too, as you usually are. When <u>did</u> you become so intuitive?"

Nathanael shrugged. "When did you become so cranky?"

William chuckled at the blatant honesty he always received from his friend and felt a small portion of his body relax. "Fair enough. That is usually Emile's department, isn't it?"

Nathanael ignored his question completely and picked up his brown suitcoat, adjusting the collar so that both of the edges would lay flat against his neck and chest before putting it on. "Will we see you both tonight at Charlotte's? I hear Michael and Hope will be there planning their wedding."

"I suppose it will all depend on Charity. If the coach arrives on time, I'll meet her around four. If not, it might not be until tomorrow before I can make it back over to the farm. Then again... that is all assuming she is still speaking to me by then," William admitted to him frankly and left the kitchen to walk over to the door. Checking for the third time this hour whether or not the sky was sunny or still decidedly inclement.

"Will I need my cloak when I leave?" Nathanael seized his opportunity quickly and entered the kitchen to make himself some buttered toast with cinnamon—his one vice on days where he cared to eat nothing substantial at all.

"I doubt it. It started snowing heavily over an hour ago. Not sleeting anymore, mind you. It did enough of that last night, but the big clumps that are still falling should keep the sun at bay for the next few hours at least." William came back over to the fire and stoked it properly. "The Farmer's Almanac is calling for a chillier winter this year. I bet we even get a foot of snow by this evening, if not sooner if this storm keeps up. Though I would hate to be anyone out in it today, let alone someone riding in a coach over these roads."

"Indeed." Nathanal shuddered at the possible prediction of the winter to come. "Now that you mention it, I think I <u>do</u> prefer summer over winter, after all."

"What? You told me you always <u>loved</u> Christmas." William placed the poker back within its stand.

"I do, but I am tired of being cold, William. At least in the summer it sort of feels warm but that's probably just my imagination." Nathanael buttered his bread before offering William a slice.

William shook his head. "I'm fine, thank you. I couldn't eat even if I wanted to."

"You <u>are</u> nervous." Nathanael took a bite of his bread and chewed slowly. "Emile said last night that you would be. I said you'd be terrified or at least close enough to it, though either way, it is probably the same."

"Scared stiff, man." William rubbed his hands together, then reached for his gloves next to the fire to make sure they were not placed too close to the flames. "What else did Emile say, if you don't mind me asking?" William searched for anything right then that would serve as a mental diversion, even something he might be irritated by.

"Well..." Nathanael looked up at the ceiling as he tried to recollect the majority of the conversation, then back down at his friend. "Nothing of consequence, really. He mostly talked about his trip to Washington. Several of our ships were attacked this month and Congress had decided to schedule a call up of the colonial militia just to be ready, if it goes beyond that."

"Are they still referring to them as the colonial militia? I thought they did away with that when they formed their own government," William inquired curiously.

Nathanael shook his head. "That might be so for some, but whether they are called the state militia or the colonial, they are essentially the same thing. A group of male volunteers from every state that serve as our military at the moment."

"I see. And would this become a required posting if they do not receive enough volunteers?" William picked up his heavy coat and buttoned it all the way up to the top before wrapping his thick navy blue, knitted scarf from Nancy around his neck twice.

"Not at this time, though I have no idea what will happen if we actually do go to war." Nathanael brushed off the crumbs that had fallen onto his coat and dusted his hands.

"It will be an absolute slaughter. Not a single one of them knows how to fight properly." William shook his head. "The generals will need to train them as a group if they hope to win anything of merit, let alone defeat a whole nation."

"Maybe so, but you or I will not be there to do it." Nathanael put on his heaviest coat as well and grabbed his gloves from the table.

"No, we will not." William picked up his own gloves he had laid by the fire and held the door open for his friend. "Are you off to the college, then?"

"Where else would I be going?" He said with a teasing smirk, then relented. "Charlotte and Emma are watching the children this morning because I have two classes this afternoon, but I will come back here and wait for you later before I head over to the farm in case you need a mediator... or someone to give you last rites," Nathanael taunted casually with a playful nod and left in the direction of the college.

"Hopefully neither." William stamped the collected snow from off his shoes and locked the door behind them, remembering the last time his friend had offered such a morose suggestion.

Having little else to do today but seek out ways to idly pass the time while he waited, he made his way east across town to the Mercantile and General Store before checking on the schedule once again. The sign posted outside still read the same arrival time, despite the rather harsh weather, so he turned southward towards Elijah's shop, hoping that his nephew would be busily working at this hour, but more importantly, ready for a visit. Over the years, Sebastian had always been a wonderful listening ear whenever he had needed a positive distraction, which made William even more optimistic that perhaps his son would possess the same gift.

Nevertheless, by the time he reached the corner by Elijah's shop, not a hundred yards away from where he was to meet Charity, he could already tell that today was not going that well for Elijah either. From the sound of the harsh words and loud clangs that were being thrown into the frigid air just as quickly as the piece of iron that suddenly soared in front of him and fell at his feet, an even stronger nor'easter could have been blowing down the street, and it would have created far less havoc.

Reaching down cautiously, while also keeping an eye out for any more projectiles that might unexpectedly come his way, William picked up the warm metal carefully and studied the length of the blade. As rudimentary as it still was in its shape and overall thickness, he could still tell that it had been wonderfully created with a definite intent towards the same Spanish folds in the steel that his father used to emulate. Yet, it did hold a definite warp near its center that pulled it slightly to one side and the balance of it in his hand felt a tad bit off center when he held it firmly, despite the excellent lines of the craftsmanship. Intrigued, William tilted his head to peer around the corner of the building, checking to see if it was safe to pass before doing so, and held up the offending article near his shoulders to the man inside. "Missing this?"

"No!" Elijah growled angrily, a scowl of definite irritation covering all his features.

"You know, Eli, you could have killed someone throwing it into the street like that," William cautioned him and turned it over once more in his hands.

"Good. Maybe then they will hang me and put me out of my misery," Elijah fumed as he pulled another piece of iron from out of the barrel and paused as he gripped it tightly in his hand, as if debating his next decision in whether or not it was worth it to continue trying.

"You, too? I thought I was the only one as intemperate in mind as this weather we are having." He laughed and took a seat on the stool near the half-open front by the street. "Have you been trying your hand at making swords again lately?"

"I've been failing at making swords again lately, if that is what you mean." Elijah shoved the new piece of iron into the red-hot coals with a grunt and waited, pumping the bellows twice to fan them even higher.

William grinned. Standing there with his muscled arm gripping the handle of the large bellows above his head, Elijah looked just like his father on the day he came to Señor Moretti's. His face, though almost a decade older at the time, had been just as stern, determined, frustrated, driven, angry, and entirely fed up with the scenario around him just as Elijah was mimicking perfectly today. And still, with Señor Moretti's help, he <u>had</u> grown to soften that will during his time with him and became a much better man and father because of it. Probably much like the same process he would often use to create a fine blade, now that William considered it fully.

Could he do the same eventually for Elijah? He hoped so. If he could endeavor to be more patient with him than he had been with Charity... then maybe. "So, what made you start making these? I haven't seen anything this nice since I saw the blade your father kept over his fireplace back in Portsmouth. I believe he said that one was his father's, but it was truly magnificent, Eli, like something made for royalty almost."

"Yes, but this one was all Thomas' idea, or rather my father's in the first place, I suppose. I don't know." Elijah placed one hand on his hip and threw his head back, exhaling slowly as he tied back his longer hair out of the way. "The truth is, Papa taught me how to do this years ago, but I haven't tried since, and now that I want to do it, I can't seem to remember all the steps."

"You will," William reassured him. "The talent is already in your blood. You just need to harness it and bring it out. It's also important to remember that you need patience to do it. Metal isn't like wood, Eli. You can't soak it and force it to do you will. It has to be coaxed gently and stretched out over time—not beaten into submission or it will crack or break."

"Huh... you sound like you have done this before." Elijah checked the iron in the fire and put it back in, as it was not quite as hot as he needed it.

"Oh, no, not in the least. Your father just told me that particular piece of advice years ago, actually. When we first came to the Colonies, I used to sit here for many hours watching him. I didn't have a job back then or really anything useful to do at the time, so I watched, and he listened. We were a good pair." William folded his hands in front of him and smiled at the memory of the countless hours he had spent sitting on that very stool, observing Elijah's father before William had received his position at the hospital. Well before Emile and Emma had returned from Charleston. And certainly before he had met Charity Bentham. In fact, he had longed so many times over these past three years for a talk with Sebastian once more even though he knew it would never occur.

He could have certainly used his wisdom and candor yesterday during his sleepless night that was for sure. William nodded at his inner comment, then snapped his attention back to reality suddenly as a tremendous realization hit him square in the face. *Sebastian would have told me that I was that same piece of steel* *that needed to be stretched out and molded as it was tempered away from its original state into something much more effective. Despite what I have been telling everyone <u>and</u> myself, God wasn't torturing me with Charity all of this time. <u>He</u> was using <u>her</u> to mold me into a finer blade.*

"Sebastian... you're absolutely right," William whispered to himself and swallowed hard as he realized once again how much wisdom the man had given him that seemed to cross the barriers of time just when he needed it most.

"And what can I do for you today, Uncle William?" Elijah walked over to him and waited patiently, obviously not noticing his contemplations or his recent comment.

"You are doing it right now actually." William chuckled lightly and tried to compose himself away from the lump that would not leave his throat at the sudden revelation. "You are distracting me from the inevitable punishment that is waiting for me soon enough, I suppose. That and I would like to borrow your wagon if you can hitch it up for me."

"Sure, why don't you come with me now while the metal is heating up." The two of them walked then to the small lean-to barn and attached corral behind the forge and worked together hitching up the team of horses he kept on hand to the buckboard wagon already waiting in the barn. "I'll need it tomorrow to pick up a load of metal that arrived yesterday, but you can have it all night if you require it."

"Thank you, Elijah. I will be sure the horses are fed properly afterwards, and that they are back by morning." William climbed up into the buckboard and was about to spur the horses towards the farm to go check on the children when a rider galloped past them at a full run towards the store and brought his horse up short at the hitching post outside.

"That doesn't bode well," Elijah said with sudden concern.

"No, it doesn't. On second thought you had better grab your coat and gloves, Eli. I am afraid you are going to need them." William watched as the man down the street ran into the building and then returned a few moments later with several other men who came back out after him, each running in a different direction. "Hurry, Eli!"

Without another word, Elijah came out of the forge, jacket in hand, and climbed up into the wagon beside him as William drove it down the street at a fast clip.

"What has happened?" Elijah yelled to the man waiting there when they had arrived and the last button of his coat had been fastened.

"The coach has rolled down the embankment by the falls...just out of town..." The man gasped; a long trail of fresh blood falling from a cut along his forehead.

"And the passengers?" William grabbed the leads tightly, afraid for what the man might say next and tried not to breathe for as long as he could manage to keep himself from being unnecessarily distracted.

"I'm not sure. I think one of them is beneath the carriage, the rest..." The man swayed on his feet, unable to continue.

Panicked that the man might faint where he stood, William called out to a random man passing by them on his left, "You there!"

"Um...yes..." The scared man answered back meekly, uncertain why someone was yelling at him in the first place.

"Take that man over to the hospital and tell them help is needed by the falls!" William commanded as he turned the wagon around. "The two of us will go see what we can do until they can arrive."

"Yes, sir!" The pedestrian ran over to the injured man who had rode into town with increasing alarm and steadied him as they walked arm-in-arm over to the hospital.

With a jolt they were not expecting, the team of horses then took off down the street, spurred on by William's powerful slap of the reins upon their backs. If the accident was even a tenth as bad as the man had just explained, time was of the essence now, and as dangerous as it was to proceed so quickly in the storm that was obscuring the view of everything around them, William knew they couldn't afford to waste a single second.

All along their way, passing people and other wagons moved quickly out of their path with a shout whenever they encountered them as William directed the horses skillfully out of town, undeniably grateful each time that none of them impeded their progress.

"You are going to kill us, Uncle William, if you don't slow down!" Elijah held on tightly to the side of the wagon for dear life, second guessing his decision entirely to have even gotten up into the wagon at all today with him, let alone loan it out.

Totally focused on the road in front of him, William ignored him. The falls were a good five miles outside of Philadelphia at least, in an area that lay along the main road, thick with pines and overgrown with other coniferous vegetation even in the winter. And as dense as it always was, it would be only too easy to miss a turn anywhere along the way in this weather with the sleet that fell this morning, not to mention the danger the overspray from the falls would cause upon the already packed snow. Many travelers avoided that area during the winter, especially for that very reason, but for some idiotic motive, the driver must have thought the route safe enough to travel on. Either that, or he did not know the true danger of it in the first place.

Whatever the reason that had served to spur his actions in taking that ill-advised route, in William's opinion, it had been foolishly chosen and horribly inept. His only hope now was that no one would have to pay the ultimate price for their driver's poor decision.

That Charity would not. He let the thought play itself out again in his head and flicked the reins even harder. "C'mon boys, just a little farther," he encouraged them as he wiped away the accumulating moisture from off of his face.

Obedient to the last, the horses raced on against the winds and driving snow even though the storm picked up considerably once they had reached the edge of town. The half-collapsed buildings that Emile had called an eyesore just last week had served to dutifully shelter them from the worst of it within the city proper but now that the two of them were exposed to the harsh gusts of the open countryside, they pelted them with almost blizzard-like conditions.

"Can you see anything at all?!" Elijah asked, sheltering his eyes from the stinging crystals that attacked him as he peered towards where there should have been a road.

"Not anymore, can you?!" William slowed the horses down to a considerably slower trot and then stopped them altogether as he tried to get his bearings and find the road again.

"Not a thing! Everything is just... white... everywhere!" Elijah brushed away the piles of snow that had been sticking in his curls and continued to scan the horizon.

"Well, they can't be much farther! I saw the post for Whitemarsh's farm just a mile ago! The bridge should be somewhere here on our left; I just know it!" William yelled over the howling wind.

"Look! There it is! And there's the coach, Uncle!" Elijah grabbed his uncle's shoulder and pointed to an overgrown area over to William's left before he jumped down from the wagon, grateful to be out of that carriage of death, if only for a few minutes. After what he had just experienced, he would definitely think twice before loaning it to his uncle again, no matter the reason. If he wanted to risk <u>his</u> life, that was up to him, but Elijah had seen enough adventure today to last him a lifetime, or so he hoped.

Eager to find Charity and make sure that she was alright, William jumped down, as well, and practically ran over to the embankment, leaning far over the edge itself to inspect the scene. To his relief, Elijah had been exactly correct, for there, not fifteen feet down, near the ragged shore of the half-frozen river lay the battered remains of the coach and the scattered belongings of its unfortunate passengers.

"Lord, no…" William swallowed hard, instantly fearing the worst.

Then, in the snow-deadened silence around them, a man's cries for help echoed back to them from beneath a tree somewhere halfway down the ravine.

"Come. We have to help them, Elijah." William's instincts sprang into action as he attempted to climb his way down over the broken tree limbs and tangled boughs, clumsily hoisting himself over them until he reached the area where the man's calls had sounded. "Hello?"

"I'm here! Help!" The man's cries sounded more desperate now.

"I'm coming." William rounded the end of the long tree and found him at last under a tall birch. As far as William could tell, he was mostly unscathed and only mildly injured, though the bulk of the tree still lay securely on top of him. "Can you move?"

The man shook his head and looked down at the tree across his leg. "I've tried, but I'm stuck."

Allowing his mind the chance it needed to jump from one idea to the next, William surveyed the tree both from the top and from the bottom before calling back up to Elijah. "Can you tie the rope that's in the back of the wagon to one of the horses and throw it back down to me?"

"Sure!" Without a moment to lose, Elijah ran back to the wagon, looped the heavy rope securely to the largest of the stallions and tossed it back down the steep incline towards his uncle, watching as it landed mere inches from his grasp.

"Good!" The doctor reached up the muddy embankment and grabbed it before wrapping it several times around the medium sized trunk and tied it off as tightly as he could manage.

"Now heave, Elijah! Heave!" He yelled up to him as he watched the tree shift just enough afterwards for the man to remove his leg from underneath it with a yelp.

"Ho!" William commanded Elijah to stop and untied the rope once he was free and had moved farther uphill from it.

"Can you manage it from here? My nephew has a wagon up top if you can pull yourself up," William inquired, grateful that the man, who appeared to be in his early fifties, was looking far better than the one who had arrived into town with the news.

"I'll try." The man nodded while shivering greatly.

"How many more were in the coach, sir? I am assuming the man who rode back with the horses was the groom."

"Yes, Robert managed to jump clear before the coach rolled. It's the only way he made it out unharmed," he tried to explain, though it was abundantly clear to William that the whole ordeal had left him entirely shaken by the experience.

"I wouldn't say he escaped injury altogether, but he did make it into town to bring aid." William helped him stand but then held him by both of his upper arms so as to help him focus more clearly on the information he desperately needed. "How many more were in the coach, sir?"

"Just a woman the same age as yourself, a younger girl about fifteen and her brother. Though I haven't seen any of them since we crashed."

William's heart fell. "Alright. You climb up to the road. I'll look below for them. No doubt others will be arriving shortly."

Still too stunned to object, the man nodded and grabbed onto several of the tree roots to pull himself up until he reached the top with Elijah's help.

William, however, left him and the safety of the hanging rope as he slid his way down the rest of the embankment another ten feet, until he reached the bottom then made his way over to the detached door from the left side of the coach that lay on the ground just before the river. Sadly, beneath it lay the remains of the young man the driver had spoken of earlier, only this patient was far beyond William's or anyone else's help. From his open eyes that stared directly up into the falling snow, William knew without checking that the life behind them had already expired. With a labored sigh, William closed the man's eyes respectfully and continued on in his search of the wreckage. "Charity! Charity Bentham!" He called once, then louder again when nobody answered.

"Will... William?" Beneath the sound of the rushing water passing next to him, a small whimper, so faint that he almost did not hear it, came from the opposite side of the coach.

"Charity!" William gasped in relief and ran around the back side of the overturned coach before splashing headlong into the foot deep, icy water. "Charity!" He almost collapsed to his knees at seeing her as one half of her body was completely pinned beneath the coach at the edge of the river, while the other half was still feebly struggling to keep herself up from drowning.

"Elijah! Help me!" William screamed in panic while reaching down to support Charity higher to get her out of the water. "I'm here, Charity. Don't give up yet."

As cold as she was, Charity could only mumble something slightly incoherent but allowed him to hold her without protest.

Still waiting near the road up above, Elijah scrambled down the embankment and froze when he saw the woman trapped beneath. "What do you want me to do?" He stood by his uncle's side, incredulous as to how either of them were going to help in this kind of situation. They were only two men, after all, and the coach probably weighed a good 500 lbs., if not more. Neither was there enough rope up in the wagon to possibly reach this far, even if they <u>could</u> use the horses to help.

"Here, take my place and hold Miss Bentham just beneath her arms. You'll need to wrap yourself securely around her back to lift her safely when I tell you." William looked over at Elijah and beckoned him towards him with the top of his head.

"Lift her! How am I going to lift her, Uncle? We can't move this coach!" Elijah argued vehemently against him but followed his uncle's orders to the letter.

"That is precisely what we are going to do!" William climbed to the other side of the woman and crouched down in the icy waters to place his right shoulder and back against the top edge. "Now, when you feel it move at all, pull, Eli. Pull with all you are worth and let's pray this works!"

"If you say so." Elijah's head bounced in acknowledgement and with a yell of intense exertion, William lifted the heavy coach an inch and then two more, his face and teeth gritted firmly into a tight line of focused strength.

Utterly stunned, Elijah's eyes widened in disbelief at what he was seeing, but just as he had been instructed, he tugged on the woman with all his might, then slid her free before William dropped the heavy wooden coach with a loud crash after, sending sprays of water in every direction.

"She's out, Uncle!" Elijah yelled triumphantly as he fell backwards into the icy current with a splash from the sudden momentum.

"Elijah!" William's heart froze, fearing he would have to save him next, if he didn't move quickly. "Get up, man! Get out of the water as fast as you can and up to the wagon before <u>you</u> freeze now!" William ran over to Charity and lifted her up easily out of the rushing current but struggled as he carried her back to safety through the water and slippery ice.

"How did you do that!" Elijah gasped, his body starting to shake all over the higher he climbed. "That coach weighed more than three men put together, maybe four."

Totally consumed with Charity's quickly declining condition, William looked down at her and tried to focus on not jostling her too much as he climbed. "Adrenaline, Elijah. Simple science," he huffed in return.

"Science my foot, Uncle!" Elijah pushed past him and climbed up the hill first to reach down from the top to help William with his load.

"Can we talk about this later?" William panted under the strain of carrying Charity up the steep embankment and the cold seeping through his clothes with every step.

Elijah didn't answer, instead he just moved over to the wagon and held the horses to steady them while his uncle placed Charity safely inside.

"What about the girl, Charity? Did you see where she went?" William rubbed her hands together within his own and took off his scarf to wrap it furtively around them. He would have happily given her his coat too, if it would have helped, but it was already far too soaked to be of any benefit to her whatsoever.

Charity shook her head, her teeth chattering against her purple-blue lips. "I th--think sh-she she is st-st-still insi-i-i-de the c-c-c-oach-ch-ch."

Another wagon and several more men rode up to them then as they spoke and dismounted, several others brought blankets and quilts over for the wagon for them to use as they huddled within it for warmth.

"Is that everyone?" A large man with a beard as thick as Saint Nicholas, though not as white, walked up to William and handed him a fresh pair of gloves.

"Thank you kindly." He put them on instantly as he shook his head, aware that his now damp hair was already freezing solidly against his head in places. "There is one more in the coach, I believe. Though sadly, her brother has already passed."

"Can you make it back into town on your own?" The man asked him gruffly while sizing up the man and his companion's condition.

"I'd like to boast that I could, but the three of us are frozen through, I'm afraid. We had to fetch Nurse Bentham from out of the river before you arrived. Do you think you could spare one of the men to drive our wagon? My nephew can ride in the back with the driver." William pulled both of his arms around himself and tried to contain whatever warmth he still had left.

"Jacob, leave your horse with me and drive them back into town. I'll see to the girl," he directed easily, clearly the leader of their expedition. "You can help Jacob up front, sir. It will be hell otherwise to stay on the road in this blizzard without someone else to help guide."

The man who was obviously named Jacob walked over to their wagon and climbed up into the driver's seat before picking up the reins.

"Can you make it a little longer?" William said softly to Charity, cupping her trembling cheeks with the woolen gloves on his hands to slightly warm them.

"D-d-do I have a-a-a ch-ch-ch-oi-sssse?" Charity tried to smile back, but the convulsions from the cold stopped her.

"Not really. We could build a fire here first, but I don't think it would be wise to wait." William wrapped the quilt around her wet body as best as he could and passed another one over to Elijah. "Cover every inch of you that you can. This wind will burn you if you don't, if it hasn't started to do so already." William climbed up awkwardly onto the front seat and looked back at the young man over his shoulder before adding, "I don't want to be the reason why you cannot lift a hammer for the rest of your life. Do you hear me?"

Elijah nodded several times or shivered; William wasn't sure which. Either way, he obediently opened the blanket with his shaking hands and wrapped every part of himself that it would cover before huddling down protectively behind the bench of his wagon like a child hiding from his deserved punishment.

Chapter Thirty-Eight

November 29th, 1811

Without another word, off the wagon flew almost as fast as the way it had come, only this time Elijah was grateful for the haste in which it had travelled. From his more sheltered location behind the driver, time passed so fast now that it seemed to be flying just as quickly as the wind blowing against them. With mile after passing mile, thick trees turned into shorn fields, which then transitioned into taller buildings as they reached the outskirts of town.

Yet it was only when Elijah began to see familiar landmarks jutting out of the almost fog-like atmosphere of the snowy squall that William called over it to the driver, giving him the instructions he needed as to where to drop them and the wagon off before taking the coach's driver to the hospital. The man who had been assigned to help them had not truly understood why William would not want every one of them taken to the hospital directly, along with the injured driver, but seeing no harm in his rather unusual directions, he did not argue with him in his condition.

Pushing the horses even harder, they arrived less than ten minutes from the time that they had entered the city limits to the moment that the wagon pulled up to the corner house with its warm candlelight shining brightly onto the street without. Exhausted by the harrowing adventure they had just endured, the horses both shook their heads wildly in protest as Elijah crawled out of the back of the wagon and trudged over to the door of his uncle's home before pushing the unlocked door brusquely open with his shoulder and falling inside.

"Bles-ss--sed fff---ire!" He practically yelled with delight as he stumbled five feet across the wooden floor inside then collapsed against the back of the settee, using the piece of furniture to hold himself upright. Suddenly grateful beyond words for the intense warmth of the fireplace that struck him forcefully as he entered.

Nathanael, who had been still waiting for his friend's late arrival, was busily heating up the kettle for some warm apple cider in the kitchen but practically jumped when he saw Elijah stumble towards him half-frozen.

"Elijah! What on earth has happened to you!" Nathanael rushed over to the young man and began peeling every piece of ice hardened clothing from off his body, frightened at what he might find underneath.

"C-c-c-oa-ch-ch-ch ..." Elijah tried to articulate the story but could not. In his decidedly chilled state, every last inch of him felt as stiff as the ice that clung to his clothes, making it nearly impossible to move even his hands to help his uncle strip off the many layers, much less stand on his feet fully.

"Is your uncle with..." Nathanael began to ask further but stopped as the man in question stepped through the entrance next carrying Charity's stiff body and kicked the solid wooden door closed behind him with his heel.

"Nathanael, we need the tub brought out here to the fire. And I require blankets, lots and lots of blankets." William laid Charity on the settee by the fire and began taking off her heavy overcoat, her upper bodice that went over her white blouse, her shoes, her long stockings, even her heavy overskirt. Yet nearly every layer he encountered was practically frozen solid and a struggle to remove.

Elijah, who was still shivering terribly, though slightly less so now, managed to grab the dry clothes tossed to him by his uncle from the bottom of the stairs and moved to the kitchen to redress. "What c-can I d-do?"

"We need to heat up as much water as we can and fill that tub. Charity needs to warm up slowly or it will send her body into an even greater shock." William pointed to the large cast iron pots laid out already by the fireplace. "You can put the largest one on first then fill all the others and whatever other pots you might find in the kitchen right on top of the coals. I know we normally hang them over the flames, but it should help them heat up faster this way."

"Good idea." Elijah nodded and used the blanket he had been wearing to dry his hair before dropping it also into the pile of semi-frozen clothing discarded by the door as Nathanael bounded down the stairs just seconds later with William's medical satchel, a leather pouch of some kind and a stack of assorted quilts and wool blankets.

"Thank you," William said gratefully, aware once again how well the man seemed to read his thoughts. "Elijah, can you find me some new clothes? I don't care what, just so long as they are dry."

"Sure." Elijah ran up the stairs two at a time and returned with a black blouse and khaki breeches from his uncle's small wardrobe.

"Will these do?" Elijah held them out to him.

William nodded before stepping behind the settee to do the same as Elijah, for he was already feeling stiff and sluggish by the exposure, as well.

"Is anyone going to tell me what happened?" Nathanael brought the metal, upright tub William always used into the room with the help of Elijah and placed it carefully in front of the fire, then began pouring the first of many kettles of steaming water into it. With a silent prayer of thanksgiving, he also expressed his gratitude to God that He had motivated him earlier in setting some to boil for washing his clothes, then prayed for what all of them wanted, Charity's complete restoration.

"The coach from Washington went off the road by the falls. Three survived. One did not. Another was still missing when we left," William explained briefly as he shed his overcoat, suitcoat, pants and shirt before putting on the dry set Elijah had brought him. As hurried as he was to tend to the woman in front of the fire, he didn't bother putting on more as the floor by the entryway was already quickly puddling up from the wet clothes that had quickly warmed to the temperature in the room around them.

"William..." Charity groaned helplessly on the settee beside him and moved her head slightly in his direction.

Grateful that she was now sounding even remotely coherent, William stepped quickly around the piece of furniture and felt the sides of her face and arms. Both were still as ice-cold as before, with the consistently worrisome purplish hue. As warm as the house was inside from the large fire blazing brightly next to her, he had hoped by this point that she would have recovered more before he had been forced to proceed further in undressing her, but clearly, she had been in the water for far too long already to avoid it.

"Charity, can you hear me?"

Not a single muscle moved now, nor a sound was heard in response to his pleading.

"Please, I need you to at least open your eyes for me," William begged next to her, his face merely inches away from her own.

Not a single eyelid even twitched to show any recognition.

Feeling utterly defeated by the knowledge of what he knew must be done next, William groaned inwardly. "I'm sorry, but I have to, Charity. Hopefully, you will forgive me later for this, though I highly doubt it." He felt the deep sense of regret wash over him again for all the many things he had said to her that might never be forgiven, then pushed them all back farther away from his mind so that he could focus on her fully instead.

Unwilling to waste another moment debating a decision that he knew was the right one, William worked methodically on the task placed in front of him, as he lifted the covering quilts he had laid upon her, before respectfully removing the other remaining wet pieces of clothing but chose to leave the clinging cotton white shift and matching bloomers underneath before cradling her into his arms.

"This is not going to be pleasant, Charity, but I <u>have</u> to do it." He pursed his lips in reluctant resignation as he prepared himself to do what he had been trained to do above all else, yet Charity still did not stir, nor did she seem to protest at all against whatever it was he was about to do next.

In the time that it took for him to draw in a sharp breath and hold it, a hesitant flicker of indecision flashed across his eyes as it mixed with the fear that was threatening to choke him. "God, I need her... please," he prayed, his whole being calling out for God's intervention as he drew nearer to the water.

Finally resolved that this was the only way possible to help her, he exhaled it out again and reached down to place her gently within the warm water before holding her there as she finally reacted and pulled away with a whimper from the pain the water caused.

"I'm so sorry... I know it must burn." He stroked the side of the woman's face to comfort her as he poured some of the hot water over her neck and head to warm her more quickly.

Attempting to give the woman every respect she so justly deserved, Nathanael looked the other way and handed William a large linen towel from the stack he had already placed upon the table.

"Thank you." William looked up at him gratefully and tucked it around the woman's small frame to cover her better in the water. "I wasn't sure what else I could do, Nathanael. She's almost frozen through as it is."

"You do what you must, William. Let God sort out the rest later." Nathanael nodded in understanding. "Now Elijah... would you like some cider or some warm stew? I happen to have both ready and waiting. And we should probably see to some warm water for those hands, as well, and maybe a little liniment." He further drew his attention towards the food waiting in the kitchen.

"Stew would be fabulous, Uncle," Elijah replied with a grin and flexed his fingers on both of his hands. "You know, I think I just now realized that I haven't eaten since lunch."

Amused by the totally mundane conversation taking place next to him, William chuckled. "I haven't eaten since yesterday."

"Yes, but doctors don't need to eat it seems." Nathanael laughed back at him, trying to do something that would distract Elijah and himself from what was happening on the other side of the room.

"They do. They just forget to," William added and continued to pour warm water over Charity's chest and arms. For five full minutes, he repeated the action again and again, and the low groan that had been the only sound she would utter since she was placed in the tub now lulled itself into a quiet murmur. Yet even in that, she still had not managed to open her eyes.

Reaching down into the small pouch Nathanael had given him, William pulled out just one of the small bottles and held it up to her lips, encouraging her to swallow. "Charity, please... I need you to drink this," his voice betrayed just a hint of the pain he was enduring at her desperate condition.

This time she obeyed tentatively to his command, and by the time that she had finished it, the paleness in her cheeks had pinked up slightly.

"That's right... drink, Charity." He gave her another bottle and waited as her breathing picked up more and her head fell back comfortably against the edge of the tub, no longer needing his support to remain upright.

Intensely curious after what he had seen earlier, Elijah watched everything his uncle was doing from the kitchen counter but said nothing. Neither did Nathanael, as he subconsciously knew from the moment they had entered tonight that their secret was going to come out eventually.

"Can you hear me now, Charity?" William coaxed and rubbed her arms gently all the way down from her shoulders by her neck to the very ends of her fingertips to encourage the circulation.

Charity tried to nod in response, but her neck still lacked the strength it needed to remain stiffly secure. In fact, the motion of her trying to keep her head upright only made her look a little bit like a child's rag doll, if he were to be totally honest. "Stop fussing, William... please."

Thrilled that she was now talking, too, William reached down and slid his hands up and down her leg from just above her knee to her ankles, massaging the muscles as he went like he would for any other patient in her condition. "Can you still feel this?"

"Yes, ouch!" Charity winced at the last and almost cried out. "I think that leg might be broken or at the very least greatly bruised."

Alarmed, William instinctively moved his hands lower and felt around her left ankle as he ran his fingers all the way up her leg to her knee before shaking his head in relief. "Not broken thankfully, but you are right about the bruise. I can see the deep purple on your shin through the water already."

"Do you have any more?" Charity asked politely this time. "My head is still spinning wildly, and I can't seem to focus on anything you're saying."

William took another bottle from the bag and held it up for her. "I'm sure it is probably disconcerting to experience it, but at least you're coherent now. So, I would call that a win."

"Sort of..." She swallowed again and this time was able to take the bottle from him at the end and manage it for herself. "You have no idea how cold that water was, William, or how long I had been lying there before you came," she said with an exhausted sigh as she handed the empty container back to him.

"I can only imagine. Elijah and I only got a short taste of it and even then, I don't think we could have stood it much longer than we did," William assured her and reached behind her head to help her draw in the bulk of her long, wet hair to the front.

"Is that where you found her? In the water, William?" Nathanael asked, clearly shocked that she had survived such an ordeal. "It is freezing out there!"

"It's colder in the water, I assure you, Uncle." Elijah took a bite of his stew and swallowed. "But don't worry, Uncle William is strong enough to lift coaches it seems and who knows what else," he replied sarcastically while glancing over at William from across the room, but not in fear or with the cautious skepticism William had half-expected, more out of an awed reverence than anything else.

"I <u>did</u> say later, Eli." William sighed in apprehension, knowing that the moment he had dreaded for the past eighteen years had finally arrived. "Do you want to know everything now or just enough to satisfy your curiosity?"

"Curiosity? Uncle William, what you did today far exceeds the definition of that word any day, and you know it." Elijah crossed his arms across his chest and shook his head incredulously. "Besides, I think anyone would be astounded by what <u>I</u> saw."

Feeling instantly guilty for the position she had obviously placed him in, Charity looked up at William from within the tub and clasped his hand beneath the water, holding it close to her covered chest with her back to the rest of the men gathered. "I'm so sorry," she whispered quietly, feeling a great sense of responsibility for what may possibly occur.

"Don't be," William replied without any remorse whatsoever. "I'd do it all over again if I had to." He fixed his gaze completely on the woman in front of him, then asked, "So what's it going to be Eli, the complicated version or just the raw facts?"

Elijah only stared back at him for a few moments to consider his answer, then cocked his head to the side closest to his other uncle before replying, "I don't think you need to tell me everything, not yet anyways. To tell you the truth, I have suspected for years that the three of you were different than everyone else I've met."

"Huh, what made you think that?" Nathanael leaned his waist against the counter casually and stared down at his mug of cider, carefully fingering the edge of it with his finger and thumb.

"Well, let me see if I get this right. You never go out in the sun unless you are wearing those ridiculous cloaks, which both you and I know must have been intolerably uncomfortable in all that heat last summer. Then there is the fact that you hardly eat anything when you come over for a meal, though I can tell that you try to make it look like you do. Not to mention the very <u>interesting</u> detail that the two of you look <u>exactly</u> the way you did the day I met you back in Portsmouth and <u>that</u> was almost twenty years ago, Uncle William. No one ages that well, not even Uncle Emile." Elijah leaned back against the counter triumphantly and waited for him to deny it.

"Is that <u>all</u> you have noticed?" William stroked Charity's fingers beneath the water, a calmness coming over him by the soothing motion of the water beside her skin.

"That depends. Who else is what you are? I am assuming Miss Bentham by the sheer insanity that you were willing to risk showing me who you were to save her. Emma too?" Elijah asked as easily as if he were discussing their business dealings at the warehouse, much like the straightforward manner of his father.

"Yes, and Emma," William answered just as easily, no longer interested in keeping up the previous pretense. "She became one of us the day Hope was born, but not before."

Suddenly feeling the same shocking revelation that William had experienced earlier that day in front of his forge, Elijah stopped for a moment and threw his head up at the ceiling above, laughing but not laughing, before turning back to his uncle across from him. "My father was, too, wasn't he?"

Nathanael and William both nodded solemnly.

"<u>That</u> was why he left us for that year! And here I always thought it was something <u>I</u> did! I spent <u>years</u> trying to make myself enough for him to never leave again." Elijah shook his head in amusing frustration.

"He stayed away to protect you, Elijah. Not because he did not love you," Nathanael explained simply. "In the end, he finally realized it was not the best decision for his family and returned when he was able."

"It was <u>never</u> your fault at all. He was stronger than the rest of us, but too afraid of losing all of you to risk hurting his family," William added with absolute understanding now. "As hard as it was for him to be away, you were worth the sacrifice."

"Incredible." Elijah smiled quickly and huffed as if the weight on his shoulders that he had been carrying for years had finally been lifted.

"So where does that leave us, Eli?" William asked him tentatively as he settled, unsure just how much more he needed to share with the young man to satisfy his interest.

"What do you <u>mean</u> where does that leave us? Except for the fact that my uncle is some kind of superhuman, how does that change anything? Unless you are worried that I am going to ask you to do all the heavy lifting for me at the forge from now on." Elijah finished his bowl of stew and set it in the basin for washing, then crossed his arms across his chest casually once again.

"It changes things a great deal," Nathanael declared without explanation as picked up his empty cup and added it to the wash tub, as well.

"I don't see how. Does the rest of the family know?" Elijah countered quickly and took a seat in one of the nearby chairs at the table.

Hesitant once again to be the one to deliver the unsettling news, William glanced over at Nathanael before answering, "A few... your mother has known for years and Hope does, too, but she was told only recently."

Surprised, Nathanael's eyebrows lifted immediately at his unexpected admission, but he did not move to comment.

"Well, I don't think you should tell Jedidiah. He never did like those mythical stories Mama used to tell us. Said they gave him nightmares. Me, I couldn't care less. I thought they were all pretty interesting," Elijah mused confidently, and William could see the boy he once knew was peeking out again from the young man's smile.

"I think that is very wise, but what about you?" William prodded further.

"What about me?" Elijah folded his hands and placed them behind his head as he leaned back comfortably in his chair.

"Can you keep our secret?" William tightened his hold on Charity's hand and felt her respond in kind.

Glancing up at the ceiling for what seemed like an eternity to everyone else in the room, Elijah thought briefly for just a moment, then turned his gaze back to both of the men before replying, "The way I see it, nothing in my life has changed at all. You are still Uncle William and Uncle Nathanael, and you always will be. I don't need any more explanation than that. But please... stop wasting all the pie at supper. It's killing me watching Mama throw it all away just to be kind."

"Deal." William chuckled at the added humor, for he knew Elijah was doing it mainly to make them all feel less stressed. "And thank you, Elijah. That means a great deal. Though, yes, you can have all my pie in the future."

"Mine, too. But I do get to eat the soup. Emma is a very good cook," Nathanael complimented her easily.

"That she is. Well, now that I have finally thawed myself out, I had best get back to the forge and close up shop. The fire has surely gone out by now, but my tools still need to be put away. Or was there some other life-altering confession I should know about?"

"No, that would be more than enough for now, Eli." William grinned and tilted his head in his direction to drink in his expression.

"Good." Elijah stood and pushed in his chair at the table. "Oh, and I should probably go find where that man has left my wagon."

"I'll go with you, Eli and help with the horses. Besides, I'd like to see what you have been working on over there. Now that I think of it, I don't think I have set foot in the forge in probably five years at least." Nathanael picked up his thick coat and gloves before handing an extra coat over to Elijah.

"Will I see you tomorrow, Eli?" William asked over his shoulder as the two men reached for the handle of the door behind him.

"Tomorrow? Well, I don't know. Are you going to turn into something crazy like a butterfly before then?" Elijah quipped with an entertaining smirk.

Totally amused by his playful analogy, William rolled his eyes at the absurd suggestion, feeling the compelling need to offer one of his own in return, one that he knew would get a rise out the man. "No, not a butterfly. But what do you think about bats?"

"Completely terrifying." Elijah shook his head, still not impressed.

"Maybe he'll turn into a bear, if he doesn't decide to eat soon." Nathanael eyed the half-full leather pouch and nodded knowingly towards it. "People who do not eat are cranky. Remember Emile?"

"Hah, I remember it well," William assured him. "I had to share a room with him back then, didn't I?"

"That man can snore like thunder, Elijah. Be grateful that we do not," Nathanael explained seriously. "Do you need anything from the hospital for Charity, William? I can stop by on my way back if you do."

"No, I think I can handle it from here, but thank you," William answered.

"Alright. Then I'll see you tomorrow," Elijah said quickly, and the two men shut the door behind them, leaving William and Charity alone in the relative silence of the room behind them.

As long as the day had been, the wind and snow still continued to blow fiercely outside, continuing to blanket the whole city in a thick covering of downy white, but the crackling fire in the hearth inside made it seem less formidable somehow to the two people within.

Feeling the last of the adrenaline that had been keeping him going for the past hour slip away, William closed his eyes and exhaled slowly. In every way imaginable, his body was thoroughly spent beyond comprehension, but even with that knowledge, he was still incredibly grateful that there was nothing today that he had been forced to let go... not Charity and not even Elijah.

With a slight tremble to his hands that spoke also of the emotional stress he had placed his mind through to accomplish it, he ran his fingers through his wet hair and tried to pull it back completely away from his face, taking just a moment to fully collect himself once more.

"That was incredibly generous of you. Not many men would have risked having to give up their lives and everyone that they loved just for someone like me." Charity looked up into the clear blue eyes of the man before her and wondered what thoughts were hidden deep within them that she had yet to discover.

"Like you?" Surprised that she would even think such a thing, William let go of her hand immediately and reached over to brush a piece of her wet hair out of her face, before tucking it gently behind her ear with the others, feeling more than a little bit grateful for her recovery. "I'd give up more if it meant you not dying. You know that, right?" William closed his eyes briefly and felt ashamed once more. "Though from what you have experienced recently, I fear I have not made that very clear, have I?"

"No." Charity blushed and snuggled deeper under the surface of the warm water. "But is that the real reason why you came? Or did you just come to rescue me?"

"I do seem to do that a lot with you, don't I?" William smirked slightly and the pleasure it felt to release just a bit of the stress he had been carrying with him felt intoxicating.

"Wait a minute, let's not forget that I had to save you, too, on at least one occasion." Charity grinned right back, remembering the day she had brought him his cloak on the sidewalk.

"How <u>could</u> I forget? I seriously almost died that day for real that time." William played with the surface of the water for a minute before glancing back up at her, "But no, that is not the only reason, though it <u>is</u> a very good one, don't you agree?"

Charity nodded, then added more hesitantly, honestly afraid of what might be the true answer to her question. "Then why did you do it?" She reached forward and drew his hand closer to her once more, placing it within her own beneath the water.

"Why, indeed..." William chuckled, then cleared his throat, suddenly realizing the very intimate situation they had now found themselves in.

Awkwardly conscious of it, as well now, Charity scanned the room around her nervously but then turned her attention back to the man in front of her, her mind entirely focused instead, on the one question that had been plaguing her since Emile had asked her days ago to return. "<u>Are</u> you still angry with me?"

"Am I still angry?" William shook his head incredulously, disgusted with himself for the many things he had said to her on so many occasions. "It seems like I have been angry a lot lately, though for all the wrong reasons."

"Yes... yes, you have." Charity reached up with both hands and drew her wet hair around in front of her to the opposite side closer to the fire, wringing out the remainder of the water before pointing to the blanket on the settee. "I think I have warmed up enough to manage standing now, William. Can I have that?"

"Of course." William turned around obediently and picked up the oversized quilt then held it up high in front of her before shutting his eyes respectfully until she had taken it from him.

Then, turning around once again away from her to give her a little privacy, he faced the paintings on the wall behind him and waited. "Can I get you anything else that will make you feel more comfortable? Nathanael said there is some cider maybe."

"No, thank you. But I highly doubt you have another dress anywhere on the premises."

"Ha... most decidedly not." William laughed at the sheer humor of the statement. "But I <u>can</u> dry yours out by the fire while you finish thawing." He began picking up her wet clothing that had been discarded on the floor beside them and moved around her to hang them closer to the fire. It would take several hours or more to dry them out enough so that they would be wearable to go back to her home, but at least she would have the proper attire when she eventually left.

"Here." Charity handed him both of her drenched stockings and her favorite cape in turn.

On the surface, the action should have been totally embarrassing, humiliating even under any other circumstances as these were her inner and outer garments, after all, but after what she had just endured, none of that seemed to really matter in comparison, or at least not in that way. To the two of them, these were simply the actions they did at the hospital with one of their patients and not the more intimate discovery that two people might enjoy in another circumstance.

Continuing to ignore everything sensitive about the entire process he was steadily performing, William took each of them discreetly from her, then reached for her hand gently to stop her from walking away, thereafter, sensing the sudden need to pull her nearer to him, blanket and all.

From the moment that he had seen her lying there in the river, his whole being had been crying out to protect her in every way that he possibly could. Yet now that the danger was effectively over, he could no longer stand enduring even a second longer without her touch or her necessary closeness beside him. "To answer your previous question, Charity... no. I am not angry with you. Despite what I have said and done, I do still love you, Charity Bentham, and I know now that nothing short of Heaven or Earth is going to change that for me. Not even you."

"Are you sure?" Charity gazed up at him, afraid, or rather uncertain if the man would be able to keep his promise this time.

"Absolutely." He kissed her hand lightly and drew closer. "You have my word, both for today and forever on that account, I assure you."

"But William, you must believe me that I didn't tell your family to force you into any of this." She took a breath and paused, her expression becoming even more serious and yet also disappointed, as she was almost certain that if she said what she needed to say right now, it just might end whatever chance she ever had with the man who was holding her so lovingly. "Though I feel that I must tell you that if you were to ask me now if I would do it all over again the very same way... even if meant losing you altogether... I can't lie and say no... because I would," Charity said the last three words with a calm assurance that came from years of continually fighting to be worthy enough to be validated and yet also with the consumingly deepest regret she had ever felt in her life, clearly hoping once and for all that she could make him understand.

"But why? Why did you come when you knew I would hate you for it?" William let go of her hand and started to step away, intending only to stoke the fire higher, and not to leave her entirely as she so quickly assumed.

"Hate me?" Charity almost started to cry by his words and his sudden absence. "That is a very strong word for doing something that you <u>know</u> deep in your heart was the right thing. You just won't admit it."

William sighed and closed his eyes, wishing he could go back and change many things about their past conversations together, chiefly being his selfish necessity to be respected by her more than his desire to give her the love she so desperately needed. "That may be so, especially when I obviously cannot make rational decisions concerning the care of my family." He shook his head in defeat. "But in that same light, I still can't get past the idea that this gift of ours is dangerous, too, if not cautiously heretical to use it."

"Heretical?" Charity stepped back slightly in confusion.

"Yes. I just don't feel that it is my right to play God, Charity." He looked over at the woman who looked as beautiful to him soaking wet and unguarded as she did pristinely attired in the hospital. "Neither is it yours. If we are to survive together, we can't keep hurting each other in order to help others. That means that we simply <u>have</u> to reach a consensus between us that we can both agree to."

"I understand." Charity reached out to him once more and drew him back closer. "But William, consider this... you give your patients medicine, correct?"

"Yes..."

"You use treatments created by others that heal even though at one time they were also deemed heretical. How is this any different? I dare say if more people knew what we could do, they would be begging for our help, not condemning us," she tried to reason with him in a way she had never done before.

"Maybe." William nodded thoughtfully, then quipped expectedly back, "Or they would be burning us at the stake as demons. You forget that not everyone accepts what we have become as easily as Elijah just did."

"Not everyone... or not you?" Charity bit her lip, hoping she had not pushed the man too far once again in her reasoning.

For several long moments, William couldn't help but just stare at her as he contemplated the truth she had just uttered, then spoke slowly and quietly as he thoughtfully replied, "When I told myself years ago that I wanted a marriage of equal minds, I had no idea then that it also meant being open to equal opinions. On the surface, I suppose I was only looking for someone I could share a common interest with, but what I found was something infinitely <u>far</u> more valuable. You. You, my beautiful, endearing, funny, sarcastic, irritating, condescending..." He continued to list off every emotion she had ever brought out in him, the good and the bad, before he was stopped by her sudden and impetuous kiss. A sweet, enduring, everything he had ever dreamt about for weeks kiss.

Forgetting everything else he had planned out so faithfully to say to her today in his epically rehearsed apology, or so Emile had sarcastically called it, he pulled her into his arms and held her tightly, knowing that from that day forward he would never let her go again.

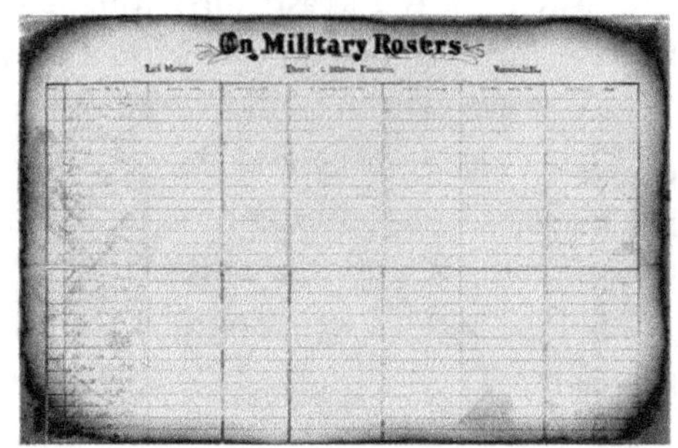

Chapter Thirty-Nine

Thursday, December 19th, 1811

"Almost noon already and I haven't even made a dent in this pile it seems," Emile tsked in displeasure at what felt like a never-ending load of work today, then sat down at his desk and picked up the correspondence the courier had delivered earlier that morning, intending to finish at least one of the items in the stack before heading to the café to meet the others. From what he had been told by the man who had left them, the paper on top was supposed to be the list of the possible state militiamen. Which meant that it only lacked his approval before the actual commissions would be sent out.

Yet even with the seemingly urgent nature of the simple request, Emile had little interest in reading it. After all, the war with England might never be declared in the first place, making the reasoning behind troubling himself with approving soldiers for such a possible battle rather pointless.

Scanning the names quickly from the top all the way down to the bottom, he saw many men that he knew and several others that he did not, which was to be expected. Most of these documents they sent him were senseless hazards of his profession, but every once in a while, on the rare chance there was always something... he paused as his gaze fell upon one very notable name in particular. One that had <u>no</u> business being on this document, or any other that might cross <u>his</u> desk other than the morning post.

"Martha, hold all my meetings for the rest of the afternoon. I am going out," he said respectfully to his secretary seated outside his office and folded the document into quarters before striding quickly out of the room, hat in hand.

When he assumed his position as the state representative to Congress two years ago, he had finally accepted, though rather reluctantly, that all men had the right to make up their own minds about their political beliefs, but this man on the list did not. He was too young, too inexperienced, too naive to have even considered it in the first place.

The change this man wanted <u>was</u> essential to life. That much was true. But careless decisions of this kind were unwarranted—dangerous even, if the consequences were higher than the reward.

Stopping at the café around the corner from the government office where he had made a reservation earlier that morning, he took his familiar seat inside by the large window that faced out onto the street and waited for his friends to arrive. With Christmas only a few days away, the café was filled to the brim with paying couples and families, all seated in every nook and cranny. From the back of the spacious room where the large fireplace sat, completely adorned in thick cedar boughs, festive ribbons and dried orange slices to the smaller tables and chairs that were spaced out in an odd circle of sorts, every inch of the room emanated the joy from everyone that was eager to take in just a moment of the peaceful charm the establishment provided.

Yet despite his sudden haste to escape his office and go somewhere where he could think more clearly, he found that he was only a mere twenty minutes early. Though with the way he was feeling now, he almost wanted to skip it altogether and march right on down to sort the man out before he made any <u>other</u> plans without his consent.

"Would you care for some tea, coffee, or cider, Mr. Deschamps? Or maybe, since it is very close to Christmas, might I suggest some festive hot chocolate?" The tall waiter, who very much reminded him of an older version of Michel, asked him after he was seated.

"Coffee please, with double cream and sugar this time, I think." Emile took off his hat and set it carefully next to him, making sure he would see it and not leave it behind like his father had done on so many occasions in the past.

"Right away, sir." The waiter left without another word and returned minutes later with a steaming cup of the richest smelling coffee Emile had ever encountered. "As you ordered, double cream and sugar." He dutifully set the drink onto the wooden table before him and moved to leave.

"I'm sorry, but is this new? It smells excellent." Emile lifted the cup and breathed in the steam, savoring the acidic blend with hints of vanilla and some kind of nut.

"Yes, just in this morning, actually, and all the way from Italy I am told. We used to serve that French kind you always like, but with the blockade outside of port, it has been harder to get it. Will this still be acceptable?" The man who had served him on many other occasions inquired patiently.

"It will do very nicely. Thank you." Emile took a tentative sip and smiled. Strangely enough, there were few things he loved more in this world than his wife, his adopted daughter, his friends, a warm fire while watching the sun set, and a large amount of vanilla cream in his coffee or tea. Though this time, he might have to add another delicious item to the shockingly long list.

"Emile, you're early!" William stamped off the snow from his boots at the doorway and made his way through the maze of tables over to him, paying careful attention not to slip on the moisture accumulating on the smooth wooden floor under his feet. "I thought Nathanael might beat me this time, but I see _he_ is the one who will arrive late. Sadly, that is usually my lot."

As if almost hearing his name beckon him, the door opened once more behind William and in walked Nathanael, shrugging off the snow from his black cloak and hat. "It is really coming down today, isn't it?"

"Quite." Emile gazed out the window beside him and watched as several teams of horses passed by pulling their sleighs and passengers. "It's looking more and more like Christmas every day by my view."

"Yes, well, speaking of Christmas..." Nathanael began the first topic of conversation after taking his seat opposite Emile at the table. "Charlotte has asked me to invite all of you for the festivities tonight."

"You can count me in. It has been all Samuel and Holly have spoken about for weeks. That and what will happen when they stay at Charlotte's after the wedding." William smiled and sat down next to Nathanael. "Believe it or not, I think this may be the first true Christmas those two have ever had. Not that I am judging their parents in the least, but whatever they did before makes our celebration look like something straight from royalty in comparison. I don't mind, of course, but it _has_ been nice seeing this time of year through their eyes for a change."

Emile chuckled. "I rather like the evergreen boughs, cranberries, and dried fruit that the people here hang around their homes. It makes the whole house smell like a wonderful kitchen and a lush forest all at the same time."

"It is a pain to hang up though, let me assure you. Sticky sap everywhere." Nathanael grimaced at the recent memory . "It took me the better part of two days to help Charlotte with the lot of them. Still, it made her happy, so I didn't mind it so much in the end."

With a slight nod towards his drink and a raised hand, Emile motioned to the waiter to bring the table two more cups of coffee and then casually stepped into the next series of awkward questions awaiting them. "From what I hear from Emma lately, it seems that you have been spending quite a lot of time over at the Fabbri's. Do you think you have formed any kind of special attachment, yet? Or is it a bit too soon to speak of freely?"

"Well..." Nathanael pursed his lips, then smiled slightly, unable to hide his true emotions about their relationship. "It isn't what I had with Elsie, but there is definitely more than a comfortable friendship brewing—something neither of us quite expected to tell you the truth. Still, it may be a bit too early to desire anything beyond that for a while, or at least not until we have sorted out Michael and Hope's wedding first. Though what I <u>can</u> say is that we very much enjoy each other's company at present, maybe a little more than we should."

"I certainly hope so, Nathanael, since you are contemplating marrying the woman," William chortled quietly, partially in jest and partially in a veiled declaration of the absolute truth Nathanael was obviously still trying to hide.

"What? How did <u>you</u> know?" Nathanael seemed utterly shocked that his friend would know something so intimate that he had not breathed a word of to anyone, except in his prayers.

"I overheard you talking in your sleep the other night." William attempted to hide his amusement over the man's apparent shock. "But what I really want to know is how will you both explain the apparent age difference when someone undoubtedly asks? I mean, we all know that you are nearly the same age, give or take a decade, but to everyone else you will start to look much more."

"That is a concern, I'll grant you. But a marriage of convenience has often been looked upon wisely by many over the centuries. I see no reason why people can't think the same of us here in Philadelphia for a time, maybe even a decade more wherever we may choose to move on to later. Beyond that, I try not to look any farther. Our lives change enough as it is to do otherwise. Besides, having our relationship legitimized by marriage will protect her from the scrutiny that comes with widowhood, and I can help them on the farm when it is needed, too. Although I will say that in many ways, we are the same, she and I. Or at least where it matters most. She lost Sebastian, and I lost Elsie. But yes, I do care for her very much, indeed," Nathanael tried to explain his very detailed reasoning behind their recent decision to join forces.

"Well, I think it is high time you were not alone in this world, Nathanael. So, I'll not stand in your way." William smiled as he looked over at his friend. In fact, it was the same smile that had not left his face for almost a month. Or rather, it was the same incorrigible grin that appeared every time he thought about drawing one more day closer to his own wedding with Charity.

"Nor I. Marry the woman, Nathanael, before someone else scoops her up before you." Emile drank at least half of his coffee, feeling the immense satisfaction that normally came when things in their lives seemed to be finally falling into some semblance of order. "And what about you William? Are you ready for Sunday?"

"It can't get here soon enough, Emile." William tried to drink his coffee but found it incredibly difficult to do so today as he struggled to control the muscles in his face long enough to accomplish it. "I'm sorry... but I just don't think I have <u>ever</u> been <u>this</u> happy."

Emile and Nathanael both looked over at each other and smiled.

"Good, because 'cranky William' was intolerable, as was 'insolent and angry William', as well," Emile stated aloofly and raised both his eyebrows at his friend in total condemnation before chuckling lightly. "It was all I could do to stand you."

The other men laughed along with him.

"No, seriously, William. It really <u>was</u> quite awful," Nathanael added and drank some of his coffee, at last. "Hey... this is new."

"Yes, from Italy I am told." Emile finished his coffee and set the cup near the table's edge to be collected when the waiter passed by.

"Mmm," Nathanael took another sip with pleasure. "You'll have to find out what ship it came from, William, and get some more. It is very delicious!"

"Yes, it is." William took a taste of it once more and swallowed. "So, on another topic, I <u>did</u> have a small favor to ask of you, Emile."

"Hmmm?" Emile glanced over at the man but was truly looking just beyond him and thinking once again of the name on the list in his pocket.

Suddenly confused by his distracted state, William tipped his head down and studied him as he tapped his fingers patiently on the table while he waited for his full attention, knowing that if he did not, he would only be repeating it all again in a minute.

"Alright already, William! Spit it out, man. What do you need me to do?" Emile blurted out, increasingly frustrated once more, though not at William, at all, more out of a deep disappointment of the position that was consistently thrust upon him.

Surprised now by his sudden, emotional response, William hesitated, concerned even more so about the reason behind it, then framed his thoughts carefully before speaking, "Would you be willing to walk Charity down the aisle,

Emile? I know it is a lot to ask, but you are the closest thing I have to a brother here, and I simply could not see anyone else doing it."

For a few moments Emile appeared slightly taken aback by the unexpected suggestion, then recovered nicely. "I'd be honored... truly. Or..." He paused before adding more mischievously, "I can be the one who remains readily prepared to help the poor lady escape. From the books Emma likes to read, I hear many brides are overly anxious on their wedding day."

Alarmed, Nathanael almost spurted his coffee at the comment onto the table, then appeared suddenly nervous. "Please don't. I can't bear another week of 'out of his mind happy William' either. I need a 'happy medium William' in order to survive."

"Indeed." Emile chuckled at the very idea.

"Well, speaking of said lady..." William let the sentence drop off before continuing, "You might be interested to know that Charity and I have that in common, too."

"What?" Nathanael appeared equally shocked.

"Her family is a little closer in line to the King than mine own, not that it really matters as neither of us will be stepping into those shoes any time soon," William replied with a slight tip of his head towards the window, not seeming to care the least bit about whatever remained in that world behind him.

"Might help the embargo, if you could," Emile muttered sarcastically.

"There's a thought," William countered right back. "With King George a raving lunatic now, his son seems to be creating enough havoc of his own to make up for his father's insanity."

"Truer words have never been spoken." Emile nodded and glanced back out the window at the snow that was falling peacefully now.

"Will I have to call you Lord when I say your name in the service on Sunday?" Nathanael inquired seriously, as if making sure he was doing everything according to traditional protocol this time.

William shook his head and laughed lightly. "Lord? No... that title is reserved only for the Earl's first son, so until my brother relinquishes his hold on this Earth, I am still just William Harvey Wells the doctor. But you <u>will</u> have to call her Lady Charity Emeline Bentham. A duke's daughter keeps that title no matter how many brothers or sisters she might have."

"Marrying up, I see, William." The corners of Emile's mouth turned upwards at the humorous thought as once upon a time that had been his own intention. "Bravo."

"Hardly in that sense, but yes in all the others. Though you should have seen her face when I told her. 'What? You're a lord?' She said in disbelief. To which I replied, 'Is that a problem?'" William tried to repeat the conversation in the same tone of voice they had each used.

"Even Sarah called Abraham 'Lord', William." Nathanael educated them quickly. "So, in that light, it only makes sense."

"Oh, she would have loved that!" William laughed loudly and almost snorted, then pleaded again more earnestly, "Please don't give her <u>any</u> other ideas, Nathanael. I am hanging on by a thread as it is."

"No, please do, but she will probably say, "I don't think so, *Monsieur*," Emile quipped with increasing diversion in the same way she might have said it.

Unable to control themselves now, they all laughed together so hard that tears were forming at the edges of their eyes, drawing more than a few other customers to chuckle along with them. For several minutes, in fact, the three of them could hardly contain themselves, before one by one, they all fell back into a quieter composure.

"But seriously, William, who would have thought that two people so much alike as the two of you are in your background, in your profession, in your lifestyle, would end up eventually together a world away from their birth? It is nothing short of miraculous to even consider it." Nathanael marveled once again at the Divine arrangement of it all.

"They almost didn't." Emile looked back at his friend across the table, his mind entirely distracted by the paper in his pocket that was now burning against his chest.

"Yes, we almost did not. Thank you, Emile, for your intervention. I will be forever in your debt." William finished his cup of coffee and set it carefully next to Emile's. "Though I never <u>did</u> get to give her my speech."

"Oh, you'll use it someday." Nathanael chuckled once more. "Knowing the two of you, I am sure we haven't seen the last of the rows between you."

"Surely not. And why don't we call it a debt finally paid. I think at long last we may be even," Emile suggested.

"Maybe... or until the next time." William raised his eyebrows quickly and smiled.

"There is <u>not</u> going to be a next time, William. You've gotten me into enough trouble as it is. No more travelling in boats with you, <u>now</u> or <u>ever</u>."

The two men who sat across from him smiled and the three all laughed again at the light-hearted banter they were enjoying on such a festive week.

"So, will Charity be able to make it tonight, too, William?" Nathanael asked once more and finished his coffee, bringing them back to his initial question when he had arrived.

"I think so," William said quickly. "She normally has tonight off at the hospital."

Lost in his own world again, Emile pursed his lips but did not answer, contemplating instead what he was going to say when he next saw Hope.

"Uh-oh, I've seen that face before. What is wrong, Emile?" William cast him a worried glance. "Something has been eating at you since the moment we arrived."

"Fine." Emile sighed and pulled the piece of paper out of his pocket before handing it over to William, not wanting to look either of them in the eye, for he was not sure just yet where he stood on the matter.

"What _is_ this?" William scanned the list of names, then stopped. "Oh, never mind... I know precisely what it is." He handed the document over to Nathanael who made the same face when he suddenly saw the unmistakable name, only this time, he let out a low whistle, too.

"And you are probably not in favor of this, are you?" William asked tentatively, knowing the answer to his question before he ever said it, yet he still felt compelled to ask it anyway.

"I am not sure what that idiot was thinking when he signed up in the first place. Doesn't he know that he could be injured or worse, leave his new wife a widow, mourning him for the rest of her life? I picked up the pieces once in her lifetime, William. I don't know if she will live through it all again." Emile swallowed hard and tried to hold back what he was really feeling.

"Well, they aren't married yet, Emile, at least not for another few months. Besides, he may never be called into service at all, despite how passionately he might feel about the British right now," Nathanael tried to reason with him and lessen his indecision on the matter.

"With his determination, he will be the first in line." Emile looked at him darkly but would not budge an inch on his position.

"He's just a boy, Emile. Don't you remember what you were like at that age," William tried to soften his mood.

"I was _never_ like that at his age." Emile took the paper seriously and folded it back up before placing it once more into his inner pocket.

William laughed at his lie once again. "No, you were probably worse."

"Alright, I concede just a little on that point." Emile shook his head and smiled, though not genuinely. "But I also didn't have a wife at home to worry about."

"You're right. You probably had three girlfriends, instead." Nathanael quipped just as quickly.

The muscles in Emile's jaw flexed several times in the silence thereafter before he looked up at them once more, his brooding melancholy coming closer to their humor. "It's almost as if we've known each other for centuries, gentlemen."

"Truth once again." William regained his more serious composure and dug a little deeper, trying to understand his particular point of view. "All joking aside, why <u>don't</u> you want him to serve his country? Aren't <u>you</u> doing the same?" He hesitated and studied him from across the table. "I know it is different for the rest of us, but America means more to that boy any day than you or I or even Nathanael."

"<u>I</u> am expendable, gentlemen. <u>He</u> is not." Emile paused, then closed his eyes, knowing that he was going to have to allow it, even if it was against his better judgement to do so.

"I think Emma might have something to say on that matter, if we were to ask her." William tossed his head back and fingered his inner pocket, searching for the correct change for the coffee.

"No doubt. But I fear that the two of you would be disappointed once again, as she most certainly shares my conviction on <u>this</u> matter. Ever since Sebastian died, we have made it our sole purpose to do whatever God deemed necessary to take care of Hope and many times that meant doing what must be done, no matter the cost was to us personally."

"I am sure that must have been very challenging." Nathanael sympathized. "And something you seem to be handling very well, I might add."

"Only barely sometimes." Emile picked up the hat beside him and pondered once again on a thought that had bothered him the past month, or at least ever since he had given Michael his permission to put that engagement ring on Hope's hand. "I know I have asked you both this once before, but <u>have</u> I truly changed all that much from the man who was conscripted so many years ago? I <u>think</u> that I have, but then there are times where I know I have not. Or better still, have I <u>at least</u> done enough for the better to outweigh all the sins of my past, or am I just returning to the same world over and over again, expecting a different result?"

"The fact that you are concerned enough to ask that question proves that you have, Emile," William answered him honestly. "But how long will you feel the need to keep track of Michael's actions?"

"Huh... someone has to," Emile answered gruffly. "And especially so when I see things like today's list."

"But for no other reason?" Nathanael asked him curiously. "I know Michael has been a handful, but that is to be expected when two people are as passionate as they both are. Though I must say that the man, though very young, does remind me many times of you, I suppose."

Emile grimaced and shook his head slightly, though he knew Nathanael was correct in every word that he had just uttered. "Maybe. Though Emma says he is much like Hope in her feisty devotion to whatever cause is presently in front of her."

"Sounds like Sebastian, too." William placed the fare for the coffee on the table and watched as Emile did the same, followed by Nathanael.

"Yes. I can still remember the look on his face when Señor Moretti said he had lived in that castle for 300 years. The man wanted to practically explode. Even I was scared." Emile laughed lightly and stood up, motioning for the others to join him outside. "And the way he looked at me when I entered the room that day. Icy daggers would have described it perfectly."

"If looks could kill, you'd already be dead again, Emile." William put both his gloves on once more and tapped Emile's forearm before holding the door open for Nathanael to pass. "Though between you and I, I would have paid good money to see the expression on your face when you woke up alone on that floor."

"It wasn't the one with which I am looking at you today, that much I can assure you. In fact, I almost did not even join you at the table at all. I heard everyone talking, or rather waxing eloquently about everything we had become, and all I wanted to do was leave. Nothing in that room interested me more than going home. Or at least not at first." Emile looked back at the café windows behind him, watching those inside sharing the same conversations they had all just enjoyed, then slowly smiled. "But then I heard William's voice, and I knew I could not leave, not immediately, anyways. We had made it that far together and something about our time on the ship made me want to stay a little longer."

"My clever wit, no doubt," William said dryly with a smirk.

"No doubt." Emile rolled his eyes. "Or maybe it was because of your great seamanship."

"Ha! I almost vomited on you then, too. Be grateful it was only on the floor that time," William defended himself once more. "How was I to know my stomach hated the sea?"

"You know, William, on a slightly different subject, I never did ask why you chose to remain as a doctor. With all the money from your family, you could have done anything you wanted after the shipwreck—toured the whole of Europe, started your own enterprise, or anything else your heart so desired. Why did you choose something so incredibly difficult, knowing how much you would be tempted in it?" Nathanael stared back at his friend curiously. The snow that had been falling steadily for hours slightly blocking his view, even though it had tapered off to a delightful bit of flurries here and there. As dense as it was before, it was not enough now to accumulate much more, but was sufficient, instead, to create a perfectly festive backdrop for the carolers outside the church across the street.

Following his gaze, William looked at the building where in just three days he would finally have everything he had ever dreamt of and more and contemplated the answer to Nathanael's deep question. "For me, being a doctor is not just about knowing what the right thing is to do when I help people who are ill. It is about making yourself sacrificially available at any given hour, for any desperate purpose. It is setting your wants and wishes aside for the greater good and knowing that when you finally lay your head down at night or morning, which is more often the case, that you are doing exactly what God has called you to do." He looked back over at Nathanael with deep admiration and cherished friendship. "It is a little like what you do, Nathanael, isn't it?"

Nathanael nodded solemnly. "Just minus the daily temptation."

"Yes, minus the temptation." William nodded. "But to answer your question, I chose to stay with you because I knew beyond a shadow of a doubt, that you, Nathanael... <u>you</u> needed me more than I needed you. And <u>God knew</u> that <u>I</u> needed <u>you</u> much more than I thought I needed anyone."

Nathanael smiled, then looked over at him sincerely. "It <u>has</u> been a long road, hasn't it?"

"Not really, friend. It has been a wonderful journey. A journey that I would take all over again in a heartbeat if you asked me to, and I would not hesitate to look back for an instant." William placed his arm around the man's shoulder. "You were never a sacrifice whatsoever. You were a purposeful choice, and I don't regret a minute of it. Not for all the riches in Christendom."

From a few feet away, Emile watched the two of them together and began to regret very much the time he had missed without them. Or rather, how different his life might have been had he never returned to France at all after the wreck. If he <u>had</u> stayed, he would have most likely never met Emma, but still... he looked away, trying to maintain his composure at the disappointing thought, however futile.

"Emile?" William glanced over at him. "Don't think for an instant that there has been anyone more important in my life than you. Your friendship has been the one thing that has kept me grounded the most since the very beginning. But you should also know that God put you in that cabin for a reason, too. So, I guess in a way, you were more <u>His</u> prisoner than England's."

Emile nodded and held his lips back tightly. "We have become quite a pair you and I—two people, worlds apart, yet joined together faithfully in one purpose."

"Yes, keeping Nathanael alive," William jested.

"Yes, indeed." Emile laughed, though William and he both knew that it was less of a joke and more of a reality. "But you kept <u>me</u> alive, too, William. You fed me with hope when I came to you after the revolution and gave me the space I needed to accept what was to come."

William nodded. "And you taught me to see... well... see the real me. I think in many ways, you might know me better than I know myself at times."

"I feel the same," Emile agreed easily, feeling the most content that he had ever felt before. "Now, if the two of you will please excuse me, I have this paper to sign and get back to the office and then presents to buy for Père Noël."

"Are you still going to have the children put their shoes out by the fireplace on Christmas Eve?" Nathanael asked curiously, remembering all the years his friend had deposited small gifts inside of them for Sebastian's children the night before Christmas.

"Of course!" Emile said boisterously and spun around on the street with a smile and a wink. "And don't you tell them otherwise. Children need a little magic in their lives, after all."

"Go already! And hurry back, Emile! I'll see you tonight!" William waved. "And don't forget... Sunday... right after the morning service. Don't be late!"

"But William, don't you know? The French think it is fashionable to be late every now and again," Emile called back to him from almost twenty feet away.

"Not on your wedding day it isn't!" William yelled in return and tried not to show how concerned he suddenly felt now by Emile's comment.

Without another word one way or the other, Emile simply tipped his hat and turned around before waving back at them while he rounded the corner.

"C'mon, Nathanael. We are <u>not</u> going to let that man outdo us again this year." William grabbed Nathanael's elbow and tugged him towards the General Store down the street.

"What on earth are you up to, William?" Nathanael tried his best to keep up with him.

"Christmas presents, Nathanael. Lots of them!" William's blissful smile quickly returned and the two of them practically ran like schoolboys down the street, stopping at store after store to buy small trinkets and toys the two children might like, as well as many other things for their friends.

With the music of the carolers floating all around them in the wind, and the light jingling of the bells ringing softly from the sleighs as they passed, William and Nathanael both knew that this was going to be the best Christmas of their existence, for every second of it was already filled with joy, friendship, expectation, and most of all, love.

Chapter Forty

December 25th, 1811

"Merry Christmas, Darling." William kissed his wife softly just once as he lay awake in bed, waiting for the sun to finally pour in through the upper window just enough to brighten the room and reveal her beautiful, golden hair once more. It had been three days since the morning of their wedding, yet he still had yet to get used to the fact that he never had to tell her goodbye ever again. Nor, quite humorously, would he ever need to figure out what he was doing for every single moment of his day either, for that matter. But that incredibly unimportant fact had not occurred to him until yesterday at lunch.

Or to put it more accurately, it might be more appropriate to say that Charity was a very diligent planner—a wonderful example of all that was good in the world of sequence and order, who truly delighted in making sure every need was allotted for before anyone had to ask. In fact, before he married her, he had often thought that <u>he</u> had been terribly exact in his ways of doing things at the hospital, almost to the point of being outwardly annoying to some of the staff at times. Yet watching her the day before their wedding, making sure the children had every single belonging they required for their stay at Charlotte's, drew him to a total amazement of her own special gift that far surpassed his any day. Or maybe that was yet another reason why they had gravitated towards each other from the very beginning.

Maybe... William smiled and moved a long, wavy spiral away from her face slightly so that he could view her delicate features better, then suddenly frowned.

There <u>was</u> still one problem that he had yet to address. Something that seemed far less pressing than everything else he should probably do to arrange things in their home to accommodate her needs, but also something that worried him probably more than the rest.

How <u>was</u> he going to be able to hide his slovenlier ways regarding the upkeep of his clothing? Not to mention the haphazard storage in his overly full closet that was heaped to the brim already with decades worth of his medical journals and various mementos? A closet that she might adamantly require once she had time to finally unpack the three trunks of clothing that had arrived before the wedding, along with her other personal effects.

Maybe I can have Elijah build some shelves in the living room for the books and store the rest elsewhere? William pondered the prospect out mentally but found himself chuckling when Charity practically hit him in the face with her free hand to push him farther away.

"Go back to sleep. It's too early," Charity groaned quietly beside him, nestling herself deeper underneath the warm quilts and sheets, but more importantly, away from the chill of the house around her.

Leaning on one elbow next to his mostly sleeping wife, he traced a single line down her slightly darker toned arm before wrapping his fingers within her own and holding her closer still. "We need to get up, darling. It is well past nine, already."

"No, we don't," Charity protested grumpily with a growl of disapproval. "It's my day off. I've earned it, so go...a... way...."

William snickered and thought very seriously about never moving another inch away from her for the rest of the day just so he could watch her. "Where do you think you are right now, Charity?"

"Trying to sleep, that's where, and my annoying roommate keeps waking me up." Charity pulled the pillow over her head in further demonstration of her total resistance and shoved him slightly away.

Especially humored now, William laughed again inwardly once more at how incredibly hard it was <u>every</u> morning to wake the woman up and reluctantly left her sleeping in the bed before getting dressed in his best pair of black breeches and white blouse. The very one he loved to wear whenever the occasion suited it, for it was far too fancy to wear on any other day. The absolute richness of the Sea Island Cotton fabric against his skin this morning sent ripples of happiness through him, as did the brown brocade vest that always accompanied it. Both had been gifts from Emile years ago during his stay in Charleston and William could not have been more pleased with his friend's purchase, even if he did have to save them for special occasions.

There would be other gifts today, as well, as it promised to be a wonderful time together with his friends, complete with games after supper, followed by carols together by the fire and then dancing. Though, according to Nathanael, that particular diversion always had to wait until well after nine o'clock due to some religious principle or tradition that he could never remember.

And yet, even with his friend's rule aside, William was quickly discovering that surprisingly enough, he could hardly wait. Like every other young man in his social class back in London, he had been diligently trained by several frustrated tutors over the years in the correct way to entertain a lady on the dance floor, as well as in the flawless execution of countless types of allemandes and minuets. All were the accepted standard of dance in those days, labeled as decidedly elegant movements that were often choreographed to a full string ensemble stationed somewhere in the room. But all of that was nothing compared to the reels Charlotte loved to dance with Sebastian and definitely far more temperate than anything Emile ever demonstrated. The bourree and gavotte both might have been the most lively dances in France during Emile's time, but they were certainly far from anything in William's comfort level to attempt without injuring someone.

Being the main form of entertainment at the time, balls were more plentiful back then, and dance cards were always meant to be filled with the names of all the most eligible gentlemen present, much like a list of would-be suitors in William's estimation. Though he had quickly found a way around that, as well. Since dancing as a whole had always been one of William's least favorite diversions, he often sought out whatever library the estate contained instead or located a secluded corner where he could steal away into and avoid the whole spectacle altogether if he could manage it.

Yet that being said... in <u>this</u> moment, with his wife sleeping peacefully in front of him holding more of his heart than he ever imagined possible, William could not think of a single thing he wanted to do other than that today. After all, he had never once danced with his wife and the prospect of doing so tonight made him smile just thinking about it.

Like so many other couples, the two of them <u>had</u> meant to do so at the meal following their wedding, but with all the guests they had needed to greet and the arrangements for the children that had seemed far more pressing to handle than something that was purely for their own enjoyment, they had not been given the opportunity, nor the time.

Then, as the day had drawn to a close, and the last farewell had been said to their friends, Charlotte <u>had</u> made him promise most fervently to at least try to arrive shortly before the noonday meal, if by not supper on Christmas Day. Yet sadly for them, it was quickly approaching that time already and promise or not, they were probably not going to arrive before lunch. The trip that would normally take them only a little over twenty minutes to travel across town in the warmest of days was most likely going to be a bit longer to navigate through the heavy winds and snow that began late last night, for no carriage would be available on Christmas Day or at least not one that did not cost a good part of their wages to hire it. Nevertheless, despite all of those details that could be adjusted here and there to accommodate whatever Charity needed, he <u>could</u> afford to let her sleep at least another hour if she wanted, maybe a little more if they were to arrive slightly later.

Newly wed as they were, it had not taken him long to realize that his wife would slumber until well into the early afternoon if he would let her, as she much preferred staying up through the late hours of the night to rising early any day. A habit that seemed to match his own in some ways as he often had trouble falling asleep at times, though always for very different reasons than he had currently now. That could all change when and Holly came back home to live with them next week, but he highly doubted it. As strange as it may seem in their little thrown together family of sorts, he might as well get used to being the only cognizant parent awake before the stroke of noon and sidestep that conversation for a later date. Or rather, it certainly wasn't anything necessary enough to delve into at the present for an alternate resolution, as happy as they both were.

With a lightness that matched the brilliance of the morning all around him, William skipped down the stairs, whistling a festive tune about holly and ivy at an uneven thump-tha-thump and grabbed several dry logs from the waiting pile to build up the fire, hoping that the warmer atmosphere would entice his wife into consciousness. For the bulk of the night before, they had spent almost the entire evening in front of it, sharing story after story about their favorite Christmas Days and memories of their childhood. Much like the way Nathanael and he had done on their first Christmas Eve together years ago. Yet when she had finally fallen asleep against his chest at last, he had lovingly carried her up to bed just as he did their dearest Holly after her bedtime story every night.

Young Samuel had often proclaimed on more than one occasion that he was far too old for such nonsense as what William often relayed, but he could tell from the boy's enraptured attention every night while he pretended to play with his toys, that the boy was still enjoying the stories of the North, Greek fables and Celtic legends, despite his dismal declarations otherwise.

In fact, it was the one thing William loved doing with them most of all after a long day at work. Why, just the thought of coming home, having dinner with his own family and watching them grow in his love for them overwhelmed him as much today as it had the very first night they had stayed together. Though not many people had managed to sleep that night either.

Having spent several weeks at Emma's after their parents' death, the children had a hard time adjusting to their new surroundings. But when Charity entered their world, all of that changed for the better, and he was grateful for it. Even if at other times he was also painfully reminded during their waking nightmares of the circumstances that had brought them to him in the first place.

How utterly terrible it must have been for them to lose <u>both</u> of their parents in an epidemic. And how wonderful it was for him to have been given such an unexpected gift. A rare chance at something he never would have been able to achieve physically on his own in this state.

And yes, though it was true that someday, they might be able to find one of the children's relatives eventually. He would be only too happy to have them both reunited with them once more, even if it hurt his heart today to even contemplate it. If Sebastian's death had served to teach him anything, it was that however possible that scenario might be, for the moment, he should simply cherish every minute he was given with them and strive to live up to the example he had been shown through so many others over the years.

Closing his eyes to thank God once again for each of the blessings in his life today, including those who were not present with him physically, William paused in his gratefulness when he felt his wife's loving arms reach around and hold him close. "You're finally awake, darling."

"Barely," Charity yawned. "Did we sleep at all, or did we spend the whole night talking?"

"You tell me. You carry on in your sleep like you are still awake most nights. Nathanael does, too, so I guess I am used to it. Though I <u>much</u> prefer your conversations any day over his."

"Why?" She rubbed her cheek against the soft material on his back.

"Let's just say that yours are... far more... oh, how can I put this politely... um... <u>colorful</u> in their delivery." William teased as he turned around and kissed her forehead. "Though we <u>will</u> need to leave in about an hour if we are to arrive for lunch as planned. Will that be enough time to get dressed, or should we postpone our plans until closer to supper? The children will be disappointed, I am sure, but I made sure that there were plenty of things under the tree to distract them until we arrive."

"No, an hour should be fine," Charity said with her head now laid against his chest, her loose, naturally wavy hair brushing lightly along the bottom of his neck as she breathed, tickling him in the process. "Merry Christmas, dear."

"Merry Christmas. The first among many." William rubbed her back gently, then released her. "How's this? I'll make our breakfast this morning while you get ready. Then we can open our presents to each other, if you like, before we go."

"My, so bossy all the time, my lord." She pushed away from him sassily.

"Why yes, m'lady. Always at your service." He bowed dramatically as he had been taught many years ago and walked over to the kitchen to start some eggs and toast.

"That's right, peasant. Fix me my coffee before I send you to the stables where you belong," she taunted right back before heading up the stairs to get dressed like she was nobility.

"Yes, m'lady. Coming right up." William put the kettle over the fire and returned to the kitchen to continue whisking the eggs. He had been right when he had asked Emile and Nathanael not to tell her about Sarah in the Bible, but that still had not stopped them from instigating their own form of mischief before the wedding. As a matter of fact, the first time she had called him that title yesterday, he had wanted to chuck his coffee at his friends just for starting such an irritating tradition behind his back without realizing how endearing it was quickly becoming. After all, once upon a time, he had signed up to travel all the way across the globe just to escape that kind of fate, and here he was... welcoming it now. "Lord and lady indeed, next thing you know, she will be wanting me to build her some kind of castle." William rolled his eyes at the very idea and added some fresh mushrooms to the eggs.

Although it <u>was</u> true that they never actually needed the nourishment of the food they always prepared rain or shine, the systematic repetition of doing the same daily rituals that had been a staple of their human lives did help to curb the insanity of their lengthy existence. In many ways, it was almost as if the simple mental exercise alone provided a stability all its own, though it did little to satisfy their actual cravings.

Glancing up at the wall across from him and the many portraits it contained, including the newest one of Charity and himself that he had drawn shortly before the wedding, he thought about his parents once more and how much he would have liked for them to have been at the wedding. His mother would have adored

Charity, if they had been given the chance to meet. Though he very much doubted such an event would occur on this side of eternity.

In every way, Charity was exactly what his mother had always wanted for him in a match. A lady of high society and stature that would elevate him by her manners alone. Which was true in a way, though William was more grateful that his wife was his equal in so many others, as well. Ways that mattered more than money and vastly more important than any title. In the truest sense of the word, she was his helpmeet both in the hospital and at home. And despite how much the complicated interactions between them had pained him, William had discovered that <u>she</u> had been the one who had pushed him the farthest towards being a better version of himself, and for that reason among others, he treasured her beyond expectation and comprehension.

"How fancy <u>is</u> this gathering today?" Charity called back to him from the top of the stairs, trying to maintain a conversation with him from above.

"If I know Emile, he will be positively resplendent, if that helps," William answered back and put the eggs in the pan over the fire while stirring them periodically to keep them from burning.

"So, the nicest thing I own then," she replied, despite sounding slightly muffled as if she was under some kind of cover.

"That about sums it up well, m'lady, and I <u>am</u> sorry. I know it is a bother for something with just family, but it's only one day a year."

From the several loud thumps on the floor and the countless footsteps moving about above him, William wondered if his wife was trying to find something at the bottom of his chaotically organized closet or fervently digging through one of the many trunks she had brought over from her apartment.

"Maybe I should just wear my wedding dress again and be done with it." Charity laughed lightly from the top of the stairs, the tone in her voice now hinting a bit of frustration. As careful as she was about literally everything in her life, she obviously was still struggling to find whatever it was that she was looking for.

Unable to control himself, William thought back to the captured image of Charity in his mind. The one created at the exact moment the doors had opened, revealing her and Emile, would forever be the last thing he would ever think of before he fell asleep every night. Moreover, just seeing his wife in her stunningly beautiful cream and gold wedding dress with its tiered and multi-layered skirt that complemented the sophisticated V-neck bodice, elbow-length sleeves and veil the had reached all the way down to the floor around her had sucked all the air sufficiently from his lungs, if not the entire room. So much so that it had taken him a full five minutes to recover from the moment enough to even blink.

Furthermore, as the ceremony progressed, Nathanael had steadily grown concerned at his assumed lack of attention and had finally felt the need to lean over and shake his arm to make sure he was still conscious when he had not answered his question during the vows.

At the time, William had no idea whatsoever that his friend had even been speaking to him, or what he had been trying to convey. The only thing that had been registering in <u>his</u> mind, at that moment and most of the ones thereafter, was how unworthy he felt to be standing there, and how thankful he was that she had finally said yes. The rest was purely semantics. A simple 'yes', and an 'I will', followed by a kiss and they were forever man and wife—never to be separated ever again, at least not in that way.

"Maybe not <u>that</u> dress... though I would happily see you in it every day if I could." William cleared his throat and tried to remember how to breathe again.

"Did you <u>really</u> like it? It took me forever to find the right fabric," Charity echoed back to him casually.

"Did I like it? It would be hard for a man not to like it, Charity." He steadied his breathing once more and pulled the eggs from the fire before setting them down on the counter to cool. "There are simply no words..."

"Good. I was rather hoping to leave you speechless."

"Well, mission accomplished. By the way, the eggs are ready."

"Thank you," she said sweetly, then entered the room once more dressed in a tightly fitted scarlet red dress with a cream, tatted lace collar overlay that wound around gracefully near the edges of her neck and fell all the way down to her delicate waistline.

Understandably stunned once again, William's mouth fell open at the mere sight of her, for he had never seen his wife in much of anything formal besides her normal uniform at the hospital and then, of course, her wedding dress.

Concerned by his overly quiet response, Charity used one hand to smooth out the few wrinkles still remaining in the skirt around her waist before timidly inquiring, "Will it do? I haven't worn it in ages, but I thought, 'it's Christmas, after all, maybe I should try something green or red'. If you don't think it will be suitable, I can go find another..."

"Will it do? Oh, darling..." William crossed the necessary few steps over to his wife and pulled her into his arms once more as he kissed her deeply.

"I take it that is a 'yes'." Charity smiled, enjoying very much the longing she always saw in her husband's eyes.

"A definite, 'yes'." William held her hand and felt the ring on her finger once more, the one that he had kept safely stored away on the rare chance that God might finally bestow upon him the greatest blessing of all.

"It _is_ beautiful William." Charity cast a glance down at their hands, then quickly interjected, "I forgot to ask... Whose ring _was_ it, William? Your grandmother's, or mother's perhaps?" She wove her fingers within his own and pulled him slowly over to the settee in front of the fire.

"Would you believe, neither?" William sat down comfortably on the familiar piece of furniture and guided her down to sit closely beside him. "Fact is, I went out and bought it the day after you first kissed me in this home."

"Really?"

"Yes," William admitted sheepishly. "I was walking down the street that day on my way back to the hospital and saw a small shop with many other expensive baubles and trinkets in its large window. Some were no doubt real and not paste by the very fine quality they portrayed _and_ their location farther back in the display to avoid theft. While others were more common items people might purchase like pocket watches and a few strings of pearls. Yet, off in the corner, almost completely hidden under a draped scarf of some kind, was this ring, in the most unassuming brown leather box. In the condition that it was presented, I doubt the store owner had any idea of its true worth, or it would not have been buried so."

"What kind of gem is it? A garnet of some kind?" Charity held it up higher to inspect it.

"Not even close. It's a rare, ruby Ratnaraj, a gem most often reserved for royalty."

"Seriously?"

"Um-hmm... Well as you might have guessed, before I could stop myself, I went right in and purchased it quickly before anyone else might discover it." William finished his rather long story and waited to hear her rebuke of his hasty decision.

Charity's mouth, however, fell open in utter astonishment, instead. "But you had no guarantee then that I would ever marry you. I know I certainly didn't."

"True." William played with the ring again, admiring how the red stones matched her dress perfectly in hue and quality. "But I knew. You drove me crazy..." He smiled in remembrance. "But I knew... or at least I dared to hope even then."

"Is that so." Charity stood up and walked over to the short table by the fire to pick up the two presents that had been placed there before the wedding. "Then do you also know what I got for you this Christmas, O Mystic Wonder?"

William chuckled. "I'm smart, but I am not _that_ gifted."

With a smirk that very much resembled one that William had seen on many other occasions, Charity turned around and handed her husband his present before taking her seat next to him with her own. "You go first. I've been dying to see if you like it since I wrapped it up."

"I'm certain I will, whatever it is. I'm not really that picky." William pulled on the twine and unfolded the paper surrounding the flat, wooden box before opening it. There within several layers of protective tissue lay what he would label as a rather dismal looking booklet that was held together only barely by its strings upon the worn spine. "Um, I'm afraid to ask, but what is it?"

"Open the cover, silly." She took the extra wrappings away from him to free up his hands.

"Alright..." William reached obediently inside and lifted the dark brown leaflet front to reveal the perfectly inscribed handwriting introducing the title. "_Exercitatio anatomica de motu cordis sanguinis in animalius,_" he read aloud. "By Mr. William Harvey, 1628," William gasped in surprise. "Where on earth did you find this?"

Charity giggled. "I didn't. Nathanael did, or rather his colleague, Mr. Armstrong, at the college did. Now, this is only on loan for the time being, but I was told that as long as it remains with you and is returned, should they ever have need of it, you are welcome to keep it in your collection, being his namesake and all." She paused before adding more appropriately, "That, and due to some kind of professional courtesy for delivering his son—both things enormously balanced the scales in your favor where they were concerned. Though I have it on good authority that this is exceptionally rare."

"It is." William shook his head in disbelief, for he knew most of the manuscripts and papers of the esteemed physician had been either burnt in the great London fire or confiscated by the parliamentary soldiers who had ransacked his home near Whitehall. In all of their destructive actions, it had mattered not that the doctor had once treated Charles I or that he was his close personal friend. All was taken and destroyed anyway.

"This _is_ the man you are named after, is it not? The one who studied how our blood flows and began the library at the physician's college." Charity set the trimmings aside to look over the manuscript with him.

"Yes, it is. He also presided over several witch trials, too, even if he never convicted any of them. But that aside, never in all my life would I have ever dreamt of holding something like this. I simply cannot fathom it." William kissed his wife's cheek, then went back once more to turning each page carefully as if they would crumble in his hands by the mere touch. "What we can learn from this, Charity!"

"Well, you'll have to thank Nathanael later, too. He was practically bursting at the seams with excitement when he gave it to me. I kind of hate that he missed seeing you open it."

William laughed. "Well, I am afraid that this book exchange has become something of a thing for the three of us. Or rather, it is a Christmas tradition of sorts that began the day I bought him the first book on the Vicar Of Wakefield. Though this gift far exceeds the other one by fathoms."

"Indeed," Charity answered with even more curiosity.

"And what about yours?" William nodded to the box sitting next to her on the couch. "Aren't you going to open it?"

"Of course." Charity rolled her eyes at the sudden imposition. "Yet, if I knew how pushy you could be, I might not have married you."

William shook his head. "There is no escaping it now, darling. You can't claim ignorance whenever it is convenient. Besides, you were <u>well-acquainted</u> with <u>that</u> fact far before we ever had our first real conversation."

"I could try," she muttered as she opened the box and placed a hand over her mouth to stifle her laugh. "A watch?" She held up the small silver pocket watch that could be hung on her blouse for easy access.

"When I saw it in the General Store, I thought it would be something very useful for you at work. Though at the time, I didn't know then what I know now."

"Oh?" Charity raised one eyebrow. "What is that?"

"That we either need a rooster, or a very loud alarm. Yet neither may be able to wake <u>you</u> in the morning," William quipped lightly and crossed one of his legs casually over his other before leaning back farther.

"That is not funny, and you know it." Charity shook her head and poked her husband playfully.

"Do I?" William closed one eye and cocked his head in her direction. "Are you certain? Because I hear roosters can make very good pets. Maybe Samuel can keep him in his room at night during the winter months."

"Stop..." Charity laughed. "I <u>do</u> love the watch though. Thank you."

"No, thank you. This is probably one of the nicest presents I have ever received." William closed the book and carefully set it aside on the circle table next to him before drawing his wife closer to him on the settee so that he could wrap his arms around her once more. "But all joking aside, I am so blessed that you married me, Charity. There is no one else on this Earth that I would rather spend the rest of my life with... no one else at all." He sighed happily and drank in the closeness the moment afforded them.

Feeling perfectly content, as well, Charity looked up over her shoulder at her husband, admiring the sharp lines of his jaw, his clear blue eyes and the comfort of his arms around her that made her feel protected even when she was angry with him. "Do you promise? There may be many years ahead of us to regret that decision."

"Well, if there are, I'll remind you each and every day of my love if I must, for I will never grow tired of saying it. I love you, Charity Wells," William pledged faithfully.

"And I love you, too, William... until my very last breath," she repeated the last line of her wedding vow just as ardently as before and turned towards him to look up at him once more.

"Til' my last breath," William repeated as if they were saying them for the first time, which in their case, they probably were, though with a much different intent than those shared within the chapel walls and with far more concentrated meaning.

Experiencing the same unexpected flush she had felt the day he had first kissed her here in this apartment, Charity turned her gaze away, suddenly feeling the need to change the subject before they became even more distracted. "Well, as you've said, we should probably finish those eggs if we are to leave soon." She moved to stand up, but he held her close, unwilling or unable to release her so soon.

"What?" She stared deeply into his eyes, trying to see beyond his actions to what he was really thinking, which was always much more than what she saw on the surface.

"Thank you for marrying me," William said finally with a voice thick with the emotion he had been carrying all morning.

"Of course, but why?" Charity touched his cheek, her fingers tracing along surface of his skin slightly.

"Because in marrying you I realize that I have been given the most important chance of all."

"Really, what chance is that?" She leaned in closer, feeling almost desperate now to be near him.

"A chance for everything I have ever dreamt and more, Charity Wells... so much more."

"I adore you, too." Charity melted into his arms once more, aware that there was nowhere else she would rather be ever again.

Feeling the warmth spreading all the way through him again at her simple touch, William leaned in closer and whispered something scandalously suggestive quietly in her ear. "I am sorry, Mrs. Wells, but I've suddenly decided that we <u>are</u> going to be late—fashionably... inexcusably... and appallingly late." He kissed her once more deeply and rose before reaching down and lifting her up to carry her back upstairs before shutting the door behind them with a flick of his boot.

Breakfast and Christmas, as wonderful as they were certain to be, were simply just going to have to wait.

Epilogue

Christmas Day 1811

Running around the great room with a squeal of delight Young Samuel played a form of disjointed tag with a very delighted Caleb close at his heels as the rest of the family watched on Christmas morning. As in years past, Jedidiah and Nancy had arrived shortly after breakfast, bringing their boys along for the family festivities, as well as some gifts and a full platter of various desserts to share. And for once, Elijah was grateful. It had been a full-time job already just keeping up with Uncle William's two youngsters since his wedding. But doing so on a day when they were even more excited than usual was exhausting.

In the beginning, he had been more than willing to give the help needed, seeing as William had promised him a full week off of work at the warehouse afterwards in exchange, but that still did not make it any less of a chore this morning. Not to mention the fact that after this experience, Elijah had determined more than ever that he was most certainly <u>not</u> ready for any such delights of his own for quite some time, as the chore of taking care of those who belonged to others was about all he could handle for the moment. Moreover, as delightful as everyone always thought their sweet little children were, he was beyond grateful to know that they could be returned to their parents at any time and not remain with him indefinitely. A feeling he obviously shared with his other uncle across the room.

From the deep lines in Nathanael's forehead to the way in which he held the children at a respectable distance away from him, Elijah could tell that his uncle felt equally inclined to his way of thinking but was trying his best to remain supportive for his mother's sake. Since the first day the two children had arrived at her home weeks ago, his mother had doted on them incessantly, adoring the pudgy, dimpled cheeks of Holly and the precocious ways of young Samuel, but the preacher was enduring it all with a stoic fortitude like anyone might do who was forced to eat cold porridge every day of their lives.

Safely tucked away from the fray in his favorite chair near the corner of the room, Elijah watched him humorously from a distance and tried not to laugh every time one of the children would helpfully bring his uncle some sticky treat from the table. In fact, by the way that he eagerly handed the dessert back to them each time and then stared with panic at the screen door for the child's very absent parents, Elijah would not be surprised if his uncle was not coincidentally called elsewhere quite suddenly after supper if the squeals and chaos continued much longer. Surely, he always had some ailing church member that was poised to rescue him in situations such as these. Which meant it was only a matter of time... or fortitude, he supposed, before the man eventually bolted.

Yet it was not until the sound of heaven-sent footfalls on the stairs just outside on the porch rang out that the atmosphere in the room increased even more in its vitality. With the knowledge that their last guests had finally arrived, Nathanael practically leapt from his seat and opened the front door wide to greet William and Charity, ready for the festivities to commence.

"Merry Christmas, William... Charity!" Nathanael welcomed them with a grin and waited for both of them to step inside before closing the outer door and walking back to his seat.

"Merry Christmas!" They both said in unison to the others.

"Thank goodness you're finally here!" Elijah exclaimed happily, knowing he could finally escape from his duties at long last. "They've been asking about you all day."

"Yes, I've been helping Elijah keep them occupied since six o'clock this morning as a matter of fact. It must be awfully wonderful to get to sleep so late, Uncle William." Hope yawned through her sarcasm, obviously still tired and more than a little bit irritated with their tardiness.

"Yes, well, we are here now, and that is all that matters." William looked over at Charity and smiled. "Did they enjoy all their presents?" He asked as he reached down and picked up Holly with one arm, then with the other.

"Oh, definitely! But we saved a few for you to open with them," Charlotte answered peacefully from her rocking chair next to Nathanael. By the smile on her face and the way the two of them sat so very close to each other by the tree, the new arrangement they had discovered appeared to suit her, as well, and William was glad for it. After everything that they had both been through in their lives so far, the two deserved a little piece of happiness for the next few decades, or maybe a little longer if the Lord allowed.

"Thank you so much for taking care of the children for us." Charity leaned down and tapped the nose of little Caleb in front of her. "I'm so eager to have them home with us once more that I can hardly wait."

"When _will_ we be coming home, Uncle William? I miss my bed." Samuel stuck his lower lip out in a definite pout at the man who was caring for him like his own father.

"I bet you do. And it won't be too much longer, I promise. Maybe two or three more nights... four at the most. Would that be okay?" He handed James off to his mother and knelt down to Samuel's level, making sure he knew that his opinion was valued, as well. Not that it would change anything that had already been planned with the others, but creating the image of its overall importance felt necessary just the same.

Contemplating greatly whether or not he could stand to be away that long from his bed and other precious items that he might desire, the boy placed one finger on his lips and nodded. "Alright, but what _have_ you and Miss Charity been doing without us? Did you have to work? I bet lots of people need you at the hospital."

"Actually, he has been passing the time telling me all his stories about when he was your age—lots and lots of them. We've been simply bored without you." Charity stepped over to the boy and reached out her arms to take his younger sister from William. "I'm simply anxious to hear about all the fun things you are doing with Uncle Elijah and Aunt Charlotte."

"We got presents in our shoes this morning, Miss Charity. So many presents!" Caleb tugged on the side of her red skirt and held up one of his freshly painted wooden blocks.

"Oh, my! How wonderful!" Charity and William both grinned at his simple thrill.

"Yes, someone was trying a bit too hard this year, I think." Emile smirked from his comfortable position leaning back in Sebastian's favorite chair that had been moved closer to the outer wall but still faced the fireplace on the opposite side.

"Did you like your new scarf?" William inquired, hoping he had selected the one that had suited his friend best. After all, it _had_ been recommended to him by Emile's tailor, so he felt fairly confident that he would.

"I wore it over here this morning actually. Though that wind is incredibly strong out there today. A regular nor'easter must be brewing along the coast." Emile looked out the window and judged the safety of the house next to the bending tree limbs that were still swaying wildly in the wind. Surprisingly enough, the rare storm had only picked up in its intensity since midnight, knocking down at least two or three of the trees along his way to Charlotte's that morning, making him more than a little bit certain that if it did not stop, several more would no doubt fall with them before the day was over. Though thankfully for all at the farm, none had come even close to any of the structure as of yet.

"Will Michael be arriving soon?" Charity asked Hope who was trying her best to appear interested in what was going on around her.

"I think so. He should have been here already, but it appears you are not the only ones running late today." She crossed her arms, clearly moping at his unusual tardiness, and held them against her chest firmly. "His family wanted him there with them this morning, so I suppose I will just have to be patient."

"Well, speaking of being patient..." William glanced over at Emile and winked. "Is it alright if we give Hope her present first? I don't think Charity will make it if we have to wait until Michael arrives?"

Emile nodded once, for they had already discussed the whole plan with him the day before the wedding and had been given her mother's approval.

"What present?" Hope looked back at the pile near the base of the tree and shifted several of them around. "I already looked before you came, and there is nothing under there for me today besides the new pair of shoes Mother bought for me and Uncle Nathanael's journal."

"It isn't under the tree, sweetheart." Charity tried to maintain the suspense of the moment a little longer, but it was killing her to lead her on so.

"Then where is it?" Hope's face shone utter confusion.

"It's back in town near Michael, actually." William followed Charity's lead, making his clue as cryptic, and yet as accurate as possible.

"Why did you leave it there and not bring it with you?" Hope shook her head in frustration. "Now I will just have to wait until tomorrow for it."

"You'll have to wait until tomorrow for it anyway," Emile said casually from his chair across the room and placed one arm around his wife to draw her closer. "And you may not share one minute of it with Michael until the end of March."

"The end of March?" Hope looked even more confused. "And why do I have to share it at all? He has enough things already. This one is supposed to be mine."

Charity giggled. "Because I am giving the two of you my apartment... if you want it. I don't need it anymore since I moved all my things over to William's house..." She tried to finish her explanation, but the girl practically vaulted from her seat on the floor and into her arms in seconds.

"Of course I want it!" Hope squealed with delight. "That is incredible Miss... I mean, Aunt Charity."

"Yes, it is," Emma added politely. "And one we know you will use with respect for the time being, correct?"

"I promise." Hope ran over to her mother, then to Emma and Emile and gave them the biggest hug she had ever given them in their lives.

"Don't you think they should be hugged?" Emile pointed over to the two newcomers. "We've done practically nothing."

"Of course! Thank you, Uncle William... Aunt Charity! I can't wait to fix it up for us." Hope hugged them both in turn and sat back down next to her mother. "Do you think you will be feeling strong enough to help me soon, Mother? We won't need very much as it is practically perfect the way it is."

"I think I can manage," she answered sweetly. "But maybe not until the week after the children leave, alright?"

"Alright." Hope beamed, too excited about the many possibilities to say more.

"Now, who is going to open the rest of these presents?" William picked up two of them and read the labels. From the manner in which some of them were wrapped, he already knew what a few of them contained, but the rest were a complete mystery to him. "This one appears to be for you, Elijah, and the other is for Jedidiah." He felt the very long package in his hands, the weight and breadth of it intriguing him greatly.

With a building sense of deepening curiosity, he handed each to their owners and watched carefully as Jedidiah peeled back the paper of his gift and gasped. On his lap lay the most brilliantly fashioned sword William had ever seen. Far more superior than the one that had hung over the mantle years ago and just as intricate.

"I can scarcely believe it!" Jedidiah held the blade up to the light and studied its angles and etching. "Who is this from?"

Humbled by the reception his gift had received, Elijah remained silent for a few moments, suddenly feeling apprehensive about revealing it.

"You finally figured out what you had forgotten didn't you, Eli?" William eyed him with great respect from his position near the fireplace.

Elijah shrugged. "I just did what Papa showed me, then I added some of my own blood, sweat, and tears—mostly tears. It is probably the finest blade I have ever crafted so far, and I wanted you to have it, Jedidiah."

"But why me?" Jedidiah handed the blade over to his wife who showed it to Charlotte and Nathanael after. "You could have sold this for ten times the worth of the steel that created it."

"More like a hundred," Emile corrected him politely. "People do not make things of this quality anymore."

"No," Emma agreed with astonishment at his obvious ability.

For the first time in his life, Elijah wanted to explain to his brother all the many reasonings he had settled upon in his heavily conflicted mind for why he had made it in the first place, but all of them seemed to pale in comparison to the one thing that had been at the center of its creation—love.

Glancing over at Nathanael with renewed appreciation, Elijah tried to hold back the emotion that he had been keeping at bay for weeks and began, "Someone told me recently that Papa allowed the two of us to choose the path we wanted, Jed. You chose the farm, and I chose the forge. But I never valued your sacrifice in taking on the farm... not really. I was more focused on trying to be everything our papa was, though he never asked me to do so. In my distraction, I never saw the real vision Papa always had for me until now. I only saw my own goals and faults."

"Huh, that's funny. I think I have felt very much the same. What a shame we spent most of our lives trying to live up to a legacy that never crossed our papa's mind once. All he wanted was for us to be happy," Jedidiah replied simply, his eyes fixed on his brother as if the two of them were the only ones in the room at that moment.

"True." Elijah smiled back at him briefly and felt the presence of his father in the words they had just shared. "I know now that though I have not always shown it, there is much I still need to learn from our papa."

"Really... what is that?" Nathanael asked, resting his elbows on the arms of his chair, intensely interested in the conversation unfolding before him.

"That a man can be strong without having physical strength, and that he can also be humble without being weak. This sword is proof of that. It is just a part of the tremendous legacy he left us, and I will <u>never</u> take that for granted again," Elijah promised, his voice thick and even.

"Nor I," Jedidiah pledged just as faithfully. "In coming to this country, he gave us all a chance of something he never had and with God's help, we will be able to pass all of that and so much more on to our own children one day."

The rest of the room nodded in agreement as all of them remembered silently the man who had been their father, their mentor, their husband and their friend.

"And speaking of passing things on…" Elijah cleared his throat nervously, then began in earnest. "There is one more gift I want to give you, Jedidiah, but you must promise to share it with Hope one day if she should ever desire it." Elijah winked at his sister from across the room.

"I'm listening." Jedidiah tilted his head, confused by the strangeness of his request.

Reaching into his inside coat pocket, Elijah pulled out a piece of folded parchment Charlotte recognized the moment she saw it.

"Oh, Elijah… are you sure?" Charlotte's eyes brimmed over with tears. "It was your legacy, as well."

"I've never been more sure about anything else in my life, Mama." He handed the folded parchment over to Jedidiah and took his seat quietly.

Completely perplexed now by the whole conversation, Jedidiah glanced at his mother and then back at Elijah before carefully opening the document and gasping audibly. "It's the deed to your half of the farm, Elijah! I can't take this from you!"

"You can, and you will," Elijah stated firmly. "Provided you keep your word about Hope. She may not ever need any of it, but I want you to set aside a few acres for her just the same. Maybe somewhere between here and Uncle Emile's house, perhaps, along the front road. Would that be too hard to do?"

Jedidiah shook his head, completely overwhelmed by the gift. "But Papa meant it for both of us, Eli."

"No, he meant it for the family. My place is at the forge, Jed. It always will be. I know that now. And your place is here, or at least until you get tired of milking those dreadful cows, which by the way, I have a bit more respect for you regarding them."

Jedidiah and some of the others laughed.

"I know it isn't enough, but thank you, Elijah, truly." Jedidiah stood and walked over to embrace his brother warmly. "Papa would be proud of you, Eli."

"He was proud of all of us. He said so, and I know it even more so now."

Then as if the silence was becoming all too much for him finally, young Samuel seized the opportunity to steal the attention and shouted to all of the others gathered, "This is boring. I want to play already!"

Many of those around the child laughed, for his stubborn and compelling nature reminded them instantly of the man of whom they were speaking.

"Go ahead, young man." William handed him another toy from the pile and placed one arm behind his wife. "Why don't you hand the rest of the presents out, Hope, since you already got your gift."

"Alright." Hope smiled once more and climbed down on the ground to fetch out the other parcels before handing them all out to the others in the room.

Before long there was ripping of paper and exclamations, ribbons untied and tears, all mixed wonderfully together with the echoes of laughter and joy. As a matter of fact, it was <u>exactly</u> what each of them had hoped today would bring and then some.

"Do you know what <u>I</u> want most of all today?" William whispered in his wife's ear as they watched their friends gathered around them.

"What?" Charity almost blushed, uncertain what the man might say next, and especially so in front of so many people.

"I want to dance with my wife." He kissed the side of her cheek and smiled, a warmth spreading behind his eyes that had not ceased to burn since she had returned after Thanksgiving.

"So, do I." Emile stood. "Nathanael, I am sorry, but we are changing things up this year." He pulled Emma up from her chair, wrapping his arm around her waist and turning her around. "Jedidiah, do you still know how to play your father's guitar?"

"No, that would be Elijah's thing, as well," Jedidiah laughed heartily at the request. "But I <u>will</u> fetch it for him, if he is willing." He left the room and returned from the upper bedroom with his father's Spanish guitar in hand. "You'll need to tune it, Eli. I don't think anyone has played it since last year."

Nodding his head slightly at the request, Elijah accepted the instrument reverently and listened closely to the pitches of each string, tuning every one of them perfectly before looking up at his mother. "Do you have a favorite, Mama?"

"The Bourree in e-minor from Bach," she said confidently without a hint of a pause before patting Nathanael's hand next to her.

"Is that your favorite, really?" Hope asked quietly, for she had not heard the song played in quite some time.

"No, but it was your father's." Charlotte smiled, then motioned for him to begin. "You should dance, too, Nancy. It has been far too long since you enjoyed yourself in that way." She reached for James and encouraged her to join her husband.

Soon, the rest of the room had paired up together, as well, and were happily dancing around the children, the presents, the table, and the scattered toys. None of it mattered. For one glorious moment, on Christmas Day in the year 1811, all was right in the world and full of unspeakable joy.

Other Resources

Brady, Ollie. "Spinel Vs. Ruby: Gemstone Showdown Explained." *Caldera Gem*, 18 Sept. 2024, www.calderagem.com/blogs/news/spinel-vs-ruby. Accessed 16 Jun. 2025.

"Federalists Vs. Republicans." *This Vs. That*, thisvsthat.io/federalists-vs-republicans. Accessed 3 May 2025.

Grove, Stephen. "The Impact and Devastation of Scarlet Fever Epidemics in the 19th Century." *19th Century Events and Developments*, 19thcentury.us/scarlet-fever-epidemics-in-the-19th-century/. Accessed 7 Oct. 2024.

Hecht, Johanna. "The Manila Galleon Trade (1565–1815)." In *Heilbrunn Timeline of Art History*. New York: The Metropolitan Museum of Art, 2000–. http://www.metmuseum.org/toah/hd/mgtr/hd_mgtr.htm (October 2003).

"History Of The Pennsylvania Hospital." *Penn Medicine*, 1 Jan. 2017, www.uphs.upenn.edu/paharc/timeline/#:~:text=Pennsylvania%20Hospital%20%2D%2D%20the%20nation's,teaching%20and%20clinical%20research%20institution. Accessed 3 May 2025.

Memon, Nazneen BHMS. "What Medicines Were Used in the 1800s?" *MedicineNet*,www.medicinenet.com/what_medicines_were_used_in_the_1800s/article.html.

Penn, Nicole. "Aurora General Advertiser." *American Enterprise Institute-George Washington's Mount Vernon*, www.mountvernon.org/library/digitalhistory/digital-encyclopedia/article/aurora-general-advertiser. Accessed 3 May 2025.